WELLSPRING OF FORESIGHT

WELLSPRING OF FORESIGHT

32 SHORT STORIES

WITH BIBLIOGRAPHY

LORENZO GARCIA TABIN, SR.

AND

SINAMAR A. ROBIANES TABIN, SR.

To order additional copies of this book, contact:
Xlibris
1-888-795-4274
www.Xlibris.com
Orders@Xlibris.com
797043

Table of Contents

Sinamar A. Robianes Tabin, Sr.

Lorenzo Garcia Tabin, Sr.

Bibliography

Dedication

To our children: Loumarie Linglingay Tabin Galvan, her husband Glicerio and their children Brigham and Bridget; Lorenzo II; Naomi and her children LeGrand Aaron Nathanael and Lindsay Jan Miona, and her husband Richard Hansen; Sinamar II Tabin Tolman and her husband Nathan and their son Gabriel Arvin; Marlo Bagnos, his wife Marcella and their children Lorimar, Enoka, and Job Enzo; and our late parents Clemente Ramos Tabin and Crispina Retuta Garcia, and Rafael Romano Robianes and Elena Alos Baradi. Also to all our brothers and sisters and their families.

Also, we dedicate to the TMI-Global (Timpuyog dagiti Mannurat nga Ilokano -Global 'Guild of Ilocano Writers-Global)—headed by the late T. Gabriel Tugade, with Aurelio Solver Agcaoili, PhD; Cristino Iloreta Inay, and the two of us husband and wife—that the main purpose is to translate the writings of the Ilocano writers.

Also, to all who treasure Ilocano literature.

Foreword

I

THIS is the first selected stories of a couple Ilokano writers with translation in English. It contains diverse forms of short fictions: humorous, crestfallen, with local and international settings, traditional and contemporary, published and unpublished, and awarded stories.

Sinamar was admired during her prime and had a bunch of fans reading her fictions, not only because of their theme that affect the moods but even with her alluring name—*Sinamar* means rays of light, that precisely allures the attention of her husband.

In the other side, Lorenzo became popular because of his first novel *Ti Imetda nga Impierno,* published by the *Bannawag* magazine when the author was 22 years old and the youngest writer who turned novelist during his time, and where Sinamar congratulated him in the *Dakami Met* or Letters to the Editor, and the start of their relationship; followed by *Ramut ti Sinamar,* then *Agus,* the sequels of the trilogy of Pupoy's life. More so when his tongue in cheek novel *Pakpakawan, Berde!* followed by more humorous novels until the publication of his award-winning contemporary novel *Adtoy, Siak ni Jesus Crisostomo: Dramaturgo.*

See the whole list of their writings in their separate bibliographies between the English (translation) and the Ilokano (original) sections of the book.

x

LORENZO GARCIA TABIN, SR. AND
SINAMAR A. ROBIANES TABIN, SR.

II

THIS anthology is divided into two sections, the English translation *Wellspring of Foresight: 32 Selected Short Fiction,* and the original form in Ilokano, *Ubbog ti Sirmata: 32 a Napili a Sarita.* The English section is divided into three chapters: **1. Sinamar A. Robianes Tabin, Sr. 2. Lorenzo Garcia Tabin, Sr.** and **3. Bibliography;** and the Ilokano section is divided into two chapters: **1. Sinamar A. Robianes Tabin, Sr.** and, **2. Lorenzo Garcia Tabin, Sr.** The stories were arranged by the date of publication and/or by the time of composition.

We want to apprise that the objective of the translation and publication of the anthology is to fulfill the main purpose of the TMI (Timpuyog dagiti Mannurat nga Ilokano Global), or Guild of Ilokano Writers Global, which is to translate the writings of Ilocano writers.

We consider four issues that we applied in developing our writing career. We embodied them every time we cope with our writing.

First: *Bannawag-style.* We were in the process of learning to write when the Bannawag magazine started sponsoring short story writing competition. Doctors, lawyers, dean, professor and editors served as judges and we considered them demigods from heaven, or demigods in literature. We examined their commentaries, and the winning entries of other demigod writers since most of them were professionals. What we reflected about ourselves during those years? We were as trifling as a mongo bean nothing to be compared to those giants—another description—who were pillars of high-sounding words.

Bannawag-style was an attribute which is so vivid in our mind, and sure enough we still remember.

That attribute was introduced by the late Dr. Marcelino A. Foronda, Jr. when he was one of the judges.

Why did he dub *Bannawag-style?*

We realized that the term Dr. Foronda used was not demeaning. Since *Bannawag* was the only 'Bible of the North' magazine the editors, or the Liwayway Publishing, compelled to the need of the readers. During their early stages they did not publish something incomprehensible by the readers or for 'literature' in that matter.

No doubt, it was the only 'melting pot' for the diligent Ilocano writers; the source of their entertainment. We comprehend that reality, so we based all the lifeblood of our writing to the perception of the editors.

We were not different from other writers. We need to follow the acuity of the editors, if we want our writings be published. Thanks God, and the editors, and for our needing of money—there were even occasions that we could collect the payment of our stories before their publication. We replicate: our heartfelt gratitude to the kindness of the editors.

Second: *Smart-alecky*. After writing for a long period of time and we were lucky to enroll for a graduate study at the University of the Philippines at Diliman, and read more books by foreign authors, we comprehended the veracity of Dr. Foronda's view. We read a lot of short fiction, novels, poetry they consider their styles modern or experimental; literary criticism, and many more that could enhance writers' outlooks. One of our compadres tried to write a poem, which style or form was diverse. It consisted several lines with one word, a frog's hum—*koka, koka, koka, koka...* Probably the editor became irritated, for he threw the 'poem' in the garbage!

Some of us tried to evade the wrapped-up method of writing—we learned that term from the late Valerio L. Nofuente, an instructor at the University of the Philippines at Diliman, who wrote his remark about [Lorenzo's] stories included in *Pakpakawan, Berde! Ken 24 a Sarita*. According to him, the stories were wrapped-up.

Smart-alecky! We won't forget that term of one of the editors—that word was not exactly aimed to us, but we heard that when we visited the editorial. Are those who were planning to change the form of writing for *Bannawag* considered smart-alecky?

But we were not perturbed. We gradually deviate from our 'old' style of writing. The style of our first story where we changed our style published by the *Bannawag* 'The Eden in Their Lives' *(Ti Eden iti Biagda)* was purely dialogue; we presumed that this was the first, if not the only one of its kind published by the *Bannawag*. Another example is '*Here in Glory: Penitentiary*,' we did not use names; and xii

LORENZO GARCIA TABIN, SR. AND
SINAMAR A. ROBIANES TABIN, SR.

many more stories. After that, we tried our best to use new form or style; we diverged our style or form from 'the old' when we participated in every competition, where some of our entries were lucky enough to pass the verdict of the judges and started winning the perception of the demigods of literature. Our gratitude to this magazine is beyond description—that was the reason why I was able to write published literary pieces, as listed in the bibliography included in this anthology.

The form of the short stories winning entries gradually improved. By altering the form of my stories, and novels like *Behold, I Am, Jesus Crisostomo: Playwright (Adtoy, Siak, ni Jesus Crisostomo: Dramaturgo)* we also started winning in writing competitions.

Third: *Balls, he partook in the competition but did not do his best!* It is still fresh in my [Lorenzo] mind that phrase by *Tang*[1] Ben—that's what the late Atty. Benjamin M. Pascual wanted us to call him; he was a very humble lawyer and dean and one of the pillars of the Ilocano literature whom we could never forget because he was so closed to us. He mentioned that when the third judge was not with us to evaluate the entries in that short story competition. We did not have any idea that time about the participants, but we were tickled and shook our heads upon knowing who the author was. We became more meticulous in writing afterwards.

Fourth: *Ask Loring, he is good in assigning titles!* We included this part though seems not that important, but it is also significant in the world of writing profession.

We had a pleasant conversation where we were nattering together with Feliciano Martin T. Rochina, the late Reynaldo A. Duque, the late Pelagio A. Alcantara, and other writers that night of awarding the first novel writing competition sponsored by the Economy Tours and Travels, Inc. (ETTI)—my novel was awarded second prize while Martin was third; the late Samuel F. Corpuz who was awarded first prize was not in our group.

---

[1]   *Tang,* an address to a middle-aged man as sign of respect.

Our topic was assigning titles for short stories and novels. Some writers could not start writing without first assigning a title for their works—we are one of those. Some complete their works before assigning a title—like Peter La. Julian: we observed that when we were in Coromina St., Quiapo, Manila together with Prescillano N. Bermudez, the late T. Gabriel Tugade, Constante Al. Domingo, and Benjamin Castillo Chua.

It was Martin who asked about the topic.

"Ask Loring because that is his forte!" the late Rey said laughing.

Most probably Rey remembered that there were books printed by the GUMIL Metro Manila that I assigned their title.

It should be evoked that the title of many of my writings when I was a budding writer were altered by the editors.

III

WE encountered some problems in selecting our short stories included in this anthology, not because of their substance but because we lost some of what was supposed to be included. We carefully preserved all our writings published by the Bannawag, including our unpublished manuscripts, but many were eaten by termites, and some were not spared by downpours during the repair of the roof of our house where they were kept—that was when we moved to America; they were forgotten, or probably neglected by the people left behind, and those who were told to repair the house; they did not put them in a safe place—nothing is better to keep articles than the owner who knows how to value literary pieces. My experience at the Filipiniana Section of the University of the Philippines, where I was assigned to keep the manuscripts and copies of the *Bannawag* magazine, where some of our writings were included, was beneficial. Some of the stories included in the anthology were reproduced from that library.

NOTE: *Man, and Time (Tao ken Panawen)* and *Face (Rupa)* [by Lorenzo] and *Jackfruit (Anangka)* [by Sinamar] were both published twice by the *Bannawag—see* the dates at the end of these stories.

xiv

Lorenzo Garcia Tabin, Sr. and
Sinamar A. Robianes Tabin, Sr.

Let's observe the first section comprising the selected short stories of Sinamar. It's unfortunate that the last of the two chapters of *Sweetsop* (Atis) and *Macopa* (Makopa) to complete her stories about fruits were not found. Likewise, in the section where Lorenzo's selected fictions, including some not published in the *Bannawag*. We planned to include our [Lorenzo's] story *Pilarica Naamitan: A Post Meridiem* (Pilarica Naaamitan: Maysa a Malem) that garnered second prize from the GETSMAIL (Governor Evaristo T. Singson Memorial Award for Iluko Literature), 1991, but we were not also able to find it.

The difference between the published and unpublished short stories is obvious. We want to accentuate that we indebted from the *Bannawag* the publication of our writings. First and foremost, we, husband and wife met each other because of this magazine. Secondly, we acknowledge that the *Bannawag* molded us as man, that brought us where we are right now.

I, Lorenzo, steadilly 'get off' from the style of *Bannawag*, where I heard from one of the senior editors the dub 'smart-alecky.' But I ignored it, instead I embedded into my mind my appreciativeness to this magazine—the reason why I was able to write more than usual, as manifested in the bibliography included in this anthology.

Probably our writings could be panned, and we expected that, but we focused on the individuality of their form; we just wanted to stimulate the readers that there are forms other than the form of fictions they usually read from the *Bannawag*, that in our opinion required further study, for there are a lot of exceptional writings written in different languages around the world.

They may not be efficacious, from the views of the readers whose intention is just to relax after a tedious work the whole day, but we did this, that these short stories may signify the purpose of the *Bannawag*, and hopefully to help the Ilokano literature. We are aware that the Ilokano language and literature is flourishing, as manifested at the University of Hawaii at Manoa.

We likewise 'courageously' translated these short fictions into English for distribution not only in the Ilocos Region but anywhere where lovers of literature live; and hopefully be read also by those who could not understand Iloco/Iluko/Iloko/Ilokano/Ilocano and comprehend the big role of the *Bannawag* magazine; and as mentioned, to accomplish the objective of the Guild of Ilokano Writers' (*Timpuyog dagiti Mannurat nga Ilokano*) [TMI]-Global. — **LORENZO GARCIA TABIN, SR.** and **SINAMAR A. ROBIANES TABIN, SR.**

Critical Introduction

Ilokano Literature and the Question of Redemption:
The Case of the Short Fiction of Tabin and Tabin

By Aurelio S. Agcaoili, PhD

A Tandem of Storytellers

In a number of works of the husband-and-wife team, Lorenzo G. Tabin, Sr. and Sinamar Robianes Tabin, we sense what Jonathan Franzen[2] has said about the power of books. He rightfully declared that books are the sanctuary of the human soul. I could not agree more.

Sanctuaries offer us a place to get away from the unnecessary grind of the everyday. They shield us from all sorts of danger and offer us protection from the ravaging effects of the unfamiliar and the unknown. Some kind of trembling before the strange could grip us. And then we lose our way, unable to return to where we come from.

---

[2]   Jonathan Franzen, *How to Be Alone: Essay* (New York: Farrar, Straus and Giroux/Picador), 2002.

xviii

LORENZO GARCIA TABIN, SR. AND
SINAMAR A. ROBIANES TABIN, SR.

The hermeneut is right about texts such as this *Wellspring of Foresight* and its original form in Ilokano, *Ubbog Ti Sirmata*, opening up a world for us to get into.

Good books, indeed, open a gate for the reader to get into and enter into a conversation with it. The "it" here is a new reading of human experiences. And those who have the gift of artistic vision are able to leave us something behind, educating us at the end about the complexities of human life.

Franzen reminds us that the author—two Ilokano short fictionists in the case of this book—is a master of the language in which s/he writes. Apart from that capacity to think and see and feel and intuit differently, the good writer is able to sense life's difficulty. Out of that understanding, the writer may start to figure out which word makes sense and which one does not in that one bold and courageous act of mediating the difficult texts of life. That act of mediation—that act of writing about it—is an act of making those difficult texts understood by those who care to know.

In *Woven Strands of Roses: Letters with Annotation That Sprung Forth from the Hearts,*[3] the first book of Lorenzo Sr. and Sinamar[4] as a husband-and-wife team, we get a glimpse of their story and history as Ilokano writers.

There is that back story of having come to know each other by that circuitous and yet delight-filled, perhaps destined, route of Ilokano literature. There is that parallelism in their love for Ilokano literature and their commitment to contribute to its flourishing and their love and commitment for each other (in the beginning as lovers and eventually as husband and wife). Their story as Ilokano writers, I would say, is their story as a couple as well.

At day's end, this we can say: they have both been sustained as individual writers and as a couple writing in the Ilokano language. The fact that even if they could write in other Philippine languages and yet

---

[3] Xlibris US (2014).

[4] Hereinafter, I shall call them this way in this essay.

decided to remain the voice of the Ilokano people and their language is itself a testimony to their commitment to a cause that so few would understand.

The history of Philippine literature is replete with acts of exclusion, the acts oftentimes systemic and systematic as these are state-sponsored and sanctioned, and are subtly incorporated in the country's educational system. Hardly we can say that there was a respect for the diverse expressions of the cultural and literary life of the many peoples of the Philippines during the last three generations starting from that imposition of a language of the center, Tagalog, as the language of the entire country.

The peripheralization of other languages of the country apart from Tagalog and English was just fairly common, and until today, the measure of intelligence and abilities of citizens remains mediated by tests in those two languages. Clearly, the educational system has been in cahoots in this wanton homogenization of an otherwise diverse languages and cultures of the country.

Let us recall that Lorenzo Sr. wrote his master's thesis in Tagalog as it was not possible for him to write it in Ilokano at that time, even within the seemingly liberal and emancipatory culture of the University of the Philippines where he finished his master's degree in Philippine literature.

Sinamar, as a teacher in one of the bigger cities of Manila, could have easily shifted to Tagalog, the language that could have opened up doors to her as a rare "woman writer"[5] of the country.

---

[5] We must acknowledge here that Ilokano literature is rooted in something called a unique case of Ilokano "patriarchy," with patriarchy to mean that some of the acts that are otherwise social and public have been dominated by men. There have been exceptions during the last one hundred years, with several women writers (Leona Florentino comes to mind here) subtly hinting what could now be termed "Ilokano feminism," but they remain as exceptions. These women writers writing with sense and clarity were few. One or two or three swallows so they say, cannot make a summer. This is a problem. Sinamar's act is certainly one of the exceptions.

XX

LORENZO GARCIA TABIN, SR. AND
SINAMAR A. ROBIANES TABIN, SR.

Whether by fate's design or by choice, the fact that both of them remained committed to the development of Ilokano literature by their act of sustained writing in that language is sufficient proof that we have in them writers who have had always their own people and their own language in mind.

I wish to go back to the mastery of the Ilokano language, a mastery that is unequivocally demonstrated in the works of Lorenzo Sr. and Sinamar.

In bold strokes, we get the drift that both have been able to create a vision in their handling of difficult life situations. Sinamar resorts to parable-like stories that almost leave us a lesson to remember for always as if she is teaching us about how to untangle the knots of our everyday life. Lorenzo Sr. utilizes a range of techniques and approaches in showing us about the sense of things including the context of the transcendent, the metaphysical. In his excursion into the unfamiliar, he tells of a myth, the *muthos* of the Greeks, and cautions us that there are other crucial things in life other than the mundane. Taken as one, this we can say about their work: there is a calculated re-visioning of reality in order to envision a newer one, perhaps, a better one. There is a promised sense of the redemptive in this book they wrote together.

Sources and Contexts

Ilokano writing in the Philippines and elsewhere is plain and simple a fool's act of making some sense in the always-already determined impoverished life in the country. While it is rooted in the oral tradition that served, in the precolonial and colonial periods, as the glue that made people remember who they were despite the demonization of the *frailes* and their agents of the cultural works of the Ilokano people, the imposition of English by the Americans by way of the imposed public education system, and the "Niponggo-icization" of the Ilokano children who were in schools and the attempt to turn the entire country into a Tagalog nation, Ilokano writing almost always became a "backyard activity" (such as the *daniw iti parparaangan* or poems created and recited in the backyard after a full day's work in the fields) and the handiwork of the poorer classes of the Ilokano people.

There was a divide—and this divide continues to split apart the various local Ilokano communities everywhere: (a) the rich and political elites ruled, and they ruled like patriarchs and pharaohs and patrons, and (b) the impoverished masses that were being ruled over, dominated, deprived, and told what to do, the poor classes remaining under the rich who have become the surrogates of the colonizers.

The *babaknang-and-gangangay* divide (the rich and the ordinary people) has remained the same to this day. Only the accidents have changed. In the case of Ilokano writing, only a few of the *babaknang* took chances with developing and enriching the Ilokano life and literature. Many of those who picked up writing and who continue to write are from the middle and lower-middle and poor classes, the *gagangay*. A handful of the middle class (more like lower middle class here from a socioeconomic metric) come from academia. But even these "acts of writing" from these academics seem to be some kind of an afterthought. Their commitment is neither here nor there.

The economic consequences of Ilokano writing, in general, are enormous. Most Ilokano writers die poor. Many of their manuscripts remain looking for publishers that are nowhere to be found. Those who have the means join others in collective publishing called *tagnawa*. Even those who showed talent in the beginning had to drop out because Ilokano writing, let this be said, cannot sustain even the basic economic need of the writer. Official state appreciation of creative writing in the country is at best a case of tokenism.

The story of the Coromina group of Ilokano writers writing with youthful vigor in the 1960s in the heart of Quiapo in Manila, a group that included Lorenzo Sr., is an indubitable proof of the real situation of Ilokano writing until today. And with the onslaught of state-sanctioned acts of homogenization by the state and its ideological apparatuses such as the schools, literature, and the mass and social media, we must document here our fear for the future and for the coming generations of Ilokanos. It is in this context that this present work Lorenzo Sr. and Sinamar finds its relevance: it will be served as their covenant to the

xxii

LORENZO GARCIA TABIN, SR. AND
SINAMAR A. ROBIANES TABIN, SR.

Ilokano language and people. This book will make it certain that the Ilokano language, a lingua franca of the northern part of the country, remain alive. Our hope is that it will not only remain alive but will thrive as well.

The Texts: Sinamar's Parables

Sinamar's approach to writing is that of a teacher, with her stories following a model, that of a parable.

I think of two sources of that parabolic orientation of Sinamar's short stories: (a) her being a classroom teacher in basic education and (b) her being engaged in the Christian faith.

Both sources of inspiration come into a fusion to mold a storyteller that is so clear in what she wants to say, her descriptions of human situations capturing and reveal difficulties.

The way she resolved them, while most often suggestive, has some twists in them. In the stories where moral resolutions are a given like those involving the test of one's love and faithfulness ("It's Under Your Discretion"), the test of faith ("God Exists, Joan"), regret ("If Life Could Only Be Bought"), and life's unpredictable nature ("In the Wheel of Fortune"), we sense here a voice of a moral actor. Sinamar wants to teach us a thing or two—or remind us about some fundamental things about character, good manners, and the need to make ethical decisions, and ethical because these are expressions of what is just and fair.

Through her fourteen stories, we get a reading of an Ilokano nation as lived in the Kailokuan. And then in one sweep, she leads us to an experience in the diaspora, in a watermelon plantation, with Ilokanos coming into an encounter with Mexicans (more symbolic here than literal, I suppose). There is some "unbearable lightness" in that intentional and funny act of "stealing watermelons" ("Livelihood Once Outlived"), the fun something earthy, something close to what could be termed as *rabrabak ken ang-angaw* (act of making fun of someone or provoking him in a way that is playful). In the days of old, the Ilokano people, despite their life of want, knew how to laugh.

There is that sense of seriousness in her mapping of the challenges of the everyday whether these challenges are individual or are public, that is, involving a group of people or even affecting a community.

For the latter, I think here of the story about a particular banana, "Aunt Rosa's Banana." The story moves from the individual, gets political when a particular local government politico comes into the picture. A politico politicizing a banana plant is something ridiculous, indeed. The community comes to an epiphany. And then that whooping resolution of the issue after a *force majeure*.

The simple village life—more of a *purok* than a *barrio*[6]—is portrayed in many of these works, and we are led back to the time when life was simpler and problems could be solved by talk and community members defining the problems together and coming to a resolution to repair relationships, bandage and heal wounds, and remember that common humanity these characters share one more time ("Jackfruit," "Once a Lourdes," and "Court Her to Teach a Lesson"). Somewhere, Sinamar invites us to get into the world of the psychologically incapacitated, and we develop sympathy and empathy for people who are not like us but could be like us except that we are a bit luckier, and the dice of bad luck did not come our way ("Glimmer in the Dark or How Are You, Dolly?"). Despite the odds, she reminds us in this story, we have the capacity to save ourselves, perhaps come to grips with reality and discover the many ways of self-redemption.

The Texts: Lorenzo Sr.'s Sense of the Transcendent

I have always suspected that Lorenzo Sr., in his past life, could have been a prophet, an angel, or a philosopher of the transcendent. Or it could be that there is no "or" here as he could be all of these. He makes comments on the sociopolitical condition of the Ilocos and the country

---

6   *Barangay* is today's equivalent of a *barrio*, a term made widespread by the Spanish colonizers but borrowed from Arabic; *purok* is a portion of a barangay and is usually made up of clusters of homes of families related to each other usually by blood or by marriage.

but in a way that is so subtle sometimes we do not realize right off the bat that he utilizes the short fiction to offer his social criticism.

I have seen his other works and always, there is that element of seriousness in the way he unravels for us the meaning of life. The telic orientation of that quest for answers is not that clear all the time, but that is the nature of questing—of looking for answers by asking the difficult questions. How he could move from the light and the comic to the serious concerns about life and its despairs, about hope and frustrations, and yet, also about that one fundamental need for redemption?

Ispal—or *salakan*[7]—is a good epistemology here to understand the deeper truths Lorenzo Sr. tries to untangle in his portrayal not only of Ilokanos adapting, like that barber coming to terms with his being a barber and then easily moving like a chameleon from behaving and speaking like a Tagalog back to his being Ilokano when the need requires.

When we do a reading of the eighteen works, he gifts us with in this book, we discover a long duration of giving voice to life as mediated by the Ilokano language. The way he does it with his Ilokano is seamless like the weavers of the *inabel* producing with their bare hands and agile movements of their eyes and bodies a design of a weave they dreamt of the night before.

Some of these works bear the dates in the 1960s and then move on to the 2000s. Many of the younger generations born after the now (in) famous EDSA People Power I and the EDSA People Power II perhaps no longer get the drift of the sentiments and sensibilities preserved in these stories.

Historians talk of the past, indeed, as "another country" and this is understandable as the one coming across the historical must be

---

[7]   Both mean redemptions. When inflected, we can account a verb *mangispal* (an infinitive, to redeem). When this is marked, it becomes a noun ('*ti mangispal*': the one that redeems). The same holds for *salakan: isalakan, mangisalakan,* and *agisalakan* are forms of the infinitive (to salvage or save). When marked, *mangisalakan* would mean 'the one that saves.'

ready to construct and reconstruct approaches on how to deal with the strangeness of the bygone years. Take the "The Flickering Stars of Escopa." There is almost a nostalgic rendition of the sense of "flickering" (into English) of the original *matimati*.

There is an elemental visual power here especially when those who have lived near Aurora Boulevard in Quezon City in those years, or of Project 4, or of the manufacturing plant of Timex (the electronics company) that has now been transformed into a temple of God could see what life was by that Rizal Street in that part of that city, when yonder from the boulevard were shanties that passed off as homes of impoverished people dreaming not of the blight they know so well but a better because fairer life.

Having gone to a university that almost always required me to pass by this place almost every day, I have a sense of this tragic story of Escopa, that Escopa that was a place of possibilities, limitless and life-filled.

But that was not meant to be. Someone had the land title to show and the land title alone is enough reason to dismiss the lives of the wretched that lived there, that imagined that they could live on that land far longer than what the title-holding owner could tolerate. These lives of the impoverished did not count in that story as the "story of the rich people." These lives, with the famed extrajudicial killings, do not still count today except when needed as numbers—faceless statistics— during elections. So much for the deficits of democracy here. And Lorenzo Sr. is absolutely right.

Escopa would go through a conflagration one day, the shanties turned to ash, some people succumbing to the fire and its hellish wrath, consuming everything it touched.

Somewhere, in the other parts of the city, there were other squatters' squares that would go the same route, one sure way of driving away the homeless of the city, of pushing them some more to the edge, and then turning the vacated burned lots into a subdivision, a commercial area, a residential place for the rich and those who can afford to pay the millions of the cost of each house.

The Philippine-United States relations is implicated in the story on US navy ships docking in Olongapo for a number of reasons at the time when the US maintained military bases in the Philippines.

The bases, this we know for certain, became a magnet for the rest-and-recreation activities of navy people who were always at sea for months and months on end and away from their families. "Deep and this Babylon" leads us to the inner lives of several navy men and Filipinos depending on ships docking and people looking for a way to forget their "loneliness in the deep." Towards the end, the verbal camera that produces a canvass on a page leads us to one person with a social conscience, Willy Shaw "(who) would never forget the workers scavenging garbage when it is supposed to be their break time… the boys under the bridge shouting 'Hi, Joe! Some coins, Joe…!'…Nat who was waiting for his mother who was working in a club… Ramon, the young Filipino man dreaming to for contentment in the other world."

We know one thing here: through Willy, Lorenzo Sr. leads us to see other lives and other alternatives to find meanings in those lives. It could be this—and this is a rejection of what Roger Briant does, he who argues, and declares that "we need to be happy" and that "we need to go with the flow." We can only imagine here what happiness there is in that aloneness that is not solitude, that aloneness that gifts you with the Babylon of sorrow.

Even as Lorenzo Sr. pans the camera, we are greeted by some subtle social criticism, the condition of blight in cities and piers and dockyards and urban streets assaulted us so and reminding us that somewhere, there is this fundamental iniquity is not only a case of inequality in one or two countries but in a global light: that one country's prosperity and joy and happiness might be the result of the deprivation and sadness and grief of another.

The exchange between Willy and Ramon opens a world for us to see, and the iniquity becomes palpable, even wounding. Ramon is looking for happiness by having money; he wants to join the US Navy—as is the case of every ambitious and able-bodied young Filipino boy in those days—and his money problem would be solved. Willy checks him, saying, among others, that once Ramon joins the navy, he would be imprisoned. We could hear Willy telling Ramon this: "You have found happiness here in your country."

One of the more poignant portrayal of this ugly reality of two lives in a country purporting to be a democracy could be seen in "The Eden in their Lives."

Banong comes alive here, that Ilokano who has learned to adjust to life's situations that are otherwise not easy to navigate. Equally alive is Hil Garcia who tries to keep his integrity amidst all the challenges every poor man faces, even poor man like him with big dreams. In his case, we get to know Hil as an aspiring writer.

But there is that caveat: his girlfriend wants to succeed as a writer as well. Situations like this one lead us to dilemmas that lead us to more dilemmas until one has summoned his courage and announce to all: "Let life come alive. Let life be lived."

A detour into the biographical approach to reading a literary work, even one that has been labeled by its author as a work of fiction circles us back to where Lorenzo Sr. was at the time of the writing of this particular piece.

When we juxtapose this biographic note against the lessons, we learned in their first book particularly from their letters to each other, and we become certain of biography-meeting-fiction. Here is what Hil told Banong: "Second year in college. I stopped because my parents could not afford the expenses. I experienced cleaning restaurant bathrooms. After that, I worked as plumber. Then as electrician. But there is no advancement from these kinds of jobs. I tried writing. The payment of my writings was not even enough to lengthen my breath. I decided to work in the factory. But the same, no advancement there. I could endure but I want to help my siblings go to school. You know, Banong, I have a teacher girlfriend—from our neighboring province. She is also a writer; she has a dream and I'll be her stumbling block if I stop doing better."

I agree that there is no one-to-one correspondence here, that what Hil has told Banong is not necessarily exactly what was happening to Lorenzo Sr. at that time. But the similarities are too glaring to ignore.

xxviii

LORENZO GARCIA TABIN, SR. AND
SINAMAR A. ROBIANES TABIN, SR.

In many of his works, I am certain about one thing: that Lorenzo Sr. has been able to deploy his own experiences and turn these into "ingredients" of his act of writing Ilokano literature.

The creative because imaginative fictionalizing of the facts of one's life, as in the case of a number of Lorenzo Sr.'s short stories, is one of the reasons why his works are relevant.

These works are an act of reading the social life of the Ilocos. And by the fact that the setting and characters and issues in these stories do not only concern the Ilocos but the entire country, these works are instruction in a lot of things. We grant that these are not entirely factual as well, but that encounter between fact and fiction is what gives shape and form to his stories. That encounter is factually fictional, and fictionally factual. The "one-ing" of fact and fiction is inaugurated in these works. There is raw talent here. And daring.

If it were the case that Hil Garcia (or Hilario Garcia in the story "Three Footprints") is the alter ego of Lorenzo Sr., the argument is plausible. Either that our author denies this claim totally or affirms it. There is no in-between here, some kind of a gray area where one can play neutral by admitting some of the things being said in the claim and denying some as a consequence. But human agency does not work this way: either one knows where ethics begins and ends or not at all. In the face of difficulty, for instance, what else is there for an ethical actor? When human choices have reduced to no-choice choices, we understand why an Edwin, a dreamer of stars, would come rise up in a god-forsaken country and call for revenge, for the righting of society's so many wrongs, for the purging of its so many ills, and for the arresting of its atrocities.

The story takes its inspiration from Bertrand Russell who philosophized about the "three passions."

The social reformer famously said: "Three passions simple but overwhelmingly strong, have governed my life: the longing for love, the search for knowledge, and unbearable pity for the suffering of mankind... Love and knowledge, so far as they were possible, led upward toward the heavens. But always pity brought me back to earth."

It appears that these "three passions" take their new form in the "three footprints" alluded to in the story and the technique of parallelism begins.

Divided into segments—episodes if you wish—we see here the elements making up the story: (a) heaven, (b) earth, and (c) visitation.

Let's extend the parallelism: we long for heaven, we come to knowledge on earth if we are lucky enough, and then we go back to earth to put a closure to an unfinished business such as memory, self-actualization, rebellion, inaction, and inability to understand in the beginning.

We follow the story: three young boys—cousins—dream of better things, of the good life, of the stars. Edwin decides to stay with his grandparents in Baybayyabas. Anong enrolls at the Philippine Military Academy to become a soldier. Hil goes to the university to become a writer.

The tragedy—the murder of Edwin's parents—was kept hidden from him for a long time. He boils over. Revenge gnaws at his soul and heart and spirit.

And then he joins a rebel group.

It was not a reactionary act on the part of Edwin: it was simply basic justice. His desire to inflict retribution is both personal and political. The knowledge about his mother and father succumbing to the brutality of others, his mother being raped, his father witnessing that rape, was just not normal human beings do. To add insult to injury, the perpetrators who are "close to the mayor" of the town, go scot-free, moving around in the town as if nothing happened.

And then he dies, Edwin, the one with the idealism, the one who has the clarity of mind about what, in fact, is happening to a society that is plain and simple unjust, its system of procedural justice reserved for those who can afford lawyers on the take and political leaders on the payroll of the moneyed.

The last—the "visitation" by Hil—is literally a return to the same barrio where the three began to follow the stars, dream big dreams, perhaps, like many young boys in the rural areas of the Ilocos, stretch their index finger and follow all the airplanes that pass by their piece of sky.

As a writer, Hil Garcia becomes the key actor in the last episode of the story.

He remembers.

And he comes to know a lot of things.

And then he finds a way to memorialize Edwin.

He gets to become a writer, his childhood ambition.

And a good writer, he says. And then this story is left with him to write and let the public know about what Edwin his cousin had to go through.

In the publication of Edwin's death, a society eager to acknowledge its faults might make amends, grow social conscience, and reform the country's justice system or how justice is being administered.

In many ways, this could be regarded as a "proletarian literature," if by that we mean that sense in which the editors of *Talugading*[8] referred to in their "From the Editors" (Manipud Kadagiti Editor) as "rissik ti proletario" (sliver of the proletarian). The editors talked about this in 1977 at a time when an experimental New Society was offered to a gullible and vulnerable people.

We must note that Constante Casabar had by then been pressured to leave the country because of his proletarian novel, *Those Who Wake Up at Daybreak* ("Dagiti Mariing iti Parbangon").[9]

Pursuit: A Redemptive Vision

One other non-Bannawag style that we see in the works of Lorenzo Sr. is an award-winning story on a family: Abraham Sr., his wife Filipinas

---

[8]   Edilberto H. Angco, Rogelio Aquino, Cristino Inay, and Lorenzo Tabin (eds.), *Talugading: Antolohia Dagiti Sarita nga Ilokano* (Manila: Gumil Filipinas), 1977.

[9]   See, for instance, this volume: Constante Casabar, *Dagiti Mariing iti Parbangon/Silang Magigising sa Madaling Araw* (Quezon City: Ateneo de Manila University Press), 1993.

Isabel, and their five children. "The World Should Stop That People Could Get Off" is a prayer, a wish, a request. It evokes a world spinning, unmindful of the affairs of men, women, and children, unmindful of the abuse of power by those who have it, unmindful of the iniquities that benefit the elite and disenfranchise the already disenfranchised masses of people.

Somewhere here in this story is a subtle dig on the bioethical. We sense here a fundamental question: What do we do when society has become so numb and callous and unhearing? What do we do when the masses have the opportunity to even experience the meaning of "three square meals" but instead are being offered cake to mask off the everydayness of hunger and want?

Abraham Sr., a painter, dabbles beautiful, the ideal. He has inclinations to go philosophical too by trying to understand more fully in the round what several Western existentialist and phenomenological philosophers are talking about life, freedom, and society.

He is trying his best to understand a number of nihilist philosophers like Friedrich Wilhelm Nietzsche. The other branch of existentialism such as the atheistic take of Jean-Paul Sartre's on the nature of man and his life mesmerizes Abraham Sr. the painter. Sartre's repudiation of essentialism makes the painter think. He is led to a theistic existentialist, Soren Kierkegaard, he who talks about the leap of faith by retelling the famous story of Abraham as he was asked by his God to take his son Isaac to the bush and with Isaac himself as the offering.

There is a certain listing of these philosophers in an attempt to link back Abraham Sr.'s gift as a painter. We know that painters paint with ideas, their canvasses another world in blank awaiting peopling.

But there is a caveat here: his wife, Filipinas Isabel, a teacher, has begun to take an active role in the resistance movement against an oppressive ruler, perhaps a despot the country has not seen before, one promising greatness but never delivered anything substantial beyond the lilt of his baritone, the cadence of his lies couched with big but empty words.

A domestic trouble ensues, the husband insisting that the wife would not go to those rallies and demonstrations, and the wife, a

xxxii

LORENZO GARCIA TABIN, SR. AND
SINAMAR A. ROBIANES TABIN, SR.

politicized teacher, telling to his face that he does not go to the market and thus, does not know how people could ever live with their inflated money. Somewhere is that accurate accusation: painters, somehow, live in their idealized world. We extend the same logic to husbands who are not in the know because they do not go to the marker: the money for food can no longer buy enough food.

Filipinas Isabel joins—even serves as one of the heads—of the resistance, her two sons took part too. She is injured, the oppressive ruler leaves and another one takes over. It appears that something came out of the "people revolution" and that both Abraham and Filipinas Isabel settle to a quiet, more laid-back domestic life later on.

We know from this story some unsaid tension in the continuing struggle that the people of the Philippines continue to witness until today despite what we might term as two "successful" people revolution, the first to oust a dictator (Ferdinand Marcos) and the second to oust an jueteng-compromised, celluloid-charged "people of the masses" (Erap Estrada). We know for certain now that both media-hyped revolutions did not produce a just and fair society. Instead, these paved the way for the full return of the same oligarchs that have ruled the country for generations, the same oligarchs who sing the songs of democracy but only in their name. The deficits of that democracy are too evident to dismiss, with a class-oriented campaign against drug addiction and with poverty incidences risings.

Final Note: The Place of Tabin and Tabin in Ilokano Literature

The place of Lorenzo Sr. and Sinamar is secure in Ilokano literature. When that Ilokano literary history will be written, their works would stand out for a number of things: these sixty-four short stories have documented the lives of Ilokanos wherever they are. Why "exile" and "diaspora" are not easy narratives as these require the ability to go epoche, that act of suspending our judgement in order to have a grasp of the sense of things.

All these stories lead us to a way of deploying short fiction as a way to offer a critique of society, with Sinamar, clearly, going the route of what may be termed "the romantic" mode and with Lorenzo Sr. embellishing his stories with ethnographic data. There is that didactic tendency in the Sinamar works while Lorenzo Sr.'s work can afford to be open to other ways of leaving behind some lessons about life by simply suggesting. We know the reason: Sinamar was, and continues to be a teacher and that is that. Lorenzo Sr. is more experimental, exploratory. His life as an immigrant reveals this streak in his works. A re-reading of his narrative as an immigrant in the United States, for instance, proves to us that we can tease out some aspects of his life in his own biography and in his reading of his Ilocos society. It does not matter that that Ilocos society of small-town life has moved to the big city of blighted Manila to the an even bigger metropolis we call Los Angeles and then eventually, Salt Lake.

The sense of the redemptive, it seems to me now, is in the parabolic structure of the Sinamar stories. The structure has followed the style of writing found in "Ilokano popular cultural form" as established in post-World War II Ilocos and as used in a number of popular magazines.

Lorenzo Sr., on the other hand, has demonstrated his ability to navigate the waters of two rivers: one that follows that same popular form and the other, one that continues to challenge that form to open up a new way of telling a good story.

Here, I am reminded of what J.R.R. Tolkien has said about redemption: "We all long for Eden, and we are constantly glimpsing it: our whole nature at its best and least corrupted, its gentlest and most human, is still soaked with the sense of exile." The sense of exile of our human nature is clearly mapped in these stories of Lorenzo Sr. and Sinamar. I can only hope that the current and future Ilokano fictionists will learn from their works.

University of Hawaii at Manoa
Honolulu, April 2019

1

SINAMAR A. ROBIANES TABIN, SR.

Jackfruit

I WENT directly where the jackfruit tree was upon arriving from the village store. Huh, its ripe fruit has gone! And there was still a sap from where it was plucked. Did Uncle Mateo drop by?

I went to wake up father whose legs were widely spread apart while snoring under the old tamarind tree. He jolted out of bed and rubbed his eyes.

"Where did you put the fruit of my Jackfruit, *'Tang?*" I asked.

"What are you talking about? I haven't found a rope to tie it. I felt asleep waiting for you."

"These are the things you asked me to buy," I threw the stuffs on his lap. "Who picked my jackfruit?"

"I felt asleep, I said!"

"If you did not send me for an errand, it was not lost!"

"Silly, if you did not stay there too long, then you should have had protected it!"

"But you were the one who was here!" I was on the verge of crying when we went under the jackfruit tree. "If you are not a sleeper, it should have not been lost!"

My father snorts. "Go ask in Eden's place. Her children were here while I was sleeping… Most probably it was wisely done by her naughty children."

Might probably. I passed by Fred and some other children when I went to the village store. Fred is *Manang*[1] Eden's son, and her brother *Manong*[2] Asiong is Lito's father.

Manang Eden was waggling her feet while seating on the mortar beside their kitchen when I arrived at their place. *Manong* Asiong was at the highest branch of an orange tree.

"*Manang*, where is Fred?"

"Why?" she even not bothers to look at me.

"I just want to ask him if they happen to see who got the fruit of my jackfruit. It was still there after lunch, when I followed my mother at the *Balo*[3]Andiang's place. When I arrived, it was gone."

She stopped her waggling. She stared at me sharply. "You're suspecting Fred, is that what you mean?"

"I passed them by with Lito… including other children when I went eastward, *Manang*."

"Oy, oy, oy, Marissa!" her chin and her eyebrows moved at the same time. "Shame on you suspecting my son! For God's sake, they had not skipped any meal time…"

"I am not exactly pointing directly to Fred, *Manang*. I am just asking."

"That's really your attitude when you lost anything! Just a little bit, nothing but my children!"

"If nothing lost, I should have not asking," I felt heated.

"You must look around first before making allegation!" she acted in arm akimbo.

I left her alone before arguing like what happened when I found my new chemise in her possession. I followed the low field towards Lito's place. *Manang* Antin, Lito's mother, was home catching lies with other women at their staircase. I told my purpose. *Manong* Asiong was not home.

---

[1]   *Manang,* an address given to an older sister, or to an elder woman.

[2]   *Manong,* an address given to an older brother, or to an elder man.

[3]   *Balo,* widower.

"Lito is not here, *Ipag*[4]. Serking came to fetch him to climb some coconut trees at the seashore. About the fruit of your jackfruit, my son is afraid to do such. He is a very good boy!"

Hope they have the worst diarrhea! I swore when I went home. My father was seating under the jackfruit tree.

"If you did not send me an errand, and you did not sleep, it should never be lost. Good if it was not its first fruit," I started sucking up by the nasal.

Uncle Mateo arrived. He is the captain in our village. He was holding a paper. He asked why I was crying. My father told him the reason. My uncle looked up the branch where the fruit was plucked.

"They probably know your being tightfisted. That you'll never share them," he said.

From the south, where the place of thick ipilipil tree is, four children were running toward where we were. Uncle beckoned them to come forward. "Do you know where the fruit of the jackfruit tree of your *Nana* Marissa, boys?" his question was low and kind.

The three looked at each other. The youngest pointed a place. "There, *Lolo*[5]. *Manong* Fred and Lito are watching for it. We are going to get a bolo to open it…"

Uncle did not let the four boys go.

"Let me give a lesson to these damn boys. They are shameful. They were proven who groped the *baki*[6] of Zoilo… Good if nobody knows that they are my grandsons…"

"Punish them the hardest!" My voice grumbled.

"Now go to the house," my father looked at me. "Your uncle and I will be responsible."

---

4   *Ipag*, sister-in-law.

5   *Lolo*, grandfather.

6   *Baki*, an open worked basket with a flat square bottom and round rim; for hens to lay eggs.

I followed him mumbling. I readied the door bar. I seated at the bench by the window. I waited for uncle and father who followed Fred and Lito at the ipilipil area.

They finally arrived! I went down the stairs. Father noticed the door bar I held as a cane.

"I told you go to the house and let me and your uncle give a lesson for these," father said.

They sat calmly side by side under the tamarind tree. Uncle Mateo was in between Fred and Lito. Father was squatting while others surrounded them.

"So, you tried to pluck the fruit of the jackfruit of your *Nana* Marissa, Fred?" my uncle started. "Then you planned to tell afterwards…"

"Yes, *lol*… oh, no, *Lolo*. It was Lito's. He tempted me."

"It was your idea when Auntie Marissa was gone."

"It should be better if you told her in advance," uncle was still calm. "Okay, Fred, go get a rope in your house, and the kerosene can your mother uses to measure rice bran."

Fred ran away then came back with the rope and the kerosene can.

Uncle Mateo tied the jackfruit with the rope after measuring with Fred and Lito.

"This jackfruit is also good as a necklet, right children? Try it, Fred."

Fred hesitated. Uncle Mateo got mad. "Collar it!" he positioned it on Fred's neck. "Hold it with your two arms…"

The children laughed at Fred after collaring the jackfruit. Father smiled one sided. Fred was teary.

Uncle pointed at Lito. "You, it is your charge to bit that can, okay?" he yelled at the boy. "We will go around in procession with the jackfruit as your necklet while shouting: *you children like us, don't do what we did who stole…*"

My heart bits faster. This is not good. The parents will be mad at me.

"We are going to do this, yes, because you won't stop stealing. You had promised many times. I am tired wrenching your ears. So, it is better for us to go around in procession… Common, let us go because there are other things that we do with your *Lolo*!"

Fred hesitated. But uncle got a stick for beating. "Shout. Shout what I taught you," he ordered Lito. He tried. "Make it louder! Like what you were shouting when you are playing!"

I stayed foot. My father followed. Like what I was thinking, Uncle Mateo stopped by the front yard of *Manang* Eden. She was very mad.

"They are your grandchildren. You were not sickened to go with them in procession!" *Manang* Eden said. She was with *Manong* Ikko.

"You do not have an assistant to teach your hardheaded children other than me," my uncle answered. "I would rather appreciate the people who will know that the stealers are my grandchildren, and I punish them, like this..."

"Why did you allow that to happen, '*Tang*?" I asked my father when he came back.

"Let those hardheaded children learn their lesson!"

"But the parents will get mad at you..."

"They should be thankful, if their children would learn their lesson..."

"But the fruit of my jackfruit, '*tang*... where will they bring it?"

"Talk to your uncle."

My mother arrives. She was in a hurry.

"What stupidity had you done, Anno?"

"Why were you so late, *Baket*[7]?" asked *Tatang*[8].

"Why did you let the children do a procession? The people are blaming you that much. Asiong was so mad. His wife was crying. Are you not ashamed what the children doing while shouting along the street while beating the can? The more so with your brother who is a captain of the village!"

"Don't give me a sermon, for your sake... Where had you gone for you were no place to look for!"

---

[7] *Baket,* a general term for an old woman; an address of endearment given to a wife.

[8] *Tatang,* father.

"If you are not really a stupid old man!" and she faced me. "Did you tell your father what to do?"

"Ah, no, 'nang. Uncle did…" I explained what happened.

"Even then. It should not be that way. It's shameful! It's shameful!" mother kept on saying.

In *Manang* Eden's place, I heard her cursing repeatedly and yelling about the past.

"They don't even remember my obedience to what they want me to do. I washed a lot of their clothes without paying me! They are rude! They are rude!"

"If you are not coddling your son, he should not be like that. You are not allowing me to teach…"

"You love your son to go in procession? If Marissa was in that situation, I don't know what uncle's feeling will be!"

"See what you and your father did?" my mother looked at me with wide-opened eyes.

"*Manang* Eden is talking about the pass and she forgot that she used to run here when they do not have something to cook!"

"Stop your mouth! Do you think you are still a child?"

I went down. From the east, *Manong* Asiong and *Manang* Antin were fast approaching.

"How dare what you did, uncle? You should have asked me to repay the mistake of my son. Or you let us punish him, not like what you did. You put us in so shameful situation!" *Manong* Asiong said at ones.

"This is what happened, Asiong," Father was calm. "Do you want your son to transform or not?"

"But it should not be that way… He was not the promoter. He was only with a group, uncle."

Manang Eden should have noticed what was happening so she approached them like an empress.

"How much, Marissa, is your jackfruit?" she said face to face.

"I don't need your money, *Manang!*"

"That's who you are after getting something from us!" she faces my father. "How much is the jackfruit, Uncle?" she gropes the pocket of her blouse and counted some wrinkled peso bills.

"Keep that, Eden. There are more things that you could use that."

"Don't be like that if you do not have any place to ask for something to cook except here!" I added.

"Marissa!" my father looked at me with sharp eyes.

"How much do I owe you?"

"Sum up how much had you not paid since I got enough mind!"

"You're acting like who you are, you egghead! You've forgotten that I washed your clothes when you were still with mucus running from your nose and your mother was sick?"

I want to attack her, but Uncle Mateo and his companion arrived. The exhaustion of Fred and Lito was evident, more so when they saw their parents. Lito's arms were so reddish holding the jackfruit fruit. Uncle fanned his hat.

"And you are all here…" Uncle said.

"They came to confront, Uncle!" I said.

"You removed our right like parents, Uncle. It was so difficult for me that you bring my son in a procession…"

Uncle's molar hardened. "It is more painful for me if your children grow wicked and hardheaded, Asiong. As much as possible, while I am the barrio captain, I don't like my grandchildren and relatives to do something against the law…"

Manang Eden was about to go without asking permission. Uncle noticed.

"Don't go away, you, Eden! We'll talk something very important," the order was commanding. "You, Marissa, go get a bolo and oil, so that this jackfruit will be cut…"

I followed the order.

Uncle cut the jackfruit into pieces. Its flesh was so fat and smells good! Uncle hold one each of his hands. He offered to *Manong* Asiong and *Manang* Eden.

"Taste what your children labored for!"

"I don't have the appetite to eat, Uncle. Give it to them!" and *Manong* Asiong and *Manang* Eden tried to hold their children.

"Get it…" Uncle was getting mad. "Don't you accept it?"

Manong Asiong and *Manang* Eden accepted the offer. *Manang* Antin was wiping her tears.

Uncle offered Fred and Lito each.

"Okay, go home! When you do it again, I will not just bring you to procession. I will hang you in the plaza…"

Uncle pick up the remaining slice when the family had gone. He laid in his mouth. They were laughing with my father afterwards.

Mother remained mumbling in the house.

I was left swallowing my saliva! –0

Bannawag: May 4, 1970; *translation completed:* June 25, 2018.

Once A Lourdes

L OURDES closed her eyes. Tightly. But she could not delete the thoughts which kept hunting her whenever she was alone. She cupped both her ears and buried her head into her pillows like she wanted to exorcise her thoughts. But even this did not help any.

Eventually she turned up and opened her eyes. She stared at the dirt-stained ceiling. Outside, she could hear the infectious rhythm of the jukebox and the roar of passing motor vehicles. She tried to ignore these. But in her mind, she could again see accusing fingers pointing at her. She could hear wild laughter. The sounds of clinking wineglasses. All these brought her back to the club she used to work as hostess. The soft melody and he whispers of a tipsy customer blend to create a romantic ambiance. Work and like that for six hours. After work, she would shift to a more decent dress revealing a very natural beauty: a well-carved nose, hazel eyes, rosy complexion, long fresh tresses, a lovely face, and a body molded for the gods. She would then pick up her books, and moments after would be in the premises of the university where she was earning a commerce degree.

She turned on one side. She saw the bed of Amore. Her young lady roommate had just gone out. It was only now that the latter had time to go out and buy her groceries and other needs. She had been very busy doing her term papers during the last few days. Amore had asked Lourdes to join her at the supermarket, but she was not simply in the mood. She wanted peace and quiet to herself. There was longing for home in her heart but there was an unmistakable hesitation to do any daydreaming. She was afraid to see a crumbing barrio house she could not bear watching a hunchback mother following muddy trails, bare feet, peddling fish and such.

Lourdes bit her lip. Her mother did not know about the clinking wineglasses, the soft melodies, and her place of work. She did not know Vener, the bank manager. She did not know Edgar, the navy man. She of course knew Rommel because he was her classmate in high school back in the province. Her mother liked Rommel. She said he a respectful and strong.

Lourdes stayed with relatives when she was new in the city. She didn't mind the small and dingy room assigned to her. She persevered. Sometimes she had to be satisfied with simply having fermented fish for viand. A hunchback mother's counsels were all insulted in her mind and heart: "Be patient, my child. Study hard. Things can be difficult but if you work hard enough ad have a strong determination you will surely succeed."

But Lourdes left her relative's house after two years. She was hurt by frequent snide by her aunt. Why was she not getting a job and then studying at night so that she would not be a burden to her mother? Why she was not joining the movies sine after all she looked very much like a movie actress. He felt flattered. But she knew the risks in the life of an actress especially for a country-bred like her. Surely, her mother wouldn't approve of such an occupation.

Rommel used to visit her then, although these were far in between. The reason, she thought, was the distance between his boarding house and hers. They were also strict in the university where he was studying. She was also aware that Rommel was a scholar.

Lourdes' daydreaming was interrupted by soft and gentle music. She looked out the window. Beggars. There were three of them. A child, a teen, and an old man. The old man who was strumming the guitar was bind. The teen was singing while the child stretched out a basket.

Lourdes saw her face in the child when she was that age. She looked very much like that when her mother would not be able to give her money with which to pay a required contribution in school. She would go to her maternal relatives for help. Thus, she promised herself that when she was old enough to have a job, she would return their kindness. That was why during her last visit to their barrio, she brought home several boxes of giveaways for them. But her own mother did not accept the beautiful blouse, skirt and slippers she had bought for her.

"I cannot wear those while selling fish, my child. I'd be a lot happier if you simply finished your course and started a career."

Her mother wept when Lourdes told her that she didn't have to worry about her school expenses anymore because she was already earning enough.

"Please, my child. Stop that thing you call a job. I can still support you. I would die from the rumors I'm hearing. They say that you are becoming worse than where you came from; that you were now living the life of the loved child that you were!"

No! No! She screamed in her thoughts.

The beggars finished singing. They were waiting for a dole out. A fat, haughty woman came out hands akimbo. She shouted at the three. "I don't even have anything with which to buy my own food, just where do you think can I get something to give you? You're all so husky. Why don't you look around for jobs?"

Lourdes fished something from her pocket. A whole fifty-peso bill. She hurried down to give the money. But the three were already gone.

The young lady suddenly felt chest pains. It was only three days ago when she and Vener met. He was inviting her to go to Baguio with him. He gave her a check in the amount of seven hundred pesos. Pay all your dues in school, he said. Until now, she did not know what to do with the remaining amount she could not possibly send it to her mother. The blind old woman would not surely accept it.

Lourdes could not understand why she hated herself today. She was comparing the old Lourdes who stayed in a small and dingy room with the present Lourdes ho no longer seemed familiar with the hardships of life.

Use your brains. Don't be weakling. These days, money was most important. This was what all the rich tell her. And she fell for it. She worked in the pub house. She ignored the touch and kisses and embraces of the men looking for momentary bliss. She revolted at first, especially when she would see the image of her hunchbacked mother in the wineglasses which she served to customers. But there was no other job available. Eventually, with all the unending ridicule and sneers of her own relative, she moved to another place.

I am still the old Lourdes! she insisted. I know my identity. I haven't forgotten where I came from. I am true to my promise to my mother. I am trying hard to attain it. I am not bad. It's true that I have sinned. So, what, I'm only a mortal of flesh and blood.

It's been a long time since Lourdes and Rommel had seen each other. Anyway, she really didn't care to hear any news about him since she transferred to a new boarding house. More so when she met Edgar, who, she thought, could help realize her desire to go abroad. But their affair lasted only during the short period that Edgar was in the country. Edgar would arrive before her graduation to work on her papers to go to California where he was based.

During this time—her last semester in school—she resolved she would reform. She left her former boarding house to share a room with Amore. The room was small but decent. It was quiet here. She could concentrate well in her studies. She had introduced herself to Amore as a regular student. Amore was very much like her. They were pursuing the same course, although Amore was only in her second year. Their schools were close to one another.

Lourdes met Vener just a few days previously. The latter did not yet know of her new boarding house, but he waited for her in school. Vener had told her a job was waiting for her in his bank. She could have this as soon as she graduated. It was during this meeting that Vener gave Lourdes the check for seven hundred pesos. She could not say no when Vener invited her. They spent a few hours in a motel together.

I am not that bad, she reassured herself in her mind it was not her dream to marry Vener. She did not even believe he was a bachelor. The truth was they did not yet know each other that well. It was Edgar who was always in her dreams. She wanted to go away. She wanted to live in California. She needed to leave the bitter memories which were haunting her. They were to marry when Edgar returned to the Philippines. They were to go together to Ilocos and have their wedding there. They would go to America. They would arrange for her mother to join them there.

She did not like Vener, but she could not tell him directly how she felt. She only needed him for his money. Hat she felt for Edgar was different.

The alarm clock rang. It was already five o'clock in the afternoon. Outside, the jukeboxes went wild. The street lights were already lit.

Amore arrived, he face-ashen. One could easily tell she was almost in tears. Lourdes knew her roommate would not say anything unless asked.

"What happened?"

"My mother" she sighed. "I met a townmate just now and I was told mom's bleeding has recurred. My aunt wants me to buy some medicine from my allowance, but I've spent all of it already."

Amore never told her of her mother's ailment before.

"Has you mother been ill for a long time now?"

"She got it from her laundering. But she got well already. It must have recurred because she was working too hard again. Even my aunts tell her not to, but she still works so hard. She was so concerned with my studies. She says she'll be able to relax only after I'm done with college. My father's gone, that's why. He died when I was still in my mother's womb." Amore wiped away her tears.

Amore took out what she bought. "If only it were possible to return these so that I could buy the medicine or my mother. . ."

Lourdes breathed deeply. Why did Amore not tell her this before? But, she herself has not told Amore the secrets of her life. Small talk was all that transpired between them.

She was touched by Amore' crying. She slipped her hand into her pocket. The fifty-peso bill was still there.

"Don't cry. Go buy the medicine your mother needs and send it immediately. Or, you might wish to bring it yourself if you have nothing important to do in school!" Lourdes opened her bag. She picked out two twenty-peso bills more.

Amore wiped away her tears. She stared at Lourdes. "How about you? You also need the money. You were graduating. . ."

"That's not what's important. Take it and don't think about having to pay for it. Pay it when you can."

A joyful Amore kissed her. "You're an angel I can never repay your kindness. But I'll surely tell my mother how good you have been to us."

Lourdes felt like a thorn was plucked off her chest. She could breathe easier now. Again, she saw her own mother in her thoughts. The blind old woman was looking more upright. There was a faint smile across her face.

When she will go home, Lourdes thought, she'll have for her mother a gift, not just her diploma. –0

Bannawag, April 24, 1972; *translated by* Lorenzo R. Tabin, II.

Testament

THIS is a different day to Criselda Robillos. She had been waiting this day since their father died. The decision of her two step-sisters with her father, Shalina and Ada, was too painful, despite that she expected this even when their father late Don Antero had been bedridden.

"Get out! You have no right to own any little portion left of the late *Tatang* because you are only his sputtered blood to the Robillos! Flotsam! Illegitimate!"

This was straight from the mouth of Shalina, the eldest, after the ninth day of the death of their father.

Attorney Rafael, who was the lawyer of their father, said: "You can't just leave, Criselda. They are the ones who do not have any more share because they all have taken their shares and they are both married. Even though you are illegitimate, as they said, you grew up under your father's care. You took care of him until the last breath of his life. If they are jealous because you finished your education, it was their fault for they did not pursue their studies when your father told them to do so. Don't go away, whatever they say. You may go away, when you wish to, because your mother is still alive, but after my reading the testament."

Criselda breathed heavily. Her eyes were focused to the open gate of the spacious courtyard. She was guessing who will come first—if it be Shalina, Ada or Attorney Rafael.

She passed on her attention to the big watch on top of the ladder. It was still early, she weighed up. She examined the archaic furniture in the living room. She remembered the day when Shalina and Ada were debating which of these will they get. Shalina will get more because she has the bigger house than Ada. They really intended that Criselda could hear their conversation. Just take whatever you want! she almost yelled out… Instead she asked: "Who will then get this old house, *Manang*?" she aimed her question to Shalina being the eldest and arguably knows how to determine what to do to all their father had left.

"Huh, I'll order to be torn down. Then make it a pigpen!"

Will this old house become only a pigpen, this house which their father repeatedly telling her that it brought different kinds of good things in his life? 'Don't ever let this house be destroyed, Elda. One of you will renovate it and make it better, or even you when you get enough money. It will be a good place for your gatherings during any anniversary celebration…

She reminded to Shalina. In return she yelled at her.

"Hoy, hoy, you have no business to whatever I like to do. *Tatang* would never know what I will do because he had been dead!"

Criselda's reminiscing was cut off when *Nana*[9] Sayyang, one of the helpers came in. She asked a little cash to buy additional food.

"Please take care of the menu, *Manang*, okay?" Criselda said. "I have a slight headache…"

The helper laughed. "Don't worry, *Ading*[10]. I'll be responsible for Attorney's favorite dish."

She cleaned and fixed the living room. She changed the curtains. Afterwards, she went to her room. A big and old suitcase was on a small table. She opened it. She found her big picture wearing toga she inserted inside the cover of the suitcase. She brought out from the back of the picture an envelope containing some documents. She closed the suitcase then read the documents one by one. She put the documents inside the drawer of the small table when she was satisfied.

---

[9]   *Nana,* an address given to an elderly woman.

[10]   *Ading,* an address given to a younger brother or sister, or whoever is younger.

Now that she was laying down, she envisaged ones more the past. The days when she studied hard through the guidance of their old father. "You have to study harder for I want you to finish your studies, unlike your sisters. They did not have interest. They instead decided to get married early."

The time that Shalina and Ada mumbled against their father. "It's not a joke to send somebody to college, *Tatang*..."

"Just let it be, for I want her to reach the issues you failed to do. She got brains!"

"My goodness, that flotsam? That's why she is arrogant because you are always on her side."

Both Shalina and Ada are now rich. They are the richest family in their town. But when Criselda finished her studies, they never gave her anything. They blamed Criselda for telling their father not to go and stay with them. But their father reasoned out that he did not like to live with them because they were too busy, and their husbands shown disrespectful to him.

When Shalina dropped by yesterday, she asked Criselda when she's living. "If you think that neither me or Ada will bring you to stay with us, no way, go wherever you like to go. And remember, you have no right to listen to the testament that Attorney Rafael will read because nothing will be given to you."

She smiled. She knew the content of the testament. She was beside her late father when he was dictating the content and he promised Criselda not to divulge to anybody. She had been thinking about the effect of the testament to the two. They would be very mad at her, with bitter curse, for she knew very well their attitude.

She is just a particle in the eyes of Shalina and Ada. She knew that upon the death of their father, everything will be different especially when they find out the content of the testament. She could foresee the distant future.

To Criselda, freedom is the most important. She could not forget what their father said. "All of these riches came from the hardships that I labored for. My parents did not give me anything except my life!"

She did not notice the time that had passed by. She was awakened by the chattering outside. She noticed those who arrived. It was Shalina and Ada together with their husbands and children. They were gabbing and laughing. If Criselda was not mistaken the husbands brought bottles of wine for lunch.

She heard the question from *Nana* Sayyang. "What? She is still here?"

Criselda got up from bed. She opened her suitcase. She brought out some dress and changed. She closed the luggage. She tested the weight of the suitcase.

There were footsteps coming up.

Criselda peeped at the window. She saw the two husbands holding their lighted tobacco under the tamarind tree at the yard. Criselda went out. She saw Shalina. Their eyes met. Shalina snorted and went to the kitchen. Ada also went upstairs wearing a very tight outfit and overly thick makeup as if she's going to a party.

"I thought you are not here anymore. Your mother had been waiting for you for a long time. If you think that there is a portion intended for you in the testament, no way. You have no right," Ada smiled sarcastically.

"Attorney Rafael told me not to leave without hearing him read the testament of father."

"What?" Ada's lips opened so widely.

Criselda went into the room.

She needs to leave before Attorney Rafael arrives.

She dressed up. Simple. She became more beautiful with her black blouse. She brought out the envelope that she put in the drawer. She read it again. Longer. She put the documents back in the envelope when she was contented with what was inscribed.

She looked out down one more time. Shalina and Ada were already beside their husbands. They were waiting for Attorney Rafael.

She carried the suitcase. She carefully and slowly walked toward the stairs. She went directly under the tamarind tree. She holds her feelings. She forced herself to smile. She handed the envelope to Shalina.

"W-what's this?" Shalina's eyebrows met.

"Father made a mistake in preparing a testament, *Manang*. You, being the children of the late *Tatang*, with whom he married, should be the one in the testament. But don't worry. It is in those papers that you are the real owners. I hired another lawyer to prepare the testament. If Attorney Rafael will not accept it, show him these signed documents. I'm living, as you've wished, but take care of this place. You know very well that the late *Tatang* treasured it very much..." She looked at each of the two one by one.

Nobody had uttered a single word. They stared at Criselda in wonder who turned back toward the gateway. –0

Bannawag: August 7, 1972; *translation completed:* June 20, 2018, 2:12 AM.

Aunt Rosa's Banana

THE Mayor's car stops in front of the house. I knew that this banana I am taking cared of was the reason of their visit. I called Auntie Rosa in the house.

The Mayor put his arm around Auntie Rosa's shoulder ones they reach the banana. The banana's three hands were already long despite out only for two weeks. What really was the wonder of this banana? Because it bears fruit without a blossom. There were only five pieces each hand and when it is ripe its fruit will reach the ground.

"Your place Labut, Rosa, is small," the *Apo*[11] Mayor said, "but your banana made it big. It is now very popular in the town proper. What variety is this?"

Auntie Rosa was puzzled what part of her body to scratched. Nobody really knows the name of the banana.

"Hmm, Mayor," Auntie Rosa said, "my daughter forgot to ask her friend who gave it to her. She said it was from the other country."

"Because nobody knows its name, I will baptize it 'Rosa's Banana'."

"Okay, Mayor!" approved by the companions of the mayor.

Auntie Rosa's smile was overly wide. The Mayor patted her shoulder. "Take good care of it and I will advise all the barrio captains to buy some shoots of your banana. We will compete to the Green Revolution contest hoping that we will garner the prize. Its fruit will then be ripe, Rosa!"

---

[11]   *Apo,* a sign of respect given to elders, master.

"That's why don't be mad, Angkuan, when the reason of sending you an errand is about this banana. You will be one to receive an honor in the contest, as mentioned by *Apo* Mayor a while ago," said Auntie Rosa ones the visitors had gone.

"And in the end, there will be no more shoots for us to plant. You always say yes to all whoever ask some, auntie!"

"You need to be wise, Angkuan. I just say yes to make the visitors happy. Nonetheless, the banana is good in bearing shoots. And, we don't ever know if that banana could bring me to where the Mr. President is. I will then see the Palace. And so, the what they call Nayong Pilipino. The Banana of Rosa, and Labut, as well as you, Angkuan, will become popular. Is it not what your dream is to see Manila?"

"That is right, auntie…"

"I am sure we could go there together. And if that happens, we owe it from the banana."

I was able to relax when I finished fixing the fence of the banana. No more visitor after the group of the Mayor.

In the dusk, I burnt the dumped smoothed part of a bamboo just under the fruit to smoke it up.

Our neighbors from the southern side of the road *Nana* Tibang and *Tata*[12] Ayong dropped by. *Tata* Ayong approached me while *Nana* Tibang went directly where Auntie Rosa was culling marunggay leaves for our viand.

"This banana you are watching is lovely, *Barok*[13], for its charmed *Apo* Mayor to visit our village!"

"He praised it that much, *tata*."

"He just flattering you, you know. That's who *Apo* Mayor is."

"He told Auntie Rosa that its fruit will be entered in a contest in Manila hoping to win a prize, *tata*…"

"Don't believe him!"

---

12   *Tata,* an address given to an uncle, a middle-aged man.

13   *Barok,* an address given to a son, or to a young man.

Many more did *Tata* Ayong dissuasion. I ignored all of them. He went where *Nana* Tibang and Aunt Rosa were.

"It was so uplifting how your plant banana made to all the visiting people, right, Rosa," *Tata* Ayong smiled one sided, "for even the Mayor who did not visit here for quite some time visited."

"I did not ask them to come and see my plant, *Manong*. But whenever what *Apo* Mayor said become materialized that it will be entered in a Green Revolution contest when it be ripened and wins, will it not be an honor to our poor village?"

"There are more beautiful and bigger bearing fruit bananas somewhere in the south…"

"According to my daughter in Manila, it does not taste good. It is sour like a *damilig*[14]!" followed through by *Nana* Tibang.

"You are right, *ipag*," catches *Tata* Ayong. "Same to what my niece in Sto. Domingo said. Its extra length size is just mystifying; my banana plants *tumok*[15] and *asukar* are far sweeter."

"It is difficult to say that because both of us had not been eaten a fruit of that kind of banana," countered Auntie Rosa. "If ever that will be the case, so be it."

"Those who are ordering shoots will blame themselves," *Nana* Tibang said.

"What's then your business about it," frowned Auntie Rosa.

"It is just a matter of idea, Rosa, natural to good neighboring," *Nana* Tibang said. "Are you mad?"

"It is not my attitude to get mad with other people, *Manang*. I am just countering you back."

"Okay, let's forget everything, *Adi*[16]," *Tata* Asiong said. "It will be good if your banana will give honor to Labut!"

---

[14]   *Damilig,* a variety of thick-skinned yellow banana.

[15]   *Tumok,* a kind of banana which trunk is short, but fruit is long and remains green when ripe.

[16]   *Adi,* an address given to a younger brother or sister, or anybody younger than oneself.

I thought the two stays longer based to their attitude when they come visit but they bid farewell when I went inside.

"Those envied the visit of *Apo* Mayor," I said to Auntie Rosa when we sit for our dinner.

"I really don't know why they are like that. Ignore them. Just plant whatever seed that could be planted. Remember that when I brought home the banana, you insisted that it will never get into life and bear a fruit, but see what happens…"

I satiated on the bamboo bed outside after our launch. I watched the shrouded surroundings. When will it be, Angkuan, that you come out from Labut? Will it be the banana of your Auntie Rosa the real cause of your getting you out to Manila?

There were still many who turns up to visit the banana. If I were to charge them five cents each, I could have saved a lot. But the thing is, Auntie Rosa was always busy outside because she was our bread winner. I was always the responsible accepting the visitors. After almost a month, the fruit of the banana became so fat and very long. They were more than two feet each and the trunk had a difficulty of handling them. By watering it in every afternoon, there came out a lot of shots.

I would rather not to fence the well, but Auntie Rosa was always telling me to do so. In one afternoon, *Nana* Tibang dropped by again where the banana was.

"I supposed, Angkuan, you could not wait its fruit to become ripe," she said.

"Why, *nana*?"

"Well, just mark my word."

"Unless you tell somebody to steal or cut it down, *nana*."

"Silly, no stealer in our blood!"

"I am just answering you, *nana*… I am just wondering, because if there is good for your neighbors, you are always there to counter out!"

It was late dusk when Auntie Rosa arrived home. She was smiling widely telling us about the result of her business. The mayor met her because there was a barrio captain meeting in town, so he invited her. The mayor told the captains about the banana. There will be an induction to be done in the nearby village the coming Sunday and the

Mayor told Auntie Rosa to attend. The Mayor will also send a reporter to interview Auntie Rosa.

"Mark my word, Angkuan, our banana will garner a prize from the Palace. Not only that, we will reach Manila without a single cent to spend because it will all be free…"

I am not used of attending inductions or ballroom dancing, because I am belittling myself that much, but I was encouraged by the invitation of Auntie Rosa. She even told me to prepare for a song just in case she would be asked to render a piece, and I will be her substitute.

The induction was illustrious. There were a lot of ladies. The barrio captains of villages were also present. Including the Mayor.

Dancing was in between. The Mayor was serious on planting activity. That was an order from Manila. The prize was big, and it was unbelievable. Not only by the hundred but in thousands. It was really good time when you win the prize.

I rendered songs the following days accompanied by the robustness of my plants especially the fruit of the banana. As requested by the Mayor, Auntie Rosa had given each barrio captains a shoot. She did not accept their payment.

"It will be my pleasure if you could augment their number, Captain," Auntie Rosa just told them. "And your tribute by including our poor village."

"Even just for buying a cigarette, Aunt," I countered Auntie Rosa.

"There will be more prizes, don't worry, Angkuan."

Since the banana was good in producing shoots, even I had transplanted for ours, Auntie Rosa even shared our neighbors a shoot each. But *Tata* Ayong and *Nana* Tibang refused the offer. They had the same reasoning. They will get some after testing the fruit and they will be willing to pay for any amount.

The Mayor had not forgotten to drop by when he visited the neighboring villages. He was so happy seeing the length and chubbiness of the fruit.

I counted the days. It will still be more than a month before the judges come as mentioned by the mayor. I was imagining myself flying to Manila.

It became so dark one afternoon. Followed by heavy rain. We learned from the radio of *Nana* Tibang that there was a strong storm coming. I was scared. If storm comes, it will not excuse the plants. More so with the banana. That's why I put a stronghold at the trunk of the banana.

"Watch the banana, Angkuan, watch it," Auntie Rosa repeatedly telling me when the wind starts whipping. "The dream will surely fly away when the banana be destroyed…"

But if bad luck comes, it will surely come. The strong wind stayed for two days and when it stops, every plant in the village were flown away by the storm. Auntie Rosa's banana was dropped down into the ground like the other plants.

Auntie Rosa wailed as if losing a child. *Tata* Ayong grinned widely watching me cutting the leaves and fruit of the banana.

"I was right… I was right," hummed *Nana* Tibang.

I felt like clubbing this old woman.

The Mayor also dropped by. "What a waste. What a waste!" he exclaimed while touching the fruits as big as an arm. "They were not even ready for harvesting."

Auntie Rosa kept on crying.

"Don't feel so bad, Rosa. Anyway, your banana had given a lot of shoots to people and they will awaken the villagers to plant. If no prize to be received right now, there will come more prizes."

My heart was heavy. I hate somebody I don't even know. "Really you don't have a good luck, Angkuan. Nothing really!" I kept telling myself. –0

Bannawag: July 22, 1974; *translation completed:* July 2, 2018.

Court Her To Teach A Lesson

I MET Frances del Carmen at the seminar-workshop for the young blood held in the North. She was the center of attraction in the workshop. She was the most inquisitive among the young blood who attended. She may be considered as the most beautiful girl among the attendees. She was half-blooded.

I am not conversational in this kind of gatherings. Not far from a knocked escargot, as said by Ernie, my companion who attended. That was probably the reason why Frances was attracted, to introduced herself in the last day of the seminar.

"I have not heard any word from you, Brad!" she said.

"Because you had asked all the questions you want to ask, *Ading*[17]!"

She extended her hand. "I am one of your fans. I thought a Jerry Penian is a very old guy, but he is young and still a bachelor!"

"Don't be mistaken, he had begotten a lot outside, *Ading*!" added Ernie.

"I know without a doubt even he does not tell," countered Frances.

"He is the one who got some, *Ading*," I pointed at Ernie. "For me, not even a one following me."

"So, it is still free to follow you if that is the case!" she laughed.

My goodness!

---

[17] *Ading*, see 10.

"It is leap year. If the one whom you are planning to marry in your office learns about it, she will summon you to marry her right away!" Ernie said when Frances moved to the other group of attendees.

I was observing Frances during our ride back to Manila. She was not easily baffled. She loves conversing with the cats.

"Speak up, Honey!" She even goads me. "Come and visit me in my dorm, okay? Or in school…okay? Or maybe I will be the one to visit you in your place, so I could research for my library work…"

She mentioned that she was enrolled at the nuns and priests' school in elementary grade and high school and she was even a scholar at a university she was enrolled in Manila.

"Sweet dreams, Jerry… Goodnight. I'm sure you could write good poems," she said when we got off with Ernie from the bus.

"One click, if you court that girl, *Lakay*," Ernie said using a friendly term *lakay*. "I suppose, if you started from the workshop, she should have been your girlfriend when we were in the bus. She even more beautiful than your Mila. Her body built is for special romancing…"

"Ouch! She is good for courting but not for marrying type! Tatler. She had said what she said, while it was only our first time to meet…"

"She will think you are a slow-witted if you don't court her. She was game. She was challenging your manliness!"

WHAT IF I court her? I don't believe that she has no boyfriend yet in her being tattler and frivolous. If I court her and she accepts me then she will never let me go, then those who got her first will surely laughed at me. One thing more, I already have Mila my officemate. She is the one I am planning to marry. I should have been a married man if she accepted my proposal to wed her because of the other suitors.

"There you'll be tested, *Lakay*," Ernie said one time.

"It is not like Frances whom I want to be my lifetime partner…" I said.

I was caught unaware when Frances visited me in my jobsite the Friday of that week. She was in a rugged attire. She was more attractive in her t-shirt and pants. She wore a jockey cap. Her chicks were rosy because of the heat of the sun. She had a companion. She said she was her classmate. They clipped each under their arms some books and notebooks.

"I have a lot of research works and I remember you. One thing more, I was waiting for your visit, but I waited for nothing," she said.

She even invited me for a party in their dorm that night. She did not leave until I said yes for her invitation.

I was baffled by Frances. She laughed at me and slapped my shoulder when I was at the door of their dorm handling her my gift. The two ladies whom she introduced as her cousins laughed loudly.

"I missed talking with you… You are so conservative, and I want to transform you," Frances said.

"*Manong* Jerry, you may not know Frances well. She is a great collector," added one of the ladies.

"Of course!" Frances pointed out the shelf full of books. "I'm a book collector…"

Not that long a while, there came two young men. They too have gifts on their hands. Frances introduced us to each other.

"We thought we were late but looks like we are kind of early," they said.

Frances smiles and told the two ladies to prepare for dinner.

Ernie did not believe me when I told him the invitation of Frances when we met again.

"Then what are you waiting for? It's so clear that she's already yours! Forget that Mila."

"We are not in vibes."

You are acting like not a man, Jerry, I also uttered to myself. Court her to give a lesson!

I called her one afternoon. She was so excited when I invited her to have a date at the Rizal Park. She even asked me what my favorite food that she could bring for us.

She brought a lot of food. Her dormmates jested us.

"Tie him up properly so, he could not fly off no more…"

"Give him a number, okay…" added the other one.

We sat closely in the taxicab. As if she intentionally strokes her breast to my arm.

While walking toward the benches along the bay, Frances put her arm around my waist.

"Are you also bringing your girlfriend here in Luneta, Jerry?" she asked while we were seating. The seashore was calm. As if the tiny waves were going through the music being played from the open jukeboxes.

"What, it is only now that I came here with you," I said.

"Was she that too conservative and you could not invite her?"

"I don't have a girlfriend."

"Don't tell me to believe you! You are handsome and a writer. And in your office, you are mingling with sexy chicks almost every day…"

"How about you? How many boyfriends have you had?"

"Do you want to be my boyfriend?"

I laughed.

She came closer to me. "You know, Jerry, you are so different to all the guys I knew. Not only tall, dark and handsome, but you are also intelligent. And I really like you for your assets."

She did not resist when I kissed her.

Why was Frances like this? Does she allowed herself to be over and done with this by every man she likes? How about the feelings of the man who becomes her husband? Her parents and her siblings, are they not condemning her?

"I know what you are thinking about, Jerry," she said keeping herself in a distance. "But see, is there no women's lib now? If you men could express your feelings to a woman you care for, why not us? Of course, we felt bad upon learning that this and that is your girlfriend, so we too, we need to express ourselves to counteract, right? For me, three boyfriends are enough to select from…"

"Are you also in favor of the pre-marital sex?"

"If you were the one to select a woman to be your lifetime partner, do you want her to be an experienced woman?"

"Of course, not…"

"That's it." She came closer again.

This will not be replicated again, I promised to myself when I was in my bed.

That made Mila zealous. Despite telling a lie, Frances's letter where she called me 'Darling Sweetheart, Jerry' she got was enough evidence. She requested me to go to her dorm because she was sick.

"If it is true that Frances is not your girlfriend, let's get married right away!" Mila said.

"That issue could not be done right away. You know very well that I am not yet prepared. I don't like you to regret afterwards…"

Ernie visited me one afternoon when he came from his office. He brought with me a letter from Frances.

"The woman was really sincere to you. She is sick. She requested with urgency that you go visit her. She does not like to be brought to the hospital. She said she wants to go only if you accompany her. Her mom had just arrived this morning and was crying. She was so concerned."

The mother of Frances permitted me to go in and sit.

"I am sure you are Jerry whom my daughter was waiting for. Please, persuade her to go to the hospital because she is too weak, my son. She's been like that for a week. My daughter loves you very much."

According to a short story by *Nana* Conchita, Frances was spoiled. She is the youngest among the three sisters, the most beautiful and intelligent. They were so strict to their first two daughters and their strictness gave them a good lesson. That's why when Frances studied in Manila, they gave her enough freedom.

Frances was weak. She smiled when I sat down at the edge of her bed. I held her palm.

"Go to the hospital… See a doctor…" I said.

Her eyes spark. "If you say so, I am willing. Accompany me. You know, I could not forget what you have said in Luneta. I know that was the reason why you were keeping yourself away from me. You were in doubt. But God knows, even though I was so close to opposite sex and not hesitate to say I like them, that does not mean that I am giving my womanhood all the way. No, Jerry. I still know how to protect myself. Not everything is a game."

Frances started crying. And I held her palm tighter. –0

Bannawag: June 28, 1976; *translation completed:* July 3, 2018.

In The Wheel Of Life

M Y cousin Lito, the one Papa toke care and sent to school, had been in my house when I arrived from school. He had grown up to be an adult. I have not seen him for seven years. I was not able to hold my feelings. We embraced each other. My three children were watching. They were both in awe.

"You were lost, I guess," I said after taking a sit.

"Uncle sent me to look for your place, *Manang*[18]. I'm glad that I found it."

"How is *Manang* Sonia?" I intentionally not to ask for Papa.

It took for a while before Lito replied. "S-she is still single, *Manang*. How about *Manong* Cesar, *Manang*?"

"He is still the same old Cesar…"

"Uncle read his published write-up in the Bulletin. He was so excited… He does not hate you anymore. You need to come to attend his birthday on Saturday!"

I was right when the promotion of Cesar from his job was published. Papa will look for us. But why not they looked for us when we were like beggars asking for their help and guidance?

"I am afraid they may be more embarrassed if we come…"

"Uncle had been changed, *Manang*. He is always praying for you. Whenever he is homesick on hearing the pieces you were playing in

---

[18]   *Manang,* big sister, or older woman.

the piano, he calls for a pianist. He was saying his plan to give you his renting apartment in Makati to make *Manong* Cesar's job closer."

"Papa would never do that. *Manang* Sonia does not allow him. They have a promise to me."

"They had changed, *Manang*. He was always saying he is very eager to see his grandchildren…"

Lito bid goodbye afterwards. I did not promise to attend Papa's birthday. It was so clear what they want to show. They are calling us to demonstrate their friends in society and say: "Here is Gloria, my hardheaded daughter and his husband who was in misery but is now an executive."

Even my Papa's friends, they veered away when I got married with Cesar. "Why do you like that misery for there are much better than him courting you?" Cesar was not finished his studies then in commerce while I was already teaching.

As if our wedding then was cursed. Despite our perseverance to work, many challenges came into our lives. I bore children every year. My mother-in-law passed away, so responsibilities were afforded to Cesar to take care his three younger siblings. I owed to all my friends. I made my faced thicker and I used 'life is like a wheel.' Cesar is kind, loving and calm.

I had cooked for our dinner when Cesar arrived home. The children ran after and hang around him and they mentioned Lito.

"We learned that we have a *Lolo*[19], 'Pang. It will be his birthday on Saturday and he is inviting us," Detdet said.

Cesar looked at me. I nodded. "Remember Lito, my cousin they took care and sent to school? Papa sent him to bring the invitation."

"What do you say? Are we going?"

"I don't know… I still remember those…"

"To avoid their idle talk, and hence Papa decided to find where we are, let's go."

---

[19]   *Lolo,* grandfather.

"Ye-he! Ye-he!" the children jumped. "At last, we can meet our *Lolo*! We can meet our *Lolo*!"

"I know what Papa have in mind," I told Cesar when we were in bed. "He wants to see us because of your progress. But if you were not promoted, I don't think he wants to invite us."

"The important is, we'll see each other. Don't show anything unhealthy to those we'll be meeting there more so with Papa and *Manang*."

To have a free time to go and back to Laguna, we should have use Cesar's office car. He did not like to avoid what the people in my relative's place may say that we are now rich. We commuted by bus.

In our way down to Laguna in the day of Saturday, many things coming back and forth in my mind. I was imagining the face of *Manang* Sonia. The last time I met her in the office she was working, as if she was a countess pointing the door. "Why don't you approach your husband's relatives and ask for a loan?"

"My child is sick, *Manang*. Cesar could nothing to do. We had approached all our friends!"

"Sorry. I am following Papa's order. Remember that if you did not marry that misery Ilokano, your life will never be like that. Endure the consequence of what you did!"

In our family, birthday is the most celebrated affair. I know well that Papa will have a lot of visitors.

We arrived early. Seven years feels like just yesterday. The picture of the house I left seemed nothing had changed. Only the plants around changed a little bit.

But not a single car in the front yard.

Cesar advised our children before pressing the doorbell. "Sing in unison 'Happy birthday, *Lolo*.' After that, kiss him!"

"Okay, Pop!" answered Leo, the second to our children.

A young lady looked down from the second floor after Cesar rang the doorbell. She came down and open the gate.

"A-are you *Manong* Cesar and *Manang* Gloria?" she asked.

I nodded. "Where is Papa? And *Manang* Sonia?"

The first thing my eyes looked in the living room was the piano. It was still in its original place, in the corner of the living room. I introduced to my children each hanging picture.

Not long a while, Papa appeared from the stairs. Attending by a servant. He wears a gray hair. Detdet led the singing of "Happy Birthday" and embraced him after taking a seat. Cesar kissed Papa's hand after my embracing him.

Papa had teary eyes. "I've been asking people to look your whereabouts since your *Manang* Sonia had an accident.

"We leave in Nueva Ecija, Papa. We just came back to the city when I was offered a higher position by our company," replied Cesar.

"How about you, Gloria, are you still teaching?"

"Yes, Pop!"

"Okay, that's good, my children, by not abandoned your professions. I was thinking not be able to see you anymore. Your *Manang* Sonia, since she met an accident, she focused her attention helping the needy. It will be late when she gets home."

I inhaled. "It's your birthday today, Pop, but seems no visitors?"

"T-that's true. This gathering is only for us. Lito had just left to get my order from the restaurant. I want the children to be satiated. What can you say, my grandchildren? I have a lot of gifts for you."

"*Lolo*, Mama did never tell me that we have a *Lolo*," countered Joey, our third child.

"Please play the piano, Gloria, while waiting for Lito," Papa said.

My fingers were very eager to hit the keys. I had not forgotten them. The tune was in line. I looked for the composition of "Happy Birthday." The whole living room was full of feeling-melting melody. My tears started dropping!

When I looked up where Papa was, he was so calm with smile on his face. I approached him. I asked him why *Manang* Sonia did not miss work only for today. I was told that it was *Manang*'s idea, so we could be given a time together.

PLEASE visit more often, Gloria, Cesar," Papa said when we bid farewell in the afternoon. He put envelope each of the children's pocket. He also gave me a letter. He gave us two paper bags full of goodies.

"Please come to our house also, *Lolo*, so you could see Mama's plants and Papa's quails," said Leo and Detdet.

I read the letter when we were in our ride home.

I hope, my children, that the small amount I gave to the children have an importance. Deposit it in the bank for their studies. Your Manang Sonia, is not really a member of an organization. She is in a Correctional Institution since killing her boyfriend. I know that what happens to your Manang was the most important lesson God had given me. In my age, I hope you could understand me. I am very grateful for the success Cesar had garnered, and I know that you will never say no when I ask you to manage our small business one day.

Please visit me more often. I missed your children!

I pitied Papa, I exhaled.

"What I told you that life is similar to a wheel was true!" Cesar said. "These are all its part now. Maybe if not because of demeaning me by Papa and *Manang* Sonia and your relatives, I may not be in my present situation. We will visit Papa as long as we have enough time."

We examined the envelops Papa put each in the pockets of the children. Checks amounting a thousand each! –0

Bannawag: March 27, 1978; *translation completed:* July 5, 2018.

Glimmer In The Dark Or How Are You, Dolly?

I WAS having a meeting with Dr. Telesforo Vicente, the psychiatrist here in Pavilion 3, when two able bodied men brought inside a woman who was struggling to free herself because she did not like to go up in the second floor.

"Shame on you! You are all demons! I don't like to go up! I am not insane! No! Ha-ha-haaay. Motherrrr, please help me from these followers of Satan! Hu-hu-huuuu!"

My bosom felt being squeezed. I felt like helping the woman. I hang my eyes unto her until she was hidden. I heard her yelling in the second floor dominating the yelling and singing upstairs.

The other women here in the ground floor were more lenient than the others I saw who were talking with the social workers. Dr. Vicente explained to me that the mind set of these patients were already straight, but they were still under observation. Those who were in the second floor were more serious.

"Excuse me, Mrs." Dr Vicente said when she was called by a social worker who guided the newly arrival.

Somebody touched me. I looked at her. Two women wearing roses uniforms smiled at me and opened their palms in front of me.

"Good afternoon, Ma'am. You are so beautiful, Ma'am. Please give us twenty cents each to buy cigarette!"

A third one approached us. "No, Ma'am. Don't give them," she said.

"Mind your own business! You envious!" one of them stuck her tongue.

"I'll report you to the doctor," the woman entered the other room in a hurry.

The two women left mumbling.

I walked around while waiting for Dr. Vicente. I turned my attention to the isle at the left toward the wide room. Here, beds without mats were in queue. Some patients were laying down. They used their arms as pillows. Some were staring wide-eyed or gamboling as if they were playing along with an immodest music. The stench of putrid urine that merged in the air was upsetting to the nose. It was retching.

I went away from the corridor. Another one smiled at me again and offered her palm.

"Whom are you visiting, Ma'am? Me, I missed a lot a somebody who could visit me. But nobody came even just to peep and asked if I am already okay."

I guessed this one was older than I am. Her hair was tousled. Her eyes were deep but smiling.

I did not know what touched my hand to open my bag and brought out my comb. I offered to her.

"Twenty cents more, Ma'am. I'll just buy a cigarette. Our bed is stinky. It makes me vomit."

"Are your social workers allow you to smoke?" I said after giving her twenty-five cents.

"No, ma'am, as long as we are not asking from them."

She was also calm while conversing.

"How long have you been here, *Manang*?" I asked when she said she was from Ilocos Sur.

"I've been here six months, *ading*. I want to go home but seems my husband and my children had forgotten me."

"Why did they bring you down here?"

"It was a long story. Family problem. My problem with my husband. Problem with my meddler sisters-in-law and parents-in-law. Maybe a mixed up. I lost my control. My mind suddenly black out. I wanted to kill them all…" She gasped then sighed. "But now, not anymore. I am very thankful for the many advices of the social workers and nurses. My mind is now clear."

"What are those similar to you doing?"

"They allow us to wash the uniforms of the patients. They send us an errand and pay us. But I am not collecting my salary. I informed my doctor that I will collect it when I have enough to pay my fare back home."

She took turn asking me why I was in the hospital while I had no relative to visit. I explained that it was a part of my assignment of being in the hospital. I was there to observe and to interview the patients. I need to know the reasons why they brought them down to the hospital.

It was on that moment that one in white passed by. She called the attention of the one I was talking with. "See you, *ading*[20], for they want me to do something," she said.

I watched the patient while moving away. Again, the clamor upstairs was overwhelming. Somebody was yelling something nobody could comprehend. One was singing; the other one was reciting a poem. Somebody was laughing. Another one was hitting a can.

Life! I said to myself. Is this the real world of this hospital?

I saw Dr. Vicente in a distance going down from the second floor. He waved at me. I followed him down to his desk. He was holding a chart.

"This newly arrived patient is number eight in our pavilion, since this morning. If you count the patient arriving every day in more than twenty pavilions of this hospital, you really got a headache. Your being here is timely, Mrs. To the arrival of the number eight patient. You may have her as your case study."

"Thank you, Doc."

"Here is her chart." He handed me the chart. "Read it so you could learn the details you needed about the patient. I just want you not to divulge her real name."

---

[20]   *Ading,* see *10.*

I nodded. I scanned the chart. Dolores de la Fuente is the name of the patient. Dolly was her nickname. She was twenty-six years old. Reason of her illness: in despair with the same sex. I frowned.

I looked at Dr. Vicente who was scanning other charts. "Doc, does it mean, the patient is a tomboy?"

Dr. Vicente smiled. "Sometimes it is difficult to understand that tomboys are also affected with the love they lost from the same sex!"

"Is there any cure for them, Doc?"

He wriggled his head. "That's other's business… if anybody could do it."

After copying the important things that I needed about Dolly, I requested to see her before leaving.

"You can see her, but you cannot go near," the doctor said.

Dr. Vicente gestured the social worker in green uniform. He told her to accompany me upstairs. He wrote something in a piece of paper that I need to give to Mrs. Bueno, the in-charge nurse.

I followed the social worker to the winding stairs. I shivered upon seeing padlocked big bars. The social worker inside unlocked the bars upon knowing that I have a business with Mrs. Bueno.

I was deafened by a mixture of bantering from the wide padlocked rooms. The stench of putrid urine once again affects deeply into my nose—stronger than in the first floor.

Why is it like this? Are these confined here human or beast?

I followed my guide social worker. We entered a clean room. There were five in white inside. Other than the five social workers. There were women and men talking with Mrs. Bueno. They accompanied Dolores de la Fuente. The man was her brother. The girl is her sister-in-law.

From this staff nurses' room, there are windows both sides looking down the wide rooms where many patients confined. From the window in the right side, I recognized Dolly both hands and feet tied on the bed. In the adjacent bed, there was a patient whose arms were tied but not her feet. She was kicking in the air as if she was pedaling. Her dress was held up to her breast. She was no panties. She was singing. Every pedal, she accompanied by her high pitch singing. Another one was acting like talking somebody on the ceiling. Another one was speaking poetically in mixed dialects. Are these people still alive? I said to myself. Why are there people like them? Was it because society is so cruel to them?

My bosom felt being pressed while moving away toward the window to peep again to another window. My eyes were met by smiling widely patients. They tried to reach my hand. Some were walking around.

Mrs. Bueno told me to seat down when the two had gone. I introduced myself and my purpose. She was so kind answering my queries.

"As you can see," she said, "it needs a lot of patience and understanding for them. The complete memories of those who are here had not been back compared to the patients you had seen downstairs. That's why they act like children. Some of them have no panties and they just open themselves. But there is no malice here for all the patients are women same with the social workers and nurses who assist them.

"The only distressing part of it, is that our society had a difficulty of accepting the patients when they are released from here. There were healed patients, that after going home, they still coming back here. Their reason, they are the laughing stuff and being demeaned by their neighbors. The negative effect is that those patients will never be cured but become more severe. Some even decides to stay here until they die. But it is not allowed.

"If there ever be people like you to come and interview or to write something about our patients, nothing we could advice except to tell the people, that patients coming from our facility, be cured and back to normal like the ordinary illnesses. And when they go back to society, they have the right to be loved, taken care of, and be understood."

I expressed my gratitude to Mrs. Bueno for a lot of information I learned about their patients. How they could be maintained and what their most important responsibility for them. I asked her a better place where I could talk to Dolores de la Fuente.

"Come back after a week hoping that her mind will be better," she said.

In my ride back home, it was hard for me to believe that I reached that hospital. This is an assignment given to me by my professor. She likes a case study. I suggested to get one of my pupils in first grade, but

I was challenged by my husband. To make sure that the report I will submit is believable, I need to go to that hospital.

My husband gave me a big smile when I informed him about my experience.

"So, you are brave, and also a solo flight!" he said.

I went back to the hospital after a week, as I had promised to Dr. Vicente. I brought with me a food for Dolly. It was exactly two o'clock when I arrived because I had a class in the morning.

I was happy because Dolly was already one of the patients in the ground floor. The social worker I asked for told me that Dolly's diagnosis had just done. There were three patients being assisted by the staff nurses. I approached Dr. Vicente and asked him a permission to talk with Dolly alone.

"Try if she wants. But I think she could not answer you thoroughly for now," he said.

Dr. Vicente advised a social worker to bring Dolly in.

"You can talk to her in the terrace," the social worker told me. She pointed out a patio in Pavilion 3.

Dolly did not want to follow me in the patio. She was familiarizing me. She accepted my invitation when I told her I am a friend and I have a very important thing to tell her.

She sat calmly. I handed her the food I bought for her.

"Is this from Naty?" she asked. Her deep eyes were probing when she looked at me. "If it is not from her, I don't like to eat it."

I did not know what to say. I just nodded.

I observed Dolly's slow sipping and chewing. Sometimes, she stared with wide-eyed. Her eyes were focused to a distant place.

"How are you, Dolly?" I said.

She looked at me. Her answer was soft. "This... sitting. Drinking. You, who are you? Why do you like to talk with me?"

"How do you feel... is it now okay?" I instead asked.

Her eyes became uneasy. "Yes... I want to go home now. I missed Naty... she is the only one who cared for me. My siblings, they are all demons! Armies of Satan! They allowed them to incarcerate me here... They don't understand me!"

I was dumbfounded. She spoke so fast. English. Tagalog. Spanish. Iluko. I let her talk. Until tired.

I took turn. "How are your parents?"

She jiggled her head weakly. Her eyes watery.

"My mother had passed away. It was long time ago. But… she often visits me. She wants to bring me with her. But I do not want to go with her yet. What I want, to be married with Naty."

"Both of you are women…"

"It could be, why not? I belong to the third generation. If two men can be married, why not with two women?"

"Your father… how is he?" I changed the topic.

She gnashed, and her fists hardened.

"My father was the reason why I became like this… My mother had not passed away early if not because of him!"

"Why?"

"He had a relationship with the youngest sister of my mother."

"Where is your father now?"

"He is in the province… he married another woman."

"He did not marry your aunt?"

"He was scolded by my siblings… She is now in Hawaii. She was married by her boyfriend."

"No more problem then!"

"Wrong! He gave a big problem to my mother. That's the reason why I hate men… and loved my same sex."

I nodded.

"Who is Naty?" I asked.

"She is my ideal woman. She told me she loves me. But… my gifts to her, she gave them to a man… I want to kill them both. But I loved Naty. If she asks forgiveness, I will forgive her… I love Naty. I really love Natyyyyy!"

I let her talk and talk.

"Let's go, I will bring you back inside."

"I'll wait for Naty to come and asks forgiveness. Mother told me last night to visit me today."

"The nurses will scold you."

"I'll strangle them!"

"That's not good... As a friend, I suggest you try your best to become healthier, so I will come and visit you in your home."

"House?" she smiled wearily. "I don't have a house!"

"The house where your brother lives," I corrected.

"Those demons? They don't understand me! They speak a lot of things I do not like. They say tomboy is not good... also smoking... drinking... wearing pants... They are all demons!"

"Are your brother and your sister not visiting you?"

"I don't care if they don't come, if they don't bring Naty with them! *Manang* Marissa is always promising to bring her... Naty had never been visited me."

I brought Dolly inside. I went directly to Dr. Vicente's desk afterwards.

"So, what's up?"

"I think, Doc, she is regaining her old self."

"When she stops mentioning Naty and her late mother..."

"How long will she be staying here, Doc?"

"Two, or three months. It depends. They are not allowed to go home just like that."

I was about to leave when a woman with about my age approaches us. She had something under her arm. She seems to be Dolly's sister-in-law whom I met in Mrs. Bueno's office.

"How is Dolly, Doc?" the lady asked.

"Under observation."

"When could we bring her home?"

"We don't allow a patient to go home until proven that she is fully recovered, Mrs.," Dr. Vicente said. He turned on me. He introduced us to each other.

"I am Marissa, Dolly's sister-in-law."

"I am Lita... I had chosen Dolly as my case study in one of my subjects." I looked at Dr. Vicente.

"Ask Mrs. about Dolly," the doctor said.

Marissa agreed when I explained my purpose. We went out from the pavilion after Marissa handed the goodies that she brought for Dolly who was already in the room. We went to the hospital's canteen. We ordered soft drink and food.

I asked questions.

"It's a long story," Marissa said after thinking. "In fact, none of us in the household permitted her becoming a tomboy, for she was not originally like that. She looked okay when she was in high school. She had a lot of suitors. We wanted her to finish her studies in any course for her good future. She is the only one, out of the six siblings, who did not finish studies. But she joined a group of tomboys. The problem is she did not ask permission before going out. For her situation right now, she had not been home for almost a month. We learned her situation when her group dropped by to tell us what was happening. She was hurt by her girlfriend."

"Before that, do you know something happened with her parents?"

"A lot… but very personal. Anyway, I learned from my husband that Dolly was loved much by their mother. Everything she wanted, have or not in hand, always be given."

"Why did she become a tomboy?" to confirm what Dolly had said.

"Caused probably of joining a group of tomboys."

"Was there any deeper reason?" to make sure.

"My husband said that probably Dolly followed their aunt's…"

I shake my head. "All people are abnormal," I said. "I believe that there are events to worsen the abnormality of an individual to make people resolve that that individual is crazy. Dolly is an example. She was not originally a tomboy. She turned out to be a tomboy. She courted a girl. When she learned that she was cheated by that girl, she is now in this situation…"

"Might have been punished…"

"It could not be judged like that, Marissa," I said. "In fact, she told me something. That I believe the cause of her becoming a tomboy."

"What was it?" Marissa looked at me.

I recapped what Dolly told me: "Their father took the youngest sister of their mother a mistress. That's why their mother became ill, and the cause of her death. That was also the reason why Dolly hate men so much. And that changed her character."

Marissa's eyes drew attention to me examining. "Dolly told you all of those… and you believed her?"

"Was it true?"

"It's up to you if you believe…"

We parted with Marissa with my queries unresolved. She was summoned by Dr. Vicente.

At that night, I prepared my report. I was challenged by my husband saying that the case study will be special if I could wait the outcome of Dolly. If she recovers in the hospital. And base upon the response of her siblings.

I visited the hospital several times after our meeting with Marissa to learn the condition of Dolly. Sometimes only a short time; asking to the social workers. I learned that the tomboy friends of Dolly had visited her three times. She was asking for Naty. Naty was not in the group. She went home to their province and there was a possibility that they married with her boyfriend. Dolly became serious. She yelled at her friends. She threw all the goodies they brought for her. That was the last time the tomboys appeared in the hospital.

It was three months past when I visited Dolly. She had changed a lot. She was then a receptionist, letting people in.

After signing the logbook, I approached her.

"How are you, Dolly?" I said.

She smiled. "Here I am." Her voice was soft.

Other patients approached us.

"Twenty-five cents, please Ma'am. Just for cigarette."

Dolly side-glanced them sharply. "You, every time you see a visitor, twenty-five cents. Shame on you. Go inside. Or else, I will report you inside. Ma'am advised me to do that, for your information!"

Her mind was already cleared up, I said to myself. I felt good.

I asked where Dr. Vicente was. He was inside.

I approached Dr. Vicente who was sleepy reading the charts.

"Are you sleepless last night, Doc?" I said after having a seat.

"One of the patients was in bad condition last night."

"Dolly had improved a lot, Doc," I said.

"It's really inspiring… And she had a promise. She will never court her same sex again."

"That's good!"

"Dolly is our first of its kind patients. Truth is, Dolly was unanimously selected by our association as case study for the Asian Conference in Japan."

"When will she be home, Doc?"

Dr. Vicente shakes his head. "That is our problem. She does not like to go home anymore."

"Is that true?"

"You better talk to her."

Dolly's face was in an aura when I approached her. I asked permission from the social worker to talk to her.

"How are you, Dolly?"

"I'm now okay, Manang," she said. "And you know, *Tatang* and his wife visited me. And so, with my siblings… But they were not happy. As if they feared me. I'm glad that *Manang* Marissa was understanding… Because of what I noticed from them, I decided to stay here to serve the people whom I felt love and caring… I heard from the social workers a lot of advices. From my siblings, nothing! I don't know, but I think, I want to serve here in the hospital… The people here taught me the right direction of life, and what really life is…"

I could not explain my feelings with what I heard. This Dolly is far different from the first I saw here in this hospital.

"Dolly," I said, "this is not your world. You will see and feel life better if you get out from here."

Dolly shakes her head. I noticed her teary eyes. "I could never repay the goodness and endearment they gave to me, *Manang*…"

"That's their responsibility," I said.

"I also want to serve the people who will come here… Maybe, one day, I could also share what happened to me… as their guiding light in the future."

Dr. Vicente smiled when I impart Dolly's explanation.

"Dolly is really extraordinary," he said. "She is our only patient like that."

I thanked the doctor before bidding goodbye. I requested Dolly's address, his brother's place, hoping that I could visit her when she is home. I also left my address.

"Feel sorry for her," my husband said after telling him our last conversation with Dolly.

"A job well done… an extraordinary report!" my professor said, and my classmates when they heard the story of Dolly after my report the next Saturday. They don't only know, but something was being touched in me. For Dolly.

ALMOST two years since I wrote the case study of Dolly, when, one Saturday morning while cleaning my garden, I did not notice the approaching couples.

"*Manang* Lita… *Manang* Lita!" the woman ran to embrace and kiss me. I was astounded. "I am Dolly, *Manang*! Can you not recognize me anymore?"

"My God, Dolly!" I exclaimed. "You're so beautiful… and sexy!"

Her hair was long up to her shoulder. Her fingernails were shiny. With light lip steak. Is this really Dolly?

"*Manang*, this is Nestor," Dolly introduced her companion.

I smiled at Nestor. I invited them in.

"I supposed you have important message," I said when we were sitting.

"I'm not going further, *Manang*," said Dolly smiling. She looked at Nestor. "We are here to invite you with *Manong* for our wedding…"

"Ha? Really?" I felt warm in my face. I looked at Nestor. He got a kind face. Dark brown complexion. They looked suitable for each other.

They nodded and look at each other.

Dolly was excited to explain how they met with Nestor. Nestor read about the story of Dolly that was published in a magazine that reached Saudi Arabia. They became good friends until their love story blossomed thru letters.

I looked at Nestor. I want to know his deeper character.

"Dolly did not hide anything from me, *Manang*," Nestor said. "We understand each other despite of… our past… After our wedding, I will bring her home. I am the only son. I will put her up a small village store from my little savings. And probably, I will also put up a small shop, for I am not going back to Saudi."

Our past, I repeated in my mind. But I did not investigate the past of Nestor.

I FELT the bristling of my hair for excitement when my husband and I were in the church to witness the wedding of Dolly and Nestor. Dolly's eyes were teary despite her smiling face. Her father and her siblings were calm in front desks.

Dolly embraced me after the ceremony. She was crying.

"You have a big part in my life, *Manang*!" she whispered. "I will never forget you…"

My eyes were teary.

I watched Dolly receiving complements when we let each other go.

I looked up my husband when he held my palm. We smiled at each other. I rested my face on his shoulder when we followed the queue out. –0

Third prize, Governor Roque Ablan Award for Iluko Literature (GRAAFIL), August 2, 1982. Published in the *Bannawag*, April 8, 1991 with a title *Komustaka, Dolly? (How are you, Dolly?)*; included in the *Batonsileng, Antolohia dagiti Sarita ken Daniw, 1992; translation completed:* July 9, 2018.

Allegedly Dwarf

I HAD not yet finish washing our dishes after that lunch time when mother called me.

"Come here and talk with this deaf timeworn man!" mother said.

I knew that it was *Manong* Peding whom *nanang* called deaf timeworn man. He was one of the old bachelors in Daang Bakal who was giving any kind of gift in our house. I overheard that he likes Bascion, my youngest sister. *Manong* Peding was a Tagalog.

I peeped out from the window. It was really *Manong* Peding. He rode on his bike and carrying a paper bag. I went out.

"Good afternoon, Teacher," he said and his golden tooth spark in the sun.

"Why did you come here in the middle of the day?" I said.

"The reason, Teacher, I was able to catch a dome fishes when we went to Wawa Dam, that's why I decided to come and give some for Sally. She always saying that she loves eating freshly catch fish." Sally is what they call Bascion here in Montana Subdivision, Montalban, Rizal, our place.

Manong Peding handed me what he was carrying in his hand. I opened it. Shrimps, crabs, and some *buntiek*[21]. I had not been eaten these kinds of fishes.

"They're so delicious, *Manong*," I said. "How much is it?"

---

[21] *Buntiek,* young freshwater mudfish.

"Common, Ma'am. I am not asking you to pay. Instead, if you want, let's have a picnic in Wawa Dam. We have a hut in the mountain. We have a lot of plants around it."

"It's only now that you mention about it. We should have gone picnicking long time ago. I want to see Wawa Dam."

"If you have time, let's go. A lot of fish this time in the river."

I noticed that *Manong* Peding was not pretending. "Let me plan about that, *Manong*," I said. "I'll let somebody to tell you when."

Nanang was sitting on a sofa pouting when I got inside.

"He gives it free, why not accept. You better go cook it," I said.

"That's why he continuously doing that because you always accept all he is giving."

"It's ruder if you let him down," I reasoned out.

"Looks like you are pushing your sister!"

Mother stood up mumbling. I continued washing the plates.

"Is it done, Mom?" I said after washing.

"Come and taste it," she said. "The taste of a freshly caught fish is truly far better than a frozen."

"If I did not accept what he offered, then we would not be eating a fresh fish."

"You better be careful. You might be the one he is thinking to court because he knows that your husband is out of the country. Tell you the truth, I don't like the face he got. Better if his hair is not completely gray."

"That's why he is for you, '*Nang*. I think, you have the same age with *Manong* Peding."

"I surely slap his temple if he ever turns his attention to me."

The sun was already cooling off but Bascion was not home yet. I visited our vegetable garden at the back of our house. I toiled on my newly planted eggplants.

There was a hubbub in the street in front of our house. It was *Manong* Peding. He was accompanied by another timeworn. They were riding bikes. *Manong* Peding's smile was so wide.

"*Manong* Peding, again, thank you to what you've given a while ago," I said.

He scratched his head. "Don't mention it, Ma'am, it's a little thing. Never mind, I'll double it next time," he looked at his companion.

"You might be going somewhere, *Manong*?" I said.

"N-nothing… We just come this way for he also wants to see Sally."

I became serious. "You mean to say, *Manong*, your companion is also a bachelor like you?"

"He was so picky, Ma'am, that's why he became like that," *Manong* Peding laughed.

If *nanang* was so angry with *Manong* Peding, and then there is another Peding to visit in our house, surely the angrier *nanang* will be.

"Ha, e, don't get mad, *Manong* Peding. I supposed that Sally is not coming home this afternoon for I told her this morning to go and sleep tonight in our sibling's place in Sta. Mesa if they have exam."

The two looked at each other. *Manong* Peding's face became tarty.

"Then we'll not staying any longer, Ma'am," they bid good bye.

I caught *nanang* peeping in the window when I got back. She immediately left from her post when she noticed me coming.

"What was again your topic with that dwarf?" *Manong* Peding was short that's why *Nanang* calls him dwarf.

"He said he is coming to visit you. He even brought him a companion who is timeworn like him for he planned to show you, but I did not allow them to come inside," I said.

"Silly… am I a lady for them to visit? I surely strangle him if he tries to visit me."

This is *nanang* when we her children ridicule her. She seems like a young lady who was newly courted. She had been a widower for quite some time.

"Is it bad when you like each other so we will have somebody that could give us fresh fish to eat?" I continued jesting.

"If you are planning to get me married to somebody else, I would rather live you alone with your children. I will go back to Subek."

It's been three months since we met *Manong* Peding. He was accompanied by Mr. Uy, the president of the homeowners who came to our house to investigate about our seven lost hens. The members of the barangay promised to look for the stealers. It was almost two months, but no result yet. *Manong* Peding volunteered to go around in our street. He was a member of the Barangay Tanod.

Manong Peding was a good man. He was respectful. He was a joker. If you ask what his job is, he will tell you it's jack of all trades. He can be construction worker, electrician, machinist, television technician, stove repairman, farmer, and fisherman. But he likes the best being a barber when he is not in his cleared forest land. All people in Montana is his client. He has no shop but doing his business by house service.

Because Bascion sometimes borrows *Manong* Peding's bike, he now likes my sister.

I can feel that *Manong* Peding is happy helping people.

It was dusk when I noticed the arrival of Bascion with overly wide smile. As if she was marching along the street.

"Why are you so late?" I said.

"Because I saw *Manong* Peding in the waiting shade with another timeworn with the same name Peding. They said they came here."

"And you prolonged your conversation, wanton," countered *nanang*.

"He introduced another timeworn."

"From now on, avoid talking with that dwarf," nanang said. "I heard that there are a lot of drug addicts here in Montana? You may put yourself in trouble."

"You're so much, Nanang. A lot of bad things entering your head. Never mind if you meet people like Manong Peding. If a guy intended for Bascion is timeworn, you must be thankful for having a son-in-law grandpa," I said.

"Frivolous! Don't ever involve me with that kind of thing. If I had plan to get married, I should have done when you were still young.

MA'AM, I have something to tell you," *Manong* Peding greeted one afternoon while I was cutting my Bermuda grass in our yard.

"Just tell me," I offered a chair but rather he instead sat on the grass.

"Am I not acceptable for you, Ma'am?"

"I can't understand you, *Manong*..."

"For Sally... if I'm worthy to her."

I breathe deeply. The timeworn was not jesting. I shook my head.

"I think, it's not yet time for her to think about those things. She is studying, and I want her to complete her studies."

"I can wait, Ma'am." I was astounded. Is this this old man as serious as he is?

"Why did you not think getting married when you were younger, Manong?"

"I feared having a family. I used to tell myself, why do I have to get somebody to fed for?"

"You did never have a girlfriend?"

"Courting by eyes, scared to speak up." He laughs.

"By the way, Ma'am, I need to go now but please don't mention to Sally what I had said." I collected the grass and leaves I cut. I put them in the garbage. I saw nanang drawing water from the well.

She was looking at the back of Manong Peding who was moving away.

"My goodness, 'Nang, he voiced out his intention, if he is worthy for you," I teased.

"Don't ever tease me like that or I'll leave you alone with your children.

"He said he is ashamed of you. I just go along with his goodness."

"I had told you not to entertain."

Bascion arrived catching her breath one afternoon. She slumped herself at the veranda.

"Why are you like that?" I said.

"There were three men following me. They forced to come and visit me. I even don't know them."

"Where were they from?"

"At Daang Bakal. They know *Manong* Peding. I just ran, and ran..."

It was on time that *Manong* Peding passed by riding his bike. He had a paper bag. He got off, and he approached us with a very wide smile.

"Good afternoon, Ma'am," greeted *Manong* Peding.

"There is no good afternoon at this time, Manong Peding. Your neighbors are endangering," fightback Bascion. I mentioned what Bascion informed us.

"I know who those are. They are always asking me if you are my girlfriend. I said no, because that is true. He told me that he likes you."

"That one who looks like an addict?" I faced the visitor.

"It looks like there is good news in that paper bag, Manong," I said.

"I came just to let you taste the fruit of our plants in the mountain," he handed the paper bag to Bascion.

"Wow, yummy!" she said. "Watermelon, papaya and jicama. It's good to eat with vinegar. Seems you have a lot of plants, Manong?"

"You will see… Had you not mentioned before, ma'am, that you want to see Wawa Dam?"

"I have been interested to see the dam," I said.

"No problem, Ma'am. This coming Sunday. I'll order for fish. Come all. Bring mother and the children."

When we finished our breakfast, was the same time when two tricycles ordered by Manong Peding to pick us up arrived.

Nanang, my two children and I rode with the other tricycle. My three children and Bascion rode in the other one.

We reached in a group of huts that looked like mushrooms. Many had been in the river swimming. I chose a hut for us and brought in our things.

There was a wide bench inside. I paid ten pesos.

I asked where a pool was. A man pointed one on his left side.

"Climb one of the mountains and you will there, Ma'am, the big dam. The dam is part of the swimming area."

My conversation was cut when the children invited Bascion to go swimming. I allowed them but told Bascion to make sure the children be in safe place.

It was not even ten minutes when I saw Manong Peding with two men.

"Were you being here long enough, Ma'am?" Manong Peding said after putting down their things.

"Not that long, Manong," I answered back.

I was about to go and call the children when I heard a yell in a direction where nanang went. "That's nanang's voice!" I said.

Manong Peding was in a hurry toward where the yelling came from. I followed him.

It was true nanang was the one sinking and floating in the deeper part of the river.

Manong Peding ran and leaped to rescue. He carried nanang who embrace him tightly out from the water.

"Why did you go to the deep?" I told *nanang*.

"As if something was pulling my legs," answered *nanang*.

Bascion and I helped nanang back to the hut. *Manong* Peding followed us.

"We are truly hungry," the two men said.

"Okay, let's consume all the food. It's a double celebration for this day," said Manong Peding.

"If not because of you, I'm dead now," nanang said when she was resting after meal. Manong Peding was not far from her.

"It was all God's will. Maybe there is still something He wants you to finish."

NOW, when *Manong* Peding come and visit us in our home, it was different from before when *nanang* calls him dwarf. She's now the one who invites him inside and to talk with *Manong* Peding.

Ah, life, I simply chant when I notice nanang talking with *Manong* Peding. –0

Bannawag: June 20, 1983; *translation completed:* July 11, 2018.

It's Under Your Discretion

PRECY had given her next subject when the children stood up in unison and greeted, "Good morning, visitor. Please come in. Please sit down!"

Framed in the door a man with a good body built, wearing ray ban, smiling and a gift held under his armpit. Precy was guessing who this giving trouble was.

"Thank you, children," the man answered.

"You are welcome," answered the children and sat down.

That was the only time when Precy shifted from where she was standing and moved closer to the door to ask who among the children was the purpose of the man.

"Happy birthday, Precy!" greeted the man and removed his Ray ban.

"Ed... you?" Precy was stunned. She did not know whether to be happy or hate boiled from her bosom. "Please, sit down," she pointed the chair in the corner.

Instead of following the order, Ed handed a gift from his armpit. "For you. Advance happy birthday. Your favorites are inside."

"Why did you come here in school?"

"Let me explain. I came here to let you know I still care for you. I came back to the Philippines because of you. I am here to pick you up."

"Your wife?"

"She had been dead for a long time. We lived together only for two years. I had already suffered a lot, Precy. I sacrificed. I had acquired all our dreams."

"Is that how you measure me, Ed?"

"I'm still the one you loved despite of everything, Precy. I learned everything how Cesar got hold of you as a wife. You don't love your husband!"

"This is not the right place to talk all of those things, Ed."

"Okay, after your class tomorrow. I'll wait for you at the Max Restaurant in Cubao."

"No more important items for us to talk about, Ed."

"I want to explain. There are a lot of things you need to know…"

"You better go. It's so embarrassing to my co-teachers."

"Then I'll wait for you tomorrow. Same time, same place."

Ed went out in a hurry. Precy was left confused. She sat in front of her desk. Why did Ed show up?

"Are you done with your exam?" Precy did not notice the entering of Marissa from the adjacent room.

"I'm done."

"Who was the handsome guy who came to your room?"

"It was Ed. He resurrected after eight years."

"What?" Marissa's eyes opened widely. "He still had face to show after what he did?"

"He said we will meet at the Max tomorrow morning. I want to express all my ill feelings."

"Have a date? What if some of our companions here in school see you?"

"Our story with Ed is an opened book here in school. They all knew how Cesar came into my life."

"I don't respect Ed. He came to destroy your relationship with your husband. Despite of the goodness of your husband, can you still betray him?"

"Look, Marissa. I don't mean that way…"

"Forget all about that Ed…"

IT was late in the evening when Precy arrived. Cesar was already home.

"I came home early today, Mommy. Go change and let's have our dinner. There is something I want to tell you," Cesar said.

Precy's head was empty when she proceeded to their room. She was thinking if it is proper to tell her husband about the visit of Ed in school. She lazed down after changing her clothes. She had a headache. She heard Cesar's slipper scraping. He sat at the edge of the bed.

"What's wrong? Are you not feeling well?" her husband asked.

"I was dizzied in my trip. And my head ached checking test papers."

"You should have brought home, so I could help you. Come let's have our dinner."

Precy had no appetite to eat because Ed's picture was coming back and forth in her forehead.

There were only two of them in the room. Precy was quiet.

"You know, Mommy," Cesar said, "I was informed that Mr. Reyes chosen me to head our company to attend meeting in America next month. It will be one week with you. Everything is free and there's even pocket money."

Precy did not answer. She did not even look at Cesar.

"Are you not excited, Mommy?"

"How… they may not allow me in school."

"I will ask your principal to allow you to come with me."

It was almost midnight but Precy was still awake. The past was still flashing back into her mind. Ed and Cesar worked together at the same office. She and Ed already been had understanding, but this did not stop Cesar to court Precy by giving gifts, roses, and visiting her in their place despite her not entertaining him but her parents did.

An opportunity came that Ed should be transferred in a different branch of their company, in the Bisayan region, because of a problem in that area. Because of this, Ed advised Precy to avoid Cesar in the office. Precy was an education graduate and passed civil service but preferred to work in an office. He followed the advice of Ed.

"Be good. Get away from Cesar. We'll get married when I come back," Ed promised.

But Ed was cornered by a different lady. Precy learned that Ed and his wife moved to America. Because of what happened, Cesar became close to the siblings and parents of Precy. Whenever Cesar followed up his feelings, Precy was frank: "My love had been dead. Never, ever could I love you!"

But Precy yielded to Cesar in the long run.

Their first son Joel came after three years. The child made them more intact. They were able to buy a house, modern appliances, car and had saved in the bank for the future of Joel.

But in the inner self of Precy, Ed was always there. She could not accept that Ed betrayed her despite their numerous promises and dreams.

The next morning, Cesar told her that he will be home late because of an overtime in their office.

"Did you tell Cesar about the visit of Ed here in school?" this was the first question of Marissa to Precy.

"I supposed, it's not important to tell."

"What if he come to know it?"

"Comes what may… That will be the time for me to explain."

Precy met Ed. He had been waiting at the Max Restaurant. He was handsome in his attire.

Precy did not have appetite to eat. Ed eat with gusto for he had not eaten his favorite fried chicken for a long time.

"Okay, okay, I feel good. I'm so happy," Ed said after their launch. "We could talk well. We could explain everything. Now there are things you need to know without prior notice."

"If it only hurts, never mind, Ed. I just want to ask, why did you do those for me?"

"Because I loved you. Criselda was in between life and death when I met her. Her parents almost kneeled to ask me to marry their daughter just to see her happy in the last part of her life. I told them I had a girlfriend, that we were about to be married. They offered me a condition. Criselda was their only child. They were the riches family in their place. The promised that after our wedding, we will stay in America because that was what Criselda's request. Criselda passed away after two years. Criselda's parents fulfilled their promise to me. All that Criselda inherits from her parents were given to me. They even told me that I could marry my previous girlfriend."

"You did that without informing me?"

"I sent a letter to Cesar. I explained everything."

"You sent a letter to Cesar?"

"I directed him to take care of you, but he did a different thing. But it was just okay for me. The most important was, all our dreams will be fulfilled to live in other country. I now have my own business there. I'm here to fetch you."

"Is that how easy it is? You came here and get me, and I just come with you just like that?"

"Cesar will not hold you back if he knows I'm here. He knows my plan."

"Ed, you are kidding. That's not true," Precy rose her voice.

"Ask him if I'm telling you the truth or not. When he arrived last night, I know he told you something."

"H-how did you know?"

"I knew because it's been a year that I am the secret partner of the company where Cesar is working."

"Ed, are you toying people because you are now rich?"

"I did everything because I loved you. I want to share you everything I have."

"Let's go out, Ed!" and Precy went out in a hurry from the restaurant.

Precy threw herself in the bed upon reaching home. She was worried. He weighed what Ed said.

Precy intentionally stayed put when Cesar arrives. But her husband kissed her.

She opened her eyes. "Had you eaten?"

"Yes, my boss treated us. We did not know the overtime he told us yesterday. It was just eating and even in a pricy restaurant. There were only seven of us. We even divided by ourselves the left overs."

What is this? Is this just Ed's trick?

"And you know, Mommy, I did not know what our boss was thinking. He said that when I come back from America, he will assign me as president of the branch our company will open."

Precy arose from bed. "There might be something behind that…"

"We are so lucky, my companion told me. Anyway, whether they give that position or not, it's just the same with me."

"I have something to tell and ask you, Ces. Sit down."

"You look like suspenseful," Cesar laughed but he did not sit.

"If I tell you Ed came to our school?"

Cesar's eyebrows arched when he looked at Precy. "Will you say it again?"

"Ed came to our school."

"Then?"

"He mentioned a lot of things. He explained a lot. Was it true that he sent you a letter?"

"That goddam bastard!" Cesar said.

"Why didn't you mention the letter in the expand of eight years we lived together?"

"Useless, Mommy. I know what he wants to do on visiting you. To fetch you as he wrote."

"Who am I? A toy for everybody? Did you know that Ed was the secret partner of your boss?"

"Well, Mommy, the expand of eight years, just like only yesterday. I know that despite what I have been trying to prove our family a model, I can't do anything if your heart and feelings still belong to Ed. It's your discretion to decide as long as Joel stay with me."

Precy remained silent for a while. "How loved Joel for you, the more for me. I won't change Joel in any amount of riches or anything else. Starting tomorrow, resign from your job. We will just put up our own business."

Cesar embraced Precy tightly. –0

Bannawag: June 27, 1988; *translation completed:* July 12, 2018.

If Life Could Only Be Bought

I ARRIVED with an unexpected news in that middle of the day. "Joey met an accident. He was in between life and death. They allegedly brought him immediately at the East Medical Center," my husband said.

"Was he serious?"

"His head was smashed…"

"His head was smashed…? How come?"

"*Nana* Marcia said that the members of their rival fraternity allegedly counteracted. They bludgeoned and dropped him in the cliff of Tibag last night."

"Jesus Christ! I've been telling Lulu that there is no good thing in fraternity. She had not given an attention."

I changed and ate in a hurry.

I dropped by Lulu's house which was not far from our house. I felt envious ones again upon seeing a semi palace building in the garden. How beautiful. I pushed the doorbell.

Teresing, the maid, came out.

"Come in, *Manang*," she invites.

I came upon *Nana* Marcia, Lulu's mother, in the terrace. I approached her.

"Please, Marissa, *Nakong*, go and accompany your friend in the hospital. My poor grandson. He was unconscious when they picked him up," she said sobbing.

I tapped the shoulder of the old lady. "God is kind, *nana*," I said.

I brought the things needed by the patient in the hospital because Lulu missed to bring them due to nervousness and in a hurry.

Many questions in my mind while in a ride. Why was this happened again to Joey? This is the third time, if I am not mistaken. He was in first year in college. He is the only boy of five siblings. He was quarrelsome. He was hotheaded. So many times, did Lulu complain to me because of her children.

"Marissa, why are my children far different from your children who are so diligent in their studies? I'm giving all their needs."

"Probably… because you lack attention to them. You are all focused to your businesses."

"I am telling them to whom my businesses are for. You know, as if I could no longer guide them especially Joey. As if he is revolting. Whatever the reason is, I don't know. He never listened to me."

"Why won't you talk to him personally? Explain your side."

"Useless, Marissa. He arrives home late most of the time. Whenever I asked him, he runs immediately into his room. Or sometimes, he goes to my in-law's place and say whatever against me."

"About Fred, what does he say?"

"He's one thing. He does not have a vocabulary except money. Come home and help me guide the children, I said, but he's always talking about his income. He wants to build a ten-door apartment."

"You already have a lot of houses for rent."

"I don't know about my husband. He is not satisfied."

"Anyway, nobody's luckier than you are. You have all the material things that we couple far from attaining. Despite our hard work, we could not save because all our earnings go to the education of our children."

"Truth is, Marissa, I am envious to you. Your children are obedient. They are not quarrelsome. They are good students. You go to church at the same time on Sundays. You are happy."

"Those are nothing compared to your standing in life. You are the owner of the most beautiful house here in the subdivision. You have an agency. You have a lot house for rent."

"I am not happy for those, Marissa. I am no different from a robot following all the caprice of Fred. Most of my best friends had gone."

"They are humbled with Fred…"

"He was not like that when his salary was nominal. Whatever Fred wants it needs to be fulfilled."

I noticed the improvement of Fred and Lulu's life. Before Fred went abroad, he had a good position in the Custom. There were lot of hearsays behind the abrupt change of their lives. But the thing I like to Lulu is she retained her friendship to me despite all those gossips.

I missed the passing of time, I arrived in front of the hospital. I approached the information. Lulu's group were in the third floor, at the ICU. So then, the condition of her son was serious.

I came upon Lulu looking down the small table. Accompanied by one of their maids and her cousins. I approached her. I rested my arm upon her shoulder. She looked at me. She embraced me.

"How is Joey?" I said.

She pointed the nurse station. "Will you go ask them. I am scared of what they may tell me. They brought him directly to the operating room."

"Fred needs to know this."

"I will tell him after his discharge. He does not like to come home anyway. "Please go ask." As if Lulu pushed me to the nurses' station.

My heart bits faster when I approached the nurses' station. I inquired. They pointed the sitting doctor. I asked about Joey. The answer was indirect. She asked my relationship with the patient, or his parents. Then she said: "The patient was not attended properly, Mrs. He lost a lot of blood before bringing to the hospital."

"Y-you mean to say, Doc, he could not be survived?"

"He had undergone surgery. He had given blood transfusion. But his brain was damaged so badly, I don't know the result of the surgery."

"Do whatever you can do, Doc. His parents are ready to pay whatever amount will be."

"Mrs., I tell you frankly. What I can say is, only God can do a miracle."

The doctor was resolute. She pointed out where the patient was. I almost yelled upon seeing Joey. His whole head was covered with bandage. Blood was oozing from his nose and ears. His eyes were closed. I went back to the doctor.

"Doc, why is it that there's blood coming out from his nose and ears?"

"Not only his head was damaged. He was beaten very badly. Internal hemorrhage." The doctor advised the four nurses to watch Joey attentively. The doctor wanted to talk to the mother of the patient. I called Lulu and let them talk together. But she did not approach the bed of Joey.

"I don't have enough courage to see the condition of my son, Marissa," Lulu said. "Please, don't go away from me. Go home when somebody arrives."

"The condition of your son is serious. You need to inform Fred."

"Come here tomorrow. Accompany me to call him."

My head seemed a big basket because of the picture I witnessed when I went to the hospital. They were helping Lulu. She was yelling. She was crying.

"You killed my son. Bring back his life! I can pay it!" she yelled.

Joey, he's dead? I inquired from the nurses' station. It was twelve midnight when the life of the youngster ended.

"The doctors did all their bests but that was really the time for the youngster. The damage in his brain was really bad."

I went back to Lulu. She was not crying anymore. She embraces me upon seeing me. She was trembling. She rested his head on my shoulder like a child. She howled again.

"Joey has gone, Marissa. I don't know how Fred reacts. Why is it like that? If life could only be bought."

I accompanied Lulu to call her husband by long distance.

If Lulu did not tell that Joey was already dead, Fred might not have promised to come home. Lulu was crying and with loud voice. "Resign! Come home and you'll never go back there!"

I gave Lulu advise after calling. She needs to strengthen herself and relied upon God everything in the future.

"Life was lost. And it only be repaid also by life!" she said instead.

Lulu paid everything needed to the hospital. She did not like the dead to be in the funeral home. She wants him to be in the living room of her big house. "For the very last time, I want to watch my son."

We went home together. Others left behind to accompany the remains. While we were riding back home, I counted one by one all Lulu's friend I had in mind. Where are they now? They all distanced themselves one by one when Lulu's life progressed, and Fred's character changed. I knew, I'm her only close friend left. If there are so-called friends, they all belong to high society nothing to do except their individual interest. The same world Lulu had. She ones said, "You know, Mar, I'm tired of my kind of world. I lost my piece of mind. I'm tired. But this is a kind of world Fred loves."

A lot of Lulu's relatives were already home when we arrived. They inquired about Joey. *Nana* Marcia and *Tata* Teban were excited to know whether their grandson is still alive.

Lulu answered them all. "No more Joey, mama, he's gone…" and ones again cry broke the stillness of the whole mansion. "It's all Fred's fault. He never gave attention to his only son." She cried with all her might.

"We can't do nothing now except to accept the fact, *tata, nana*," I said to Lulu's parents. "The most important thing to do now is to haunt for the criminals."

"We knew already, *Anakko*[22], who they are. Their parents dropped by last night and offered their help for the hospital. But what now… the child had gone."

"Fred will decide when he arrives," I said.

I assisted Lulu when she could not cry anymore. "Strengthen yourself. Whatever you do now, the life of your son could no longer get back."

"If I could only buy life in return to my son's life, I'll do. What's the use of Fred's dream now? That if you have money, you are powerful and

---

[22]   *Anakko,* a term of endearment to a much younger individual, or a son or daughter.

fearless, and nobody is luckier and happier. But I could not feel those. I'm scared. I'm scared to death even in the middle of the day."

"It's enough, Lulu," I said. "We'll fix and prepare the place for the boy."

I bid to go home when there were enough people.

"That's why it is not good to be braggart and high headed," my husband said several times when I informed him what happened. "Death comes like a robber. I supposed this is a lesson to your friend. Since they had their business, she misled her children. There were a lot of helpers they could hire, but Joey was looking other things. He was thirsty with the love and affection of his parents."

Fred arrived the next day. We all witnessed the reaction of Fred crying and yelling like crazy embracing the coffin.

I was not able to attend the funeral of Joey because we had exams for the third grading period in school. Same with the next days. I had not seen Lulu. Every time I planned to visit them my husband halts me.

I received a letter after the thirtieth day after the funeral of Joey. It was Saturday. "Marissa, I invite you, that we all go to the house of Joey my son," wrote Lulu.

My husband had no power to stop me in accepting Lulu's invitation. Lulu was smiling when she embraced me. She informed that the case of her son had reached the court. Fred was sitting calmly.

In the kitchen, there were scrumptious food being prepared. "Your visitors are only numbered but why do you have to cook a lot?"

"There are a lot of visitors waiting in the house of Joey."

"House of Joey?"

Lulu nodded. "You will see."

Joey's home as said by Lulu was not a tomb nor mausoleum. It was a beautiful granite building that excelled over all the mausoleums in the cemetery. There were two big rooms. There was a bathroom, living room and kitchen. Modern and complete appliances. There was a television set. There was a fridge. With soft leather set. The living room was carpeted. The corps of Joey was in the other room. In the other room, there was a cushion bed and big dresser. All the things of Joey were there. He looks like alive in his enlarged picture in the living room.

According to the workers, the building was done in a hurry. The price of Joey's house was more than three million including the appliances. A lot of money! How wonderful!

"This is just a portion if I fulfill all I had promised when he was still alive. I intended to do like this because if we visit him, as if Joey is still with us. We can eat and sleep here," this was how Fred explained when we were eating.

I could hardly swallow my food. There was a silent prayer in my bosom. I hope, Joey, that you could reach the presence of the Lord. Hope you can have the endearment you were looking for when you were here on earth. –0

Bannawag: June 26, 1995; *translation completed:* July 14, 2018.

Tata[23] *Basil's Dream*

THE neighbors and relatives who came to welcome me and my sister Grace on our arrival have just left when somebody spoke from the foot of the ladder.

"Gasiiinggg! Where is my present."

I trembled. "Who was that, *'nang*?" I looked at my mother, who was desperately wringing her hands on the chest at the corner of the room.

"It's your *Tata* Basil. I'm sure he got word of your arrival."

"*Ipaaaggg*! {*ipag*[24]}. Gasiiiinngg! Mariiisssa!" The voice was getting increasingly louder and he was now also tugging harder at the ropes that served as handrails for the ladder.

"Foolish old man… what an embarrassment!" murmured Grace. "He chooses a time like this to disturb people. I'm tired. The mob has just left!"

"He won't stop unless you let him in," said Bella and Pedro, the couple who lived with mother. They too were wringing their hands desperately.

"Well, should I let him in?" I looked at mother.

"No!" Grace spluttered. "Let him come tomorrow when he was sober."

---

[23] *Tata,* an address given to an uncle, a middle-aged man.

[24] *Ipag,* sister-in-law.

"*Loka*[25], he came from seven mountains away. I'm sure he heard about your arrival and misses seeing you as well," mother simply said.

"Let him come up," I said.

"He'll make a scene. He won't give us peace," Bella warned. Pedro went to lie down with his five children at the corner of the throwing out his stub. Grace covered herself up and snuggled on the floor.

Mother brandished the bean after opening the door. I heard *Tata* Basil laugh.

"Good evening, my sister in law. It's nice to see you still have such a nice heart to welcome me unlike my relative down at the *tianggi*[26] who shoos me away like I was a dog."

The rungs on the ladder squeaked.

"Hold fast or you might fall," mother cautioned. "You and your insistence on getting drunk at such an hour. The children were tired."

The doorway silhouetted the crouched and swaying figure of *Tata* Basil. His clothes were rags. His pants were patched and holey. He wore a rope belt. Long haired. He reeked of *basi*[27]. I kept quiet where I sat. I was still studying in college the last time I saw *Tata* Basil.

"Hello, *tata*," I said after he settled himself on a bench, looking around. I knew he was searching for Grace. Grace was his favorite among all his nephews and nieces when they were small.

"Oh, were you Marissa? Just fine, my dear. Left behind. Pitied. Ridiculed!" Whoa, now he was crying. He's sobbing.

"Uncle stop bawling, c'mon. The kids might wake up," Bella interrupted. "Go home now, go on. Come back tomorrow when you're sober."

"What did you say?" He faced Bella like he wanted to punch her. "You're all the same! I'm just arrived, I've just sat down, and now you're sending me home!"

"Just leave him be. You know how he was when he was drunk."

---

[25]   *Loka,* crazy.

[26]   *Tianggi,* village store.

[27]   *Basi,* sugarcane wine.

"My presents, my dear," he said. "Some pants and a shirt will do. Just look at me, will you, I'm in rags."

I nodded.

"And some extra for *basi,* my dear. . ."

"Not that. Enough for that already, you poor thing."

Grace pinched my side. "You and your patience talking to that drunk. Send him home already, I said!"

"What did you say, Gasiiing?" Looks like he overheard. "Sending me home without a present? I've just arrived, and you send me home already. Just see, foolish girl, if you don't end up a monster like your uncle."

"But just look how drunk you were, uncle. You're so embarrassing to look at."

"Basil the drunkard but I know south from north. Come now, tell me who else can endure living in the seventh mountain? If I'm embarrassing you as you say, why do people still flock down to my hovel?"

"Go home, uncle," Bella persisted.

"Take these so you have something to munch on your way home," mother said, handling over some wrapped bread.

"Where do you go home, *tata*?" I asked.

He waved his arms and swatted away the plastic bag that mother held. "I don't like bread, *ipaaagg*!"

"Why you devil! Just go home then and cease disturbing us."

"Where does he live then?" I asked mother.

"In Burador. At the seventh mountain. . ."

I looked at the watch on my wrist. Ten thirty. "If he goes home, what time would it be when he arrives?"

"Roosters would be crowing by then, of course."

"Oh no, let him be, how dreadful. Let him sleep in the kitchen. He might not reach this Burador that you're saying."

"I disagree! He will break the plates. He broke one of our earthen jars when we let him sleep in the kitchen one time when he was drunk," Bella flared.

"He won't give us any sleep," mother added.

Tata Basil stretched himself on the bench. "You Bella, the lies you tell. Why shouldn't I break your plates when you won't feed me? My dear relatives don't be stingy with e so that your lives will remain peaceful. If you won't give me some presents, I won't go home."

I fingered the fifty in my purse and placed it in his hands. "Your present from me, *tata*," I said. "Tomorrow, when you're sober, come back so I can give you some new pants and shirts."

Tata Basil arose and kissed the money I gave him repeatedly. "*Tenkyu! Tenkyu beri* mats. . ." He stood up. He stretched. "I'm going home then, and I would just be on time for moonrise when I reach Maramramot Dam. . ."

When *Tata* Basil was gone Pedro and Bella stood up and berated me for giving *Tata* Basil so much.

"That type of person should be locked up in an institution," Pedro said.

"But he's not a lunatic. . . He's quite conversant in fact."

"Embarrassing uncle," insisted Grace.

GRACE and I dressed up to go to town after breakfast. I prepared my camera. There was a lot of pictures I needed to shoot. I wanted to see a lot of people who would take parts in the book I was going to write. Truthfully, I would have chosen to stay in town at my late father's house, and would have gone there directly yesterday, but I couldn't convince Grace, who said she was shy. And since mother still lived near the sea, and it's been a long time since I last saw her, we went there instead.

We passed by a *tianggi* or village store on our way to get a tricycle to town. They recognized me. They invited us over. They called me all sort of names. Teacher or Master Writer! The said it was nice I could remember to come and visit mother.

At the Town Hall, we visited Ralph, the youngest son of my late *Manang* Seniang and favorite grandson of my father. I haven't seen him ever since he was elected as mayor of our town. He saw me.

"Your husband, where I he?" he asked.

"He's overseas. . ."

We exchanged news. How he was managing the town. The town has prospered since he assumed the mayorship. They even now had a College of Fisheries, the airport was almost finished, and a lot of scenic spots were opened by Tourism for local and foreign tourists.

"That's great," I said. "I can see that if father was alive, he couldn't ask for more, in the fulfillment of his dreams for his beloved town."

"You're a writer but you never written about your hometown," remarked Ralph.

"It would be a book but not today."

I directed the tricycle to where I grew up. Our original house was gone though I can still see my childhood-self playing in the wide and spacious yard.

I didn't expect that Grace and I would find *Tata* Basil waiting for as at the yard when we got back from town. He was sober. His face was bright. His clothes were clean although patchy.

"Good afternoon, mu daughters. O came by to bring you some samples of the fruits from my papaya trees. And, to ask if you would like to bring back some vegetables with you to Manila."

"Of course, I'd love to, *tata*. Give us some and I'd pay for them."

"That's so much more weight to bring home, *Manang*. There's a lot of vegetables there," Grace whispered to me.

"I won't have you paying for them, my daughter. I give them freely. If you could make it to Burador, of course, it would be so much better, so you could choose what you like. . ." He said he had a lot of vegetables planted.

"Shall we go?" I asked Grace.

She shook her head. "I didn't come here to climb mountains, but to swim in the beach. I don't know why you put up with that drunk."

I promised *Tata* Basil that I would drop by his place since I've never attempted any mountain climbing during my childhood. And mother and Bella kept saying that Burador was beautiful where *Tata* Basil lived with his teenage son.

That evening, I asked mother about *Tata* Basil's life and why he became a drunk. I learned the cause: his wife ran away with another man, his rich compadre. Their three eldest daughters were now living as house helps. One remained in Isabela where his in-laws lived, and the last one, was left with him. They say he was the only one who could put up with *Tata* Basil.

The following morning, we climbed the mountain. Grace remained to look after Bella's kids. Bella and Pedro accompanied us. Mother insisted on coming though I was worried because of her cough.

We crossed a dry riverbed. We climbed one side of a cliff. A sign was stated: **This way to Maramramot Dam**.

"We'll climb hand on hand. "Be careful where you place your feet," my companions cautioned.

We were nearing the valley. We could just see the flowering plants that were placed to fence that looked like stairs, that led to something like a conference house or a guest house. My companions said that if I wanted to see the waters of the dam, we needed to enter the fence.

I breathed a little easier when we reached h top of the seventh mountain and I could see the valley and the occasional nipa huts.

Tata Basil was truly waiting I n us hut's yard. I directly sat down when we reached it and asked for water. My companions entered the house and there they drank their water. Bella brought out some for me. After drinking, *Tata* Basil directed them to go pick vegetables among his garden around them. My eyes were attracted to the papaya trees with their many ripe fruits north of the hut. I couldn't believe a sight like this could exist in the middle of the mountains.

Tata Basil probably noticed where I was looking and said, "Wait here and I'll bring you some more of what I brought to our place yesterday."

He quickly entered the hut and when he came out, he was holding a sliced papaya fruit on a big platter. I enjoyed the sweetness of ripe papaya.

I asked *Tata* Basil why he stayed in such a solitary place, and why he couldn't stop drinking once he began.

"I've promised, my dear, ever since your aunt exchanged me, that I would stay here. Many told me to hunt them down and kill them, but no thanks. Let them be. Your father, who was my first cousin, how he ridiculed me. Instead of pitying me, he cursed me saying I was embarrassing the clan. He just didn't know how I felt whenever I remembered this part of our life. Besides, I couldn't face the thought of becoming a criminal. It was so easy if I chose to. I knew where they lived. I could easily dynamite it. But I still think of your aunt and even though he did that to me, she was still my wife who gave me five children. So, I turned to gin and *basi* whenever I remembered my fate. If I don't drink, I plant anything. A lot of relatives do drop by here who do nothing but ask for vegetables. Sometimes, somebody comes by and would buy a huge quantity. That was how I and my son get by.

His son wasn't home that time because neighbor came by and brought him to hunt boar at the next mountain.

I told him to stop drinking because it would bring him nothing except destroy his body. And it didn't help to solve his problems.

I saw his eyes turn watery.

"If all the advice I heard was like that, my dear, I'd have stopped drinking a long time ago. But all right, then I can promise not to drink again . . . but there's something I'd ask for in return, my dear. . ."

"What was it, *tata*?"

"Could you ask our mayor, please, to give me a carabao to take care of. A matched pair would be best. I hear that the Bureau of Animal Industry has a program where they give livestock to those who were willing to care for them."

"Why don't you tell your barangay captain?"

"My dear, they don't treat me like a person down there. Especially my rich relations. Not even a dog could bear what they say whenever I pass by there for a visit."

"What I know about the program I that they bureau will give livestock, but they must be well-cared for. The female should produce young. But if you go on drinking like that and you forget to care for them, they surely won't give them to you."

Tata Basil's eyes flashed at what I said.

"I will never drink again, my dear, if only you can secure me a pair of carabao."

"The mayor will give you carabaos as long as he can see your efforts. Ask him to come here for a visit as well."

"Accompany me, then, my dear . . ."

I wasn't prepared for that request. What if Ralph refused to grant his request? I looked at *Tata* Basil. He was groomed. But how can I believe that he can stop drinking when it's already a part of his system?

But when I mentioned *Tata* Basil's request to Bella and Pedro, they flared up like dry grass.

"He will embarrass you, Marissa, just wait and see!"

Why were they like this? Why wouldn't they help *Tata* Basil when they were more than eager to ask the vegetables in his garden?

"*Tata* Basil was like that because you couldn't understand him when he said that nobody understands and cares for him among his relatives. Don't worry and I'll try to approach our Mayor with his request. I'll try to get your barangay captain's help."

"If so, you're serious about this?" Pedro ascertained. "Then would you also ask Mayor to grant me a pair of goats."

Darn it, now I'm stuck. Oh, well, let me try it at least. They'd have a lot to thank me for if their requests were granted.

I thought Ralph would say no to the requests of *Tata* Basil and Pedro. But instead he was happy to learn about it and that people like them were the ones he would really like to help.

THAT was a long time ago, but until now, when I remember, it's like I couldn't believe that I was able to help transform somebody like *Tata* Basil. He would always repeat to the people how grateful he was to me and that he would never forget me if he leaves. The last I heard he was no longer in Burador. He and his son have managed to erect a house near his brother's and they have increased the number of livestocks the Bureau had given them. —0

Bannawag: June 17, 1996; *translated by* Lorenzo R. Tabin II.

Resia's Demigod

THE voice of Ester, our guidance counselor in school, was smooth when she invited me to her desk. "Please, Marissa," she said, "go directly to Resia's house when you go home. "Inquire what hospital is she confined for even a moral support could we ever impart to her."

I was shocked. "Why? What happened to her?"

"Serious… it's between life and death. Somebody called here in school very early this morning."

How could I go for we had not been talking personally in almost two years?

Many of our co-teachers were listening this morning. All of them pouted and murmured. "Is a usurer got sick? But the illness of a usurer is cancer!"

"Good for her! As if she is a queen when collecting payment!"

"Marissa, I want to hear from your lips if you go Resia's place or not."

"Yes, I'll go…"

"Thank you, Marissa. I know you have a godly insight. Unlike some of the members of our group. Why they hate Resia, I really don't understand. She was not forcing them to borrow."

I was already in my class when Rose and *Manang* Libring, both belongs to our Grade One group, dropped by. I did not expect what *Manang* Libring said. "Don't go to Resia's place. If Ester wants to know her condition as she said, why, there are janitors she could send? You, if you go, I'll hate you. Never in my mind would I forgot what she did to me. Had you forgotten how terrible she talked to us?"

"Only now that I heard she became sick," countered Rose. "But sick or not, she does not have a problem. She got a lot of money. The only problem is, if she really got a cancer at last!"

The good Lord forbids! What I knew, Resia had a one-month vacation so she could focus her attention for the building of the ten-door apartment, her long-time dream before her husband arrives from abroad.

I was still in the jeepney ride home, but not decided yet if I go to Resia's house or not. If I don't go, Ester will get mad at me. If I go, *Manang* Libring, whom I considered my elder sister, and I usually ran for help whenever I got a problem, will also get mad at me.

Resia and I were classmates at the Northern Luzon Teachers College, now Don Mariano Marcos University, in Laoag City. She was from Ilocos Sur, I was from Ilocos Norte. We were both candidates for secretary with the student council. We first met at the campus advance meeting. She rendered a beautiful song while I recited my message without reading it. I did not expect to win. Resia approached me with a congratulatory embraced after the election and told me she was reading my writings in the *Bannawag*. Then she said, "I think your ambition in life is not really to become a teacher. Like me, I was only compelled."

I just countered her with an appear.

During the times where we were in the campus, she never mentioned about her parents and siblings, except her favorite topic for her dreams. She wanted to become rich and with a lot of money and jewelries deposited in the bank. She even dreamt to become an international singer if she could focus her attention in singing. She did not like to become a teacher after graduation.

That was true because not so long after our graduation, I received a letter from Resia that she planned to test her luck in Manila but not to teach. We wed with Larry. Despite my promised not to teach after graduation, my husband challenged me to use my course since I was able to pass the civil service. He said I could learn to love my profession.

I followed the advice of my husband and I was just surprised one day when Resia suddenly appeared in school as replacement of a retired teacher.

"O, what a small world!" we said after our tight embrace watching by our co-teachers. "My best friend in college," I just told them.

Somebody asked. "Is she also a writer like you?"

"A singer," I said.

"Not anymore," Resia said. "A dream that didn't come true. I married after graduation."

"We are the same," I said.

But why did she like to teach after all? "Crazy! To fulfill my dream to become a millionaire!" she countered.

My eyes opened overly wide. "How? You know very well that teachers' salary could hardly sustain themselves."

"Marissa, listen to me," she said. "Before deciding to teach I learned a lot of technique to fulfill my dream. I'm not going to tell you now, but you will know sooner or later."

She said she worked five years in an office filled with teachers going back and forth to loan. Gerry was her only child. Gerald her husband was going back and forth in abroad.

"Until such time that my dreams be fulfilled, the pain my two siblings planted to belittled me. I want to reciprocate their throbbing greediness."

"That's not good," I said. "Only God have that right to do."

"God?" she laughed. "Is there God during these times? Money is people's God now. Money is God for my two siblings and my relatives who seemed like dogs grabbing a lot of money by means of politics."

"You only, but me, no. There must be God in every teacher, Resia."

"You're now a saint of every saint, my friend. Okay, forget what I've said. Let me learn the ins and outs of our school. Do me a favor. Help me."

"Okay, but I don't like you to make money your demigod… for old times' sake. I'll help you, okay?"

Resia's attitude became more perplexing by the passing of days. Introducing Resia's self was not difficult by her own style. Spendthrift.

She uses jewelries and appliances. I confronted her one day. This is what she countered: "Those are ways of camaraderie. You know, there are a lot of things I am after for."

"Is it business? Monkey business?"

She laughed. "Keep guessing… But this is not yet the time. Just keep quiet of what I'm doing."

As if it was intended during that time, Larry playfully applied in an advertisement for Saudi. Hallah, there arrived a telegram as an answer telling him to go to their office and bring the documents needed. And we even needed to look for a place for us to move because we were given only a month to stay to the housing of the company where Larry was employed once my husband flies to Saudi. Resia offered to Larry a house and lot in a subdivision close to their place. She even loans us three thousand for the processing fee which we gave it back when my husband receives his separation fee from GSIS.

I learned more about Resia the longer we worked together in school. She said they have two house rentals in the adjacent subdivision. Aside from the ten-bedroom apartment to be started the soonest time. She said she got a lot of expensive jewelries from Saudi. And she got deposits money and jewelries in different banks in Metro Manila.

And there exploded a news in school that Resia did start and manage a Teachers' Loan in our school so that we do not have to go to other loan agency.

"Let's do it together," Resia invited me. "It will be better because your husband is in Saudi."

I shake my head. "Resia, sorry, we could not help to our co-teacher's in this kind of business."

"We will ask only ten percent interest unlike other loan companies asking fifteen to thirty percent."

And there were lot of teachers approached Resia to borrow. Not only my co-teachers, but even the parents but many of them got mad because of her strictness to collect payment. One of them was Manang Libring. "Your friend is too much, Marissa. I was late only for two days, she blubbered left and right. That if not because of her money, my son would never be gone to abroad. Marissa, don't ever do what your friend is doing."

I STOPPED the jeepney near the place of Resia. Whatever, I said to myself. I calmed down my temper. I pushed the doorbell in front of the big two-story house. Resia had surely reach her dream to become such.

A youngster opened the gate. He kissed the back of my palm. "Come in, *Tita*," he said. Gerry is already a young man. I had not seen him for quite some time.

Two women were in the living room. "*Tita,* they are my aunts. They are Daddy's sisters. They are the one assisting Mommy with two nurses."

"Where is you Mom?"

"I'll go see if she is awake, *Tita.*" Gerry entered a big room at the basement. I talked with his aunts. I asked what really had happened with Resia and why did they not bring to the hospital. They shake their heads.

"They advised us to go home, Ma'am, and Resia does not like to stay in the hospital anymore. And her illness is so serious. Her cancer busted inside. She did not care before. The doctor told us not to tell anymore."

I shuddered. Her cancer busted inside? So that means, she had been suffering for that long and the reason why she got a leave of absence? "Her husband, he knows already about Resia's condition?"

"Yes, Ma'am, we are waiting for his arrival. We started waiting for him since last week, but he could not just leave without his replacement."

"Can I talk to her?"

"Yes, she can talk. She complains the pain in her bosom when it occurs. There is always pus and blood oozes when she coughs."

"Is there any doctor looking for her?"

"There is, Ma'am. Just left some minutes ago. There are even two private nurses, but they are sleeping upstairs because they luck sleep. Her doctor advised to just stay home because she got complete needs."

Gerry came out. He signaled me to go inside. I did not expect what I saw. There was a dextrose connected to Resia that beside her, a big oxygen tank. She was assisted by three big pillows. Many emptied bottles of medicine on the table.

"Resia, what happened?" I was holding my feelings when I sat by the edge of the bed. I held her hand on the air. "Why did you neglect yourself and became like this?"

Her voice was calm and tottered. "Thank you for visiting me. I've waiting for you… I don't know, I don't know why this suddenly happened to me. I was suddenly fell down and then they brought me to the hospital… but I'm glad you dropped by, Marissa… I know you had forgiven me… You know what I've been asking many times to the Lord? Give me new life so that I could repay my shortcoming to Him. He probably punished me… Remember what I was always telling you that there was no God and money was my demigod? Despite of having a lot of money when a challenge like comes, it easily disappears. I had paid a lot of money to the doctor, and my very expensive medication. My savings in the bank is almost drained."

"Just toughen your mind. Pray to Him. Ask for forgiveness. God is always mindful!"

She pressed my palm tightly. "It's only now that I realized my grave mistake. Please… help me pray. Please ask forgiveness to those whom I inflict pain in our school. If I survive this, I don't like to go back to school. I will focus my time to serve God!"

Probably her medication was for sleeping. Resia got asleep after taking the medication. I was not able to hold my tears. I was thinking that she probably won't stay long. I prayed silently beside her.

RESIA had not stayed long since my visit. Many attended her funeral. Two of her siblings arrived including her relatives with positions in the province. What Resia described about them was totally different in real life. In fact, they offered Gerald to shoulder the funeral's expenses—or if what Resia told me was true, what these people shown to us was fake and they just wanted to prove that Resia was in fault. —0

Bannawag: July 15, 1996; *translation completed*: July 15, 2018.

God Exists, Joan

"MA'AM does God really exist?" Joan asked. She was fifteen already. She was almost as tall as I was.

"God exists, Joan. Why? Do you doubt it?"

"Well, if God does exist, ma'am, why was this happening to me again? Why did Sister Didi leave? She said and promised to give me light, so I won't be lost again."

"But of course, she's left, her missionary days in the Philippines were through. And that means, her promise to bring you to America will soon be fulfilled. She'd come back for you like she told me in our last conversation. That's why you need to study hard."

"Sister Leona was sending me away from the boarding house, Ma'am…"

"Did. . . Did you do something?"

"She insists that I stole the shades and wristwatch that I'm using, but they were given to me by Sister Didi before she went home."

"Didn't you tell her?"

"I did, Ma'am, but she doesn't believe me. She said Sister Didi wasn't fool enough to buy me expensive things. She insists I stole them because one of her friends lost something when they visited the boarding house. So, I answered back. I don't understand why she's like that. She's so different from Sister Didi. She's even saying bad things about Sister Didi, even though she's a missionary like her."

"Bad things? Like what, Joan?"

"Mostly about the book that Sister Didi wrote about me. Sister Leona's saying that Sister Didi wrote it to gain a lot of money from our church members."

That was the first time I heard about the book. "A book, Joan? Did you bring a copy with you?"

"I did, ma'am. . ."

Joan pulled out a blue-covered book. And there was Joan's picture on the cover. I accepted it silently and scanned the first pages. . .

"There's a lot here that I didn't know about you, Joan," I said at last.

"Well, you never asked me, ma'am. You send me home right away after classes. It's been a long time since we last got to talk. Now Sister Didi's gone, I hope I could talk to you more."

"I knew you had a lot to do in the boarding house that's why I sent you home immediately. . . Joan, can I borrow this book? I'll return it tomorrow."

"I might not be here tomorrow, ma'am."

"Why?"

"I'm moving to a different house, one of our church member's."

Noon struck. I've finished my tasks. It was time to go home. The afternoon teacher who shared the classroom with me was absent. I looked at Joan. She hadn't moved from where she sat.

"Was there something else you want to tell me? Let's talk about it and maybe I can help you," I suggested.

"Until now, it's still a mystery to me why I had to be born, why my father hates me so much, and why all these misfortunes happen to me. That's why my doubts about God's existence just surfaces sometimes. And even if He's real, He plays favorites. Some He cares about, and others He just ignores."

"God exists, Joan. Erase those doubts from your mind. If misfortunes happen, they occur because there's something to learn from them. No father hates his child."

"Then I am that child, ma'am. My father's simply the opposite. He's not actually insane, but he hates me because my Mom diet birthing me. My father never took care of me. He gave me away to a blind old woman, Lola Basilia from Badoc. But before she died, she sent for my father and returned me to him. I was seven. I wanted so much to be loved as his daughter, but I never felt it. The whore he lived with made me her slave. She h me raped when I was eight for some gambling money. When I told my father, he hit me and said I was lying.

"I ran away. I had nowhere to go I was crying. I even wanted to jump down a cliff. But Lolo Asiong and Lola Tina found me. They pitied me. They took me in. they treated me like I was family."

"Why didn't they send you to school?"

"The school was far, ma'am. Besides, they said that if one was industrious, they get rich, even without an education. Even if you study everything there was to learn, if you were lazy you won't get anywhere. They were farmers. They tilled a wide plot in Trinidad Valley. They took me wherever they went. We sold produce at the market. If there was too much vegetables, we'd sell them wholesale."

"Where were they now?"

"They've been dead a long time, ma'am. Armed robbers entered our house one night. Their faces were covered. They called Lolo and Lola and took all the money they could find. They didn't see me hiding under the bed."

"After the funeral, nobody else took you in?"

"Nobody, ma'am. They said I was the cause of the couple's misfortune. At the market, I shared my problem with one of the girls my age and she invited me. She said I could stay with Ate Celia. She took care of many children. She taught us how to pick pockets, slash bags, snatch necklaces and sell Shabo!"

I trembled as Joan explained. So, the warning one of the parents gave me at the start of the school year as true after all. "Beware of your tallest student, ma'am. That girl from Baguio was a topnotch snatcher and thief!"

"Did you enjoy that kind of life, Joan?"

"Oh, no, ma'am, none of us did. But we had to do it. Nobody else would take us except Ate Celia and her husband who we rarely saw. Ate Celia told us that people were cruel. What they did to her made her use children for revenge."

"Did she give you a lot of money?"

"Just barely enough for a little snack, ma'am. She said it was all right since we never missed any meal and were well-fed anyway."

"Didn't the police arrest you?"

Joan pointed to the scars on her arms and forehead. "The first time they did, it was horrible, ma'am. The scars on my forehead were from cigarette burns and a 2"x2" caused these scars on my arms. That's 'coz I resisted. After that, they didn't bother us anymore because Ate Celia gave the police protection money. They would lock us up whenever we get caught, then the police would call Ate Celia and she would come bail us out. The police even tell us where to go to pick pockets."

My lips thinned at this revelation from Joan.

"How did you meet Sister Didi?"

"She was walking near Burnham Park, ma'am. There were three of them. They passed my beat. I grabbed her bag and hightailed it from there. She screamed. But a highway patrol just happened to pass by at the time. . . They caught me. I was locked up. Worse, the police on duty were all new. I tried to call Ate Celia, but a companion told me she was also caught and sent to Manila by the NBI because surveillance found out she was delivering drugs there. I was trying to think of a way to get out. My hatred against my father and stepmother flared up. If not for them, I wouldn't have been there.

"One day, I was surprised when the guard told me someone paid my bail. When I came out to see who did pay, I recognized Sister Didi standing there with my papers, and my hairs stood on end. She smiled at me while I felt like melting like salt.

"She introduced herself. 'Joan, I am Sister Didi. I'm a missionary from our church assigned here to the Philippines. I will help you change your life and return to God.'

"That was the first time I ever heard an advice that touched me deep inside. I cried in front of Sister Didi and begged forgiveness.

"She brought me to the boarding house where she lived, in Quezon City. She kept her promise that she would treat me like her own sister. She never wearied giving me advice. She promised to send me to school until I could finish a course. I was thirteen when she enrolled me in kindergarten. I wasn't shy because I wanted to return her kindness."

"Joan," I said, "Sister Didi was God's way so you can see the light and feel His true love."

"Then why won't Sister Leona believe that I have changed?"

TWO ladies were waiting for me outside my room one morning. From the nametags pinned on their lapels, I saw that Sister Leona was one of them.

"What can I do for you, Sisters?" I asked with a smile after greeting them. Their faces remained impassive. I know at once that Joan was their reason for being there.

"Were you Teacher Marissa, Joan's teacher?" asked Sister Leona.

"Yes, I am, Sister."

"Our reason for coming was very urgent, Mrs. Del Prado. We want to know directly from you whether Joan was still coming to class or not."

"Joan was never absent, Sister," I said.

"It's been a week and Joan hasn't returned to the boarding house. She left after I told her about the wristwatch and shades."

"Sister Didi gave her the wristwatch and shades as a gift before she left."

"No missionary was crazy enough to give someone like Joan such expensive gifts. One of our companions who visited the boarding house has been missing her wristwatch and shades for some time now."

Could it be that Sister Leona didn't know of Sister Didi's plans to bring Joan to America?

"You picked out Joan as the culprit, was that it, Sister?"

"She left without saying anything after our conversation; wasn't that clear admission that she took them? And for your information, you're hiding one of the most cunning thief and cutpurse from Baguio! That's why I came by, to warn you, and to ask for your help if possible, to get back the wristwatch ad eyeglasses from Joan."

"I thought you helped people like Joan to change and face life again, Sister? Don't you want to know what has happened to Joan who was once a thief and cutpurse?"

"I don't tolerate the likes of Joan like Sister Didi did. You should be aware, ma'am, that if not for the mission, Joan would not even *be* a person! I will help when I help but I will choose who I help."

My anger rose when I heard this. What kind of missionary was this? Even so, I kept my tone level.

"Sister Leona, to tell you the truth, Joan never stole any eyeglasses or wristwatch. Sister Didi bought them for her as a gift. And for your information, Sister Didi was coming back to take Joan to continue her studies in the States. Sister Didi was an only child and her parents want to take Joan to adopt her as their own daughter."

"I see that even you have been brainwashed by your thief of a student!"

The image of Sister Leona blurred. "A foreigner like Sister Didi was better because she knows how to care for one of our countrymen like Joan. It's good for her that with her mission she carried a heartfelt desire to serve not only God, but also her fellowmen. You can leave now, Sister Leona, if you have nothing else to tell me!"

Sister Leona and her companion angrily turned around and left.

IT has been seven years since that morning; it was only through Joan's letter that I found out she's been in the United States for four years. I've all but forgotten about Joan ever since Sister Didi returned to the Philippines to process Joan's papers. Oh, and Sister Didi married a Filipino who was also a missionary like her and they have two children. –0

Bannawag: November 11, 1996; *translated by:* Lorenzo R. Tabin II.

Livelihood Once Outlived

I WAS going out and in at the wide-opened patio of a small trailer where we were staying looking far away waiting for the arrival of Marla from Coachella. I was mad for instead of seeing her at the gate of their house, I saw their big black bulldog.

"Once your niece made a mistake, I will surely expose what I'm hiding!" I said to my timeworn husband last night, and I repeated when I woke up. "If not because of her chattiness, Siding and Ibing should have not gone. Probably that was how *Manang* Asiang your sister taught her!" *Manang* Asiang's house was in the third street away from us.

"Don't ever include that woman, *Baket*[28]. She is not touching you," my timeworn said. "And it is not Philippines her anymore… they will capture cantankerous here!"

"I see, mark my word, *lakay,* I will surely expose what I'm hiding, I said so. Perhaps, Marla believes that, because I am just a lowly woman being related to your family, this is what she talks about me, something not even eaten by dog. If she does not have mouth like that, Siding and Ibing should have not gone unnoticed. What kind of living they have right now, I surely don't know. Probably tomorrow, or the next day, some police officers will drop by here to say they met an accident or had been abducted and raped. Or procured by drug addicts. God forbids!"

"Lot of nonsense. You better pray for their good condition under a rightful hand. Marla, even she is a cantankerous, she is kind. She gave

---

[28]   *Baket,* wife, also old woman.

you a microwave oven, and many more foods. Alright, you better pray, it's far better than letting your mind fly anywhere else."

"I had forgotten how to pray! My tears had dried out. Do it by yourself. It's good for you because you are always here in the trailer crossing your feet the whole day long!"

My timeworn was already eighty-one years old but because I was only forty-one years old, his eyes are still twinkling when satiated over me.

I noticed Alona not so far away carrying on her hand a bucket walking with feet apart from each other toward us. I surely know that there is something fishy this potbellied woman who was also renting one of the trailers of Marla come to divulge to me. When I was still in the Philippines, I did not know what a trailer was. I learned that it was a house like a bus with wheels that it could be hauled and moved anywhere you want to park, unlike a trailer used by businessmen of tobacco in the Ilocos Region.

"You look like Good Friday again, why? It's still too early in the morning, you should be smiling instead," she said. She dropped the bucket she was carrying. The tilapia fishes flounder. "Okay, get some. Andy had fished a lot by hook this past dawn and I'll go ask *Nana* Orang to sell some."

As if I did not hear Alona. I placed my arms akimbo and stood up from where a was sitting. "You know what I was thinking?" I pointed my index finger to her. "If there is no good news from where Marla went, I will talk to her with words not good enough for dog's food. I will expose my being cantankerous. Nobody could have overplayed me in Nagbakuitan for your information!"

"What happened?"

"I have been sleepless for how many nights now thinking where Siding and Ibing are to be found."

"You are thinking so much? I heard that they went with their companions picking grapes in Moreno. There probably no telephone where they are staying that's why they could not call you."

"Even so! I will fight with Marla if she comes home without bringing good news!"

"You better get tilapia because it's getting late. I'm warning you; you could not win over Marla. Nobody had won over her. Despite of her cantankerousness, she got body like a giant dresser. Ones she catches you with her two big arms she will browbeat and weigh you down, see if she could not squeeze you? More so because you are not far from a bamboo branchlet!"

"Just try me and I will bring her to court. Don't she ever think that I do not know my right. And I am paying my monthly rental! If I say I will bring her to court, I will!"

"I see, never mind. Just go get something to put your tilapia. Common. It's getting late."

"I do not have money to pay for. We don't have money yet."

"You will pay when your timeworn husband receives his pension."

I sighed when Alona had gone. She is also an Ilokana like me. She was from La Union. She was able to come to America because his father was a veteran like my timeworn husband. Unluckily, his father found a Mexican far younger and more beautiful than her mother. They don't know where in the corners of California they are hiding now. When Alona luckily land a job in a clinic in San Diego, she met Alejandro who was also a Filipino, and they decided to live together. They married just recently in Las Vegas. Alona was already loaded when she discovered that there were two women stayed with Alejandro prior to her. One was an American whom he begot a child and left in San Jose. Alejandro promises everything when Alona starts complaining. Anyway, she was the only one he married.

My reminiscing was cut off when somebody tapped my shoulder. My husband called me. "Had you prepared our breakfast, *Baket*?" he blinked at me. If he had that kind of posturing, there are two meanings.

"I had cooked rice. I had even cooked the viand. Just eat if you are hungry. I'll wait for Marla."

"Hey, those tilapias are still fresh. They are still frisking like me. I missed eating *sinigang*[29], *Baket*."

---

[29]   *Sinigang,* a meat or fish dish mixed with vegetables cooked in water and seasoned with sour ingredients like tamarind.

"Why don't you cook *sinigang* if you missed it? Stop bothering me when my head is as heavy as a wickerwork!"

"Put it down, *Baket*, to make it lighter."

"Hey-hey, don't ever cajole me you timeworn for my head is really in bad shape!"

"You go then prepare the food because I am very hungry."

It was about time for us to start our breakfast when we heard a resound coming into the wide courtyard. It was really Marla. She was touching tenderly her bulldog. The bulldog was like a human who could understand words. It was the guard in the big house of Marla. I was about to stand and confront Marla but my timeworn stopped me.

"Eat properly so that you have enough strength when she whirls and throw you down," he said.

"Hey, that niece of yours should not make a mistake for she could she what I'm hiding!"

"Keep it easy, *Baket*. Remember that we had not yet paid our loan to her. And you should not show her what you are hiding for I am the only one who had the right to see."

"Timeworn philosopher!" but instead of getting mad at him, like the past my feelings was melted by his smooth communicating. The only thing I am against with this timeworn is that whenever Marla say anything, everything is yes, as if he does not know how to say no. He did never contradict or reprimand his niece.

Soon afterwards, a cracking sound by the trailer we were in attracted our attention. I peeped out. It was Marla with an overly-wide smile.

"What's news, *Nakkong*?" I said. I called her *nakkong* to tone down my feelings that about to explode again.

"Let me in first, auntie, before answering you."

She went inside with very heavy steps. The chair she sat on cricked. I was scared the chair may break down. My eyes focused to Marla's cackle. It was serious. It almost reached her bosom.

"You don't worry nothing. Siding's job in Moreno is now secured. The reason why they were not able to call was that there was no telephone in their new boarding house of one week. But now they have telephone because they moved to *comadre* Isang's."

"Were you able to talk to them, *Nakkong*?"

"Yes, the two of them, auntie. They will call you on Sunday. They said they really planned not to call."

I was able to breath freely. "How many months are they staying there, *Nakkong*?"

"They are staying there forever!"

"W-what?" I covered my ears because my voice resounded acutely.

My timeworn husband's chin dropped.

Marla laughed out loud; her cackle swung freely.

"Not really… Two or three months, they said, auntie. They will complete the picking period of grapes so that they could bring home something to recompense your homesickness!"

"Your auntie worried a lot," the old man said.

"Auntie, never mind, for your problems had been solve, and accompany me this afternoon. You and Alona."

"Where are we going?"

"Let's go steal watermelon," she chuckled.

"King of balms. I really don't like that idea!"

"Don't worry. I'm just very eager to eat newly sliced watermelon."

Stealing is Marla's sayings. Many times, did she lead us with Alona to pick bitter melon, string beans, and jute at the yard of whoever *pulano*[30] or *pulana* we don't know but same Filipinos like us. The owners were not home. The problem was, only me and Alona did she like to get off from her car and pick those things. When we go home, she had been laughing with gusto.

I told her before to tell the owner to share their vegetables instead of stealing. As if those fruits taste better when it is stolen.

"If you ask for, do they share?" she countered and leaned her head.

"What do you think, am I going to do what she asked for?" I asked my timeworn when Marla had gone.

"Either you like it or not, she will always be followed," my husband said. "Just go to avoid misunderstanding."

---

[30] *Pulano or pulana:* a colloquial name given to a male or female person.

"For God sakes! I did never try to steal my whole life. But I'm stealing here in America! I doubt if I could ever present myself to the good God when I die?"

"Never mind, you will not be alone, *Baket*. It will be the three of you with Marla."

"Ay, ay, ay! Never ever!"

"Then just keep quiet, *Baket*," the palm of this timeworn as thick as a carpet groped my thigh. "The good is the daughter of God," he squinted his left eye and twisted his lips while looking at me sideways.

I wagged my index finger to my husband. "Remember this, you timeworn," I said while my feelings which was about to boil cold off. I can't understand my feelings because I feel like losing everything by the softness of his voice. "If your good niece put me in trouble, she could wait something bad!"

"Then let's go rest, *Baket*, before anything else…"

It was around three o'clock when I heard Marla yelling. I was just awakened from my nap beside my husband. I arose and went out from the room in a hurry. I peeped how Alona waggled while walking beside Marla.

I was hesitant to go if not because of my husband's enticing.

"Just go to avoid hearing words," he pushed me.

Marla's red pickup was almost raspy when we traversed the street between the wide-open field, seemed unending. We passed by the wide grape yard then the Sunkist area where the yellow fruits were sparkling under the flaming sun. Next month, pickers will be like ants under the flaming desert. The heat in the Philippines was nothing compared to the heat here. Peaking at the grape yard, where I was with has ended. I collapsed many times because of the heat. I cried a lot before. I cursed why I moved in this inferno.

Marla stopped her car between the thick Sunkist trees and watermelon area, where we were going. The ripe watermelon fruits were huge scattered all around the area.

"Alright, get off, auntie, and load this pick up. Bring this knife."

Me and Alona were hesitant.

"What if somebody see us?" Alona said. "I might give birth to my baby at no time!"

"You won't give birth yet. But if you give birth, I'll let you do it at once. I know how to be a midwife, to tell you the truth. Alright, go ahead. I'll take care of you!"

"You are here but we are the one picking and loading," I said. "If ever they catch us and bring us to jail, what?"

"No coward Ilokano! If they put you in jail, I'll come to redeem you. I know the chief personally."

Alona went out first. I followed her. We were in a hurry cutting the fruit from their vine. They were heavy. Loading had not hold her desire. She opened one of the fruits. She shared me. It was sweet and cold. We enjoyed our large bite. The sweetness of the watermelon here were different.

"Hurry up, let's go!" I said when I counted our pick twenty.

I breath heavily after loading the last two in the pick-up.

"I felt like giving birth!" Alona's eyeballs rolled up while holding her tummy after loading her last load.

Marla smiled very wide. I watched the swinging of her cackle.

"That's life here," she said. "Cunning is livelihood when outlived!"

"Could be deadly if unlucky!" I seconded.

Marla was about to start the car when we heard a siren away from behind.

"Somebody had seen us!" I said. My bosom started drumming.

Marla's face colored like a cooked crab. She was not able to speed up because the black pick-up was already behind us.

"Why did you pick watermelon without asking permission?" one of them was mad. They got off from their car. Two men. They were Mexican.

"Your watermelon's fruit were good looking that's why we were enticed to pick, handsome." Marla's smile was overly hanging. "My companions were so good in picking. It's sweet, they said, for they even ate some while picking."

"M-Marla!" I exclaimed. My God, she had imperiled us!

Alona looked like a fish soaked in vinegar.

"*No comprende Inglese?*" one of the Mexicans pointed out the signboard NO TRESPASSING.

Marla's face turned into normal. "Hey, wait!" she said as if something clicked as an electric bulb in her forehead. "You are not the owner. I know the owner. Let me see your green card?"

The man looked at his companion.

"You too, where is your green card?" Marla got off and hands in akimbo looking sharply at the two. "All right, you don't have a green card. Do you want me to report you?"

"No *senorita*… no *senora*!" The two were scared to death. They hurriedly back to their pick-up.

Marla drove directly in *Manang* Asiang's, her mother. "Let's share her. So, she wouldn't complain," Marla said.

That's what I like to Marla. She was kind.

Manang Asiang got a wide smile upon seeing the watermelon in our arms with Alona.

"They are so big!" *Manang* Asiang appreciated. "Where did you get it?"

I pointed at Marla. "She ordered us to steal, *Manang*," I said.

"You silly! I don't like to be involved with your sin!" she jiggled herself. "Bring back to your car!"

Marla was about to come near. Her eyebrows arched.

"You, Marla, you instructed them. I did not teach you to do that…!"

"You should be thankful for we are here to share you," yelled Marla. "Don't believe to auntie. We asked those from the Mexicans!"

"So be it!" *Manang* Asiang's smile hanged eventually. Alona was about to laugh and followed Marla in the car.

"Regards to *Manong*," *Manang* Asiang said and put a green buck into my pocket. "I won a little bit last night in the Casino," she whispered. "Don't tell Marla."

We reached Franz, Marla's husband, in their house. He was walking back and forth in their front yard. He was boxing the wind.

"Where have you been, you woman for you did not locked the gate?" he said looking to Marla. His eyes were sharp.

"What for?"

"Bulldog has gone. With his chain!"

"What?"

Marla was wiggling to run around the side of their house. She probably left her bulldog there. Afterwards, she cried loudly. She cursed whoever stole their dog. She had nothing to point out except the drug addicts who was taught by the Filipinos to eat dog. Eating dogs in America was strictly prohibited but many are still doing it.

Marla came back to where we were. She looked at Franz. "You might be the one who taught them to roast Bulldog!" she yelled. "You are voracious in eating dog. You told your friends to steal him!"

Marla faced us. "Auntie get your watermelon with Alona and I go to report to the chief!"

"No more Bulldog to guard!" Franz also said as if he was talking to somebody else.

"She did not survive, *Baket*," my husband smiled widely while pianoing on my thigh when I mentioned what happened. He blinked at me. —0

Bannawag: August 6, 2001; *translation completed:* July 17, 2018.

2

LORENZO GARCIA TABIN, SR.

Man, And Time

*A*MA[31] Valentin had almost than smoothing out a horizontal wall of a calesa when Manolito arrives.

"I thought you are not coming back?" *Ama* Valentin said.

"Because I took a bath first, *tata*[32]," the man said.

It was the same time when Herminia went down from the stairs, the only child of *Ama* Valentin, who was going to draw water from the well. Manolito blinked the young lady. Herminia pouted the young man.

"Please attach the roof," *Ama* Valentin voiced out. "Check if it is short and cut a piece from the other sheet of galvanized iron if ever." He did not stop what he was doing, and he had not notice Manolito followed his eyes toward Herminia.

"By the way, *tata*," Manolito said while doing what it was told, "I passed by *Mang*[33] Castor. He wants to withdraw his order. He said he have no money for he had spent his savings."

"He had spent it?" the old man's forehead furrowed.

"Kind of, *tata*... I noticed that it was only his alibi because they were chatting with *Mang* Timot about building a calesa. They adore the design of Cardo. They said it's a contemporary model and the assembly is better. They had not said anything against our handiwork. Cardo is

---

31 *Ama,* an address of respect given by younger men to older men.

32 *Tata,* an address given to an uncle, or a middle-aged man.

33 *Mang,* an abridged of *Manong,* a big brother or older guy.

our strong competitor. Let's see, he had not even a year in the business, but his designs are at present well-liked."

"Ever since in the beginning, I've been building the source of their income." *Ama* Valentin stopped his smoothing. "All the calesas here, I built them. They all passed through my hands. And if they did not like my handiworks… Alright, Cardo is now here, as you had said. He is creating a new model. It will be beneficial if it's true."

"They said our handiworks are weighty, *tata*. The wood parts are too broad, and because of that, the horse are hard ups in hauling the calesa."

Ama Valentin smiles. "They ever knew that I do not like brittle. Things that they could not use long term. See our handiworks, it takes a lot of years before needing repair. But nevertheless, I am delighted."

Manolito was astounded to what the old man said. He did not expect that despite of having a competitor, he is still delighted. He knew there are truth what *Ama* Valentin had said. But he also knows that their creation has a big disadvantage: the old model of handiworks against the creation of Cardo—who had just newly graduated carpentry.

Manolito arrived not long time ago from where he helped farming in Isabela, the place of his cousin Mauro. He stayed there less than a year. They originally feeling the same with *Ama* Valentin that's why when he came back, the old man asked him to be his helper.

It was already late in the afternoon when they stopped working. Before Manolito went home, he first went where Herminia was cooking. He stood by the door for an extended time, for he was not noticed by Herminia.

Manolito cleared his throat to signal his presence. The lady was startled, and she almost dropped the knife she was using to cut the eggplant she will cook for viand.

"So, you're easily startled," laughed Manolito.

"Because of you. I thought who was at my back."

"Sorry, Herming. May I have a drink?"

"Just go and dip what you need," Herminia said.

Instead of going to where the drinking vessel was, Manolito sat at the bench near the lady.

"You are becoming more beautiful as the days pass by," he said.

"I thought you want to drink?"

"It seems I am bothering you too much. See you then…" Manolito stood up and turned back.

After getting down, he looked back and noticed Herminia peeping toward him.

MANOLITO and the old man were almost done with what they were assembling but they had not yet received a new order. Unlike the past days. Many from other villages even came to order.

Manolito noticed the stillness of *Ama* Valentin. The old man was not usually like this. Sometimes, he stops from what he was doing and lay down on the sled.

"Do you remember those times when we did not enough time to finish our job?" asked *Ama* Valentin.

"Yes, *tata*. There were a lot of…"

"But now it is in the contrary," intervened by the old man. He smiled and nodded.

Manolito stops his smoothing and looked at the old man.

"Do you know that this never came up to my mind?" *Ama* Valentin talked again. "But here it is. And it is only now that I realized that all people, whatever he is doing or condition in life, his reformation will come. In the passing of time, or even the days, there is already rectification."

Manolito did not talk.

"This needs to be happened," continued *Ama* Valentin. "And by doing what I think is important thing, I can feel happiness and contentment because of the services I had given to them. But in the side, I feel sad because I did not plan to prepare the coming of this event. This will not harm anything if I'm alone. But I am thinking about Herminia. She is still single. She does not know anything except to house chores. She will experience hardship…"

MANOLITO bid farewell again to go to Isabela where his cousin Mauro was.

"Are you leaving again?" the old man was saddened.

"Yes, *tata*. It's harvesttime again and *Manong* Mauro impressed upon me to go and help because he does not have anybody to help him."

The old man kept silent, silence that Manolito understood.

"I am sorry for leaving you, *tata*. Please don't ever think that I am going away because of what happened to our job. It's really true that *Manong* Mauro had no helper, *tata*."

"Had you not told me that you do not have a plan to go back there?"

"That was true, *tata*. But a letter from *Manong* Mauro had just arrived where he impressed upon me to go."

"When are you going then?"

"This afternoon, *tata*."

"Please don't ever forget us, Manoling…"

"I assure you, *tata*. If not because of the inculcation of my cousin, I would not go back there anymore."

THE stay of Manolito in Isabela had been over a month. Harvesttime is over. One dusk while laying down on a sled under a blackberry tree after dinner, he remembered Herminia. He was forcing himself to forget the lady. In fact, he should be in the Ilocos Region if not because of what he thought self-centeredness of Herminia. He likes to forget the lady.

He received a letter from his house. His mother informed him the death of *Ama* Valentin.

Manolito prepared himself to leave at ones. He needs to go home. He will go and see Herminia. He got hold of Herminia who was sitting mournfully beside their window.

"Condolence," Manolito said when they were on face to face with Herminia.

Herminia was not able to hold her feelings. She sobbed and covered her face by her palms.

"I heard that you are planning to go to Manila, Herming," Manolito said when Herminia stopped crying.

"Yes," the voice of the lady was bitter, "I'm going to look for a job, even just a housemaid."

"If *tata* still alive, he does not agree with what you are thinking."

"If he is still alive. But my father has gone. And I need to live."

"Don't continue your plan. If you agree, if you don't think otherwise, I will invite you in Isabela, the place of my cousin Mauro. I could look for a field to till there."

Herminia rose her face still wet of tears.

"I won't speed you up. I know you are still in mourning. In the meantime, will you please accompany me to the cemetery? I would also want to visit *tata*."

It was almost dusk when they walked out from the cemetery. Herminia was still looking down while crying.

"I promised to *tata*," Manolito said. "And it is up to you the fulfillment, or otherwise, of my promise to him."

"My father liked you very much. In fact, he was always thinking about your departure. He felt so much the drifting of his customers."

"Did he also felt bad with me because I left him alone?"

"No, because he knew that you are coming back."

"But he's gone… and I am coming back for you, if you allow me."

"Let me clear up first, Manoling."

Manolito looked Herminia eye to eye. "Yes," his right hand found the palm of the lady, "we need to clear up." –0

Bannawag: first published in October 4, 1965; reprinted in August 27, 2018; translation completed in August 26, 2018.

Deep And This Babylon

IT was almost the same time when the siren rang to inform that it was five o'clock in the afternoon and when Willy Shaw stood upon the gangplank of the ship. He noticed the workers running after the others from the building being built at the foot of the mountain thirty meters away from the water, toward the dumpster from the ship. Four big steel, two square feet, side by side were the dumpsters. He looked steadily to the workers running after the others to get the white uniform from the ship; some of them collect any kind of food, like apples, Sunkist, bread, eggs and meat the cooks had just thrown away for they might have been lazy to bring them back in the freezer; and, whatever they could eat. All the items they collected; Willy Shaw know for sure that they do not need them in the ship anymore. Whenever a cloth got stained, they just throw it away and ask for a replacement—their sustenance arrive as member of the American army. How many uniforms Willy Shaw had thrown? There was even a civilian shirt he bought outside which he had not even wear, he just threw away because it did not fit with him. There is a big difference between the Americans and the Filipinos, he observed. So, their attitude here is like this. They had just landed in Subic not quite long ago.

"Let's go, Willy," he was distracted when Roger Briant, his friend, called him. "Don't pay attention to those people," he added when he noticed where Willy's attention was focused.

"I pity them," Willy Shaw shook his head.

"They are really like that. We better go."

There was only one exit at the gate. And, also, one entrance, aside from the exit and entrance of cars. The people walking was in queue. They all have passes. They were all inspected before allowed to go out.

Outside the gate, several meters away, there was a concrete bridge not that big.
Willy Shaw noticed some women that looked like comforters. They were short compared to them. The height of most of them were only up to below the White's armpit. They smoke a lot, and every time they puff a cigarette, there is red left from the tip of it. They were not good looking. But that did not surprise Willy Shaw why they Americans were attracted by them that much.

The attention of Willy Shaw was caught by the children under the bridge. They were completely naked. Some of them used a small booth. They each have scoop net. They were competing in offering their scoop net while shouting "Hi, Joe! Some coins, Joe!" There were kind Americans smiling while throwing ten or twenty-five or fifty cents—some just pass by. If the coin they throw does not go inside the scoop net, the children were competing to dive for it. The water was dirty—Willy Shaw felt nauseated.

One black and curly-haired boy attracted his attention. Upon seeing this, something touched his feelings, without knowing what it was. More so when he noticed the pitiful condition of the boy. His eyes were so lonely. He was the smallest among the children and could catch money the less. Unintentionally Willy Shaw groped his pocket and threw fifty cents to the boy. The boy was so happy when the coin drops into his scoop net. "Thank you, Joe. Thank you, Joe!" he shouted. Willy Shaw smiled at him.

At that very moment, he felt nostalgic upon remembering Ram, their five-year old son with Sally. He was as well homesick with Sally. It was about a year since the last time he visited them. Ram's small voice was ringing again to his ear, saying, "Don't stay away long, okay, Pa? Bring me home a toy, okay, Pa?" As if he was looking Sally smiling in front of him. That vacation was not even a week. His wife and his son were lonely when he bids goodbye. "We will be so lonely again, Willy," Sally said that time.

Willy Shaw exhales so deeply upon remembering these.

His imagining was cut short by the nuisance. They were already at the other end of the bridge. It was so noisy and no clear message except those asking somebody to get change their dollar.

"Change, Joe… Change, Joe!" met a chubby woman by the left side of the road. "Here, Joe," said a skinny woman from the other changing store and pulled Willy Shaw inside.

Roger Briant decided to change his twenty-dollar bill. Five dollars only for Willy Shaw.

"That's not enough, Willy," said Roger Briant. "You're not satisfied."

"This is enough."

Jeepneys were in line in the other side of the road and they were competing to ask passengers to ride. Willy Shaw and Roger Briant got a ride. Clubs were everywhere. The buildings were huge and the lights with different colors were bright.

Roger Briant asked the driver to stop in front of *Paradise Club*. Roger Briant did not get the change of a peso he handed to the driver.

Inside the club was dim. The band players played joyfully. The dress of the woman singing was vibrant. Many of the sailors like Willy Shaw were already drunk. Most of them had women under their arms. They were so noisy.

Willy Shaw and Roger Briant got a table for four in the corner of the club. Two over perfumed and beautiful ladies approached them at ones.

"Enjoy with us, Joe," the two women gleefully offered themselves.

"Oh, yeah, honey!" countered Roger Briant and put his arms around the shoulder of the one wearing a dress with roses. The one with yellow dress approached Willy Shaw.

Roger Briant appealed a waiter. The guy knew at once what they needed.

"This is the way of living here, Willy," Roger Briant said. "Just get what you want!"

The two women laugh.

"As long as you have this!" his partner clicked her forefinger.

They laughed with gusto one more time. Willy Shaw was just smiling.

Roger Briant had downed several bottles of bear. Willy Shaw had just downed two.

"Dance with the music, Willy!" Roger Briant said upon noticing the silence of Willy Shaw. He tossed his glass one more time. He did not put it down until emptied. "It will be another long time when we are back in the ship. Enjoy while you are here."

Willy Shaw smiled sheepishly. When the strength of the drink overpowered, he felt the warmth all over his body.

"Are you not happy by my side, Darling?" his partner teased him. She moved out from her chair and sat over Willy Shaw's lap. Willy Shaw smelt the fragrance of the woman. Without farther ado, he kissed her.

Roger Briant and his partner whispered sweet nothings. Not long awhile, they left Willy Shaw and his partner. They went up the stairs. That was also Willy Shaw and his partner did.

ROGER Briant's wallet had been emptied when they went out from the *Paradise Club*. Willy Shaw still had five pesos. While enjoying their time, their partners secretly picked their wallets. They were not able to say no when the two women were laughing emptying their wallets. "Money first, honey!" that's their litany.

Nonetheless, Roger Briant was satisfied. "That's the way life is, Willy," he said. "We need some pastime. "We only have a very short time to enjoy, out from the ship." He tapped his friend's shoulder. "We'll come back tomorrow night. We need some amusement!" he crackles.

They passed along the street many of their countrymen who were drank and wiggling with dirty white uniform. They put their arms together over their shoulders with unsteady footing, not knowing where to go. Some of them were selling their wrist watch in a bargain price.

In front of them, a guy was being surrounded by people in side street. When they were able to come closer the incident, they noticed that the guy was blooded and full of dust; he was one of their countrymen. One of his eyes turned black. Blood oozing from his mouth, his clothes was also full of blood. Some of their countrymen help the guy to put into a jeepney. Willy Shaw and Roger Briant learned that their countryman was ambushed by some Filipino guys because of a woman.

Willy Shaw and Roger Briant were about to reach the bridge when the latter noticed the black boy whom he saw by the bridge earlier. He was by the barbecue stand. He looks like hungry.

Willy Shaw was surprised when he talked to him because he was fluent in English.

"What's your name?" asked Willy Shaw. "Why are you here? It's already late, are you not going home yet?"

"My name is Nat," replied the boy. "We have a small house, but I prefer to stay here. I don't have a companion there… What's you name also, Joe?"

"Willy Shaw… don't you have a mother and a father?"

"I don't have a father. My mother is in the club."

Willy Shaw tapped Nat's shoulder after giving him a peso.

"Be good," he said.

WILLY Shaw could not sleep. Nat, the black boy, was still in his mind. He was also thinking Ram and Sally he left in California. Upon remembering Sally and what happened to him in the club, a black image came across his mind. What if Sally would also look for somebody to give her happiness that he could not give while he's away?

"I'm lonely, Willy, while you're away," Sally did always tell him when he was on vacation. "I'm bored waiting…"

But he was tied here. They were living because of here. "Let us endure," that was his litany. But where does that enduring be ended?

Willy Shaw noticed that Roger Briant could not sleep as well.

"Roger?"

"Hmmm?"

"Are you still awake?"

"We are about to move again," Roger Briant said instead. "A boring movement. We are heading to Japan. When we go back to America, that will only be the time for me to see Windy," what he had in mind was his wife.

ONE time, Willy Shaw met a young man, a Filipino. Ramon, that was the name of the young man, in the bridge. He was waiting for

Americans offering something to sell. Willy Shaw brought his camera with him.

"How much are you selling, Joe?" Ramon asked in English.

"I don't sell."

Ramon was good looking, noticed Willy Shaw. By his observation, the young man was different from what he met before. Ramon's clothing was in order. He must be educated.

"Are you in school?" asks Willy Shaw.

"Not anymore. I stopped. I don't have money."

Willy Shaw and Roger Briant invited Ramon for a dinner.

"You are happy here," Willy Shaw said while they were eating.

"That's what you think. Life here is tedious, Willy. You know, I'm also dreaming to become a navy, like you."

"That's good, Rammy!" countered Roger Briant. "You can taste a lot of different food!" he crackles.

"Money is what I need, Roger," said Ramon. "Satisfaction in life. I want to get away from our poor country."

Willy Shaw taps Ramon's shoulder. "The contentment you are looking for, Rammy, is in your country," he said. "You can't find in other places."

"I can't find happiness here, Willy. All but frustration…"

"You know, Rammy, you become a prisoner once you entered the navy."

"I want to look contentment in other places, Willy. I can't find any peace of mind here."

Roger Briant laughs. "You're amusing me, Rammy," he said. "You have a lot of pastime around… You don't have money? Come follow us."

"That's not the one that make me happy," Ramon wiggled his head.

WILLY Shaw and Roger Briant did not go out together. Roger Briant was not feeling good—Willy Shaw also need to forget sometimes. He needs to sway away some painful feelings.

While waiting for another bottle, he brought out a wrinkled letter from his pocket. He just received it a while ago. It was from Sally.

"Ram was always calling you, Willy," said Sally in one part of the letter. "Why are you not coming home? Even on his sick bed he was saying: 'Doctor, why Papa's not coming home? Is he bored with us with Mama? Doctor, please tell Papa to come home,' then he looked at me, Willy, and said: 'Mama, when Papa is home, I'll get fine immediately.' He repeated that again and again, Willy. And when he was about to go, he said: 'Papa is about to come home, right, Mama? He's almost home, right?' He was hopeful that you were coming home, until he got sleep, sleep that…"

Willy Shaw's fist closed tightly. The letter got wrinkled. His jaw locked. He poured his glass once again. He tossed.

HERE comes one more time a boring journey—they're living the Philippines.

Willy Shaw would never forget the workers scavenging garbage when supposed to be their breaktime… the boys under the bridge shouting "Hi, Joe! Some coins, Joe…!" Nat who was waiting for his mother who was working in a club… Ramon, the young Filipino man dreaming to look for contentment in the other world.

"We need to be happy, Willy. We must go with the flow. We need some pastime…" Roger Briant said repeatedly.

But he feels pain every time he remembers Sally saying, "I am lonely, Willy, while you're away. I'm bored waiting…"

Little by little the ship was moving away. The size of Olongapo becomes smaller and smaller in the eyes of Willy Shaw. He threw his attention to the seemingly unending deep. —0

Bannawag: June 5, 1967; *Napili a Sarita dagiti Ilokano (**Selected Stories of the Ilocanos):** pp.103-108, 1968.

The Eden In Their Lives

1

H I, handsome, do you need a haircut? Come in… Ha! Ha! You looked like a pole there. Don't mind those playing checker. They're always like that when they don't have customer… Come, my friend. Only fifty cents…"

"Are you really good?"

"What kind of haircut? Flat top? Army cut? Beatles… Twiggy, or what? Yeah, I know what's suited to your friendly face, my friend."

"I like the best haircut. The one that made the ladies inside swallowing their saliva. Specially the nurse with sugary smile, with a hairy thigh appearing when seated. And the lady by my side in the winding department."

"Ha! Ha! I can do everything anybody ask me to do, friend. What's your name?"

"Hilario. And you?"

"Banong. Hep, not there, Friend. That's the post of that guy with wide temple and bearded and big tommy like a buddha sitting in cross-legged. Here… Like that. You know, Friend, you're the most handsome this white shawl ever caped…"

"Those who consider you a moonstruck are wrong."

"They are right… like you. Ha! Ha! You know, Friend, life is floating in the air."

"How long have you been here?"

"A year… I've been a barber for less than twenty years."

"Are you Ilocano?"

"If I'm in our town, yes. But I'm Tagalog here. Wherever I be stranded, I am… Ha! Ha! Wanderer, according the divers in Mindanao, Samar, Palawan… Aha, I have a long story about my experiences. You may not believe me."

"Do you like your life story be written?"

"My life stories? Ha! Ha! No idiot writer bothers to write about me. Ha! Ha! It's better to live without any worries."

"You are extraordinary, I would say, but nobody is extraordinary as long as he knows how to treat his situation."

"Maybe you."

"Why?"

"You should be an actor. Or you would have gone to school. See your image… The factory you are working at is not suitable for you."

"Just say I am lost… But there is no job not fitted to anybody who desires to live. Like you. Ask yourself why you remain a barber while you could have a different job."

"This is better than those who are hauling money in the night. There is something for everybody. Crazy are those who dream beyond their reach."

"You can't blame them. Let them dream if that's the end of their talent. If you do not have dream, you don't have a future."

"Everybody has a future. You… who are you?"

"A man with many dreams… A boastful prophet. Handsome insane. Ugly wanderer. And tearless cry some… But I'm happy…"

"Ha! Ha! If you have a lot of money, yes. The women… ah, look at those. Their buts seem plunging in the ground. And, my goodness! Half of their thighs are shining, and something seems peeping in between! I just don't know where they are going in the night."

"To their jobs, where else? I want you to be my friend. Where are you renting?"

"Just beside the creek. In the north. The house by the old acacia tree…"

"Is it done?"

"Yes. Wait for me outside, if you want to come…"

"Alright. Keep the change."

"Hey, handsome… Have you been out for quite some time? Had you collected your salary?"

"I've even done with my haircut… I guess the wide-forehead old man kept you on hold?"

"It's because the queue. It's already time for collecting salary, still hard to collect. You're really… Ahem… don't ever look at me like that because I'm melting by your eyes! Don't ever smile at me because your lips gobble me up!"

"Who is that, Hil?"

"A, Banong. She is the one in the winding I mentioned… She's Lily. He is my barber friend, Lily."

"Ha, I have seen a boar many times… He! He! Tsk! Tsk! Any angle I look at you, no doubt, you're handsome, Hil! If you want to visit me, I'll wait for you in my place. Okay, boy?"

2

THIS is my world, Hil. Sorry. I woke up late. See, my things are tipsy turbid. Nobody keeps them.

"Why won't you get a companion?"

"It's better to be alone. I just talk with those pocketbooks. I observe them ones I got home. I don't even clean sometimes. My nose is familiar with the smell from that pig den—that one by the door. I'm also a swine. Ha! Ha! I'm not taking a bath most of the time because it seldom has water here."

"So, you are reading books."

"Only those entertaining and can make head big. Those writings of Hemingway, Tolstoy, Melville, and other big shot novelists."

"I thought you said that writers are crazy? Are you educated?"

"I'd just started college. I stop when I was drained out of money. I have a minimal income in barbering… I preferred to continue my profession rather than look for another job. Reason is it's clean. And I guess it's my destiny. Did you also go to school?"

"Second year in college. I stopped because my parents could not afford the expenses. I experienced cleaning restaurant bathrooms. After that, I worked as a plumber. Then as electrician. But there is no advancement from these kinds of jobs. I tried writing. The payment of my writings was not even enough to lengthen my breath. I decided to work in the factory. But the same, no advancement there. I could probably endure but I want to help my siblings go to school. You know, Banong, I have a teacher girlfriend—from our neighboring province. She is also a writer; she has a dream and I'll be her stumbling black if I stop doing better."

"I was right from my guess—you're a writer. Your girlfriend… Are you sincere with each other?"

"Only time can tell for that matter."

"I don't have parents, I don't have siblings, I don't have a girlfriend, I don't have relatives… Nobody endears me—I'm not preparing for anything. But I'm always happy, Hil. You know, I had somebody lived with, a woman I loved and cared for. We had a child… a child I found out dead when I got home one afternoon—I'm not sure if Lita killed him. Lita has gone. She went away with another guy but… Ha! Ha! Forget the past. Forget the other questions."

"I'm bored in my present job, Banong. Non-stop walking. I feel pain in my chest, more so when the thread snapped off. I have a hard time catching my time. Some of my co-workers are mean. They are hard up but still have time in jobbing jokes. I guess they are contented. Especially those who are working there for almost twenty years. I admire their endurance. They are scared with strike. They are scared with the balding Jew."

"I have a lot of neighbors who are good to that Jew, Hil… But I want us to be happy tonight. I know a good place to kill time. Only three pesos each. We can spend the whole night; you can't spend your whole salary. I had a lot of customers today."

"I don't like that, Banong."

"It's up to you. There's another place for us to go. But we better have our dinner first. I always have good viand, Hil. If not squid, sardines. If not sardines, any kind of canned food. These are better, so I only cook rice. I'm lazy, Hil. I'm lazy. Ha! Ha!"

"Okay, but we need to drop by in my place."

3

HERE is what I told you, Hil."

"My, there's no difference from the thirty per."

"Ha! Ha! You need to experience all kinds of living, Hil."

"Oy, Hil… are you lost?"

"Ernesto, Lito… Lino… Jim!"

"Ha! Ha! Here is paradise, Hil. Only two times a month… Ah, Banong, you brought him?"

"I want him to be baptized, Lino. Ha! Ha!"

"Okay, common, come in, Lito, Lino, Ernest. We need to welcome Hil."

"The bottles of beer are waiting on the table, Hil… Banong, come in."

"Wait for a while, I need to go somewhere."

"Don't spend so long, Lito. Bring with you the heavens."

"Ha! Ha! You're still a hot blooded, ha, Ernest?"

"I need to forget Mila ones in a while, Banong."

"Why are you shaking your head, Hil?"

"I remember the two children of Ernest, Jim. How many days did they pay you today, Ernest?"

"Twelve days… But why do you think about that? To stay young, you need some rest… Heaven is here, Hil. Never mind those who are waiting!"

"We are so tide up in the fabric factory and we just spend all our earnings for how many days in just a night?"

"Ha! Ha! Ha! Don't show up that you're newly born, Hil. There is a very rare opportunity."

"We have different world, Jim."

"Here are the heavens, my friends!"

"Ha! Ha! You selected some juicy beauties, ha, Lito. But we need one more."

"They're all yours. I'll go get one for me."

"Never mind, Lito."

"Ah, that can't be, Hil. Aha, it's on time. Lily's just arrived... Lily, take care Hil... Comrades, the music is sweet..."

"Hil, you surprised me!"

"Banong brought me here in Hell! Look at them, as if the five of them were in heaven. You, why..."

"Ah, honey, it's boring in the factory! It's so dull there... I'm about to resign... It's Hell there! Come and I'll make you happy. My lips are burning... my bosom is lovely."

"Lily..."

"Can you see your companions? They went up. They went to heaven. Ha! Ha! They selected those who are sweet. Poor guys! Ha! Ha! Do you like it, Honey? For you, it's free. I like you..."

"L-lily... L-lily..."

"In heaven, Hil..."

4

OY, Hil, why?"

"I'm leaving, Banong."

"Where are you going?"

"I found a branch of government institution in Manila; the Board of Technical Surveys and Maps."

"Good for you, Hil. Me, I'll stay here forever. A barber until the end. But... Ha! Ha! I don't have a future... I'll just be happy... Poor me, it's my luck. I'll always be a crazy Banong... You're going away, we probably won't see each other again."

"I will always be thinking of you, Banong. Goodbye."

"Goodbye..."—0

Bannawag, June 17, 1968. *Talugading,* 1977; *The Quezonian, MLQU School Organ,* Ang Eden Sa Kanilang Buhay, a Filipino translation, 24- June 7, 1971.

Face

"WHAT causes her late," *Baket*[34] Sepa said and glanced the clock on the table. Eight o'clock in the evening, she looked sideways by the lamp the list of her creditors from her fish bending. "My poor daughter…"

Baket Sepa lives alone in the room she was renting for twenty-five pesos. The room was small; there was a small dresser and cushioned bed. Her eating table was small. She arranged her kitchen utensils in the window sill.

In the small store below, arrived a tall and muscular man. His haircut is white side wall and looked like Japanese. Around twenty years old. He smiled at the store keeper with a baby and ordered for a bottle of beer. While waiting, he glanced ones and a while the stairs going up to where *Baket* Sepa was.

"She is upstairs," the store keeper said.

"Later," the man answered.

He drank the liquor as if water. His face was gloomy; he only smiles when their eyes with the store keeper met.

From upstairs, *Baket* Sepa came out from her room; she entered the other room where a couple were. A skinny man was lying strait on his bed while reading a magazine. The woman was facing their newly washed clothes. The old woman was always gabbing with them during the early afternoon.

---

[34]   *Baket,* old woman.

"Engineer is very kind, Totoy," she started her vice ones again. She called the man Totoy. She sat in front of the table of the couple. "Every time I ask something, he always give… I hope he will come tomorrow." She always winks when talking.

"How about the skinny old man who was here the other day? And the half-blooded who was here some days ago?" the eyes of the man remained pasted to what he was reading.

"Skinny has no money… half-blooded is cheater," the old woman pouts. "Engineer is better, despite his age… he is summoning me to marry him, but I don't like," she pouts. "I'll be tied up if I give way. Must be better if he does not have children."

"You also have children, *nana*." The pregnant said. She put their box of clothes under the bed.

"Yes, my children. Clarita is recuperating; she got a lot of children. My poor daughter, she was widowed early… how about Rogelio? Has he been promoted? How about his wife Cena, and their two children? How about Nestor the navy… ah, probably he's home now… My grandkids… poor them… But don't ever tell Rogelio and his siblings about Engineer, okay 'Toy?" she strokes her hair.

"But why?"

"You already know… they don't like that. But they could not give what makes me comfortable, right, 'Toy?" she touches her finished eyebrow. "I was also beautiful…"

She went to her room. She gets hold of her picture from the small room on top of her dresser. A smile played on her red lips.

She went back to where the couple were. "This is my picture when I was still gorgeous! Look at it, 'Ne, was I not also beautiful?"

"Yes," the pregnant inattentively looks back.

"I was also an actress! Though only an extra," she always shows and tell her pictures. "I was also a WAC under President Quirino… But the most enjoyable part of my life was, when I was in Olongapo. The 'Cans were wise! But they had lots of money. Only a few acts of charming, here comes the two hundred dollars. But poor them!" she laughs. "Money first before anything else!" she giggles.

The pregnant stood up. She reaches out the uncut watermelon from the pan. She cut it into pieces.

"I thought you had cut it in the noon time, 'Ne," the old woman said. "The other one I got was sweet. It was bargain where I bought it…"

They ate.

"I had delivered Rogelio then," the old woman said. "If you are looking at this picture, do you ever think that I had three children?" she looked at the picture through the bulb; she half-closed her eyes. Then her face turned gloomy. "Rogelio's father was a devil. After begetting Rogelio, he disappeared like a smoke! I did not know where inferno he is now. Maybe he went back to Japan, or eaten by bullets…" She looked up her gloomy face. "Nestor's father, he's another one. Maybe he went back to America…. been drowned by his compatriots. But the late Jones got money. A hundred bucks a night was too little." She smiled then became serious and turned her face to the pregnant. "You know, 'Ne, the archaic Spaniard father of Clarita was so kind. I did never taste his hand. But he was then so scrawny." She laughed. "But he was never behind from the devil father of Nestor when it comes to money. He gave me all I needed…"

The magazine being red by the man on the bed produced rustling sound.

Down below, the man had consumed three bottles of beer. He ordered one more. He looked up the stairs one more time. Then looked back the store owner.

"Really?"

"Yes," the store owner said. "And not only one; not only Filipino."

The man toasts up his glass. He brought out a paper from his pocket. He opened in front of the store owner.

The store owner's eyes were wide-opened. "But—"

"Clarita promised that she comes today, but not here yet," a shadow of yesterday was visible ones again in *Baket* Sepa's face. "Maybe, there was something wrong, or her youngest son is in tantrum ones again… My poor daughter! She loses her husband so early. She got so many children…"

"Has she not had a source of income?" the pregnant said.

"She's working in Balara. Her income is not far behind from her big brother Nestor. You know, Nestor is a navy." She mentioned that many times. "Rogelio on the other hand is a PC... But that Rogelio is stupid. From all of them siblings, he is the only one who could thwack me. I was so bunged-up in sending him to school..."

"There was a good reason why he was like that," countered the one reading.

"What does he need more?" *Baket* Sepa's eyes were wide opened. "Was he ever got a job without my recommendation? Then he still mistreated me... What if I killed him when he was still in my tummy, had he ever protected himself? Right, Totoy?"

She remembered the Engineer ones again. She had mentioned him many, many times that he was the one paying for her rent. "He needs to be here tomorrow because it is paying time again," she said.

They did not notice the one coming up. The yellowish man like a Japanese was reddish. There was something bulging on his waist. He winked the man on the bed, who also winked at him.

Baket Sepa's eyes were wide-opened ones again.

"Bless me, *Nanang*," he kissed the hand of *Baket* Sepa.

"God blesses you."

They went to the room.

"Had you eaten?" the old woman asked.

"Don't worry about me."

"You had drunk again! What is your problem? Why are you here? Are you not assigned in..."?

"I'm now catching sinners."

"Hmm, had you caught some?"

"You better go get a bottle..."

"You're already drunk!"

"Is there a drunk PC? And you know what, I'm now a lieutenant."

"Why are you not in uniform?"

"It's easier to entrap..."

"No drunkard could entrap anybody."

"It's all a part of it... It's still eight o'clock, why are you home early?"

"And where would I go? The fact is I am waiting for your big sister Clarita."

"That's the reason why you're early… That's right," Rogelio nodded several times. He looked for something to eat. He pinched from the boiled fish in the earthen pot, then drunk water. "Clarita… heh!"

"Occasionally it's only seven o'clock, I'm already sleeping."

Rogelio's shoulders shrugged while laughing. He looks at his mother sideways.

"You know, Mother, there's another woman again in my life. I don't like Cena anymore. Disregard our two children… Look at the picture of my new customer."

"Have pity with your children, Rogelio… Your wife."

Rogelio's eyes spark. "Pity her? Ha-ha! Do you have a little amount of pity to a child? Did you have any empathy on me?" he looked at the cushioned bed. "Where is he, Mother?"

Old Sepa threw a sharp look to Rogelio. "You're drank, Rogelio… better sleep."

"No courageous that is drank… no sleepy veteran! Where is he?"

"You're mistaken, my son… I'm already old…"

"But you're not done with your vice…"

"Don't say that!"

"Don't make me blind…! Do you want me to arrest you?"

The old woman's eyes sharpened. "Before you arrive, I was happy… Better sleep, or you better go?"

"For I'm not your son… Because Clarita is only your child. Pwue!"

"Go away!" the old woman flared up. "I don't need a son who doesn't know how to honor his mother… Get lost! You probably don't know who's in front of you. Ha! This is a general's wife! General Santos…!" trembling, the old woman was in a hurry in bringing out a picture from her briefcase. "Look at this… recognize him. Do you know him? He is my boyfriend! You couldn't scare me. Wherever corner of the world we will go… Do you think I'm afraid of you? Hah, how many times had I been in court? I always be the winner. All the police officers are my friends. Just one word for them, you're done! Do you want me to tell them to get rid of you from your job right away? You're only my son—"

"Yes, I'm only your son. I'm your son but you don't consider me as one… I'm only your son now that I'm grown up… But did I grow up with you? No! Had you given me anything during my growing up period? Nothing! You gave me away!"

"The reason why I gave you to that family was to earn something for you with your siblings. I just left you to them, not to give you away. I gave them money for your education. But they change your name… they used theirs… Was it my fault if I needed to earn for your sustenance, you, my children? Ha? Ha?"

"Don't make me a fool! If you really cared for me, why did you love big sister Clarita the best? You couldn't even love my wife Cena."

"You're the one who forgot your wife, stupid! Only yesterday, I again sent your wife twenty pesos. How about you, had you given her a single cent? When Clarita undergone a surgery, you hadn't even bother to lend her some amount to pay off her hospital bills…"

"Enough!"

"Monster! You're like your cobra father! I should had better kill you when you were still in my tommy!"

"See?" Rogelio's jaw hardened. "Are you consider me your son? But come with me, we'll go somewhere."

"You want to arrest me? For what did I do wrong? What do you have to be proud of? You may not know General Santos… you may not know who my boyfriends are." She spread out pictures. "There they are! Identify that President… that Vice President… that congressman… that senator…"

Rogelio's jaw hardened. "Wait for me." He stood up. He winked to the couples when he went out. The whole neighborhood had been awakened. Many were murmuring. There were many faces in the windows.

Old Sepa's mouth was popping like corn when Rogelio had gone. She mentioned a lot of bad things about Rogelio and good things about Clarita and Nestor. She even went down and told all people around. But nobody bothers to take notice. "Yes" was the only answer of the couple upstairs.

She was still boiling when Clarita arrives. Clarita was tall and with fare complexion. She looks like Spaniard.

"O, why, what happened?"

"Your shameless brother Rogelio dropped by to make trouble!" the old woman squeals on. But she cooled down. "Had you eaten your dinner...? How are my grandkids?"

"I escaped from them, just to drop by. Boy is enrolling tomorrow."

"How much does he need?"

"Fifty pesos. But... I came from some places to buy..."

Rogelio and Nestor arrived. They have the same height. Nestor was bulkier but softer. He got a pointed nose; with blue eyes. He looks like an American. He held Old Sepa's hand and kissed it. He smelt strong liquor.

Upon seeing Rogelio, the old woman flared up again.

"What are you doing?" there was pain in the voice of Nestor. "Roger dropped by in our place... it's shameful."

"He was the one who came and made trouble."

"What you are doing is shameful. Look at the people. What would they say about you?"

"Hah, and you're ashamed for me? You're so good! After bringing you into the world and rearing you, this is what you paid for? Get away!"

"Calm down!" Nestor's whisper was hard. "It's so shameful, I said! We want you to transform. You're so old..."

"Am I doing something?"

"We heard that many men are coming here... Just imagine, what face do we have for our friends?"

"That's what I was telling a while ago," countered Rogelio. "As if what we are concern about is not for her good."

"You, Rogelio, if I say I kill you, I kill you!"

"Don't yell!" Nestor controlled his temper.

"Am I doing something? I just go out in the morning to sell fish... Is it bad to earn a living? If you do not like me to go out... You can't give my sustenance. What I need... I am not doing anything... If I was bad before, because of you... because of your future."

"I've been telling you to come to our place," Nestor's voice was hard. "But you prefer to brood here… for you are open…"

"I come, so I would be tied up to the kids? The kids… the kids…" the old woman looked down.

"You don't need to hurt mother," countered Clarita. "She's already old… why are you denying her happiness…? You're overdressing her up…"

"Too much!" groaned Rogelio. "Is it too much in preventing something shameful?"

"Your brain is like a catfish's, Rogelio," breathed Clarita.

"You can say that because you are digging up from her!" minced Rogelio. "Do you think I don't know what you have in your basket? What mother had been digging for, you're the one consuming… And she said you're her only child. She does not consider us with our big brother as her children because your father Spaniard married her! How about my father? Why, is there nothing a Japanese could be compared to a Spaniard? And the father of big brother, because he was an American…"

"You should understand our mother…"

"Stop it!" Nestor's fists hardened. "Don't ever agree to mother's animal desire. If you're not ashamed, it's up to you!"

"Mother should be given a lesson…" Rogelio said.

"Stop it!" yelled *Baket* Sepa.

"Our fathers were gone," Clarita said with teary eyes. "And you should not be mentioning them anymore. We are siblings; we have one mother. Was her fault of becoming like this? Was it her fault in bringing us to the world? Was it her fault of having war that brought us here?"

Baket Sepa's teary eyes were reddish pointed to Rogelio and Nestor. Her tight-closed lips were trembling. She turned back, and the door of the room made big sound when she slammed it. She stomps her feet in the room of the couple.

Their lips were tight-closed, the couples followed their eyes to the old woman swallowed by the stairs down below.

"Give me a bottle, 'Ne!" her hard voice was broken turned to the store owner holding her baby down stairs

The store owner obliged silently.

"Those shameless sons of devils' cobras!" she gulps the content of the glass. "They don't know how to repay!"

When she finished a glass, she ordered more. "They don't know how to pay back!" she punched the showcase. —0

Bannawag: June 23. 1969; March 12, 2018; *Tagumpay,* Mga Mukha Sa Basag Na Salamin, a Filipino translation, March 17, 1971; *Napili a Sarita:* 1969, pp.43-50.

Here In Glory: Penitentiary

THIS constricted room where he comes home every dusk was no different from a pigpen. His feelings were not acquiescent in going home because he hated the whiff of the spoiled food, mice and cockroaches' dung, malodorous scattered clothes, stinking water in the corner where a stuck broken conduit where the fess of those who were living in the second-floor runs. He was fed up with the unkept things he just lives in the morning for he was in a hurry to his job; to the dirt from the second floor caused by heavy stumping. His body was itching because he seldom has time to take a shower. For even he wakes up early, if not before four o'clock, he has no chance in the bathroom for those workers in the restaurant in front of his room were very busy using water and not even a single drop could reach his faucet. His eardrum could hardly hear because of the non-stop music from the jukebox, the noisy diners, the laughter of those who were drinking even in that very early morning. The pong of wine and beer was dizzying.

Before entering his room, he turned his attention to the restaurant, he feels the stumping in the second floor.

How could he gain peace of mind in this kind of world? He smacked lightly when he switched on the light. If they notice the light, they would surely come but is he going to grope in the dark? He dropped the empty container of his provisions he brought with him to work in the small table where two dented old aluminum plates placed upside down, a cracked cup, a bottle of coffee, empty bag of sugar, empty can of sardines, empty pack of cigarette, empty pack of matches, empty bottle of pomade used as ashtray, and a setting cracked mirror. There was an old gas stove in the corner. He beat repeatedly his bed to undashed it. It cricked when he sat on it. He removed his shirt. He removed his worn-out shoes. He leaned on the cold concrete. He covered his face with his palms and breathed heavily. A rotten life! He snorts. Dumb!

He reminisces the clean room in Espana Extension, the scent of air to inhale, the laughter of the children running after each other on the shiny floor, bread, meat, newly cooked rice, stereo. Their woman relative who was expert in telling something to their two helpers what to do, and to bring their children into the bathroom for showering. Her skinny husband who was always looking down the plans on his desk nobody was disturbing him except his dry coughing ones in a while.

If we eat, then, you also eat, they remind him. All your earnings are yours alone. But when payday is approaching, the woman starts enumerating the expenses bothering her. He will give then a ten, a twenty, or even more, then their woman relative starts commending and comparing him to the gallivants mixed with flattering. They never tell him to help but he collects their garbage in the evening never waiting to be told to do so and do anything without even told despite his tiredness in his job, for he could not stomach the heavy implication which is much heavier than a yell when they supposed to send him an errand.

He brought an empty cigarette pack from his pantaloon's pocket. A single stick was almost smashed. He reached the match from the table. There was a single matchstick. He lit the cigarette. He reached a broken mirror and smirked his boney face, his moustache, his long hair, his deep-set eyes, his long neck, his boney chest…

My god, you looked like a ghost! He exclaimed. He put down the mirror. He went to stand by the door.

In front of the room, at the back of the restaurant—this is the only building in the corner of P. Paterno in the south and Evangelista in the west with a division separating the restaurant and the crown shop in the west side of his room, in the inner side—the three men arranging, bundling, cording, watering, and mixing the flowers and branches for wedding, or for the dead were so busy. They were teasing each other.

Are they not bored to what they are doing? He thought.

The jukebox suddenly bursts into a deafening sound. He recalls the Visayan manager of the restaurant. The Kapampangan who owns his room and her beautiful daughter whom he accidentally pepped one day when she was taking a shower—how attractive nipples she had, a belly button, a hypogastrium! The Ilocana lady who owns the small store in the west side of Evangelista. His debt from them...

He turns back from the door. He puffs his cigarette. He laid down the bed. In the darkening ceiling, a *ginggin-ed* [or dancing] spider was dancing on her web. There were two house lizards preparing to pounce on a small gnat. He closes his eyes. He found his self in a store of books, papers, pens, all kinds of office supplies. He overheard a stout blind old woman telling them what to do. He could see his co-workers sweating profusely. He feels dizzy when he was confused what he needs to do first. He feels better when he sides glance a good looking, sweet voiced, kind and not arrogant lady.

He had been working in the bookstore which he considers a penitentiary for two years. He perseveres, with six, eight a day pay. Eight pesos was listed in the payroll, but a two-peso deduction was probably for the unknown demon! How many tens of pesos a week? And some other deductions for unknown contributions. Plus SSS.

He stopped schooling. He tried to save. But he pays thirty pesos for this world where he was catching his breath. His food. His unavoidable friends. He was becoming lighter and lighter. A coffee without milk and ten cents pan de sal in the morning. He cooks half of a chufa of rice and a salted broken tomato, and ten-cent dried fish for his provisions in his job. He could only eat good food when newly received his salary. If he does not control his spending, the end of his life.

"Were you bored here?" he could hear once again their old relative. "Or were you offended?"

"No, *Nana*," he said. "I just want to be closer to my job. A-and I want to experience the difficulty of being alone..."

"It's up to you," said the old woman. "But if you need us in the future, you are free to come back anytime. And whenever the people in the province complain, don't ever blame anybody..."

Yesterday, he received a letter from his father. His brother is preparing to enroll the next school year. Please, we need your money, Son… he had told them that he could not send money for a while for he was saving for his tuition. Imagine, when his brother went to school last year, they asked him to shoulder his expenses. How much money is needed in going to high school? Please carry on, Son, they said, for you're the only one we could ask for.

He puffs again. Why is it like that? He closed his eyes. He could remember once again their woman relative saying: "Are you bored here? Or were you offended?" The blubbing of his siblings. His sniveling cousins: they haven't been eaten their breakfast while it's lunchtime again; they hadn't been taken a bath for they had just gone from the reef area; they were in tattered… His aunt whose back has almost broken because of her skinny stature while weaving mats or basket that she may have an extra source of covering the misfortune of her husband's fishing in the Puro. His mother who was sickly but still moves no matter what. His father who's limping because he lost his leg when he used dynamite in fishing, but still dives, and still lights a dynamite every now and then.

The door was knocked. He recognizes the four knocking in succession. Here comes the witch! He clenches his teeth. He should have not switched on the light. It's Saturday today, but they were not paid. Devil capitalists! he groaned.

The knocking was repeated, heavier, more. He gets up from bed. He opened the door.

"Ah, *Nana,* I thought it was somebody else" he pretended rubbing his eyes. "I had a little nap. I was thinking to come up, for I knew you were waiting for me. The truth is, before going out this morning, I had decided to give all my salary to you…"

"That's good so I could buy the thing that unchaste annoying me for!" the eyes of the fat blind old woman were wide-opened.

"The reason why I came home early is that I was almost in trouble in my jobsite. I was very mad at the capitalist, my god! Imagine, you were hoping, and I was so abashed to you, but they did not pay us. In fact, we are planning to go on strike…"

"Hey, you need to pay! If you do not have money to pay, move out!"

"If I only have a big salary... I did not intend not to pay. But I really don't have money..."

"If you could not pay until tomorrow, move out!"

The jukebox made a bursting sound that reaches into his room. There was rumbling upstairs, and a lot of dust started dropping down.

You all devils!

If you get mad, you whistle or whirr, they say. And he whistles. His tummy rumbles. The rice container clanked when he opened. There was only a handful of rice grain. There was no left over in the cauldron. No matches. No coffee. Nothing that he could swallow.

"Pansit... adobo... gisado... mami... siopao!" the laughter of the drunkard was so earsplitting.

His room was knocked twice in twos. Here comes the manager! He mumbled.

"Eh, how are you, Boss?" he said smiling. "You probably come to ask for my payment, right?"

"You had eaten my food long time ago. You already had pooped and sweated it. But up to now, I had not received from you a single cent."

"Boss, you see..."

"Why won't you tell that you don't like to pay anymore what you had wolfed down, and I may give you food? There are a lot of cooked and uncooked... Not like that that you promise, and you could not abide... That's what you are Ilocanos!"

The Visayan turned his back whining.

He closed his eyes tightly, breathed deeply, closed his fist hardly.

He computed his bills in the *tianggi* in the other side of the street. A lot! But hope they could lend them more. Anyway, the owner was an Ilocana.

The three men in the flower shop were still busy. They were making dead's crown. The light bulbs in the ceiling were dim. Many passers-by still look for a while at the crowns.

He greeted them. He smiled the crumbling of his intestine. The concrete ground was wet and the cut off branches and leaves and rotten flowers were everywhere. He smiled at the puffer fish-liked bulging short man.

He stood by the gutter. The lights of the cars in the street were as sharp as eyes in the dark. In his left, the aroma of the food in the dining area make his stomach grumbling, the clinking of spoons and plates, the voracious eating of customers. In his right, the queued shops of gravestones, and other kind of figurines shrieking incessantly. Many people buy figurines—rich, whom the numbers of sniveling, tattered children extend their tiny palms.

There were many people in the *tianggi*. When cars became sparse, he crossed the street. He approached the Ilocana *tianggi* owner.

The eyes of the store owner twinkled. She says it's good he arrives, that means she was not going to his place anymore. She could add the payment for buying her goods.

He needs to be an actor, if not, he will not have food for dinner. "It's so nice in the Ilocos," he added to his explanation, "for even you run out of things, the neighbors are readily share their kindness. We Ilocanos are like that, right?"

He was able to get a ghanta of rice, a can of *ligo* sardines, a pack of Bataan cigarette, a match, and other kind of little things he needed. He was able to barrow ten pesos because he promised his pay the next Monday. Just enough for a partial payment to his rental.

He was able to breathe easier upon reaching his room. He cooks. He eats. He smokes.

After satiating, he went up. He was adamant to proceed because of many people around the big table where the renter and visitors were gambling, but the blind old woman and her daughter saw him. In front of the visitors, the blind old woman inquired his purpose. He said he was going to pay. Ten pesos.

"Ten?" the eyebrow of the blind old woman arks. "It's not even enough for a one round bet!"

"That meager amount, Mama, never mind!" the young lady pouts.

"I want to accept, but I'm afraid you may not eat anymore. Just keep it for now!" the blind old woman said.

He was blinded by anger. His fist hardened. His whole body heated up. But he held his temper. His arms trembling in pocketing the ten pesos and immediately went down without looking back the puckering mother and daughter.

His chest turned heavy when he sat on his bed. His mind spins.

"Are you bored? Or were you offended?"

"Please, your money, Son…"

"I'll lend you, but remember to pay on Monday…"

"Why won't you tell if you don't like to pay anymore what you had wolfed down, and I may give you food?"

"Ten? Not even enough to place a bet in one time!"

He breath heavily. After a while, he was putting his clothes in a traveling bag. It will be easier for him to decide upon getting out from this room. –0

Bannawag, June 28, 1971; *Pakpakawan, Berde!* pp.129-135.

A Creek: Once Upon A Time

S HE WAS mumbling. Her eyes were twinkling under the brightness of heaven while looking up the university. She was excited watching the students looking down the creek. Sometimes she laughs with their crunchy laughter. She was trying to recognize the boys and the girls putting their arms around each other's shoulder. More so when they puff their cigarette one by one, or when they put food in their partner's mouth. She hates the boys for their hair was even longer than hers. And their clothing was wobbly.

But she was most attracted by the books and notebooks carried by the students in their armpit. Sometimes she mimics and walks as if there was a book under her armpit, then sits and looks like she was opening something on her lap. She suddenly looks up over the window when she hears the university's bell rings proclaiming the changing of time. She watches the students going in and out. She could imagine herself mingling with the students. She laughs with them. She does the utmost against them.

"Ting... Ting? Are you there, *Apok?*"

"They're coming out, *Lola*[35]... had you heard the bell?" Ting's voice was like an angel's voice. she felt the groping palm on her shoulder.

"Are there a lot of them again, *Apok?*"

"Yes, *Lola*... hey, those who kissed last night are there!"

"In the same place?" the blind old woman slumps beside Ting.

---

[35] *Lola,* grandmother.

"Yes, Lola, and they are hooking their arms to each other."

"Pity for their parents."

"Are not only the poor being to be pitied, *Lola*? They are very rich, see! Their dress and pants are so beautiful…"

"Who are those roaring again?"

Some were shouting something the girl and the blind old woman could not understand. The shouting was in unison. After a while, Ting noticed the students scrambling in going out from the school's gate, by the bridge. A guy with a blue uniform and a truncheon stumbled on the ground. Ten students thrashed him down.

In the west, a flock of students crossed the wooden bridge. They wrapped their heads with a fragment of cloth. They have a red banner. They were attacking the school's gate. They were hollering.

"Are they here again, *Apok?*"

"Yes, *Lola*. And they are more today. They are more aggressive than yesterday."

"They are probably becoming worse."

"Maybe. Some are picking up stones. They want to go inside the school. What's their reason, *Lola?*"

"The demand of the students as said by your mother had probably not granted yet. She said it's about a tuition fee. All prices are going up."

The bell rang incessantly. The students went out in a hurry. Windows were closed. The gates. The guards left. The yelling of the students subsides outside the school. But they did not go away.

Ting's forehead wrinkled. She looked up the sun. It will be a bit longer before setting. Before the last bell the dusk had been spread a while, and the bright lights had been on by the time. But why is it early today? Ting was saddened. She presumed that the lights will not be opened this time. And there will be no glow of light in the shanties.

"Are they going to cut the classes, *Apok?*"

"Yes, *Lola*."

"Pity is the students."

"Lola, when will *Inang* brought home *Amang*[36]?"

"I see, my *Amang* is home just say when your Inang bring him home…"

"Every time she goes out, she says she's bringing home Amang. Maybe she just kidding… You know, *Lola*, I really want *Amang* to come home so I have somebody to send me to school."

"You can go to school even your *Amang* is not home. Didn't you say that you want to go to school: you want to be like Doctor Rizal, the late Marcelo H. del Pilar, the late Emilio Jacinto, the late Mabini…"

"And the late President Quezon, *Lola*… and everybody you mentioned their brightness. I want to become wise. To become a president. When I become a president, we become rich, *Lola*. Every politician… you said before, become rich, am I right, Lola? I'll also be known by the people. You also mentioned that that is the school where Mr. Mayor studied. Even Mr. Senator. And you also mentioned that there were a lot of wise people studied there…"

"Then you need to grow fast. Don't be hard headed. Follow everything we told you with your mother. You know, your mother really wants to send you to school."

Ting sat in the tiny extension of their shanty. She faced in the south where her mother comes every time. The blind old woman lit a small lump in the tiny living room.

"I missed Inang very much," whispered Ting. Where her mother coming from, she was not sure.

Whenever small children ran after each other in the narrow-improvised bridge made of two narrow slogs of wood, laughing with gusto, Ting also laughs. She pouts when the pregnant with a not-even-a-year-old child on her waist yells, or that skinny wearing a tattered dress shout. Ting shrinks whenever that short-sleeved tattooed man attempts to hurt the child with her age. In the other shanty, Ting saw the sisters the older being bigger than her, holding a flattened aluminum plate. There was a piece of burnt rice from the bottom of a cooking pot they

---

[36] *Amang:* colloquial but intimate address for one's father.

were after each other. When the younger cried of disappointment, a mother went out with a black cigarette in her mouth and hit the older hard enough that made the young shrank painfully.

Only the shanty by their side was quiet by that time. Ting thought that the young woman sometimes being followed by some young men was not around. Her mother was not around either. They might probably not home yet.

The Angelus was sounded by the bell in the plaza in the west. Ting ran to the living room. She kneeled beside the blind old woman. She did the sign of the cross, like what the blind old woman did. She prayed that her mother will bring home a lot of money for her studies. She added that her mother will bring home her father. After she finish, she kissed the hand of the blind old woman.

"God bless you, *Apok...*"

Ting decided to cook. But the rice container was empty. They went in the tiny terrace-liked area of their shanty to let the time pass. The blue sky was full of glittering stars. There were few people in the narrow-improvised bridge. The students in front of the school were gone.

"You know, Ting, breeze in the province was like we have here right now. During the dusk in the barrio like this, the children playing hide and seek under the full moon were so happy..."

"Is it true what *Nanang* said that the barrio is beautiful, *Lola*?"

"That's true. There were a lot of guavas, dragon fruit, oranges, mabolo, *kulkulang*[37], manzanita, *allagat*[38] ... all fruit bearing plants. When I was a little girl, we were satiated with food. Here as well, I learned. There were also a lot of plants before the arrival of the Spaniards. It was so peaceful. That school was not there yet. This creek was wide. It was clean. Full of fish. A lot of children swimming."

"Was it true that the people in the barrio were nice?"

"Of course, yes. If somebody got a problem, it's a problem of the whole barrio."

---

[37]   *Kulkulang:* a small plant in the shrubbery with yellow edible fruit.

[38]   *Allagat,* a vine with long, soft leaves and red flowers which fruits are edible.

"Why then we came here...? And you came from a different of Inang's place?

"That's true. I am not related to your Inang. But we were close. You know, your Inang's family were happy... under your Lola and Lolo's wing. Your Lola was a Visayan. But when the problems of land occurred, they were included to those who were killed. Your Inang decided to come to Manila. That's why you were born here."

"And how about you, *Lola*?"

"I'm from Laguna… we were poor. I am ugly, nobody dared to court me. I came here to look for my destiny. My parents died without seeing them… I experienced a lot of hardship. Until I lost my eye sight… When you grow older, you will discover all the secrets of life…"

There were a pair approaching from the narrow-improvised bridge. Ting recognized the young woman who lives by their shanty. The man was much older. The youngster was giggling when they went inside the shanty.

"Was that the young woman, *Apok*?"

"She was, *Lola*. She and an old man."

"Poor little girl."

Ting felt the shuddering of the shanty. Then heard the whining of the young woman. Then a long silence.

"Poor little toy," repeated the blind old woman.

Her Inang arrives. She was holding hands with a man. They stopped in the entrance when they saw Ting. The man deep sat and disappeared in the dark.

Ting ran to meet her Inang. She received a paper bag. They walked hand and hand through the narrow-improvised bridge.

"Why did you arrive late in the night, *Inang*?"

Her Inang just smiled and mussed up her hair.

They entered. Ting and the blind old woman ate pancit. Her Inang watched while talking with them. After a while, her Inang reached the broken mirror and analyzed herself.

She told them she was going out. "Take good care of Ting, *Nana*, okay?"

"Of course, … Are you staying out late?"

She did not hear the respond of her Inang. Her mouth was still full of pancit. It was yummy, and she forgot to ask something.

SHE was awakened by the hubbub in the university. When she rose up, she noticed her Inang sleeping soundly in the corner. She went out slowly. In the *Bangsal*[39], she reached the blind old woman groping on the wall.

Ting's eyes were wide-opened. There was a multitude of people in the school building. Many of them waggling red ensign. There was a wide and long piece of cloth where big letters were written. She could not understand what the students were bellowing. They were pointing at the old American with big goiter and the skinny tall old Filipino who were owners of the university. They were looking down from the third-floor lobby. It was here where the chemical laboratories were.

The American and the Filipino disappeared.

They hubbub of the students became more aggressive. There was an explosion in the school building. Those who were inside ran without any direction. The explosion burst in succession. Followed by roaring and screaming.

In the west, the siren exploded. Three police jeeps arrived. The students ran in different direction.

In the afternoon, the rallyists return. In the *bangsal*, Ting's Inang also watches.

The students became more aggressive. Her Inang said there was a mixed different group other than the students'. They were paid according to a source. Her Inang also said that the students were demanding not to increase tuition fees. But the American and the Filipino owners were hard headed. The Filipino follows everything the American wants to do.

It was about three in the afternoon when a big explosion occurs from the third floor. The laboratory exploded with fire and spread the warmth in the afternoon. The students ran in all directions.

---

[39]   *Bangsal:* an annex to the kitchen without roof or wall.

Ting's eyes were wide-opened watching the flaming fire. The debris flew into the sky. Big pieces flown down into the creek.

Ting's Inang became worried. The residents in the shanty area were shouting. Flake of fire continues.

"Prepare… Ran away…!" somebody shouted up.

Ting's Inang gathered their clothing. They went out. Prayers of the blind old woman who was holding Ting's hand was not in order.

They were in the narrow-improvised bridge where people were hustling and jostling when the flaming wood dropped straight down the creek. They screamed. The narrow-improvised bridge collapsed. They dropped into the creek. Ting and her Inang were able to hold the dangling part of the narrow-improvised bridge. They groped up into the wall. The blind old woman left in the creek. And the young woman who was accompanied by an old man last night.

The big flake of fire dropped unto the shanties. The fire ate the cardboard wall and roof. The fire spread all over the shanties.

A fire as big as a house dropped down the creek. The watchers screamed. Those who were under the clay were drowned by the fire. Ting closed her eyes because the blind old woman was one of them.

Ting looked up the university where her dreams were molded. Ting was in the verge of crying. Her eyes were reddened. Tears glided on both of her chicks.

It's gone, she loses her voice. It's gone…

She felt her Inang's palm on her shoulder. –0

Bannawag: June 19, 1972; *Pakpakawan, Berde! ken 22 a Sarita:* c1977, pp.147-153.

Three Footprints

"Three passions simple but overwhelmingly strong, have governed my life: the longing for love, the search for knowledge, and unbearable pity for the suffering of mankind... Love and knowledge, so far as they were possible, led upward toward the heavens. But always pity brought me back to earth." – Bertrand Russell.

I want you to write a novel settled in a modern technique, Hil," these comments of Valerio Castillejos, the publisher of Mata, were impinged in the sense of Hilario Garcia. "Describe the totality of the people squirted by the vicious system of power. How the vengeance of fast in the edge whacks down the iron machinery that puts up the shutters of freedom. What the possible reaction will be if the faux pas of both sides was not prevented. I want you to enforce the sharpness of your pen with full force the soonest time possible so that the truth will prevail. This was now your chance to validate your upstanding attribute!"

It was a very challenging remark for Hilario Garcia. But Valerio Castillejos' remark has an arid upshot. Why, does Castillejos believes he does not know what was happening?

His attention was concentrated at the lampshade on his table.

Hilario Garcia opens the drawer of the table. He takes out the blue notebook. He opens it in the first page...

I. Heaven

ANONG, Edwin, and I sit cross-legged delightfully in the *bangsal* one starry early evening.

"That biggest one is my star!" Anong pointed his finger to the star in the east.

"It's my star!" Edwin said.

"It's my star!" Anong said.

"Then that one right there is my star!" Edwin pointed the isolated star in the west.

I am looking at the star cuddled by a comb-liked moon.

"And you?" I did not pay attention Anong's touch. I am thinking that I am in the cuddle of the moon.

"Hey, are you asleep?" Anong touches me again.

"I am thinking," I said, "why a star is in the cuddle of the moon? What if I have wings and I fly up to the moon? They say the Lord God is in heaven. Maybe He is in the moon. I will talk to Him if ever. I ask Him to put water into our well so that we do not have to go to Kinwang to fetch water. I will borrow, if ever, Uncle Aling's thing for taking pictures and take pictures of the Lord God…"

"For me, I will ask many firearms!" Anong said. "I will follow, if ever, with *Manong*[40] Iyac to shoot birds!"

"If I ever see you, I will hit your anus with my pointed fingers!" Edwin said.

"But… why?"

"I pity the birds!"

---

[40]   *Manong, n.:* a call to a big brother; or older male, as sign of respect.

In the patio, Grandfather Iroy was twisting *lapnit*[41] by the spinning wheel causing a sharp sound. Grandmother Andiang was moving around in the *sagumbi*[42].

By the cogon field in the west after the newly plowed field, there was a loud whistling of Mona Liza. Uncle Aling was coming home; he came from Kinwang where he fetched two earthen jars of water by a sled.

Anong's, Edwin's, and my father were brothers. The parents of Edwin had been dead. Anong's mother had also been dead; his father Uncle Moding was in the city away from us and got another wife. My father and my mother were in San Marcos where they brought my little sister to cure her illness.

The three of us were almost with the same age, month was only the difference. I am the oldest, Edwin was second, Anong was the youngest. We stay in the house of our grandfather on top of the Mount Baybayyabas where they decided to have a homestead up in the east outskirt of Santa Monica.

"You, three hanging balls, come and sleep now!" grandfather's voice when he called our attention was like the sound of the bonds of white bamboos being pulled by a sled.

One morning while we were feeding chickens Edwin and Anong were laughing with gusto while making two cocks fight. I escaped from them and I ran to climb a corkwood tree by the north side of the house. As if I am in heaven again. I settled myself on a branch and watched the River Parsua down below by the foot of Mount Baybayyabas. I let my eyes follow the flow of the water from the Candle-liked Gushing Fountain from Mount Bullagaw in the east. My attention was focused at the Pangasaan Elementary School by the foot of Bullagaw. The sparkling light of the galvanized iron of the school's roof looks like pricking by

---

[41] *Lapnit:* a bark of jute plant made into ropes, or thin strips for bundling rice stalks.

[42] *Sagumbi, n.:* an extension or annex of a bamboo-and-cogon house which was used as a storeroom.

the Candle-liked Gushing Fountain. I thought that time: when I turn seven, I will also go to Pangasaan to study.

"Hey, you, hanging balls, you're there again!" I almost lost my grip when Edwin looks up.

I jumped down and ran after them. They went for rescue behind grandfather who was repairing the bindings of the earthen jars on the sled.

"What are these, you, scrotums, doing!" grandfather got mad and he wrings their ears.

"Good for you!" I stuck my tongue out toward them.

"You, too!" grandfather said but I managed to run away.

"We are going to fetch water in Kinwang," grandfather said one humid morning. "Put Sawak on yoke on the big sled, Edwin. You, Anong, Pango was yours. Be careful not to let the sleds turn upside down for we do not have reserve earthen jars anymore. You, Ayong, ride on Sikkubeng."

"Yahoo; I love it!" Edwin skips like a frog.

"You are so excited because you are about to pass by Adela's place again!" Anong said.

"You, swashes, your eyes were not opened yet, but you already want to court!" grandfather gave a side-glance smiling.

We went down the hill in the south. The wide cogon field was waving like an ocean. We passed by the branchy manzanita with a lot of ripe fruit. I stood up from the back of Sikkubeng and I reached up for a fruit from the branch and I threw it in my mouth. Anong followed thru. He lost control and felt down the ground.

"That's what you earned for!" grandfather said. "You seem not having some meals."

"Do you like guavas, Dela?" asks Edwin when we pass by Adela's place where she was uprooting yam by the foot of Mount Kimmabalio, the homestead of the Ollieros.

"That was rotten!" Anong said. "He just picked it up from the ground!"

"Don't believe in him, I just picked this from the tree!" Edwin threw a sharp-glance to Anong.

"Your grandsons seem trying to court, old man!" grins Adela's father.

"Not really, sir," Edwin said. "I just like Adela."

Rainy season was fast approaching; we did not notice the passing by of summer. It had been thundering deeply more frequently. The cuckoos had been also cuckooing in the field of *samsamon*[43]. Grandfather and uncle were already busy uprooting stumps and slashing and burning a tract of forest land for cultivation.

"Let us see who could carry more stumps," challenged Anong one time.

He had just carried five stumps when he quits because he accidentally drops a stump to his foot.

Ipil-ipil were more common in the forest land. We compete to get the sharpest bolo. Our skins were thick; we ignored the itch of the *sabawil*[44].

"I do the igniting," I said when the leaves and everything had been dried after several days. We cleaned the edges so that the part which was not cleaned will not be burnt.

As if there was a song in my bosom with the leap of flame in the withered leaves and I felt as if I was going to heaven with the curling tongue of fire emitting black smoke. I inhale the pleasant smell curling into my nose.

And during an early evening when stillness prevails in the house, I enjoy listening to the whistling of uncle, if he was not murmuring, while following the slow moving of the clouds as if within my reach. Edwin and Anong were joking and exchanging pleasantries.

The sky had been collecting clouds and not long before, it shows the first sign of rain. During this moment in time, many of our relatives, young women and young men, come to help us plant so that they will have reasons to come back during harvest time. There were lots of asad[45]

---

[43]   *Samsamon, n:* themeda triandra, an erect leafy grass used as fodder.

[44]   *Sabawil, n:* a climbing vine with purple flowers and hairy stinging pods.

[45]   *Asad, n.:* a pointed stick like a dibble to make holes in the ground used in planting rice grains.

and tubes of white bamboos prepared by grandfather and uncle for this occasion.

The men and the women were winking and elbowing lightly each other, accompanied by the soar of their mouth. As if their eyes were full of stars.

Uncle arrives early one occasion.

"Have you not conquered Caring yet?" asks grandfather.

"Almost there."

"You were always saying almost there… probably you do not know how to cozy up. Be careful, somebody may take ahead over you… Just tell me, if I need to do it for you," grandfather said.

"This stinky old man, as if he was the best!" grandmother said. "He did not even know how to court for himself!"

"Oh, common, blind old woman…"

Edwin and Anong were playing bad jokes too much one time. They boxed each other. They had lumps. Grandfather did not intervene. From that day forward, they did never play bad jokes anymore.

My father and my mother came home not so long afterwards. But my small sister was not with them anymore. My father built us a home nearby grandfather's home. Sometimes I oversee my mother crying.

But heaven was always near in Baybayyabas. As if I am reaching it. Then again, I climbed up the corkwood tree and look over the Pangasaan Elementary School.

THERE was a knocking at the door of Hilario Garcia's room.

"Papa, mama says it's time to eat," a voice from his youngest.

Hilario brought down the blue notebook. "Okay, I'm coming," he said. He focuses his attention to the lampshade on the table.

He opens the notebook; he skips some pages…

II. Earth

AFTER our graduation from the sixth grade at the Pangasaan Elementary School, we parted from each other. Uncle Moding brought Anong with him in Manila. We went to San Marcos with my parents. Edwin was left behind with our grandparents in Baybayyabas.

I studied at the San Marcos Institute. Edwin stops schooling for he decided to study at the back of a carabao. I could not blame him for he got a passing grade when we graduated. I seldom heard news about Anong. But he was in school.

Thieves and criminals who usually prowl at night multiply all over. The prices of commodities rose up. The news about the restlessness all over the country became frenzied. My parents became restless as well.

When I graduated from high school, I went to Manila. I studied journalism at the University of the Philippines. I looked for Anong from the address he sent me. I was not able to meet him because I was informed that he went to Baguio, to enroll at the Philippine Military Academy.

Edwin did never go out from Baybayyabas. Our grandparents were too old, and he did not like to leave them alone. Uncle was then there but there were times that he was too quiet since his lady of his dreams got married. I was informed that Edwin continued to court Adela Olliero. I said, I hope they were meant to each other. I even told them I will attend their wedding if ever.

One time when I spent a vacation, I intentionally visited Edwin in Baybayyabas.

"I knew now why my father and my mother died," he said. He was sad. Even so when I handed him a pair of t-shirt and blue jeans as my present, his response was as tasteless as a viand without fermented fish. "It's done by people!" he continued. "Those son of…!"

I tapped his shoulder. "Forget it," I said. "Could you bring back what had happened in the past?"

"No. But I can do something. I know them. I often see them. My blood boils up when I see them!"

Somebody said they raped my aunt. Uncle had witnessed personally. He became outrageous. They killed them both. Why those who did it were not sent to prison, they had a connection with the former mayor.

"Don't ever forget this, Hil," he said before we parted. "If the present condition goes on, blood will flow in the Parsua River!"

"Hey!" I said. "What a pity, Cousin, you should have continued your studies. That's a poet's line!" I tried to ease his burden.

"I'm serious!" he said.

The misunderstanding between the government and the activists became more and more intense. There were more rallies. Even at U.P. often that classes were suspended because of the problem between groups. Then the group against the law became more popular. The explosion of pillbox and the spurt of teargas became more frequent. Along the streets there were heavy hoof beats of students; their shouting became louder and louder. Their group became thicker and thicker. Their stomping produced a cloud of dust. The earth seems riddled all around the campus.

Many of my schoolmates tried to entice me to join them. But I could not swallow their ideology. My mind was focus in a different direction. I wanted to be a prominent writer. I drew knowledge from the erudite of different world of wisdom. I made the U. P. Main Library as my second home. There were times that I almost locked up when the janitor was about to close because I am still in a corner digging for more knowledge.

I have not completed my studies yet when I started writing for my brain had been overflowing with wisdom. I had drawn a lot of knowledge and it needs to be topped off.

One time, when I called with Uncle Moding's place, Anong, now Jan, happens to be there. We were about to complete our studies and both of us were amazed for the huge changes of our physiques. Jan's stature was then a real military built. He said he got a high rank in the academy and he was hoping to be given the best rank commensurate to his ability upon graduation.

"I have something I want you to read," he said when our feelings subsided. "I'm sure you'll like it."

He brought out the autobiography of Bertrand Russell. He handed it to me and borrowed the lines of Russell at the same time. the three passions of Russell: *longing for love, search for knowledge*, and *unbearable pity for the suffering of mankind*. This part was impinged in my mind:

love and knowledge, so far as they were possible, led upward toward the heavens. But always pity brought me back to earth.

"Service, Hil," Jan said. "I learned that during my stay in the academy. Laughter was not enough to boost the personality; our joy in Baybayyabas, now they were only reflection that could not be visited… Let's see what's happening. What can we do?"

When I went back to my boarding house one day, a letter from my parents was waiting for me.

"Edwin was gone, son," the letter says. "He went in the refuge of the mountains… he went with the leftist. Not long after Adela Olliero commits suicide because the brother of the mayor raped her…"

I remember what Edwin mentioned during our last conversation: if the present condition goes on, there will be blood to flow in the Parsua River!

I felt something cold creeping up in my spinal cord.

My mind flows smoothly more than ever when I graduated. If I ever had more extra-curricular activities, I should have garnered higher than cum laude. But that was not the most important. I have articles published almost every day in the daily papers. Some papers were enticing me to join them, but I preferred to remain free lancer. I am free to roam. I am not in box. I can do everything I want. Anyway, my earning was not bad.

Jan was commissioned as lieutenant at first. But he was promoted almost instantly. Not even quite a year when he was promoted captain. Captain Januario Garcia! He was assigned in Northern Luzon. We got married almost simultaneously. My family lives in the city.

"Edwin was now a commander, son," my father writes to me one day. "He was not just a commander. He was very popular. He was being hunted by the law because he was not afraid to anybody else in the North. They had killed a lot of army officers in their territory. Nobody could go closer. Your grandparents were very sad… Your uncle became more serious…."

"Edwin was too much," Jan said one day when we had a time to chat. "I hope it won't happen. But I already overheard that the law had given him an ultimatum. I cannot do anything if they assign me to confront him."

I decided to talk with Edwin. I want to help them.

I asked somebody from the valley to drive me by cart to the foot of Baybayyabas. I do not know where the camp of Edwin's group was, but I was sure my grandparents know where. I know that my grandparents were dear to Edwin and he could not take for granted not to visit them.

The corkwood tree was still at the north side of my grandparents' house. But it was already old. I noticed that the yard became more constricted than before. The white bamboos were still dense in the south and in the west. The cogon field was bushy. If there any changes of the place, probably the fact that no children playing and laughing.

My grandmother had teary eyes when she embraces me. I had also a painful feeling inside because that was the only time when we see each other after so many years. Her eyes had still some sparks. My grandfather was seating silently in a corner. He was already week; he could not recognize people any longer. I was informed that uncle was in Kinwang.

"Your cousin… oh, my grandson!" my grandmother asks when I mentioned Edwin.

"Is he ever visits you?"

"Monthly… but he had not come this month."

My grandparents do not know where the camp of Edwin's group was. It was only several days before the month ends and I decided to wait for him.

Edwin was surprised when they arrived one night. I almost did not recognize him because of his long beard. I told him my purpose; and the plan of the government.

"It's too late," he said. "Many lives had been sacrificed, because of the greediness of the powerful. My surrender, as you've said, it's easy to tell. But do you know my feelings? Do you know the feelings of the harassed? Was forgiving just as easy as to chew betel nut? What they did to my parents… and to… Adela… I surrender just to be laughed at?"

"For the welfare of the land, Ed," I said.

"…or for your own good?" Edwin's smile was appalling. "You were already well-known, Hil. Anong as well was popular. I know. So then, the government was planning to arrest me. I will not be stunned when I meet Anong. But you came ahead to show people that you were more vigilant. If I go with you… I am not selfish. I can give that as a present to you. But do you know the reason why people like me exist? Hiding, running away and running after, like cat and mouse. You were a renowned personality. You had written a lot. But had you tried to contemplate on our status? If you had done, who are we by your standard?"

"The cause of all of these is just a matter of misunderstanding," I said. "And I believe that it is up to us, that we could be instrumental in resolving problem."

Edwin shakes his head. "Do you believe that if I surrender, the movement still goes on?" he said. "Do you remember what I said about the stream of blood in Parsua River? I don't like it to come to pass…"

"That's why I came… that I looked for you," I said, "to ask your favor. We help each other. I believe that what we could do, it will be a key in solving the problem…"

There was an approaching heavy hoop beat. Edwin's curse followed when he recognized the sign. His eyes were sharp when he looked at me.

"You're a traitor, Hil!" he said.

"That's not true, Cousin," I said. "I knew nothing…"

"My grandsons…" my grandfather's voice was soft and trembling. Grandmother stood by his side with tears on her eyes.

Edwin stood in front of our grandparents. He put his palms on their shoulders. Then he turned back in a hurry. He flicks his rifle from the corner.

"Don't get out from here, Grandmother," I said. I went down of the house.

The moon was bright, and I saw the shadows in the surroundings hiding by the trees. Edwin crouched for refuge in the north forehead of Baybayyabas looking down the Parsua River. I looked refuge by the big trunk of the ipil-ipil. I readied my camera. It doesn't matter how much could I get. In that very moment I did not know what I should do. I was thinking my grandparents. I could feel the presence of Jan; that he leads the attack; probably they smelled the presence of Edwin in Baybayyabas. But I was not sure.

In the far west, I saw the off and on light. The sound was soft at first. It became louder and louder. Helicopter!

"Edwin! I know you are there! Surrender!" I recognized the voice from the megaphone from the foot of Baybayyabas. "I promise not to leave you alone. Just for the sake of our grandparents…"

"It's too late!" shouted back Edwin. "You better go home!"

The shooting continued in the west. It was late when Edwin ordered his group not to shoot. Jan also shouted not to shoot but his words were swallowed by continuous shooting from up above and down below. In the space up above, the helicopter was coming closer. Suddenly it emits sharp light followed by gunfire in the distance.

The last I could remember was I witnessed the flame all over the house of my grandparents. I closed my eyes. Gunfire and moaning continued; it became softer in my hearing…!

THERE was a knocking on Hilario Garcia's room's door.

"'Pa were you not hungry yet?" voice of his wife.

"I'm coming," he said. He put down the blue notebook. Her eyes were focused on the lampshade on the table.

He flicked the notebook once more, in some pages…

III. Revisiting

I WENT back to Mount Baybayyabas after so many years to revisit, and to see the best that I could do in a place of my youth that was neglected after the flame.

It was the same Parsua River, where Edwin said blood will flow, only it had eaten a lot a part of the foot of the mountain.

It was the same forehead of Baybayyabas. There were old ipil-ipil tree, but many were downed by the past years. On its foot, men were killed. I did not see but I heard that one of the shadows of the ipil-ipil tree was where Captain Januario Garcia lost his life. Yes, Jan, or Anong.

I thought I could no longer climb the forehead of Baybayyabas. I was no longer the young Hilario who even ran to climb up.

I climbed up still. And there, in the distant, I positioned myself to hide, listened the shooting, aimed my camera. I noticed then the coming of the helicopter from the west. Followed by non-stop shooting from up above and down below the forehead of Baybayyabas. And I witnessed the tongue of fire in the house.

Yes, Edwin, Januario, blood flew. Your blood; my blood; our grandparents' blood; the blood of the Garcias! Our uncle...

You all had gone. And I was left behind. Probably it was my fate, to be left behind after the flame. When I awoke, I was already in the hospital. You were gone...!

And I stood by the remnant of the corkwood tree. The place where the house erected was already grassy. The noisy chickens in the morning were no longer there. No more yelps from the carabaos and cows. The Mona Lisa of my uncle was no longer there; the field of white bamboos became thicker. The cogon field which was waving seemingly a withered garden now. The nurtured field of peanuts and watermelons now a field of *samsamon*. The guava tree by the south side of the well which was had water only when it rains, was no longer there as well.

The Candle-like Waterfall was too far, its water could not reach the Parsua River. The head of the Pangasaan Elementary School was no longer shining as well. Were there still studying right there?

"After the encounter," said the old man whom I asked for in the Parsua River, "nobody dared to climb the Mount Baybayyabas. The late... so I learned that he was your uncle... he did not go back at all. Was he not given a chance to get out from Mandaluyong?"

"Not anymore. He died inside..."

I felt the emptiness of my world, the vanity of knowledge I drew from different sources for many years.

And the affection between our jokes with Anong and Edwin that always bursting, the true knowledge we drew from our everyday climbing the Baybayyabas... But the past Baybayyabas was no longer there; the heavens were nowhere to find. How could I go back?

THE words of Valerio Castillejos were embossed in the attention of Hilario Garcia: define the entirety of the people squirted by the vicious system of power.

And he observes the surrounding… as if many immeasurable objects were wriggling!

He suddenly remembers the lines of Bertrand Russell: *but always pity brought me back to earth.*

He remembers the monument he was planning to erect in Mount Baybayyabas, where the corkwood tree stood: Captain Januario Garcia facing west; *Ka* Edwin in the east, by their feet an old man and a woman were embracing while in sitting position looking up the heavens.

"'Pa, come now…" voice of his wife.

Hilario Garcia closes the blue notebook. –0

Bannawag: December 19, 1988; 1ˢᵗ Prize, *ETTI,* 1988; *Daton,* 1991, pp.237-246.

The World Should Stop
That People Could Get Off

Prologue

THE fullness of life Abraham, Sr. wants to depict in the canvas was indistinct. What kept on swaying in his mind is the disarrayed imagination highlighted by Kierkegaard, Sartre, Nietzsche, Jaspers and Merleau-Ponty in their writings included in, *Reality, Man and Existence: Essential Works of Existentialism* edited by H. J. Blackham. Abraham, Sr. wants to concentrate the belief of Kierkegaard on God, the reason of Nietzsche in saying that God is dead; he wants to unearth the meaning of love illustrated by Sartre, the equivalence of phenomenology adapted by Merleau-Ponty from the perception and emotions he extracted from his own experience. And many more reasonings of these philosophers. He wants to exhibit in the canvas the extent of the viewpoints of these intellectuals so that by the canvas, appears the overburden of the citizenry he could imagine and feel. He wants these pigments to be distinctive so that the society recognize at once the blood of the citizens flooding his vision. But it seems like a firefly on and offing the delineation of reality, the man, and the creation where existentialism moves about. The activities of Filipinas Isabel, his wife, is occupying some space in his temple. Sometimes, there is a motivating factor for him to paint the whole image of Filipinas Isabel where existentialism evoked by Nietzsche, Sartre, and others be mixed together.

156

ABRAHAM, Sr. took a sit on an armchair and closed his eyes tightly. His vision casts aside the pictures coming in unison into his temple. Those who were running after and over to hung unto their ride going back home in a late afternoon or dusk. Those who are wriggling at the big malls as if they were not short of money shopping the merchandizes—he assumes that they just go there to cold off, or to satiate their eyes for their pockets could not afford the weightiness of prices. Those happy go lucky students could not feel what their parents carrying on their shoulders for their education because of the high prices of their needs. Those who were yelling each other. The overly exposed news in newspapers— killings here and there, NPA here and there, ambushed soldiers and police officers here and there, loaded women here and there... The city where those who came from the province found a refuge because the powerful Leftist is now too congested. Especially Filipinas Isabel who is fed-up for she believes that they, teachers and other lowly government employees were oppressed. Sometimes Abraham, Sr. feels the freezing of his palms and feet when he thinks the activities of his wife against the present powers: she is one of the leaders of the activist teachers.

Abraham, Sr. was getting concerned with their five children, Filipinas Rosal, Abraham Joselito, Abraham Solomon, Filipinas Linglingay, and Abraham, Jr. whose ages ranging from seventeen down to eleven... their future.

1. Domain

ARE you really not listening at all?" Abraham, Sr. looked at Filipinas Isabel arranging her things for teaching. Abraham, Sr. hang his newly fixed framed family picture.

"I had told you," Filipinas Isabel said. She faced the mirror and looked at her face.

"Why are you still involving yourself?"

"What did you say?"

"You might be steering your movement," the face of Abraham, Sr. soured. He faces the small library in the living room and started arranging the books. He removed the book of Nietzsche, Sartre, and others.

"What's wrong about it?"

"You're not the one responsible…"

"And who would be? The politicians? The army? The NPA? You might have no feelings."

"Why won't you focus in your teaching?" Abraham, Sr. said. He put down the book on the table. He got a duster.

"Why, what do you think I am doing? Am I not teaching?"

"In the streets?"

"'Pa, when will we be awakened? It's even a little bit late. See this… unending promises… without any result. Those who are in power are like dogs nothing doing except to bark and bark and bark. Those who are outside are also barking even louder. How about the whimpering of those who were persecuted? You might be pretending you do not know that the two separate powers are ignoring the condition that is exterminating the whole nation. Sometimes I am pondering, that the belief of men to God is empty because when I am passing by the chapels or churches, many are attending masses, but I do not know what they are praying for. I guess, if they are praying for peace, there is no problem like this in our country. It is a pity, there are lot of religions but…"

Abraham, Sr. shakes his head focusing his attention to his wife. "I am thinking," he said, "that too many people and as if there is a power forcing us to eat one another… we the brothers. That power is using us as a machinery of evil dreams!"

"Then, what will you do?" Filipinas Isabel side-glanced him.

"I feel that you are influencing your children…"

"Good to awaken them with truth. And join the movement. I don't like them grow unmindful what's happening around them until they become insinile. I want them to join in molding the future. I want them to stand fighting for their right!"

"Really?"

"You should be the one in my side. You are brilliant… a frustrated writer and artist. But you do not have an inkling with the present situation. As if you do not belong to the society.

"Ma…"

"You just don't feel the hardship of being insufficient because you are not the one buying daily needs. Prices of commodities are sky rocketing. We teachers really are worn-out… but the authorities did never mind us. They forgot that they made us servants during election. They said they raised salaries. But why people are not contented? You probably don't know these for what you are focusing is your canvas. You can't even take care of yourself; you are more than eremites. You are appearing as a toy of the elitists, 'Pa. The elitists who were made crazy by their canvas… well and good if they honor you. But seems nobody wants to look back to your paintings."

"Because I woke up late. It was late when I realized that art is a silent expression of peace. There are some lines of Nietzsche, Sartre, and others, despite others consider they only show hollowness. For me, without that hollowness or skin if it is human… then, there is nothing being covered. I believe existentialism is within the people themselves. Then, if there is skin there is also flesh, and if there is flesh, there is also bone, if all of these is present, it's a human, then there is life within."

"What's the use of thinking all of those Nietzsche's and Sartre's? Despite of unearthing those nonsense in your soul, can it lengthen your life? 'Pa, look at all around you!"

"I've been telling you that I do not have in mind except peace… tranquility? Can't you understand that I don't like to be involve with unrest in the world? You don't even know; I want to be separated from this world. If it's a ride, I want to alight. But I do not like to die yet! What's happening is maddening. Brothers, eating each other. Why is it like this? There are many other outside the country to go to. But I do not like that way. I even prefer to go back to the province. But there is no good news there either."

"Then?"

"Let's face the truth, 'Ma. Our nation is in turmoil. But remember that you are in public service. You are a government employee, whatever angle you look at. You should be one of those who are supposed to control the welfare of the citizenry, especially the children who will be the guidepost of the next generation. Stop your plan to strike. Don't intensify the problem of the country."

"It's too late," Filipinas Isabel said with no intense.

"Nothing is late."

"Just live me alone. I had started, and I need to finish it. Anyway, it is not only our group who like this. A lot. Even we don't move, others are prepared. I think, not far from now, there will be bloody revolution."

"Then how about your children?"

"They will always be my children."

"And I will always be your husband?"

"What else then?"

Abraham, Sr. exhaled when his wife gone. His eyes were focused to the book of Blackham, where Nietzsche, Sartre, and others are.

2. Getting Off

ABRAHAM, Sr. was about to dip his paintbrush in the palette when Junior, the youngest, ran towards him.

"Daddy, Daddy... Mommy is in the tv!"

He smacks, put down the paintbrush and followed his son to the living room. His four other children were there open-mouthed facing the television set, they are Filipinas Rosal, Abraham Joselito, Abraham Solomon, and Filipinas Linglingay.

"Daddy, look at Mommy," Filipinas Linglingay's voice seem hang in the air.

There was no excitement in Abraham, Sr.'s face. Before Filipinas Isabel went out early dawn, Abraham, Sr. warned her not to go. But there, in front, and she is one of those who are yelling and waving a piece of red rend cloth while the red marked in a white ensign of the demonstrators where their demands had written. They were dense in the middle of the day, in the street toward Malacañang. Those were teachers, they were in uniform... elementary, secondary and college. They were in unison, thought Abraham, Sr.

The camera had changed the direction to the left. Huge number of students. They were also yelling. Another big group in the other side, then in the back section, a group of government employees. Impenetrable was the armed trench of the government in front.

Abraham, Sr. noticed the turning back of Filipinas Rosal and Abraham Joselito. They are second year and first year in college. With gloomy face.

Abraham, Sr. dialed to another station. The same program. Every station has the same program. It came to his mind; it means one thing: the issue is serious.

He switched off the television.

"Daddy, I want to watch Mommy," Junior said.

"That's enough," said Abraham, Sr. "You better play Atari."

He faced the canvas again. What he witnessed in the television has a serious effect and the sound image in his temple he wanted to exhibit in the canvas before had flown away. He had connected all together a while ago the images tried to exhibit the anthology of Blackham where he brought to life Nietzsche, Sartre, and others.

He picked up the palette. The fullness of the country once again back into his mind. The people in the city. The occurrences that made the civilization zany, the vision being sculpted. Those innocent citizenries being sacrificed. The slain members of the armed forces. The beating of the bosom of the country. He wants to reveal all of these in one big canvas.

This is the last challenge; he had reflected again. If he fails, he will drop art forever and probably he will just be an eremite. But he needs to probe his wife, Filipinas Isabel that there is beauty in life outside of society by own point of view, in a silent boarding on a vision; portray that the world had ceased and the seniors, yes, the seniors who had been exhausted travelling...

Here comes again the yelling of the demonstrators in the television set.

Abraham, Sr. stood up.

"I told you to play Atari!" he said and looked at sharply the three in the living room. He switched off the television set.

"I-its Mommy, Daddy," Jr. stooped.

"Forget your Mommy."

"They are rumbling," Abraham Solomon said.

"Let them rumble."

"There are a lot of soldiers," Filipinas Linglingay said. "There is burning...they are even firing their guns..."

Abraham, Sr. gritted his teeth. He went back to the canvas.

The colors in his temple had gone. He put down the palette and laid down to the armchair. This will be the last. This will be the last! His temple felt breaking up because of the whirling views.

Where is peace? The freedom? The exquisiteness of life? How could be alienated from this world of the puppets? The pretenders... the greedy... the wicked?

Abraham, Sr. closed his eyes. Lord...

He was awakened by the commotion in the living room. He rubbed his eyes. He stood up. He went to the living room. He saw in the television the scurrying people; explosion, and blazing. Reporters and photographers were on the go. Cameras were non-stop flashing. Abraham, Sr. was not mindful what the announcer was saying. His eyes were looking for Filipinas Isabel where the cameras ran at. The demonstrators were like army of red ants and they did not have focus where to go, but they were not moving out from in front of Malacañang. Sometimes, other groups shown in front of the Congress, in EDSA, around television stations. There was an incoming blaze in almost every corner. There was yelling.

Lord, is this it? Abraham, Sr. thought. And he was weekend sitting beside his three children. In the television, turmoil is becoming serious. The demonstrators had occupied the channel they were watching. No more program in other channels. They were showing the consequence of greediness.

Cold swarms over Abraham, Sr.'s palms upon seeing the teachers being attacked and then rumbling. He saw Filipinas Isabel, his wife, in front, with other leaders and looked like Gabriela Silang raising their arms.

Piling! Abraham, Sr. exclaimed within him. Piling!

In a group of students, Abraham, Sr.'s eyes looked for Filipinas Rosal and Abraham Joselito.

He stood up, hurriedly changed.

"Don't ever go out, okay? Whatever happens, don't ever go out from the house." He glanced the clock; it was almost six in the evening. "Just take your dinner. You, Linglingay… prepare for your dinner. Just be careful. Don't wait for me. Don't ever allow other people to come in."

"Where are you going, Daddy?" Junior asked.

Abraham, Sr. just mussed up the hair of the youngest.

He was almost not able to take a ride going to Cubao. No more rides. He got a taxicab in Cubao and ordered to drive him to Sampaloc. The driver was hesitant.

In the Rotonda, they met a bunch of rowdy people.

"The Malacañang… The Malacañang!"

In the atmosphere above Malacañang, tongue of flame sticking above.

The driver did a lot of turning the taxicab until reaching Legarda. From there alone, uproar everywhere. Abraham, Sr. paid the driver and mixed himself with people without one direction.

Non-stop explosion under flame. When he reached Mendiola, he noticed that the Malacañang starts crumbling. The firefighters could not rescind the maddening flame. Bodies everywhere in the streets were being cleared by the authorities. Teachers and others were among the fatalities. Abraham, Sr. was scared to death identifying the uniformed teachers. He was searching for Filipinas Isabel. His wife was nowhere to find. In the group of the fatalities among the students, Filipinas Rosal and Abraham Joselito were not among them. Where did they go?

Malacañang was exploding like a volcano. The skeleton of the buildings prying the bosom of heaven were glowing. Then, there was explosion from the nearby building. And flame is spreading relentlessly. Abraham, Sr. ran away feeling the heat of the flame's tongue.

Every time he met an ambulance, or any kind of car carrying victims, he tried his best to know whether Filipinas Isabel, Filipinas Rosal, and Abraham Joselito were included.

He called a lot of hospitals. He wants to know where his loved ones were. If they were in a hospital, he knew for sure what happened. If they were not, he does not know if they had gone home, or they went with those who escaped, or whatever or whoever. He does not like to be like that. Whatever their differences with his wife, or reprimanded his children, Abraham, Sr. can feel right now that he still cares for them.

He found his wife at the Medical Center. They had just brought her to the emergency room when he arrived. He could not talk to her; the doctors did not allow him. She was in serious condition. They just allowed him to peep for her. Filipinas Isabel was under dextrose. Her eyes were closed. There was a bruise on her right cheek. There was blood on her temple and her left leg.

His children, Filipinas Rosal and Abraham Joselito, were nowhere to find.

There were many patients and even the hallways were full of waiting for a space in rooms. The smell of medicines is diffusing.

He called to their house and informed that he could not go home. He asked their condition. Abraham Joselito and Filipinas Rosal were not home yet. Abraham, Sr. gritted his teeth. Where did they go? He prayed nothing injurious had happened to them. He could not leave Filipinas Isabel; he just waits for a news from his children.

Many news arrived. Injured still coming. This place had been downed. In the north. In the south. This building had been downed into ashes. This one and that one had died. Raging flame was unstoppable in the city. The authorities could no longer stop the fuming citizens. Groups from all over the country were in unison to attack. Even the camp of the armed forces had been attacked. The secretary of defense had been held.

The whole citizenry had revolted!

And this was the primary news: The President disappeared!

Lord! Abraham, Sr.'s eyes closed tightly from where he was sitting while waiting. Why is this happening?

The citizens should stop, he mumbled. The time should stop, the moment…

The world must stop…!

Epilogue

AT first, Abraham, Sr. hardly believes what it was in front of him: a huge canvas where a seemingly real life is moving, and ruins or skeletons—at first there were few who criticized his work, but he did not object them, then came those who have positive views and understood his message. The right hand of the mother whose entire body was bath with blood was holding the whole world as if she was forcing to stop it so that people could jump out. In the whole part of the body of the mother, there were the various events who wrapped up the last half of the history of the country in the twentieth century.

Now, the last one who loved paintings has just left, who bargains and begging to buy the canvas in whatever amount he wants. He had only one answer: "I am sorry, I am not selling this, my only Masterpiece."

He had not counted the canvases he had sold since his first solo exhibit where he first displays this biggest, and he believe it as his Masterpiece, a canvas after the that revolution. Every exhibit he did, this canvas is always there as display, which he believes gave him luck.

He had received a lot of awards. Until it became as just an ordinary one, and sometimes, he assigned his wife Filipinas Isabel who just retired from teaching to receive for he does not have time, and as just to honor her what he believes a big responsibility of his beloved for her involvement in the recent revolution. And despite Filipinas Isabel limping, her face is bright, and she could not forget to mention the reason of her husband's success.

Considering the fact, Abraham, Sr. has no complain anymore. Their five children, Filipinas Rosal and Abraham Joselito who both survived from their serious involvement with the revolution; Abraham Solomon, Filipinas Linglingay, and Abraham, Jr. had settled with their individual families. Their professions as siblings could be proud of. And they already have a lot of grandchildren.

But he always feels emptiness in his life, more so when his eyes catch the book where Nietzsche, Sartre, and others, could be read, which he did not removed from the old shelf. He is uneasy waiting for the start of losing the sweetness of the country's sleep. Many years had passed since the revolution that imparted dumbfounding silence. But again, something being awakened, which is being awaited like the crowing in the early dawn.

At the corner of Abraham, Sr.'s mind, there is the President who changed the lost President—it was known afterwards that he was abducted and killed by the leftists—who had not been changed since he was appointed for the citizens are satisfied for his leadership.

As if Abraham, Sr., wants to paint a new image of the present century, where the President is acting. Now that he could still hold his paintbrush.

And he once again in front of a huge canvas, who is thinking a different angle; his arm is over Filipinas Isabel's shoulder while his eyes focused what has written at the foot of the huge mother in the canvas: 'GOD IS DEAD'—Nietzsche.

Demigods were dead! Abraham, Sr. thought.

In his mind, at the foot of the other canvas, written: "RESURRECTION"—Abraham, Sr.

Resurrection.

Abraham, Sr. pulled Filipinas Isabel close to him. –0

Second Prize, ETTI, *1989; Bannawag:* December 25, 1989; *Daton,* pp306-314; *translation completed:* July 19, 2018.

The Flickering Stars Of Escopa

I. We were Here, Dalen, In Escopa

*A*ND *I say again, Dalen: the world was truly blind for it cannot see the groping beggars;*

Yes, its eyes were open, but it seems to be feigning blindness to the dripping putrid venom of the fanged in this land who were ready to gobble us up.

For this was the truth, I say again, Dalen: the blind can see, and it was the ones who have eyes who were truly blind.

Again, I say, Dalen: the world was swimming in a sphere of wickedness.

Have faith, my love: the blind will rise, and they will be able to see in the pitch-dark which dims the stars of Escopa;

Then they will grope for the truth, and they will not regret having been born in Escopa, despite their endless misery;

And woe, my love, to those who can see but feign blindness. Woe to this world...

Chapter 1

ONCE again, Escopa was awaken. Kosep was awake. And Dalen. And Djona. Forty, thirty, thirteen. Father. Mother. Child.

They were perhaps the first to wake up. It was not even sunrise yet. Orion was not yet sleepy. Nor was the Big Dipper. Kosep and Dalen talked. They whispered to one another. Kosep stroked Dalen. In the

smooth parts of his beloved. While Dalen's eyes were fixed in the hole where the stars were bidding goodbye. Those flickering stars. Her breath was deep.

Djona turned to one side. She looked in their direction. Then turned around. To face the wall. She crouched. Her eyes spun around the punctured wall. Where would she be going again today?

Where were they going again today?

From Escopa, they would go to J. P. Rizal. Julian Manglicmot, the one-eyed, also go out.

All of them would go out.

Again. On this hazy Monday morning, the first day of the week, they would go out. Light steps would be heard between residential houses which were mostly ramshackle patchwork, some made of cracked hollow block base patched with rusty and punctured galvanized iron. And old cardboard…

The sound of their steps would be the rhythm of the early morning. Or, the break of day. There were those who already had something to eat; many had not yet taken in anything.

Kosep had eaten something. So, had Dalen. And Djona.

And so, had Julian Manglicmot. For he was never wanting in food.

In pairs and holding hands, they traced the western exit with cautious, sometimes hesitant steps. And they find their way to J. P. Rizal. There were smiles on the faces of those whose hands were held and led; there were apprehensions in the minds of those who served as guide. Those who were led, patchwork; those who guide, rags.

In the mind of Kosep, Dalen's words were imprinted. In fact, they were the world. They were the patchwork and rags. In this paradise. In Escopa. They were all this…

Man, and child. Woman and child. An aged pair. Perhaps, father and child. Perhaps, mother and child. Perhaps, husband and wife. Eyes were the guide. To the father, to the mother, to the better-half, the eyes were the light of those who ask to be guided.

Says Kosep: All of us were of the same world; we were one world; only one place in which to move around; we live the same way. The only difference was that in our misfortune, we have no sun nor stars to enable us to see through the thick darkness that surrounds us; ours were but wishes and dreams which will never see fulfillment. In your case, your dreams were attainable…

There were faces that were always smiling. There were those which were always sad.

But there were more sad faces. No day passes by when they were not in bitter mourning.

For Escopa was a dark world. And the story of Dalen and Kosep was just as dark. And so was the story of Djona. Escopa was a world in the dark.

Only half of Julian Manglicmot's world was dark. The other half was bright. This was the perception of Kosep and Dalen.

Because of so-called freedom, the whole place was enveloped in darkness. Darkness which Kosep perceived to be two arms' length thick. So thick, even the sharpest of eyes could not penetrate. Which Djona wanted to pierce open, so she can see the view of a different world; which freedom was no different from an isolation room which was always pad locked. Which was surrounded by freedom. But not to Julian Manglicmot. For he has a Pajero to watch out for. All were free to throw away dead cats. Dead dogs. Dead rats. Sometimes, dead or aborted fetuses. And whatever. Which was a fuse of life…

Freedom, for it was a retreat for snatchers. Kosep has seen them around every so often.

Freedom, for drivers were free to speed away to their hearts' content on J. P. Rizal. Along Aurora. Along Katipunan. If they ran over someone being led—once Kosep almost got hit—only God (or, should it be Satan?) would have to deal with the owner of the Pajero.

Freedom. For at Escopa, people were free to come and go; free to pursue their prey with a shiny Batangas knife, or with a rod, or a *paltik*[46]. And shortly thereafter, blood freely flows and then dries up in the dust and blackened streets.

---

[46] *Paltik,* A home-made revolver in the Philippines.

No chocolate boys [47] may dare come close. Who would not be afraid of a sharp *Batangas*[48] knife, Kosep thought, especially during this age where the medal of courage had become worthless? Poor us, says Kosep, as he throws up his gaze to the high heavens.

Freedom still, Dalen, says Kosep, and Djona, he adds, for the Pajero that Julian Manglicmot was looking after and always followed by Whistle was free to come and go. Oh, yes, Sergeant Angel Guardiano was Whistle. The engine of the Pajero was revving up; Whistle's head was up high; one-eyed Manglicmot was always watching the surroundings.

Ah, they were free. All of them.

Dalen and Djona will leave Kosep at an intersection buzzing with people. There he'd sit down. Or, stand up. Begging. Asking for heaven's blessing.

But there were many with whistles; and they were irritated by the likes of Kosep. Anyway, Kosep perseveres. Until he was fetched by his loved ones.

And where did Dalen and Djona go?

Kosep does not even ask. He just trusts that they would fetch him. There was always a sampaguita[49] garland that Djona would place around his neck.

"My father whom I loved very much." If only she knew the truth.

"My child who was my sole light," Kosep knew this was not the truth. But to him and Dalen, it was.

The sampaguita continues to exude its fragrance. In Djona's embrace. In the child's embrace for the father.

And Dalen?

She would put on a lot of scent when she went out. But the smell would have been gone when she returned. Kosep could not complain. What was there to complain about? They were there to care for him.

---

[47]   *Chocolate boys,* Police officer.

[48]   *Batangas* is a province in the Philippines where sharp knives were manufactured.

[49]   *Sampaguita,* Philippines' national flower.

They came into his life as a miracle. Dalen was rife with problems of the world. She was brought by fate just outside Kosep's paradise.

"You were a sincere person, Kosep," said Dalen. "You do not pretend. You can perceive what can't be seen by those who pretend to be blind."

Why do I need to pretend? Kosep thought. But he did not say this out loud. He had only one worry. So, what if they were lost?

Chapter 2

DALEN is that you?" Kosep set his right ear to the direction of the door.

"Shit!"

"So, what happened?"

Dalen slumped her body upon the punctured chair. "Nothing was worse than that monster."

"Was it Whistle again?" Kosep remembered Angel Guardiano.

There were wrinkles on his forehead as he stood. He held his waist. His feet searched for his worn-out slippers. He approached Dalen. He groped for the woman's shoulder and pressed them gently.

"I'm fed up talking with him. He does not run out of excuses. Why don't they just tell us frankly if we could expect anything or not."

"Come now. Let it be. They can't see what happened to me. Look, even Manglicmot who was our leader can't do anything. The glitter of the Benz which bumped me was so blinding they can't see me anymore... So, let it be."

"If you can only see how they look..."

"I can see all of them, Dalen. Even those which Whistle cannot see, and Manglicmot. Just like Mr. Pajaro, who always bothers us... His henchmen, can they see us?"

"The devil even threatens!"

"Which was why they are being devils, wild boars, too."

"What should I do then?" Dalen lit a cigarette. "Will I just spread my legs and display it like dried beef?"

"Why should you do that?"

"But it's what he's asking for!"

"You never grow tired of smoking. You're aggravating the pollution...."

"Don't change the topic... Shit!"

"Oh, World. Oh, Man. Oh, Escopa."

"The beast was even enticing me..."

"To leave me?"

"Of all the things you were, you're not a devil like him."

"Which makes me wonder how you can bear with me. But each man must accept what he was."

"Even when he was abused?"

"It's difficult to accept."

"I said so."

"But one must."

"No! Everything has an end. They were abusive because no one dares face up to them!"

"Do we have anything to fight them with? We can't even unite."

"I'm not thinking of myself alone. Djona, she's already a young woman. It's not nice how Whistle looks at her."

Kosep stopped massaging the shoulders of Dalen. He groped for a chair at the corner.

II. What Now, Escopa?

I AM Kosep, hinged as a door into a cadaver-smelling world, my world with Dalen and Djona.

The nauseating odor exuding at high noon was so gross to the nostrils.

You're no different, Escopa, from a wretched life eaten up by flames.

    I am edgy... I can't understand.

    Was it because the ones dear to me were not here?

    My world was getting hotter... do you have a fever, Escopa?

    My chest was burning;

That's why my loved ones made me stay... they said I should rest.

Chapter 1

I WILL give you several days!"

"Why should it be that way, Mr. Pajaro?"

"You were really idiots. I own this land, don't you understand? Angel Guardiano… come here, Sergeant."

"Y-yes, Mr. Pajaro?"

"This was the government's land, Mr. Pajaro. But it's ours now since we have been staying here for so long."

"Law of the psychotics!"

"Law of the blind who could see… Most of us were born here. Our ancestors lived and died here. For many years now."

"I don't care about your ancestors. You follow what I said. When I tell you to prepare, you prepare! If not…"

"Blasted thinking!"

"We won't leave the place."

"Over our dead bodies."

"You, selfish ones, who were wild boars of the city… Where's your conscience?"

"Julian Manglicmot… Julian Manglicmot!"

"S-sir…"

"Look at these."

"Brothers…"

"Horns of Satan!"

"Fangs of Dracula!"

"Crocodile!"

"Be careful. I am here as representative of the law."

"You, Sergeant Whistle?"

"Calm down fellows. The problem can't be resolved with anger."

"Ah, Kosep. Use your head!"

"Remember your Dalen… and your Djona."

"We must uphold our rights."

"Escopa was our problem… What will we do? Mr. Pajaro was there."

"Pajaro… Baldomero Caesar Pajaro!"

"Begging your pardon, Mr. Pajero, I mean Pajaro… But please let me be the spokesman of my fellows…"

"That can't be… Julian Manglicmot was your president."

"Julian Manglicmot?"

"Yes, fellows… I am here. Don't worry. I will talk with Mr. Pajaro."

"Those were words of a blind who has eyes!"

"If you don't listen…"

Chapter 2

DO you believe Juan Manglicmot?" Dalen's voice was heavy, and her eyes fixed at the slightly opened window. It was getting dark outside. Smoke was swirling lazily on the rooftops. The smell of dried fish being fried at the neighbors' kitchen was very strong. A few of those squeaking carts could be heard from the alleys.

"How about you?" Kosep stroked Dalen's back.

"Me? I think I've lost trust in people. They were all bastards!"

"There were a few good people left."

"The morons. They don't get tired of being abused. Can't you hear the radio? If it were only possible, I would fly way up high where I could see none of the devils of the world."

"Will you leave Escopa then?"

"Shit!" Dalen breathed deeply. "I suppose Mr. Pajaro will not stop bothering us. He was so close to the people in power."

"If only Escopa can unite."

"If only Escopa unites! When will there be unity? When even Manglicmot was held by Pajaro by the neck…"

"Let's continue to have faith in God, Dalen."

"Forgive me. I suppose God sides with the powerful. Remember this: Pajaro has started it and it won't be long before he will hand down his judgment upon us. Remember that!"

"Oh, my. Was there no more hope? Can't you see something good around us anymore?"

"Where was that hope? The world was rotten, Kosep. If only you can see it."

"I can smell… Djona…"

"Djona, yes. You remember Whistle? Angel Guardiano? He really won't leave me in peace. It's Djona I'm so concerned about."

"I'm going out also tomorrow. So, I could help you."

"Remain in the house a little while longer. Maybe some good fortune will come upon Escopa."

Chapter 3

THEY did not listen. The hand-to-mouth creatures of Escopa.

Nobody could stop them!

Not even a full army of Pajaros.

Of Angel Guardianos.

Of Juan Manglicmots.

Chapter 4

THIS morning, Dalen and Djona left the house early.

Kosep did not join them. He was not yet strong enough.

Thought Kosep: Am I lucky? Even if he sometimes cannot understand why Dalen loved him so much. What qualities does he possess?

"You don't know?" Dalen asked him once. "You have the eyes that the powerful ones do not have. You don't understand? Let it be. I alone will understand. You know, there were so many things in this world which were difficult to understand. You, do you understand why I talk like this? There were many things that you will never know about me. You want to know? No, you had better not. I don't even understand myself sometimes. Often I'm a riddle—but let me remain that way…"

It was very hot. And it's even getting hotter. The heat can explode into flame. Kosep thought: What if Escopa suddenly bursts into flame?

He shrugged off the disturbing thought.

There were those who passed by. Kosep, how were you? I'm fine. What's new? It's almost judgment day! Blasphemy be careful. Was that so… but they say He judges daily.

Kosep's belly grumbled. I don't think the two will come home soon. There must be still some food somewhere.

So, he poked around. The rice was cold, but it was something.

He rested afterwards. It was hard being alone like one were dead but still living, he thought. If only I were a writer, or a painter. He remembered the news he heard from Dalen. He would have shaped the world he was moving in. But why did Dalen know about these?

Kosep, how were you? Still waiting. They might not come home anymore. Hey, don't pass by here again. But what if it comes true?

Don't let it happen, God!

The heat softens up. The sounds in the alleys start. The smell from the kitchen of the neighbor's teases Kosep's nose.

The news was out from the transistor radio. Hey, it's getting dark.

His wife and daughter were not home yet.

He began to worry. This was unusual!

He groped around the kitchen. He will cook rice and be done with when they arrive.

But what he cooked has cooled off. Kosep stayed awake. The door was still open.

Wife and child were not yet home. My God don't let anything happen!

Chapter 5

KOSEP had just closed his eyes when he was awakened by shrieks from the door. He raised his body from where he sat.

"You were still awake?"

"I waited for you... Where's Djona?"

"Sorry, Kosep. It's all because of that bastard Whistle."

"W-why?"

Djona sobbed.

"Your daughter... Whistle's really evil."

"It's the like of him who should be damned!" There was bitterness in the chest of Kosep.

"I have judged him," Dalen's voice was law and hard. "I have condemned him."

Suddenly, flames engulfed the east, and then the center of Escopa. There were splashes of water. But the flames were hungry and fast in consuming the walls.

Escopa was awakened.

The whole place screamed.

"Fire! Fire!"

"Somebody poured gas!"

"Get him!"

Suddenly, gas bathed Kosep's house. Blaze followed.

The fire was laughing wildly in the dawn.

III. Your Burnt Smell Was Pungent, Escopa

THE burn was so painful, Escopa!

They have taken away our only paradise, and here now was your skeleton. What a pity.

We can see you, Escopa, even with your flickering stars;

Here, dear ones… here we were watching but you cannot see us anymore;

Arise, dear one, embrace us, wipes away this pain with the balsam of your warmth;

The smell of that swirling smoke was incense…

Chapter 1

THE sirens sounded. The firemen came. Cameras clicked. The radio transistors awakened. Those who were rushing the news items were distressed. Who did it?

Chapter 2

THEY hugged one another. The three of them. Kosep, Dalen, Djona. In the ruins of Escopa.

Dalen looked up. The stars were flickering. The burn was so painful. Ah, it radiated to the very bone.

They were ferried by ambulance.

The ambulance wailed. Their lights blinked all the way.

When the sun was up the next day, the newspapers carried these news heads:

Sergeant Angel Guardiano was waylaid… organ slashed.

Julian Manglicmot was arrested… in the yard of Mr. Pajaro.

Chapter 3

WHEN Kosep closed his eyes, he saw the flickering stars in Escopa, just as Dalen had described them.

He saw the sweet smile of Dalen.

He saw the sad smile of Djona.

He saw himself, and Dalen, and Djona, in three white beds.

They were relaxed. They were fast asleep. —0

Bannawag, February 22, 1989; *Lingka:* 1994. pp.100-110; translated by Lorenzo R. Tabin II.

What If The World Ends, Taraki[50]?

e-mail 1: prologue

IT was past the middle of this century when computer was introduced. Since then, the world had changed a lot. Philippines had also sloughed from the ashes of war. My Father Taraki I had not been planning to run away from the Philippines and come to the cuddle of America, the land of Milk and Honey so they say, and we suspected a fascist and the reason of our strikes, we, the radical students from the Universities of Metro Manila, like the University of the East, University of the Philippines, Polytechnic University of the Philippines, and others.

Presidents of the Philippines had changed several times since the start of the century that was about to bequeath but there were only few who remain worthy to be remembered; most of them were blamed because their promises turned into stinky fish sauce of the Ilocos Region or wriggled pickle delicacy of Pampanga.

Schools sprang like mushroom, students multiplied in number—they were scared to be abused when their time comes. Some sold their carabaos. Many went to Manila to serve as servants. Some learned to be snatchers in the dark corners of streets in Tondo and Quiapo, and to spread their legs in the stinky rooms in Sta. Cruz and Misericordia

---

50   *Taraki,* Handsome.

and Felix Huertas and Pandacan and Malate, Culiculi and Calumpang, and crossing their arms around the neck of their lovely partners in Luneta then afterward go behind the bricks in Intramuros where their only white dress be torn apart. Many became lawyers, doctors, teachers, politicians—many turned into avaricious for they were influenced by the crocodiles they met in the city. Others who graduated from their studies, they choice jobs—why, I am a graduate, why do I work in this kind of job? But in the end, they became street sweepers.

But still many remain under the camachile trees enjoying their stench; or in the groin of creeks and bosom of rice fields, and they were still newly bloomed compared to flowers and still green compared to fruits but they had already learn to take care small babies because thick were the young night in Abbarit and with sweet songs of crickets and cicadas cuddling their feelings looking up the flickering stars behind the heavens—forget education, grandfathers were able to live only by embracing the harrow and the plow tail, and spring from the brooklets was what they assuaged their thirst, not cola with caffeine. A child here. Another child there. Nothing to harvest, no rice to cook. But young evening was always sweet; there were teasing dollar cannot buy, though they kept swallowing upon hearing the green smile of Uncle Sam—but their dreams was always behind the heavens.

Many images, many films of the real life. Because the world, uneasy. Barrels of blood streaming and breathing skeletons full of flies flying over the black corners and slain over the creeks in the groins of the mountains and the authorities who were assigned to look over were blaming each other. Nothing to throw into the mouth because crisis has arrived in the world. No jobs. Empty mouths were multiplying incessantly, unaccounted perforated stomach. And come timely calamity in the nature—earthquakes, volcanoes, floods, el nino: the world seems mad!

Some are day dreaming to get out from the inferno where they were put into. Especially when dollar revalued, and peso devalued, many planned to become traitor to their mother land. They flew over the place that can ignore their assailing stench...

II

DID I also bring assailing stench when I arrive where I am right now, using the education I drew from the wells of the University of the Philippines? I, Taraki San Diego II, am I not worthy to call Pinang my Mother? My late Mother whom my Father Taraki San Diego I left in Abbarit when he decided to take advantage the offer of the government that they can become a citizen of America. Do not go, my kind Mother Pinang said. If you go, I don't come with you; if I die, I will die in the soil where I was born.

And that's what happens. My Father became a brown American. My mother was left behind in Abbarit and my father missed her remains when she was buried.

My employer sent me to study at the Brigham Young University in the State of Utah as scholar of the nation. I returned to the Philippines after my graduation, but I did not stay long for I took advantage the position as programmer offered to me by Microsoft in Orem, Utah where we were engulfed to solve the problem of the y2k. In a different point of view, maybe I became a traitor to my job in the Philippines. But a beneficial chance was very seldom to come into your life. Was a man be blamed if he goes to a place where he could use his God given talent?

Here, I was able to learn things I missed in UP. Knowledge I obtained by mingling with different peoples from the four corners of the world. If the rotten way of running the government, the increase of politicians in number without thinking except their own good, that becoming not far from a vampire in sipping blood of their countrymen; if injustices of own blood was rampant, killing between siblings, the resurgence of the leftists, the distribution of illegal drugs in Manila and suburbs, the soaring of prices of commodities because of the devaluation of peso under dollar and the negligence of the authorities to the citizenry, there were also big issues facing the UN and the Americas, like the war against Sadam, war in Bosnia, tension in Chechnya, Ukraine, war in politics, and different kinds of domestic and world problems shown in the newspapers and social media.

If we mix these altogether, there is a sure possibility that the world would stand still!

e-mail 2: three Tarakis

From: Taraki San Diego II /sandiegota@worldnet.att.net\
To: sandiegoba@mail.asiandevbank.com
Date: Thursday, March 4, _____, 8:40 pm
Subject: Letter of Taraki II

Dear *Manong*,

Your jab in your editorial in the *Rainbow* was effective. Your words were as sharp as the shark's teeth. Your description of the leader sounds like a big bellied crocodile in the land. Teary-eyed politician who was carrying with both arms a young skeleton gasping because of the nauseous smell of wine he gulped, the leader, last night celebration of Rizal's Day—dripping was tears (or nasal mucus?) in his beard. You think, he was a good actor—was there anyone like him who doesn't know how to act? That's surely the reason why the citizenry—or the world—was gasping because of them. Their unrestrained laughter was enough to deafen the innocent angels. The shower of their breath was not far from Pinatubo's lava—where can we find somebody who was different from them? Those who were in the left, do you believe that they expect nothing other than be given power to smash the world? The painful feeling in the chest nothing to cry for except the stinky odor of putrefaction of promises of the parting century. Will there still be Moses or Christ standing between December and January? Or will the world be standing still at the last tick of the computer era? How do you embrace the worldwide promises and clothed it with a shining white, you the editor, who was bringing to your people the words that will awaken their sleepy hope? You were giving them hope, but do you believe that there was still hope in the world you described in your paper? The rainy season there in Manila, were they still similar with the times we were fish tackling with mudfish and catfish in the paddled rice fields and creeks in Abbarit, and ar-aro and gourami fishes in Limas, our entrapping of wild doves and turtledoves and wild doves in Labut? Or was already been encircled with black wind of summer and the world was now gasping its last breath? Or the circling imagination in my forehead was too much, because of your awakening me?

I like the jolt of the articles you published in your latest issue. If only they could be weapons to demolish the palace of the powerful. But I have a question: were those powerful want to read, or they don't have time, or do they have hide like rhino and words were not enough to hurt them?

Poor people!

But before my mind be jumbled up into the air—I'm afraid I couldn't finish my novel where I focus the termination of this century—let's go awhile to a lighter topic.

I had mentioned that *Dayag*[51] had miscarriage three times, and now, at last, by the end of this retiring century, we finally produce another one. If nothing could impede, it will be in the 7th of April in this Spring Taraki III comes out to be tempered into this world. Yes, Taraki III will be his name because we already know that what *Dayag* conceiving will be a boy, based to the ultrasound. We are very excited waiting, me and *Dayag*. But more so with *Tatang*, yes, Taraki I. *Dayag* was now on maternity leave in preparation to the birth of Taraki III, for she still has a lot of sick leave.

Yes, about *Tatang*. Just the same. His palms become itchy if he stops doing anything. As if he has something to probe or overcome. He has nothing to do now that winter was over except to go around back and forth to look something to do. What I observe, this were behind the house which was almost an acre was not enough for him to till. He had tilled haft of it and only waiting for the proper time to plant eggplant, tomatoes, radish, pepper, squash, white potato, okra—yes, we look like we were in the Ilocos when we start harvesting fruits of his plants. What was interesting, once again he asked when your sister-in-law delivers her baby—when I told him the name of his grandson will be Taraki III, he

---

[51]   *Dayag,* beauty.

looked at me then turned his eyes to the last droppings of snow outside the window in the west.

He is also asking how his grandchildren in the Philippines right now—sometimes he stops as if he reminisces. Notwithstanding the evident signs of time in his face, you still notice his unwavering decision to come here first. But we know very well that time is inescapable. Now that Winter is fast going behind—lilies that hid under the soil while waiting for this time are starting to sprout. Not long from now, the surrounding will turn into green and flowers and leaves with different colors, like the rainbow, will come into blooming. It looks like paradise! Then comes Summer, Fall, and then Winter.

The coming of Taraki III into this world is fast approaching!

Like the fast approaching ending of this century, and the y2k.

But unluckily he will be borne into this foreign world; far away from where we were borne, and where *Tatang* was borne.

But we, his parents, will be close to him. We will watch him sprout. Like the sprouting of the young shoots and blooming of flowers in the spring. I know that the path he will follow will not be sure because nobody could tell that although notwithstanding, it could be guided, now that it was still early, into his best result. Like a young branch of fire tree that lives here in four seasons—spring, summer, fall, and winter— he will also live within these seasons away from the pollution there in Cubao that lives in a year. Away from the influence of unmindful authorities—notwithstanding the guarding of the puppies in the palace of their masters, the stench of the stinky petrified fish will lose its essence; there will surely nobody of them accepts what you exposed in your editorial, but it could not be hidden to the citizenry because they no longer blind that could not distinguish the image of an actor compared to the people in real life.

Nevertheless, I have unending ideas to write, notwithstanding the length of the time I spend in the e-mail only to express all I want. But there will be more time for I still have a lot to do waiting for me right now.

I guess I don't have any more time to be homesick there in our motherland—only our family was always in my heart.

I presume that there will be more e-mail you receive from me before the century ends.

Your small brother,
Taraki San Diego II

e-mail 3: Bagnos San Diego

From: Bagnos San Diego /sandiegoba@mail.asiandevbank.com\
To: sandiegota@worldnet.att.net
Date: Wednesday April 7, _____, 9:40 P.M.
Subject: The nation is sinking!

It's been quite some time since my last e-mail, Taraki II, my *Ading*. I don't need to explain one by one. I was so busy the past weeks. And my e-mail got some viruses. I suspect that there were piglets from the palace who was able to peep on what I was sending. I presume that they blocked their distribution. I don't know. You know everything about the computer. It was good that they had not censored the newspapers. I hope nobody could read my letter to you. To censor. That you will know what I want to write.

By the way, I remember. You mentioned that Taraki III will come to the world today. I hope the mothers will be okay. That my nephew will come to try his luck in wriggling here in this perturbed world.

We may have different point of views in life's face. But in other side, we don't have differences. Our styles were similar. We both understand every strand of words we were using. We both love to use flowery but poisonous words. But the worlds we are wriggling at are not the same. This might be better. For our writings become bolder. But you're right. We're not sure if the authorities I'm attacking at read what I'm writing. But I know many of the readers' conscience were being peppered. They surely curse what I am describing.

How could they be blinded by what's happening around them? They could no longer breath freely by the souring up prices of commodities. How could they be dumbfounded by the sobbing of their young fruits?

They're over worked by their hardships scratching something to lengthen the breath of their loved ones. They can see it. Without reading. By their hollowed eyes. The flying dust everywhere...

Once again somebody was butchered the other day...

The trusted source of the news said. That the butchered was a father of six small children. He told his wife that he was going to look something for dinner. But he found death. Some say they found him stealing a kilo of rice. But there was no evidence.

Kidnappers are still around. As if the chocolates could do nothing. Some evidences show that one of them accompanied the criminals. That's the reason why nobody being caught by the law enforcers. They're good only in looking for pleasure. They say, what the fathers do the children will follow. That's why there are many gamblers. Many womanizers. They couldn't remember how many children they begot outside. Many are telling them that they are their child's father. But they could not remember when they enjoyed each other with the mother of that child.

That's why the underprivileged were aloof from the palace. It seems that the country's house was only a dream. They might even sicken in thinking of it. That there was a building like that in their world. If only easy to separate Abbarit from the sickening city. It was supposed to be easier to dream there with the twin rainbow. But where to find twin rainbows now a-days? Even during the sleeping time, many images come. Everything is bloody. Hollowed eyes are transparent. Cheeks squared off. Sagging shoulders. Empty stomachs. Curved legs. Dried hair...

When I'm in front of this computer, I could imagine pictures seem skeleton in my writings. There might be time when you are in front of your computer that your characters will bulge up from the monitor and attack you before hitting the delete key.

You mentioned y2k. they said it will produce calamity between December this year and January the next century. Whatever will be that calamity they were talking about; it is the focus of my attention. Computer is powerful, as if like God sometimes. I'm thinking if I'm worried, why don't they use this as a weapon to destroy the overzealous unmindful authorities? Not just like the robots in films. But it should be used to exterminate the atrocious crocodiles in the land.

I suggest you make a program like this. Anyway, you are in the ground of Microsoft. Invent a chip that will oversee the world. That wherever the demons hide it will look for them. And bring this demon in the plaza where people could watch him shouting, he is the cobra of the nation. And receive whatever punishment the citizens give him...

What am I thinking, Taraki II, *Adingko*[52]? If you were here, you could see that I am telling the truth. Alright, I can describe the people squirming in every mall. An image of progress. For you could not feel that they have problems. As if all of them are eating three times a day. As if money was not their problem for, they are gleefully shopping expensive merchandise. Or are they only viewing these items? There are also twin rainbows in the pupil of their eyes! They are watching those lovely ladies counting their crunchy cash money. For the payment of the golden pants or t-shirts. They might have in mind: why do they have crunchy cash money and I do not have? What if I snatch it?

I've gone so far...

Your *Manang Sam-it*[53]... Yes, she's been mossed in her teaching profession. Her salary? She stops thinking about it for all the promises for them had flown away by stinky promises. They who are the heroes of the nation. The pillars of the supposed fortress of the nation. And it turns out that they could not guide the young ones properly and instead of becoming good, many of them are in the dark corners sucking the wick of their lives. These six nephews and nieces of yours, they're now grownups. But thank goodness, they also honor the meaning of my name. None of them went to a different direction or gone with those who were sucking the flavor of their death. They are all about to graduate in college. Some of them are now working. Like you, two of them are being queasy in computer. As if they could not live without these so-called masters of the people. Me too, the old typewriter which was the source of my life is now in the garage. Computer was easier to use now...

---

[52] *Adingko,* my small brother.

[53] *Sam-it,* Sweet.

Mention also to *Tatang* Taraki I not to worry about his grandchildren he left here. Girl or boy, they inherit his vigor. Same to brother Taklin, and Angie's children. They are truly Taraki nothing more nothing less. That's what we could brag about. I can say that our father Taraki I was successful in rearing his family. Unlike his siblings' children, our cousins, who were not nurtured properly because they turned into idlers. I can say now: what our Tatang did was not worthless. His principles will be in concord when he goes back to mother earth.

Yes, we are preparing the next issue of the *Rainbow*. More and more writers are now joining happily. They now realize that they need to sharpen their pens to make our weapons more effective in fighting the corrupt enemies.

Yes, it's not yet time for us to write sweetened lines. When that time will be, I can say that it will be when the nation is ready to be offered poetical lovely lines. The sweetened lines will be useless if the greedy gulf them hungrily. But I know that time will come. If not, these will be left as footsteps in the history of this departing century. It's not my plan to be a hero like Rizal. I just want to be like a mote for those sharp but sleepy eyes.

I'm far beyond. But I still have a lot of things I want to bring into your attention. Many more times to come. The end was still far ahead. But I also need to prepare…

Here's you, *Manong*,

Bagnos

E-mail 4: spring and winter

From: Taraki San Diego II /sandiegota@worldnet.att.net\
To: sandiegoba@mail.asiandevbank.com
Date: Thursday, April 15, ____; 9:30 p.m.
Subject: Taraki II's reply

Manong,

No doubt that Taraki III was handsome! He copied from us and Grandfather Taraki I. But there is also a resemblance to Dayag, like her eyes. His face was both from us his presents. Right now, his vigor was evident—I hope my reckoning will come true.

The three of us were so happy—me, *Tatang*, and *Dayag*—to accept him in this world. But the past few days, I noticed the lukewarm feelings of *Tatang*. As if he had something wrong but he said when I asked him that there's nothing to worry. In the past when Spring comes like this, he was so glad to give attention to his vegetable plants. He was so happy to talk with his green garden as if they understand him.

Yes, it's spring again. The shoots of sloughed plants in the neighborhood were so green again. Green were now the remains of branches that make the view soft and cold. Many flowers bloomed. It looks like paradise!

I'm excited to your comment about computer. It's probably true the programmers, and the technicians like us may have to ability to hold the future of these components, but there is a limit of our knowledge. Maybe we could invent like your idea, but it's not time yet. I think, men, like the politicians, were making their own future. If we do what you said, there is a great possibility that the computer will comment against to all our wrong doings and it will throttle us. But I'm not saying your idea is not valid. That may happen. But it needs a lot of time to spend before it gains a fruitful result. In the meantime, we the programmers are trying our best to fix the errors of the first program. They said in Texaco that not all that were feared for in the world about the capacity of the computer, like the y2k, were valid. There had been errors fixed though it's true that there are more to fix.

I don't know the real feelings of the Filipino people there in the Philippines about this case of the computer. Here in America, especially here in Utah, there is a silent preparation of the residents. Although their diligence in preparation, or their wearisome is not clear, there are leaflets being distributed, especially in the congregation of faith, teaching, or warning their members, to prepare. Although nobody is seating and talking over the mortar or in front of a bonfire about the problem, there are also those who do not like to take chance and they rather follow the advice of their leaders. They say, there's nothing bad in preparing their needs for the unexpected calamity, besides they can use their preserved food in case what they are preparing for doesn't come. Some say they need to prepare a year supply, or a month, like water, dried food, fuel, and other needs, especially here under winter of December and January, for nobody could tell if there will be strong snow. It doesn't mean that we are scared, but we decided with Dayag that we follow the flow.

But many are heedless. There are radio announcers laughing, saying that those who are scared with the y2k are insane. Nobody knows what will happen really is, all are guessing. But we in the computer, we have a little knowledge, although we are trying to avoid, or to escape the coming of that calamity, or little problem.

I remember when we were still in Abbarit. Many were whispering about what's happening in the neighborhood, like the spreading of the lefties, or barefooted killing their political enemies anywhere, or those living in the night. I was still young, but those whisperings were scary, as if there were surely be left dead in the middle of the road in the next morning, they left them under the dew under the wattles tree or climbed up a pensioner. Sure, there were whisperings turned into true hearsays. There was even spreading news that the judgment day of God was fast approaching, how many times, but it did not happen. We even heard here, that a group of faith in the Philippines spread that the judgment day was about to be fulfilled and they prophesied the exact date of that momentous day. They sold their important belongings, anyway they won't need them anymore. But what they were scared the most did not come true and they committed suicide because of their shame. But there was story in the scripture about the wise virgins. They prepared oil for light whenever darkness comes. Some laughed at them because they did not believe them. But it happens, and nothing bad happens to them because they were completely prepared.

That's why it depends upon the people to follow their will. And he will pay the consequence. If so happens that he lives longer because he followed the best thing to do, well and good. But if he dies because he was pigheaded, sorry for him.

That's all for now because *Dayag* was calling for me. She needs me to mix milk for Taraki III—that's life here, no helpers.

Your *ading*,

Taraki II

P.S.—I'm half through with the synopsis of my novel, but no title yet; I am thinking to use **Last Century**.

Regards to the *Rainbow*. Hoping the sharpness of your pens be as good as ever.

Still me.

e-mail 5: many were blind

From: Bagnos San Diego /sandiegoba@mail.asiandevbank.com\
To: sandiego@worldnet.att.net
Date: Saturday May 1, ----; 9:32 p.m.
Subject: Many were blind

Taraki II,

Two things may happen: you, computer wizards will be successful in blocking the things that may happen. Or what was scared for in the technology becomes successful.

The guardians like you are busy in the silent war of science. You mentioned that this problem was worldwide. It will affect all the computerized gadget in the world. Like banks. Power. Water. Airlines. Ships. Telephone. Television. And many more. We who are in the city know the possible outcome of this problem. Although many are still unbelievers. Many are acting deft and blind. But others, really are innocent in this matter.

One thing I know was real: those who are in the provinces are unmindful. Especially those who are in the countryside. Whatever happens to those I mentioned above. For many of them doesn't have equipment like those. Probably many still oblivious about computer.

Upon my observation, the citizenry is not that busy. Even it means the loss of the computer. The more important for them is where to get something to put into their mouth in the next meal. They are more concern on the high prices of commodities. I mean those are running after a food to prepare every meal. I think, many are missing a meal or two. The thickness of people roaming around in big stores or mall is confusing. As if people have more than enough money. In fact, many of them are scratched from their jobs. Probably they are in those places only to dream. Or envying. Many are jobless because they were removed from their post in the government establishments. Or were forced to quit from their private jobs. For the employers could no longer afford to pay them.

The people are hungry, Brother. Especially the children. They are supposed to be the hope in the future.

Can you blame if there was news in the papers about ambushing or robbing?

Who is to blame?

Were all these happenings part of what they call the warning of the second coming? Calamities in all corners of the world.

But discotheque houses were always full. The passenger jeeps are always full of commuters even hanging just to reach their destinations.

As I have said, more things are concerned for by the people. For their daily needs.

Savings? What do the people save? Where do they get? Probably they don't like to save for it may be the reason of those who were more hungry people to kill them.

If I think too much about the situation here, I can't help but to breath heavily. As if I am being choked. I may ask: was this already the Pearl of the Orient?

If you have savings there, you are lucky. Here, nothing. Many are unfortunates. Your departure was timely. You escape from the time of scarcity. But I'm sure you could not escape from your shadow.

Many meet untimely death. But more so to be borne.

But pity for those who come to earth because they come in the wrong time. They should have borne when the mudfish aplenty. And freshwater catfish. And blackwash freshwater. And gourami fish. And frog. And different kinds of vegetables in Abbarit. They should not be starving. But now, they come to eat pollution. They eat broken thorns of salted fish. They suck stubs of banana trunk. Good if they still have rice to cook. Or wild yam to uproot. Or wild jicama. Or raw young eggplant fruit to eat. Like what the Japanese soldiers did during the second world war.

Okay, we write. Heaps of writings. Hoping that those books or magazines or newspapers be our food when real time of scarcity arrives.

We write hoping we could survive these challenges in the end of the century. To have something to read when the knotting of our intestines ends. We will have something to raise into the sky. And shout into the heavens: THIS IS THE RECORD OF THE PAST CENTURY!

I don't know how many blind people are there. I don't know how many deaf. But many are there wriggling in the streets. We only need to become prophets. So that we can see what we are talking about. So that we can hear the sobbing of the world. We the writers. For nobody could understand us. In the real sense. Hoping people could realize the reason of being here on earth.

Yes, our Father Taraki I. You the Taraki II. And Taraki III. We have our own times. To wriggle in. We are all fragments of the whole century, this parting century.

A lot of things, Taraki II, my Ading, we need to accept. So that we will become the complete man. Continue your novel. Finish it. Print it into a book form. Not necessarily to be read today, it will be read in the future. It will be left as your footprint.

That's all. I'll see how we could prepare this next issue of the *Rainbow*.
Your Big Brother,
Bagnos San Diego

P.S.: There's news they flashed in the t. v. There is war in the south. Many died but the battle is still going on. Soldiers and civilians. And at the same time flood. Flood in summer. –Still me.

e-mail 6: Inkling

From: Taraki San Diego II /sandiegota@worldnet.att.net\
To: sandiegoba@mail.asiandevbank.com
Date: Saturday, May 22, _____, 9:44 p.m.
Subject: Inkling of the Fall

Manong,

Happy birthday, my beloved brother—no matter how old you are, it is not being counted by the passing of years but by means of footprint you left, and I say that you have done a lot because the pages of the *Rainbow* was not a joke. I congratulate you, my beloved brother.

Spring is nearing to its end. The young branches, and leaves and flowers, are almost ready for the approaching challenges of weather. The nature is busy preparing its strength for the coming Fall.

It's just more than a month since the birth of Taraki III but his grip is tight. His fists are now hard. He is starting to distinguish people. He knows how to defy when he needs milk. He has no patience. He makes me sleepless sometimes. But I like him because in his whimpers there is promise for the future. I am not tired going to Food-4 Less, or in Sam's. whenever he needs additional milk—I don't like him short of milk. He is now our focus of attention, our untiring perseverance with Dayag. I can say he is the face of the San Diego in the next century. If he smiles at me, twin rainbows spark in his eyes. His feet are still raw but there is already lucid Ilocano blood running into his veins.

Taraki III is our future with Dayag! If we play him during our golden moments, we feel as if we are out of this world and we forget that there was a threat of the parting century. That threat signifies the images of preparation in the queue throughout Salt Lake City. You can't hear a single word but was written. Dumb warning! Yes, nobody was talking about that warning of the century. But there were letters. Like the letter I just received from my bank. Informed us that nothing we need to worry about—I just presume that they also sent letters to others—for it's been quite some time they were preparing for that fateful night.

Nevertheless, that negative thinking was always coming back and forth, like the unavoidable arrival of Fall or illness notwithstanding how careful men do.

Tatang, Taraki I, reminded to me. He really was strong because as if he does not like to give way to the passing of time. But this morning I was ready to go out, but he was still in his room. He used to be the first to get up from bed and was already tilling his garden, talking with his plants. I went to see him in his room before going down. He said he feels as if his veins were shirking.

"Tell me if you need some check-up, Pop," I said. I remember that yesterday he was slightly coughing.

"I can withstand this… no matter how many doctors you have if your time is over, it's over."

That's all. I'll write you again.

Your brother,

Taraki II

e-mail--: epilogue

MANY days had passed—it's now in the middle of Winter and snow falls continuously; the shower brought by the freezing wind benumbs the feelings, but the white surrounding depicts a paradise in between two mountains cuddling Great Salt Lake—but it's abundance opposes the scarcity of letters I received from my Brother Bagnos, where he relates the numerous Filipino who are going home, based to the spreading news, for the approaching y2k. They would prefer to wait the possible event between December and January, which is the separation of the old and the new century. They want to be in their love one's side in the Philippines before that event. I am not sure about the news because based on where we are here in Utah, our countrymen are silent. We probably don't like each other to know we are scared; each and everyone likes to show that we are already in America, a land being looked up by the whole world. He also mentioned that *Rainbow* was not in good shape because of the unexpected rise of prices of printing materials; especially the interventions of those who are in power. He said that there was cobra among the staffs of his publication and his mouth might have been stuffed by the Leader's head. But still many of them are standing for, but nobody knows how far they could survive and how strong they are in fighting for their right.

The ending of the old century was far spent but the history has not been repaired. Wars are on-going. Nobody wants to stop. Nobody wants to give way. Nobody wants to be a loser.

How months old is Taraki III? He is starting to stand. He can say mama. But I worry a little bit because he might notice the commotions in the world. I worry that he might first notice the sounds of war around.

Our father Taraki I, he was confined in the LDS Hospital in downtown Salt Lake City. We brought him this afternoon, but I needed to leave him and drove under strong snow at the I-15 going south to Orem for important matters to do in our job, for the y2k. All Microsoft programmers and technicians were under red alert. I left Dayag and Taraki III at home but ones and a while, I call her, and advising my wife, to keep calm.

I'm away from my family.

I'm away from the bedside of Tatang, who is fighting for his life.

I'm in my job for we are waiting the parting of the old century.

We had done all our best for the computer. We think, the world is ready whatever happens. We fixed all that needed to be fixed. Based to the news from my Brother Bagnos, many are also preparing in the Philippines. Or waiting for whatever happens.

Sometimes, I'm asking: What then if the world stand still, Taraki? In the middle of the benumbing Winter?

I should have completed the **Last Century…**

While waiting for the expected moment, I'm writing this. I may use it as the ending of the **Last Century.**

What might the world look like when darkness comes in the middle of night? What would happen in hospitals, notwithstanding they believe they were prepared?

My Father, who was fighting for his life…

And Taraki III…

Again, and again, I looked up the big wall clock in front of me. It's pendulum swings peacefully. There is silence in the office. As if nobody wants to listen the radio. Again, and again, I called up Dayag. Again, and again, I called up the LDS Hospital. But when I was about to call Dayag one more time, I decided not to. I wanted them with Taraki III to be asleep when the old and the new century meet.

How many more hours?

I thought: the time in the Philippines comes first.

I faced my computer... —0

Saluyot: December 1999.

Wadsapani

HER NAME: Policarpia Camangeg. Her nickname in Kilkillabot: Carpia. When she arrived in Indio, California: Claire—Carpia was stinky, she was told by the relatives of her husband, and nobody in America named stinky; that's why she did not know at once those whose names were Josh, Susie, Ernz, Madz, Nesty, that in Kilkillabot, they were hardened Kosep, Simang, Wastong, Inyang, and Sintang. Her voice: shrilling in the high pitch and she was the queen of big mouthed women in Kilkillabot—it sounds like an automatic rifle when started. Her complexion: darker than dark brown—it's too much if compared to the back of a frying pan. Her height: her husband *Apo* Tabs (Gustavo or Usting) Camangeg was only up to her neck and she could easily carry him both hands up to the ceiling. She walks like her feet were being scorched, or like a cut tailed bird. What *Apo* Tabs attracted to her? Maybe her single dimple when she smiles like the scarcity of the fall moon. What blinded her parents to entice her to marry *Apo* Tabs, who was even older than her mother? The pension of the old man who was a veteran during World War II for they did not know that his pension was almost not enough for his monthly sustenance. Then afterwards, a lot of different kinds of medication that stimulate his withered feelings.

Because of *Apo* Tabs citizenship, his family was strayed in America, they who were coupled, and their three daughters, namely: Gretzie, 18, Totzie, 17; and Latzie, 16 that in Kilkillabot, Trudis, Sitang, and Saling—they spent two years in Mecca, California and they're now almost three years in West Valley City, Utah.

When they were newly arrived in Indio, California where they first stayed from Kilkillabot, Claire's eyes climb and grope in every part of the house of *Mang* Rosie, her sister-in-law who's younger sister of *Apo* Tabs. She felt strangled with the constricted of the rooms and living rooms and had difficulty of breathing because of the dark brown carpet. Their house in Kilkillabot had only a concreted floor. She was not able to count the number of those whom they reached but dizzied due to their wriggling.

Mang Rosie cooked *pinakbet* bitter melon, eggplant, okra, and white sweet potato seasoned with fermented fish of Dagupan they bought from the Oriental Store in San Bernardino. She might want to surprise the newly arrived for they might think that there was no jute in California. But when they face their dinner, the old woman was open-mouthed because of what she observed though she knew they were so hungry.

"Why don't you eat?" *Mang* Rosie was open-eyed.

"Because they are not eating vegetables, *Manang*," Claire said in high-pitch. "They don't even like fish. They always eat pork or beef…"

"Hey, were they not born in Kilkillabot?" *Mang* Rosie's eyes were opened wider. "You're the first Ilocanos I ever knew who do not eat pinakbet! Why did you allow them like that, *Manong?*" the old woman turned to her brother.

"Because that's what they like, *Kabagis*[54]," *Apo* Tabs said insipidly. He speaks rarely like the appearance of the fall moon.

What happens in that afternoon spread with the *Pinoys* in Indio and Mecca as fast as an epidemic, especially that Maribel, the eldest among *Mang* Rosie's children whose house was in Mecca next to Indio in the boundary of California and Mexico was the first to learn about it. Notwithstanding her size as big as close to a woven bamboo basket, with a high pitch voice as well like Maribel and like Claire, she speaks rapidly.

The gape of Claire's mouth was too wide, and her eyes seems protruding when Maribel spoke rapidly while her mouth seems emitting

---

[54]   *Kabagis,* big or small brother or sister.

bubbles. *Apo* Tabs looks up his wife, with mouth also agape, as if he was saying: now you've met someone, old woman, beware!

Before they went to bed that night, Dennis, the eldest son of *Apo* Tabs, who just left from Indio because he got a job in West Valley, Utah, called up. Claire should have told a lot of news, but *Mang* Rosie unceasingly turn her bracket fungi-like ear toward them, so they just greeted each other.

When they finally went to bed, Claire uses her high pitch voice to her husband: "Hey, I'll die with untimely death, if we stay here longer! Your niece as big as an earthen jar, I really don't like the shape of her mouth!"

Slowly, *Apo* Tabs looks at Claire's mouth then slowly threw his eyes away from his wife.

"Don't ever say that, Honey, or she might call you something else also…"

"She just tries, that she may find something she had not seen before!"

In the next morning, Maribel called Gretzie, Totzie and Latzie and her other nephews and nieces together to go and help to clean the house of Wally, her boss in Palm Desert, and at the same time to seek help to find jobs for the three.

"To clean?" as if Claire's face was covered with thick cloud.

"Hey, no place for lazy people here, Auntie!" catches Maribel who notices the refusal of Claire. They were about the same age at forty-seven.

"Those children do not know any job… In our house, they did never do anything."

"Then, you should have not come here! Nobody lives here in America without knowing how to work…"

Claire's ears felt flipped lightly. Her mouth was opened but before she could say a word, Maribel spoke rapidly again.

Claire's blood rose to her head. In Kilkillabot, nobody had a courage to talk to her like that. She was the mouth of the whole neighborhood.

When those who went to clean got back, Maribel spoke the faster. She mentioned the sisters fingering their ways of cleaning, and the crying of Totzie when she taught her clean the toilet, and her refusal to be the housemaid of Wally's family.

"Why, are you rich, and have a right to choose a job?" yelled Maribel.

They stayed only for a day in *Mang* Rosie's house. The next day, Maribel transferred them in the house of the dead mother of Wally in Mecca close to her house. They agreed to rent one of the rooms. Maribel shouted them to be patience if they want to live, for when the time comes that they receive the green cards of Gretzie, Totzie, and Latzie, and land for a job, hopefully their lives will improve.

Claire and her family planned to call Dennis in Utah, but Maribel yelled them up. Telephone bill was expensive. Suddenly Claire felt her head busted and she almost uprooted Maribel's curly hair and thrush her face in the burning desert, but *Apo* Tabs stops her.

"Just be calm, Honey," he patted Claire's buttock. "Just be calm…"

"Telling you, I want to lacerate the face of that earthen jar!" Claire snorts.

The surrounding was sweltering because it was almost in the middle of summer in Mecca. It seems the environment was blazing, and *Apo* Tabs was untiring in fanning himself with a cardboard because Maribel does not want them to use the cooler. She said the power was too expensive.

"I did not know that America is like this! I'm being roasted alive!" Claire talked out of control one night while she and her husband were almost swimming with sweat on a bed for one. Gretzie and Totzie laid down on the carpet, while Latzie laid down on an old sofa.

Many boxes full of assorted things left behind by the late old woman who owned the other part of the supposed to be big room. The room of the late old woman was in the middle of the train-shaped house and her belongings were not touched, and Maribel advised to always be cleaned because it was used to be Wally's office—Claire learned afterwards that Maribel was doing that because she was expecting a big inheritance, or else Wally, the only child and heir of the late old woman, change his mind. Claire and her family sometimes awaken in the middle of the night when they hear heavy footsteps, or somebody tries to open the room without somebody doing it. Surely, it was the ghost of the old woman, Claire chewed angrily towards the face of Apo Tabs.

Claire discovered, and made her angrier, that Wally was always going to their place and they were losing their privacy. Not long afterwards Maribel assigned her to cook because Wally loves her cooking. She was so regretful for telling that she knows how to cook. More so because they only have time to eat when Wally has gone home almost in the middle of the night. They just huddle up in the corner pressing their stomach, and ones the man gone, they were like a hangry cat to face the leftover dinner.

Maribel knows a lot of people in Mecca and Indio and she asked them help to find jobs for Gretzie and Totzie ones they receive their green cards. It was Gretzie who first employed as grape picker. Not long afterwards Totzie was also employed. They were assigned a distance away from their place, in Delano close to the navel of California faraway in the north of Los Angeles. At first, Claire was adamant in allowing her daughters, also Apo Tabs, for they were not been away from them, but Maribel yelled them out. Latzie was left behind because she needs to continue her high school studies in Mecca.

"You will never live if you always remain together! Let them go, Auntie, for them to learn how to live!"

Ones they started receiving green bucks, Maribel started also to charge them their loan for their fair from Kilkillabot.

Because Apo Tabs always saying like a prayer the narrowness of the room for them, Maribel suggested them to rent one of the trailers in the compound around her big house. Not a problem anymore because the Old man's pension had been transferred from Kilkillabot.

Ones their transfer was finalized, Maribel connected them a telephone line. Mang Rosie called them immediately just after the telephone was connected.

"What we were now, was not far from a sparrow, *Kabagis*," jokes Apo Tabs trembling and non-stop fanning because of too much heat. The trailer was long with small windows. "The toilet was inside. In Kilkillabot no toilet inside…"

Mang Rosie flared up immediately like irascible black sea water fish. She threw her anger to Claire because of her fear that her brother become high blood. She was the owner of the trailer.

"As if you were that rich!" her voice was trembling because of anger. "It was good if I did not know and saw your place in Kilkillabot. Your house was so little and very old!"

"My husband was just joking, *Manang*," Claire tried to hold her temper. She hates being yelling at.

Maribel was more irritated.

"We were helping you to live, and you were speaking like that. For your information, many more people live here in America harder, for they were sleeping in side streets. As if you didn't owe nothing!"

"Don't talk like that, Maribel. Not because we only came here from a faraway countryside, you need to know we also have feelings to be offended!" Claire was not able to hold her temper. "Surely, we made a mistake in coming to America! For your information, nobody had ever talked to me like that! This is what you need to remember: if you have a big mouth, mind is bigger!"

Maribel left wide mouth-opened. She did not expect that Claire has the same big mouth.

Claire wants to earn money, so she could also send some amount to her siblings left in Kilkillabot. The reason, she's receiving letters and telephone calls asking some money. Their tone sounds flattering, that's why she felts something in the corner of Claire's heart. Yes, it's true, she's already in America, meaning to her relatives, they're already opulent—some say those Filipinos in America saying their lives was difficult were tight-fisted.

But every time she discusses her plan to live *Apo* Tabs during the day so to go to work, the old man trembles and he feels a lot of pain every part of his body. He feels very week and feels dying.

"You'll not die yet, Uncle!" Maribel yells some time. "You still have a lot of sins for you to repent!" follows with empty giggle. The old man was mischievous even when his kind late first wife, whom he begot all professional children, was still alive.

Mang Rosie also said that her brother was scared with his own shadow. She said her brother was so caring with Claire, as if she was not unsightly.

Apo Tabs suspicion almost came into effect because one of the inopportune days he allowed Claire, his wife told him that somebody joked her and tapped her buttock.

"And, you also allowed him, Honey?" he said indirectly to offend, shaking, as if he was thinking when he touched their young girl helper when his first wife was still alive.

"Hey, don't compare me to those who were easy to get, Honey!"

Apo Tabs kept silent, but in the next morning, he strongly refused not to allow Claire to go picking Sunkist in the wide field in the east.

"I'm going to die if you live me today, Honey," whispered *Apo* Tabs in his sweetest ever whisper, and he even touched Claire's tail end. And, when was the last time he ever touched his wife? "And if I die because of you?" he even closed his eyes a little bit like a sleepy rooster. "I'm not the one who'll come to haunt you, but your conscience itself."

So, Claire was forced to say an alibi to the one who tried to fetch her that *Apo* Tabs was so sick that's why she could not go with her.

The time they stayed in the trailer that long, notwithstanding the fighting of their tongue with Maribel, they go in good terms again when they were not attacked by their vicious habit, and because of that, Claire learned a lot of stories about her husband's niece's experiences with different men who sipped her beauty. That her oldest daughter's father was not really the one whom everybody in Kilkillabot knew but rather the Mexican who owns their neighboring store in Mecca. And the doctor who wedded her in America so that she could get a green card, she divorced him because she really did not have a single hair stood up because she could not forget her first boyfriend. And during her seemingly unbearable problems come into a pile, she got a relationship with the husband of her close friend, before she lives with the father of her two other children.

Sometimes when Maribel and Claire go together picking up tin cans or cola's bottle, Maribel taught her to pick up anything scattered in the ground, not far from stealing, then she immediately goes away when she notices somebody was coming to their way.

One time when Maribel and Claire went together to bring *Apo* Tabs to his doctor for check-up in Indio, the old man's niece thrusted a hospital blanket in the wheelchair under his tail end and told her uncle not to move his buttock. Sometimes, in other chances when Claire and Maribel go to K-Mart or Wall Mart, the latter gets some items out from the store without anybody noticing it.

That's why when their tongues fight again, Claire mentions to *Apo* Tabs: "Your good niece don't ever try to fight with me for I will strew her whole stink all over Kilkillabot. I know everything about her hollowness!"

"Don't tell me, you're going to poison the whole Kilkillabot, Honey," *Apo* Tabs said.

"I'm not kidding! If she got a big mouth, mine is bigger, to tell you the truth!"

"You're right because I can see it…"

Claire was able to breath loosely after paying off their loan from Maribel. They talked together as family and planned to go to West Valley in Utah where Dennis is so that they could distance themselves from Maribel. Claire could no longer stomach Maribel's mouth. And they learned that it was easy to find a job where Dennis is, unlike in Mecca that you were sunburned during picking time of grapes or Sunkist, and after picking season, no more job available.

Gretzie first went to West Valley. Then Totzie. Latzie finishes her studies in Mecca before the three of them with Claire and *Apo* Tabs follow Gretzie and Totzie.

THE tail of Summer was almost gone, and Fall was about to come when they arrived in Harvey Street in West Valley, Utah. They were specially welcomed by Dennis, his wife Marie, his daughter Rina, and his son Joshua but Claire's face was as dim as if she was under the sun in the desert. The reason was that Dennis and his family rented only an apartment with only two rooms, a kitchen, a toilet, and a not too big living room.

"We are more than a canned sardine, Honey!" Claire whispered to her husband as if she was gobbling pickled hot pepper with the sourest vinegar from Vigan.

Dennis introduced Gretzie and Totzie to the Deseret Industries for employment. He enrolled Latzie at the Granger High School where she continues her studies. At first, they so happy because it was their first experience to be able to work in a better place in America. Nevertheless, Claire was not contented. She noticed a lot including the environment, around their apartment for there were a lot of people roaming around like garbage, people with different races in Harvey. Afterwards, she complained to her husband why they went to Utah.

"If I only knew beforehand that the condition here was like this, I should never come here. I didn't understand, the invitation of my niece in Modesto, California was so good, but we came here!" she mulched in front of Marie.

"For all I know, we didn't force you to come," Marie said as if she was heartened.

Dennis was able to find a better job and he left Gretzie and Totzie in the Deseret Industries. But the two did not stay long behind for they were able to land a job at the Salt Lake International Airport at the cafeterias. Their income became better and Claire didn't wait long, and she enticed her family to move in the neighboring apartment.

Not so long afterwards, Gretzie bought a car for she needs for transportation in going to her work. Claire's chin became longer for her daughter's car was much newer than Dennis' car. But in the first night just after buying the car, drug addicts from the neighbor broke the win shield of the car. Claire yells like an automatic rifle but nobody mind her because they could not understand her using her dialect, because she could not speak a single English or Spanish word. Luckily, an insurance paid for the repair of the car.

Hence, they decided with Dennis to look for a house to buy. One of Dennis' friends help them look in the neighborhood. But he advised that only Dennis and his wife will sign the contract as the law required.

Claire felt bad for Gretzie was not included to sign the contract. But they didn't like to be left behind in Harvey, so they were forced to go with Dennis. The condition, they would help pay the monthly mortgage as if they were renting for it was more economical than what they were renting in the apartment. And the place was much better.

At first, their five children were happy for they were about the same age and they knew each other since they were in the Philippines despite Rina and Joshua grew in Montalban.

Claire might have been bored watching *Apo* Tabs for she didn't have nothing to do except to watch television and to feed and help her husband in the shower and not long after she complained a lot. Because it was cold in the basement where they occupied. Because people upstairs were so noisy. Because they were paying a lot for water and power, half of the bills. She became mad to her children whenever she couldn't control her feelings.

"Living here was useless!" she gobbles. "Can't even touch a single penny. Always roaming around in the house. Servant in the house! I'm going to look for a job also, Honey!"

"Please don't, Honey. Don't leave me alone. When I'm dead, okay, go to work whenever you like."

"When will it be?" said Claire with wide-opened eyes. "If my condition was always like this, probably I'll die first ahead of you!"

"No, Honey, I'm almost there… That's why please have patience."

"How, you have a lot of medicines… and you still have time to touch."

Sometimes, she and all her daughters yelling each other in the basement. Claire was so irritable. Sometimes she got mad with Dennis. The whole family upstairs understands each other for Dennis's children were good, and Marie was a good mother as well.

Again, and again, Claire asks her children to look a job for her.

"How could you land for a job for you don't know how to speak English!" Gretzie got mad one time.

"I'll go to school!" yelled at Claire when she learned that there was a school near their place for elderlies who were not gone in school. "Enroll me for I want to study. For it's just an hour a day, and in the evening."

Gretzie and her sisters were forced to pay for her tuition. Then, she often asks Marie to teach her for Marie was a teacher in Quezon City before moving to Utah.

But Claire's brain was as dull as a dull blade for she could hardly stuff into her brain the lessons. Sometimes, Marie makes an alibi that she was busy and doesn't have time to teach her. Claire gobbles sometimes and tell *Apo* Tabs that Marie was stingy.

After finishing her first lesson, probably she learns and remembers around than ten words.

"I'll continue!" she forced her children.

And she enrolled again. The same rotten potato, only few words added in her vocabulary. She even blames her teacher for they don't know how to teach. "They're just teaching without knowing anything!" she gobbled.

But Gretzie and her sisters were fed up spending for her studies because she could hardly learn anything. They instead look for another job and they lost any time to see each other with their mother. Latzie likewise look for a job while going to school.

Not long afterwards, there came a White guy tailing Totzie when she goes home late in the evening and visiting her during Sundays.

"She was my customer in the airport," she explains when asked.

They learned afterwards that the White guy was a divorcee, and his age was almost a half as with Totzie's. He was even bald and have three children.

Not long afterwards, not only to visit, but to even sleep during the night. Marie ones asks her, for Dennis didn't like that thing to happen in his house. But Totzie told him he was only her friend.

"Here in America, this was nothing, *Manang*," she explained.

"Your *Manong* doesn't like that way in this house," Marie said.

Claire reacted like a fish with sharp pins upon learning what Marie did.

"My daughter is not an easy to get type. My daughter is clean. She did nothing wrong in the world, for your information!" she yelled even Dennis and Marie were not in front of her.

Dennis himself talks with Totzie. The thing was, Totzie responded him negatively.

"I'm not prostitute! I know what I'm doing!"

Instead of answering, Dennis held his temper and went to their room. From then, he avoided talking with his half-sister.

There was a couple friend of Marie who pleaded to rent one of the rooms upstairs. Because they were good at first, Marie and her husband accepted them. Pam became a good friend of Marie. If Claire doesn't get mad, the three women were close as sisters.

Sometimes only Claire and Pam were talking when Marie is out.

Suddenly, one early evening of Thursday, Pam bid farewell the next morning, that they follow Claire's family for they were able to buy a house not far from Marie's family's place.

Dennis and his family were surprised but couldn't do anything. But they came to know in the long run that Totzie doesn't like being reprimanded to her doings and asked to the White to look for a house for them to buy.

"You transfer, and just transfer without telling in advance," he said.

Nevertheless, the relationship between Marie and Pam was not that affected. The only thing that she did not like was the treacherous act of the mother and daughters.

Not because they were already separated, the actions of the mothers could not reach to Marie's family. If the White was always sleeping with them when they were with Marie's place, more so when they have a new house.

They went to the Philippines for vacation. And when they came back to Utah, Marie's family learned that the wedding of Gretzie and her boyfriend whom she left in Kilkillabot had been decided.

"The one who will marry Gretzie was rich," conceited Claire, that reached Marie.

But not long afterward, the news spread like fire that Totzie and White were getting married. They did not have a plan like that for Gretzie was supposed to be first.

"That's better like that," they learned that Claire said, "for she might become pregnant untimely!"

Whenever White goes home late, Claire was so eager to see him.

"*Wadsapani*," she says sometimes.

She cooks good food for her son-in-law, that sometimes, especially in Saturday and Sunday, her three daughters accompany him to eat. They seem very hungry and most of the time, nothing even left over for Claire. But Claire never complains. Probably because her son-in-law was White.

Claire was so strict collecting the rent of Pam. She even minding the usage of washing machine and water and power.

"This was how to wash, Pam," she teaches Pam who was much older than her, and much richer in the Philippines.

"Don't use the dryer, Pam…

"Don't switch on the light in the stairs, Pam…

One time, Pam might have been dying to eat salted dried fish, so she fried some. She was not even half cooking when Claire was running to go down.

"*Wadsapani!*" she yelled.

Pam left with mouth wide-opened. "What did you say?"

"I said, *wadsapani!*" Claire said in akimbo. "The children said, *wadsapani*… Troy could not breath with your fried stinky fish!"

"Oh, I see… what's up, honey!" Pam said with wide-opened eyes.

The *wadsapani* of Claire reached the other Filipinos in Utah.

Gretzie befriended a Filipina in Beehive Clothing and Claire forced them to let her work in the sewing factory. Despite *Apo* Tabs yearning not to leave him alone, nothing the old man could do. Even she could not speak English, because she knows how to sew, they accepted her. Not long afterwards, she kicks Pam away from their house. She does not need their rent anymore.

Not long after that, Gretzie was able to bring her husband from the Philippines and they separated at once Claire. She said her husband doesn't like to live with many people.

Claire's White son-in-law disappeared like smoke, and probably that causes the untimely death of *Apo* Tabs.

Claire spent many early evenings alone as if losing her mind looking outside the empty window. —0

Bannawag: December 3, 2001.

A Spherical Sun, A Slice Of Moon, And Five Litters Of Stars

Happy heart and happy faces,
Happy play in grassy places
That was how in ancient ages,
Children grew to kings and sages.
—Robert Louis Stevenson
"Good and Bad Children,"
The Book of Virtues, pp. 23

NONI. Not a small subdivision. Not big either. It's in the middle, like a tiny flat stone being use in playing pitching pennies. It's easy to find. It's not also hard to go to. If you know how to catch frogs, you can find for sure. Ones you see a lot of noni trees, that's what you were looking for. It's a small place. But densely populated. Which was most of them were children. They, who were all happy.

Their laughter was shallow. And if they laugh, all their eyes also laugh, and as if there were plenty of stars dropping down from their bright pupils. Even the pouting on-the-way mother, or a basin-liked laboring with quadruplets, be laughing with gusto. It seems the residents doesn't have any single problem.

They probably were always full; they never be starving. Probably they were so industrious. More so with the mothers. For their bellies were always stuffed. Their husbands were probably so anxious to eat

211

noni. Even probably the mothers. For there were none of them gifted with only three children.

They were not originally like that, you know. In fact, the elderly men were not used to eat noni. For it smells laundry detergent. Not even a carabao or cow want to smell it. But when one of them tried to eat a single fruit, one came after him, and another, and another, until the whole neighborhood learned about it. And the holding hands of the husbands and wives became sweeter and sweeter. And the lamps were put off very early since then. And the vomiting of the mothers became regular, for they even use make up every day. The running back and forth of the fathers became more regular, carrying their wives with both arms to a tricycle and always in a hurry before the water balloon pups out in the center where Doctor Palpaltot's clinic was, whose smile was overly wide because God gives him another good blessing for he was able to build his clinic that big because it was too much to say that almost every day many approaches him to deliver their babies. That when his patients go home, as if he begs when saying: "Come back again next year, okay?"

It's usual that even before the camachile leaves or dangla tree leaves drop under a bamboo bedstead where a nursing mother was confined after bearing a child, to say exorbitantly, the ever-thirsty father was already allowed to climb up the bamboo bedstead.

But Noni will never ever be full. Like a drum when it was full of water, it will overflow. If one was accidentally gone out, it seems they forgot their way back home to Noni. They probably found somebody who works better during the night in a paradise (or inferno) where they were thrown out, and they don't like to get out from there! There they wallow forever.

But many decide to be mossed in the Noni Subdivision. They probably could not keep their pants away from the trunk of the Noni tree. And they always looking up a slice of moon, or look sharply to the full sun, as if they were mumbling, oh how slow you were to dive in the dusk!

Okay, going in and out, that's what they say, for man was like that. If somebody goes out, somebody will come in. And in Noni, more were coming in. Babies.

But there is a special family in Noni. The family Paraiso. Consisting their Papa and their Mama, and Bingbing, 12; Bongbong, 10, Dangdang, 9, Tingting, 8; and Yengyeng, 6.

THE family Paraiso was not big, not small either. But the number of their children is not far from other families who were all conceived in the early dusk. Once their Papa stood up from his tired typewriter, especially when he had taken noni and their Mama was there roaming around after arriving from the other town where she was teaching first grade—she's been teaching more than ten years in first grade, but as if she doesn't like to get out from taking care the children—he couldn't hold his yearning touching their Mama, and if only she had not yet undergone ligation, it might be more than five had they been conceived in the cuddle of dusk. Their Papa, he is always at home—they're saying, he is doing chores at home. That the whole day, his attention is to his typewriter, almost becoming hunchback. He had made cry many blooming ladies and newly bloom teenagers. And made the newly crowing young men or men already with cockspur dreaming day and night. And he was able to make the string beans old men and fibrous old women who were listening and reading his stories laugh with gusto. His brain flows like cooking oil and he could type with close eyes, for his fingers know where to grope, as if they were also making love.

Notwithstanding that news spreading around that there were lot of gold (that's what they say) outside Noni, their Papa decided to cower under the noni tree, instead of going to a place where he could not smell even a rotten fruit of the source of his life.

Their Papa's dream was not that high; a low-slung dream was much easier to reach. When the eyes of their litters with their Mama brighten, it seems that what he was crunching was liters of stars and their bungalow that look like a turtle will be filled of crunchy laughter. The full sun seems brighten up after the slice of moon covers it when their eyes with their Mama waggle to each other.

One lazy Saturday morning, when the sun was already smiling at the inner canthus and lachrymal caruncle of Mount Bestride and half of the liters in the Noni Subdivision had cleaned their eyes, their Papa's typewriter was again cranking at the end of the extension of their kitchen at the west-north side while their Mama was again ever busy in the middle of their kitchen. Although she was still sleepy, Tingting was already around with their Mama watching her cooking. In the living room, Bongbong's legs were still open-wide in the sofa where he slept. A fly was flying around his open mouth, and sometimes he smiles, and his axed-size teeth protrude, and maybe mistaken that he was awake because his eyelids could not cover his protruding eyes: as if there were stars dancing in his pupils against the light. He was embracing his thick book that he reads until every dawn break, as if to guard against whoever tries to get it.

In the second room of their turtle bungalow, you may have misconstrued that Bingbing and Dangdang's intertwining legs were caressing on the wooden bed which has no cushion and as old as Bingbing's. In the upper deck of the double deck in the same room, Yengyeng's eyes had been roaming around the dim ceiling, embracing his Gameboy.

"You should have awakened your lardy piglets!" high-pitched their Mama who peeps through a blackwash curtain of their Papa's office.

Their Papa seems deaf and could not hear her wife for he was busy bending over his typewriter and sometimes acting as if going along with the sound of his typing. His spinal cord seems protruding but still smiling widely, then sometimes got mad and again smiles.

Their Mama approached him slowly. Her head leans left and then right watching their Papa.

"Had you encountered a bad spirit, Papa?"

"My goodness, the ginger footed shark, my goodness!" as if their Papa accidentally sat over an ember when he lifts his buttock suddenly. "You, ginger, I mean sweetheart... The flower, I mean carabao I was catching had bolted away!"

Their Papa suddenly became silent when his vigilant eyes caught by the front of their Mama's skirt. Little by little his eyes grope the rich bosom of their Mama. He spreads his boney arms acting to embrace. The three pieces of noni fruits he gobbled in the early evening still in the go. He opens and closes his eyes rapidly and make his lips pointed acting like a hungry male breeding pig.

"Oh, oh, what's up again? You'd done a lot last night already…" their Mama acts to move back. "That's what happens because you always eat noni… Go awake your piglets, it's getting late."

"Never mind… it's time for them to grow. Just come with me, Mama."

"Go awake your *Manong* Bongbong, Tingting," told their Mama when Tingting approach them. "Hurry up for it's becoming late. Also wake the three up."

Tingting met Yengyeng in the extension holding his Gameboy.

"I was told to tell you to go and wake up *Manong* Bongbong, Yengyeng," Tingting was serious.

"Why, are you afraid with *Manong* Bongbong? He is not going to eat you."

"Look at his eyes," Tingting pointed his lips to Bongbong when they reached him. "Is he awake or still sleeping?" she looks at him examining. "Wait," she said. She tiptoes going to the kitchen. When she gets back, she brought with her a bottle of salt. She handed to Yengyeng. Tingting focuses her eyes to Bongbong.

"Hey, you do it!"

Slowly from the back Tingting approach Bongbong who was so quiet. She places the bottle of salt in front of Bongbong's eyes.

"Hoy!" Bongbong suddenly stood up.

Tingting and Yengyeng stampede toward their Mama who was coming out from the office of their Papa. Bongbong ran after them.

"They tried to pour salt in my eyes!" answered Bongbong when their Mama asks. His eyes were popping out.

"I did not tell you to put salt into his eyes!" she reprimands Tingting and Yengyeng.

"Because they looked like peeping escargot… They probably taste good with salt, right, *Manong*?" Tingting smiles widely.

"Hey!" Bongbong's eyes protrude the more. He scratches his buttock at the same time.

"Okay, go and wake the two up and we'll have our breakfast. It's Saturday today, there are lots of things to do in the house... Nobody goes out to play."

Tingting and Yengyeng ran into the room.

"Don't yell anymore... we're already awake!" met by Bingbing and Tingting and Yengyeng left open-mouthed before shouting. Dangdang stretched out from her bed.

Not long afterward, they were already facing their breakfast of fried rice with garlic and sliced pieces of hotdog. A soy with milk replacing coffee was steaming. The four ran after each other, except Bingbing, to thrust their spoon. But their Mama stopped them, and their spoons left hanging in the air. They need to wait for their Papa.

Their Papa came over, as if counting the five, all their eyes focus on the steaming food. Under the table, Bronson was wiggling his tale and his tongue hanging while watching his masters, as if saying, please drop some bones!

After their Papa got his place at the end of the table, the four were about to get their food, while Bingbing was still watching quietly, but their Papa stops them.

"Bless the food first, Bongbong," their Papa said.

Their Mama asks who will be washing the dishes before finishing their breakfast.

"It's Dangdang's turn today," said Bongbong who was still busy eating. "It was my turn last Saturday, she was today, next time will be Tingting." Monday was the eldest's turn, down to Friday. Each of them has Saturday and Sunday assignment.

Dangdang remains silent. but she finished first. After finishing all their breakfast, they could not see her anymore. Their Mama called her many times before answering. She was in the bathroom.

"She stays there again forever!" said Bingbing, holding her journal, which she could not left behind. She might be writing every event, moment by moment in her life.

It's an exaggeration if we say that everything that she does in the bathroom was written.

BINGBING'S eyes followed Dangdang, Tingting, and Yengyeng going out the door. They invited her to go with them, but she refuses.

When Bingbing went inside, she noticed Bongbong straddling, while scratching his groin, the book he was glaring, and sometimes giggles and he could not tear off his protruding eyes the more. He did not even notice Bingbing passed in front of him.

Bingbing closes the door. She was adamant to pick up her journal. But regardless, she glances her notebook, and her album in the bed's corner. She could not decide which one to pick up. She does not like the teasing of her siblings. But when she daydreams Jerry, she even ashamed herself, for there was truthfulness in their comment. She could not understand her feelings. It was just lately, but she could feel warm groping on her face whenever Jerry smiles at her, and that warm feeling spread all over her body. Sometimes she even asks herself if she was worthy to partake the sacrament during their Sunday meetings. She does not like to ask, even to their Mama, for she feels embarrass that much.

Bingbing was just transferred from their primary class. She was now in the Young Women Organization, while Jerry also now in the Young Men Organization.

They belong to the same section in Six Grade at the Noni Elementary School. Bingbing was trying hard to study because she doesn't like to be log behind Jerry. She likes to show she's better, and hopefully she could catch the interest of the young man. She notices that the same with Jerry to her. They were fighting for the first place. Sometimes, she notices the young man staring her, then look to other side, and asks herself: does he likes me? Was he ashamed? Sometimes, she tells herself: we are still young.

Sometimes, they go home together, if they couldn't wait for a ride. But it's seldom because their classmates joke them.

Bingbing's daydreaming was disrupted when the door opens. It was their Mama who came in. She closes her journal at once.

"So, you're there making your vulva big. You should be outside sweeping," their Mama said. "A lot of caimito leaves dropped. You could never help me, now that it's vacation time… What were you hiding?"

"Huh, nothing…" Bingbing hid her notebook at her back.

Bingbing feels like bashful mimosa when their Mama get the notebook forcefully.

Their Mama smiling looks at her sideways. And she said: "You're still young, little girl… I'm not mad… But you're still young." Their Mama sat beside her, then taps her palm the shoulder of Bingbing. "When I was like you, there was also a young man… But I did not focus my attention to him… I focus to my studies until I became a teacher, and met you Papa, who was already a writer that time. That's why we reached this kind of life… Focus to your studies. When you reach the full maturity, like a fully bloom flower, when you find somebody, or somebody likes you, tell me and I will help you to choose. Like your Papa…"

"Ay! I don't like somebody like Papa! Hunchbacked! And bald!"

"I was not originally hunchback!" their Papa said who has been listening by the door. "And I was not bald. Your Mama made me hunchback and bald!"

"You talk a lot old man. You better go take a shower, or you may forget again; and you'll have a lot of dandruff falling again!" their Mama stood up. They went out with their Papa hand in hand.

IT'S already late in the morning but Bongbong still busy reading a book of dungeon. He was still scratching his groin once and awhile. The smell of the chicken being cooked by their Mama, with a fermented fish mixed with leaves of pepper garnished with ginger and tamarind, make that spot itchy. His mouth becomes watery and his stomach rumbling. It had been a while from the last time they ate chicken. They only have a chance to eat good food when their Papa receives payment of his novel being aired in the radio or published by the Dawn. But he doesn't like to put down what he was reading, and he doesn't like to go closer to their Mama cooking or he will surely be sent an errand again. It was Tingting who was always by their Mama's side. Bongbong loves the best reading, even the whole day or night. That's probably the reason of him having bulging eyes.

He did not notice Dangdang coming from outside, who had been watching him scratching. Dangdang's mouth was wide-opened and her eyes were directly focused to what Bongbong was scratching.

"*Manong*, why do you have black groin?" Dangdang's mouth was still wide-opened while squatting in front of Bongbong. "You have exanthema!"

"Shut-up!" glared Bongbong and stood up angrily.

"Ma, *Manong* Bongbong have exanthema!" Dangdang said running to their Mama.

"That's enough," their Mama said. "He was not always taking a bath that's why."

Bongbong approach Dangdang slowly at the back with watery mouth because of the viand being prepared by their Mama. He suddenly kicks the back of Dangdang's knee and seems ignoring what he did while looking over what their Mama was cooking. Dangdang tripped but she did not stumble.

"He taught, it's funny!" pouts Dangdang. There was also sparks in her eyes.

"Hmm, it's yummy, Ma!" Bongbong said, turning his head side to side. There were again stars in his eyes. "Be sure not to mix that pepper's leaves with fruit, Ma, okay?"

"Prepare the table, Tingting…" their Mama said.

Bronson had been wiggling his tail under the table. Again, he looks at Bongbong, then smells and yawn.

The three were joking while roaming around the kitchen.

"Go call everybody and we'll eat," their Mama said.

Bongbong, Dangdang, and Tingting had not open their mouths to call, Yengyeng was already running from the yard, holding his Gameboy. He went directly to his place. Bingbing also came out from the room embracing her journal. She went directly to her place at the left side of their Papa, followed by Bongbong. Their Papa sits at the end of the table, who was still busy tapping his typewriter in his office. At the right side of their Papa sits Dangdang, then Tingting, and then Yengyeng. Their Mama's was at the other end of the table.

Every time they eat chicken or fish, they know for sure who will be served the head. Their Mama said, because their Papa was the head of the family. And to give him ideas to write where they will get money to buy good viand. Even Bongbong likes head very much he could not complain only for their Papa. He was telling his mind, there will come a time that I'll also be the head.

They were all facing the food. Except their Mama who was keeping something in the oven. Their viand was already divided. Each of them has a bowl. All their choses were given. Their Mama, whatever was the leftover, it's her share, like the heart or the gizzard. Their eyes look like protruding and the table was full of stars. They were only waiting for their Papa coming out from his nest. Bongbong was about to call him louder because his mouth was watery. They could not eat first if they were not complete in the table, if they were all home. But their Papa was already bending and holding his lower back approaching the dining table.

Not long after that, the kitchen utensils start producing jingling sound in the dining table. Bronson keeps on waggling his tail under the table.

Bongbong suddenly stood up. He ran to climb the sink. He jumps up and down.

"Puah! Puah! Puah!" His snivel and tears meeting together.

"What are you doing?" their Mama stood up about to help Bongbong.

"Ha pep pe… ha pep pe! It's fuut!"

"Ay, ay, fuut, should say, hey Bongbong! Only a devil's pepper… you look like a monorchid," their Papa said. "Or did Dr. Miguel removed your testicle when your Mama brought you for castration, or I would say for circumcision?"

The four laughed with gusto. Their Papa watched them: as if he was watching a lot of stars gushing forth from their eyes. He caught Dangdang secretly bite the share of Tingting looking at Bongbong. And returns it immediately.

Tingting frowns when he notices what happens to his viand.

"You got some, right?" Tingting looks at Dangdang sharply. He snatched Dangdang's viand and bites.

Bongbong returns to his place when the fire of the pepper subsides. He continued biting the chicken thigh. He was very hungry. He uses his two hands in biting. Suddenly, he accidentally drops the thigh. He stoops. His forehead hits the table. Before picking the thigh, Bronson catches it. Bronson ran the thigh outside.

Bongbong ran after Bronson the latter was able to hide. He went back pouting.

"You like chicken, *Manong*?" said Yengyeng. He offered his share. But when Bongbong tried to reach, Yengyeng put into his mouth leaning his head left and right making his eyes wide-opened.

"Don't worry, I'll give you another one," their Mama said.

Bingbing, who was not saying anything, who was focus eating, and laughing with the group, sometimes looks at Bongbong.

DANGDANG didn't mind whether her voice goes beyond somewhere or not, she loves singing while taking a shower.

She loves imitating the style of Jolina Madrigal. Then, she changed her song.

"*Diatdiatteng arigodon, Manong* Bongbong got exanthema!" Dangdang did a prolonged rasping while robbing her back.

"Giddy!" countered Bongbong who was going to take a drink in the kitchen. "She's unduly greedy to sing. Might produce earthquake!"

"*Diatdiatteng arigudon,*" seconded Yengyeng who entered at the back door of the kitchen.

"…Yengyeng puckers something!" continued Bongbong. "Hurry up and I'll take a shower also," he shouted to Dangdang.

"Tell you, *Manong*. Even you spend the whole day showering, your whole exanthema will never be torn apart," Dangdang said. "Go gather taro leaves or ripe fruit of devil's pepper then crush and rub it to your itching!"

"Stupid, it puckers up the most!"

"After puckering up, your whole skin will be torn apart, and then your exanthema will completely disappear!"

"You better pour boiling water, *Manong*!" countered Yengyeng with wide open grin. "Tell me after pouring and I'll help you tear your skin apart, because I pity you that much. Hey, no, sorry, I don't like to be infected!"

"You'll be infected. I used your brief!"

"Ay-ay!" Yengyeng wry-mouths.

Dangdang had changed her clothes when she went out from the bathroom. She walks joyfully when she went to their room.

When she went out, she gathers Tingting, Yengyeng, and other children from the neighbors.

"I have a gimmick," she said, while the other children gather around her. She was short compared to two bamboo-pole-like tall of the children, but they listen her.

"What's that again, Dangdang?" said Tingting. Tingting calls Dangdang that way even she was a year younger. "I know what you have in mind, okay."

"I will never be Dangdang if I cheat you. It will then be my sweetest name. Dardanella the Beautiful!"

"Beautiful your pan-shaped face!" pouted Tingting.

"Can you see that tree in the east?" Dangdang said. "The fruit is sweet."

"The fruit is sweet!" catches Yengyeng, leaning his head left and right as if showing he knows everything. "I had eaten a lot of its fruit."

"Yengyeng is right. It does not matter if there's only one Yengyeng as long as he is the right Yengyeng the youngest!" Dangdang said. "Do you know what I have in mind? No, because I had not told you yet..."

"I already knew!" Tingting said.

"I said you don't know because I have not told you yet. Just what Papa's saying, which I was listening sometimes, it is as yummy as God's recipe..."

"Then what are we going to do?" Tingting is bored.

"We'll go pick some fruits. Old Tanas is not around… Whoever does not follow is not God's child. I guess you do not like not to be a child of God, right?"

"We are going to steal?" Yengyeng's eyebrows move up.

"No. That's bad. We'll just go ask for some."

"You said they are not home. How could we ask for?" Tingting said.

"We'll tell them when they get home."

"Do it yourself," Tingting said.

"You are very eager to eat, right?"

"Y-yes…"

"Whoever follows me he is not coward."

"I'm not coward," everybody says.

They followed Dangdang in queue.

"Common, climb," Dangdang said ones they were under the manzanita tree.

"How about you?" Tingting said.

"I'll stay here and watch," Dangdang said. "Don't you worry. When Old Tanas arrives, I will tell him about asking for some."

The children seem hungry monkeys climbing after the other. The branches where they hang were almost broken. Their munching sounds like melody in the forest, followed by filling their pockets.

Dangdang was enjoying her humming under the tree, again and again, asking for fruit but nobody was listening her.

"Tingting, that one, very red… Yes, that one there… Yes, yes… Yengyeng that one above your head." She points different directions. "Pick a lot… fill your pockets. My goodness, I know it's yummy! "Share me some… Hey."

"You climb yourself, not just instructing what to do!" Tingting threw her two pieces.

"That one… the-there…" Dangdang's munching abruptly stop because from the north side, she notices Old Tanas waggling to their direction. She feels scared. My goodness! She exclaimed to herself.

She did not look up for those who were in the branches. She secretly went away.

Old Tanas was walking like a wiggling mango tree approaching the manzanita tree. He was pointing his finger toward the children.

"Hey, you, pilferer children!" his voice sounds like thunder.

Tingting was frightened. "Oh, my Mama, Satan, I mean Old Tanas is here!" She was confused. She wanted to jump but he was in a high branch.

Old Tanas was fast approaching.

They slid down the tree one by one. They plunged down heavily in the ground. One massaged her knee, the other one her elbow, or whatever painful. Tingting's buttock hit the bulging soil. She blew repeatedly in succession holding her butt while running. The sweet fruits in her pockets were scattered in the ground.

"Wait!" Old Tanas said. He was mad and at the same time feeling funny with the children's situation.

"You're pert, Darangdangdang!" Tingting confronts, breathing heavily, when she got home, still holding her butt. Dangdang humming joyfully while sitting cross-legged while reading comics.

"You're so slow… Where is my share?" Dangdang said.

"Your share in your face!" countered Tingting. She feels her pockets. She picks out some red fruit and selects one and threw it in her mouth. The pain in her butt disappeared while enjoying the sweetness of the manzanita.

"Hey, see the house lizard!" she pointed out the ceiling.

Tingting suddenly enfolds her arms to protect the fruits on her cuddle. He did not look where Dangdang pointed at. "I know your stroke, you!" he pouted, munching again. "Hmm, really yummy!" he looked up Dangdang sideways.

"Hope you choked up!" Dangdang chewed air in her mouth.

ALL of them five were in the living room. Bongbong sat cross-legged while reading his dungeon book. Bingbing was writing in her journal. Dangdang was wiggling her head left and right while following by humming Jolina Madrigal's cd. Yengyeng was looking up a hanging electric wire attached in the doorbell.

Tingting was uneasy, like a cat laboring with difficulty. Tingting was looking down as if looking a needle in the dark carpet. She walks up to the extension. Then in the kitchen. She looks up here and there. Her eyes stop at the cabinet where their Mama keeping her kitchen utensils.

Tingting opens one of the cabinets. She puckers up and put her hand in front when a winged cockroach flew over her nose. Bottles of fermented fish, soy sauce, black pepper, salt, v-chin, garlic, and whatever seasonings Tingting found out. She opens the other one. There were small packages of flour, seasoning for cake, mixing utensils, and others. She reached a box. She puts on the table. She looks for what she needs. From the oven's drawer. The places where her Mama keep her tools. She also looks for eggs. A tool for mixing. Sugar. Oil. Afterwards, she starts singing facing the oven.

Somebody was tiptoeing from Tingting's back. She stops singing. Then proceeds.

"Hey!"

"Hey your face!" pouted Tingting.

Dangdang's he-he was cut. "Why does the octopus, said Papa, when startled it emits black blood then straightens its tentacles and runs?" pouted Dangdang. Tingting's complexion is similar to an octopus.

"You want me to pour on you oil?"

"Hey, you're cooking, smells good, Ting…"

"Mm, mmm, you'd just smells food, and you made my name sounds good… Tse! Tsuen!"

"Oh, my Ting! I'm not a puppy… Share me a small piece, please."

"Share your face!" Tingting flips Dangdang's hand when the latter tries to get some cooked pieces. But Dangdang had pinch a small piece.

"What do you call of this?"

"Bibingki."

"Bibingki?"

"If it's big, *bibingka*[55]. But because it is small, bibingki, you silly!" Tingting explains her term for her small pancakes.

---

[55] *Bibingka,* soft, round glutinous rice cake.

"If it is big, Tangtang; if it is small, Tingting... Hmm, it looks like yummy. One more piece... Hmm, your bibingki is really yummy. You're a good cook, Ting," Dangdang pinch one more time. It's now bigger. "Whom did you learn to cook?"

"I'm just copying Mama's... Your hand!" Tingting flips Dangdang's hand one more time.

Dangdang felt pain. After putting Tingting's last pancake into the plate, Dangdang secretly ran the plate away, saying in her mind: "Octopus!"

Tingting shouts when she discovers that the plate disappeared. When she went to look in the living room, the four had gobbled up the content.

"Is that all you have, Tingting?" Bongbong said, still munching greedily.

"One more piece, Tingting," Bingbing said putting down her journal and put the pancake into her mouth with two hands.

"Go cook more, Manang Ting," Yengyeng said putting his finger into his mouth to remove the sticky pancake.

"You have no manners! You've gobbled it all! I didn't cook for you!" Tingting was munching air when going back to the kitchen.

"Bring more!" said the four in unison. Then laugh.

Tingting brought their Papa a piece into where he was bending over his typewriter. Their Papa seemed unmindful with Tingting because of the unrelenting tapping of his typewriter.

Tingting was enjoying her last piece, pinching little by little before putting in her mouth, as if saying, I'm already good in baking!

When their Mama arrives, in a hurry, Tingting offered her a piece of the pancake she kept.

"Ma, she what I cooked. Taste it, it's yummy!"

"Yeah, you're right, my child," their Mama said after putting a little pinch in her mouth. "Learn faster how to cook so that you can do the cooking when I'm busy. Your siblings, the only thing they know is to make their groin bigger and bigger..."

"How does the groin grow big, Mama?"

"Hey!"

Tingting joined the four. They enjoyed their half-repressed laughter in the living room, where they talked whatever topic under the sun, and when they laugh in unison, as if there were liters of stars twinkling out from their eyes and their house will be fall of light. Their Papa also in his nest, he as well laughs in unison with them and the trrrrrrrk of his typewriter disappears. Likewise, their Mama working in the kitchen, also laughs, and when they do it together with their Papa, as if the light of the full sun and the slice of moon mixed together. Their house seems a paradise in that very moment.

But their laughter suddenly cut off when their Mama raised her voice. Their Mama seldom raises her voice, and when she raises her voice foreboding follows. The five opened their mouths in unison. For sure one of them committed a sin. They waited for the next scene.

Tingting readied to go out, for she foreseen the next event. But their Mama raised her voice again.

"Tingting!" said their Mama in a high pitch voice. "Where did you put the flour?"

"She cooked it into a bibingki, 'Ma!" countered Dangdang, meaning, a small pancake. "I told her not to touch it, but she still cooked it bibingki…"

"You're a liar!" pouted Tingting. She looked Dangdang sideways. "They ate, 'Ma, Dangdang and all of them. She told me to cook… They ate all, 'Ma."

And as if pointing finger has no end.

"I planned to cook a noodle… but you'd eaten it…"

"Never mind, you loved it also, their Mama," smiled their Papa.

"Because of that, you don't have a viand for dinner. Dip with a *bugguong*[56]!" their Mama said, meaning, a fermented, salted fish.

"No way!" Bongbong suddenly feels irritation with his exanthema upon hearing *bugguong* and he stops his reading. He scratched his exanthema with both hands. "It's your fault, you, octopus!" he looked at Tingting with a sharp eye.

---

[56] *Bugguong*, fermented fish with salt and water used in seasoning vegetable dishes.

THEIR Papa and their Mama had not been home from where they attended writers' meeting. Bingbing, Dangdang, and Tingting were lying flat on their bed after tired playing scrabble. Bongbong went back to his place to read; he was not scratching that much because their Mama bought something for his exanthema. He won from their game; he always wins and the four do not like to play with him. But it seems nothing to Yengyeng, for he was always the loser. The reason was he always focusing to his Gameboy, when he was at home, if he is not outside catching dragonfly, butterfly, or picking up ashtray kitten along the streets, or thrown away by the owner.

When he was tired playing his Gameboy, he went out with no exact place to go.

He visited his two friends, Leo and Bimbo. They did not have plan to do. They just talked about anything under the sun. Afterwards, they decided to walk around the Noni Subdivision. They were giggling. Kicking bottlecaps of soft drinks, or anything they found along the street. Sometimes, they race over each other. Afterwards, they sat along the road gutter. Or lay down on the grass and look up the blue sky. Or walking with one foot. Or racing with one foot. Or walking with their arms over their shoulder while leaning their heads side by side and sing incomplete song. They do a lot of unplanned things.

There were number of castor oil tree at the east end of the subdivision. It has some ripe fruit. Playfully Yengyeng picked one. He peeled it.

"Hey, look at it," he said. "It looks like a fruit of the almond tree," he said comparing to an almond.

"You're right."

"Is it also good to eat?"

"Let's taste it," Yengyeng said.

A little bit at first. The taste was good; they liked it. And they ate a lot.

Not long afterwards, Bimbo invited his friends to go home. He ate more than his friends.

"Yes," Yengyeng said. "I'm sleepy…"

And they parted from under the castor oil tree.

Once reaching home, Yengyeng went to the bathroom immediately. He made a loud sound in the toilet. He went there many times. Not long afterwards, he felt bad. He felt cold. He felt dizzy.

The arrival of their Papa and Mama was timely.

"Who told you to eat castor oil fruit?" their Mama said upon knowing what they ate.

"Because it looks like peanut… almond," said Yengyeng. "And it tastes good."

"It's not all delicious are delicious, I mean, good to eat," their Papa said.

Leo had also loose bowel movement, and excessive vomiting in their home.

And Bimbo, they ran him to the hospital and gave him dextrose.

One day, Yengyeng went out again. He looked for Bimbo and Leo. But he could not find the two. When he decided to go home, he passed by a crying kitten. The kitten looks pretty with its spotty hair, looks like a Himalayan he saw in a book.

Yengyeng picked it up and brought it home.

When he arrives home, he saw an electric wire, dangling in the kitchen. Their Papa fixed the iron and forgot to keep it safe because he went back to his typewriter.

Yengyeng focused his attention to the electric wire for a while and looked at the outlet in the wall. Then looked at the kitten he was holding onto his chest which was so quiet after feeding it.

"You have a beautiful kitten," said Bongbong who was going to the kitchen to have a drink. "Where did you still again?"

Yengyeng seemed not noticing Bongbong. He picked up the electric wire. He plugged it to the outlet in the wall, and the two ends to the kitten.

"Hey, hey, what are you doing?" said Bongbong with wide-opened eyes.

The kitten flutters and struggles and its hair bristled. Yengyeng was thrown down to the floor.

"What are you two doing?" their Papa said and stood away from his typewriter.

"Yengyeng electrocuted the kitten, Pa!" Bongbong said.

Yengyeng made a wide smile rubbing the kitten softly.

"You're so silly! If you're not careful you may electrocute your balls instead!" their Papa said.

One day, Yengyeng might have bored enough looking at the dangling electric wire by the doorbell. He slid a chair close and reached the wire for he tried to fix it. He put two wrong ends together and the fuse funnel busted. All bulbs shut off, including their Papa's electric typewriter. All the other members of the household yelled in unison while Yengyeng dropped on the floor because of the impact of the current that struck him.

They all scolded Yengyeng. Yengyeng just giggles.

"Hey, what you're doing is not funny!" their Mama said. "Next time, you may be the next to be roasted alive! The Lord forbids!"

SUNDAY evening. Bingbing, Dangdang, Tingting, and Yengyeng reached Bongbong to his place reading in the living room. He was no longer scratching, but thighs wide opened and Dangdang was peeping his darkened groin; is your exanthema now healed, *Manong*, she wanted to ask but she does not like to give joke at this very evening. They were all quiet, as if they were all angels plunged on earth. The books they needed were all on the small table in the middle of the living room, including the hymnals.

They were waiting for their Mama who was still doing something in the kitchen.

And their Papa who was making noise in the bathroom.

Not long after, their Papa and Mama came to the living room. The five looks like pried escargots. Ones in a while, they look each other. But they did not like to look each other too long because they did not like to start laughing that make all the stars fall from their eyes.

"Who is the conducting tonight?" starts their Papa.

"It's *Manang* Bingbing, 'Pa," Dangdang said.

"Alright, start, Bingbing," their Papa said.

"Good evening… nice to see you all. I am conducting to our Family Home Evening. Papa is presiding. Dangdang will give the opening prayer, Bongbong will give scriptural thought, Tingting is the chorister, and Yengyeng will give the closing prayer... The opening hymn is *There is Beauty All Around*, and the closing hymn will be *Count Your Blessings*..."

Their Papa's part is to give some advices, the more the silence of the five. Not even one of them rose their faces. As if they were all sinners to be given punishment. Instead of telling them their errors the past week, their Papa asked them what good or bad things they had done. He started from Bingbing.

"I was not able to help Mama in the house," starts Bingbing. "And, I also ate the pancake of Tingting, for I did not know she stole Mama's flour..."

Yengyeng was about to complain but their Papa was looking at her, so she just looks down.

"I don't know any bad thing I did," Bongbong said. "I just read. And I forgot, I also ate some pancake Tingting cooked..."

"I led Tingting and the rest in stilling manzanita," Dangdang said. "But they also enjoyed eating..."

"I cooked what Mama was keeping," Tingting said. "But you all enjoyed eating."

"I electrocuted a kitten..." said Yengyeng.

Their Papa advised all the five. "You all need to repent," he said. "What you did the whole week, will give lessons for you. Promise not to do it again."

"And tell them to help me, Papa. Your children are growing fast, but they're becoming slothful."

"Had you heard your Mama?"

One by one said yes.

When Yengyeng finished giving the closing prayer, their Mama told them she prepared some snacks.

"Yippee!" all of them rose their arms in unison. "It doesn't matter if there's only one Mama as long as she is like Mama!" they said in unison.

"Hey, stop flattering me!" their Mama said.

"It's not flattery, Ma," Dangdang said. "Corny!"

"Who washes the dishes?" their Mama asks.

"It's Papa!" the five said in duet.

"Very good, children!" their Papa said. "Now, you need to repent twice!"

"Ayyy!"

Not long after, tiny laughter over powered everything, and like other moments when they laugh together, seemed more liters of stars culled off from heaven one more time, and the house of the Paraisos was fall of light and cracking laughter.

And while stars were culling from the eyes of Bingbing, Bongbong, Dangdang, Tingting and Yengyeng, their Papa winks their Mama with one eye.

Before their Mama enters their room with their Papa, she said: "Go to sleep for you are going to school again tomorrow morning."

Their Papa went to his nest while typing. When he went out, he was eating ripe noni.

Their Papa enters the masters' bedroom with their Mama.

When the eyelids of Yengyeng's eyes were about to close, he stood up and approached the masters' bedroom of their Papa and Mama.

"Hey, they're already sleeping!" blocks Bingbing.

"I'll just go and say goodnight," Yengyeng said. But he went back with wide-opened mouth.

"Why?" asks Bongbong.

Yengyeng shake his head. He scratched his nape.

"Let's go to sleep," Bingbing said.

The four walked in queue; Bongbong continue reading in the living room. When they reached the locked bedroom of their Papa and Mama, they slowed down. They listen confusedly.

"You're impolite!" Bingbing drove the four in to their room.

Moments later, they're all in peaceful mode. The liters of stars in their eyes hid, like the sun and the moon of their Papa and Mama. —0

January 1, 2002, 2:11 p.m. (draft)
January 6, 2002, 12:12 a.m. (final)
Bannawag, June 24, 2002

Patriarch

1. Last Day

HE was alone once again. He could no longer sleep since the early departure of his wife in his second marriage to her job—he married the second time a year after the death of his kind and understanding first wife. His breakfast was waiting on the end table by his bed's side. He will just take his breakfast when he was hungry, if he ever feels it. His medicines as well had been prepared on the table.

It was winter and chilly outside more so after a snowfall like this. Nevertheless, the venetian blind and the curtain of the window by his feet were opened. His shaking subsides when watching, even a shadow, the lovely cradling of the breeze the green leaves of the weeping willow tree in the middle of Spring, the whole Summer, and in Autumn when the leaves change their colors into different colors before the coming of Winter that brings snow once-in-a-while. But it looks frozen this time with cloaked snow by the crossing of Market Street and 3800 South and seems ice oozes from his breast. He was bleary waiting for a shadow of a bird, but nothing even a transparent of it alighting on the naked branches, unlike during Spring or Summer or Autumn that many of them singing and sometimes alighting on the window sill and peck the glass and look inside. When his muscles were still strong, he sometimes throws crumbs of bread or rice at them, probably the reason why they always go and visit him.

No bird visits him this time. He could not even hear the moaning of the heater, especially the wind embracing and rocking the branches of the weeping willow tree.

His eldest son with his first wife in Yorkshire, how were they now? When was their last visit with his daughter-in-law, and his grandchildren? If only he could stand, and able to walk for a distance, he must visit them often because Yorkshire was not that far from Market Street. But he could not even move his right foot for his thigh was plowed by a Japanese bullet during the second world war and sometimes, it was painful and as if he loses his breath when it tightens, more so when he was alone, like now.

Tatang[57]?

There were times that he could not hear his second daughter with his present wife, where he was able to have a White son-in-law. His daughter watches him during the day until his wife arrives and takes turn—his daughter goes to work in the evening. The eldest works during the day, like their *Nanang*[58], and the youngest works during the day and go to school in the evening. Whatever his daughters do with him, it all like a dream and let them do whatever they want to do with his vegetable body.

There were times that he could grope by the wall in joining with his three daughters in the living room, together with their *Nanang,* but when times their arguments heated, he just gropes again by the wall going back to their room with his wife and there he broods to reminisce his lustrous days. His mind flies and flings up and away. Sometimes it flings up and away in Pagasa, then in Poblacion Sur, or in Labut and in Panay-ogan, or in Baybayabas, or in San Isidro, or Guimud Sur, or in Abbarit. Sometimes it flings up to Tarlac, or in Bataan, or Corregidor. In the Death March, or when he was courting his first wife. His first wife looks like a morning star in Guimud Sur and flowers of his dreams, since he met her during harvest time in the golden rice field in Cabanayan.

---

[57] *Tatang*: father.

[58] *Nanang*: mother.

Yes, he could not feel any weariness in flinging up and away and when his mind is in the horizon, he forgets everything around him and the rays of the dawn smile at his face, and the kiss of the sun bidding goodbye in the afternoon was as smooth as a Spring breeze. There were also times that he flies swiftly in the horizon and goes on high to smile with the stars. Anytime he flings up and away he sees the open valley and ocean bellow, the houses that seem sleeping turtles, rice field with golden rice, green forest and scaly pearly ocean. He feels awesome mingling with the birds looking down the wholeness of the world. The frown of the surrounding, and the shouting of the wanderers was unfamiliar: as if they were preserved remains of the world.

But when an excruciating pain from his thigh seems unbearable, he was drawn out from where he was flinging up and back to his real world. When the pain subsides, his recollection shuffles into a different world but many times a painful view appears in his pupil. He hears the news from the very lips of his children: the happenings in the nucleus of his beloved motherland; the restless society, the throbbing in the bosom of the citizenry caused by the negligence of the caretakers. They sacrifice their lives for the welfare of their beloved homeland, during the Second World War, but was this the expense of the blood that flows in the jungle of Bataan and in the sugar plantation in Tarlac; the unaccounted lives that were sacrificed in the Death March? Was this the crop of the past? This slough brought by the modern time? The self-exiled good citizens to look for a better place to live, like what happens with his life? The second half of his family was here because of that negligence; that if the gods of his homeland were not negligent, his family did not go astray and there will be no problem for him to depart from his loved ones. The lives of many Contemplacions were not sacrificed in places where they look for scratch to feed for their loved ones. His homeland should not be like a cadaver butchered by vicious eagles in the city. The reason why youngsters in almost all schools in the city, and many fed up citizens, held some revolutionary actions. And the worsening restlessness of those who were living outside, likewise those who were cacklers who were showing to the public that they were sympathizers with the illness of society but give nothing for the welfare of their homeland but problems, causing unavoidable sky racketing prices that strangles the life of the whole citizenry. There will be no mistakes if not because of these counterfeit and negligent individuals. There will be no sin. There will be no temptation. He should not be led in a problem like that. Yes, he who is the patriarch… the patriarch…

2. Guilt

IT was my fault, **Inada**[59]*.*

> *It was my fault.*
> *It was my fault.*
> *It was my fault!*
> *I did not ask for your forgiveness.*
> *Because I knew you could not forgive me.*
> *And I am here right now.*
> *Although there is another bosom I am leaning on, you are always in my mind.*
> *I love our children. I love them very much, because they were your living embodiment. But how pity, only one among them is close to where I am.*
> *I miss those who are in the Philippines very much.*
> *Again, forgive me for I left them. Some say, I need to prepare for the future of these three children we had with your substitute. They say, they do not have a future in the Philippines. I am receiving some news, Inada, regarding the hardship our children were experiencing, especially the two who were not as lucky as their other brothers. Our son in Yorkshire had given an opportunity to come here in America. But they also have number of children with your good daughter-in-law.*
> *You have a lot of grandchildren in the Philippines, but according to the spreading news regarding the problems down there, I feel so bad to imagine their depressing opportunity. How pity. But what will I do? I lost all my energy, Inada. There is always pain in my thigh plowed by the Japanese bullet, but doctors see nothing, many of them, causing them to give medication. Sometimes my neck stiffens, and I could not swallow my food*

---

[59]   *Inada*: their mother.

because something I do not know plugs, even the liquid I drink. They say that according to my doctor, my food goes directly to my lungs. That was how my eldest daughter with your substitute explains because she understands and speaks English and I just keep my mouth open and receive whatever they tell me. Even probably when they say I am dying; I will just say yes because I can do nothing. What I feel with my body and my condition here in America was like a robot or a withered vegetable. If I ponder my condition here, I am like a living aborted fetus being kick by time every now and then. It was just lucky, and I am grateful, that the sharpness of my memory did not change; to exaggerate, I remember everything, probably the reason why my mind goes everywhere.

Yes, Inada, they say America is a paradise. But is it a paradise for somebody like me? My biggest world is nothing but this small four-cornered room, which I cannot observe properly in the distance because my surrounding looks like misty. But your image, Inada, remains still the same. Even in my sleep, in my dreams, your image often comes into view.

They say, the surrounding of Utah was beautiful, especially during springtime, and summertime, and the whole year round. Your son in Yorkshire says time here is not far from life. That during Spring, it conveys the coming back into life the buried plants and they start growing shoots and flowers start to bloom and they grow fast to make the surrounding like a paradise; the sky was clear, the wind caressing and people all over were all smile every day. Then comes Summer and it tempers the leaves, it makes other colors stronger, like the contrasting races who were now citizens here— when my eyesight was still good, I also noticed the stunning different colors of the leaves, why they were like that, I do not know. Afterwards, comes fall or autumn. Sometimes, I feel that I am oppressed. Because when I watch the smooth shuffling of the falling leaves on the bosom of the environment, as if my body was also shuffling in that environment—but although it was painful for me to think that my flesh will be mixed in foreign land; I wish, Inada, that my corpse will be put to rest by your grave. But, oh! Yes, Inada, the leaves shuffle and soon after, there comes in view the naked branches and they look like many skeletons begging for compassion from heaven. Yes, Inada, the environment looks like wearing veil as seen thru the stillness of the people. As if they worry very much for the coming of winter. Winter brings snow that burry the heap of leaves. That was how clear your son explains, your son who was gifted with keenness of nature. I do not know. I also wish to see the beauty of nature, as they say, but now I see nothing but mist. The laughter all around, it seems come from a deep hole for even my ears were selfish enough to give me chance to savor the kindness of the world.

But then there was something very sad being done to our countrymen here, Inada. Instead of helping each other, because there was only one reason that drove them to come here, no because they almost eat each other by attacking themselves. There were those who does not like to listen demeaning topics, and could not stand foul odor by slandering each other, and avoid meeting with these good countrymen. Not all of them of course, but a lot of them. I'm thinking, Inada, they brought here their bad attitude in the Philippines. And I am also thinking, that was probably the reason of being stagnant of our beloved land of origin because of this attitude.

Yes, Inada, many things are coming back and forth in my mind specially when I am alone here in this world where I am wiggling. As if my mind does not have anything to do except to go around and round and many insignificant things cramming in my head.

That must be the reason why in my present world, Inada, there were times that I could hardly breath. I am mildly delirious, then my world seems going upside down and the four corners of the wall around me met together and they compress me. I scream sometimes, and my body stiffens, but when I realize that I am alone, that your substitute was not around because she went to work, I am strengthening my mind for as much as possible I don't like to be lost in this foreign place. My world, Inada, it is still the world we built, full of laughter, we were satiated with the newly harvested vegetables. We did not have enough money, but we were happy. Here, a lot of food, but there is no newly harvested I used to have in Abbarit. There are marunggay, and okra and jute and bitter melon and eggplant but most of them are stone-liked. They froze the leaves, but our co-Ilocanos love them all the same for it is better than not to eat something like those.

I don't know, sometimes I want to blame the Creator for throwing me down here. But do I have the right to blame the one who create me, specially the untimely separating you from me? Or was that my punishment for my many shortcomings for you? Why did He allow me to be tempted, *that I sinned you? Was it His fault, or mind? My heart is sobbing when I remember you, Inada. But even I drink my tears, can I still bring back our verdant days?*

Yes, Inada, I am telling myself ones in a while, that time threw me here in this strange place. I could not understand a single word of their language. Not even I do watch in the television, I could only understand a little bit thru their action, when my vision was still good. My heart is heavy, Inada, but so hard, so hard!

Are you happy where you are right now, Inada? Our bourns who are now there with you, how are they? Your grandchildren who passed away early, are they now big? Are happy there? Me, I can say that I am not happy. My companions in the house are always laughing, and I am just smile not understanding their topic. I am no different from a scarecrow or puppet of no worth in the world where I am wriggling right now. Or am I still moving, Inada? Or maybe I am already a moving carcass?

Where are you, Inada? Why won't you answer me, or appear to me even a single moment? I missed our produces in the Philippines, but I missed you the most. I do have a lot of sin, but can you forgive?

Where are you, Inada, where are you?

My heart is so heavy, Inada. I can't breathe. As if something is chocking me. I am being chocked. My chest, it feels like compressing. What's happening, Inada, what's happening? Please extend your hand and assist me. If I have the right to be assisted by you, Inada. I could not...

3. Within the Rim of the World – 1

WHAT happened to him?

I don't have any idea, he just screaming when I was in the living room watching
DVD. When I came to see him, his left arm was waggling a lot and his right hand was holding his thigh. He was bellowing ouch repeatedly.

What's painful, Daddy? Was your wound the cause?

Are we going? Are we going?

Where are we going?

Are we going? Are we going?

My God! How goad. Had you called your big brother?

Nobody's home. Brother will be home late.

How goad. Your big sister went to Wendover… didn't you call her cellphone?

That's her cellphone.

Your small sister?

They have their finals… Hey, *Tatang* is mumbling!

Listen what's he mumbling… His grip is tight…

Tatang, Tatang… He's not responding… Hey, look at him, *'nang*, he did not touch his food... and his medicine.

That's why! Why didn't you see?

How should I know, for he is not the only one I'm attending?

3. Sin

MY children, please forgive me, to whatever mistake I made… My children… my children, can't you hear me? Please listen to me. I know I sinned unto you, more so with your Nanang.

Yes, your late Nanang. Your Nanang who was so kind. I committed a very serious misdeed to her.

I bring with me my misdeed to her wherever I go. I did not tell to any of you. Also, your younger siblings, Barok, they do not know; also, to the youngest whose age was only two that time, I'm not sure if he understood what was happening. If you remember, your mother came to Manila several times, and she made her homesickness as the reason, more so with her elder grandchildren, who were your children with my good daughter-in-law. She was the one who had visited your place in Balara, where she came to help in taking care of your second. Then after that, in Times, in Sampaloc—I always remember although I had not given a chance to step on those places where you lived while preparing for your future. I did not plan to come for a vacation, or just to see you. It was always my alibi to your Nanang that I was flighty to travel, and many things just to stay in Labut. But the truth, there was a bigger thing that I could not left. That was the big temptation. That I could not express not even today. I felt the negative feelings of two of your siblings who were young women then, but a disregarded it.

It was a serious sin, Barok, and I am embarrassed to face wherever I want to go. I don't have enough power to knock on the big white door, for it seems something was holding my feet.

Was it because I did not ask for your forgiveness?

I am not so sure if your Nanang had mentioned something, yes, your kind Nanang. I remember now, and my mind melts to reminisce, and I am ashamed of myself. Yes, there were instances that she caught what I was doing, but I did not hear any hesitancy in her mind, and chance to chastise that temptation, who was a fruit of her sister. She just let her tears drop while preparing food, or to carry your youngest brother who was not asking to be carried up. I caught the dropping of her tears while doing even the littlest thing. I knew I was the reason, my deed, but my mind hardened, and I did not ask for understanding, or intend to explain the affairs; for what should I explain? Or how could I explain?

4. Enticement

I am already old, Barok, what still be the reason of going to America? he said while talking with his children from his first wife on the bamboo bench under the young mango tree beside their house in Poblacion Sur. His children made a vacation from Manila that summer.

The condition of living here is too tough, his eldest son said. There might not have much importance to you. But it is very important to these three... They don't have good future here.

That's true, seconded the next to the eldest. So, you would petition us also. I would not like as much as possible that your grandson grows in this impoverish life.

I have been telling him, the stepmother said. He does not like. Citizenship for them veterans is free. I am tired of feeding pigs and taking care cows. I also want to touch green bucks as they say.

Think it over, Brother, his doctor friend and a veteran like him said. Your children have the right idea. If you stay here forever, hardship will your three young daughters inherit—they might have husbands who would inherit the same. Anyway, we were given a chance to become Americans, why should we not take advantage of it? If only my health is still good, I might have been in the cradle of Uncle Sam.

When his oldest son went home from America where his work sent him to observe, where he had given a multiple indefinite visa, he decided to go back and seek for a better future. This was his son whom they arrive at with after the easy approval of his petition for citizenship. He was accompanied by his wife and three young daughters.

5. Within the Rim of the World – 2

I called you up, Barok, because your father is no longer talking. He is always whispering 'are we going, are we going.' But if you talk to him, he does not respond.

Does he still have medicine?

We bought him already.

You bought him? Does he had not under Medicaid?

They stopped it because I already have a job.

Are we going? Are we going?

Is that him?

He might be hallucinating, Barok.

Send him to the LDS Hospital, where his doctor is. Your siblings are not home to drive us there… it's supposed to be your children,

Your siblings are not home to drive us there… it's supposed to be your children, but they are not home also…

I could not live my job because we are so busy. It will be nine o'clock when I go home.

So, what's up now, Barok, you are all busy? I could not even speak English, and we do not have ride.

What a coincidence. Okay, I'll see what I can do.

7. Farewell

I want to bid farewell while on your side.

Don't think about that.

But I also want to spend my last moment beside the children in the Philippines.

Can you divide yourself?

I want to be buried in the land of my birth.

8. Affection

Although my body left here, my spirit will come to you, my beloved Inada!

9. Within the Rim of the World – 3

ARE you all around?

We are complete, Barok.

Prepare your computer… Open your monitor, or your television which is bigger… let's do conferencing… okay, come closer… they're waiting in Manila.

Do they have gadgets, *Manong*?

I bought them when I visited them.

Are we going? Are we going?

Who are you talking with, Daddy?

Are we going? Are we going?

They are already here, *Manong*…

Good… you in Manila, are you all there?

We are all here, *Manong*. Including our children, we are complete…

Good. We are doing this because we don't know what will be next to happen. As you can see… can you see us, right? This is *Tatang*. He is breathing but look at his feature. His doctor said…

Are we going? Are we going?

What did he say?

That's his only word.

When did he start like that?

He started yesterday, although he had been bedridden for quite some time.

Does he have medicine?

Complete, of course… remember, he is here.

Then how?

When he was still able to talk, he always telling us that he wants to come to the Philippines.

Why didn't you allow him?

It was not that easy… We understand his feelings. But the distance between America and the Philippines is not like adjacent rooms.

How come?

We did everything, children. Not because I'm living him during the day, one of your sisters are here to look for him… we are taking part. When I arrive in the afternoon, that's the time when she goes to work.

How we wished to see him during his last moments.

How many of you in Manila who doesn't have work? How many of us here in America are jobless? We all have works. Our children here, they work during the day and they go to school in the evening. We are all busy. We might have time to bring him to a care center, but we choose to keep him by our sides. I know that we all love him, despite what… the past.

10. Nostalgia

I'M going home!

Where? This is your home!

I have a house there.

You don't have a house there. It was arrogated by your good nephews. All you had left behind, now owned by other people.

There's no evidence that they are the owner. There's no document. If you don't have document, you don't have something to show the court proving that you are the owner.

Documentation is no longer needed there. If they want to get your property, they can do it anytime.

That's not true!

Whatever you say. You are already an American no more no less. You're no longer a Filipino. Being a Filipino had been dissolved when you signed the document proving that you are now an American.

I did not sign anything.

You thumbed mark.

Am I already an American while I am still brown, and my nose is still flat? Don't I have anymore right to go back to the land of my birth? Don't I have anymore right to gain my being brown? My heart and my soul, I'm an undisputed Filipino. My being an American, it's only in the paper and even they turn the world upside down, they could never change the color of my skin, what I have in mind, the blood oozing in my veins. My heart still throbbing its borne loving, caring, culture, and every custom a natural born Ilokano like me could be proud of.

But you are already in America, 'Tang. What's the importance of going back to the Philippines? You are already on the warm cushioned bed; you still want to go back on the hard and cold floor.

I can't feel any tender care here. I don't know anybody in my neighbor. I can't hear any barking. I can't hear any crowing of rosters flying down in the dawn. I missed the laughter I used to. I missed a balled cooked rice I deep in to tomatoes with salt in the rice field during harvest time.

You're senile.

I'm not senile. I can still remember all my, all the smallest part of my life, they are still verdant.

Go there and your life be shortened. There's no doctor there like your doctor here.

If it's your time to die, you die for sure notwithstanding how good your doctor is. The doctor has not fault when his patient dies.

Whom do you miss there?

Your siblings... I pity them.

They are all married... Are they more important than we are here?

Do you want to live me being the youngest and still unmarried?

11. Within the Rim of the World – 4

AND we are concern about the situation of medicine there. If you don't have money, you die with untimely death. They even give you medicine which is not for you… you are the witness about that; they skinned you and sip your blood even you're bloodless. That's the reason why many come here for medical purposes.

We have a minimal savings… we'll not let him suffer.

Are we going to reverse what's happening? *Tatang* is in the condition needing the best medicine, can they provide there? Say, you can afford to pay, can you stand for those who own the hospital?

Your father is so weak. I am afraid his life be shortened on the way. We want to see him…

We want to witness his last moment.

That's his biggest problem. He loves you all there very much. He loves us here the same. How could he divide his body?

He's been with you for a long, long time. Excessively speaking, you owned the last half of his life. We are asking to see only his last moment. If the problem is his travel expenses, we all here help each other. We just want to see him.

12. Voiceless Word

TO all of you who are by my side… I nurtured you. I gave you opportunities. I brought you here where you can find your future. You can now stand alone without assistance from anybody. Your siblings, those two pities for them… they don't know where to get something for their pot. I know I don't have a child who doesn't care for me. But that is more painful to think about. You know, I don't like to be separated from you. But same to them. When I go down from this house just in case, you better think that I've been dead for long. I cared for you, my children…

To you who are in the Philippines… I want to talk to you, but what is the use because you can't hear me? We are far apart from each other, my children, we are far apart from each other.

13. Decision

MY children allow me to express my humble perception. I'm not your real mother, but I also loved your father, if not more than how your mother loved him, at least I tried my best to give all what he, your father, needed during our togetherness. Probably you did not accept me completely as a replacement to your mother, but I did not mind for please believe me, and I say now, that I cared for your father because that was really from within me. How I could explain, I don't know, I just feel it and that's enough. I heard a lot of comments of people, because he was receiving a monthly pension as a veteran, that was the reason why I accepted him. Probably in the first place, that was the intention of my parents for we originated from an impoverished family and I understood that nothing in their mind, like other parents, but for the future of their children. I just followed their decision. But as time goes by, I learned to love and care your father, and believe it or not, I felt as if my flesh was torn into pieces when he is hurt emotionally, more so these past parts of his life. It is not easy to decide, my children, and that saddened him a lot. He mentioned many times how he loved you all, how he loved us in the other side, to your half-sisters. How he wished to go back to the place he grew up and there he rests, in his beloved land, where he poured their blood with his companions who served the country. But again, and again, he looked at your half-sisters with teary eyes… It's hard to contemplate, my children. Myself either, I could not decide. That's why please help me. Help me follow your father's last wish. Whatever will be your decision, I oblige with all my heart, for you are also dear to my heart, for I considered you true children from my blood. I have only one wish. We don't make this a very difficult to accept this condition. We can't do anything but to accept our allotted destiny. We know that whether we like it or not, your father will surely go to his allotted worth…

Brothers and sisters, what can you say to what we had heard? You in the Philippines?

It's up to you, *Manong,* whatever your decision.

About you here… you three?

It's up to you, *Manong…* whatever your decision…

14. Conceding

HE was not blinking. His eyes were in one direction. After a while, mumbling. After a while, some whispered words come out from his withered lips, but nothing except *are we going? Are we going?* And his arms move as if he was reaching to whoever or yearning to go along. His second loved one who could not have kept herself away from his side.

There four engenders, the eldest among all of them in Yorkshire, and their three daughters with the second. They were so tranquil; as if nobody wants to break the silence. His son's children were also there, and his daughter-in-law, their mother. These grandchildren who sometimes, elbowing, as if they develop a shortness of breath due to the stillness of their world. They sometimes want to create laughing stuff but their mother looked at them meaningfully and so they just look down.

Probably they have the same in mind while waiting for the words of his doctor. He does not allow him to travel.

But he allowed him. As if he doesn't like to have a patient died in his custody. If he is not in his custody, he is free from any responsibility.

As if he was in the deep hole, or well, hearing the measured words. Even the last word of his doctor, where he mentioned about the latest mild stroke that attacked him, it did not register in his ears, more so because he could not understand the language of the physician. Even his eyesight, it was blurred foggy surroundings. But it was wonderful, for him, if that could be said that way for, he could not feel shortness of breath. He felt so empty. Even his thigh that always painful, as if it was weightless. As if he was floating in the firmament. That sometimes, an image was smiling at him, if that was an image, as if waving at him.

He did not know that they were sending him to the Salt Lake International Airport. That they boarded him to the airplane, accompanied by his second loved one, and the eldest among their children. He was not aware that the eyes of those who were left behind were following him until entering the world that was the gangplank of the airplane, until it closes…

15. Forgiveness

GOODBYE, Tatang. May you not feel loneliness anymore. Probably we won't see each other anymore but I will remember you as an exemplar patriarch, despite of little things that you had done. I accept that it took me a little while to amend that what you had done was not a little sin, that soiled your supposedly untarnished record. I also accept that I lost my respect to you during those times. Not because of us your children, but specially to our loving mother. Betrayal… is there any explanation to the immorality made? If you still remember, our late Nanang visited us in Manila many times—probably the number of places we moved to be the same number she visited us. In one of our boarding houses in Manila, that was infested with bed bugs, if I say it was full of bed bugs, no more no less. In that place that we stayed at where Nanang visited again, where she mentioned when there were only the two of us, that you were doing something fishy. This is what she said, no more no less: 'I guest your father is doing something fishy, Barok.' I understood a little bit what she wanted to say, but I did not put any deeper meaning, and I just said: Don't think about it. If I remember right, I did not mention to any of my siblings to what Nanang's observations. I was afraid to poison their young mind, for I was in doubt to the veracity of what Nanang said.

But her observation was true. It was manifested when she had gone, and when you brought the one you were tempted in our place in Balara. It seemed that a bomb was dropped in the home we were shaping, and it almost wrecked the family you built. There were situations that hindered that plan, until you met the substitute of Nanang.

Yes, Tatang, those incidents had been folded. More importantly, I had forgiven you.

Yes, I had forgiven you, Tatang. I can now bid you farewell definitely. I hope it will give you a hint and immerse into your bosom the warmth I am feeling right now. Now that you have been separated from us, it's the time that I really feel your value. The twilights that full of your good stories before we sleep, they will forever be verdant in my mind, and I will embed them to your grandchildren. The trait of the Ilocanos you grafted into our mind we will also implant to the awareness of your grandchildren and they will grow a true Ilocano here in this foreign land where they will also build their own world. Notwithstanding their distance from the land where their ancestors originated, they will always be Ilocanos hailed from your blood, in your heart and your soul. I hope we could do the best and it could be seen from them the image of their ancestor...

God be with you, Tatang. God be with you...

16. Let Us Go, Papa

HE felt the tight grip of his beloved on his arm.

Let's go, papa, *Tatang* has gone.

Yes, let's go, 'pa. we're not done watching Spielberg's A. I.

Let's go...

And he watched intently the airplane until gone beyond the white cloud.

17. Final Push

SUDDENLY there seems something pulled his right thigh. His beloved on his side was awaken.

My child, what's your father doing?

Why?

He looks different! Nurse... miss... My God...!

18. Let's Go, Beloved

HEY, are you that one, Inada? It's good that you are now here.

Hey, what's this looks like a white string... is this a string, or what, like a string keeping me afloat? What is this?

Never mind, Amada. Just come with me.

Are we going? Are we going?

Yes, let's go.

Where are we going? I felt difficulty…

Let me hold your hand.

I can't breathe, Inada. This one seems being stretched… my white string… see, becoming thinner… and thinner, Inada…

Don't be afraid.

You're so beautiful, Inada. You're so beautiful…! –O

First Prize, *Palanca Memorial Awards for Literature;* **Bannawag**: October 21, 2002.

Footpath

1. In the Beginning...

. . . MY father begot me, and I was born in this world. He also begot my siblings. My father-in-law begot my beloved. I begot my children...

I wandered in twenty-eight places from my origin, from the place of my birth, then in different places in a long span of time and my hope to end is like a thick fog in a long winding road—if this is the last—my pathway in the navel of the city having seasons divided into four, although it was clear in my forehead that the biggest thoroughfare in the world has no starting point and end. I dug from those places a lot of experience like a treasure desirable to many if not all the people with vivid vision to bloom from the first smile of light in the forehead of the newly born infant.

I can't remember how many full moons and stars I had counted in so many dusks but still seemed the nights were not enough for it blooms and blooms again the days that interrupt the fluidity of fishing visions, for the simple reason that the stars conceal during the day for the sharpness of the sun's smirk and it drives foresights that smoothly playing around the quiet world of amity.

I have plenty of dreams. Some of them fulfilled. Many more still hanging in the air.

I might be so different from the living stone being mildewed in a seemingly breathless rivulet going to the blue sea—for it never go up the stream. I fight against all odds in every page of the copious book of my generation's life. And I proved that the most difficult thing to do is how to look back while fighting against the bloodshed: I had a lot of slithered flailing.

6:00 P. M.: In Front of the *Computer*—1

THE cursor was disappearing at the end of the last word in the screen; waiting for a command from the wide-eyed monitor. The bulb attached in the arm-liked was becoming hotter pointing the keyboard. The timer was running at the right lower corner of the screen. Again, and again the monitor blinks and the screen saver appear. He immediately hit the space bar to go back to the screen.

From the right side of the monitor, seated was an unfolded Black Book: being blinked by the cursor in the screen the final letter from the line: ***there will be a wide pathway for the remaining people of the Lord...***

On the left side, mixed were the scattered SanDisk and PNY. Under the table, softly whispering was the tower. Beside the tower, the printer's green led was on, that on its mouth inserted about an inch thick of white paper.

He was so peaceful on his seat in front of the computer: he seems sleeping, but his eyes were glued on the monitor. Then suddenly his fingers dance on the keyboard accompanying *We've Only Just Begun* of the Carpenters from the media player. Words appear in the twinkling of an eye running after the cursor. His right little finger strikes the delete key whenever a coarse or wrong letter that form a word. Again, and again he revolves his swivel chair, then suddenly stops in front of the computer, and his boney fingers dance ones again on the keys of the keyboard, as if racing in culling seconds...

We've only just begun to live. So many roads to choose... velvety was that whispered melody.

1. Arrival

YOUR journey from the other side of the world had ended ones again.

You and your companions flew over an arched rainbow as if passing over the wide blue sea joining both the place where you came together with the place where you are heading; as if half of the rainbow was at the bottom of the earth making the world into one accord...

You are not sure what feeling you had in your first step on the land of your birth after so many years of separation. Your mind was divided: to your children, and the complete form of the country you arrive at. And you spread your views, as if your loved one was not by your side: what was the difference between the place you left with the place you are visiting? How are your children?

If not only the completion of your son's mission—he is the last among the five—you may not have time to visit.

Your mind flies outside the airport, to those who will meet your group. How would your three children with your wife, came in your mind again, who were not able to go with them because of over age, and only the two of the youngest were able to come? Was there a change from your son in eight years of not seeing each other?

Then come those who meet your group.

Not only your three children with your wife who appeared to meet. Your brother who owns the pick-up, and other relatives. Your wife was teary-eyed embracing each other.

You embraced your son.

How are you doing? You tap his shoulder.

I was burnt in the road for two years, 'Pa, he said. But fruitful.

O, you, you said when your eldest daughter embraces you. You're just remain a fish sauce?

Too much, Papa! That is my next mission. How do you know, maybe I'm going back to catch the rich guy in my mission field!

How about you? You look at your daughter in between.

You better get me, so I could catch a White guy! She smiled widely.

How is your business? You ask your brother while driving along the congested road.

A little slow because of the present condition of economy. It was affected to what happens with the WTC. But still breathing. It's just a little dancing with the transaction. It's funny because I did not complete my studies, but they are calling me engineer. I just remain unspoken... See, that building in the left side, we built it.

You're lucky.

As I've said, you need to know how to apply oil to your contacts to keep you close to the kitchen, as they say. We're just thankful with my wife for our present situation. For sure many don't believe. But I kept silent about them. Truth is, I have people to work all what we need, I'm only giving instruction.

You see what life is, you said to your brother. You even better than us graduates.

You looked like a shaft when the pick-up stops in front of your orphaned house.

You were informed that many of your belongings, and many of your magazine and book collections, where some of your writings published were consumed by termites. But the shelf you built some years before you left, was not touched by termites. The books and magazines and your manuscripts, they are still intact in their original place.

The cleavage in the center of the living room was no difference to a big crack caused by the root of the caimito or star apple you planted alongside the house. But it was covered by a carpet you brought home in one of your vacations from Dhahran where you worked for several years.

Your old small office in the extension, its ceiling was about to plunge and the table you'd been writing on has no use at all. The steel cabinet where you kept your records, that you could no longer remember, had been eaten by rust. There were some things inside, but everything in your office, they were more than a garbage. You disliked the whiff in the room that wriggled into your nose, so you did not go inside, you just pipped in, and you did not even investigate the content of that rusted steel cabinet.

Is this the house I left years ago? You reminisced.

There was a big difference between the house you left behind which was always cozy during stormy or snowy weather, or during summer time that the forest outside is burning with heat because of too much heat; you are not lucking of food to feed yourselves, clothes to wear, car to go around...

What were you been doing? Blamed your lovely wife to your children.

We did not have money for the renovation, your eldest said.

I've been sending money every month. And you have jobs.

Not even enough for our sustenance.

That's true, 'Ma. I even have a good position in my office, but salary is minimal, and a lot of deduction.

In my side, my salary is not even enough for my fare, the third said.

What then is the use of your education? Our tongues were almost hanged out bringing you to school, only to be what you're in right now!

The percentage of graduates are almost double to the number of job vacancies, said the eldest. Consider this, there are so many graduates every year—there parents were almost braking their backs shouldering their education of their children. But jobs are stagnant, not enough for the graduates. Even janitors, college graduates. There were even a lot of graduates who accept manual labor, or helper in the restaurant, or FX driver. More so the high fare, and every daily commodity. And you may have forgotten our brother was out for two years.

You better bring us, we've been telling you, said the third.

I've just arrived, your son said. But don't you worry, whenever I got a job, that will be my priority…

II. Alleviate

A temporary warmth could I share to soothe those who are in need in those places. How I wish to share even a drop of honey to moisten their withered lips. How I wish to share a piece of wool for them to huddle up.

Who should be blamed?

My heart is being throttled for every side glance under the sun; to every snow being spread in my world; to every blooming flower in the parks and in the yard; to every blooming leaf and deepen colors, because of the coming back and forth embodiments in other part of the world…

Because in the mirror of my memory there were the deprived individuals; that probably their bowels had never been lubricated the whole year; that probably they could only go to upbeat places for tourists via their dreams; that they can come to this place where starvation, and chilliness, and restlessness only via a dream.

For because sometimes I caught the groping tears on the wrinkling face of the mother when she was focusing her attention to the pictures on her bosom.

7:30 P.M.: In Front of the Computer—2

HE went back in front of the computer. He hit the space bar and the screen saver disappeared. The blinking cursor appears at the end of the last word in the program of Microsoft Word. He blinks several times inspecting the written lines.

He noticed the Blue Book by the right side of the monitor. After a while, the cursor starts blinking the new line behind it: **when the children be guided in the right footpath to follow, they will never be bewildered.**

His fingers dance in the left side, by the side of the keyboard, going along with *Top of the World* of the Carpenters from the media player.

There was a scent brought inside by the one approaching, two palms sat atop of both of his shoulders and feels the weight of the boney fingers.

The four tired stars met.

From those stars the past came back.

And the future.

I'm on the top of the world lookin' down on creation, pleaded the media player.

b. Place to Ascend-descend

YOU had three choices to go before you started your journey going north. The choice of the eldest was the place where she served a mission, that for her was a paradise; the place where she served a mission was the choice of the third; in the city in the mountain, where he also served a mission, was the choose of your son. You decided to go to the last for you will pass by going to the north. For there was a very important reason going to that direction: this might be your last chance. Your son was delighted for he could go back and get his things that left behind when he was released.

It seemed that the main road has no end going north. Just after your ride deviated from the main road, you noticed the vegetables, corn, sugarcane, rice, and many more in the field. Carabao, cows, goats, chicken, and many more domestic animals. The surroundings were green, but in between towns, our eyes were caught by the small and old houses—you missed those views because they were scarce from where you came from.

You looked at your children. Your two daughters were kidding each other, your son's head was caught by the views you passed by and telling what those were.

The zig-zag and ascending road was cemented. From the warm weather below, the breeze was becoming cooler while your car goes against the wind. From the withered view, as if the green trees in both sides were reaching the sky. The side of the mountain was stiff and the cliff on both sides were scary. The speed of the car was not fast compared to where you came from, but your feeling was like coming out every time you look at the cliff or when the do some zig-zagging and as if going down into the cliff. Sometimes you could follow a big track irking to get its luggage up. You noticed the heavy motor of your ride for it was mostly in second or third gear. Sometimes you look back where you came from and as if you are not moving forward from the zig-zagging road. Your daughters were terrified that much.

Is it not like a paradise? Your son said. You will see the place where I was climbing…

In one curvature, cars going up were heavily traffic, and in far up above, you noticed a burning truck. You did not know how far the closest fire station was, but it took you some hours before you get off from that situation. The views and proceedings in this place that probably no importance to your children but for you one of the miracles of humankind was being written in your mind. Just for example the buildings in the cliffs that look like patches in a rotten canvas of a painting. Many of the buildings seemed built over the other. Big and small. Buildings that much older than you in your sixties, but they looked like still strong enough to fight against the challenges of the nature.

When you stood up over the rim of a cliff by a park where many native products for sale, your feeling was at the rim of a paradise: the benched mountains, green and being embrace by fog, that houses or buildings on their side or the peek seemed masterpiece paintings.

Your son toured you in some places: ascending-descending. He introduced you to his friends and his mission president—different races.

This is a paradise, your son said as if he read what you had in mind. But there were also unpleasant events. Can you see those cliffs and buildings? They are remnants of earthquake…

Yes, you realized: a masterpiece of two different views!

That proved what you were hatching in your mind: in that paradise, it has a dark rim.

You were alarmed when you felt that the surroundings were becoming dark and cold: it was almost dusk. You need to go down and continue your journey. The footpath still long.

But it seemed that place did not allow you to get off from its bosom. The cars were so congested blocking all directions. As if they were drowsy where they were that time, as if this was the end of their footpath…

You were off from the congested traffic. You followed a direction different from where you ascended. But they were both stiff. The descending road was already dusky.

Even you were reminding your driver to be careful, you felt that your ride was going down like a spear, and the wheels screech when the brake pedal pushed hard when meeting another car in the curves by a cliff. You were avoiding thinking but still appears in your forehead: what would happen to the bodies drop from the cliff? Likewise, your loving wife and your children, they were soundly asleep, perhaps like you they do not like to think that they were in a ride in that moment of time in that likelihood and in that kind of place.

You catch up another car but seems unwilling to be left behind that was why your driver did not mind overtaking.

Suddenly the gallivanting of your mind ended by a sharp cracking in front. Your ride also suddenly brakes, and you almost dropped into the open cliff.

In the curve, you noticed below by the light of your ride the broken branches in the cliff and down below deafening scream and whimper, swallowed by explosion and flame tattered the thick darkness.

My God! Your loving wife exclaimed.
Your children open-mouthed.
The bus was full of passengers and they were all killed except three who
were in critical condition and brought to the hospital.
You thought: ascending... descending...

III. Back Side of the Face

WHY in the sense need to look back—that question was coming back and forth to my forehead, notwithstanding an answer was off and on, I was not contented. Sometimes I know the answer of my question but again I ask the same question, as if it was a nightmare. Sometimes I envy the youngsters for it seem they do not have in mind what I have in mind. Or am I guiding my mind too much to the things that never enter to the youngsters' mind?

Too much images are coming back and forth to my mind more so when I lay down and close my eyes—they smiled dancing from unknown corner of my brain and as if they were flippant enticing many other embodiments.

And then they come, gamboling: the past, the present, and the future. My mind become tired and I could not sleep.

Come and come the faces...

9:00 P.M.: In Front of the Computer—3

THE Black Book is on the left side, facedown and the binding was like a spinal cord of an old hunchback. The letters at the spinal cord and the face of the book but still looked like determined to fight against the whiplash of the transitory of time.

His eyes were focused to the blinking cursor: Face.

His face being warmth by a bulb connected to the arm-liked as if reaching the monitor was becoming stretched. The whisper of the tower was sleepy that makes the computer alive; the printer's led was still on, which was open for the collection of the fed paper being arranged by the right side of the monitor, on the head of the keyboard. More diskettes were scattered on both side of the monitor.

There was a light sound approaching: one wearing a duster holding a steaming cup. She put down beside the Black Book. Her attention was challenged by the screen where she read a line at the tail of the cursor: *a man who walked in the dark will see light.* She pressed both shoulders of the one seated then walked away.

His fingers ones again danced over the keyboard that accompanied *Solitaire* of the Carpenters from the media player and the letters raced each other to catch the cursor in the screen.

There was a man, a lonely man, supplicated by the media player.

c. Foot

THROUGH the light of your vehicle, you observed that the narrow road toward your father's village was newly cemented. A vehicle could hardly pass into the yard with many fruit bearing trees, and where ten houses were almost piecing together.

One by one people appeared from their doors. They were all your relatives. You did not expect their number. Why did they stick together in your father's area?

The house of your father, it was located at the end of the around ten meters long lane or front yard. The hasag lantern hanged by the mango tree beside the door was bright.

Your father stood upright looking at you all.

My son, Lord! muttered from his withered lips.

Do you still recognize your daughter-in-law, 'Tang? And here are the three eldest among your heritor. Two of them left…

Your children kissed the hand of your father.

Some say you looked alike your Father. You were only taller, more so that he was about to face back the heavens. Only as if he does not care the time consuming him. His muscles were still tough being challenged by the sun and rain along the dikes and rice fields. As if there were no signs of his sleepless nights and hardships and blood that he poured out in the war zone during the second world war. In his over eighty years of existence, time seems not strong enough to subsume him.

Your father said when you were alone that his neighbors came closer one by one when their lives turned tougher. You understood right away what he means, as answer to your question.

Your father had a young helper accompanying him, a son of one of your cousins at the end of the country in the north. He was the one who fished with a hook some mudfish, catfish they prepared for your group. There are now few fishes to catch but there are still some if you have enough patience. You enjoyed the roasted mudfish you dipped on a pickled pepper.

You noticed the framed picture of your father and your mother by the foot of the bamboo bed in his room.

The picture was already brownish but the eyes of your mother, who was not able to survive when she brought to earth your youngest brother, were still lovely.

You just learned: you could not go ahead northward that evening.

If only you could spend that night with your father.

For it might not be followed up any more.

The wooden floor you laid down was hard and despite your difficulty stretching your back at first, you missed the bed you used to—in the house you left behind, you have a queen size bed with your wife. Your father brought out a woven Iluko blanket from an old trunk and you remember those immediately despite of many years had passed. Your mother took good care of those, and notwithstanding its old smell you missed it and you embraced it tightly—you did not use it because it was warm.

You were awakened by the crowing, followed by repeated cock-a-doodle-doo, and you enjoyed it for it sounds like a melody brought about by the blossoming of daybreak.

Before you left, your father toured you in the rice field.

Your father was speedy in front, followed by your son, passing over the dikes of the field after taking your breakfast and as if he feels lightly pointing over the green rice field. Your wife followed behind you while your daughters were joyfully who every now and then snatch bowed stalk of grains then peel with their teeth.

You stopped in the middle of a dike and feast your eyes around where the rice expanded in the east. The essence brought by a morning breeze in your nose, made it fresh the times you were at the back of Sikkubeng during the planting and harvesting season. Your feelings flew you away and as if you were in a small paradise unreachable by the daily glitches. Those dikes, they were also footpaths being walk on by the awaken feet every morning, differed from the crossroads in the city where you shouldered your daily baggage.

How could you say goodbye to your face-like father? How could you live your origin alone shouldering his days? If you were him, where would smiles appear in your lips? Will there be left smile blossom in his withered lips?

Will this be the end of his own footpath in this life?

Go, my children, he said when you bid goodbye. Go now so that you could reach your destination. Don't worry about me. My world... here. Your world...

You could not express a word at the tip of your tongue.

You embraced your father tightly. Just think if you could see each other again you feel molten. Why was it this way?

IV. Smudged Image

TWO images were smudged but coming back and forth in the pupil of my eyes. On top of the mountain full of guavas there was a dwelling built of cogon grass, white bamboo, and floored with thin bamboo strips tied together. In the middle of the upland field in the north, a corkwood tree was fully bloomed with flowers. In the south side, a thick white bamboo going down below—climbed by vines of green edible yam fall of fruit and with roots rupturing soil.

The sun had just risen from the east. Beside the dwelling, there were two big earthen jars full of water drawn from a well in the far south. A Saint Mary-faced whom I first met in that occasion used to bathe me. She had a kind voice; more so by scrubbing my thick grime.

The leaves of the calendar dropped one by one and another smudged image came flying. In a certain village from a faraway place, there was downcast shouldering five children left behind by the lost one.

I tried to remember the face after several years. Was she still the same Saint Mary-faced? I'm no longer there, my son, she wrote me one time…

10:30 P.M.: In Front of the Computer—4

A cup where a drink was steaming has gone from the side of the keyboard. The Black Book has transferred to the right side, but its leaves were still open. The cursor was dancing the last line: ***narrow was a footpath going toward life.*** Nobody was sitting in front of the computer; water was dripping in the bathroom. The tower was still breathing and the printer's led was still on. Suddenly the screen saver dominates in the monitor, views were changing.

The arranged paper from the printer became thicker by the keyboard.

In the adjacent room, in the master's bedroom, not even a single sound.

The door of the bathroom was opened, then closed. The door of the room where the computer was opened then next the open-eyed monitor. Sweet was the *Only Yesterday* by the Carpenters.

After long enough of being alone, supplicated by the media player.

d. Sister of the Mother

IT was still early, but your daughters were already drowsy while your loving wife was silently focusing her attention to the views around; your son was touching you every now and then pointing the views you passed by. One of them was a bridge undergoing renovation for according to people was destroyed by a big flood or earthquake, or whatever catastrophe. Then afterwards, you now pass by a village consumed by fire during the wrathful politics. Then the church on top of the hill. Not long afterwards, comes the fields filled with vegetables. You remember that around a hundred percent of the part of the country were named by different saints.

You are telling all of these to your children, so that, you said, they be given an idea about the place where ancestors originated. Your son's eyes were bright listening while your daughters were just going along.

My world, son… here. Your world… *those were your father's words.*

And you reached the town where you need to stop by. That town you stop by is where your father hailed from. But you do not know anybody at all, if ever there were left from the leftovers. You did not have any news from them. You had heard only when your grandfather that this time was where he hailed from. But they gradually moved from one place to another: in the north, east, south. Afterwards, in other countries. Hey, we are relatives, suddenly you meet somebody to say. You're right, you just countered for your ancestors were all short people.

Here in this town was where some of the great writers and war veterans originated.

The reason of why you stop by was not because of his ancestors. The only living sister of your mother, who was flown here accidentally for she was born in the next town, was the reason.

You found her in the eastern part of the town proper. The face of the original Saint Mary-faced you had in mind, was completely different from what you have in front of you. She had already withered by time, squeezed by countless challenges saddled to this mother.

How bright were her eyes and smile on her shriveled lips and she embraced you upon seeing you!

Oh, my son, Lord, my son! Her eyes swam with tears when she looked you up.

Our grandmother is so beautiful with teary eyes! Your son said.

Your aunt responded with held up smile; your daughters gave back a shortened smile.

Your memories tightrope in many years that folded. She was a respected handmaid in the city, she did not work for her husband was earning a big sum of money being an Electrical Engineer. Go to school, even in a vocational school, her husband enticed her, but she did not listen. When her husband was defeated by tuberculosis, that their children were still small she was forced to grope in the dark and moved in a little village. There she was forced to crawl in taking care of her small children. She sold everything left by her husband, and when all gone, she experienced to miss enough sleep, and her tiny fingers were compelled to gather, and twine sticky strong-tinctured tobacco leaves. And she was taken advantage by a drunkard and slothful and they lived together until a bullet pierced his gibberish skull. You did not know a lot of events for it take so long for you to know everything. There were only tiny pieces of news you received.

There came a bridge between you when she read one of your writings where she read your address, and she sent you a letter. How many decades had you not seen each other?

I was praying for you, my children, asking the good Lord to let us see each other again. I was praying for your grandfather, and your grandmother, and your uncle. More so with your mother, your kind mother. To whom do I lean to for I am the only one left among us siblings? Your cousins? They could not even take care of themselves.

Those words of your aunt melted your feelings. True to truth your mother was so kind, but so with this left behind, and her mother who was your late grandmother. But time, if it was only possible, they won't sleep so they work, work, work, and work until their tongue's dangles.

Yes, this withered Saint Mary-liked, the reason why she was here, for she wants to live longer. She was doing her very best in serving other people just to lengthen her life. She was already more than seventy years old, but still active, or probably she was not thinking any hardship or any kind of whiplash of time for her reverie was to wake up the next morning.

V. Wave

HOW many years had I not seen that place? More than thirty? If I did not move out, what had it been my situation? Had I been molted or burnt by the salty water? That will also be my only place to wriggle at like a blindfolded carabao bringing the sugarcane mill round and round, my path had not changed, and I did not know a picture of other world except the few news I gathered. Probably our path with my loving wife had not met and most probably different souls had entered to the lives of my children. I should had been left behind looking up the stars and the moon and the sun through the

fissures and only a piece of tilapia-shaped fish *ar-aro,* or catfish or different variety of seaweeds like *ragragutirit,* or *pukpuklo,* or *balbalulang,* and *kulot* had I used to soothe the hanker of my children. But who had been provided me warmth on my mat? One that had been nibbled by the reef and rocky shoreline and mouths in the porch on the stairs to scratch uncombed hair in the afternoon or in the morning or noon time. I might have been singing the full moon with an out of tune not able to reach paradise...

11:59 A.M.: In Front of the Computer—5

A drink in the cup by the left side of the monitor had gone and on his right side was the Black Book.

At the back of the cursor stretched was: ***the earth will be full of the Lord's wisdom, like the water filling the whole sea.***

The mouth of the printer with led on its temple that always open was again filled with paper,

Smooth was the softer melody of the Carpenters' *'For All We Know.'* The direction of his temple was divided.

But he prefers that way for aftermaths come blending each other making the pictures more colorful being printed at the tail of the cursor.

So much to say and as we go from day to day, whisper was the behest of the media player.

e. Deviated

YOU advised the driver to speed up. You still have a long way to travel, you still have one to ascend before descending and continue traversing the long Camino real. You will pass by later where your mother was buried at the east side of the road before turning west and in that curve, the secondary school where you studied looks like not eaten by time, it seems bigger and became more arrogant on the hill it was erected. The public market at the western side of the school, and you could not recognize any of the buildings you passed by before entering the road going to the setting place of the sun. There, no more calesa, horse and rig driver you had seen. Instead, only tricycles and some jeepneys were waiting for passengers.

The road was concrete. It has sloughed, you said. But when you descended from a branch going to the right, you noticed concreted was not continuous. And most of its parts were potholed.

You graduated from sixth grade the school you passed by where you were met by teachers for one of them recognized you when you stopped to take pictures for the school and learned that you were her favorite writer. She asked your group to stop by.

You went directly to the reef edge for you passed by the village where you mold your younger years, and you felt the smile of the rocky shoreline and the reef where you wallowed when you don't have classes in high school. You did notice nothing changed; as if the waves you left still the same lovingly meet your eyes. You wove a lot of dreams within the waves.

When you stopped by the village, a lot of moon's smile and blinking of stars came back while scrutinizing the sloughed of the village in a new spotted view of the dug in destitute. The fissured dwelling where you hatched many visions had gone. The dwelling that replaced was like a sleeping turtle.

The tattered fried by saline attacked your group and your children acted to go back. There was tears in your lovely wife's eyes.

See what you left, my children, your boney uncle said. You left… you forgot the village you grew from. We were left behind sensitivity despite the impoverishment of those you left behind, they also have feelings to perceive.

Was it true, 'Pa? his eyes were focused in front of the car when you proceed to the east. You hold his shoulder close to you.

I. River

I used to answer my question *I don't know* before I think. As if I'm avoiding lengthening the moment of my mind inactivity.

Wriggled? Probably. If I'm visualizing, the events woven by my ancestors appear like a wriggled thread. The river of our lives differed from the Karayan Parsua that from the Candle-liked by the side of the big mountain in the east, its flow continued directly to the sea in the west, except its small branch connected to the creek in the north and then again connected in the west.

Our lives? It has a different direction. Like for instance a sparkler bursting like a flower up above then drop like petals detached from its stem.

We were thrown in many direction… We were scattered.

1:43 P.M.: In Front of the Computer—6

THE Black Book was put beside the newly gathered papers from the printer.

The cursor remains open-eyed at the end of the last word of the last line in the screen: *a good tree bears good fruit; a rotten tree bequeaths bad fruit.* The tower whispering smoothly. The melody smoothly whispers *(They Long to Be) Close to You* by the Carpenters from the media player.

The brightness of the bulb atop the monitor still the same…

f. Breadfruit Trunk

YOU focused your attention in both sides of the main road. You were observing the changes of familiar places. If there were changes made by time. The growth of buildings. And wrecked. The same road. the same acacias— how durable they were fighting unnumbered ruthlessness of time.

This is the town where your kind mother was born. Where its head in the east standing the Candle-liked, there was the origin of your memories: in the Pangasaan Elementary School.

You are telling all of these to your lovely wife and to your children.

You pointed the market in the right side. There I first eaten a sorbetes, you said. Ice cream, you corrected for probably they could not understand sorbetes. That you gave back the destroyed ice cream cone because of your licking then you ran away to look for your mother fearing that the vendor might get mad of you.

You reached the river of the creation. You asked the driver to stop the car at the molar of the bridge and you explained that you went up and down through that river connecting the place full of guavas up stream with the small village down below. There was a part of my young life in there, you said, more directed to yourself.

Shall we go see it, your son said.

Can you walk? Said your daughters.

We don't have time, your lovely wife said.

Your group became silent when you reached the entrance of the road going west.

Slightly cemented—looks like a splash of a leftover cement. It is narrow because it was hardly fitted for two cars going different direction. Warm was the wind caressing by the trees and bamboos in both side of the road. how many years had gone? You tried to remember. Were the barefooted still around; those who were left under the dewdrops when politics was in its prickliness? Was there anybody who would remember this crevice of the world? Its children who deviated, where were they now, you tried to think. But where were you as well? You remember it many times, but, how did you?

In your contemplation the road and the desiccated river in the north were in the same elevation. It came into your knowledge that when the river turns into stronger current due to heavy raining it will cover the whole site and the whole rice field, and it will meet the water heaved by the big creek in the south.

In the south side of the road you left behind the village where one of the parts of your life was written, but you suggested to pass it by in the meantime then you will stop briefly when you go back nonetheless you were not staying long. There was the most important part of your existence that you want to see right away, which was the reason of your going north.

That place where you first see the light. That place which had been in your vision for a long time. The image that had been woven in your temple, was so different to what you had witnessed. The river kept on moving to the south. The surroundings were verdant. But the road, my goodness, it looks like a narrow passage for you. The four dwellings, nothing has left. It's now grassy.

The breadfruit, you sow it, through the direction of the man you asked for. The blacken trunk where it was down being bigger than both hand meeting together in the act of embracing.

For your amazement, the trunk was still there. After less than six decades, that dropped trunk of the breadfruit was still there. And it was only a breadfruit, not considered as durable or struggling against the period. But there it is.

Under the old breadfruit which was that breadfruit, there a hut, or shed stood, and inside that dwelling, you behold the first light. It was there where your voice first heard by the world. And where your emerging days were almost stolen by a Japanese big flying bullet pierced in to the open window that stuck by the foot of the three-stepped stair. Even your mother was almost lost in that moment for she was getting you off from the cradle when a big ember which was that bullet flew by her face.

They, those who show you the trunk of the breadfruit, were your relatives. The people they mentioned, were the ones that make old names meet, that many of them had gone for a long time.

Those people whom your father had mingled with. They knew your father very well because he was a World War II veteran. He was hiding against the enemies during those times. He carried your elder brother running along the riverbank in the north. Along the row of bamboo trees in the east, your mother ran you also and even your whorl was hit by a bamboo thorn because of her attempt to keep you away from the Japanese and spies all over the area.

You closed your eyes to recollect and the views in your forehead became more verdant with the cold breeze that stroked your face with precedent time imprints. If only you were alone, now, you lay down under the shade of the tree at the south side of the broken trunk of the breadfruit and you let your grade studies back in your mind; the time when your leader bit the ear of the leader of the opposing group. The time when your group stole turnips, or full down stripe, vanilla, or ordinary sugarcane when you go home from school in lunch time or in the afternoon.

Were you really born here, 'Pa? your son said.

Wow, the views were so green! Your daughters exclaimed. But why were no houses?

You captured pictures before going eastward. Your son even takes you a solo picture beside the trunk of the breadfruit, with exuding emotion within your soul.

In your dropping by in a village which was part of your existence, you noticed its big transformation. The two big lychee trees at the southern part of the small piece of land. The houses you've known were gone. Replaced by small dwellings as well, like hiding chicks. You did not notice any sign of improvement.

You met some of your old acquaintance, whom you could hardly recognize despite you're the same age, because of a lot of signs of old age in their faces.

Life is too hard, one of them said.

There were only few of us left, countered the other one.

Those who left, they never bothered to look back…

Nobody listened to our yearning…

They were deaf…

There will come a time that the two rivers met to carry away this place…

How pity, it dwelled in your mind.

VII. Misleading

I was trying to hold back the aftermaths. But exasperating because it was stretched in a long line. My time would had been consumed but the thread will still be long that I doubt if my children would have courage to unwind because my world was dissimilar from their world like the dissimilarity of my father's world from my world. They would meet a deceiver like what happened to me.

3:51 A.M.: In Front of the Computer—7

THE cup ones again emitting steam by the side of the Black Book by the left side of the monitor where the cursor bopping: ***God will lead us to His pathway, and we walk through His footpath.*** Soft and lonely was the melody of *A Song for You* by the Carpenters from the media player. The cursor was gamboling perkily running after by the painted images in the screen.

G. Branched Off

YES, you've gone to the places you visited images of the past.

You looked at your children immensely.

The main road you traverse going back was long. You were all unspoken.

You were caught up by the dusk in the middle of three branched off the road: in the left, in the right and in the middle.

You missed the right direction, which was supposed to lead you where to go. It has been quite some time since the last time he drove to the north, and it was even night. This road was lengthy to get misled, you thought. It was not a joke the exhaustion for the driver, and gas to be used. You shake your head thinking you were now misled in your old route... for you were already a foreigner. Shame on you, you reproached yourself.

You spent a long hour zigzagging where you were misled. When you reached the right way, a patrolman stopped you because your taillight was busted. And you paid and confiscated the license of your driver.

Yes! Your son rose his two hands when you reached home. It was already daybreak.

Hey, thanks! Your daughters exclaimed. Your loving wife exhaled deeply.

VIII. The Kindness...

...MAY the kindness of the Lord be with you all...

It was very difficult for me to think of being away to you, my children. It was a heavy burden in my daily existence. But shall we just imagine that, we are upshots victims of all times. You are the reason of our being here right now. And you are nothing else the restlessness of our moments with your mother. Your documents are now on the way. But when it reaches the designated time, only God can tell...

There were parts of life that are difficult to comprehend. In our weaving of the future nobody could tell if we are doing the right thing—we just hope that we could reach whatever we want to obtain... in the soonest time possible.

5:00 A.M.: In Front of the Computer—8

The Black Book was kept in the shelf at the head of the monitor, beside the arm of the electric bulb looking down the keyboard but in the screen the cursor was blinking: ***the branch of the Lord was beautiful and glorious.*** The melody of *Where Do I Go from Here* by the Carpenters from the media player was softer. The printer's led emitting papers was still on like a big eye. The diskettes by the monitor were already arranged and there was only one being inserted in the mouth of the tower as being evidenced by its protruding button. The lines were also fast in going up, as if they were catching up times before filling up the paper…

Where do I go from here… tell me, the media player was asking?

h. Departure

YOUR group are here ones again. In your last day. You will be yearning again. You leave your children with twinkling eyes following your departure. They could not send you up to your flight, but in their minds, and in your minds, they will meet in your dreams and visions.

You will see the breadfruit. The river. The rice fields. Your father. The picture of your mother. You will hear the sobbing of the waves. You will see the walking skeletons. They will all upset your twilights.

Within the four corners of the house your group will destine at, within the four seasons that will toughen your inner souls, every epoch will become colorful. For the colors of the images in both ends of the rainbow will always be transparent.

In your vision, branchy streets people were incessantly wriggling, and cars were densely scampering, but National Roads will always be there where people travel in a hurry. Airports will be there flying different races of people to their different destinations in different time. There will be written stories of each one…

You have children waiting for your arrival, but more children you left behind who were incessantly begging under the sun.

You fly one more time. Where your path will end, nobody could tell.

But you will always be listening the melody of love that will douse your longing that will fly your soul that will help you forget that you were one of those who were uneasy, because your heart was full of unspeakable kindness, even your most understanding lovely wife.

You will never forget the almost same bidding goodbyes of your children: thank you, 'Pa, for touring us—we will treasure it forever.

I know you now, 'Pa, your son said.

And you always open that Book where the power of your soul spring forth.

Your group will fly as if you will be walking over the arched rainbow in a wide sea that bridged the place where you came from and the place of your destination—as if half of the rainbow was in the bottom of the sea that will bundle the world.

How long will you be flying, you know very well that it will end, and you know why… why you are where you are…

You held your loving wife close to you and you were tenderly let her head lean on your shoulder ones your ride was safely flying in the horizon.

You softly expressed the last line: the kindness of the Lord be with you all…—0

1/19/03, 5:51 P.M; 1/23/03, 12:52 P.M.; 1/28/03, 10:58 A.M.; 2/9/03, 11:49 A.M.; 2/10/03, 1:23 P.M.; 2/11/03, 11:8 A.M.; 3/9/03, 7:49 A.M.; 3/12/03, 10:49 A.M.; 3/14/03, 2:25 P.M.

Angels In The Cuddle Of Bundled Hay

I. Christmas 1962

THE sudden looking back of Ayong when he noticed Angela coming from behind was as swift as a slingshot. It was difficult to understand why at his age of about nine years, his heart feels jumping every time his eyes catch the two deep dimples of Angela. That feeling of jumping leaps up and suddenly his left eyebrow starts winking. Angela who loves to wiggle her butt stick her tongue toward him, and Ayong's feelings was like a touch-me-not when touched and seems like his jumping heart crawls in every part of his bosom.

"Why are you winking at me?" glanced Angela sharply upon reaching where Ayong, Abat, and Ansit beside the *karraang*[60]. For Ayong the sharp glance of Angela was like a newly bloom flower of touch-me-not.

"I… don't know," Ayong forced himself to smile. "Because when I remember the wink of *Manong* Boni to Manang Paring when they meet, my eyes do the same!"

"They say winking eyes produce ulcer on the eyelid as big as a fist!" Angela pouts still.

---

[60] *Karraang:* an underground furnace used in toasting white bamboo cake made of powdered glutinous rice with coconut milk and sugar and other ingredients.

Abat and Ansit snickered.

"Why are you winking Angela, Yong?" giggled Abat and his ax-sized coupled teeth showed.

Ansit prepared to sing and he looked up the sky using the tune of *Manang Biday.*

"*Manong* Ayong, wi-winking…winking… your eyebrow is very bushy!"

"These three dangling!" barks Ayong's father Isio smiling. "Don't be fling here…"

As if the four were deaf. Again, and again, Ayong, Abat, and Ansit pounce on the overspills of the bamboo-tubed rice cake being toasted over the *karraang* fired dug hole on the ground; Angela was just watching, laughs a tiny one then wiggles her butt a little bit, and her fingers met on her back. Again, and again, Ayong's eyes catch Angela's tiny starry eyes. Angela just stuck her tongue out toward him. Again, and again, Ayong's father Isio, Abat's father Masong, and Ansit's father Kanor bark at them. Isio and Kanor were brothers; Masong is the brother of Pinang the wife of Isio. Angela's mother Ibiang was helping Pinang keeping things used in mixing powdered rice (Angela's father Bantor disappeared like smoke when he went with others harvesting rice in Pudtol and nobody knew if an old Igorot woman was fascinated by him and hid him in the forest of Santa Maria.) The four were about the same age. They were neighbors in a dry field north edge of Abbarit. They were schoolmates in San Isidro Elementary School.

Ayong touched Abat, still his eyes stuck on Angela.

"'Bat, why is it that if Angela looks at me, I feel uneasiness below my navel?" Ayong munched.

"Better ask her," Abat did not look at Ayong. He continues munching an overspill he catches from the bamboo-tubed rice cake.

"H-hey, A-Angela," Ansit did a combination of squinting, athwarting, and puckering simultaneously. He was conceived by his mother to an *ariwaiw*[61] fish from the reef of Timmippang that's why he

---

[61] *Ariwaiw:* a variety of *bunog;* greyish, found in the reef area, around two inches long, with protruding eyes.

was squinting and athwarting, and fragmented when talks. "A-yong… yong s-said… why, w-when you l-look at him, he f-feels di-discomfort b-below his n-navel?"

"How do I know; I'm not touching his navel!" pouted Angela.

"You foolish!" barks Masong with wide smile. "You haven't had a cockspur yet; you already have a lot of nonsense in your minds. You probably heirs of the one who'd passed away!"

"Get away, don't fling here!" repeated Isio. "Go there… or you'll be roasted in the *karraang*…"

The three ran away toward the sled under the robust longan tree in the south. Ayong and Abat greedily munching the overspills they had grabbed. Ansit ran toward his banjo made of lizard's skin hang at the bamboo enclosure of their house.

Despite his athwarting and wide-opened eyes, Ansit is very good in playing banjo with nobody taught him. He could also compose songs while singing copying a tune of popular songs, or whatever he remembers. His voice is not abstracted when singing.

Ayong was about to throw an overspill into his wide mouth one more time but he glanced Angela looking at him.

"Do you like it?" Ayong offered the overspill to Angela.

"N-no,'" said Angela, but she kept her eyes to the overspill.

"Don't be shy!" Abat smiled widely and his ax-sized teeth appeared when he threw the overspill into his big mouth. "Beware, Ayong easily got mad when somebody disappoint him. He will never offer you when you ask… or do you like something from me?"

Before Abat's offer, Angela accepted Ayong's offer, with a side glance.

"She like Ayong the most, *yos*!" Abat said.

Angela stuck her tongue toward Abat then she sides glanced Ayong.

Ayong's heart wriggled. In his mind, a newly bloom flower of touch-me-not smiled when their eyes with Angela met in the air.

Ansit ran toward the three.

The three laid down to the sled. Their heads used the other side of the sled s railings, and the back of their knees on the other side of the railings. Angela sat on the yoke over the head of the sled's runner.

Ansit strung his banjo. The banjo sounded sweet mixing with his waving voice.

"*Pamulinawen*[62], *Yong surely was stiffened*," Ansit was athwarting and opening and closing his eyes extra wide with distorted lips. "No matter how you crush it…"

As if Ayong had step on a live coal when he stood up. "Crybaby!" he hit Ansit s head.

"*He will never have softened!*" tailed Abat.

"You too!" Ayong pinched Abat's ear.

Angela laughs with gusto watching the three.

"I know something," Ayong said. "Let's go caroling tonight, agree?"

"Oh, yes!" Abat said.

"I-I'll be the singer… you'll be the carrier, Bat," Ansit said.

"I'll direct where we go," Ayong said. "You, you want to come with us, Angela?"

"No…"

"We'll share you with whatever stuff we could collect… We'll go carol Old Marta… we'll give you everything we get from her."

"Hey, just go by yourselves!" the more Angela declined to go. "I heard that she is a witch!"

"Ayong will never wink you anymore… if you come with us."

Angela stuck her tongue.

"You're really a rotten egg, Bat!" Ayong hit Abat by his palm at the back of the latter's head. "The more Angela won't come with us."

Abat giggled. His ax-sized teeth spark.

"Sure enough, nobody will wink at me anymore," Angela said. "My mother said we will move out…"

"Where are you going?" Ayong said. He stops throwing something in his mouth.

"She said we will go to… Capay-odan."

"A-ay, p-poor, poor, A-ayong!" said Ansit with overly opened eyes and overly athwarting head left and right. He struck his banjo and sang

---

[62] *Pamulinawen:* folk song in Northern Luzon, Philippines.

in tuned of *Manang Biday*: "Angela, why you go away, ay; we will lose a companion, ay; Abbarit will be in veil, ay; and Ayong will be crying well, ay!"

"Crocker head, Ansit!" Ayong sharply looked Ansit sideways. "It's far better if we go to practice our Christmas songs… Let's go… now!"

"Want to come, Angela?" Abat said. "Guess you have not seen our hut made of bundled hay…"

The four went in queue. Ayong went first. Followed by Abat. Third was Angela. Ansit was in the tail-end and his leaning was unnoticed because it was accompanied by his practicing Christmas song. Accompanying with skipping walk. Even the first three, they are seconding the singing of Ansit.

The hut was in the middle of the dry land a little west of the tiny village, nearby Ayong's house. It has a small door, covered with two bundled hay. It was carpeted by thick hay, covered by old woven mat. Its roof was also covered with bundled hay, but there were spaces in between to let them pip the stars when they were lying down and joking. Ansit was always singing toward the stars, seconding by Ayong, and Abat in the third voice. They seldom lit the small lamp on top of two rocky soil away from the bundled hay and no spread hay under. Their father is always reminding them not to forget to put off the lamp to avoid being barbecued in no time.

"This is our precious kingdom, Angela!" bragged Abat. "Come inside," he swung his hand like a knight.

Angela obliged adamantly. She covered her nose upon getting inside.

"Stinky!" she pouted.

"Probably because of those blankets… those are Sit's blankets," Ayong pointed the unfixed dirty sawed together sock of flour. "That old Iluko-woven blanket was Bat's… I don't have a blanket," Ayong said when Angela feasted her attention round. "It's too sweltering for me that's why I'm not using blanket."

"He is not taking a bath that's why he uses his thick grime as a blanket!" giggled Abat.

"They are the ones who are afraid of water, that's why they had not taken a bath for almost a year… that's why their blankets are too stinky!" Ayong said.

"W-water i-in Chri-istmas time i-is very cold, d-don't you know?" Ansit struck his banjo.

"Is it nice to sleep here?" Angela asks.

"It's far better than in the house!" said Ayong. "Ansit is always serenading the stars, and the moon…"

"*O, very bright hole!*" sung Ansit. "*Surrounded by… stars.*" He played his banjo looking up the sky. "*What is our future, we are looking up above.*"

"*…Ansit the stinky!*" Abat seconded in out of tune.

1. First Caroling

BE careful," advised Pinang, the mother of Ayong. "Don't go near by Old Marta the witch."

"Don't you worry, Auntie," Abat said. "I have an oil to counter her…"

Ayong wore a sunhat. Abat in cap. Ansit in *bistukol*[63] with a timid tie, so it won't drop when he slants his head and squinting. Ayong brought with him a basket made of woven dried palm leaves which he uses when going to school. Abat carried on his shoulder a big suck which his father Masong use to put unhusked rice when they harvest. Ansit carried his banjo, and again and again, he played it; but Ayong stop him so that people they go carol at would not notice them beforehand. The moon was bright, stars were blinking. There few Christmas lanterns hanging on the windows were bright.

They walked side by side in a narrow path southbound to the housing area. Ayong was in the middle, Abat was in the right and Ansit was in the left side. In the far west, and south, and east, heard some caroling. There were even groups of drummers.

---

63 *Bistukol* is another term for *kattukong*, which has a wide-brimmed hat made from bottle gourd; widely-known traditional Filipino accessory of Ilocano culture.

"We go first in Uncle Kilin's place," said Ayong. "Prepare the suck, Bat. I'm sure they will give more than enough. They brought home a lot of white bamboo from the mountain."

"Auntie Pasing is too tight fisted," said Abat.

They call almost all their neighbors in Abbarit uncle and auntie. Most of them were relatives.

Their Uncle Kilin's Spotty barks continuously when they reached the ladder.

Ansit played his banjo. Ayong and Abat readied. The dog barks more angrily.

"Jingles bells," started Ansit.

"Jingle," Ayong seconded.

"Bells," Abat third.

Then they sang rapidly.

"Jingle bells, jingle bells… Our uncle has big… big thing."

The dog hauled.

Ayong hits Ansit's side.

"…Big heart," corrected Ansit.

"Oh, how… sack-fall of gifts," Ansit didn't listen Ayong. And he did it by himself. "They give to us."

The dog had nothing to do except to moan.

"'Christmas, Uncle," bellowed Ayong.

"Abat is… Abat is, waiting for a gift," tailed Ansit.

"Go sing in the next house and we'll wait for whatever they give," Ayong said.

Before Ansit attempts to go away, their Uncle Kilin appeared wearing underwear made from sack of flour. He handed three long bamboo-tubed cake. He sports a long smile.

"Your song is beautiful," he said. "Will you sing it one more time?"

"No bonus, Uncle," Abat said. "And we are in a hurry. But if…"

"Okay, I'll give you more," their Uncle Kilin said.

Ansit harrumphs. He played his banjo. And he aired his ringing voice. Seconded by Ayong and Abat. As if they were trying to harvest the twinkling stars and the ever brightly moon.

Their mouths were over-widely opened after singing.

"Be-autiful…!" their Uncle Kilin claps. "You're really good singers. You are the best singers' children," their Uncle Kilin said when Ansit finished singing. "Alright, I awe the bonus of your gift. Come back next Christmas and I'll double your gift." And he closed the door.

"Cheat-ter o-old man!" Ansit's eyes overly opened and athwart his head.

The dog whines and wiggles his tail and hangs his tongue as if it was smiling. Abat kicked it. "You, crazy dog!" he said. The dog cried.

"Never mind, for we got three bamboo-tubed cake," Ayong said. "We still have a lot to go caroling."

They went southward to the Farinas area. They passed by three houses. They selected the not so big.

"We'll try this," Ayong said.

Abat looked up toward the house. The lump's light in the living room was lazy.

"Maybe Mang Itok has been sleeping," Abat said. "See, they're so quiet."

"M-maybe t-they're not home," Ansit said. "T-they're newly m-married."

"If there is light, there are people," Ayong said. "Just play your banjo, Sit!"

"Wait," stops Abat. "Did you hear what I hear?"

"What is it?" said Ayong. "Your ears are like dog's ears!"

"Listen!" Abat said. "Look, hey, the light of the lamp of Mang Itok is dancing! Maybe there's an earthquake! Their house is cricking…"

Ayong and Ansit listened intently. They looked at each other under the bright big moon.

"Maybe they are caroling each other," Ayong said. "They are making a younger sibling."

"How did you know?" asked Abat.

"I heard one night when Father and Mother were talking."

"That Mang Itok and his wife are making a younger sibling?"

"'Let's make a brother of Ayong,' whispered Father to Mother. Then came the earthquake."

Ansit giggled. "E-earthquake, e-earthquake!" his eyes over-widely opened.

2. Second Caroling

THEY stopped at the first house they approached. There were lots of dogs in the neighborhood and they bark continuously.

"Take care of your legs for the dogs may bite them for Christmas!" Ayong said looking left and right.

"I would eat their liver raw!" Abat said.

"Be ready for the sack, Bat. I am feeling that Tang Bosyong will give a lot. Sing the most beautiful song, Sit."

"You seem like Ma'am Insiang telling all what to do, yos!" Abat said. Ansit played his banjo.

"*This house*," he started. "Second it," he told Ayong and Abat.

"*This…*" Ayong seconded.

"*…house*," Abat third.

"*…that we're approaching*," continued Ansit, and every time his song ended, Ayong and Abat seconded and ended. "*…the house of handsome Tang Bosyong, this might be where we could get more gift… Alright, Abat…*"

"Don't mention my name!" Abat hits the side of Ansit.

"*…come closer*," Ansit didn't listen to Abat, "*and accept what Nana gives. If it is small, ask for more. If it is a lot, same ask for more.*"

"Wonderful! The three hanging balls!" the old woman said in surprise handling her gift banana-leaves rapped rice cake. "We did not prepare white bamboo-tubed rice cake… we only have this," she said.

"Our name is not hanging balls, *nana*," Ayong said. "I am Yong, Bat is our carrier, and Sit is our guitarist. Our group is called Yong-Bat-Sit…"

"O, yes, the three hanging balls!" repeated the old woman.

"That wrinkly old woman!" murmured Abat after turning away.

"H-her face is l-like a batt of a f-frying pan!" Ansit said and played his banjo very hard.

"Just keep quiet," Ayong said. "They said it's not good to be temperamental during Christmas."

"Who told you again?" munched Abat.

"I dreamt of it," Ayong said.

"D-dream of A-Ayong the stinky!" hummed Ansit.

"You cracked! I'm not stinky!"

Abat guffawed.

They slowed down in the third medium-sized house they approached. They looked up it. Ayong stops.

Then he walks again.

"Why?" Abat said.

"Can't you remember?" Ayong said. "Apo Bantor's family is not giving anything on Christmas day."

"W-why m-maybe?" Ansit said.

"They are tightfisted," Ayong said.

"Who said?" said Abat.

"I told you so! Why, you two don't believe? The truth is, they don't have Christmas!" Ayong said. "*Nanang* said, they don't… I forgot what she said… they just don't have Christmas."

3. Third Caroling

AYONG, Abat, and Ansit approached the newest house in the south. The windows in the first and in the second floor were decorated with lantern. This was the first house with galvanized roof in Abbarit. The three don't knew very well the owner. Their parents said that they were relatives, but they were out from Abbarit for a long period of time because they went to Hawaii and they just came back after *Apo* Porong retired from his job in the sugarcane plantation. People were adamant to approach them because they feel humiliated by the rich people.

"Do you think *Apo* Porong gives some Christmas things? Ayong Said.

"Why, don't they have Christmas as well?" Abat said.

"M-maybe they l-left in H-Hawaii," Ansit said. He played his banjo very hard then stopped it by his palm.

"Will we try?" Ayong said. "If they don't give…"

"I-I'll sing the '*leaves of noni, merry Christmas, stingy, come down you t-tightfisted and I hit you with a walking stick!*'" Ansit said.

"Then we'll come back and burn it!" Abat said.

"That's not good, you cracked!" Ayong said.

"The tightfisted, they are not children of God. That's why they need to be burnt alive!" Abat said.

"Who said that?" Ayong said.

"I said so!" Abat said. "*Nanang* said, they'll be sent to hell. The hell, they said a flaming fire. That's why we will roast them alive!"

"*Roast him yes, roast him alive!*" whines Ansit in tune of *Hark the Herald*. "*Apong Porong the tightfisted!*"

"Let's go then!" Ayong said. "Sing the song you are hiding under your stinky blanket, Sit. Do your best…"

Ansit played his banjo with gusto. He looks up the sky, as if he was harvesting the stars and the moon. His eyes were focus to the constellation in the middle of heaven. He shouted the Christmas song he composed in tuned of *O Bright Moon*. Before seconding by Ayong and ended by Abat, Ayong asked why the tune was like that.

"I composed it," Ansit said. "I-if you don't l-like, d-don't sing!"

They did not have choice but to sing with him.

"*O, star that's twinkling, which appears in Belen, our sing please listen, then our gift be given; when Apo Porong gone to bed, please, please, let him awake, to hand us his green bucks, and fill the suck of Abat.*"

Abat hits Ansit's side. He did not sing the last line.

"*When they are awakened,*" continued Ansit, "*Abat is speeding, to receive the money green, a gift that is given; many things they are giving, Apo Porong is very rich, they give a lot of gifts, to make their lives better, and much longer on earth.*

"*We are now very grateful, they are sharing their riches, so that we are also blessed, during this Christmas of Jesus!*"

Ayong has not yet yelled Merry Christmas, Sir, but the wide door had opened at ones. There displayed a tall, bald, semi-big-eyed old man who worn oversized flowered shirt. The edges of his lips almost reach the lower tip of his ears because of his wide smile. He challenged the three to go in.

"I like your song," *Apo* Porong's high-pitched small voice sounds like a tiny bird busy catching something. "Come in!"

The three were adamant. They were open-mouthed, eyes overly wide-opened slowly investigating every part of the house, they walk as if counting every step.

"O, my God! O, my God!" because of wonder Ayong's voice sounded like a whisper. They use fluorescent light, big soft sets in the living room waiting for the kisses of their butts. The flooring was made of sandstone. Hanging curtains were white.

Abat and Ansit were speechless. Ansit might have even forgot his mannerism.

"Praning," Apo Porong called his wife.

The old woman came out from the door in the right wriggling her butt like a duckling. "Yes, Dear?"

"We have three visitors… angels!" *Apo* Porong said. His smile was still playing on his lips where his lower edge of his two ears were hanging. "Give them something to make their tummy warm… what are your names, and your parents?"

"I am Yong the son of Isio and Pinang," Ayong said. "I am the head of the three of us…"

"Because he got the biggest head," added Abat. "And I am Bat the son of Masong and my late *Nanang*… If not because of my uneven teeth, I'm surely the handsomest of the three of us and in the whole Abbarit."

"M-my name is A-Angsit, I, I should say Ansit," Ansit said. "M-my f-father p-produced me…"

"The name of our group is Yong-Bat-Sit, sir," Ayong said.

"So, you are still my grandsons!" *Apo* Porong said. "You're so shy, so we do not know each other!"

Apo Praning came back holding on her palm a tray with three cups where aromatic chocolate was steaming. From its smell only, the three started swallowing.

"Don't be shy," *Apo* Porong said.

Abat sips at ones. He was on tears spitting out the hot drink in the cup. He covered his mouth. "My tongue is blistered!" his whisper to Ayong was almost unheard.

Ayong brought the cup close to his mouth. He sips very little. He blew the cup. He sips again a very little. He enjoyed it. He blew a bigger one. He sips a bigger. It tastes very good, Lord! He said to himself. But my good boy, it is too hot!

Ansit was so careful bringing the cup close to his lips, using his mannerism of making his eyes big and leaning his head side to side. Again, and again, he brought the cup away. Again, again, he brought it closer. The aroma of chocolate was penetrating his flat nose. He is producing a cupful of saliva. He blew it very little. He blew it the weakest. It again penetrated his nose. He closed his to enjoy the sweet aroma. He blew again. And again. And again. Every blow followed by smelling the aroma. Then his exhale-inhale-exhale–inhale. Afterwards, not only exhaling and inhaling, he even swallowed his abundant saliva. He had forgotten the mannerism of his eyes and his head!

Ayong hits Ansit's side. "What are you doing, nuts!" he said. He had drunk half of his drinks.

When Ansit noticed that his drink had cold, he tossed it at once!

They were sweating profusely looking at *Apo* Porong smiling with a half-of-foot-long smile that made the corner of his lips and the tip of his ears met together.

Apo Praning brought each of them packs of chocolate as big as their palms. By Ayong's estimate, probably there were twenty pieces per pack.

"You are good," *Apo* Porong said ones again. "From whom you learned your talents of singing and… to play banjo?"

"It is Sit, Apo, who is good to sing and to play banjo," Ayong said. "He got it from his great, great grandfather. And Uncle Kanor his father taught him as well."

"You as well… I like the blending of your voice."

"We are not saying thank you, *Apo*, for we will come again next time!" Abat's smile hang out.

The old man laughed. The old woman smiled.

"Just say Grampa, you silly… Because you were the first children who visited us this Christmas, you have some gifts… that bags of chocolate your Gramma gave you."

Many more stories relayed by the couples before letting the three go. They have children left in Hawaii, and some grandchildren. They even asked them to sing, and the better the blending of their voices, with even action as there was something they were harvesting from heaven. They sang one more time *Naraniag a Bituen*. Apo Porong and his wife gave more packs of chocolate as Christmas gift.

The three had not yet gone that far, but they let their subdued feelings ones and for all. They jumped, and jumped, and jumped! They yelled and yelled and yelled. "Yos! Yos!" they said and embraced each other. And then Ayong said: "I will also go to Hawaii! Promise! Nothing could stop me… I will go to Hawaii!"

"Wait," suddenly Abat became serious, covering his bubbled lips. "We have one each with Sit, why do you have two, Yong?"

"I will give one to Angela," Ayong said looking up the sky.

"But she did not come with us…"

"Poor little girl. Nobody gave her a gift; her mother not even prepared a *tupig*[64] or white bamboo-baked rice…"

"You're moving our hair whorls again… I did not hear nothing from Angela… Did you hear something, Ansit?"

"N-not e-even a lizard's whisper!" said Ansit.

4. Fourth Caroling

THEY reached the big dike in the eastside of the village. They sat at the edge of the dike facing east looking down the wide rice field spread by rice with ovum in the bosom of Kabanayan. The breeze was cold in the dash turning old bringing the fragrance of the rice field in their noses.

---

[64]   *Tupig:* a glutinous rice rolled up in banana leaves and roasted in the oven or over hot ashes.

The attention of Ayong was focused to the small hut in the southeastern side of the village. The lantern in the window was as big as where it was hanged. "Is the suck already fall, Abat?"

"Not yet, but it is already heavy," Abat said. "We'll use your basket next…"

"Can you see that?" Ayong pointed the small hut.

"House of *Apo* Marta the witch," said Abat and Ansit almost simultaneously.

"Let's go a-caroling her," Ayong said.

"Hey, just go by yourself! Your mother said…" Abat said.

"I-I d-don't like t-to die y-yet!" Ansit said.

"You have antidote, right…" Ayong said. "See, her lantern is so big and bright. No doubt it is the biggest in Abbarit. She is waiting for us."

Abat grope his pocket. "I left it!"

Ayong thought for a while. "Let us go," he insisted. "Who doesn't want to come, he doesn't have testicle! And I already said she is not a witch."

What Ayong said is final, he pursues it; nobody could stop him.

"You don't believe it?"

"Only when she had done it to us."

"How, when you are dead already?"

Ayong quivered upon remembering the cemetery.

"I-I don't l-like to be b-buried y-yet!" Ansit's voice trembled. "How does it feel t-to b-be buried, Lord?"

Despite of having been scared, Ayong walked ahead. Followed by Abat. Ansit was behind by two meters, murmuring: "I-I don't like t-to die yet! I do not like yet!"

"Sing beautifully, Ansit," Ayong said. "If not, *Apo* Marta will inflict you with black magic!"

Ansit accompanied the Christmas song he composed and based to the tune of *One Night I Galloped a Horse.*

"Why is it like that again?" Abat hits Ansit's side.

"I-I am t-the composer, n-not you!" Ansit said. "If you don't sing, you will b-be the one B-Baket Marta inflict her black magic!"

So, they sang *I Galloped a Horse.*

One night, we went caroling, house of Apo Marta our neighbor; twinkling stars our guide, so that we will not be inflicted with black magic...

"Your mouth!" Ayong hits Ansit's side.

"So that we will not stumble in our way..."

They have not sung half of their song, but the old woman had opened her door.

"Come up, my grandchildren! Come up!" she invites them.

The three looked at each other. Abat and Ansit were about to run away, but Ayong held their arms. In the corner of Ayong's mind, he prayed: "Lord,

have mercy on us!"

"Be seated, my grandchildren, be seated," the old woman pointed the dwarf dining table in the kitchen. "You know, I cooked a big potful of chicken congee. I killed my only chicken. The rice I cooked was harvested in the mountains of Kinwang. And I also cooked *patupat*[65]!"

"As if we do not know!" whispered Ayong to Abat and Ansit.

"She feeds us before inflicting black magic!" Abat's whisper was so soft.

The tiny and skinny body of the old woman was in highspeed in preparing the cake. She used oversized coconut bowl, and the spoons she used were also wood. Her deep eyes were smiling, as well as her tiny lips.

"Okay, eat, my grandchildren," the old woman said.

The three looks at each other. The chicken congee smells enticing and Abat's tommy was inviting.

"Don't be afraid... I will... not inflict you with black magic!" the old woman's voice was burbling.

The three were about to ran away.

But the old woman sobbed. "Common, my grandchildren, eat."

Abat and Ansit spooned simultaneously. They feed themselves simultaneously.

---

[65] *Patupat:* soft pudding made of glutinous rice and sugar carefully wrapped in plaited buri palm leaves.

Ayong uses his spoon. But he did not put into his mouth. He watched Abat and Ansit.

In the corner of his mind, if Abat and Ansit die, he run home to tell what happens.

Abat and Ansit loved the chicken congee. They munch in highspeed.

"Why, my grandchild, are you not eating?" the old woman said to Ayong. "Are you afraid of me?"

"Y-yes… n-no, 'Amma," Ayong said and he closes his eyes when he fed himself. Have mercy on me, Lord! His mind said.

"My husband and two children died simultaneously in Tiktikrubong. They were still young," the old woman said. "That was probably the reason why they called me a witch."

The three stop their spoon in front of their wide-opened mouth. Their eyes were focus to the old woman.

"The people had twiggy tongues. The mongering followed me up to here in Abbarit. If only I were a real witch, I had killed them all!"

The three eat faster. They finished almost simultaneously; burped big. The old woman was in an act to give them seconds, but they burped the bigger, then they said almost simultaneously, they were already full.

The old woman gave them a lot of *patupat* when they went home. "I prepared those for you," she said.

The three were observing themselves while walking slowly along the dike northward. They had the feeling to throw the *patupat* away but Ayong's forehead said no.

"Beware if tomorrow I won't wake up anymore, Yong!" Abat said. "If I say I'll come to spook you, I'll come!"

"If I say nothing will happen to us, nothing," Ayong said. "If ever, slash my ear!" But inside of him, he said: Please, Lord, don't let it happen!

"W-we s-slash your ears, Yong-yong!" Ansit widely open his eyes and nodded.

5. Last Caroling

LET'S stop by Angela's place," Ayong said. "Let's go wish them Merry Christmas."

Abat and Ansit were hesitant but Ayong drugged them.

"I-I don't like to sing anymore," Ansit said. "I-I'll just a-accompany you."

Ayong fixed his stand and looked up the heavens. He massaged his throat, then let his voice fly: *Sa-aylint nayt, ol is brait, ol is kam, ron yon birdyin mader en tsayld, oli empan so tender en mauld…*

"I don't know its continuation anymore!" Ayong hits Ansit's side.

Before Ansit able to continue, the window was opened, and Angela and her mother appeared. They let them up.

"We did not prepare," Angela was coy.

"That's true, my children," her mother said. "Because we did not have something to cook…"

"We are not here to ask for gifts, *Nana*," Ayong said.

"Ayong is here to give Angela a gift, *Nana*," added Abat.

Ayong was timid to offer a bag of chocolate to Angela. "Your share from what we collected in our caroling from *Apo* Porong's…"

"This *patupat* also," Abat offered to Angela. "We got it from…"

"…From uncle Kilin's," Ayong was faster than wind to add.

"You are so kind, children," Angela's mother was teary eyed. "We will miss you when we're gone."

"Is it true that you are moving, *Nana*?" Ayong said.

"After the New Year. Maybe…"

"Y-Yong's heart will b-be c-crying, *Nana*," Ansit strung his banjo. And sang: *"Bannatiran, your feathers… white. You are going away; you don't have p-pity… at all!"*

"It's not white!" Ayong secretly hits Ansit's side.

6. In the Cuddle of Bundled Hay

AYONG and his friends dropped the gifts they caroled to their respective houses. His mother saw the *patupat* and eat at once because she loves that much but they were not able to cook. Bless my mother, Lord! he whimpered in his mind.

Abat and Ansit were enjoying in munching their piece of chocolate. Ayong nips his share like a mouse. They joyfully laying down in the cuddle of their bundled hay hut.

"It should always be Christmas, right?" Abat said.

"It could not be," Ayong said. "There is only one Lord Jesus, the son of Virgin Marry."

"Virgin Mayyang should bear a lot of Jesus so that there will always be Christmas," Abat said.

"W-who is M-mayyang?" Ansit said making his eyes big.

"The mother of Lord Jesus. The old Maria in Bacsil, they call her Mayyang, then the mother of Lord Jesus is also Mayyang."

"Your father will tear your ears when he hears you, silly!" Ayong said.

"W-why not all d-days are Christmas?" Ansit strung his banjo.

"So that we are always happy," Abat said. "Father said, if it is always Christmas, there will be no old women grabbing each hair and chopping old men… And don't you like us to always eat *tinubong*? And probably Apo Porong will always give us chocolates…"

"… And *patupat* of *Apo* Marta," added Ayong.

Abat and Ansit tap their tummies.

"I think my tummy is aching," Abat's voice is inaudible.

"I-I think m-mind too," Ansit said.

Ayong laughed. But shortened because he remembered Angela and her mother who ate *patupat*. If *Apo* Marta is a real witchcraft, we will all die, Lord! his inside trembled. He wanted to change his mind, but his head is firm.

Ayong pipped the stars from the spaces of the bundled hay. Lord, please don't allow Angela and her mother to move out…

"Yes, my son, I will not allow them to go!" the voice from his side was like a thunder.

His neck was like sprung looking to Abat.

"Abat the uncircumcised!" Ayong hits Abat's skull.

Ansit giggled and at the same time he strung his banjo.

They awaken in the morning when the sun was already pipping unto the spaces of the bundled hay when the entrance was opened widely.

"Wake up you, sleepers!" a voice coming from outside was small and sweet.

The smiling face of Angela met the big eyes of the three. They looked at each other.

They simultaneously touched their belly.

"It's not aching!" Ayong's voice was inaudible.

"It's not aching!" Abat opened his eyes widely.

"I-I f-feel like pop… a-ay, no it's not p-painful!" Ansit opened his mouth and forgot to close.

"Ayoooong!"

Ayong got a very long smile upon hearing the voice of his mother.

And they woke up simultaneously. They stood up simultaneously. And jumped.

"Merry Christmas!" they yelled.

"I have something to tell you," Angela said. "The chocolate was yummy… and the *patupat*, mother loves it. And said, we are not leaving… because she said she was thinking of you."

"Yippi, yippi!" Ayong jumps and jumps and jumps. Abat and Ansit watched him, a little while then followed through.

The bundled hay was shattered and the three were shrouded. Angela laughed at will when the three got their heads out from the rubble of the bundled hay, with lengthy smile.

II. Christmas 2003

MERRY Christmas, Bat! How is Seattle? Your family? You Sit, how are you in Canada? The stupidest of stupid, you are expanding like a Hippo!"

"Hey, Yong, Merry Christmas! Had your first grandchild with Angela been borne? How are you in Alaska? By gully, seems you are frozen for you always have good health!"

"Do you need bundles of hay there in Alaska, Yong? My youngest, by gully he is the heir of my being Ansit! But he is a computer wizard, mind you!"

"See what lucks gives. Who knew we could come to where we are right now? And see, we are meeting and conversing to each other through the computer!"

"MERRY CHRISTMAS AND HAPPY NEW YEAR!" they greeted each other in unison.

(Yong-Bat-Sit whispered that where they are right now is a blessing! He! He!) –0

2nd edition, 12-28-02, 3:07 p.m.
3rd edition, 01-05-03; 5:04 p.m.
Bannawag, May 26, 2003
Translation completed: May 26, 2018; 10:50 p.m.

West

Voice I

I know you arrived in this life around seventy years ago. But this came into your realization only by a gradually blossoming of your mentality. I followed you wherever you travelled. Whatever you do. All your laughter. All your sorrow because of misery. All your triumph. All your happiness. From the bosom of your caring mother. In the cradle of your loving land of birth.

I did never leave you alone in your lives.

But there were a lot of times you did never realize my presence by your side. Perhaps seldom did I come into your mind. More so when at times you were enjoying bundles of blessings.

For I do not have a voice you could ever hear. I do not have an image you could ever see. For you to remind me always.

For it is not my duty to portray my own image. I am not the one to let my voice be heard.

You should be the one to build my image, even just in your imagination. You be the one to listen to my voice, becoming a song or melody in your heart and in your mind. For my image and my voice, be your guiding spirit in every moment in your whole life.

But what are you doing?

Introduction

AS if there was a voice whispering me… so it was true that you had not taken a shower yet!" *Tang*[66] Mike was nailed down by the doorway of *Tang* Dave's room. "You must be reading Playboy again?" he peeped above his palm the magazine *Tang* Dave reading by his half-closed eyes by the edge of his bed. The venetian blind of the window in the east was fully spread and he noticed the tinning gray hair of his friend whose back was by the window.

"*AARP Modern Maturity,*" *Tang* Dave rubs his eyes. "This is a good article about the generation of Kofi Annan. He said: '*You don't hit a man on the head when you've got your fingers between his teeth.*'

"Who is that Kofi Annan?"

"He is the Secretary General of the United Nations. It is his second term. He is also aged but he was unanimously voted by the UN members after receiving his Nobel Peace award. He is taking care of us…who had been in this life for quite some time… You should also read once in a while so that time will not pass you by. You are far behind, Miguel…"

"Mike, just call me like that because we are already here in America. The previous Miguel is no longer in the paper. I guess they call this period computer age… and just say old man. Why, you could no longer hide that you are already an old man. You are already seventy."

"Kofi Annan is thinking about the future of the worldwide aging…"

"Do you think, can he still control the aging? Can he bring back your seventy into the time when you were younger?"

"No, but he can give you hope to be happy in traversing the remaining days of your life."

"O, my, you better go take a shower because we go somewhere. Don't say you had forgotten." *Tang* Mike scratched his nape and turned back.

Tang Mike stares at what he was reading seriously before closing. He laid the magazine on top of his bedside table. He inhaled looking eastward where the window of his room is facing. He had opened the

---

[66]   *Tang,* a contraction of *Tatang,* term of respect to elder man, or a father.

venetian blind earlier, but he did not unlock the lacked glass window. Nevertheless, he could clearly see the clear sky in the east. And the globe willow tree in the southeast side of their apartment. The robust tree had become leafy and its global shape is now in the exact form.

It was just in the first week of April and Spring which was one of the four categories of seasons in America was about in the midpoint.

Tang Dave stood up. He spread his feet and stretched his arms sideways. And kept on jumping. He counted. Then exhales repeatedly.

"What are you doing again…" *Tang* Mike aimed up his head. "My goodness, Lord, why aren't you tired exercising!"

"To make life longer, Mike. To make it longer," *Tang* Dave said without looking back Tang Mike.

"What do you want? You want to reach the age of Methuselah? Crow's feather needs to turn white first!"

"What do you know, it becomes a miracle?" *Tang* David continued what he was doing.

"Jesus!" *Tang* Mike scratched his nape. "You know why I still have patience on you?"

"Because I still have patience on you!"

"No! No! Because you are a *Saluyot*[67] like me! And we have the same luck. Had you not been thinking why we followed the same path and met in the crossroad despite the width of America? If not because you looked like so miserable the first time, I saw you at the City Park… If I did not invite you, where were you stay? When your White wife disposed you like a garbage… But forgot the past… we'll just pretend that we are both lucky when our pathway met. Do you remember that I told you, that many wanted to come and stay with me, but I was choosy of people? Even in the first time I saw you, I knew at once that we were in the same ship. But, hey, it's becoming late. You haven't taken your breakfast…"

"Why is it, Mike, that the old people love to think over and over again their past?" *Tang* Mike side-glances *Tang* Dave.

---

[67]   *Saluyot:* Jute, a sobriquet given to Ilocanos.

"Hey!" *Tang* Mike side-glances *Tang* Dave sharply. "I said, move...! You're like a deaf child."

"It's not good to be in a hurry, Mike, more so when you are already old," *Tang* Dave said. "Preserve your remaining strength for the coming days."

"Okay then, just to make you stop… Go take a shower. After taking a shower, go directly to the kitchen because I am going to prepare our breakfast."

"Thank you very much, Mike. Because of what you are doing to me, I am reminded about my lost first wife."

"Stupid old man!" *Tang* Mike said and turned away toward the kitchen.

Tang Dave brought clean clothes for changing. He went into the bathroom. He was so careful to turn on the faucet of the bathtub for he did not like the water to be too hot or too cold. It is hard to become sick, he always reminding himself.

When they face the fried rice with garlic, a piece of egg and hotdog for each of them prepared by *Tang* Mike, *Tang* Dave inspected the food before eating.

"Our food intake should be balanced, Mike," *Tang* Dave's voice was soft. "It should not be egging every day. It should not be meat every day. As well as it is not good to be vegetable every day."

Voice 2

I am always awake. I know the meaning of every rustling sound made by unfolded pages. I know if the printed words are light or dark. I am in your pupils, Dave which was David when you were in Sabang which you decided to change when you became an American. Despite becoming an American citizen, you are still the newly borne David I followed ever since. Your mind was hatched by your successes and failures. Whether in work or in love. Despite the rolled days and spread nights, you always wake up the next day and face east. Where the sun rises. In any season.

You seem like twins, Dave and Mike, which was Miguel in Saud, since your pathway met. When you go out together, you look like the only people in the world. If one of you have something to eat, you eat together.

There was probably a single strand of your veins not joint: no specific place you face, Mike, when you wake up, either east nor west, south or north. You both sleep on your back. As if you are looking up the ceiling of heaven. That every night your bed cradles your bony back, as if the blooming early morning was being hatched. It was not hidden to me that you have something in your mind, as if you are waiting many days still to bloom. You, Dave, you face every direction except westward; if you could do it you do not like to face west...

2. Springtime: Main Street Plaza

TANG Dave let *Tang* Mike drive his Thunderbird 77 car. *Tang* Dave does not like to drive this time because his White wife who left him was in his mind again. Like the shooting of sprouts and the blooming of flowers, his memory to the White is always fresh coming back and forth in this kind of season.

Tang Mike turned to the right eastward in Lancer Way from their apartment in Harvey Street. Springtime is no longer be hidden by the blossoming of different sprout of trees queued along the street, likewise the verdant views of the tulips producing flowers in yellow, violet, white, or red in the flower garden of every house. The cold left by the past winter could still be felt (time of ice, generally known by the Filipinos in America as snow, not as ice), making *Tang* Mike's feeling fresh.

Tang Mike loves to drive and his favorite is driving along side streets for his ability to drive is being challenged. And enjoys the places, despite driving the same place continually.

Tang Mike turned northward at 2700 West between City Hall and Valley Fair Mall, then turned east at 3500 South toward Freeway I-215 circling the county. They went northward at I-215 then followed I-80 at the right going inside the city then followed 600 South and went north at 200 West. *Tang* Mike parks at the parking lot of the Dee's Restaurant at the North Temple and they walked eastward toward the Main Street

Plaza between the Salt Lake Temple and the Church Office Building. At the north side of the North Temple, Conference Center was strongly built looking down the Temple Square at the south side and as tall as the capitol building northeast. When *Tang* Mike looking around this view, especially in springtime, he always comparing Saud which surroundings is woodland. Saud was molded by nature while this city which is now their world was built by human.

In that Saturday morning, *Tang* Dave and *Tang* Mike, there were already a lot of people enjoying the beauty of the man-made plaza. The dwarf trees were verdant and made more beautiful by the colorful tulips in the surroundings. The tourists love to stroll here in the Main Street Plaza which was built two years ago. People roaming around were from all corners of the world.

From where they were seated which is made by a concrete bench, *Tang* Dave's eyes were focused to the people going north and south in the plaza. Going different direction. The children are giggling while being guided by their parents. There are morning stars in the eyes of the young partners strolling around.

"A boxed life," *Tang* Dave said, with no particular focus.

Tang Mike looked at him, but his lips kept tightly closed.

"Mike, do you know that our lives are also placed in box?"

"You may even say it's in a casket?" *Tang* Mike said without looking at *Tang* Dave.

"Where are those people coming from and going to?" *Tang* Dave looked at the people around with no subject.

"Just like you. Why are you here? Why did you not remain in the mud of San Juan? There are so many reasons why people roam. But like you, like me, I don't understand why we were tossed out here by luck. After the death of my beloved, living without a child to help me live, I did not have specific direction in America. California, Delaware, Florida, then here in Utah…"

People in the plaza became denser. From the Salt Lake Temple, the newly wed White Bride and Black Groom coming out from the building and out to the plaza, accompanied by their relatives in both sides. They shoot pictures, and it was not only one taking videos.

"It is a perfect combination of races," exclaimed *Tang* Dave.

The groups of the newly wed proceed to the temple silently.

Tang Dave and *Tang* Mike moved to the western side of the Main Street Plaza, being called Temple Square, at the edge of Salt Lake Temple in the south side. At the side also of the Tabernacle Building which was look like an upturned world—it is over than a hundred years old. Like the plaza, the tulips and other plants were verdant and lovely. The music coming from the Tabernacle Choir members practicing in that building to be aired every Sunday morning in the television was so sweet.

"This place gives a feeling like you are in a paradise Mike!" *Tang* Dave closed his eyes enjoying the melody being aired from the Tabernacle Building.

At the South Temple, outside the Temple Square, there was a small group offering a pamphlet of a religious sect differed from the belief of the members using the Salt Lake Temple. Slow but heavy was the sound of the feet of the black horse hauling carriage along the South Temple.

Voice 3

I don't have the power to stop your desire, Dave. There were revelations in your mind, small voices, that I like you to listen. But you should be the one to listen that power. There is a law in life where my duty is focused and that is the limit of my power.

If you desire to reach the stars twinkling during summer when new experience is being molded, I do not have the power to block. I know that there is a limit of everything you wish to reach. But if you have the power to fly in the horizon, all right, I will follow you wherever you go. Anyway, your outlook is becoming clearer and sharper because of my presence.

It is daintier for me to suppress you, for if you were a kite, you flew too low. Whatever food is available you are satisfied. You are no different from a matured leaf in the summer ready and waiting for the kiss of the next day.

1. Summertime: Timpanogos Cave

AS part of the preparation of *Tang* Dave and *Tang* Mike in going to Timpanogos Cave National Monument on Saturday, they went to buy their needs in the NPS. *Tang* Dave bought a Noni Gold, a bottled noni juice which he learned made in Hawaii, to make him stronger, aside from the bottled water as advised by somebody he asked from.

He tried to beguile *Tang* Mike to buy anything for him, but the latter did not respect his advice. He is not interested in climbing Timpanogos and if not because of the ever beguiling of *Tang* Dave, it was far from his mind going to that place.

It was almost at the middle of summertime and the bite of the flame of sun was hurting. The different colors of leaves are turning brunette—yellow, green, violet, red, and even blue, and white. The ever-green leaves of the globe willow tree alongside their apartment, being swung by the breeze, likewise turned browner by summer.

Tang Dave woke up early. He takes a shower early. He prepared for his essentials early—he even prepared for *Tang* Mike, just to entice him to go with him. It was *Tang* Mike who used to ask him to go but it was opposite this time.

"You will not regret your coming with me," *Tang* Dave said while driving southbound along I-215. Sometimes, he looks on both sides. He just allows the fast drivers to overtake him; one more thing he was scared that his Thunderbird 77 got in trouble. He was trying not to be drowsy, for he could not avoid when driving a long distance. He did not force *Tang* Mike to drive, for he did not like to give him any reason not to go with him.

He got a full tank before they started but almost half had consumed upon arriving the reception area of the Timpanogos Cave National Park which was sandwiched by two big mountains. The road was snake-shaped and that was what he knew the reason of consuming that amount of gas.

They reached the area with already a lot of tourists waiting for their turn to watch the videotape about the Timpanogos. The reason of their viewing: to give the tourist a chance to backout if they think they could not climb. But the explanation of the tourist guide was so enticing and nobody backout except *Tang* Mike.

"I don't believe I can still climb," he said when they were told that the distance of the narrow path upward is one mile and-a-half. Around three thousand feet high. "Just go ahead, Dave. I'll just wait for you here. I have no doubt that I could not climb."

"We are already here," *Tang* Dave said. "Let's climb. If the women can do it, why can't we?"

"They are young. How about us?"

"We can do it, I am sure!"

And *Tang* Dave bought tickets for them before *Tang* Mike says no. He went back to the car to get two bottles of water for each of them and he let *Tang* Mike carry the two bottles.

"Bear in mind that you can do it." *Tang* Dave said before they start climbing. "And do not think the length of the path upward."

The narrow path belted at the mountain beheld like a line. Rocks and some trees were on the left side that if you look up your neck feels like cracking. In the right side is a cliff with trees that when a stone rolls it is impossible to know where it drops.

They had not even stepped for twenty. *Tang* Mike's knees had been creaking. *Tang* Dave's knees had not been creaking, because probably he was exercising every day, but he could also feel the shrinking of his muscles.

"Let's stop for a while!" *Tang* Mike was breathing heavily. He looks up to where they were going. "Seems unreachable!"

"Don't look up," *Tang* Dave said. They continued climbing. "Focus your attention to the pathway. Don't look down… in the cliff."

There were assigned stations saying how many more feet to climb. They met some people.

"Still far?" ones in a while *Tang* Mike asks to those they meet.

"Still far!" they answered. "But amazing!"

They were caught by a skinny man with a guitar on his shoulder.

"Hello guys!" he said. "Are you okay?"

"I'm dying!" *Tang* Mike gasped.

"It's about there, right?" asked *Tang* Dave.

"It is still a way to go," replied the man. "But you will reach the place. Me, I climb twice a week."

"Why do you have a guitar?" asked *Tang* Dave.

"There is a lady up there who loves me playing guitar," said the man. "See you later." And he climbs faster.

Tang Dave left open-mouthed. The way the man walks, as if he was only walking on a flat ground.

They had not been walking for ten steps when *Tang* Mike again stops.

"I can't do it anymore, Dave!" gasped *Tang* Mike. "I'm running out of breath!"

"Drink," *Tang* Dave said.

They were caught by a chubby woman. "Hi, guys!" she greeted. "Are you okay?"

"Yes, we are," *Tang* Dave said.

"No, I'm not!" *Tang* Mike said. "I'm dying!"

The woman laughs. She said it's just a matter of doing regularly. She said she was climbing three times a week.

"It needs be," *Tang* Mike said following his eyes to the lady as if she was about to run climbing. "She had a lot of things to lost!"

Tang Mike feels nauseated when he accidentally looks down the cliff on his right side. He gropes on the left hoping to get something to hold on.

Tang Dave's knees started creaking and was also starts gasping but there was a voice in his mind saying: *you can do it, Dave, you can do it!*

They had been climbing for almost two hours because they stop more often than usual. Many had passed them by climbing and met going back. It was almost noontime and the surrounding were becoming warmer, except the parts which had still ice that had not been melted by summer. For the first time, it entered to *Tang* Mike's mind that the end of his life was approaching. His mind accused *Tang* Dave, but he also blames himself for he did not insist to resist to the enticing of his friend.

They reached the bathroom which was almost hanging in the cliff by the starting point of the remaining third part of the pathway. *Tang* Dave's sweat was becoming cold and it was not new that feeling to him.

That was the foreboding of a bad feelings. He wanted to sit flat in the bathroom, but the smell was more dizzying. He drank more water. He did not show his feelings to *Tang* Mike when he went out.

"I heard we are approaching the finish line!" he said smiling. In his mind, he cried for more strength.

Tang Dave sat outside of the bathroom while waiting for *Tang* Mike who went next to him. He spread his attention in the north, east, and in the south. In the north, the mountain was lower than where they were. In the east, the cliff was stiffer, and what he thought the tip, he noticed the tail of the pathway they were tracking. In the south, the seasoned trees hanging by the cliff were defying. If ever *Tang* Dave look at the west, he could see the end of the two mountains and where they started, there was the valley of Timpanogos and where the Jordan River swelled. And where the sun sets every day. He could look down the whole west to where the rolling day rests.

He does not like to think about it although he knew that Jordan River was there—why they named that river after the Jordan River in Israel, they were part of the things he was avoiding to reflect.

Sitting on the wooden bench helped *Tang* Dave while waiting for *Tang* Mike. When they followed the other tourists, they regained a little strength in counting their steps. They were about to consume their bottle of water. But *Tang* Dave did not like to touch the second bottle in preparation for their going back down.

He tried not to think about their climbing. Instead, he focused his mind to the Noni Gold where he drank three spoons before they get out from their apartment. And his happy yesterdays. And he avoided looking up and down. But ones in a while he turned his eyes to *Tang* Mike. He always telling him they are closing to their destination. But he knew he was lying to himself for he also was very eager to reach the tip. They had been climbing more than two hours. How long will they still be climbing? He wanted to look up the sun, but he did not like to know it was about noon time. Nevertheless, he knew it was so, for he could see his shadow, meaning, the sun had come out from the nipple of the mountain they were climbing. Not long afterwards, it will past noon; the sun will slowly be hiding to the west.

They stopped several times more. They could not remember how many more who passed them by climbing and met who went down. It is now that *Tang* Dave asked in his mind: what had he got in insisting himself to climb? To go and see the popular cave at the tip of Timpanogos? Why is it that, that cave situated in the tip of the mountain? What is really something important in that cave?

Tang Dave looked back *Tang* Mike. It looks like the latter was counting his steps, looking down, as if nobody around him.

"Welcome to the Timpanogos Cave National Park!" *Tang* Dave observing *Tang* Mike reflecting was cut off by a warm welcome of the smiling lady.

They had reached the tip!

"See!" *Tang* Dave's eyes twinkle patting *Tang* Mike's shoulder whose eyes look like a sleepy fighting cock.

At the mouth of the cave, *Tang* Dave felt the cold breath coming from inside. There were wonderful things explained by the tourist guide. The three caves contained hundreds of different shapes of calcites or drips turned stones or rocks silvery or golden color. They were sharp-pointed. More importantly the discovery of the cave. There was a group that discovered this state of the Americas. There was no water around and they looked for a source until they reached the foot of the Timpanogos Mountain. From there, they found lion's footprints; there was a belief that if a lion looks for water, they even climb mountains. They followed those footprints until they reached where they were right now. At first the entrance was narrow, but they widened. To make easier for the tourists to walk or enter. They decided to add or widened the hole of the cave. They even attached electric light. One of the wonders of man's intelligence was their bringing up their materials. There were a lot of tektites mentioned by the tourist guide that found only in this place.

Notwithstanding the wonder of that place, *Tang* Dave had not understood a single message of what he heard. What was important to him, his plan to climb that mountain had fulfilled.

They went out to a different gate. After bidding goodbye with other tourists who climbed, and the people who managed the cave, *Tang* Dave went ahead.

He stopped at the entrance of the pathway downward—it was different from the pathway they followed when climbing with the pathway that met them out, but they met not far from the place. *Tang* Dave stood in akimbo facing west: for the first time. And as if the separation of the two mountains seem a wide smile that met his eyes.

Tang Dave said to *Tang* Mike: "See! See!"

But by their going down, the cliff looked like an open-mouthed jailbird ever ready to crunch them into pieces.

Voice 4

IT was good that I had a different responsibility. In the world where I was wriggling time does not move and I do not mind my growing old like you, Dave and Mike. I do not have complain, in every moment mingling with you. I won't mind tiredness and wiriness, when you are snoring or even laughing.

No man is an island, they say. What if I invert it, no island is a man? Hmm. It was not important to you good friends, but I know that you know it was like that, because sometimes you listen to my small voice which only few knows how to listen. Or knew that there was a voice like that, that only the inner self knows how to listen to it.

I understand why you were uneasy. But I just don't know if you understand that the law of nature should be followed. Was it hard to accept the turning of time? The chance to be separated from civilization?

2. Autumn: Antelope Island State Park

THE leaves of trees along the freeway had been ripened before the middle of Autumn or Fall or falling of leaves, in the last part of October. Even the leaves of the globe willow tree beside their apartment had been matured and not from then they will start falling. In the four divisions of time in America, this is the time *Tang* Dave hate the most. He does not have interest to go out, he prefers to stay sleeping in their apartment, but three months is too long not to go out. His every morning exercise is not enough to sway away the uneasiness trying to hatch in his forehead. And the chilly feelings engulfing his palms and feet.

Tang Mike was observing the 65 m/hour speed limit along Freeway I-15, but *Tang* Dave desires to be slower.

They were not talking to each other, *Tang* Dave pretended to be sleeping. If possible, he does not like to spend some hours, or the whole day of Saturday, like now, in the Antelope Island State Park. But it was Tang Mike's turn to entice him to go with him. It was about ten miles the distance of I-15 from their apartment in Harvey before turning west to the small road toward the seven-mile-long bridging Great Salt Lake between the park and the city of Syracuse.

What was special in this park that attracts tourists? *Tang* Dave thought. Antelope Island State Park is in the middle of the Great Salt Lake. There was no verdant view during any of the four seasons. Most of its parts were desert, except some grass that loves living in that place. But there was a pasture place, or a ranch, which is the Fielding Garr Ranch. There was even a visitor's center. There were tourists visiting in the middle of spring until the end of autumn.

Tang Dave's reflecting was disrupted when the Thunderbird 77 resounded and shuffled. He noticed the opening of *Tang* Mike of the window and handling something to the guy in the gate. They reached the tollgate.

"Enjoy your stay!" the man said.

Enjoy? Thought *Tang* Dave.

The Thunderbird 77 resounded one more time. Sometimes it hiccups and almost lost its breath.

"Your Batman seems not able to bring us to our destination!" jokes *Tang* Mike.

"Better so we won't continue," *Tang* Dave didn't smile. "We have not reached the destination, but I'm already tired!"

"You're tired? If you go home by foot, will you not be tired? Remember, Harvey is more than twenty miles away from here. Good if there's a Greyhound or UTA that pass by here. Nobody wants to hitch hike anybody they don't know."

Tang Dave remained silent. He got a sour-faced throwing his attention in the south and sometimes in the north side of the bridge— they were traversing a different kind of bridge; no posts and railings for the builders decided to stop up its length. He purposely not to look at the west they were facing, just to let *Tang* Mike feel his hesitance in going.

"It was your turn in Timpanogos, now it's my turn here," *Tang* Mike smiled one sided. "We're now quits, my friend. As what they say, give and take."

"What more could I say?" *Tang* Dave said. "If only I have a brother, or a relative nearby, I don't have a second say, never to be your companion!"

Tang Mike laughed with gusto. "That's right!" he said. "You don't have a brother, nor a relative… like me. So, we don't have a choice except to be the brothers. Either I like, or you like it or not."

"Unfortunately!"

"Hey, no. we are lucky instead. Why, you say? If you're short, or me nothing, you are there to help or I am here for you to lean to. Remember when you lost your pension in the mail? And when they cut my SSI because of the government's fault? How could we live without any of us?"

When they reached Antelope Island State Park, they made round and round before reaching the Visitor's Center. *Tang* Dave was surprised because despite the isolation of the park, that is not what the ones in the center show. It was not different to the buildings found in the city. The needs of the tourists were complete.

And many people. Isolated place but many people? Young, adult, and there were partners with women displaying their bellybuttons. *Tang* Dave frowns. No man is an island?

Tang Dave more surprised when they went to the Fielding Garr Ranch. From his observation, there were no enough grass in the places they passed by but the visons, mule deer, water buffalo and horses were fat. How do these animals live in this kind of places? He thought. Or were there people bringing them food? How do they live during winter?

They proceed to a waiting shed and took their lunch. The heat of the sun was piercing but soothed by breeze as sign of the approaching winter. The breeze was enticing to sleep, and it drops the eyelids of *Tang* Dave, added by the sparkling back of the water. The surrounding was so quiet, which was seldom disturb by the clinging laughter of children from the other waiting shed.

Tang Dave thought: Antelope is past asleep in the cradle of Autumn in the bellybutton of Great Salt Lake!

Voice 5

THERE was snag in the bosom being warmth of every bit of time. I could also feel the coolness in the depth of your soul. Dave and Mike, in a sense that seems nobody felt your importance if not only the two of you. My voice I am trying to instill in your deepest self for you really need the warmth from each of you. I am instilling in your deepest understanding that you need to unite the mind and your feelings for you only can understand yourselves.

Until the important time arrives. I want you to understand my revelation that there are only thirty-one days in December.

2. Winter time: Park City

THIS place I am planning to go, it is important that it is not only me who decide," *Tang* Dave said in one day they were watching with *Tang* Dave a television show. "We need to plan together. If you do not like, it will not be pursued. But you need to suggest also where we will go. Whatever you say, write your plan on a paper, and so with me, then we will compare. By that means nobody is giving ways."

That was what happened. And in one of a rare result of their decision, they decided to go to Park City.

Both had never been in that city which was the most popular skiing cite during winter, more so when there was a snow storm.

For *Tang* Mike, he wants to see personally the professional skiers. He had been in this so-called state of snow but had not seen any personally.

For *Tang* Dave, he wants to experience skiing. Every time he watches skiers on the television, his desire to try enlivening. For he feels so good when watching, and in his mind, it must be better if he himself was there flying. He believes that nobody is too old to anything one wants to do if he is desirous to fulfill his dream. He wants to prove that it is not yet late for somebody like him.

"You drive in going up," *Tang* Mike said.

Tang Dave did not hesitate. He wants to show *Tang* Mike that he is not scared of driving not even the thickest of snow. That he could manage to guide his Thunderbird 77 despite the oldness of his car.

In the day of their climbing to Park City, *Tang* Dave went to the Deseret Industries to buy a second-hand ski boot. He did not tell *Tang* Mike; he did not show. He decided to surprise his friend.

Despite that they had different things in mind, both were exited in readying themselves. Both were exited hopping to the Thunderbird 77. While *Tang* Dave was traversing I-80 eastward to Park City, they hummed *Top of the World* of the Carpenters being played in the stereo. Again, and again, *Tang* Dave slows down when he feels the complains of the car's tires upon hitting black ice, which was hard and slippery. Many motorists met an accident when they made a mistake.

The sun peeping through the clouds from the past snow last night signals that it was about noontime when they reached Park City. There were already a lot of tourists and most of the convenience stores were fully packed in front of the park.

While *Tang* Dave and *Tang* Mike watch the skiers being brought by the electric operated hanging trolley up and down, the latter noticed the back pack of his friend. *Tang* Dave kept silent, as if he was so focused watching the flying skiers.

Most of the tourists brought sky paraphernalia, aside from their hoodies making themselves warm.

The two old men brought also themselves jackets but differed from the others. Aside from their hoodies, they also wore gloves.

When a skier flies, *Tang* Dave's body also moves, as if he is in the act of skiing. Next time, he found himself bringing out the ski boot he bought and change his rubber shoes.

"Hey, hey! Don't ever do that!" *Tang* Mike was scared to death.

"I'll just try," *Tang* Dave said. In his inner self he was determined to say: *I can do it, why not!*

And he walked in the ice. At first, he tested himself. Good! He was around ten feet away from the foot of the iced area.

"No, Dave, no!" *Tang* Mike scared to death when *Tang* Dave slides.

But *Tang* Dave had gone to his dream.

Voice 6

OKAY, Dave. Okay, Mike. In this very moment I know it's clear in your mind what I am.

    Listen to my voice. Listen: I am with you; I am in every individual…

II. Closing

TANG Mike was so silent watching his friend who was so calm sleeping on a bed where he was wrap with white blanket. It was his second day at the LDS Memorial Hospital. His right arm which was clubbed on a heap of ice when he slid was heavily wrapped. His doctor was not sure how grave was his neck. Worse comes worse, the spinal cord of his neck might had been affected. If that was the case, he will be paralyzed his whole life.

"Bless my friend, Lord!" *Tang* Mike's voice was raspy, and he massaged the left palm of *Tang* Dave.

The sun was about to set in the west when *Tang* Dave moves. It caught the attention of *Tang* Mike, who was drowsy on his sit. He slept a little since yesterday the day his friend was brought to the hospital.

Tang Dave opened his eyes.

"Dave… Dave!" *Tang* Mike's eyes were watery.

Tang Dave's smile was dry. "Don't you worry, Mike. I can manage," his voice was soft but confident. He looks at the open window on his foot side facing west. As if he heard a small voice who was telling him: you also have a west, Dave.

"Get well soon, Dave…"

"West is beautiful, Mike," *Tang* Dave's smile was appealing. —0

*December 31, 2002, 3:45pm; January 5, 2003, 1:46am; January 5, 2003, 4:37pm; April 26, 2003, 10:11am. June 16, 2015, 2:51am. First published by **Rimat**, May 2003. Translation completed: June 12, 2018, 1:45am.*

Where Is Your Resting Place, Felipe Abraham?

Introduction

Where have you been, Felipe Abraham?
Seems you traversed a long way for you looked like exhausted.
Or are you going home, where do you live?
Or are all places you stopped by your home?
Do you have a family to go home with?
Or cherishing you and waiting for your return?
Who are you in the world where you wriggled at—
A wandering flotsam or neglected?

I

A S if we are heading to the same direction, brother," said the brown guy who looked up the one in front of him. It looks like the traveling bag he was dragging was heavy. "Guess we came from the same place…"

Seems the one being followed who stooped when he entered the entrance of the airplane was not listening. He was catching his breath. He walked a long way from where he got off at the Delta Airlines in Los Angeles International Airport, where he transferred to the Philippine Airlines. He looks like so haggard and as if he was sleepless for a couple of days. The knapsack on his back was small but still looks like too heavy for him to carry.

"Brother… Brother." The one who was following made three steps faster for his desire to catch up the one being followed.

The one being caught up looked back the one who was already walking with him side by side who seemed like a bulldog. His sleepy eyes were deep in his oblong face. "Am I whom you are talking with… brother?"

The one who was following laughed a brief laugh. He looked up whom he caught up. "You're funny, brother. Where are you in the Pinas, Brother?"

The one being caught up shrug his shoulder; he moved his head a little bit.

Where am I in the Philippines? Where did my mother give birth to me? I was born outside Metro Manila, according to my father. My late father, a native Ilokano. Also, my late mother, yes, my mother—I don't know where she is, if she is still alive. Both were flotsams where they met…

"Your attention, please. Reminder to the passengers: only a hand carry is allowed for every passenger." The order from the boarding area was loud and clear.

"Why are you like that, you had allowed us in our check-in?" the complaint outside sounds mad.

"Have you heard that, Brother?" Miguel Arcadio touched Felipe Abraham. "They complain while in fact they do not know how to follow the law. Do you know how their hand carries passed? They did not bring in the check-in area. They left to those who accompanied them. Cheaters, really. Real Pinoys!"

The one being stood beside turned right and passed the stewardess who greeted him. The one who was walking alongside followed him.

"By the way, I am Miguel, Brother. Miguel Arcadio. Mike here in America. I'm Ilokano… from Norte." The one who stood alongside said. "Sorry if I'm so persistent. Because I am looking for somebody who could understand me… How about you?"

"Felipe Abraham," the words of the one being walked beside were deep. He coughed dryly.

"Felipe Abraham… beautiful name. Are you from Norte also, Felipe?"

"I can speak Iluko."

"Very good… Where is your home or where do you live?"

Felipe Abraham moved his left shoulder.

Where is my home? Where do I live so I know where I am going home? Where could I find a home? Where are those who are waiting for me? But is there anybody waiting for me?

Felipe Abraham walks in between people who are looking for seat.

"Good morning, sir," a stewardess greeted Felipe Abraham. "Here is your sit, sir," she said upon seeing the boarding pass.

"Thank you," he coughed dryly.

Felipe Abraham stops when he noticed Miguel Arcadio.

"Any problem. Miguel?"

"Sorry, brother. Am I giving you a problem?"

"I want to be alone…"

"But I want a companion…"

Felipe Abraham shakes his head slightly.

These are all Filipinos. There probably no White who wants to ride with a Filipino? Or are they not allowed to ride with a PAL? It's been a long time. Had the Philippines changed a lot?

This brother who is following … Is he always going home? Where is he going home? Has he had a wife or a family waiting for him? You are lucky, brother, if that is the case.

You had not gone home or spent a vacation in the Philippines, Felipe Abraham for more than twenty years now. Can you still remember why you came to the Americas, and why you went to Utah and hid yourself in Provo when you were tired in Upland, California? Do you still want to reminisce those days? Okay, never mind. Forget those events as scars… if you can.

"They are already inside, they are still in a hurry, Brother," Miguel Arcadio elbowed Felipe Abraham lightly who noticed the other passengers.

These people had no patience. They are all in a hurry. They have numbers, and nobody could take their seats for sure. Why is it that people are always in a hurry to reach their destination? Why are they so in a hurry? Why don't they wait for their time for it will come for sure?

What if their ride drops into the deep, then they had also caught their death? Real people. Where are these people going? Do they always have money? Or do they have a lot of money?

"What is the number of your seat, Brother?" Miguel Arcadio elbowed Felipe Abraham.

"13-A..." Felipe Abraham coughed dryly.

"Good, we sit side by side! Mine is 13-B... How bad our numbers are, brother! I don't like number 13. I was not born in the ancient time, but I don't like this number..."

"Are you afraid of dying, Brother?"

"Don't be foolish, brother! You know, I seldom get a vacation in the Philippines because of that. I feel like dead when I am up here."

"Are you afraid of being shredded by sharks in the deep?"

"My gosh brother... I am not joking!"

Are you not scared to die also, Felipe Abraham? Is there still a reason for you to be afraid of dying, while you are already worthless? Is it not? Do you still consider yourself worthy of living, Felipe Abraham? What is the use? Do you believe that man is being consumed during his lifetime? Do you believe that after a man is born his death follows? Okay, if you do not believe, there is a great reason why. But whatever that reason is, it just demonstrates that a man weakling. But there is no weakling Ilokano; you the genuine Ilokano, you are not supposed to be here, or you were not able to reach all the foreign places if you did not have a strong will, right? Is there any other reason? Unless there was something you were running away from, a grave sin you had done... But what kind of sin? Did you kill somebody? Some of the bad elements in your country of origin? Well, you are a hero if that is the case, according to the nationalist minded, or radicals like your term during your time of running and hiding in the corners of the universities in Metro Manila, then spit the back of those you considered puppies and big-stomached in the palace. You said that what you were doing was not a sin. Then what are you hiding from? Women? A lot of women? Once, or how many times did you curse the women for they were the ones destroying the manhood of the fathers? You forgot that your mother was also a woman…

"Here is the thirteen, brother. Where are you going?"

"Sorry, Brother." Felipe Abraham was pestered with a whooping cough.

"It's a huge aircraft but with few passengers. I asked one of the stewardesses the capacity of this and it was 474. But there are only 121 passengers today. That was the reason why this is a direct flight despite having a stopover in Honolulu… better so we could reach the Philippines earlier… I want us to arrive there right away!"

What does the old place look like now? Is there a big improvement?

Your home was full of laughter, Felipe Abraham. There was no difference from a small paradise. Your father had a minimal income from the university printing press and he did not aspire for a bigger income. Anyway, there were only three of you he needed to feed. Your mother had no complain either for she did not dream big dreams. There was a small television set in a corner of your small house in the eastern side of Metro Manila. Small radio. Small electric fan being used during the hottest time of summer. You were not short of food although prices of commodities had started to go up.

Your mother was beautiful. She became a beauty queen in their place and many envied the good luck of your father. Even the leaders of the land who knew them. Why your father and your mother met, your father could not explain. Love was blind. Your mother said: your father was the most dignified man I ever met…

Your father was a good storyteller in the evening before sleeping. He had a lot of interesting stories, and even your mother, also glad to listen. Just perhaps because he works in a printing press, he read a lot of books where he adapted his stories.

Then, you noticed that there were men visiting your father. When the men had gone, your mother's face was so sad and looked mad. But despite of sadness in your mother's face, she still was beautiful. She was the most beautiful woman you ever known. You did not know then but you heard one evening when they were talking with your father about a politician in the province. You were still innocent how a mad man looked like, but it was only the time you heard your father had cursed.

Not long afterward, the politician suddenly came with bodyguards and in front of you and your father, he raped your mother. When your father fought back, they hit his nape and went away with your mother. Probably you were lucky for they forgot you and left you in gape.

Your father had not able to complain. Nobody listened to him. Probably all who had witnessed had given muzzles. People had no power. But after that, he was then always looking far beyond, then suddenly cries, like an infant.

That was the last time you had seen your mother. Your father brought you away from that place and he raised you up in the city. Your father did never marry again. But those days full of laughter had never came back...

Those imps!

"What did you say, brother?"

"Huh?"

"Ladies and gentlemen... welcome aboard. Thank you for using the Philippine Airlines."

Felipe Abraham looks at where the voice came from. If she was not the one, they had the same voice with the beauty he left...

Rarely a moment that you had a peaceful world with Agrippina, Felipe Abraham. You were always in the crossroads despite the stinging flame of sun at noontime. Your arms seemed untired lifting the ensign of entitlement for the poor and under privilege. Despite the harshness of your voice yelling what you call rights, despite the burning heat in the surrounding because you were starving, your legs were still steady standing for the principle you were fighting for in challenging the decaying law of a rotten society. For you, time was far from spent and chances were still abundant for the altering of time and the world; the valleys were still spacious where a new world will be built to cuddle the needy in a peaceful cradle of life. You, Felipe Abraham, as one of the leaders of an antecedent you were standing for, and as if you did not have enough time with Agrippina to gaze at each other tenderly and smile to each other under the moon during the full moon and half-moon in the east and the breeze was so gentle.

You had some members in your group saying that the ideology hoisting for your group and the feeling that brings life in your hearts could not go hand in hand. But that tremor was so powerful for it could topple down any principle, but it did not mean that if that flame burns the hope will turn into ashes that bringing force the tenderness to those who were waiting for the protection against the claws of a cruel society.

"My heart is heavy thinking the situation of the deep eyes and boney innocents in the crossroads and those who were hiding behind the open fissure in the ground of the dried field," your voice was heavy, Felipe Abraham. "But that feeling is apportioned equally when I am by your side, Agrippina!"

"I have no strength to tear off the love blossomed from my heart, Felipe," Agrippina's bosom was warm throbbing in your bosom with her arms on your neck. "We have an obligation to them, but we also have obligation to each other that we need to give meaning… can you do it, Felipe?"

The moments throbbing in your world, Felipe Abraham were so melodramatic, but can you discount it? The feelings were so powerful to enslave you. And that is the feeling to divide the principle you were standing for. Can you endure it?

When the enfolded moment turns into flame, all the moments were yours and let yourselves be drowned with the overflowing endearment of each of you.

"My beloved, only you!" there tears of endearment from the stars in Agrippina's eyes that drowns you completely.

"Only you, my beloved!"

Those were the most precious moments in your lives.

But those moments were robbed. For the flame of the ideology you stood for ever burning until the forested society be cleansed to let the forgotten garden flourish again. When the flame between you settled down, another flame inflamed again to incinerate the wicked. The lost roster had not done crowing but you were ready to walk in Mendiola or Bonifacio or Ayala or EDSA depending on what area the members of your group had decided…

Where are you now, Agrippina? The newborn how is he now? Had that bosom cold off? O, Agrippina, Norway was so far. The distance is unreachable, My Beloved!

"What do you want to drink, sir?" the smile of the stewardess looking at Felipe Abraham was so sweet.

"Hey… is it already dinner time?" Felipe Abraham was again attacked by whooping cough.

"Yes, sir… Are you okay?" the deep dimple of the gorgeous was so magnetizing.

Felipe Abraham ordered a diet drink. He jiggled his head slowly while his eyes tailed the buttock of the stewardess. He gulps the bitter soft drink that soften his dry throat.

Miguel Arcadio was snoring heavily on the front seat—he was reassigned for there were enough vacant seat. The stewardess did not wake him up.

Felipe Abraham looks out thru the window close to him. The yellowish color of the setting sun divides the horizon—black at the bottom and yellow on top, as if a contraption of a black pan and a golden bowl.

Those bloody evenings. Those gloomy night.

"There was bad news, Felipe…"

"I can feel it, Agrippina. I can feel it."

"Jun disappeared."

"That is probably a forewarning… The devils!"

"Cesar maybe their next target… then… hope not, I am scared. It is only this moment that I feel this. Whenever I have this feeling, it surely happens."

"You are already toughened by this kind of events… are you in doubt of yourself?"

"I am only a human with feelings… what if what I am feeling comes true?"

"Do you lose faith in God?"

"Felipe… Felipe!" somebody knocks the door.

"Who is that?"

Agrippina peeped. "It was Dario…"

Agrippina opened the door.

"Felipe… there was something wrong with your father. They looked for you from him. They did to him which was for you."

"Those devils… those devils!" your eyes inflamed, Felipe Abraham.

"Felipe…" Agrippina held your arm, Felipe Abraham.

"The movement had decided, Felipe. You need to stay aside for a while."

"Why now? Why now that the movement needs me the most? If I will die, this is the most appropriate time."

"No. you are more needed in the future… not this time yet… everything you needed had been prepared. Remember, you are so important to be lost this time. There is time prepared for you. You will return…"

"Ladies and gentlemen, fasten your seatbelts," voice of the captain.

Miguel Arcadio was jolted out from his seat. He ran towards Felipe Abraham.

"Brother, t-this is the end!" Miguel Arcadio was trembling. "I-I know, t-this is it… We should go back!"

"Where are your balls, Brother?" Felipe Abraham did never face on Miguel Arcadio. His smile was hanged for he was caught again by a whooping cough.

"F-Felipe… I-I'm not joking… a-are you sick?"

"Hey, Miss, give my friend a sedative," Felipe Abraham did not answer Miguel Arcadio. "He probably left his thing in Utah!"

"Fasten your seatbelt, sir, if you still like to live!" the stewardess was laughing when she turns away. When she came back, she brought with her a cup of water and a medicine.

Not long afterward, the aircraft brought back to normal. The lights that signaled a warning were switched off. The aircraft was now peacefully cradled again by the dark.

Felipe Abraham could not sleep. Again, and again, he looks out the window, that nothing could see except a thick darkness, or on the television in the middle. But he could not understand the film being played. His eyes sometimes play on the stewardess going back and forth at the isle of the aircraft. Again, and again, he was bothered by a whooping cough.

What is this for? Where does it ends? He had taken a lot of medication. These medical practitioners are nonsense. They just collect your money. It could be better if… Where are you now, Agrippina? The child, where is he?

"This is what I hate most, Felipe," Miguel Arcadio's voice is now mellow.

Felipe Abraham held his coughing. He turned on Miguel Arcadio.

"I seldom go home to the Philippines… for a vacation, and I always have a companion," continued Miguel Arcadio. "I have an aerophobia, more so for there is a little problem with my heart, and my blood."

"Sorry for jesting you," Felipe Abraham said. "I did not know that you are sick." He focused ones again his eyes outside the window.

"I was still young when my aunt brought me in Provo, Utah," Miguel Arcadio said. "Pinas was then in trouble. My father and my mother and two of my brothers were left. My father was a farmer and his harvest from the fertile field he was tilling was more than enough to fed us. But there came a cruel ordeal for the farmers. Many two-legged grasshoppers appeared, and they grabbed the land of the farmers… are you listening, brother?"

"Keep on."

"Many unscrupulous vices had those grasshoppers did. Do you know why they were called grasshoppers?

"I know."

"They lend. They gained interests. They got anything from the poor farmers when they could not pay. The roof of their houses where shining while the cogon roof of the shanties of the poor farmers were dripping…"

"Can't you tell something good about the Philippines?" Felipe Abraham's molar hardened. He was about to cough again. "Like for example…"

"Rice Terraces? Buracay? Mount Makiling? Baguio? Hundred Islands? Taal Volcano? Chocolate Hills? Ha-ha!" Miguel Arcadio's laugh was dry.

Felipe Abraham had whooping cough again.

"You want to listen stories about the beaches where the modern grasshoppers were running after each other? Ha-ha? What, are you still listening, Brother?"

Felipe Abraham breathed heavily. He was ones again looking at the black window.

They were the only one awake—the passengers were all composed. Except the none-stop movie on the television, and the soft sound of the engine, nothing more was moving giving life in the airplane. Even the stewardess, they stopped moving around.

"When my father had no longer stomach the stinky grasshoppers," Miguel Arcadio continued, "he decided to move his family to America, thru the long enticing of my aunt. He sold every source of our living and was ready to fly. Getting visas those times was so easy."

"Like you, he used his tail as G-string and ran away from his enemies?"

"He was not able to run away from them!" Miguel Arcadio's voice was heavy. "They followed them up to the airport—they did not do by themselves. There were lots of them who ride in that voyage. Remember, or had you heard about the airplane that exploded before it got in to the air? They planted a bomb…"

"I had a lot of friends who were in that aircraft…"

"Nothing part of my father and my mother's body had found. But what could the innocents do? Now, I'm the only survivor… I am the only one!"

"The devils!"

"What did you say?"

"Many lives were sacrificed…"

"The movement had been scraped, Felipe," Dario's letter you received in Amsterdam said, Felipe Abraham. "We are now like rats being watched by mustang in the night. Many had been lost. I had contacted only few of them. Many of them ran away. They went hiding in different parts of the world. Those who remained with the ideology stood for by the movement, they remained within and lucky for not haunted by the fishers in the land. We are being swept away, Felipe Abraham. Just in case my luck is up to this moment, bear in mind that I did not forget my responsibility as citizen. As I had said before, it was decided by the movement to let you go and you will come back when you have a good chance to continue flaming the movement. My days are almost over… I am not sure if I could ever write you again…

Postscript: Agrippina has gone. We were not able to talk before she disappeared. I heard that she was brought by a Norwegian when he went

home to Oslo. The child was robust—he copied your feature—whom she
brought with them. The details were incomplete how it was happened.

"I should not be taking a vacation," Miguel Arcadio sounded ones
more. "I heard that it is challenging there right now; revolution might
erupt anytime… But my aunt called me up, the one I mentioned who
brought me to Provo. She's old. She is the one who is always taking a
vacation. She is now in the Pinas. Something happens so I need to go
fetch her, to accompany her back to Provo. She is my only remaining
relative. That's why I need to go fetch her."

"You are lucky, Brother…"

"For having a single relative?"

"You asked me where I am going to sttle down…" Felipe Abraham
ones again coughed unceasing dry and deep. "There is no place for me
to go," he continued after coughing.

"Good!" Miguel Arcadio clicked his fingers. "Come with me. I'll
bring you to Paoay Lake… wherever you want. You have not been home
for quite some time, I guess. My aunt will surely be glad to know that I
met an Ilokano friend… in Provo. I can't say I have a close friend. There
were only few Filipinos there. I never met an Ilokano."

"Thanks a lot, Miguel. But…"

"Don't worry where to stay. I'll be responsible for you!"

"I am sick, Miguel…" Felipe Abraham ones again coughed
unceasingly. "My days are numbered."

"W-what?"

"My days are numbered, maybe hours. Nobody could tell. I am
going home because my father was buried there. And I like to be buried
there. And I learned that my mother is still alive. Who knows, hoping
that God will extend my stay, so we could still see each other. My poor
mother…"

"Don't you have anybody left in…"

"…Logan, Utah… Nobody…"

**In Amsterdam, when I was deeply mourning my separation
from my loved ones in the Philippines, there was a sweet lady who
enamored with me. She understood my problem. She offered her
help. Including her body. She was a good lady; she was also an**

activist. I forgot Agrippina for a while. I did not send any letter following the advice of the movement for their fear that somebody could detect where I was hiding. But those were short moments. Despite of no contact with Agrippina, she was still what I had in mind. She was my driving force.

But I did not stay long there. Some years only. I moved from one place to another in Europe. I had written a lot, nonetheless, and some were published. Yes, I learned to write while staying in foreign land for I need something to use in forgetting my homesickness. Good for me as past time. Except the women who came and go in my life.

When you are in foreign land you need to think something that can help you forget your burden. Many things come to your life and because you need something to lean on leaning to anything you think could help. Whatever.

As time goes by, while waiting for my chance to go back to the Philippines, I realized I could hardly do so without sacrificing a principle. More so when I received Dario's letter, the late Dario, that Agrippina had gone, I totally lost my interest to go back to the Philippines. To whom would I offer my sacrifices when my only driving force has gone?

When I was given a chance, I used America as my recourse, bringing my heavy burden. Hoping, in my mind, that I could find there a broken piece of my hope. I was one of those spitting the image of America. But the principle and ideology when life had been ripened everything you are fighting for will also be ripened and it changes the leaning of belief. I was one of the leftists as the belief of the movement where I poured gallons of sweat and time.

I sought something in America... In California. In New York. In Florida and in other places until l reached Utah. During those times, women were garlands of my life. They were my past time. Or I was their past time. In America, fall of challenges. Fall of immigrants. You may know, it could be considered that all people in America are immigrants. Different races. The Whites, wherever part of the world their parents haled from, they were free to do whatever they wish to. Their moves were all theirs, even their parents could not touch them not even to touch their pinky when done wrong. No women stayed long in my life. Or none of them had the guts to keep me afloat. They probably used me as experiment. Or are we all objects in the world for experiment?

One of them stayed in my life for several years. Three, four years. We had two children. Afterwards, she divorced me. I lost the case and the children were awarded to her. A girl and a boy. My money goes to them. Alimony.

I don't have a permanent resident. I don't have a house. But I could not escape from the American law. It follows you wherever corner of America you go.

I was infected with an illness, several years ago. Or in short, I did not know that I was sick until they brought me to a hospital and I was informed that I have a terminal illness... I can go anytime from now...

"Ladies and gentlemen..." all were almost awakened by the voice from the captain. "I am sorry to inform that we could not land in Manila International Airport."

"What!" the passengers were almost in unison.

Miguel Arcadio's mouth was agape.

Felipe Abraham's lips were tightly closed, holding his cough. That not long afterwards he let his very dry whooping cough and he even dropped his head in front covering his mouth.

"I am sorry," the captain continues. "There is an ongoing revolution there and all flights were cancelled. Nothing can land. I was advised to go back..."

"My goodness..."

II

THE PHILIPPINE Airlines was going back. Wherever it stops, not any more in Felipe Abraham's mind. His chest was now so heavy.

Miguel Arcadio was teary.

"My aunt... my aunt!"

Felipe Abraham closes his eyes. Tightly. He did not like his eyes to be watery.

My mother…

Agrippina…

The… what's the name of the child, Agrippina?

Those children of alimony…

Felipe Abraham coughed unceasingly. Too heavy coughing. His shortness of breath was almost unbearable. Blood oozed from his nose and mouth…

It is so sweet, Agrippina… I'm going home. I am so homesick to my promised home. You also have a home, Agrippina. Nobody could tell where everybody will go home. If we are going to the same place, very good. If we go home to the same place, I would be the happiest. But I want to go home in a garden fall of flowers never to be withered. In a valley when winter is covered by a cottoned-like snow—I considered a paradise, Agrippina—its coldness soothing to a cut. Yes, I am going home, Agrippina. You will also go home. We all go home. Junior—is his name Junior, Agrippina? I want to put my arms around his shoulder… Agrippina, oh, Agrippina!

The stewardesses were all in a hurry. The airport was still far but an ambulance was already there waiting.

Postscript

God be with you, Felipe Abraham
Wherever you go
You had traversed the narrow path
A lengthy time you did ever walked
Say goodbye to a dense humanity
Say goodbye to everyone you rode with
Say goodbye to the thick snow in Logan
Say goodbye to many beauties you passed by
Say goodbye to the scarecrow in the horizon
Say goodbye, Felipe Abraham, say goodbye

Wherever you go for as a home
Hope that you could present yourself without obstruction... —O

Rimat: February 2004; 1st Honorable Mention, *Sirmata Literary Award,* 2001; *translation completed*: June 15, 2018.

Here I Am, Tranquilino Tacneng[68]: In A 28-Story World

9:50 A. M., May 22, ----

SO MANY people… as if all the employees of the Cosmopolitan Office Building are present. The big Conference Room here in COB 26 is full but there are still standing outside. It is breathtaking.

…Who are we that much, retiring?

Who am I included with these Whites?

Ilokano… Brown American, who was born in 22nd day of May sixty-five years ago, in a virtually shanty under a big breadfruit by the edge of the Life River at the north side of the narrow pathway headed to the National Road in the east that splits Bacsil. The narrow path ending up to San Isidro close to Saoang being outflowed by the waves in the west.

Why do we need to wear a coat and tie? As if I am being chocked to this inane necktie! As if I am being prepared to be executed, that they give all the food that wishes.

These two by my side were luckier for they looked like much contented. They look paler with their black coat, against the completely white hair of this one, and the shining head of the second—luckier that

---

68 *Tacneng (takneng)*, virtuous.

my hair still intact after thirty years of going up and down here in this twenty-eight-story building… that became my world…

Thirty years of residence in Heber…

And how about here in Cosmopolitan Office Building, or COB? Thirty?

How is Abbarit nowadays?

Just dance with the music, Kilin?

I'm going to look for my destiny there, Inang. I'm envisioning a dim future here… hopefully be better there.

I'm not growing younger, Barok. And your father had gone either. I feel bad if you going away…

I also feel bad departimg from Abbarit, Inang…

Please forget what happened between you and Idot. It was a stroke of luck that you were not mean for each other… she was rape by that… maybe she did not like you to be the patcher…

Because Teodoro was a seaman… But Idot was a pragment of the past, Inang; she is not the reason… As I've said, I don't have a good future here… Good that somebody with good intention is willing to help me… I will always remember you, Inang. I will always send you a letter. I will take a vacation after a year…

"Congratulations, Quiel!" he received a tight handshake from the boss yesterday. Quiel here; Kilin in Abbarit.

Is he one of the three Distinguished Employees of the Year? Out of approximately three thousand employees?

Distinguished?

"Thank you, sir…"

Anniversary? May 22…

After COB, where?

Tomorrow will be the last day …

9:52 A. M., May 22, ----

"Are you okay, Quiel?" the gray haired.

"Ha, e… What do you think?"

"You looked like lost in the desert!" the shining crown.

"Enjoy! This is our last hurrah!"

Last?

"Are you happy? What is your plan after today?"

"We will travel around the world with my wife… we will spend all my savings!" the gray haired guffawed.

"I will go and look for Bin Laden… even in your place… in the Philippines!" the one with shining crown. "Kidding aside, I really don't know. I don't have enough savings. Probably I will look for a part time. I still like to work, to lengthen my life… how about you, Quiel?"

"Me…?"

I probably miss the mail room… the 1LL—upper underground I suppose they say in the Philippines, not First Lower Level?

Thirty years… some days' vacation. Headache? Fever? Stomachache? Oh, a lot of medicines. Two capsules are enough to let any illness fly. You could still go to work, the whole day going up and down in a 28-story COB, sure enough by means of the freight elevator.

Whom did they give the unused vacation live? What a pity… the extras, they should have included in the retirement pay. Anyway, sometimes it's good for it helps the needy. Were there five hundred hours? More than?

How much money is still in the bank?

Your nephew is not at the bottom of their class, Manong…

A hundred… two hundred… how much was the biggest? Five hundred? It was the wedding of Manuel the youngest brother.

Almost monthly. Sometimes, twice a month.

Uncle…

Cousin…

Sister-in-law…

Brother-in-law…

Be patient, Uncle. We'll pay you back. When I pass the board exam, you'll have an engineer nephew next year! Uncle Salaknib…

Who was then the one graduated in education? And nursing? And commerce? How many of them? Five? Eight? Ten?

Who were they then? Couldn't even remember their names. Where are they now? There might be one who went to Hawaii. And, in Alaska.

Was there anyone who went to Canada? Might also be in Australia. How many of them had got married? Four of them might had sent something for their wedding.

How about Salaknib's children?

How are they now? Can't even remember the last time they sent a letter; or had heard news about them. Or anybody of them sent a letter after graduating... their wedding?

O, yes, their cousin sent an e-mail the other day. Another hundred again.

But how then?

"It's a company's policy, Quiel... We have to lost you, but we have to give way to younger generation..."

65, is he an old man already?

Uncle then...

Uncle now...

It will be unending uncle...

Oh, then nothing could be saved for a ticket for even a single vacation!

But... those children of Salaknib, they don't even bother to send a letter. Were they been told by their parents to do so? Notwithstanding their indifference, they should...

I missed you so much, Kilin, my son. Your siblings are here, it's true, but they are one by one going away. One went to Mindanao... When would you be coming home for vacation? I'm so weak. I am always dreaming your late father. We were so happy walking along the most beautiful garden. I felt myself so light, as if I'm free from any illness. O my, sometimes, when I wake up and feel the pain in my joints, I would rather not to be awakened from my dreams. But I really don't know, my son, if that was a dream for it seems very true. The surroundings were so verdant...

Yes, I received your gift for my birthday. But nothing is better than you yourself is here for me to see you personally and hear your voice. Your letters...

Are the environs there more verdant than the wide rice field, or vegetable field between Limas and the River Life? Was there no waving rice stalk there?

Was there a newly caught mudfish fingerlings, sweet small crabs, blackfish, mudfish, shrimps? Turnips, watermelon… Horseradish, is there? Jute? Frog?

Does it rain there also, or just unending snow? Pity you, Kilin, my son. Lucky you if not every parts of your body benumbed by the severely cold weather? O my God… Would be better if you are married. Why don't you not get married so that you have a helpmate in time of hardship?

Yes, if you state you can eat all the food the reach will eat there… here, the only free is the harvest of your siblings from a piece of land they are tilling, but the important things to buy, my god, my son, their prices soar up to the heavens as they say. Sometimes when I feel like going to the market and go with somebody else to buy something, I could hardly bring home myself because of giddiness because of too many people. My goodness, for there are still a lot of squabbling, men and women.

By the way, Captain Ladio had gone to rest. They found his dead body by the flank of River Life. They have a suspect… but his relatives were so quiet. You know, then, what they were thinking. O my goodness, my son, it's too much.

But I am not telling you not to come home… Your younger brother Salaknib, never had he moved to another place. You know your brother very well. If he said stay here, nobody could alter it. He said, if there are not faithful to their place of birth, reason is they don't know how to love it. He said: me, I will never uproot my roots for I was born here, and I move back to this dust the same… If you could come to visit, you could see what he is doing; he warned me not to mention to you in my letters. But… he is the one who doesn't know how to give up from hardship. He is always in his farm. I just don't know; he even attended some seminars.

I remember Idot. She will be having two children. When she supposed to meet me, she tried to avoid me. My, Kilin, my son, her figure looks like a shrunken house. Her husband attained all the type of vices… and he is no longer a seaman. He is being fed by Idot, and he always hurts her… merciful life, right, my son?

O, that's all for now because the compassionate youngster who is helping me write a letter for you is going somewhere…

9:55 A.M., May 33, ----

Yesterday:

"Howdy, Quiel?"

"Ha-e... I'm fine, Kellie...!" That was not true.

Thursday. Paper delivery day at 3WW—was there also Third Floor West Wing of the buildings in Makati? And 4WW... and that side in 1NW. how many cases do they need? Five in 4WW. One... two... three... four, five... six in 3WW and how about in 1NW? Four as well. It was good, nothing in 2EW.

There were still three 6-wheeler carts. For sure Don had not gone delivering in his route. Kevin, it will be ten when he arrives.

Ooops! This lower back feels like cracked. Just imagine ten rims per box? How many pounds? Twenty?

It will be good for Lynn is arriving at 9:10... there will be no problem because he seldom brings a lot.

Eric will arrive at 9:40. He is the one bringing a lot of packages, to be distributed here in COB, and in different departments outside the building. Almost the entire 28 storeys be distributed with different kinds of packages. This lower back is painful...hope Eric will not bring a lot of boxed computers. When was the day they deliver hundred computers?

But he surely brings not less than ten boxes or small boxes of micrographics for Gloria Frances there in COB 2. And FCH for Adriane Candelaria there in COB 5. In COB 25, Roberta Appell had a daily delivery. In COB 28, and COB 12, COB 3 are surely nothing for the renovation is not yet completed.

Why now... these legs feel like affected. Feel like stiffened while spring has just over. My, this elevator is too slow, as if as slow as the waddling vehicles in Manila even in EDSA. Had the traffic condition not improved, or maybe worsen?

How many packages for COB 4? Is it only this one for Linda Clawson? In COB 6? Is it only this one for Julie Aldridge? They had been working here for quite some time. Linda had probably been working for 20 years. Julie, maybe 15 years. Where had been the ones I have been contemporaries? Almost yearly people are moving. They are going up and down like the elevator. Many had been gone.

COB 4 already.

"Hi, Linda…"

"How're yah doing, Quiel?"

"Great…" Again. Why is it that great and fine is the answer even you feel the opposite? What do they say when you say not so good? Sorry! Do they really feel sorry?

"I heard that you are retiring, Quiel, is it true?"

"I… I am not retiring. I was asked to retire. They said I am already old. Is 65 already old, Linda?"

"You look like still strong… But, don't you like so that you could have a rest? Go places. Around the world. Go to Israel… in Jerusalem…"

"In Afghanistan…"

"Go look for Bin Laden? No way, Quiel! You're making me laugh…"

Around the world? Even Park City, I had just gone there one time. The Lake Powell, only a news. Antelope Island, one time… That Great Lake, yes, for you could only look down from COB 26…

From COB 26…

According to Salaknib: mother, Manong, she'd gone…

He had been in Heber for twenty years that time. First visit in Abbarit. The transformation of abandoned Abbarit was wonderful.

She had been mentioning your name, Manong, before she stops breathing.

Why, I always sent her a letter, and stuffs.

Salaknib again: she was hugging your letters. Those you sent to her, probably they were not important to her… she looked at ones then look up and say: your brother, poor him. Again, and again, she asks: does he not thinking to get married, to come back here? And then answers herself: he said he had found his world where he is right now. Poor him.

Mother forgive me. Nobility, I found out that it is everywhere as long as you know how to treasure your public figure…

According to Miguel: you did never visit her even ones, Kabagis[69].

The other sibling: as if you resented like a damper, Kabagis. You've totally forgotten Abbarit.

His sister-in-law on this: What then the use of your being here, Kayong[70], for your mother could no longer see you?

We should not be discussing that besides Nanang's *body... But do you know why? I did not have savings for a fare. Do you know why? Do you know? Ask yourselves... But where are your graduated children? Where are they? This should be their last chance to see their grandmother... Where are they? Where are they? And you, where were you during the days she longed for you?*

Who could understand me?

All of them went home after the funeral...

Hey, a lot of plaques? Salaknib Tacneng... those are all yours, Kabagis! You did never mention to me.

Was it important, Kabagis...?

Hey, were you not be happy, Kabagis?

You know what, Kayong, he even got mad when I tried to mention to you.

It was far better if you did not notice...

See, he went to receive an award only ones, Kayong. Aside from that Distinguished Filipino Farmer of the Year plaque, where he was even hesitant to receive, she let me receive all the others. Outstanding Citizen of the Year. Distinguished Farmer of San Juan. And those...

I can't understand you, Kabagis.

For me, the honorable citizen is the one who does not trade his persona with anything—riches, honor... What then be the plaques if you are not true with yourself? Notwithstanding a heap of plaques or certificates over you if you do not know yourself, and if you do not know how to serve by all your means despite of receiving no education, what is the significance?

Those awards you received, are the not enough to show your services...?

---

[69]   *Kabagis,* brother or sister.

[70]   *Kayong,* brother-in-law.

Are those the onlhy reasons why you serve? Serve notwithstanding honor you receive...

9:56 A. M., May 22, ----

LADIES and gentlemen, we are honored to gather here in recognition of these three distinguished associates for their unceasing services with the Cosmopolitan Office Building. . ."

Poor Nanang... poor...

Uncle...

Brother-in-law...

Cousins...

Idot... how many grandchildren she got? Her children did not attend school. They left her husband Doro dead under a big acacia tree. Was it true that her third child was fathered by a rich man in town?

Hey, that part is verdant. How many hectares is that?

Approximately five, Kabagis. Including that approximately a hectare of fishpond by the Cabanayan.

There is also... is that a poultry? And piggery?

There are over a thousand chicken separated by each breed—white leghorn. Local... Those swines, there were more or less two hundred.

Don't tell me you are the owner of those...?

I was able to achieve it by the help of the government. I also attended training... I would like to have our siblings to help me, but like you, they went to some places.

What is that open space by the western part of your house?

I said, ready to anybody who want to build a house... if anybody want to come back for even your nephews and nieces dream to follow your footsteps.

During the night:

Who are those, Kabagis?

The brothers outside.

Are they still around? Why... why did you hand them...?

I did not hand them. They just get whatever they want...by themselves.

Often?

Whenever they desire.

Why don't you notify the authorities?

I may not be here anymore if I did that. One more thing, whenever the authorities need something, they also come and solicit...sort of. I don't ask any favor from them. Sometimes, they offer any amount. I am not giving them price. They give whatever they desire.

Your neighbors know this?

They are aware.

Unbelievable. Are you kidding me...?

It is unbelievable. But it is occuring. Believe it or not.

You are already a stranger in Abbarit, Kilin... with your siblings. You do not know any longer your brother Salaknib...

10:00 A. M., May 22, ----

YESTERDAY:

"By the way, congratulations, Quiel! You deserve your award."

"Thank you very much, Linda. That's what they usually do to everyone they execute, right? They give him any thing he asks for. They ask him what he wants before they execute..."

"As if you are not excited? There were only few who are bestowed an award for being loyal. Imagine, how long have you worked here?"

"Thirty... I went up and down the twenty-eight story of the COB for thirty years... You know, Linda, I am thinking Salaknib, my brother. He never left Abbarit. He did nothing except to farm... Ooops! I still have a lot to deliver!"

"Good luck, Quiel."

COB 16? Who is this Karilyn Moore?

Hey, why is it Wendy Maugham not here anymore?

"Good morning..."

"How are you... Quiel? I'm Karilyn Moore. We switched places with Wendy. They transferred her to JSMB."

"Wendy got a package, Karilyn."

"Thank you very much, Quiel. Just live it and I will give it to her. You know, Wendy told me a lot of things about you. You are the best among the mail carriers."

"Thank you very much, Karilyn. But because my late mother during our growing ups, that we need to take care our being Ilokano. Wherever we go, we need to show who we are… my late mother was so industrious. Even my late father. All their siblings were hard workers…"

"I'm sure your family is lucky…"

Really…?

Hey, I almost passed by COB 25. How many packages do Roberta Appell had? Four? Hey, all of these belong to her. Nothing for 27 where DTA, and 28 which is the Security Department.

"It's good you dropped by, Quiel. My vacation starts tomorrow."

"I thought… you're moving out also, Roberta."

"No. I haven't reach thirty years here! It is still a long way to go before reaching my 65."

"You are lucky."

"You are luckier, because you are retiring."

"You already knew it?"

"Who doesn't know, Quiel? You're so popular, nobody doesn't know you in COB. I think, you know every corner of the building. Every office. Everybody."

"Many are already new, Roberta. Employees had been coming and going. Like the passing of days, like the elevator going up and down that I could not remember every event, the same with the people here."

"I will not be here tomorrow, Quiel. Sorry. But take this. As sign of our gratitude for your nobleness… for your goodness to us. Nothing was lost, or even delivered late packages during your services. My bosses here, they know very well your goodness. Accept this."

"A w-watch?"

"So that you will always remember us when you look at the time…"

10:05 A. M., May 22, ----

LAST but not the least, Tranquilino Tacneng…"

"During these times, because of so many challenges in life, especially in economy, not only in America but we all know a global problem, there are few if any like these, our three brothers, who served this long and given the opportunity to serve with the COB this long in their department. Twenty, twenty-five, thirty years until they retire.

"Because of their perfect record, it is but appropriate to offer them recognition. We are not sure if there ever be more praiseworthy than them.

"Not to give preference, but as you can see, Tranquilino Tacneng is the only foreigner among the three. Based from his record, his record was never been tainted during the expand of his service. I don't know how he did, but I respect his durability... Are all your Filipino bloodstreams same as you are, Quiel? I urge you to recommend somebody to take over you!"

Resounding applauds.

"I am then honored to hand them their certificates and medals... Don Green, twenty years of service..."

Applauds.

"Eric Barkbuster, twenty-five..."

Applauds.

"Tranquilino Tacneng, thirty..."

More resounding applauds.

"Ladies and gentlemen, thank you for giving us the opportunity to express what in our minds.

"There is a Chinese saying, like this: More talks, more mistakes; less talks, less mistakes; no talk, no mistake. That's why as I've said, I have a short message.

"Man, his responsibility in life does not end after his retirement. His venture continues every passing day. Thank you very much for giving me the opportunity to serve in the COB, as well as the trust you've given to me.

"Specially, I am very grateful to my late mother who single handedly mold my character because my late father passed away early. My mother taught us siblings to listen to the voice of our inner selves; she molded us with the true character of an Ilokano, the Filipinos whose ancestors live in Northern Luzon. Her advices served as my nourishment and strength in coming to venture in America. I suffered tremendous homesickness for being separated from the land of my birth but because of the advices of my kind mother that rooted in to my mind, thirty years has not managed to destroy the essence of my being an Ilokano. Despite my being American citizen, I was born Ilokano, I will remain Ilokano to go back to the dust of my origin...

"Hey, I said short, but this one is extended.

"Thank you very much for considering me as your brother. That is more important than honoring me. I will bring this treasure when I go back to the land of my origin..."

10:30 A. M., May 22, ----

COB 26.

This will be the last. There will be no more other chances to come here after this event. Here is intended to receive tourists. In that eastern side where many small buildings, be looked down. The State University included that at the side of the mountain engraved a white big letter U which is the sign of the university.

In the western side where to look down, there is the three-year-old big Conference Center near the foot of the COB. In the southwestern side, different buildings including the Delta Center, the Marriott Hotel, and the Salt Center. In the far north, in the side of the mountain, the robust State Capitol seems like looking down the environment. In the far west, we notice the landing and flying aircrafts at the International Airport. Behind this is where the Great Lake.

It was interesting to come here in this level whenever time permits. When time of winter, the environment is too white and almost nothing to see other color for everything was covered...

It will only be in dreams to look under the airport... those airplanes scheduled to fly...

Those scheduled to fly...

O, yes, Abbarit. Your verdant rice fields. That fishery in your bosom. Your remaining kind people... yes, the breadfruit, the mother had gone, but the River Life … is it still gnawing your flank? The narrow road belted with the river, is it still alive?

My brother Salaknib…

Idot…

Your entirety…

I wish to come and rest my life on your cuddle, Abbarit… I wish to come and rest my life… —0

First Prize, RFAAFIL, 2005; *Bannawag*: November 7, 2005; *translation completed*: June 19, 2018, 2:15 a.m.

Bibliography

Published in the Bannawag magazine
unless otherwise noted.
Chronologically arranged.

1. SINAMAR A. ROBIANES TABIN, SR.

Novelette

Till Death//Tungpal Tanem. January 24, 1966-February 21, 1966
Sweetsop//Atis. May 26, 1969-June 2, 1969
The World on His Shoulder//Ti Lubong iti Abagana. November 9,
    1981-December 28, 1981

Short Story

Always Be My Guide//Bagnoskonto Iti Agnanayon. April 20, 1962
My Father, My Sister and Our Home//Ni Tatang, ni Manang ken ti
    Pagtaenganmi. June or July 1962
I Should Have Come to Say Goodbye//Immayak Koma Nagpakada.
    1963?
One Who Cares//Maysa a Mangipateg. 1964?
Drying Your Tears is Not Enough//Ibusenyo Man Dagiti Luayo. 1965?
Now I Know//Ammok Itan. September 13, 1965
Here is the Riddle//Isu Daytoyen Daydi Burburtia. September 27, 1965

Time//Panawen. August 8, 1966

How Many Have You Conveyed? //Manon ti Nangibagaam? February 26, 1968

Cooling Like a Roaster//Tumarektek, Agpakawitan. December 9, 1968

I Envy You//Ap-apalankayo. February 2, 1970

Jackfruit//Anangka. May 4, 1970

On the Edge of the World//Iti Ngarab ti Lubong. August 31, 1970

Load//Imet. September 13, 1971

When Lucia Falls in Love//Idi Agayat ni Lucia. December 30, 1971

The Ocean Between Them//Ti Taaw iti Baetda. February 14, 1972

Testament//Testamento. August 7, 1972

Curse in the City//Lunod iti Siudad. February 26, 1973

Will Surely Be Awakened//Mariingto Laeng. October 8, 1973

Do You Know Marilou? //Am-ammom Kadi ni Marilou? December 10, 1973

Malay Apple//Makopa. June 24, 1974

Grandmother Delang//Ni Lela Delang. July 2, 1974

Grandfather's Dreams//Dagiti Arapaap ni Lelong. August 12, 1974

Marianne, you are a Riddle//Marianne, Maysaka a Burburtia. September 16, 1974

Miguela's Love//Ti Ayat ni Miguela. October 14, 1974

Time Can Wait, Child//Makauray ti Panawen, Nakkong. January 6, 1975

Life in the City//Ti Biag Ditoy Siudad. February 3, 175

Sadiwarek. March 10, 1975

If You Really Love Me//No Pudno nga Ay-ayatennak. April 14, 1975

When Would You Understand the Truth? //Kaanonto a Maawatam ti Kinapudno? August 4, 1975

Measures of Tenderness//Panimbagan ti Pammateg. September 8, 1975

Nana Baak's Desire//Ti Sapsapulen ni Nana Baak. December 1, 1975

Auntie Rosa's Banana//Ti Saba ni Anti Rosa. July 22,1974

Tell Them That I Am Now Good//Ipadamagmo a Nasingpetakon. 1975?

You Will Also Feel These//Mariknamto Met Dagitoy. January 26, 1976

The Idol//Ti Idolo. April 19, 1976

Court Her to Give Lesson//Armem Man Ketdi Tapno Agnakem. June 28, 1976

One Who Cares for Them//Ti Mangipatpateg Kadakuada. August 23, 1976

Sotera's Crush//Ti Crush ni Sotera. 1976?

The Return//Panagsubli. 1976?

Once a Lourdes//Daydi Maysa a Lourdes. April 24, 1972

In Every Direction//Iti Tunggal Direksion. July 4, 1977

The Collector//Ti Kolektor. 1977?

Nimfa's Love//Ti Ayat ni Nimfa. 1977?

It's Not Written in the Blackboard//Saan a Naisurat iti Pisarra. January 9, 1978

In the Wheel of Life// Iti Pilid ti Biag. March 27, 1978

Whom Do You Know? //Asino ti Am-ammom? July 14, 1980

Virginia is Going Overseas//Agabroden ni Virginia. April 4, 1983

Allegedly Dwarf//Ansisit Kano. June 20, 1983

It's Upon Your Discretion//Adda Kenka Daytan. June 27, 1988

How are You, Dolly? (see *Glimmer in the Dark*)//Komustaka, Dolly? (see *Rayus a Nasipngetan*). *Ban.* April 8, 1991

Hidden Ray//Rayus a Nasipngetan. *Batonsileng, 1992*

If Life Could Only be Bought// No Magatang La Koma ti Biag. June 6, 1995

Tata Basil's Dream//Ti Arapaap ni Tata Basil. June 17, 1996

Resia's Demigod//Ti Diosen ni Resia. July 15, 1996

God Exists, Joan//Adda Dios, Joan. November 11, 1996

Livelihood When Survive//Pagbiagan No Malasat. August 6, 2001

Feature Articles

My Most Precious Christmas Gift//Ti Kapatgan nga Aginaldok. December 18, 1967

Do You Believe in Palm Reading? //Mamatikayo Kadi iti Palad? August 5, 1968

Music is Their Lives' Color//Musika ti Maris ti Biagda. July 7, 1975

God Listened to Me//Inimdengannak ti Dios. December 22, 1975

Model. Manang Pacing: Idol//Ulidan. Manang Pacing: Pagwadan nga Ina. *Rimat Magazine*, October 2004.

Poems

Being a Writer//Kinamannurat. *Ban.*?
February//Pebrero. *Ban.*?
In This Life// Iti Daytoy a Biag. *Ban.*?
Beloved. *Ilokano Magazine*, May 1967
Many a Moment. *Normalite Bulletin*, October-November 1967
My Sweet Alegria. *N.B.* 1967
My Promise. *N.B.* 1967

Awards

Glimmer in the Dark or How are You, Dolly? //Rayus a Nasipngetan wenno Komustakan, Dolly? *3rd Prize*, GRAAFIL, 1982.
Lifetime Achievement Award, TMI America/Global and TMI Filipinas, 2010.

2. LORENZO GARCIA TABIN, SR.

Novels

Ti Imetda nga Impierno (Their Load Inferno). March 14, 1996-May 30, 1966.
Ramut ti Sinamar (Source of Rays). September 12, 1996-February 6, 1967.
Agus (Flow). July 10, 1967-December 25, 1967.
Pakpakawan, Berde! (Over My Dead Body; *literal translation*: Never Ever, Verde!). September 16, 1968-November 4, 1968.
Virginia. November 18, 1968-June 9, 1969.
Balay ti Katawa (House of Laughter). Co-authors: Genaro R. Sumaoang and Jaime R. Luzano. February 17, 1979-September 8, 1969.

Darudar (as is—Third Night of the Full Moon). July 14, 1969-December 29, 1969.

San Sandi Morning (Some Sunday Morning). January 5, 1970-June 22, 1970.

Dadapilan (Sugar Mill). June 29, 1970-December 14, 1970.

Agpadigoka Man, Kabagis (Please Share, Brother). December 21, 1970-22, 1971.

Dakami a Daksanggasat (We the Unfortunates). October 18, 1971-April 17, 1972.

Mangwaksi Met ti Langit (Heavens Also Unveil). June 18, 1973-August 6, 1973.

Ta Annak Ida ti Dios (For They are God's Children). May 18, 1981-September 21, 1981.

Burayok nga Apuy (Blazing Burayok). September 10, 1990-July 22, 1991.

Adtoy, Siak, ni Jesus Crisostomo: Dramaturgo (Behold, I am, Jesus Crisostomo: Playwright). May 4, 1992-September 28, 1992.

Poems

Allon ti Biag (Waves of Life). December 10, 1962.

Ulep, Tapok, Asuk, Langit (Cloud, Dust, Smoke, Heaven). January 13, 1964.

Tallo a Saning-i (Three Entreaties). March 9, 1964.

Ladawan (Scene). December 28, 1964.

Naibinggas iti Kanta (Intermingled in a Song). June 27, 1966.

Sika ken Siak (You and I). August 7, 1967.

Gapu 'Ita Libnosmo a Nagpaiduma (Because of Your Extraordinary Beauty). In: GUMIL Filipinas, November 27, 1967.

Nupay Adayoak Kenka (Distance Never a Factor). April 29, 1968.

Masakbayan (Future). Pen name: Liwayway Gabino. July 14, 1969.

Ti Sangalubongan Agur-uray (The World is Waiting). December 17, 1973.

Sabong ti Bato (Stone's Flower). May 10, 1974.

Ayat ti Mangngadilian (Love of a Fisherman). December 10, 1974.

Tallo a Daniw (Three Poems). May 10, 1976.

Adda Sakit iti Alas Tres (There is a Three 0'clock Sickness). October 18, 1976.

Dakesen, Paskua Manen! (My Goodness, It's Christmas Again!). December 20, 1976.

Magnakayonto, Annakko (You Will Walk, My Children). January 29, 1979.

Agapon Met ti Billit ti Dhahran (Dhahran's Bird Also Goes Into the Coop). August 9, 1982.

Yanmo Kadin, Ilokano? (Where are You, Ilokano?). November 28, 1977.

Iti Dormitorio (In the Dormitory). October 11, 1982.

Paskua iti Dhahran (Christmas in Dhahran). December 26, 1983.

Maregreg ti Panawen (Time Will Fall). March 26, 1984.

Noche Buena. December 23, 1985.

Agbalkotkan, Kabayan (Wrap Up, My Countryman). April 21, 1986.

Didiosen (Demigod). July 21, 1986.

Kalpasan ti Maikawalo (After Eight O'clock). December 12, 1988.

Ngatangata (Confounded). May 24, 1993.

Kastoy ti Agdaniw, Nakkong (This is the Way How to Write a Poem, My Child). July 24, 1994.

Yan Dagiti Bituen? (Where are the Stars?). February 27, 1995.

Sakbay a Marunaw ti Niebe (Before the Snow Melts), April 17, 1995

Siak ti Agnanayon (I Am Eternity). August 28, 1995.

Innak, Kunam, Mapanka Lattan (You Said You are Going and Just Like That). November 27, 1995.

Agtedted 'Ta Atep. Lakay (The Roof is Leaking, Lakay). July 29, 1996.

Salmo 1. October 19, 1998.

Bulong ti Panagreregreg: Salmo 2 (Leaves of Fall: Psalm 2). January 25, 1999.

Salmo 3: Libnos (Psalm 3: Beauty). March 1, 1999.

Iti Pagurayan (In the Lobby). May 31, 1999.

Ina, iti Disierto nga Eden ti Indio (A Mother, in Indio's Eden of Desert). July 5, 1999.

Salmo 4: Ikupinnakan ni Taraki (Psalm 4: Taraki is Folding You Out). August 23, 1999.

Anniniwan (Shadow). February 21, 2000.

Biag a Kasla Takiag (Arm-sized Life). April 3, 2000.

Inton Bigat Idinton ti Ita (Tomorrow Now Will Be Yesterday). May 8, 2000.

Salmo 6: Napankan: Dios-ti-kumuyog, *Manong* Severino A. Lazo (Psalm 6: You're Gone: God Be with You, *Manong* Severino A. Lazo). May 22, 2000.

Kigaw (Young Calves) December 11, 2000.

Agtutuglep a Malem (Drowsy Afternoon). February 5, 2001.

Atiddog dagiti Aldaw, Ababa dagiti Rabii (Days are Long, Night are Short) March 19, 2001.

Saligemgemen ti Lubong ni Taraki (Taraki's World is Chilling). December 1, 2003.

Agmanoka iti Patneng nga iti Niebe Nagramuten (Amen to the Native That Rooted in the Ice). 2005. (see **Awards).**

(More poems under **Anthology).**

Short Stories

No Di Agunget ti Akin-aywan (Once the Guardian Permits). March 4, 1963.

Ni Apong Sabel (Grandmother Sabel). August 5, 1963.

Ditoy ti Nakainaigan ti Ayatna (He Left His Love Here). January 6, 1964.

Kadagiti Agraem a Mata (For the Becharmed Eyes). February 10, 1964.

Kaimudingan (Importance). May 18, 1964.

Nalabes a Panagrambak (Too Much Wallowing). November 30, 1964.

Ti Isagsaganana a Masakbayan (The Future in His Mind). March 8, 1965.

Tapno Maliklikan ti Agus (To Avoid the Issue). May 17, 1965.

Tao ken Panawen (Man and Time). October 4, 1965; August 27, 2018.

Nagbukaren ti Rosas (The Roses Had Bloomed). October 18, 1965.

Saosao (Gossip). November 8, 1965.

Sukat ti Napukaw (Proxy for the Lost). November 15, 1965.

Maikadua a Paraiso (Next Paradise). January 3, 1966.

Law-ang (Cosmos). February 21, 1966.

Maysa Laeng Kadakuada (Just One of Them). August 8, 1966.

Ita Ta Simmangpeten ni David (Now That David has Arrived). *Ilokano Magazine*: May 1967.

Taaw ken Daytoy a Babilonia (Deep and This Babylon). June 5, 1967.

Perlas (Pearl). January 8, 1968.

Langit iti Dayta a Lubong (Heaven in That World). January 22, 1968.

Nagsangalan (Shaping Place). February 26, 1968.

Ti Eden iti Biagda (Their Lives' Eden). June 17, 1968.

Dadakkel a Mata iti Babassit a Tawa (Big Eyes By the Small Windows). July 15, 1968.

Kaanonto, aya, Dungngo? (When will it be, Beloved?) August 19, 1968.

Annay! (Ouch!) September 16, 1968.

Rupa (Face). June 23, 1969; March 12, 2018.

Lumba iti Agmatuon (Race at Noon). July 7, 1969.

Iti Eden dagiti Inosente (By the Innocents' Eden). March 16, 1970.

Ti Suako ni Lelong Belong (Grandfather Belong's Pipe). July 6, 1970.

Ditoy Gloria: Pagbaludan (Here in Glory: Penitentiary). June 28, 1971.

Ladawan: Biblioteka (Sight: Library). September 6, 1971.

Nailet ti Lubong (The World is Crowded). May 8, 1972.

Estero: iti Maysa a Panawen (Creek: Once Upon a Time). June 19, 1972.

Naparmek iti Ayat (Defeated by Love). July 24, 1972.

Iti Maikadua a Gundaway (Second Time Around) November 5, 1973.

Abat. January 28, 1974.

Mayat nga Agimmamadi (Wavering). September 30, 1074.

Akkos Bayugaw. October 28, 1974.

Ket Nagpaskua Dagiti Anghel iti Paraangan da Mister Ligaya (And the Angels Celebrated Christmas in Mr. Ligaya's Yard). December 16, 1974.

Tata Ubing (Mr. Young). February 24, 1975.

Isu a Makilumlumba Kadagiti Darikmat (He, who is Racing with Time). April 28, 1975.

Keppeten ti Rabii ti Agbukar nga Aldaw (The Evening Shuts Up the Blooming Day). August 25, 1975.

Nangrugi Tapno Aggibus (Compeled to be Concluded). January 5, 1976.

Agriingkan, Tatang Godo (Wake Up, Tatang Godo). January 19, 1976.

Sabali a Sukog ti Puso (Uncommon Shape of Heart). January 26, 1976.

Mano ti Alice iti Lubong? (How Many Alices in the World?). November 8, 1976.

Maris (Shade) 2nd Honorable Mention, GUMIL Hawaii, April 22, 1984

Nalabaga ti Init iti Dhahran (Red is the Sun in Dhahran). November 19, 1984.

Adayo ti Belen (Bethlehem is Remote). December 9, 1985.

Tallo a Tugot (Three Footprints). December 19, 1988.

Meri Krismas, Pacul (Merry Christmas, Pacul). January 2, 1989.

Agsardeng Koma ti Lubong Ta Dumsaag ti Tao (The World Should Stop that People Could Get Off). December 25, 1989.

Pilarica Naamitan: Maysa a Malem (Pilarica Naamitan: A Post Meridian). August (?), 1991.

Mangmatimati dagiti Bituen iti Escopa (The Flickering Stars of Escopa). February 22, 1989.

*Reggaay (Landslide). 4th honorable mention, Gov. Luis Singson Literary Award (unpublished?). 1992.

Uray Maysa Laeng (One is Enough). January 4, 1999.

Kasanon no Agsardeng ti Lubong, Taraki? (What If the World Ends, Taraki?). *Saluyot*. December 1999.

Wadsapani! (What's Up, Honey!). December 3, 2001.

Sangabukel nga Init, Sangkailgat a Bulan, ken Lima Gantilia a Bituen (A Spherical Sun, a Slice of Moon, and Five Liters of Stars). June 24, 2002.

Puon (Patriarch). October 21, 2002.

Dagiti Anghel iti Saklot ti Kinerker a Garami (Angels in the Cuddle of Bundled Hay). May 26, 2003.

Laud (West). *Rimat,* May 2003.

Pagawidam, Felipe Abraham? (Where is Your Resting Place, Felipe Abraham?) *Rimat,* February 2004.

Adtoyak, ni Tranquilino Tacneng: Iti 28 Kadsaaran a Lubong (Here I Am, Tranquilino Tacneng: in a 28-Storey World). November 7, 2005 (See also: **Awards**).

Articles

Ti Naipablaak a Daniwko (My Published Poem). June 8, 1964.

Maysa a Purgatorio iti Biagko ti 'Ti Imetda nga Impierno' ('Their Load Inferno' is a Purgatory in My Life). August 22, 1966.

Mayor Victorino A. Savellano: Pinagluposna ti Cabugao (Mayor Victorino A. Savellano: He Changed the Image of Cabugao). November 21, 1966.

Dra. Fe del Mundo: Adda ti Pusona Kadagiti Agasanna (Dr. Fe del Mundo: Her Patients are in Her Heart). 1967.

Pinarmekda dagiti Dalluyon (They Trounced the Waves). January 1, 1968.

Pabaknangenna ti Apit (It Increases Harvest). March 25, 1968.

Mapa: Ammom ti Kaipapananna Kenka? (Maps: Do You Know Its Significance?). April 22, 1968.

Saan a Kas iti Ullaw (It is Not Like a Kite). December 30, 1974.

Agsebbada Gapu iti Ayat (They Sacrifice for Love). February 17, 1975.

Ti Pasion ni Jesucristo (The Passion of Jesus Christ). March 31, 1975.

Ti Samiweng 'Ta Pusom (The Music in Your Heart). June 23. 1975.

Ania ti Pagsursuratmo? (What are You Using in Writing?). December 8, 1975.

Ubing ti Adding Machine (Adding Machine is a Child). January 10, 1977.

Naulpit ti Gimong Kadagiti Agballa (Society is Unkind to the Mentally Ill). December 7, 1981.

'Eid Mubarak, Sadik' (Merry Christmas, My Friend). December 27, 1982.

Kastoykami Ditoy Saudi (This is How We are in Saudi). February 1983—December 1984.

Naimut ti Iisemanda; Salip iti Sarita 1988, GRAAFIL (They are
    Egoistic; Short Story Contest 1988, GRAAFIL). September 26,
    1988-October 3, 1988.
Adda Estilo ti Panagpakatawa; Salip iti Sarita 1989, GRAAFIL (Style in
Writing Comedy; Short Story Contest 1989, GRAAFIL). October 9,
    1989.
Kanito ti Panagpakada (Time to Say Goodbye). July 19, 1994.
Iti Abroad: Ania, Nagasatak? (Abroad: What, I'm Lucky?). February
    26, 1996.
Kastoykami Ditoy. . . (Here We Are). *The Philippine-Maui Wave
    Bulletin.* March 1996, May 1996.
Adda Balligi iti Likud dagiti Pannubok (Success Behind Trials - written
    by Lorenzo G. Tabin, named for Severino A. Lazo). October 12,
    1998.
Agregreg ti Niebe iti Winter (Snow Falls in Winter). December 21,
    1998.
**Ti Tulbek ti Panagballigi ti Maysa a Mannurat (The Key for a Writer's
Success). *Saluyot,* January 1999.
Apay, Martilio Kadi ni Baketmo? (Why, is Your Wife a Hammer?).
    February 1, 1999.
Ditoy Idi ti Lubongmi (This Was Our World). *Saluyot,* April 1999.
Dakami Met (Letter to the Editor). February 28, 2000.
Ne, Addaakon Ditoy America, Kaka! (See, Finally I'm Now in America,
    Brother!), *Yloco Journal,* January-March 2000.
Ay, Dinanonda ni Jojo! (Boy, They Reached Out for Jojo!). February
    10, 2003.
Abrod: Paliiw: Iruruk-at (Abroad: Reflection: Setting Self Free). *Rimat,*
    February 2003
Literatura: Kinamannurat: Naisangayan a Lubong (Literature:
Authorship: Amazing World. *Rimat,* April 2003.
Libro: Sagumbi: Maysa a Gameng (Book Review: Sagumbi: A Treasure).
    Rimat, June 2003
Elehia (Elegy). *Rimat,* November 2003.
Genealogy: Puon ti Kaputotan (Genealogy: Family Tree). *Rimat,* May
    2004.

Halloween: Adu ti Mangmangkik Ditoy America! (Halloween: Many
are Witch Here in America!) *Rimat,* November 2004.

Timpuyog: Tangguyob ti Panagkaykaysa (Unity: A Call for Harmony)
Timpuyog Journal April 30, 2014.

RFAAFIL 2014: Adu ti Makaay-ayo Ngem Adu Latta Met ti Saan
(RFAAFIL 2014: Many are Pleasing but Same with Unpleasant)
RFAAFIL 2014.

Gapu Ta Maysaak nga Ilokano (Because I Am Ilocano) March 4, 2019.

Anthology

Ti Bin-i nga Agnagan Ferdinand (The Seed Named Ferdinand), in:
Ferdinand E. Marcos: Kalasag ti Filipinas, GUMIL Filipinas. 19--.

Naibinggas iti Kanta (Blended in a Song), poem, in: *Ballatinaw,* edited
by Godofredo S. Reyes and Pelagio A. Alcantara. 1967.

Taaw ken Daytoy a Babilonia (Ocean and This Babylon), short story, in:
Napili a Sarita Dagiti Ilokano, edited by Juan S. P. Hidalgo, Jr. 1968.

Ulep, Tapok, Asuk, Langit (Cloud, Dust, Smoke, Heaven), poem, in:
Angalo ken Aran, edited by Godofredo S. Reyes. 1969.

Rupa (Face), short story, in: *24 a Napili a Sarita Dagiti Ilokano,*
edited by Juan S. P. Hidalgo, Jr. 1970.

Ayat ti Mangngadilian (Love of a Fisherman), poem, in: *Pamulinawen,
Dandaniw,* edited by Jose A. Bragado, and Benjamin M. Pascual. 1976.

Gapu 'Ita Libnosmo a Nagpaiduma (Because of Your Extraordinary
Beauty), poem, also in *Pamulinawen, Dandaniw.*

Sabong ti Bato (Stone Flower), poem; also, in *Pamulinawen,
Dandaniw.*

Ti Eden iti Biagda (Eden in Their Lives), short story, in: *Talugading,*
edited by Lorenzo G. Tabin, Edilberto H. Angco, Rogelio A.

Aquino, and Cristino I. Inay. 1977.

Pakpakawan, Berde! Ken 21 a Sarita (Never Ever You, Verde! [a novel]
and 21 Short Stories). Lorenzo G. Tabin. 1978.

Burayok nga Apuy (Blazing Burayok), excerpt from a novel, in: *Lahi,
Philippines Multi-Lingual Creative Writing Journal,* edited by
Alejandrino J. Hufana. 1979.

Mga Mukha Sa Basag na Salamin (Face in a Broken Mirror), a Filipino version of Rupa (Face), story, in: **Kurditan,** edited by Reynaldo A. Duque, Jose A. Bragado, and Linda T. Lingbaoan. 1988.

Tallo a Tugot (Three Footprints), story, in: **Daton,** edited by Dionisio S. Bulong. 1992.

Agsardeng Koma ti Lubong ta Dumsaag ti Tao (May the World Stop and the People Alight), story, also in: **Daton.**

Mangmatimati Dagiti Bituen iti Escopa, The Flickering Stars of Escopa, story, in: **Lingka, Anthology of Ilokano Literature in English,** edited by Honor Blanco Cabie, Clesencio B. Rambaud, and Placido R. Real, Jr. 1994.

Ti Kanta ni Pinang (The Song of Pinang), poem, in: **Talibagok,** edited by Benjamin M. Pascual, Jose A. Bragado, and Clesencio B. Rambaud. 1987.

Busel ti Rosal (Rosebud), poem, also in: **Talibagok.**

Silaw (Light), poem, also in: **Talibagok.**

Ti Freud ni Damian (Damian's Freud), poem, also in: **Talibagok.**

Aragaag nga Imahinasion (Transparent Imagination), poem, also in: **Talibagok.**

Agawidkanto (You'll Go Home), poem, also in: **Talibagok.**

Awards

Rupa (Face), short story, 2nd honorable mention, **Bannawag Short Story Contest,** 1969.

Babilonia ni Kayumanggi ken Dadduma a Daniw (Brown's Babylon and other Poems), 3rd Prize, **DPI-GUMIL Ilocos Sur Poetry Contest,** 1975.

Virginia, Imnaska a Nagpaiduma (Virginia, you are an Extraordinary Beauty), epic, 1st honorable mention, **Governor Roque Ablan Award for Iluko Literature (GRAAFIL).** 1976.

Maris (Color), short story, 2nd Honorable mention, **GUMIL Hawaii Short Story Contest. 1984.**

Tallo a Tugot (Three Footprints), short story, 1st Prize, **Economy Tours and Travel, Inc. Short Story Contest.** 1988.

Agsardeng Koma ti Lubong ta Dumsaag ti Tao (May the World Stop and The People Alight), short story, 2nd Prize, *Economy Tours and Travel, Inc. Short Story Contest.* 1989.

Tatlong Bakas ng Paa (Three Footprints), Filipino version of Tallo a Tugot, short story, Special Award, *Carlos Palanca Memorial Award,* 1989.

Adtoy, Siak, ni Jesus Crisostomo: Dramaturgo (Behold, I Am, Jesus Crisostomo: Playwright), novel, 2nd Prize, *Economy Tours and Travel, Inc. Novel Contest.* 1990.

Pilarica Naamitan: Maysa a Malem (Pilarica Naamitan: A Post Meridiem), short story, 2nd Prize, *Governor Evaristo T. Singson Memorial Award for Iluko Literature.* 1991.

Reggaay (Landslide), short story, 2nd honorable mention, *Governor Evaristo T. Singson Memorial Award for Iluko Literature. 1992.*

Mangmatimati dagiti Bituen iti Escopa (The Stars in Escopa are Flickering), short story, 2nd Prize, *Kokua Lima Hawaii No Awards.* 1993.

Labasanka Laengen, a, San Juan (Let Me Just Pass You By, San Juan), poem, 3rd Prize, *Ulopan Literary Awards.* 1995.

Sakbay a Marunaw ti Niebe (Before the Melting of Snow), poem, 3rd Prize, *Ulopan Literary Awards.* 1996.

Labut, the Wizened Utopia, poem; Honorable Mention, *Iliad Press, The National Author Registry.* 1996.

Editor's Choice: Award for outstanding achievement in poetry. *The National Library of Poetry,* 1996.

Pagawidam, Felipe Abraham? (Where is Your Resting Palce, Felipe Abraham?) short story, 3rd Prize. *Sirmata Literary Awards.* 2001.

*BUCANEG AWARDS, highest awards given to an Ilokano writer. *GUMIL Metro Manila,* 2002.

Puon (Patriarch). Short story, 1st Prize: *Palanca Memorial Awards for Literature.* 2002.

Dagiti Anghel iti Saklot ti Kinerker a Garami (Angels in the Cuddle of Bundled Hay). Short story, 2nd Prize, *Pacioles Literary Awards.* 2003.

Adtoyak, ni Tranquilino Tacneng: iti 28 Kadsaaran a Lubong (Behold, Here Am I, Tranquilino Tacneng: at the 28-Storey World), short story, 1ˢᵗ Prize: *RFAAFIL (Reynald F. Antonio Award for Iluko Literature.* 2005.

Agmanoka iti Patneng nga iti Niebe Nagramuten (Kiss the Hand of the Native Who in the Snow Had Grown Root), poem, 3ʳᵈ Prize: *RFAAFIL (Reynald F. Antonio Award for Iluko Literature.* 2005.

Lifetime Achievement Award, TMI America/Global and TMI Filipinas, May 29, 2010.

UMPIL (Unyon ng mga Manunulat sa Pilipinas) Gawad Pambansang Alagad ni Balagtas 2014. [Filipino Writers Union]

Service Award, 15 Years of Service to Deseret Book Company, July 27, 2000-July 27, 2015.

Pammadayaw iti Maika-50 nga Anibersario ti *GUMIL Metro Manila*, Disiembre 11, 2016.

Authorship in Filipino Language

Alikabok sa Duguang Kalansay (Dust in Blooded Skeleton). Poem, *Tagumpay*, 1970

Mga Mukha sa Basag na Salamin (Faces in a Broken Mirror). Short story, *Tagumpay*, March 17, 1971, and *Kurditan*, 1988.

Awitin sa Tigang na Noo (Melody in a Barren Forehead. Poem, *Asia-Philippines Leader*, August 13, 1971.

Ang Eden sa Kanilang Buhay (Their Lives' Eden). A Filipino version of Ti Eden Iti Biagda, Short story, *The Quezonian:* May 24 and June 7, 1971, and *Asia Philippines Leader*, January 21, 1972.

Isang Butil ng Ulan sa Labi (A Droplet of Rain on a Lip). Poem, *Asia-Philippines Leader*, March 3, 1972

Ang Migrasyon sa Maikling Kuwento at Nobelang Ilokano (The Migration in the Ilocano Short Story and Novel), a thesis for the completion of a Masters' degree in Literature, *University of the Philippines*, Diliman, Quezon City, 1980.

Authorship in English

Abbarit, My Abbarit, poem, in: ***Windows of the Soul,*** The National Library of Poetry. 1995.

My Brothers My Sisters, poem, in: ***Famous Poems of the Twentieth Century,*** Famous Poets Society. 1996.

Bye-bye, Baybayyabas, poem, in: ***Spirit of the Ages,*** The National Library of Poetry, 1996.

Oblivion, poem, in: ***Poetic Voices of America,*** Sparrowgrass Poetry Forum. 1996.

Labut, the Wizened Utopia, poem, in: ***Meditations,*** Iliad Press, 1996.

Floating in the Firmament, poem, in: ***Reflections of Innocence,*** The Library of Poetry, 2001.

The Birds and I, poem, in: ***New Millennium Poets,*** Famous Poets Society. 2002.

Translations

Dagiti Kaarruba (The Neighbors) by Marie von Ebner-Eschenback, in: ***Dagiti Napili a Sinurat iti Literatura Aleman,*** edited by Juan S. P. Hidalgo, Jr. 1974.

Ti Stechlin (The Stechlin) by Theodor Fontane, also in ***Literatura Aleman.***

Sakbay a Lumgak ti Init (Before the Sun Rises), by Theodor Fontane, also, in ***Literatura Aleman.***

Ti Scheuderump (The Scheuderump), by Wilhelm Raabe, also in ***Literatura Aleman.***

Mabaliwan Ngata dagiti Mannaniw ti Lubong? (Could the Poets Change the World?) By Gottfried Benn; also, in ***Literatura Aleman.***

Ti Lalaki nga Awanan Kalidad (The Man Without Quality) by Robert Musil, also in ***Literatura Aleman.***

Libro ni Mormon (Book of Mormon), published by the Church of Jesus Christ of Latter-day Saints. 1990.

Ti Pammaneknek ni Propeta Joseph Smith (The Testimony of Prophet Joseph Smith). Published: by the CJCLDS. 1990.

Pagbasaan a Mangiwanwan iti Kaamaan (Family Guidebook). Published: by the CJCLDS. 1990.

Pagbasaan a Mangiwanwan iti Sanga (Branch Guidebook). Published: by the CJCLDS. 1990.

Pagbasaan a Mangiwanwan iti Dadaulo ti Kinasaserdote (Priesthood Leaders Guidebook). Published: by the CJCLDS. 1990.

Pagbasaan iti Libro ni Mormon (Book of Mormon Guidebook) Published: by the CJCLDS. 1990.

Dagiti Estoria iti Daan a Tulag (Old Testament Readers), illus. Co-translator: S. R. Tabin. Published: by the CJCLDS. 1990.

Dagiti Estoria iti Baro a Tulag (New Testament Readers), illus. Co-translator: S. R. Tabin. Published: by the CJCLDS. 1990.

Ang Ilog na Walang Tulay (The River with no Bridge, by Sue Sumii), Published by *Solidarity Pub.* 1992.

Books

Pakpakawan, Berde! Ken 21 a Sarita (Never Ever You, Verde! [a novel] and 21 stories). 220pp. c1978.

Naabel a Linabag ti Rosas (Woven Strands of Roses), letters. Co-author: Sinamar A. Robianes Tabin. 538pp. X-Libris: c2014.

Review/Comment

Sikolohiya ng Pagkasakal sa mga Kuwento ni Lorenzo G. Tabin (Psychology of Being Sucked in the Stories of Lorenzo G. Tabin) by Valerio L. Nofuente. *The Philippine Collegian,* May 12, 1975.

Salukami Met E-mail Korner (Our E-mail Corner), *Saluyot,* July-December 2002.

Palanca Awards 2002: Namsek a Bin-i Narpekan nga Ani (Palanca Awards 2002: Golden Harvest). *Saluyot.* July-December 2002.

LORENZO G. TABIN, Gawad Pambansang Alagad ni Balagtas 2014—Unyon ng mga Manunulat sa Pilipinas (**UMPIL**) **Writers' Union of the Philippines,** translated by Ariel Tabag, in *Haraya* by Dr. Michael M. Coroso. *Liwayway,* September 29, 2014.

About The Authors

Lorenzo Garcia Tabin, Sr. (b. May 22, 1944, San Juan, Ilocos Sur) and Sinamar A. Robianes Tabin (b. April 20, 1945, Pagudpud, Ilocos Norte) are longtime translators and interpreters of the Church of Jesus Christ of Latter-day Saints; Lorenzo is currently a Temple Sealer at the Jordan River Utah Temple; and retired from the Church Office Building, and from the Deseret Bookstore in Salt Lake City, Utah. Lorenzo authored dozens of novels, short stories, poems, and a lot of feature articles published in magazines like the Bannawag, Rimat, TMI Journal, Asia Philippines Leader; garnered prestigious writing awards including UMPIL, the highest award given to a Filipino writer; Pedro Bucaneg award, a highest award given to an Ilokano writer; Palanca, ETTI, GRAAFIL, RFAAFIL, and other award giving bodies (for their writings,

LORENZO GARCIA TABIN, SR. AND
SINAMAR A. ROBIANES TABIN, SR.

366

awards, etc. see their bibliography included in the book). He is a lifetime member of the GUMIL Metro Manila (Ilokano Writers Guild in Metro Manila, Philippines) for being a president of the organization for a term. He and Sinamar are co-founders with T. Gabriel Tugade, Cristino I. Inay, Sr. and Aurelio Solver Agcaoili, PhD. of the TMI Global (Guild of the Ilocano Writers Global). He graduated AB Journalism from the Manuel L. Quezon University and MA Literature from the University of the Philippines, Diliman. Sinamar, likewise, authored dozens of short stories, novelettes, poems, and feature articles in the Bannawag magazine, was a writer of the Normalite Bulletin, the school organ of the Northern Luzon Teachers' College where she graduated BSEEd; was Ilocano editor of the Ilocos Courier at Laoag City, won some awards, once a school organ editor of the Bangui Star, of the Bangui Provincial High School. She retired as grade school teacher. Lorenzo's first book is *'Pakpakawan, Berde! ken 21 a Sarita.'* They co-authored their book *'Woven Strands of Roses / Naabel a Linabag ti Rosas'.* X Libris, 2014. They were blessed with five living children: Loumarie Linglingay (Banking and Finance, and Business Administration), Lorenzo II (physicist and trainer), Naomi (accountant), Sinamar II (Interior Designer) and Marlo Bagnos (Master of Business Administration). They live at West Valley City, Utah 84120 USA.

CPSIA information can be obtained
at www.ICGtesting.com
Printed in the USA
BVHW07091705061 9

550220BV00001B/3/P

9 781796 035551

UBBOG TI SIRMATA

32 A NAPILI A SARITA

NAIRAMAN TI BIBLIOGRAPIADA

LORENZO GARCIA TABIN, SR.

KEN

SINAMAR A. ROBIANES TABIN, SR.

ADDAAN KRITIKAL NGA INTRODUKSION NI
AURELIO SOLVER AGCAOILI, PHD

Addaan kritikal nga introduksion ni Aurelio Solver Agcaoili, PhD
Desenio ti akkub ni Lorenzo Garcia Tabin, Sr.

ISBN: Softcover   978-1-7960-3555-1
               eBook   978-1-7960-3554-4

Naimaldit daytoy a libro iti Estados Unidos ti America.

Petsa ti reb.: 05/29/2019

No agorder iti kopia daytoy a libro, kontaken ti:
Xlibris
1-888-795-4274
www.Xlibris.com
Orders@Xlibris.com
797043

Ti Linaonna

Sinamar A. Robianes Tabin, Sr.

Lorenzo Garcia Tabin, Sr.

Panangidaton

Kadagiti annakmi: Loumarie Linglingay Tabin Galvan, ni kaingungotna a Glicerio ken dagiti annakda a Brigham ken Bridget; Lorenzo II; Naomi ken da LeGrand Aaron Nathanael ken Lindsay Jan Miona nga annakna, ken ni Richard Hansen a kaingungotna; Sinamar II ken ni Nathan Tolman a kasimpungalanna ken ni Gabriel Arvin a bungada; Marlo Bagnos ken ni Marcella a kaingungotna ken dagiti annakda a Lorimar, Enoka, ken Job Enzo; ken dagidi dadakkelmi a Clemente Ramos Tabin ken Crispina Retuta Garcia, ken Rafael Romano Robianes ken Elena Alos Baradi. Kasta met kadagiti amin a kakabsatmi ken pamiliada.

Idatonmi met iti TMI Global— nga indauluan daydi T. Gabriel Tugade a kaduanakami nga agassawa ken da Aurelio Solver Agcaoili PhD, ken Cristino Iloreta Inay, Sr.—a kangrunaan a panggep ti timpuyog ti agipatarus iti sinurat dagiti Ilokano.

Maidaton pay kadagiti amin a mangipatpateg iti literatura Ilokana.

Pakauna

I

DAYTOY ti umuna ken kakaisuna, ken kangrunaan a libro a nakatipunan dagiti napili a sarita ti agkasimpungalan nga Ilokano a mannurat, a naipatarus iti Ingles. Linaonna ti nadumaduma a porma dagiti saritada nga abbaba ken atitiddog, a makaparay-aw, naliday, napasamak iti lokal ken internasional, tradisional ken kontemporario, ken premiado a saritada.

Nalatak ni Sinamar idi panawenna ket adu ti naay-ayo kadagiti saritana, babbaro ken naasawaan pay ket ngata, saan la a gapu iti tema ti sursuratenna a makasagid iti rikna ngem pati payen iti makaawis a naganna, nga isu met ti immuna a nakaawis iti imatang ti kaingungotna.

Iti sabali a bangir, limmatak ni Lorenzo gapu iti immuna a nobelana a *Ti Imetda nga Impierno*, nga impablaak ti Bannawag idi agtawen ti awtor iti 22 ket isu ti kaubingan nga Ilokano a nagnobela; ken puon ti nangkablaawan kenkuana ni Sinamar iti *Dakami Met* a nakaigapuan ti panagam-ammoda; sinaruno ti *Ramut ti Sinamar*, sa ti *Agus*, ket nagbalin dagitoy tallo a nobela a trilohia a biag ni Pupoy. Ad-adun ti nagrukbab kenkuana idi rimmuar ti makaparay-aw a nobelana a *Pakpakawan Berde*, a sinaruno pay ti ad-adu a makaparay-aw, agingga a nangabak ti kontemporario a nobelana nga *Adtoy, Siak, ni Jesus Crisostomo: Dramaturgo*.

Kitaen ti pakabuklan ti gapuananda iti agsinsinda a bibliograpia iti nagbaetan ti orihinal nga Ilokano ken ti patarus iti Ingles.

viii

LORENZO GARCIA TABIN, SR. KEN
SINAMAR A. ROBIANES TABIN, SR.

II

NABINGAY daytoy nga antolohia iti dua a benneg, ti **Ilokano** nga *Ubbog ti Sirmata: 32 a Napili a Sarita,* ken ti patarus iti **Ingles a** *Wellspring of Foresight: 32 Selected Stories.* Dua a paset ti benneg ti Ilokano: **1. Sinamar A. Robianes Tabin, Sr.** ken ti **2. Lorenzo Garcia Tabin, Sr.** Tallo a paset ti benneg ti Ingles: **1. Sinamar A. Robianes Tabin, Sr. 2. Lorenzo Garcia Tabin, Sr.** ken **3. Bibliograpia.** Naurnos dagiti sarita babaen ti tawen a pannakaipablaak ken/wenno pannakaisuratda.

Kayatmi nga ipakauna a naipatarus ken nailibro dagitoy a sarita, kas panangtungpalmi iti kangrunaan a panggep ti TMI (Timpuyog dagiti Mannurat nga Ilokano) Global a pannakaipatarus dagiti sinurat dagiti mannurat nga Ilokano.

Uppat a paratignay ti ibilangmi a nagsadaganmi bayat ti panangmulimi iti kinamannuratmi. Dagitoy ti nagsarminganmi tunggal sanguenmi ti agsurat.

Umuna: *Naimbannawagan.* Kapadesmi ti agsursuro nga agsurat idi rugian ti Bannawag ti agpasalip iti sarita. Dodoktor kada abogado kada dekano kada propesor kada editor ti naghurhurado ket kurang la tumukno iti langit ti nangibilbilanganmi kadakuada, wenno didiosen iti literatura. Inad-adalmi dagiti komentarioda, ken dagiti nangabak a sarita dagiti sumangkadiosen a mannurat ta kaaduanna kadakuada ti mamaestro. Ti nangipaspasanganmi iti bagimi kadagidi a panawen? Arigmi iti bukel ti mustasa nga awan a pulos ti kaipasanganmi kadagiti higante a teddek dagiti balikas.

Maysa a balikas ti nakatingtingra pay la iti panunotmi: *naimbannawagan.*

Nagtaud dayta a balikas iti daydi Dr. Marcelino A. Foronda, Jr. iti naminsan a panaghuradona.

Dimi idi naawatan a dagus ti kayatna a sawen. Apay a naimbannawagan? Inulit-ulitmi pay a binasa dagiti naagapadna a sarita, a nangimuntaranna iti paliiwna. Naawatanmi idi agangay a saan la a dagiti naisalip a sarita ti kayatna a sawen, ngem ti kita ti sarita, ken nobela, nga ipabpablaak ti Bannawag; adu pay ngamin idi ti ipatpatarus

dagiti editor manipud iti sabali a pagsasao: narasay pay ngamin idi ti mannurat nga Ilokano.

Apay a *naimbannawagan?*

Naamirismi a saan a panangumsi wenno ania man ti inaramid ni Dr. Foronda. Gapu ta paset ti 'negosio' ti Bannawag, nasken nga ibagay dagiti editor wenno ti Liwayway Publishing iti kagaten dagiti agbasbasa. Saanda nga agipablaak iti 'di maawatan' dagiti agbasbasa, wenno para iti 'literatura.'

Kasano ket maymaysa met laeng piman ti magasin a 'pagbagasan' dagiti naanep a mannurat nga Ilokano. Isu a maawatanmi no apay a kasdiay, ket 'impasurotmi' met ti panagsuratmi iti pagrukodan dagiti editor.

Saankami a naiduma kadagiti dadduma a mannurat. Masapul a surotenmi ti pagrukodan dagiti editor, no kayatmi a maipablaak dagiti suratenmi. Kaasi ni Apo Dios, ken dagiti editor, ken iti panagkasapulanmi iti kuarta—adda dagidi gundaway a di pay nais-iskedyul ti iruruar ti saritami, mabalinmin a singiren ti bayadna. Ulitenmi: dakkel a yamanmi kadagiti editor!

Maikadua: *Aginlalaing.* Idi bumaybayag ti panagsursuratmi, ken idi napagasatankami a nangala iti masteralmi iti UP Diliman, ken immadu ti nabasbasami a libro a naisurat iti ganggannaet, ad-adda a limmawag iti panunotmi ti kapanunotan daydi Dr. Foronda. Adu ti nabasbasami a sarita, nobela, daniw, a kunada a moderno wenno kontemporario ti pannakaisakabna; kritisismo iti literatura, ken dadduma pay a makapalawa iti imatang kas mannurat. Adda maysa a kompadremi a nangpadas a mangsurat iti daniw, a talaga a naidumduma ti estelona wenno pormana. Mano a linia wenno binnatog a pasig a kokak kokak kokak kokak. Nakasuron ngata unay ti editor, ta imbasurana ti 'daniw'!

Sumagmamano kadakami ti nagpanggep a sumiasi iti 'dekahon' a porte ti panagsuratan—naadalmi dayta a termino iti daydi Valerio L. Nofuente nga instruktor iti UP Diliman, a nangsurat iti obserbasionna kadagiti saritak [Lorenzo] a nairaman iti librok [Lorenzo] a *Pakpakawan, Berde! Ken 24 a Sarita.* Dekahon kano dagiti saritak.

Aginlalaing! Dimi malipatan dayta a balikas daydi maysa nga editor—saan a dakami a mismo ti nakaiturongan dayta a balikas, ngem

nangngegmi ta nairana a simmarungkarkami iti editorial. Aginlalaing dagiti agpanggep a mangbaliw iti porte ti panagsuratan?

Ngem saankami a nangrikna. Inin-inutmi nga 'insiasi' ti estilomi nga agsurat. Immuna a saritami nga impablaak ti Bannawag ti *Ti Eden iti Biagda,* a pasig a dayalogo ti pannakaisuratna—panagkunami, daytoy a sarita ti immuna, no di man kakaisuna, a kastoy ti pormana a sarita a naipablaak iti Bannawag. Sabali a pagarigan ti *Ditoy Gloria: Pagbaludan,* nga awan ti nausar a nagan; ken dadduma pay a sarita. Kalpasanna, inkagumaanmi a tunggal makipartisiparkami kadagiti pasalip, isaluminami ti porma wenno estilo, a nakasagatan ti dddduma iti pagrukodan dagiti hurado. Pinagturaymi ti dakkel nga utangmi itoy a magasin—isu nga adu ti nasuratmi, kas makita iti bibliograpia a nairaman itoy nga antolohia.

In-inut met a nagbalbaliw ti porma dagiti sarita a nagab-abak kadagiti pasalip. Iti panangbaliwmi iti porma dagiti sursuratenmi a sarita ken nobela (Adtoy, Siak, ni Jesus Crisostomo: Dramaturgo), nangrugi met a nagabakkami kadagiti pasalip.

Maikatlo: *Lokdit, nakisalsalip pay laeng, dina met linalaing!* Diak [Lorenzo] malipatan dayta a binatog daydi Tang Ben—kasta ti kayat daydi Atty. Benjamin M. Pascual nga awagmi kenkuana—nga abogado ken dekano a napnuan pakumbaba ken maysa kadagiti teddek ti literatura Ilokana a diminto malipatan gapu iti kinasingedna kadakami. Nasaona ti kasdi idi duakami kadagiti tallo a napusgan a hurado iti maysa a pasalip iti sarita. Dimi pay idi ammo no asino ti akinsarita iti ad-adalenmi, ngem makakatkatawa nga agwingwingiwingkami idi naduktalanmi a maysa kadagiti kanayon a makisalsalip ti akinggapuanan. Isu nga insardengmin ti makisalip amangan no addanto met hurado a makasao kadakami iti kasta!

Maikapat: *Agdamagkayo ken ni Loring ta paglainganna ti agpaulo!* Iramanmi daytoy ta bassit no ar-arigen ngem napateg met iti lubong ti panagsuratan.

Mayat ti saritaanmi iti maysa a lamisaan a nagsasanguanmi kada Feliciano Martin T. Rochina, daydi Reynaldo A. Duque, daydi Pelagio A. Alcantara, ken dadduma pay a mannurat iti daydi rabii a pannakayawat ti gunggona dagiti nangabak iti umuna a salip iti nobela

nga inesponsoran ti ETTI—maikadua a gunggona ti nobelak [Lorenzo] idinto a maikatlo ti nobela ni Martin; awan iti grupomi daydi Samuel F. Corpuz a nangyalat iti umuna a gunggona.

Topikomi ti panagpaulo iti sarita wenno nobela. Adda dagiti mannurat a di makasurat iti ania man no awan nga umuna ti paulo ti suratenna—maysakami kadagita. Sabali met dagiti suratenda nga umuna ti obrada sakbay nga ipanunotanda ti paulona—maysa dita ni Peter La. Julian; napaliiwmi dayta bayat ti panagkakabbalaymi idiay Coromina St., Quiapo, Manila, kada Prescillano N. Bermudez, T. Gabriel Tugade, Constante Al. Domingo, ken Benjamin Castillo Chua.

Ni Martin ti nagdamag no kasano ti agaramid iti paulo ti suraten.

"Agdamagkayo ken ni Loring ta paglainganna ti agpaulo!" agkatkatawa daydi Rey a nagkuna.

Nalagip ngata idi daydi Rey nga adda sumagmano a libro ti GUMIL Metro Manila a dakami ti nangisingasing iti paulona.

Maipalagip a kanayon a baliwan dagiti editor ti paulo dagiti saritak idi nabiitak pay nga agsursurat.

III

NARIGATANKAMI a nangpili kadagiti sarita nga inramanmi itoy nga antolohia, saan a gapu iti bugasda ngem gapu iti pannakapukaw ti dadduma nga urnongmi a kayatmi nga iraman. Saankami a naglibtaw a nangurnong kadagiti sinuratmi a naipablaak iti Bannawag, ken kadagiti manuskritmomi, ngem inugmokan ti anay, ken di pinakawan ti nepnep idi pinatarimaanmi ti bubong ti balaymi a nakaidagusanda— napanawanmi idi immakarkami iti America ket saan a nalagip, wenno di ngata ketdi intagipateg dagidi napanawanmi, ken dagidi nabagaan a naglagda ket dida man la impan iti di nakaangutan ti nepnep— awan la ngamin ti kas kadatao a mangipateg kadagiti kakastoy a banag. Naimbag ta iti panagtrabahomi iti Filipiniana Section ti University of the Philippines, a nakapusganmi a nagidalimanek kadagiti manuskrito ken kopia ti Bannawag, nairaman ti dadduma a gapuananmi, nga isu ti nakaagsawanmi iti dadduma a nairaman ditoy.

Pakaammo: Agpada ti *Tao ken Panawen* ken ti *Rupa* (sarita ni Lorenzo), ken ti *Anangka* (sarita ni Sinamar) a namindua nga impablaak ti Bannawag—kitaen dagiti petsa iti gibus dagitoy a sarita.

Kitaentayo ti umuna a benneg a nakatipunan dagiti napili a sarita ni Sinamar. Sayang ta awan ti maudi iti dua nga isyu ti 'Atis', kasta met a dimi nasapulan ti 'Makopa' a mangkompleto koma kadagiti saritana a naibatay kadagiti bungbunga. Kasta met dagiti napili a sarita ni Lorenzo a nakairamanan dagiti di naipablaak iti Bannawag. Dimi met nasapulan ti sarita [ni Lorenzo] a *Pilarica Naamitan: Maysa a Malem* a maikadua a gunggona iti GETSMAIL (*Governor Evaristo T. Singson Memorial Award for Iluko Literature*), 1991, a kayatmi koma nga iraman.

Madlaw ti dakkel a paggidiatan dagiti naipablaak ken saan a naipablaak. Kayatmi nga ipakauna a dakkel a yamanmi iti panangipablaak ti Bannawag kadagiti gapuananmi. Umuna unay, daytoy a magasin ti nagam-ammuanmi nga agkaingungot. Maikadua, ti Bannawag ti bigbigenmi a nangmuli kadakami kas tao, nga isu ti nakaigapu ti kaaddami iti agdama a kasasaadmi.

Inin-inutmi, kas nasaomin, ti 'dimsaag' iti pagrukodan ti Bannawag, a nakangngeganmi a kinuna ti maysa kadagidi nataengan nga editor iti balikas nga 'aginlalaing.' Ngem dimi rinikna, ketdi pinagturaymi ti dakkel nga utangmi itoy a magasin—isu nga adu ti nasuratmi, kas makita iti bibliograpia a nairaman itoy nga urnong.

Nalabit a mababalaw dagiti putarmi, ket ninamnamami a kasta, ngem impangrunami ti pannakaidumduma ti sukogda; kayatmi laeng a riingen dagiti agbasbasa nga adda met pay sabali a sukog dagiti estoria a panagkunami masapul a maadal, ta adu ti kasta kadagiti nadumaduma a lengguahe iti lubong.

Nalabit a saan a nabagas, iti panirigan dagiti agbasbasa nga aginana laeng ti panggepda nga agbasa kalpasan ti pannakautoyda iti nagmalem a trabaho, ngem inaramidmi ti kastoy, a biningaymi iti dua a benneg, tapno agpaay a pangamirisan iti panggep ti Bannawag, ken sapay koma ta makatulong iti literatura dagiti Ilokano. Ammomi a dumurdur-as ti lengguahe ken Literatura Ilokana, kas maimatangan iti Unibersidad ti Hawai'i Manoa.

Kasta met nga inkagumaanmi nga impatarus iti Ingles tapno saan la nga iti Kailokuan ti pakaiwarasanna, ken bareng no masirig met dagiti di makaawat iti Iluko/Iloko/Ilokano ket makitada ti dakkel a nagapuanan ti *Bannawag*; ken pangtungpalmi metten iti panggep ti Timpuyog dagiti Mannurat nga Ilokano (TMI)-Global. —**LORENZO GARCIA TABIN, SR.** ken **SINAMAR A. ROBIANES TABIN, SR.**

Kritikal Nga Introduksion

Ti Literatura Ilokana ken ti Saludsod Maipapan iti Pannakaispal: Ti Kaso ti Fiksion da Tabin ken Tabin

Ni Aurelio S. Agcaoili, PhD

Agbimbinnulig a Mannarita

Kadagiti adu nga obra dagiti agassawa ken agbimbinnulig a Lorenzo G. Tabin, Sr. ken Sinamar Robianes Tabin, Sr. makitatayo ditoy ti kuna ni Jonathan Franzen[1] maipapan iti bileg dagiti libro. Umisu unay ti deklarasionna a dagiti libro santuario ti kararua ti tao. Sisasarurongak iti kastoy a kapanunotan iti wagas nga awanan iti surok ken awanan iti kurang.

It-ited dagiti santuario kadatayo ti maysa a disso a pakapanawantayo kadagiti di unay nasken a banag a mangit-ited kadatayo iti pulkok iti aginaldaw a panagbiagtayo. Mangted dagitoy kadatayo iti kalasag a mangsarapa kadagiti nagkaadu a peligro ken kasta met nga ik-ikkandatayo iti proteksion kontra kadagiti makadadael a bunga dagiti

---

[1]   Jonathan Franzen, *How to Be Alone: Essay* (New York: Farrar, Straus and Giroux/Picador), 2002.

banag a ganggannaet ken ditay unay ammo. Manamnama nga agtennag iti bibineg ti kintayegtayo iti sango ti maysa a banag a di nakairuaman. Iti kasta, mayaw-awantayo ken ditay makasubli iti naggapuantayo.

Umisu la unay ti maysa a hermeneut iti kunana maipapan kadagiti texto a kas koma iti *Ubbog ti Sirmata* (ken ti patarus daytoy iti Ingles, *Wellspring of Foresight*): luklukatan dagiti texto ti maysa a lubong a serkentayo.

Pudno unay a manglukat dagiti nasayaat a libro iti ridaw a pagserkan ti agbasbasa ken pamkuatanna a makitungtong iti lubong nga iparparangarang kadatayo ti maysa a texto. Maysa dayta a lubong a baro a panagbasa kadagiti padas-tao. Kadagiti addaan iti parabur nga artistiko a sirmata kabaelanda ti mangibati iti maysa a naimbag a sursuro, banag a mangyadal kadatayo kadagiti komplexidad ti biag-tao.

Ipalagip kadatayo ni Franzen a ti maysa nga autor—dua a fiksionista iti kaso daytoy a libro—addaan iti masterado iti lengguahe nga usarna iti panagsuratna. Malaksid laeng iti kapasidadna nga agpanunot ken mangsirig ken mangrikna ken mangawat iti nakayanakan a wagas ken nainsangsangayan, addaan ti nalaing a mannurat iti abilidad a mangipulso iti kinarigat ti biag. Manipud iti kasta a panagawat, mabalin a rugian ti mannurat ti mangkalkula no ania ti balikas a mayannatup unay ken no ania ti maisiasi; napateg daytoy nga aramidna iti nainturedan a panagibaetbaetna kadagiti narigat unay a texto ti biag. Daytoy nga akto ti mediasion—ti akto a panangisurat iti mainaig iti daytoy—ket maysa nga akto a mangaramid kadagiti wagas tapno dagiti texto ni rígat maawatan dagiti addaan iti gandat a mangammo iti daytoy.

Iti *Naabel a Linabag ti Rosas* (*Woven Strands of Roses: Letters with Annotation That Sprung Forth from the Hearts)*[2], ti umuna a bilingual a libro a nagbuligan da Lorenzo Sr. ken Sinamar Sr.[3] a kas agassawa, masirigtayo ti sarita ken pakasaritaanda a kas mannurat nga Ilokano.

---

[2]   Xlibris US (2014).

[3]   Manipud ditoy nga awagak da Manong Lorenzo Sr. ken Manang Sinamar Sr. iti daytoy a sibubukel a salaysay.

Adda daytay immun-unan nga estoriada a mainaig iti panagam-ammoda babaen iti ruta ti literatura nga Ilokano, ruta nga addaan iti panagpalpalikawkaw ngem napnuan met iti panagganas a ti panagkunak naitani a kasta. Adda daytay paralelismo ti dua a klase ti panagayatda: (a) iti panagayatda iti literatura nga Ilokano ken ti karida a mangiburay iti laingda tapno iti kasta agtultuloy a mapasantak daytoy a literatura ken (b) ti panagbinnuligda iti maysa ken maysa (nga iti rugi kas aginnayan-ayat ken iti udina isu ti panagbanagda a kas agassawa—a kas esposo ken esposa). Makunak a ti estoriada a kas mannurat nga Ilokano estoriada met a kas agassawa.

Kastoy ti makunatayo: agpadada a nangitakder iti lengguahe nga Ilokano. Ngem agpadada met a nangitakder iti dayta a lengguahe babaen iti panagtultuloyda a mannurat iti daytoy a lengguahe iti man akemda a kas individual wenno kas agassawa. Ti kinaagpaysuanna kabaelanda ti agsurat kadagiti sabali pay a lengguahe iti Filipinas ngem nagdesisionda nga agtalinaed a kas timek dagiti Ilokano. Ti agtultuloy a panangusarda iti lengguaheda ket pammaneknek iti kasta a panagkumitda iti bukodda a pagsasao nga ita manmano laengen ti makaawat ken makaapresiar gapu iti agtultuloy a homogenisasion ti pagilian.

Addaan ti pakasaritaan ti literatura ti Filipinas iti madagdagullit a pannakaipapaigid. Kaaduanna a sistematiko dagitoy nga aramid gapu ta is-isponsoran ida ti estado ken kasta met a mapalpalugodan dagitoy nga aramid ti di panangipirpirit ken di panangiraman. Kasta met a nalimed a naigamer iti sistema ti edukasion ti pagilian. Narigat a makuna nga adda panangipirpirit ti estado iti kastoy nga aramid nga agtamed kadagiti nadumaduma a kultura ken literario nga expresion dagiti nagduduma nga etnolingguistiko a grupo iti Filipinas. Iti las-ud ti tallo a henerasion sipud inyetnag ni Quezon ti Tagalog a kas "nailian" a sao, nagbaliwen ti panagkita dagiti dadduma nga Ilokano iti pagsasaoda.

Ti pannakaipapaigid ken pannakaiwalinwalin dagiti dadduma pay a lengguahe ti pagilian malaksid ti Tagalog ken Ingles nagbalin a gagangay nga aramid, ken agingga ita, ti pagrukodan ti kinalaing. Kasta met a dagiti abilidad dagiti siudadano ket kaskadi nga ibabaet dagiti pagrukodan kadagitoy dua a lengguahe. Nalawag ngarud a makikunkunsaba ti

sistema ti edukasion iti nakaro unay a homogenisasion ti maysa a pagilian nga addaan iti agduduma a lengguahe ken kultura.

Lagipentayo nga insurat ni Lorenzo Sr. ti masterado a tesisna iti lengguahe a Tagalog gapu ta idi—iti dayta a panawen—saan a posible nga isuratna daytoy iti Ilokano uray no makuna a ti universidad a nagadalanna, ti Universidad ti Filipinas, addaan iti liberal ken mamagwayawaya a kultura.

Kas maestra iti maysa kadagiti dadakkel a siudad iti Kamanilaan, kabaelan koma ni Sinamar Sr. ti bumallasiw iti Tagalog, ti lengguahe a posible a nangilukat kenkuana kadagiti ridaw tapno mabirngasan ken mairaman a kas "mannurat a babai" iti pagilian.

Gasat man daytoy wenno bunga ti panagpili, ti kinaagpaysuanna ket nagtalinaedda a nakakumit iti panagdur-as ti literatura Ilokana babaen iti maysa nga aramidda: ti agtultuloy a panagsuratda iti dayta a lengguahe. Naan-anayen dayta a pammaneknek tapno maibagatayo a kadagiti aramidda ipeksada ti kanayon a kaaddada iti sibay dagiti padada nga umili ken ti panangitandudoda iti lengguahe nga Ilokano.

Kayatko a sublian ti naan-anay a kabaelanda iti lengguahe nga Ilokano, kinaan-anay a nalawag nga ipakita dagiti adu nga obra da Lorenzo Sr. ken Sinamar Sr.

Iti nawaya a panagsao, maawatantayo nga agpadada a nakapartuat iti maysa a sirmata iti panangiladawanda kadagiti nakarikrikut a situasion iti biag. Aramaten ni Sinamar Sr. ti wagas ti parabola: pagbalinenna dagiti estoriana a kas parabola ken ibatina kadatayo ti maysa a leksion a kanayon a malaglagiptayo a kas man la sursuruannatayo no kasano a warwaren dagiti singgalot ti aginaldaw a panagbiagtayo. Usaren met ni Lorenzo Sr. dagiti agduduma a teknik ken paripirip iti panangipakitana kadatayo ti pakaitarusan dagiti banag a pakairamanan ti konteksto ti transendente, ti metafisikal. Iti exkursionna iti disso a di-familiar, isaritana kadatayo ti maysa a mito, ti *muthos* dagiti Griego, ket ballaagannatayo nga adda pay dagiti napateg unay a banag iti biag iti laksid daytoy a lubong. No kitaentayo a sibubukel daytoy nga obrada a dua, daytoy ti maibagatayo: adda kalkulado a panagsirmata manen iti realidad tapno iti kasta ket makasirmata iti maysa a realidad a kabarbaro

ken posible a nasaysayaat. Addaan daytoy a sinuratda a dua iti kari ti pannakaispal.

Dagiti Pamuidan ken Kontexto

Ti panagikur-it nga Ilokano iti Filipinas ken dadduma pay a disso maysa nga aramid ti maag gapu iti maysa a kinapudno: a daytoy ket kankanayon-ken-nalpasen a determinado nga aramid iti maysa a biag nga addaan iti panagkurkuranges.

Numan pay nakaramut iti tradision nga oral a nagpaay, kadagiti prekolonial ken kolonial a panawen, a kas pamegket a nangaramid kadagiti Ilokano a sindadaan a manglaglagip iti maipapan iti bukodda a kinaasino iti laksid ti panangirurumen kadakuada dagiti *fraile* ken dagiti pasurotda kadagiti kannawidan dagiti Ilokano, ti inkapilitan a panangisuro dagiti Amerikano iti Ingles babaen iti inkapilitan met a panangipatungpalda iti publiko ti sistema ti edukasion, ken ti "Niponggoisasion" dagiti ubbing nga Ilokano nga adda idi kadagiti eskuelaan ken ti panangpadasda a mamagbalin ti entiro a pagilian a kas nasion a Tagalog, ti panagikur-it nga Ilokano nganngani nagbalin nga aramid iti parparaangan babaen iti makunkuna a *daniw iti parparaangan* ken nagbalin nga aramid dagiti nababbaba a dasig a tao, a dagiti Ilokano.

Daytoy a pannakabingay—ken daytoy a panaggudua ken agtultuloy a mangisinsina kadagiti nadumaduma a lokal a komunidad dagiti Ilokano iti amin a disso: (a) dagiti babaknang ken politikal nga elit, ken ti panagturay dagiti patriarko ken paraon ken patron, ken (b) dagiti mangurkuranges a masa nga iturturayan, domdominaran, papaidaman, ken mabagaan lattan ti aramidenda, dagiti pobre a dasig nga agdadata nga adda iti babaen dagiti babaknang a nagbalinen a kasukat dagiti kolonisador ken konkistador.

Daytoy a pannakagudua—dagiti babaknang-kontra-dagiti-gagangay—agtultuloy a kasta agpapan ita. Dagiti laeng aksidente ti nagbaliw. Iti kaso ti panagikur-it nga Ilokano, manmano laeng kadagiti babaknang ti nagpadas a tumulong a mangpabaknang iti biag ken literatura dagiti Ilokano. Adu kadagiti nagsursurat ken agingga ita agsursurat pay laeng ti naggapu iti nagtengnga, iti makimbaba a

nagtengnga, ken iti nababa a dasig, dagiti makuna a gagangay. Adda sumagmamano a nagtengnga a dasig (akimbabbaba a nagtengnga a dasig no ibatay daytoy iti metriko a sosioekonomiko) ti naggapu iti akademia. Ngem uray dagitoy nga "akto ti panagikur-it" manipud kadagitoy nga akademiko kasla man laeng aramid a mapilpilit. Awan nalawag ken nalimpio a panangikumit nga aggapu kadakuada.

Dagiti ekonomiko a bunga ti panagikur-it nga Ilokano, iti sapasap a panagsasao, ket nakaro unay. Kaaduan kadagiti mannurat nga Ilokano ti matay a pobre. Adu dagiti manuskritoda ti agur-uray ken agbirbirok kadagiti pabliser a narigat met a mabirokan; manmano ngamin dagiti tumaktakder a pabliser. Iti kaaduan a panawen ket awan met a talaga. Kadagiti addaan bassit iti rekursos, kumapkappengda iti makunkuna a kolektivo a panagilibro, ti *tagnawa*. Uray dagiti nagipakita iti talento iti rugi ket pinanawanda ti panagikur-it nga Ilokano. Maysa ti nalawag a rason—ket masapul nga ipeksatayo daytoy. Saan a mabaelan ti kastoy a panagikur-it a sungbatan ti ekonomiko a kasapulan ti maysa a mannurat. Ti ofisial a panagipateg ti naimpartuatan a panagikur-it iti pagilian ket maysa a klase ti makunkuna a pamalbalasang, maysa a klase a panglamlamiong ta "tokenismo" daytoy. Tokenismo ta simboliko ken pammarang laeng.

Ti estoria ti grupo dagiti Ilokano a mannurat—ti grupo a Coromina dagiti agkabannuag kadagiti tawen ti 1960 iti puso (ken puseg metten) ti Quiapo iti Manila—maysa a grupo a pakaibilangan ni Lorenzo Sr., ket maysa a pammaneknek a di mailibak maipapan ti justo a kasasaad ti panagikur-it nga Ilokano agpapan ita. Ken babaen ti nakaro nga aramid iti homogenisasion ti estado ken dagiti ideolohika nga aparato daytoy a kas koma dagiti eskuelaan, ti literatura, ken ti media a masa ken sosial, masapul nga idokumentotayo ditoy daytoy a butengtayo para iti masakbayan ken para kadagiti sumuno a henerasion ti Ilokano. Iti kontexto a kastoy a makitatayo ti pateg daytoy nga obra da Lorenzo Sr. ken Sinamar Sr. gapu ta testamentoda a maited kadagiti Ilokano ken iti lengguaheda. Ipanamnama dayta a libro a ti lengguahe nga Ilokano, ti linggua frangka iti amianan a paset ti pagilian, agnanayon a sibibiag. Ti namnamatayo saan laeng nga agnanayon a sibibiag daytoy a rekursos ti puli no di ket agsantak pay koma.

Dagiti Texto: Dagiti Parabola ni Sinamar Sr.

Ti wagas ni Sinamar Sr. iti panagikur-it ket kas iti maysa a maestra. Suroten dagiti estoriana ti muhon ti maysa a parabola.

Adda iti panunotko dagiti dua a pamuidan daytoy a paraboliko a nakaimuntaran dagiti ababa a sarita ni Sinamar Sr.: (a) ti panagbalinna a maestra iti klasrum iti basar nga edukasion ken (b) ti panagkamengna iti maysa a klase ti pammati a Kristiano.

Agtinnulong dagitoy dua a pamuidan ti inspirasionna tapno buklenna ti maysa a manarsarita nga addaan iti nabatad a pannakaawat no ania ti kayatna nga ibaga ken addaan kadagiti palawag a makabael ken sipupudno a mangiladawan kadagiti situasion a para iti tao a mangiparparipirip kadagiti adu a pagtutuokan iti biag.

Ti wagas ti panangrisutna kadagitoy a pasamak, ken nupay mangisingsingasing, addaan dagiti sinuratna iti nabileg a pangellaat. Kadagiti estoriana nga addaan kadagiti moral a resolusion, mangngegantayo kadagitoy ti timek ti maysa a moral nga aktor: kas iti pannakasubok iti panagayat ken kinapudno iti dayta nga ayat ("Adda Kenka Daytan"), ti pannakasubok iti pammati iti Dios ("Adda Dios, Joan"), ti panagbabawi ("No Magatang La Koma ti Biag"), ken ti di pulos pannakaammo iti masakbayan ti biag ti maysa a tao ("Iti Pilid ti Biag"). Sursuruannatayo ni Sinamar Sr. iti sumagmamano a leksion—wenno palagipannatayo kadagiti basar a banag maipapan iti kinatao (wenno naimbag a kinatao), naimbag a panaggargaraw, ken ti pannakasapul kadagiti pangngeddeng nga etikal, ken etikal dagitoy gapu ta panagyebkas dagitoy kadagiti banag a nainkalintegan ken addaan iti kinaimbag.

Babaen kadagiti sangapulo ket uppat nga estoriana, mabasatayo ti maysa a nasion nga Ilokano iti Kailokuan. Ket iti maysa a wagas, itundanatayo iti maysa a padas iti diaspora. Iti plantasion ti sandia, kas pagarigan, makaengkuentro dagiti Ilokano dagiti Mexicano (mas simboliko daytoy ngem literal, ti panagkunak). Adda daytay di masbaalan a rikna iti pannakabasatayo iti inranta ngem addaan iti bassit-usit a katkatawa iti "panagtakaw iti sandia" ("Pagbiagan no Malasat"), a ti katkatawa kas man la naggapu a mismo iti kinaawan panaginkukuna,

a kasla man la kapada dagiti am-ammotayo unay a rabrabak ken ang-angaw dagiti Ilokano a minuli dagiti away ken kataltalonan. Kadagiti duogan a panawen, iti laksid ti kinakisang nga adda nga agdadata iti aginaldaw a panagbiag, ammo dagiti Ilokano ti agkatawa. Ammoda a katawaan ti kasasaadda. Maysa nga ugali daytoy a mangpasalun-at iti panunot ken isip.

Adda kinapasnek ti panangimapa ni Sinamar Sr. kadagiti karit iti aginaldaw a panagbiag iti man pakarukodan daytoy nga individual (wenno personal) wenno iti pakarukodan daytoy a publiko a pakairamanan dagiti grupo ti maysa a tao.

Para iti naud-udi, pampanunotek ti estoria ti maysa a partikular a saba, ti "Saba ni Anti Rosa." Aggaraw ti estoria manipud iti maysa a tao, agbalin a politikal daytoy iti pannakairaman iti estoria ti maysa a politiko iti lokal a gobierno. Ti maysa a politiko a mangaramid a kas politikal a banag ti maipapan iti saba ket maysa a pagteng a makapabusor. Ket maaddaan ti komunidad iti makunkuna nga epifania, ti pannakaammoda iti maysa a sitsitik a kinapudno a naiparipirip iti estoria. Marisut iti udina babaen ti nabatad a pagteng, ti *force majeure*— ti bagió. Awan nailemmeng dagiti mananggundaway.

Dayta simple a biag iti away—ad-adda a mayannatup ti *purok* no idasig iti *barrio*—ti mailadawan iti adu kadagitoy nga estoria ni Sinamar Sr. Isublinatayo iti panawen a nawaywaya ti biag ken marisut dagiti parikut babaen iti tungtongan ken nalapat a panagtutungtong: makidap-ay dagiti kameng ti komunidad ket babaen ti wagas a panagkaykaysa maitudo ti problema ken maipaayan daytoy iti umno a pangrisut tapno iti kasta, iti udina, matarimaan dagiti narakrak a relasion, mabendaan ken mapaglunit dagiti sugat, ken maipalagip kadagiti agbibiag kadagiti estoriana nga addaanda amin iti di agbalbaliw a kinatao. Iti sabali a panirigan, awisennatayo ni Sinamar a mapan iti lubong dagiti addaan iti sikolohiko nga an-anayen ket makitatayo ti panagbalbaliw ti rikna ken pannakaawattayo kadagitoy ken maanagtayo a medio nagasgasattayo bassit ken agyamantayo ta ditay naipaayan iti kastoy a padas iti biag ("Rayus a Nasipngetan Wenno Komustakan, Dolly?"). Iti daytoy ken iti kastoy nga estoria ipalagip ni Sinamar nga addaantayo iti kabaelan a mangispal iti bukodtayo a bagi. Makitatayo

iti nawadwada a wagas no ania ti biag ket matuntontayo ti dana ti pannakaisalakan.

Dagiti Texto: Ti Anag ti Transendente
Segun ken ni Lorenzo Sr.

Nabayagen a pagduaduaak a ni Lorenzo Sr., iti napalabas a biagna, maysa a profeta, maysa nga anghel, wenno maysa a filosopo kadagiti banag a transendente. Wenno posible a saan a rumbeng ken husto daytoy "wenno" kadagitoy a pagpilian iti kasta a napalabas a panagbiag: posible ngamin nga isu amin dagitoy: a profeta, anghel, ken filosopo. Mangted ni Lorenzo Sr. iti komentario a mainaig iti kondision a sosiopolitikal iti Ilocos ken iti pagilian babaen ti wagas a padamgis ken artistiko a no dadduma ditay mapupuotan a kasta gayam ti turong dagitoy.

Nabasakon dagiti dadduma pay nga obrana ket kanayon nga adda kadagitoy a gapuananna dagiti elemento a serioso. Serioso dagitoy ta warwaren ni Lorenzo Sr. ti bugas ti biag. Klaro ti wagas ti panangwarwarna—ken maawatantayo. Ti tekniko nga orientasion iti kasta a panagbirbirok kadagiti sungbat dagiti adu a saludsod maipapan iti biag ket saan a kanayon a nalawag. Ngem kasta met a talaga ti naturalesa ti amin a panagbirbirok ken panagsalsaludsod iti no ania a talaga ti bugas ti biag ti maysa a tao. Adu dagiti narigat a saludsod iti biag ngem nabaelan ni Lorenzo Sr. a balabalaen dagitoy tapno iti kasta maipatarusda kadagiti balikas.

Ti ispal—wenno salakan—ket maysa a nasamay unay nga epistemologia ditoy, maysa nga epistemologia a mangtulong kadatayo tapno maawatantayo dagiti naun-uneg pay a kinapudno a warwaren kadatayo ni Lorenzo Sr. babaen ti panangiladawanna kadagiti Ilokano nga agad-adaptar, segun kadagiti karit a dumteng kadakuada. Makitatayo ditoy ti maysa a barbero a mangaw-awat iti kinabarberona, ken kalpasanna ti panagbalinna a kasla bannagaw a makabael nga agtignay ken agsao a kas Tagalog ken agsubli nga insegida iti kinailokanona no kasapulan.

No basaentayo dagiti sangapulo ket walo nga ababa a fiksionna a sagutna kadatayo iti daytoy a libro, maduktalantayo ti nabayagen a panawen a panangipekpeksana ti maipapan iti anag ti biag ni Ilokano nga ibabaet ti lengguahe mismo nga Ilokano. Nakaan-annayas ti wagas ti panagestoriana a kunam la no maysa kadagiti mangngabel iti maysa nga inabel. No kitaen dagiti mangngabel, adda naisangsangayan a paragsit dagiti imadada. Adda met paragsit iti panaggunay dagiti mata ken bagida. Dayta a paragsit ti mangitunda kadakuada a mangpartuat iti maysa nga inabel a ti disenio daytoy naggapu iti darepdepda iti napalabas a rabii. Kasta ti paragsit ti panagpartuat nga ikut ni Lorenzo Sr.

Napetsaan dagitoy nga obra kadagiti tawen ti 1960 agingga iti 2000. Ammotayo nga adu kadagiti ub-ubing ken agdama a henerasion ti saanen a makaawat ken makalagip iti makunkuna itan a di-famoso nga EDSA People Power I ken EDSA People Power II—a didan maarikap dagiti naitalimeng a sentimiento ken sensibilidad nga adda kadagitoy nga estoria.

Ibagbaga dagiti historiador a maysa ti napalabas a "sabali a pagilian." Ti maysa a tao a makaengkuentro iti historia nasken a masindadadaan a mangkonstrak ken mangrekonstrak kadagiti ipaip a mainaig iti no kasano a maawatan dagiti baniaga a pasamak kadagiti naglabas a panawen. Kitaentayo, kas pagarigan, ti "Mangmatimati Dagiti Bituen iti Escopa." Adda ditoy ti dandani nostalgiko a pannakaipakita iti anag ti "panagmatimati", daytay panagkiraykiray ti maysa a lawag wenno silaw. Wenno dagiti bituen iti kaso daytoy nga estoria.

Adda basar a bileg a visual ditoy a disso iti peligroso a siudad kangrunaanna kadagiti nagindeg iti asideg ti Aurora Boulevard iti Siudad Quezon kadagidi a panawen, wenno iti Project 4, wenno iti planta ti Timex (ti kompania nga elektroniks) a nagbalin itan a templo ti Dios. Maimatangantayo no ania a klase ti biag ti adda dita idi—iti dayta a paset ti siudad, iti panawen nga iti asideg laeng dayta a boulevard ket dagiti barungbarong a kunkunaen dagiti agindeg a pagtaenganda. Pagtaengan dagitoy dagiti mangurkuranges nga agar-arapaap iti nasaysayaat a biag a saan ketdi a biag a nagpupuniponan ti pannakarakrak.

Nagadalak iti maysa nga universidad a nganngani kada aldaw a malabsak daytoy a lugar, daytoy nga Escopa. Ammok ti pakabuklan

ti tragiko nga estoriana ken dagiti posibilidadna koma nga awanan iti limitasion, nga addaan iti pannakatun-oy ken pannakaipatungpal. Ngem sabali ti nagbanaganna.

Adda maysa a tao a mangtengtengngel ken mangig-iggem iti titulo ket dayta a titulo mismo ti naan-anay a rason tapno dina pulos ipirpirit ti biag dagiti mangurkuranges nga adda dita, dagiti mangurkuranges nga agar-arapaap a mabalinda nga agindeg pay koma dita iti naun-unday pay a tiempo. Daytoy nga arapaap dagiti taga-Escopa, siempre, ket maisupiat iti pagayatan ti makunkuna nga akinkukua iti dayta a kaiskuateran. Iti estoria ti biag dagiti babaknang a kas iti mangig-iggem iti titulo, awan kaes-eskan ti biag dagiti marigrigat. Awan a pulos ti pakainaiganda kenkuana. Awan a pulos bibiangda. Dagitoy a klase ti biag dagiti awanan, dagiti marigrigat, dagiti mangurkuranges ket kasta pay laeng agpapapan ita: kas met laeng dagiti biag dagiti maipatli iti wagas ti makunkuna ita nga EJK wenno "extra judicial killing." Awan a pulos mamaay dagiti kakastoy a biag malaksid laeng iti panawen ti eleksion a ti kaibatogan dagitoy ket numero—ti awanan rupa ken lasag ken dara nga estadistika a pakaibasaran dagiti makunkuna a nangabak gapu laeng iti bilang dagiti nagbutos. Ipakita dagitoy ti makunkuna a pagkurangan ti demokrasia, daytay panagkurang mismo ti demokrasia a panagbiag gapu ta dagiti benefisio mait-ited laeng kadagiti sumagmamano ken saan nga iti sapasap. Pudno unay ti pagtaktakederan ni Lorenzo Sr. iti daytoy a banag.

Iti maysa nga aldaw, agpasar ti Escopa iti maysa a nawaras ken dakkel a puor ket dumapo dagiti barungbarong a taeng. Sumagmano a tao ti lamuten ti apuy a kas man la apuy iti infierno, apuy a manglamut ken manggayebgeb kadagiti amin a masagid ken madalapusna.

Adu pay a kolonia dagiti iskuater iti sabali a paset ti siudad. Agkakaingas dagitoy. Padapada a biag, padapada a disso dagiti peligro ken pannakigubal tapno laeng koma makabirok iti maysa a nabunga a panagbiag a nabayagen a birbiroken dagiti agindeg. Normal dagiti kunkunada a bunggoy dagiti demolision. Uray ti balikas a demolision mangiparipirip iti poder dagiti agdemolis ken ti bunga daytoy a kinakakaasi iti biang dagiti tao a mademolis dagiti taengda a tugpatugpa a sim, lawanit, karton, ken putedputed a kayo. Gagangay ti kastoy a

di normal a panagbiag. Daytoy a panagdemolis—malaksid laeng ti inggagara a panagpuor—ti awan duadua a wagas tapno dagiti kakastoy a kolonia maipasubli kadagiti addaan iti titulo kadagitoy. Kalpasan ti demolision, agtaud a kas uong dagiti subdivision, dagiti komersial a pagtagilakuan, wenno dagiti maramansion a pagtaengan dagiti addaan iti kabaelan a gumatang kadagiti milion ti gatadna a balay.

Ti relasion a Filipinas-Estados Unidos mayannatup iti estoria maipapan kadagiti barko ti US Navy nga agsanglad iti apagapaman iti Subic wenno Olongapo kadagidi a panawen nga addaan ti Estados Unidos kadagiti base militar iti Filipinas.

Nagbalin ti aglawlaw dagitoy a base militar a batobalani para iti makunkuna a rest-and-recreation dagiti kameng iti navy. Maawatantayo ti situasion: adu a bulan dagiti bilangen dagiti kameng ti navy tapno iti kasta makakitada manen iti makunkuna a *terra firma*. Iti apagapaman ti pannakawaknit ti pulkok nga inimpenda isut' gapuna a masapul daytoy kunada nga R-and-R, dayta panagpallailang ken panagragsak kadagiti club. Iti "Taaw ken Daytoy a Babilonia," awisennatayo ni Lorenzo Sr. tapno sumrektayo iti akin-uneg a biag dagitoy a kameng ti navy agraman dagiti Filipino nga agdepdepender kadagitoy sumanglad barko. Iti udina, ipaunor ti mannarita ti kamerana a kamera-dagiti-balikas tapno yam-ammona kadatayo ti maysa a karakter iti daytoy nga estoria, ni Willy Shaw. Maysa a puraw a navy ni Willy. Addaan iti pamilia a pinanawanna. Kasta met nga addaan iti ubing nga anak a lalaki. Addaan iti konsiensia sosial, kastoy ti panangiladawan ti mannurat iti daytoy nga agbibiag iti estoria: "dinanto malipatan a pulos dagiti obrero nga agsuksukain kadagiti basura no panawen ti panagsardengda iti apagbiit iti panagubrada…dagiti ubbing a lallaki nga adda iti sirok ti rangtay a mangipukpukkaw iti 'Hi, Joe! Some coins, Joe…!'… ni Nat nga agur-uray iti inana nga agub-ubra iti club… ni Ramon, ti ubing a Filipino nga agar-arapaap iti maysa a pannakapnek iti biag iti sabali a lubong— iti sabali a pagilian."

Ammotayo ti maysa a banag: a babaen ken Willy, iturongnatayo ni Lorenzo Sr. kadagiti sabali pay a biag ken kadagiti alternativo a kayulogan dagitoy sabali pay a biag. Mabalin a kastoy daytoy—ket posible a di panangawat iti kunkuna ni Roger Briant (a kadua ni

Willy iti barko) a mangipappapilit ken mangidekdeklara a "masapul nga agrasaktayo" ken kasta met a "masapul a sumurottayo iti agus." Mapanunottayo ditoy no ania ti ragsak nga adda iti panagmaymaysa a di met klase ti maysa a soledad, daytay a panagmaymaysa a mangidaton kenka iti maysa a Babilonia ni leddaang.

Iti panangigaraw ni Lorenzo Sr. iti kamera tapno ad-adu ti makitatayo, bumalandra kadatayo ti maysa a kritisismo a sosial, ti kondision dagiti mangurkuranges a siudad ken pier ken pagsangladan dagiti barko ken kalsada dagiti siudad. Patigmaanannatayo dagitoy a kritisismo a dagiti kakastoy a kaso ti disegualidad ket saan laeng a kaso ti disegualidad iti maysa wenno dua a pagilian no di ket kaso ti disegualidad a global: a ti kinadur-as ken rag-o ken ragsak ti maysa a pagilian ket posible a resulta ti pannakaipaidam ken luksaw ken ladingit ti sabali a pagilian.

Ti sinnungbat da Willy ken Ramon luktanna ti maysa a lubong tapno makitatayo a ti disegualidad ket saan nga ang-angaw, a pudno daytoy, a makadadael daytoy iti salun-at, isip, kananakem. Ken pudno a makadunggiar iti kinatao. Agbirbirok ni Ramon iti ragsak babaen iti kunkunana a kaadda iti kuarta: no adda kuartam, naragsakka. Iti kasta a kapanunotan, kayatna ti kumappeng iti US Navy—maysa a tagainep amin nga agkabannuag a lalaki a Filipino a kayatna ti agragsak ken maaddaan iti kuarta ken makapanaw iti pagilianna a di met makaited iti nasayaat a masakbayan. Ngem bagbagaan ni Willy ni Ramon, ket ipatigmaanna ti kastoy: "Nabirokamon ditoy pagiliam ti kunkunam a ragsak."

Maysa pay a naldaangan a panangiladawan iti naalas a realidad a mainaig kadagiti dua a biag iti maysa a pagilian a mangibagbaga a demokrasia daytoy ket makita iti "Ti Eden iti Biagda."

Nabiag ti pannakailadawan ni Banong ditoy, ti Ilokano a makaammo a sumala kadagiti situasion iti biag nga iti maysa a banda ket narigat a danggayan. Nabiag met ti pannakailadawanna ken Hil Garcia a mangpadpadas iti panangsalaknibna iti integridadna a kas etikal a tao.

Ngem adda imas ti kastoy a panaggiddan nga agtagainep dagiti agayan-ayat: masapul a maysa kadakuada ti mangted iti espasio tapno maysa kadakuada ti agballigi. Kadagiti situasion a kakastoy, adda

dagiti makunkuna a dilema a no ania man ti aramidem adda latta masindadaan a di nasayaat a bungana. Masapul ditoy ti tured tapno maideklara ti kastoy: "Masapul ti panagbalin ti biag nga agnanayon a sibibiag. Masapul nga ibiagtayo ti biagtayo."

No kitaentayo ti biografia a wagas ti panaganalisar iti maysa nga obra a literario uray kadagiti obra a ti autor mismo ti nagkuna a maysa a fiksion ti aramidna, nalawag a pasubliennatayo dagiti obra ni Lorenzo Sr. kadagiti datos dagiti obrana, datos a mangipakita iti relasion daytoy iti aglawlawna, iti pakasaritaanna.

No kas pagarigan ta yabaytayo dagiti nota a biografiko ken idasigtayo dagitoy kadagiti leksion a maagsawtayo iti umuna a libro da Lorenzo Sr. ken Sinamar, manamnamatayo ti panag-engkuentro ti biografia ken fiksion. Ngarud, adda kinapudno a ti biografia ket maysa met a fiksion, ken ti fiksion ket maysa met a biografia. Kastoy ti kuna ni Hil ken Banong: "Addaak iti maikadua a tukad ti kolehio. Nagsardengak ta di kabaelan a bayadan dagiti dadakkelko dagiti gastos. Napadasak ti nagdalus iti kasilia iti restauran. Kalpasanna, nagtrabahoak a kas tubero. Sa elektrisian. Ngem awan dur-asan kadagiti kakastoy a trabaho. Pinadasko ti agbalin a mannurat. Ngem ti bayad ti panagsurat di pay umanay a pangsuldong iti anges. Nagdesisionak nga agubra iti faktoria. Ngem kaskasdi nga awan met dur-asan dita. Kabaelak met ti agsakrifisio ngem kayatko a tulongan dagiti kakabsatko tapno makaadalda. Ammom, Banong, adda nobiak a maestra—a taga iti kabangibang a probinsia. Maysa met laeng a mannurat. Adda darepdepna ket agbalinak a lapped no kasta nga isardengko ti agarapaap a dumur-as."

Mamatiak nga awan ti makuna a pudpudno a korespondensia iti ibagbaga ni Hil ken ni Banong wenno iti iburburay ni Banong a datos ken ni Hil. No agsurat ti maysa a mannurat a ti ramenna ket ti padasna, saan nga amin a ramen ti padas ket mainayon iti sinuratna: adda ta adda dagiti di mairaman ta kasta ngarud ti kidkiddawen ti pannakaurnos dagiti pasamak iti maysa nga estoria. Ngem dagiti banag a panagpapada, adda kadagiti padas ti mannurat ken kadagiti datos iti sinuratna. Ti pudno a mannurat a mangidukdokumento iti kabibiag ti maysa a gimong kanayon a mangrugi kadagiti pammaliiwna iti dayta a gimong.

Kadagiti adu nga aramid ni Lorenzo Sr., siguradoak a naimballigian ti panangaramatna iti lagipna kadagitoy adu a padasna ket inggamerna dagitoy kadagiti estoriana. Biografiko met ti makunkuna a fiksion. Ken ti fiksion ket adda linaona, uray bassit laeng, a biografia.

Daytoy a wagas ti panagsurat ken panagikur-it ni Lorenzo Sr.—daytay panagaramat kadagiti datos mismo ti bukod a biag—ti maysa kadagiti agdadata a rason no apay nga adda kinautentiko dagitoy nga aramid daytoy a mannurat.

Maysa dagitoy nga obra ni Lorenzo Sr. nga akto ti panagbasa—ken iti panagamiris—iti sosial a biag iti Ilocos. Ken gapuna ta ti disso dagiti pasamak, dagiti agbibiag, ken dagiti isyu nga adda kadagitoy a sinurat nalawag a mainaigda iti Ilocos, agdadata ngarud dagitoy nga instruksion ken dokumentasion kadagiti adu a banag iti gimong nga Ilokano. Siaammotayo a saan nga enteramente dagitoy a pagteng kadagiti sarita ket pasamak nga agdadata. Ngem siaammotayo met a sinukog dagitoy ken inikkanda iti forma dagitoy a wagas ti panangited kadagiti kayulogan ti biag. Fiksional ti engkuentro nga adda iti sinurat, ngem adda kinaagpayso dagiti makunkuna a fiksion. Daytay "panagkayammet a panagkamaysa" ti pudno a pagteng ken ti fiksion ket mainaguraran kadagitoy a sinurat daytoy a mannurat. Makita ditoy ti awanan-akkub ken nasadiwa a talento. Ken addaan dagitoy iti kinatured a mangiladawan iti agdadata a kinapudno a mapaspasamak iti maysa a komunidad nga am-ammo unay ti mannurat.

No pudno a ti kaso ni Hil Garcia wenno Hilario Garcia iti "Tallo a Tugot" ket alter ego ni Lorenzo Sr., addaan iti nalawag a logika ti argumentotayo. Adda dua a mabalin nga aramiden ti autor ditoy: ti dina panangawat iti daytoy wenno ti panangpaneknekna. Ti etikal a panagtignay awan iti tengnga; ketdi, adda iti klaro a posision. No dagiti panagpili a makuna a para iti tao maipideg iti situasion nga awan a talaga panagpili no di ket panagpili gapu ta awan sabalin a mapili, nalawag nga awan wayawaya iti kastoy, ket ngarud, maawatantayo ni Edwin, ti managarapaap kadagiti bituen. Tumakder ni Edwin ken agalsa ken dumawat iti panagibales, dumawat iti pannakakorehir kadagiti amin a palso ken madi nga aramid, iti pannakapurga dagiti adu nga

ag-agalen ken sakit-nakem, ken iti pannakaaresto dagiti adu a brutal ken nakarit nga aramid. Dumawat iti hustisia.

Bubon daytoy nga estoria ti maysa a paset ti filosopia ni Betrant Russell a maipapan iti kunkunana a "tallo a pasion" wenno nairteng unay a karirikna.

Kuna ti nalatak a reformador iti gimong: "Adda tallo a pasion (wenno nadagsen a rikna) a simple ngem ingget pigsa a nangituray iti biagko: ti pannakailiw ken ayat, ti panagbirbirok iti sanut, ken ti nakaro a panangngaasi iti panagtutuok ti sangkatao-an. Panagayat ken sanut, la ket ta posible dagitoy, ket itundanaka nga agpangato agingga iti langit. Ngem daytay panangngaasi ket insublinak iti daga."

Kas makita, dagitoy a "tallo a pasion" maaddaanda iti baro a sukog iti "tallo a tugot" a madakdakamat iti nasao nga estoria, ket ti teknik ken pararelismo ket talaga a nabatad.

Nabingaybingay kadagiti episodo, makitatayo ditoy dagiti elemento a mangbukbukel iti estoria: (a) langit, (b) daga, ken (c) isusurnad.

Ilayontayo ti paralelismo—bennatentayo: kailiwtayo unay ti langit, maaddaantayo iti sanut iti daga no adda gasgasattayo, ket ti sumaruno agsublitayo iti daga tapno iti kasta iringpastayo amin dagiti kunkunada a ditay nairingpas nga aramid a kas koma iti aramid iti lagip, iti panangipamatmat iti bukod a bagi, iti rebelion, iti di panagtignay, ken iti kinaawan iti abilidad a mangawat kadagiti banag iti umuna a gundaway.

Surotentayo ti estoria: tallo nga ubbing a lallaki—agkakasinsin— dagiti agdardarepdep kadagiti nasaysayaat a banag, ti nasayaat a biag, dagiti bituen. Nagdesision ni Edwin a makipagindeg kadagiti appona a baket ken lakay iti Baybayyabas. Agenrol ni Anong iti Philippine Military Academy idinto nga agenrol ni Hil iti unibersidad tapno agbalin a mannurat.

Ti trahedia—ti pannakapapatay dagiti dadakkel ni Edwin— inlimedda kenkuana iti nabayag a panawen agingga a naduktalanna daytoy. Ngatngatngaten ti kararua ken puso ken espirituna ti maysa a rikna: ti panagibalesna. Ti panagdawatna iti hustisia.

Kimmappeng iti maysa a grupo dagiti rebelde.

Saan a nagbalin a reaksionario nga aramid daytoy nga inaramid ni Edwin. Ketdi, kaso daytoy ti makuna a basar a kinalinteg. Ti panggepna a makaibales ket personal ken politikal. Ti naammuanna a pannakapapatay dagiti nagannak kenkuana iti wagas a brutal, ti pannakaaradas ti inana, ti pannakasaksi ti amana iti dayta a pannakaaradas ti asawana saan nga aramid dagiti makunkuna a normal a tao. Ket kasla panangigagara a manayonan pay ti dunor ti isip, makitkita ni Edwin dagitoy nga agwarangwarang ta am-ammo ken papagayam ida ti nabilig a mayor ti ili.

Ket matay ni Edwin, matay nga addaan iti idealismo, ni Edwin nga addaan iti kinalawag iti panagpampanunot, panagpampanunot a mainaig iti no ania a talaga ti mapaspasamak iti gimong, no ania ti mapaspasamak kadagiti kriminal a makabayad kadagiti de-kalidad nga abogado, ken dagiti politiko nga addaan iti kuarta.

Ti maudi, ti "visitasion" wenno isursurnad (mabalin pay ti "isasarungkar") maysa ni Hil a literal a nagsubli iti isu met laeng a barrio a nangrugianda a tallo a nangsursurot kadagiti bituen, nagarapaap kadagiti dadakkel nga arapaap, ken, kas kadagiti ubbing a lallaki kadagiti disso nga aw-away iti Ilocos, ket babaen dagiti tammudoda, sinursurotda ti uttot dagiti eroplano nga aglabas iti ngatuenda a langit.

Kas mannurat, agbalin a kangrunaan nga aktor ni Hil Garcia iti daytoy maudi nga episodo ti estoria.

Manglagip—malaglagipna dagiti amin a pasamak iti panagubingda: Ni Edwin, ni Anong, isuna.

Ket maammuanna dagiti nagkaadu a banag nga awan idi a pulos ti pamalpalatpatanna.

Iti udina, nakabirok iti maysa a wagas tapno maikkan-pategna ni Edwin—tapno di mapukaw ti lagip kenkuana.

Nagbalin a mannurat, ti ambisionna idi ubing pay.

Saan a maysa laeng a mannurat no di ket maysa a nalaing a mannurat, kunana. Ket daytoy nga estoria naibati kenkuana tapno iti kasta maisuratna, tapno iti kasta maammuan ti publiko ti pudno a napasamak ken nagpasaran ni Edwin ken dagiti nagannak kenkuana.

Ket iti pannakaipablaak ti pannakatay ni Edwin, ti maysa a gimong a mangawat kadagiti nagkamtudanna masindadaan koma a mangatur

kadagiti biddutna, a maaddaan iti konsiensia, ken mangaramid kadagiti wagas a mapabaro ti sistema ti hustisia wenno no kasano a matarawidwidan a mismo ti hustisia.

Mabalin a makuna a mairaman daytoy nga estoria iti kategoria ti "literatura a proletariano," no ti kayat a sawen dayta ket ti anag daytoy nga adda iti panunot dagiti editor ti *Talugading* idi insuratda iti "Manipud Kadagiti Editor" ti kunkunada a "rissik ti proletario."[4] Imbaga dagiti editor daytoy idi 1977 iti panawen ti makunkuna nga experimental a Baro a Gimong, maysa a gimong a maididiaya idi kadagiti umili nga alisto a malamlamiong, kadagiti umili a babalatungen.

Ditoy nga inotariotayo a ni Constante Casabar mismo ket dimmalan iti kastoy a pannakapabutbuteng gapu iti makuna a nobelana a proletarian, ti *Dagiti Mariing iti Parbangon.* Napabutngan—wenno binutbutengda ni Casabar gapu iti kasta a sinuratna. Iti di nagbayag, nagdesision a pumanaw iti pagilian tapno iti sabali a disso nga agbiag ken agsardeng nga agsurat.[5]

Panangtunton iti Maysa a Sirmata a Mangted iti Pannakaisalakan

Maysa pay kadagiti kunkunada nga estilo a di-Bannawag a partuat ni Lorenzo Sr. ti estoriana (a nangabak iti maysa a pammadayaw) a mainaig iti maysa a pamilia: ni Abraham Sr., ti asawana a ni Filipinas Isabel, ken dagiti lima nga annakda. Ti "Agsardeng Koma ti Lubong ta Dumsaag ti Tao" ket maysa a kararag, maysa nga araraw, maysa a kiddaw. Ipakitana ti maysa a lubong nga agwerwerret, di mangikankano kadagiti pagteng dagiti tao, di mangikankano kadagiti abuso iti poder dagiti addaan iti kastoy, di mangikankano kadagiti adu a disegualidad

---

4   Edilberto H. Angco, Rogelio Aquino, Cristino Inay, ken Lorenzo G. Tabin (dagiti editor). Talugading: Antologia Dagiti Sarita nga Ilokano (Manila: Gumil Filipinas), 1977.

5   Kitaen ti Constante Casabar, Dagiti Mariing iti Parbangon/Silang Magigising sa Madaling Araw (Quezon City: Ateneo da Manila University Press), 1993.

a mangmangted iti benefisio kadagiti elit ken mangdisdisenfrangkisa kadagiti disenfrangkisadon a masa.

Ditoy—iti daytoy nga estoria—ti panangpatama ni Lorenzo Sr. iti isyu a bioetikal. Adda ditoy ti basar a saludsod: Ania ti aramidentayo no ti gimong ket agbibinegen daytoy, no paliadon, ken no sulpengen? Ania ti aramidentayo no dagiti masa ket dida mismo maikkan iti gundaway a mapadasan ti makunkuna a "mamitlo a pannangan iti maysa nga aldaw"—nga imbes a kasta ti ipaay kadakuada ket nangina a pastel (wenno keyk) ketdi ti maidiaya kadakuada tapno iti kasta ket mamaskaraan ti aginaldaw a bisin ken kisang a mapadpadasanda?

Dagiti napipintas a banag ti pagduyosan nga ar-aramiden ni Abraham Sr. a kas pintor. Agduyos pay kadagiti banag nga ideal. Kasta met nga agduyos kadagiti banag a filosopikal tapno iti kasta ket maawatanna dagiti makalaud a filosopo iti existensialismo ken fenomenologia, isuda nga agyeb-ebkas kadagiti kapanunotan a mainaig iti biag, wayawaya, ken gimong.

Padpadasenna nga awaten dagiti sumagmamano a nihilista a filosopo a kas koma ken Friedrich Wilhelm Nietzsche. Ti sabali pay a sanga ti existensialismo a kas koma iti ateistiko a pagtaktakderan ni Jean-Paul Sartre partikular iti maipapan iti naturalesa ti tao ken ti biagna ket pagsidsiddaawan ni Abraham Sr. Ti posision ni Sartre—ti panangetchapuerana ti esensialismo—ket banag a namagpanunot iti pintor. Nakagteng iti teistiko nga existensialismo—simmurot ken Soren Kierkegaard—a nangidasar iti idea maipapan iti pammati. No mamatika, tumappuakka lattan. No adda pammatim, saan a masapul ti rason—kas impakita ni Abraham iti panangsurotna iti pagayatan ti Diosna nga idaton ni Abraham ti anakna a ni Isaac.

Sarsarmingan dayta a teknik ti panagilista kadagitoy a filosopo ti panagpalpallayog met ti isip ni Abraham Sr. a kas pintor ken mangmennamenna iti kasasaad ti Gimong, a gimong idin ti riribuk, karibuso, ken kinaawan urnos. Ammotayo nga agipinta dagiti pintor kadagiti idea. Ammotayo a maysa dagiti kambasda a blangko a lubong nga agur-uray kadagiti tao ken kadagiti imahe a mangiparipirip iti panagwayawaya.

Ti imasna dadaulo ti maestra nga asawa ni Abraham Sr. iti maysa a progresibo a tignay. Iti kasta nga aramidna, adda kadagiti nagduduma a panagtignay ti grupoda tapno iti kasta mapadisida ti maysa a dadaulo a linamuten ti binabarrairong a wagas ti panagidaulo, maysa a dadaulo nga iti rugi ket nagkari iti kinatan-ok ngem idi nagbalaw sawaw met dagiti saona, sawaw met ti baritono a timekna, ken awan met mamaay ti kinalaingna a manglimlimo kadagiti umili.

Dumteng ti di panagkinnaawatan dagiti agassawa. Ipapilit ni Abraham Sr. a di kumapkappeng ni Filipinas Isabel iti kasta a tignay, a di mapmapan kadagiti rali ken demonstrasion. Ngem edukaran ti maestra nga asawana ti husto a mapaspasamak iti gimong, ket bagaanna ni Abraham Sr.: gapu ta dika mapmapan iti tiendaan dimo ammo ti mapaspasamak iti gimong.

Saan a maipapilit ni Abraham Sr. ti kayatna. Makikappeng ni Filipinas Isabel iti tignay ket agbalin a dadaulo. Iti maysa a demonstrasion, masugatan ken mayospital. Ngem dimteng ti makunkuna a "people power" wenno rebolusion dagiti umili ket napadisi ti barrairong a dadaulo.

Ammotayo a naggapu daytoy nga estoria iti tension ti agtultuloy a panagirupir dagiti umili kadagiti basar a kalinteganda. Dua a makuna a nagballigi a rebolusion dagiti umili, ti makunkuna a people power ngem kasla awan met a pulos ti nagbanagan dagitoy. Ti umuna isu ti pannakapadisi ti diktador a Ferdinand Marcos ken ti naud-udi isu ti pannakapatakias ni Erap Estrada a dadaulo iti korapsion ken panagjueteng. Siaammotayo a kasta unay ti panangibando dagiti nadumaduma a media maipapan kadagitoy dua a rebolusion. Imbagbaga pay dagiti dadduma a kaso kano ti grasia nga aggapu iti langit, a maysa kano daytoy a milagro, a maysa a bendision. Ngem iti udina isu ti agdadata a kinapudno: awan mamaay dagitoy dua a rebolusion dagiti masa ta dida met pulos naaramid a sapasap ti nalinteg a panagbiag. Ketdi, nagsubli dagiti isu met laeng nga oligarko ket itan kasta manen dagiti agar-ari.

Final a Nota: Ti Lugar da Tabin ken
Tabin iti Literatura Ilokana

Awan duadua ti lugar da Lorenzo Sr. ken Sinamar Sr. iti Literatura Ilokana. No maisuratto ti pakasaritaan a literario nga Ilokano, mairaman a maitampok dagiti obrada gapu iti sumagmamano a rason: dagitoy innem a pulo ken uppat nga estoria dinokumentoda ti biag dagiti Ilokano sadino man ti yanda. Numan pay saan a makaay-ayo a narativa dagiti "exilo" ken "diaspora" gapu ta masapul dagitoy ti abilidad iti *epoche*, daytay aramid a mangtengngel iti panaghusga tapno ad-adda a mabaelantayo nga awaten ti anag dagiti banag iti biagtayo.

Itundadatayo amin dagitoy nga estoria iti wagas ti panagusar iti ababa a fiksion a makaited iti panagkritikar iti gimong nga iti kaso ni Sinamar Sr. adda iti modo ti makuna a "romantiko" idinto ta iti kaso ni Lorenzo Sr. iti modo ti makuna a "kritikal." Iti kaso ni Sinamar Sr., adda dita ti tendensia nga agbalin a didaktiko—a mangisursuro. Iti sabali a bangir, iti kaso ni Lorenzo Sr., aglayag daytoy iti wagas nga exploratorio ken experimental. Ti biagna a kas imigrante iti Estados Unidos, kas pagarigan, maysa a pammaneknek a mabalintayo a buloden dagitoy a ramen ti biagtayo tapno iti kasta mabasatayo dagiti mapaspasamak iti aglawlawatayo, ken mayangklatayo ti biografiatayo a kas paset ti dakdakkel pay a biografia, ti biografia mismo ti maysa a gimong. Daytoy a panangiladawan ni Lorenzo Sr. iti Ilocos saan laeng a mismo nga Ilocos ti ipakpakitana no di ket Ilocos pay kadagiti sabali a lugar, ti Ilocos, kas pagarigan a makitkita kadagiti dadakkel a siudad, ti Ilocos iti Los Angeles, ken ti Ilocos, iti udina, iti Salt Lake a pagindeganna itan.

Ti anag ti makuna a makaited iti salakan, ti panagkunak, ket adda iti paraboliko nga istruktura dagiti sinurat ni Sinamar. Ti istruktura ti panagsuratna ket sinurotna ti makunkuna a "forma ti popular a kultura nga Ilokano" a naimuntar idi kalpasan ti gubat a maikadua, ken nangsemento metten kadagiti estilo ken forma a makitkita kadagiti popular a pagbasaan agraman kadagiti popular a magasin.

Iti sabali a bangir, immuestra ni Lorenzo Sr. ti abilidadna a mangnabigar iti agus dagiti dua a karayan ti panagikur-it nga Ilokano:

umuna ti panangsurotna iti diktasion ti makunkuna a "popular a panagtimpla ken panagraman ken panaggusto" dagiti popular nga agbasbasa—dagiti masa; ken maikadua, ti aramidna a mangkarit kadagitoy a forma babaen iti panangdaliasatna iti sabali nga agus iti bukodna a wagas, babaen iti panangitedna iti kritisismo a sosial, ken babaen iti naynay a panagek-experimentona kadagiti kabarbaro nga estilo ken forma ti panagsurat. Iti agpada a wagas, nagballigi ni Lorenzo Sr. a nagestoria. Agtultuloy ti obrana ken isu met laeng nga isu a panagbirok kadagiti banag a makaited iti pannakaisalakan.

Ditoy a maipalagip kaniak ti kuna ni J.R.R. Tolkien maipapan iti redension, ti pannakaispal: "Mangnamnamatayo amin iti Eden, ken kanayon a masirsiriptayo daytoy: ti sibubukel a nakaparsuaan a saan unay a narakrak, ti naturalesa daytoy nga addaan iti kinaimbag ken addaan iti pudpudno a kinatao a napasagepsepan iti anag ti panagbalin nga exilo."

Daytoy nga anag ti panagbalin nga exilo iti naturalesa ti kinataotayo nabatad a nakamapa kadagitoy nga estoria da Lorenzo Sr. ken Sinamar Sr. Sinanamaak a makasursuro dagiti agdama ken dagiti umay pay a henerasion kadagiti obra dagitoy a fiksionista.

Universidad ti Hawaii iti Manoa
Honolulu, Abril 2019

1

SINAMAR A. ROBIANES TABIN, SR.

Anangka

NAGTARUSAK ITI yan ti anangka idi sumangpetak a naggapu iti tianggi. Ne, awanen 'tay naluom a bungana! Ket adda pay la tutot iti nakapurosanna. Immay ngata ni Uliteg Mateo?

Napanko riniing ni Tatang a nakakayag nga agur-urok iti sirok ti duog a salamagi. Nabaringkuas a nanglidlid kadagiti matana.

"Nangipananyo 'tay bunga ti anangkak, 'tang?" sinaludsodko.

"Sasawem? No diak pay nakasapul iti tali a pangsingdanko. Nakaturogak met a nagur-uray kenkan."

"Dagitoy dagiti pinagatangyo," impasab-okko kenkuana dagiti pinaalana idiay tianggi. "Sinnot' nangala 'tay anangkak?"

"Nakaturogak, kunak!"

"No didak binabaon, di koma napukaw!"

"Loka, no dika naglumlom iti napanam, nabantayam koma!"

"Dakayo ti nabati!" agsangitakon idinto ta napankami iti sirok ti anangka. "No dikay' naturog, saan koma a napukaw!"

Nagbang-es ni Tatang. "Inka agdamag dita yan da Eden no asino dagiti ubbing nga immar-arubayan ditoy itay nakaturogak. . . Amangan no dagiti ket alikuteg nga annakna ti akinsirib."

Amangan nga agpayso. Nalabasak da Fred ken agraman sumagmamano nga ubbing itay nagpatianggiak. Anak ni Manang Eden ni Fred, ket ni Manong Asiong a kabsatna ti ama ni Lito.

Nadanonko ni Manang Eden nga agkuykuyyakoy iti alsong iti abay ti kosinada. Adda ni Manong Asiong iti tuktok ti sangapuon a sua.

"Manang, ni Fred?"

"'Pay, 'ya?" dinak pay tinaliaw.

"Damagek koma no nakitada ti nangala 'ti bunga 'tay anangkak. Adda pay la itay leppas ti pangaldaw, itay innak suroten ni Nanang iti yan da Balo Andiang. Itay sumangpetak, awan metten."

Nagsardeng ti kuyyakoyna. Minulagatannak. "Ni Fred ti pabasolem, kasta kadi?"

"Isudat' nalabasak ken ni Lito. . . agraman sumgmamano nga ubbing itay agpadayaak, Manang."

"Oy, oy, oy, Marissa!" nagkumpas ti timid ken kidayna. "Agbainka a mangpabasol iti anakko! Kakaisuna a kaasin' Apo Dios ket dida pay limmangan a nangan. . ."

"Diak ideretso a ni Fred, Manang. Agdamagak koma laeng."

"Kastakay' ketdi no adda mapukawyo! Awan la ket bassit, dagiti annakko!"

"No awan ti napukaw, saan koma datao agdamdamag," bumaraakon.

"Agsapulka pay a nalaing, sakanto agpabasol!" nagbannikes.

Pinanawakon ta amangan no agapakami manen a kas idi naduktalak kenkuana ti baro a kamisonko. Sinurotko ti alog a kumamang iti yan da Lito. Nadanonko ni Mang Antin, a nanang ni Lito, a makikinkinnuto iti agdanda. Imbagak ti gagarak. Awan ni Manong Asiong.

"Awan ni Lito, ipag. Itay pay la leppas ti pangngaldaw a dinagas ni Serking a napan nagburas iti niog idiay baybay. Ket no dayta bungat' anangkam, mabuteng nga agaramid 'diay anakko. Nagsingpetan!"

Agburisda koma iti uray la nga! intabbaawko idi agawidak. Agtugtugaw ni Tatang iti sirok ti anangka.

"No didak binabaon, ken dikay' natnaturog, adayo a natakaw. 'Bag koma no dina damo a bunga," agsansaninglotakon.

Simmangpet ni Uliteg Mateo. Isu ti kapitanmi. Adda iggemna a papel. Dinamagna ti pagsangsangitak. Imbaga ni Tatang. Tinangad ni uliteg ti nakapurosan ti bunga.

"Ammoda ngata, a, ti kinaimutmo. A dimonto met la ikkan ida," kinunana.

Iti abagatan, iti yan dagiti napuskol nga ipil-ipil, uppat nga ubbing ti agtartaray a sumungad. Pinayapayan ida ni uliteg. "Diyo la ammo ti

yan 'tay bunga ti anangka ni nanayo a Marissa, ubbing?" naalumamay ti saludsodna.

Nagkikinnita dagiti tallo. Nagitudo ti kaubingan. "Idiay, Lolo. Bambantayan da Manong Fred ken Lito. Inkam mangala iti buneng a pangpisimi. . ."

Saanen a pinalusposan ni uliteg dagiti uppat.

"Ba'am ta ikkak ti pagnakman dagiti diables. Mangibabainda. Abusta isuda idi ti natakuatan a nangkurimes iti baki da Zoilo. . . 'Bag koma no di ammot' tao nga appokok ida. . ."

"Mansuenyo ida!" inkiraudko.

"Inka idiay balayen," kinitanak ni Tatang. "Dakam' ken ni ulitegmo ti makaammo."

Ngumayemngemak a nagtungpal. Insaganak ti balunet. Nagtugawak iti bangko iti abay ti tawa. Dadaanak da uliteg a nangsurot kada Fred ken Lito iti kaipilan.

Addadan! Immulogak. Nakita ni Tatang ti pinagsarukodko a balunet.

"Inka idiay balayen ta bay-annakam' ken ni ulitegmo a mangted iti pagnakman dagitoy," kinuna ni Tatang.

Nagsayaat ti panagkakatugawda iti sirok ti salamagi. Adda ni Uliteg Mateo iti nagbaetan da Fred ken Lito. Nagmasngaad ni Tatang idinto ta nagaribungbong dagiti kaduada.

"No kasta, pinadpadasyo a pinuros ti anangka ni ikityo a Marissa, Fred?" nagsao ni uliteg. "Sayo met la ibaga iti kunayo. . ."

"Wen, lol. . . ay saan, Lolo. Ni ngamin Lito. Sinugsogannak."

"No sikat' nakalagip itay nakapanaw ni Auntie Marissa."

"Nasaysayaat koma, a, no imbagayo," natalinaay latta ni uliteg. "'La, Fred, inka mangala iti tali idiay balayyo, ken daytay lata a pagsuksukatan ni Nanangmo iti tuyo."

Nagtaray ni Fred sa nagsubli a bitbitnan ti tali ken lata ti gas.

Insingdan ni Uliteg Mateo ti tali iti anangka kalpasan ti panangirukodna kada Fred ken Lito.

"Napintas met nga ikuentas daytoy anangka ket. Di ngamin, Ubbing? Ipadasmo man, Fred."

Madi ni Fred. Nagunget ni Uliteg Mateo. "Ikuentasmo!" inyusongna iti tengnged ni Fred. "Sarapaem iti dua a takiagmo. . ."

Naggarikgik dagiti ubbing idi naikuentas ni Fred ti anangka. Bangbangir ti isem ni tatang. Ni Fred, makaluluan.

Intudo ni uliteg ni Lito. "Sika, bagim a patiten ti lata, a?" imbugkawna. "Aglibuttayo. Agsublatkay' a mangikuentas iti anangka ken mangipukkaw iti: *didakam' tultuladen a nagtakaw, pada nga ubbing. . .*"

Nagtibbayoak. Madi daytoy. Kaguradakton dagiti nagannak.

"Aramidentay' daytoy, a, ta ania ngarud, ket dikay' met maminnga nga agtaktakawen. No namin-anon a nagkarikayo. Naumaakon a manglaplapigos kadakayo. Isu nga agpasiartayo laengen. . . 'La, intayon ket addanto pay obrami ken Loloyo!"

Madi ni Fred. Ngem nangpidut ni uliteg iti pagbaut. "Agpukkawka. Ipukkawmo 'tay insurok," imbilinna ken ni Lito. Pinadasna. "Ipigsam! Kastay panagpukpukkawmo no agaayamkayo!"

Nagbatiak. Ni tatang ti simmurot. Kas iti panangipapanko, napasardeng da Uliteg Mateo iti paraangan da Manang Eden. Kasta unay ti tabbuga daytoy.

"Appokoyo ida. Dikay' la maarieken a mangilibut kadakuada!" kinuna ni Manang Eden. Kaduana ni Manong Ikko.

"Awan ti kaduayo a mangisuro kadagiti barisuweng nga annakyo no saan a siak," insungbat ni uliteg. "Kaykayatko pay nga ammo dagiti umili nga appokok dagiti mannanakaw, ket dusaek ida a kas itoy. . ."

"Apay met a nayatkayo iti kasdiay, 'Tang?" dinamagko ken ni tatang idi agsubli.

"Ba'am ta agnakem dagiti annak ti diables nga ubbing!"

"Ngem kaguradakayonton dagiti nagannak. . ."

"Agyamanda ketdi, a, no agbalbaliw dagiti annakda. . ."

"Ngem ti bunga ti anangkak, 'Tang. . . pangipanandanto ngaruden?"

"Agsaritakayonto nga aguliteg."

Simmangpet ni nanang. Kasta unay ti karakattotna.

"Ania a kinamauyong ti inar-aramidmo, Anno?"

"Apay, 'ya, a nagbayagkan, Baket?" sinaludsod ni Tatang.

"Aniat' nangpailibutam kadagiti ubbing? Kasta unay ti panangbabalaw dagiti tattao. Kasta unay ti pungtot ni Asiong. Agsangsangit ni baketna. Dikay' mabain iti itsura dagiti ubbing nga agpukpukkaw iti kalsada sada patiten ti lata? Simmangkautro daydiay kapitan a kabsatmo!"

"Dinak sersermonan tapno nalaingka. . . No napnapanam ketdi ta dika metten sumangpet!"

"No dika ket ung-ong a laklakayan!" ket siak ti sinangona. "Binilinmo ni amam?"

"A, saan, 'Nang! Ni uliteg, a..." Impalawagko ti napasamak.

"Uray pay. Saan koma a kasta. Nakababain! Nakababain!" inulit-ulit ni nanang.

Iti yan da Manang Eden, nangngegko dagiti agsasaruno a tabbaawna ket agisidiren.

"Dida la pampanunoten ti kinatulokko a baonenda! Adut' linablabaak a lupotda a didak tinangtangdanan! Mangirurumenda! Mangirurumenda!"

"No dimo kunkunsintiren daydiay anakmo, saan koma a kasdiay. Dinak met ita ik-ikkan a mangisuro. . ."

"Gustom ti pannakailibut ti anakmo? No ni Marissa komat' nailibut, diak ammo no ania koma met ti rikna ni uliteg!"

"Makitam ti inaramidyo ken ni amam?" pinasgarannak ni inang.

"Agisidir ni Manang Eden ket ditoy met ti pagbagasanda no awan ti isaangda!"

"Husto 'ta ngiwatmon! Kunam sa ketdi no ubingka pay?"

Immulogak. Iti daya, simmungad da Manong Asiong ken Manang Antin.

"Apaunay ti inaramidyon, Uliteg? Diyo pay la kiniddaw ti umayko panangikaro iti biddut ti anakko. Wenno pinadusayo, a saan ketdi a kasdiay. Imbabaindakam' met la unayen ket!" impasungad ni Manong Asiong.

"Kastoy, Asiong," naalumamay ni tatang. "Kayatyo nga agbalbaliw ti anakyo wenno saan?"

"Ngem saan koma a kasdiay. . . Saan nga isut' akimpanunot. Naibunggoy laeng, Uliteg."

Nakita ngata ida ni Manang Eden isu nga immay a kasla emperatris.

"Mano, Marissa, ti bayad ti anangkam?" imparupana.

"Diak pagbibisinan ti kuartam, Manang!"

"Kastakay' ketdi ta nalpasyon ti kaykayatyo kadatao!" sinangona ni tatang. "Mano ti bayad ti anangka, Uliteg?" kinautna ti bolsa ti paldana ket binilangna ti nalukonlukon a sagpipisos.

"Idulinmo dayta, Eden. Adut' nasnasken a pakasapulam."

"Dikay' kad' agkaskasta no ditoy met la balay ti pagbagasanyo no awan ti isaangyo!" insuldongko.

"Marissa!" kinusilapannak ni tatang.

"Manot' utangko kadakayo?"

"Bilangem, a, ti dimo nabayadan manipud kaaddat' nakemko!"

"Kaska la kalaingan, Loko! Dimo ammon ti panangilablabak kadagiti lupotmo idi sikat' bassit nga agbutbuteg ken masakit ni inam?"

Kayatko a duklosen, ngem addan da Uliteg Mateo. Nailadawan ti bannog ken buteng da Fred ken Lito, aglalo idi makitada dagiti dadakkelda. Nakalablabbasiten dagii takiag ni Lito a nangsarapa iti anangka. Impaypay ni uliteg ti kallugongna.

"Addakay' met amin. . ." kinuna ni uliteg.

"Immayda rimmaut, Uliteg!" kinunak.

"Inikkatyo ti karbenganmi a nagannak, Uliteg. Nasakit unay kaniak ti panangilibutyo iti anakko. . ."

Nagkutitem ti sangi ni uliteg. "Nasaksakit pay kaniak ti itatanor dagiti annakyo nga itta ken barisuweng, Asiong. Agingga iti mabalin, no siak pay met lat' kapitan, diak kayat a dagiti appoko ken kakabagiak ti agaramid iti maikaniwas..."

Agarudoken a pumanaw ni Manang Eden. Nasiputan ni uliteg.

"Dika pumampanaw, sika Eden! Napateg ti pagsasaritaantayo," naturay ti bilin. "Sika, Marissa, inka mangala iti buneng ken lana, ta daytoy nga anangka, mapisi. . ."

Nagtungpalak.

Pinisi ni uliteg ti anangka. Unay a lukmeg dagiti lasag ken gunnotnan! Nagsinsin dagiti dakulap ni uliteg. Inyawatna kada Manong Asiong ken Manang Eden.

"Ramananyo ti nagbannogan dagiti annakyo!"

"Diak agraraman, Uliteg. Kukuada laeng!" ket ginandat a guyoden da Manong Asiong ken Manang Eden dagiti annakda.

"Alaenyo. . ." makapungtoten ni uliteg. "Diyo alaen?"

Inawat da Manong Asiong ken Manang Eden. Pumpunasen ni Manang Antin dagiti luana.

Inyawatan ni uliteg da Fred ken Lito.

"Ala, agawidkayon! No ulitenyo pay, saanto laeng a libut ti malak-amyo kaniak. Ibitinkayonton iti tengnga ti plasa. . ."

Pinidut ni uliteg ti nabati a pisi idi nakaadayon dagiti agiina. Nangisakmol. Agkatkatawadan ken tatang.

Tumanabutob ni nanang iti balay.

Nabatiak a makatiltilmon! —0

Bannawag: Mayo 4, 1970; Marso 2017 (?).

Daydi Maysa A Lourdes

NAGKIDEM NI Lourdes. Nairut. Ngem dina maiwaksi dagiti saludsod nga umuk-ukuok iti mugingna. Dina kayat a lagipen wenno panunoten ngem umayda latta a kasla manga-alia no agmaymaysa. Inapputna dagiti lapayagna sa nagpakleb. Ngem sumuknor latta iti panunotna.

Nagdata sa nagmulagat. Minulenglenganna ti nalitem a bobeda. Iti ruar, mangmangngegna latta ti ariangga ti jukebox ken daranudor ti lugan. Ngem awan ti nakemna kadagitoy. Kasla makitkitana dagiti ramay a mangitudtudo kenkuana. Kasla agaw-aweng iti lapayagna dagiti garakgak ken kanakliing dagiti agtutupa a kopita iti klab a pagpapaayanna a kas hostes. Ti nalamuyot a tokar ken ti arasaas ti nabarteken a parokiano iti danggay ti nalailo a musika. Agawid no malpasen ti innem nga oras. Agsukat iti desente a kawes ket rumimbaw ti libnos nga ik-ikutanna. Madlaw ti natundiris nga agong, bugagaw a mata, dumerosas a kudil ken atiddog a buokna. Igpilanna ti libro, ket di mabayag, mabilbilangen dagiti addangna iti pasilio ti unibersidad a dandanin pagturposanna iti komersio.

Nagsikig. Nakitana ti kama ni Amore. Karuruar ti balasang a kakuartuanna. Ita la nga adda met wayana a rummuar nga aggatang kadagiti masapulna. Nakumikom a nagaramid kadagiti term papers kadagiti napalaba nga aldaw. Aw-awisen itay ni Amore ngem awan ti gartemna a rummuar. Kayatna a bukodan daytoy nga ulimek. Adda iliw iti lansad ti barukongna. Ngem adda gawid a dina maawatan. Kasla

8

kaaliawna a makita ti marmarpuog a balayda idiay away. Ken ti kubbo nga inana nga agisursor iti lakona nga ikan.

Nakagat ni Lourdes ti bibigna. Saan nga ammo ti inana dagiti kanakliing ti kopita, dagiti nalamuyot a tokar. Dina ammo ni Vener a manager ti maysa a dakkel a banko iti siudad; ni Edgar a navy. Ngem ammona ni Romel, ta kinaadalan ken kinagraduaranna iti sekundaria idiay probinsia. Magustuan ni nanangna ni Romel. Nadayaw ken natakneng kano.

Kabagianda daydi immuna a nakikaseraanna ditoy siudad. Nakapaganus iti nailet ken nasalimuot a kuarto. Nagsilamut iti bugguong. Iti pusona, naimula dagiti adu a pammagbaga ti kubbo nga inana. Agan-anuska, nakkong. Igaedmo ti agadal. Uray kasano ti rigat, no adda la ketdi arapaap a buyogan ti panangtun-oy, saan a dinto maragpat!"

Ngem pimmnaw kalpasan ti dua a tawen. Nakidag ti riknana kadagiti pasagid ti ikitna. Apay kano a di sumrek iti trabaho sa agbasa iti rabii ta di pay isu a dagensen ni nanangna. Adda kano tipona nga artista ket amangan no maala nga agparang iti pelikula. Mayat ti riknana. Ngem ammona ti kinapeggad ti biag ti artista aglalo ti maysa a probinsiana a kas kenkuana. Ken madi la ketdi ti inana iti kasta a pagsapulan.

Sarsarungkaran pay idi ni Romel nupay naballaway. Adayo ngamin ti pagkaseraanna iti yanda. Ken estriktoda iti unibersidad a pagbasbasaanna. Eskolar ni Romel.

Nariing ti arapaapna iti nalamuyot ken naumbi nga aweng; napan simmirip iti tawa. Makipalpalama. Talloda. Ubing, agtutubo, ken lakay. Bulsek ti lakay, isut' mangkurkurengreng iti gitara. Agkankanta ti agtutubo ket inyabaday met ti ubing ti basketda. Bumambannayat ti pasakalye ti lakay, tumibtibong ti boses ti agtutubo. Nakitana ti langana idi ubing, no kasdiay nga awan ti maited ni nanangna a kontribusionna iti eskuela. Mapan kadagiti kakabsat ni nanangna. Kunkunana idi nga apaman a dumakkel ken addan pagsapulanna, supapakannanto ti ayatda kenkuana. Isu nga iti naudi a panagbakasionna, adu a kinarton ti insangpetna. Pinasarabuanna amin dagiti kabagianda a simmabat kenkuana. Ngem saan nga inawat ni nanangna daydi napintas a kimona ken pandiling ken sinelas. "Diak mausar dagitoy iti panagisursorko

iti ikan, nakkong. Umanayen a sarabok ti pannakakitak kenka a naturposmon ti karreram."

Nagsangit ti inana idi ibagana a saannan a pagdanagan ti busbosenna ga agadal ta dakkel ti sueldona.

"Pangngaasim, Anakko, ta idiam dayta kunam a pagsapulam. Maisakadka pay laeng. Matayak kadagiti damag! Ti kunada a no ania ti nagtaudam isu met laeng ti pagbalinam. Sursurotem kano ti kinabastardom!"

Saan! Saan! imkis.

Nalpasen ti kanta dagiti makipalpalama. Ur-urayenda ti ited ti bumalay. Rimmuar ti nalukmeg a burangen a babai sa nagbannikes. Binugkawanna dagiti tallo. "Awan pay igatangko iti lamutek, addanto ketdin ipalimosko kadakayo? Nagdadakkelankayo a karne. Dikay' koma agsapul iti trabahoyo!"

Kinautna ti bolsana. Nabukel a sangapulo. Nagdardaras nga immulog tapno ikamakamna ti kuarta. Ngem adayon dagiti tallo.

Nasaem ti panaas iti barukongna. Idi la kanikatlo nga aldaw a nagsarakda manen ken ni Vener. Yaw-awisna a mapanda idiay Baguio. Impilitna nga inted ti tseke nga aggatad iti pito gasut a pisos. Bayadam aminen nga utangmo iti eskuela, kinunana. Agingga ita, dina pay ammo ti pamay-anna iti sobra ti inted ni Vener. Dina met maipaw-it ken ni nanangna. Dinto met la awaten ti baket.

Dina maawatan ngem mariknana a kasimronna ita ti bagina. Pagdasdasigenna daydi Lourdes a nagan-anus a nakipagnaed iti nailet ken nasalimuot a kuarto ken ti agdama a Lourdes a kasla di nakananam iti rigat ken sikor.

Usarem ti utek. Narigat ti agkapuykapoy. Kuarta ti kaskenan kadagitoy a panawen. Kuna dagiti nalang-ay a maasitganna. Ket nasulisog met. Kinidemanna ti simrek iti nasipnget a pagsasalaan. Inturedna ti apros ken agek ken arakup dagiti lallaki nga agsapsapul iti lingay. Agtukiad idi damo aglalo no kasla maanninawanna ti ladawan ti kubbo nga inana iti kopita ti arak a yawatna kadagiti lallaki. Ngem awanen ti kamanganna. Nabainan kadagiti saoao ti asawa ti kabagianda a pakidagusanna. Immakar iti pagkaseraan.

Siak pay la daydi a Lourdes! impettengna. Diak malipatan ti naggapuak. Ammok ti kinaasinok. Napudnoak iti karik ken ni nanang. Inkarigatak a tinun-oyan. Saanak a dakes. Pudno a nagbasolak. Ngem ania ngarud, taoak met a nagtagilasag.

Nabayagen a dida nagkita ken ni Romel. Linikliklikanna ti nagdamag ken nangammo maipapan kenkuana manipud idi sabalin ti kaserana. Aglalo idi maam-ammona ni Edgar ken maipeksana iti daytoy ti nalayog nga arapaapna a mapan iti ballasiw ti taaw. Binalakadan ni Edgar nga agan-annad ket nagkari met. Nasangal ti ayatda iti ababa a panawen a kaadda ni Edgar iti Filipinas. Sumangpet ni Edgar sakbay nga agturpos tapno umayna itrabaho dagiti papelesna a mapan idiay California a nakaidestinuanna.

Iti iseserrekna iti daytoy maudi a semestre iti eskuela, nagsapata nga agbalbaliwen. Pinanawannan ti naranga a kaserana idi maam-ammona ni Amore a kakuartuanna. Bassit ti siled ngem desente. Naulimek ditoy, nawaya a makapagpanunot. Gagangay nga estudiante ti panangyam-ammona iti bagina ken ni Amore a kas met ken ni Amore kenkuana. Agassideg dagiti kolehio a pagad-adalanda. Agpadada iti kurso. Isuna laeng ta adda pay la ni Amore iti maikadua a tukad.

Saan nga ammo ni Vener daytoy a kaserana. Ngem nagkitada ken ni Vener itay nabiit. Inuray ti baro iti pagadalanda. Imbaga ni Vener nga agur-uray ti puestona iti banko apaman nga agturpos. Sana inkarawa ti tseke. Saan a nakapagkedked idi inawis ni Vener. Ket pinalabasda ti sumagmamano nga oras iti maysa nga otel.

Saanak a dakes! kinunana manen iti panunotna. Dina arapaap ti paikasar ken ni Vener. Dina patien a baro pay. Ken awan ti naun-uneg a panaginnusigda iti tunggal maysa. Ni Edgar ti agpatpataw kadagiti arapaapna. Kayatna idiay California. Iti adayo. Nasken a panawanna dagiti nakarimrimon a lagip a mangbatbatibat kenkuana. Agkasardanto kanon no agsubli ni Edgar iti Filipinas. Agkuyogdanto nga agpa-Ilokos tapno sadiay ti pakaangayan ti kallaysada. Agkuyogdanto metten nga agpa-America. Ayabandanto ni nanangna no addadan sadiay.

Dina kayat ni Vener ngem dina maiparupa ti riknana. Kayatna la daytoy gapu iti kuartana. Saan a kasta ti mariknana ken ni Edgar.

Nabatingting ti pagorasan. Maikaliman iti malem. Iti ruar, timmibong ti ikkis dagiti jukebox. Kadagiti poste, addadan sumagmamano a sisesegged a bombilia.

Simmangpet ni Amore. Ngem nalidem ti rupana. Arinsangiten. Ammona, dinto met la ibaga ni Amore no saan nga agdamag. Kastat' kababalin daytoy.

"Apay?" dinamagna.

"Ni inangko, simro kano manen ti panagpadarana, kuna ti kalugarak a dimmagasak. Paibagbaga kano da ikit a no diak pay nagasto amin ti kuarta a pinaitulodna idi lawasna, igatangko kan' ti agas ta impaw-itda ti reseta. Ngem nagastokon."

Ita la nga ibaga ni Amore ti maipapan iti inana.

"Nabayagen a masakit ni nanangmo, Amore?"

"Naalana iti panaglablabana. Nabayagen a di dimmikar, ngem siguro, nagtrabaho manen iti nadagsen. Uray iparit da ikit, sige met latta. Kababain kadakayo, kunana kada ikit a tumultulong iti panagadalko. Naimbagto kano laeng no makapagturposak. Awan ngaminen ti tatangko. Natay idi inawnak pay la ni inangko." Pinunas ni Amore ti luana.

Sinaggaysa ni Amore a binukaitan dagiti insangpetna. "No mabalin la koma a maipaisubli dagitoy ta adda igatangko iti agas ni inangko. . ."

Immanges n Lourdes iti nauneg. Apay nga ita la a madakamat ni Amore dagitoy? A, ngem uray isu, nadakdakamatna kadin ken ni Amore dagiti palimed ti biagna? Umdasen ti bassit a sarita ken kinnomusta kadagiti leksionda no addada iti kuartoda. Saan unay nga aglutluto ditoy. Pamrayanna ti tumaray a gumatang iti kanen ken sidana iti restauran.

Naluyaan iti panagsangit ni Amore. Kinarawana ti bolsana. Adda pay la ti nabukel a sangapulo.

"Saankan nga agsangit. Inka gumatang iti agas a kasapulan ni nanangmo ta ipaw-itmo a dagus. Wenno sikan a mismo ti mapan dumaw-as no awan la ketdin ti nasken nga asikasuem iti eskuela!" Linuktan ni Lourdes ti bagna. Kimmaut iti dua a sagduduapulo.

Pinunas ni Amore ti luana. Pinerrengna ni Lourdes. "Sika ngaruden ngay? Kasulam met ti kuarta. Agraduarkanton. . ."

"Saan a dayta ti nasken. Alaemon ket dimon pampanunoten ti pagbayadmo. Bayadamto latta no adda. . ."

Binisito ni Amore iti nalaus a ragsakna. "Maysaka nga anghel. . . Diak makasupsuapak iti kinaimbagmo. Ipadamagko la ketdi ken ni inangko!"

Kasla adda puris a nasuat iti barukong ni Lourdes. nakaanges iti nalukay. Nakitana ni nanangna kadagiti arapaapna. Inton agawid, ikuyognanto ti kapatgan a sagutna kenkuana. . . ti diplomana. —0

Bannawag: Abril 24, 1972

Testamento

MAIGIDIAT DAYTOY nga agsapa ken ni Criselda Robillos. Daytoy ti nabayagen nga inur-urayna kalpasan daydi nga ipupusay. Makasugat ti pangngeddeng dagiti dua a kabsatna iti ama, da Shalina ken Ada, nupay ninamnamanan daytoy idi sidadalit pay laeng daydi Don Antero nga amada.

"Pumanawkan! Awan ti karbengam nga agtawid iti uray sangkaballing a napanawan daydi Tatang ta naiparsiakka la a darana kadagiti ag-Robillos! Gabat! Bastardo!

Prangka daytoy a sao ni Shalina kalpasan ti maikasiam daydi tatangda.

Kuna met ni Att. Rafael nga abogado daydi tatangda: "Saan a basta pumanawka, Criselda. Isuda ti awan karbenganna nga agtawid ta naalada metten ti bingayda ken naasawaanda payen. Ken uray bastardoka a kas kunada, dimmakkelka iti sidong daydi amayo. Nagpaayka kenkuana agingga iti maudi nga angesna. No agimonda iti panagadalmo, basolda, a, ta dida nagadal idi pagadalen daydi Tata ida. Dika pumampanaw, uray ania ti sawenda. Pumanawka no pumanawkanto man, ta sibibiag pay met la ni nanangmo, ngem kalpasan ti panangibasak iti testamento."

Immanges iti nauneg ni Criselda. Nagintek dagiti matana iti silulukat a ruangan ti nalawa nga inaladan. Padpadtuanna no asino ti umuna a sumangpet—da Shalina ken Ada wenno ni Abogado Rafael.

Imbaw-ingna dagiti matana iti relo iti ngatuen ti agdan. Nasapa pay gayam, nakunana. Kinitana dagiti daan a muebles. Malagipna daydi panangsungkasungka da Shalina ken Ada no papananto dagitoy ken

kasdiay a muebles. Ad-adu kano ti mapan ken Shalina ta dakdakkel
ken nalawlawa ti balayna. Inggagarada la ketdi nga impangngeg ti kasdi
kenkuana. Kukuayo laeng! nagistayna imbugkaw. . . Dinamagna ketdi:
"Asinonto ngarud ti agtagikua iti daytoy balay, Manang?" ni Shalina ti
nangituronganna iti saludsodna bilang inauna ken makaammo kano
nga agdesponer iti amin a napanawan daydi amada.

"A, parakrakkonto. Paaramidko nga ubong dagiti baboymi!"

Ubong la kadin ti kaikarian daytoy daan a balay a sangkaullit
daydi tatangda a nangisangbay iti agduduma a nam-ay iti biagna?
'Diyonto parakrakrak daytoy, Elda. Pabaruen ken papintasento ti maysa
kadakayo, wenno uray sikanto lattan no makastrekka iti pagsapulam ket
makaurnongka iti umdas a kuarta. Naimbagto la a pagtitiponanyo no
adda ragragsak wenno anibersario a maselebraran. . .'
Impalagipna daytoy ken ni Shalina. Binugkawan ketdi daytoy.
"Oy, oy, awan bibiangmo iti kayatko nga aramiden. Ammo pay, aya, ni
tatang ti kayatko nga aramiden ket nalpas metten a natay!"
Nasinga ti panagpampanunot ni Criselda idi sumrek ni Nana Sayyang,
ti maysa kadagiti katulongan. Dimmawat iti nayon ti igatangna iti
lutuenda.
"Dakayo la ti makaammon kadagiti potahe, Manang, a?" kinuna ni
Criselda. "Arinsakiten ti ulok. . ."
Nagkatawa ti katulongan. "Dimo pakadanagan dayta, Ading. Siak ti
makaammo iti sidaen a paborito ni Abogado."
Nagdalus ken nagurnos iti salas. Kinaptanna dagiti tawa iti kortina.
Kalpasanna, simrek iti kuartona. Sipaparabaw ti dakkel ken daan a
maleta iti mesita. Linuktanna. Nakitana ti nakatoga a ladawanna nga
inlukipna iti kalub ti maleta. Dinutdotna iti likudan ti ladawan ti
sobre a naglaon iti sumagmamano a papeles. Inrikepna ti maleta sana
sinaggaysa a pinalabsan dagiti papeles. Inkabilna iti kahon ti mesita idi
mapnek a nangbasa.

Ita ta agid-idda, makitkitana manen ti napalabas. Dagidi aldaw a
panagan-anusna a nagadal babaen ti awan sardayna a pammalakad daydi
tatangda. "Agawaam ta uray no sika la ti makaturpos. Awan essem da
manangmo idi. Kinaykayatda ti nakiasawa."

Daydi panagsublat da Shalina ken Ada a nangtanabutob iti amada. "Ang-angaw, aya, ti agpaadal iti kolehio, Tatang. . ."

"Ba'anyo kadi, uray isu la ti mangilalaem kadakayo. Adda sariritna!"

"Sus! Dayta a gabat? Isu a natangsit ta kanayon nga ayunanyo!"

Babaknangen da Shalina ken Ada. Dakkel a nagpuonanda iti negosio ti inted daydi tatangda. Ngem dida sinagutan ni Criselda idi nagturpos iti kolehio. Pinabasolda pay ketdi nga isu ti nangsugsugsog iti daydi amada no apay a dina kayat ti makitipon iti uray maysa kadakuada. Rason met daydi tatangda a dina maanusan ti kinalaing nga agtanabutob dagiti kabsatna ken ti kasla awan a panangikankano kenkuana dagiti manugangna.

Idi dimmaw-as ni Shalina idi kalman, dinamagna no kaanonto ti panaw ni Criselda. "No kunam nga alaendaka iti maysa kadakami ken Ada, nungka. Inka iti kayatmo a papanan. Ken laglagipem, awan ti kaes-eskanna a denggem ti ibasa ni Atty. Rafael a testamento ta awanto met laeng ti agpaay kenka!"

Nakaisem. Ammona ti linaon ti testamento. Adda iti sibay ti masakit nga amada idi idiktarna iti abogado ti maudi a bilinna ket pinagkarida a dina sasawen iti uray asino. Inad-adalna idi pay laeng no anianto ti ibunga dayta a testamento kadagiti dua. Isunto la ketdi ti pagballatekan ti pungtotda, a kabulonto ti lunod, ta ammonan ti kababalin dagitoy. Makitkitanan ti adayo a masakbayan.

Puling lat' panagkitkita da Shalina ken Ada kenkuana. Iti ipupusay daydi tatangda, ammona a naggibus metten ti panaglalangenda nga agkakabsat nangruna idi maammuanna ti linaon ti testamento. Idi ikeddengna nga ipabus-oy ti tawidenna kada Shalina ken Ada, ammona a maudi daytan a panagkikitada ken maruk-atan metten iti kinadangkok dagiti kabsatna.

Ken ni Criselda, napatpateg ti kinawaya. Sitatalimeng iti kaunggan ti pusona ti dinagdagullit daydi tatangda: "Pinataudko amin iti bukodko a ling-et dagiti namataanyo a sanikua. Awan tawidko kadagiti nagannak kaniak, malaksid ti biagko!"

Dina napuotan dagiti naglabas nga oras. Nariing kadagiti anabaab iti ruar. Naitimkanna dagiti simmaangpet—da Shalina ken Ada a kinakuyogda dagiti lallakay ken annakda. Nasarangsang

ti panagsasaritada ken panagkakatawada. No saan nga agbiddut ni Criselda, imbalonan dagiti kayongna iti mainum dayta a pangngaldaw.

Napigsa ti saludsod a nangngegna ken ni Nana Sayyang. "Ania? Adda pay laeng?"

Bimmangon ni Criselda. Linuktanna ti maletana. Nangiruar iti pagsukatanna sana rinikpan. Tiningitingna ti kadagsen ti maleta.

Adda arimpadek nga umul-uli.

Simmirip ni Criselda iti tawa. Nakaplastar dagiti kayongna nga agpaypayubyob iti sirok ti salamagi iti paraangan. Rimmuar ni Criselda. Nakitana ni Shalina. Nagsalip dagiti matada. Nagbang-es a nagpakosina ni Shalina. Simmaruno nga immuli ni Ada a nagsapin iti nakipet ken napuskol ti polbosna. Impababana nga impangato a kinita n Criselda.

"A, kunak man la no pimmanawka pay la idi kalman? Di met nabayagen nga ur-urayen ni inam ti ipapanmo kenkuana? Wenno adda namnamaem a tawidmo iti testamento?" manglalais ti isem ni Ada.

"Kuna met idi ni Abogado, Manang, a saakto la pumanaw no maibasana ti testamento daydi tatang!"

"A-ania?" Nagbusingar dagiti bibig ni Ada.

Simrek ni Criselda iti kuartona.

Masapul a makapanaw sakbay a sumangpet ni Abogado Rafael.

Namles. Simple. Ad-adda a pinabusnag ti nangisit a bestidnona. Innalana iti uyosan ti sobre nga inkabilna itay. Binasana manen. Nabaybayag. Insublina dagiti papeles iti sobre idi mapneken kadagiti nailanad.

Timman-aw pay naminsan. Addan da Shalina ken Ada iti abay dagiti lallakayda. Padpadaananda ni Abogado Rafael.

Binagkatna ti maletana. Natimbeng ken nainayad dagiti paddakna a nagturong iti agdan. Nagturong iti sirok ti salamagi. Tinipedna ti rumkuas a riknana. Pinilitna ti immisem. Intanggayana ti sobre ken ni Shalina.

"A-ania daytoy?" nagsabat dagiti kiday ni Shalina.

"Nagbiddut daydi tatang a nagpaaramid iti testamento, Manang. Dakayo, bilang anak daydi tatang iti inkasarna, ti rumbeng a pagpaayan ti adda iti testamento. Ngem dikay agdanag. Adda kadagita a papeles ti panagtagikuayo. Pinaaramidko iti sabali nga abogado. No kas

pagarigan dinto akuen ni Abogado Rafael, ipakitayonto la kenkuana dagitoy napirmaan a papeles. Pumanawakon, kas kunayo, ket diyo koma baybay-an daytoy a disso. Ammoyo no kasano ti kinapategna iti daydi tatang. . ." Pinagsinnublatna a kinita dagiti dua.

Awan ti nakatimek. Minulenglenganda ni Criselda a timmallikud a nagturong iti ruangan. —0

Bannawag: Agosto 7, 1972

Ti Saba Ni Anti Rosa

NAGSARDENG ti kotse ni Apo Mayor iti batog ti balay. Ammok a daytoy saba nga al-aladak ti umayda kitaen. Inawagak ni Anti Rosa iti balay.

Sinallabay ni Apo Mayor ni Anti Rosa idi makaasidegda iti puon ti saba. Atitiddogen dagiti tallo a sapadna nupay dua a lawasna pay laeng a naibuang. No ania la unay ti kinadatdatlag daytoy a saba. Gapu kano ta nagbunga a di nagsabunganay. Saglilima la a bukel ti tunggal sapad ket inton maluom dumanonto kano dagiti bungana iti daga.

"Bassit 'toy lugaryo a Labut, Rosa," kinuna n Apo Mayor, "ngem pinadakkel dayty a sabam. Pagdidinnamagandan idiay ili. Ania ti awag daytoy a klase?"

Nangudkod ni Anti Rosa. Awan nga agpaysot' makaammo iti nagan ti saba.

"Kua, Mayor," kinuna ni Anti Rosa, "saan kano a malagip a dinamag ti anakko iti gayyemna a nangted kenkuana. Naggapu kano iti ballasiw ti taaw dayta."

"Gapu ta awan ti makaammo 'ti naganna, buniagak iti 'Saba ni Rosa'."

"Areglado, Mayor!" insarurong dagiti kadua ti mayor.

Kasta unay ti lawa ti isem ni Anti Rosa. Pinikpik ni Mayor. "Taraknem a nalaing ta bagaakto ti tunggal kapitan nga umay gumatang 'ti subual. Makisaliptayo iti Green Revolution bareng makayalattayo 'ti premio. Maluomton 'toy bungana, Rosa!"

"Isu a dika agmurmuriot, Angkuan, no maipanggep 'toy saba ti pangibabaonak kenka. Mairamankanto a maidaydayaw iti salip, kas kuna ni Apo Mayor itay," kinuna ni Anti Rosa apaman a naisibet dagiti sangaili.

"Pagangayanna, datayonton ti maawanan 'ti subual nga imula. Wenem met amin a mangibaga 'tattan, Anti!"

"Sinniriban, a, Angkuan. Wen, kunak lattan tapno maparagsak dagiti umay. Uray ta nagaget nga agsubual. 'Gasem, sangsangapuon dayta ket dandani duapulon san dagiti agrusing a subualna. Ken ammota, aya, no dayta saba ti makaidanonto kaniak iti yan ni Apo Presidente. Makitakton ti Palasio. Sa ti kunkunada a Nayong Pilipino. Maidaydayawto ti Saba ni Rosa, ken ti Labut, ken uray sika, Angkuan. Dimo met, aya, kayat a makita ti Manila?"

"Saanman, Anti. . ."

"Sigurado a makapagkuyogta a mapan. Ket no pumudno, utangtanto iti saba."

Nakaangesak iti nalukay ta nalpasko met laengen nga inaladan ti saba. Awanen ti naidaw-as kalpasan da Mayor.

Iti sumipnget, pinuorak dagiti naigumpo a nagkayasak iti apagisu a maisuob iti bunga.

Dimmaw-as da Nana Tibang ken Tata Ayong a kaarrubami dita abagatan ti kalsada. Inasitgannak ni Tata Ayong idinto a nagtarus ni Nana Tibang iti yan ni Anti Rosa nga agimarmarit iti dengdengenmi a marunggay.

"Nakaay-ayat met 'toy saba a bambantayam, Barok, ta nakalagip ni Apo Mayor a bimmisita iti lugartayo!"

"Kasta unay ti panangdaydayawna, Tata."

"Patpatiray-okannaka laeng, a. Kasta ni Apo Mayor."

"Imbagana ken ni Anti Rosa a maisalipto ti bungana idiay Manila bareng mangabaktayo 'ti premio, Tata. . ."

"Patpatiem!"

Adu pay a pangublag ti dinaldalam-it ni Tata Ayong. Diak inkaskaso. Napan iti yan da Nana Tibang ken Anti Rosa.

"Nasayaat unay ti panaamagbalin nga ignorante 'toy mulam a saba kadagiti umay bumisbisita, 'nia, Rosa," nagngirsi ni Tata Ayong, "ta pati ni mayor a nabayagen a di immay bimmisita ditoy ket bimmisita pay."

"Diak ibambando nga umayda kitaen 'toy mulak, *Manong.* Ngem no agpaysonto ti kuna ni Apo Mayor a maisalip iti Green Revolution no maluom ket mangabak, di kadi pakaidayawanto 'toy nanumo a lugartayo?"

"Nagaduan a napimpintas ken nabumbun-as ti panagbungbungana a saba iti Umabagatan. . ."

"Saan kano met a naimas a saba, kuna 'tay anakko idiay Manila. Umalsem kano a kasla damilig puro ken bulan no maluom!" insaruno ni Nana Tibang.

"Husto ti kunam, Ipag," inyallawat ni Tata Ayong. "Kasta met ti kuna 'tay kaanakak a taga-Sto. Domingo. Mangallilaw lat' kaatiddogna; nasamsam-it met lat' bunga dagidiay mulak a tumok ken asukar."

"Narigat pay la a sasawen ti kasta, a, ta agpapadatay' met pay la a di nakaraman 'ti bunga ti kasta a saba," insungbat ni Anti Rosa. "No kas pagarigan kastanto, a, ket ania ngarud."

"Mailawlaw-an laeng, a, dagiti agibagbaga iti subual," kinuna ni Nana Tibang.

"Ania ket ti pakaing-ingkitaranyo itatta, a," nagmuregreg ni Anti Rosa.

"Masarita lat' kasta, kadawyan ti agpipinnasig nga agkakaarruba, Rosa," kinuna ni Nana Tibang. "Makaguraka, 'ya?"

"Diak bisio ti gumurgura iti padak a tao, Manang. Sungsungbatankayo laeng."

"'La, awan aniamanna daydiayen, Adi," kinuna ni Tata Ayong. "Nasayaat met no daytoyto sabam ti mangidaydayaw iti Labut!"

Kunak no agbayag pay dagiti dua kas kadawyanda no umallatiwda ngem nagpakadadan idi sumrekak.

"Umapal dagidiay iti yaay ni Apo Mayor," kinunak ken ni Anti Rosa idi mangrabiikamin.

"Diak la ammo no apay a kastada. Ba'am latta. Agitukitka latta kadagiti bukel a mabalin nga itukit. Malagipmo nga idi isangpetko

ti saba, ipappapilitmo idi a dinto agbiag ken agbunga, ngem ania itattan. . ."

Nagpalpaak iti papag iti ruar kalpasan ti pannanganmi. Binuyak ti nagmanto nga aglawlaw. Kaanonto, Angkuan, a makaruk-atka ditoy Labut? Ti ngata saba ni antim a Rosa ti talaga a mangitayab kenka a mapan idiay Manila?

Aduda latta a sumarungkar iti saba. No agpabayadak ngata iti sagninikel, adu koman ti naurnongko. Dakesna, saan a makasarsardeng ni Anti Rosa ta isu met ti parasapul iti kanenmi. Siak ti ad-adda a sumarang kadagiti sumarungkar. Iti dandani makabulan, nakaluklukmeg ken nakaat-atiddogen dagiti bunga ti saba. Nasuroken a dua dangan ket agarup saanen a kabaelan ti puon. Iti minalem a kasisibogko, immadu dagiti subual.

Diak la koma al-aladan ti bubon, ngem sangkaulit met ni Anti Rosa. Iti maysa a malem, dimmaw-as manen ni Nana Tibang iti yan ti saba.

"Panagkunak, Angkuan, saanyo a mauray a maluom 'toy bungana," kinunana.

"Apay, Nana?"

"Ayna, basta tandaanam 'toy saok."

"Malaksid no patakaw wenno papaadyo, Nana."

"Loko, awan pulimi a mannanakaw!"

"Sungsungbatankayo laeng, Nana. . . Masdaawak ketdi, ta no adda pagimbagan dagiti kapurokanyo addakayo latta a mangub-ublag!"

Rabiin idi sumangpet ni Anti Rosa. Naisem a nagipadamag iti naggapuanna. Nakita kano ni Mayor ta nairana nga adda miting dagiti kapitan iti ili, inayabanna metten. Indaydayaw kano ti mayor ti sabana. Addanto kano maaramid nga induksion iti kabangibang a purok iti sumaruno a Domingo ket inggunamgunam ni Mayor nga umatendarto ni Anti Rosa. Addanto kano pay agiwarwarnak a baonen ni Mayor a makiinnuman ken ni Anti Rosa.

"Uray pupuotem, Angkuan, yalat 'toy sabatayo ti premio nga aggaput' Palasio. Saan la a dayta, makadanontantot' Manila a libre amin. . ."

Diak ruam ti dumardar-ay kadagiti induksion wenno paspasala ta bassitek unay ti bagik, ngem naparegtaak iti awis ni Anti Rosa.

Pinagsagananak pay iti maysa a kanta ta amangan kano laeng no pagkantaendanto ket siakto laengen ti mangisuno kenkuana.

Nadaeg ti induksion. Adut' babbalasang. Adda dagiti kapitan ti bario. Adda pay ni Mayor.

Maibalballaet ti sala. Talaga a serioso ni Apo Mayor iti panagmulmula. Bilin dayta a naggapu idiay Manila. Dakkel ti premio ket kasla di nakappapati. Saan la nga aggasut no di ket agribu. Good taim a talaga no mayalat ti premio.

Kinankansionak dagiti simmaruno nga aldaw a dinanggayan ti kinabun-as dagiti mulak aglalo ti bunga ti saba. Kas dawat ni Apo Mayor, naikkanen ni Anti Rosa ti tunggal kapitan ti kada bario iti subual. Dina inawat dagiti ibayadda.

"Dakkelen a ragsakko no mapatan-ayyo dagita, Kapitan," kinuna laeng ni Anti Rosa. "Ken pakalaglagipanyonto kaniak ken ti nanumo a purokmi."

"Uray para sigarilio koma met laeng, a, Anti," sinidirko ni Anti Rosa.

"Ad-adunto ti premio, dika madanagan, Angkuan."

Gapu ta nagaget latta nga agsubual ti saba, uray nakayakarakon iti bagimi a mula, inikkan met ni Anti Rosa dagiti kapurokanmi. Ngem nagkedkedan da Tata Ayong ken Nana Tibang dagiti para kadakuada. Agkaarngi ti rasonda. Sadanto la kano mangala no maramananda ti bungana uray bayadandanto kano.

Saan a maliwayan ni Apo Mayor ti dumagas basta sumarungkar kadagiti kabangibang a purok. Maragsakan iti kaatiddog ken kabun-as ti bunga.

Binilangko dagiti aldaw. Nasurok pay a makabulan santo umay dagiti hurado a kunkuna ni Apo Mayor. Makitkitakon ti bagik nga agtaytayab idiay Manila.

Kellaat a naglulem iti maysa a malem. Simmaruno ti bayakabak. Nadamagmi iti radio ni Nana Tibang a napigsa ti bagyo a sumungad. Nagdanagak. No bagyo ti umay, dina pakawanen dagiti mula. Ti saba la unay. Isut' gapuna a sinurayak a nalaing ti puon.

"Bantayam ti saba, Angkuan, bantayam," sangkaganetget ni Anti Rosa idi sumapliten ti angin. "Awanen ti serserbi dagiti arapaap no maperdi 'ta saba. . ."

Ngem no malas ti umay, umay latta. Dua nga aldaw a nagpaut ti napigsa a bagyo ket idi agkalma, awanen ti serserbi dagiti mula iti purok. Natukkol ti saba ni Anti Rosa a kas met kadagiti dadduma.

Nagdung-aw ni Anti Rosa a kasla nagpasina iti anak. Nakangirsi ni Tata Ayong a nangbuya iti panagpaadko kadagiti bulong ken sinapad a saba.

"Husto 'di kunak. . . husto 'di kunak," inrayok ni Nana Tibang.

Makamalmaluenak itoy a baket.

Dimmaw-as met ni Mayor. "Kailala. Nakail-ilala!" kinunana bayat ti panangbidingna kadagiti binukel a kasla takiagen ti kaatiddog. "Di pay met ngarud natangkenan."

Agsangsangit latta ni Anti Rosa.

"Dika unay agladladingit, Rosa. Uray ta adut' nawarasan 'ta sabam ken isut' nangriing kadagiti pumurok nga agitukit. No awan ti mayalat a premio ita, ad-adunto pay dagiti sumaruno a premio."

Nadagsen met ti barukongko. Agpabasolak a diak ammo ti pabasolek. "Talaga nga awan lat' gasatmo, Angkuan. Awan latta!" kinunkunak laengen iti bagik. —0

Bannawag: Hulio 22, 1974

Armem Man Ketdi Tapno Agnakem

NAGAM-AMMOKAMI KEN ni Frances del Carmen iti seminar-workshop para kadagiti agdadamo a mannurat a naangay idiay Amianan. Isu ti center of attraction iti workshop. Isut' kauntonan kadagiti young blood nga immatendar. Mabalin met a kunaen nga isut' kapintasan. Pangmestisaen.

Diak unay matimtimek kadagiti kastoy a tallaong. Kasla kinukkokan a bisukol, kuna ni Ernie a kaduak a dimmar-ay. Dayta ngata ti nakatukayan ni Frances, a nakiam-ammo iti naudi nga aldaw.

"Awan met lat' mangngegko a timekyon, brod!" kinunana.

"No nasaludsodmo metten ti amin a kayatko a saludsoden, ading!"

Inyawatna ti imana. "Maysaak kadagiti agrukbab kenka. Kunak no lakay a laklakaddogan ti Jerry Penian, ngem young and bachelor met gayam!"

"Patiem, adut' putotnat' ruar daytan, ading!" insuldong ni Ernie.

"Uray dina ibaga, a, ket ammok lattan," imbales ni Frances.

"Isut' addan, ading," intudok ni Ernie. "No siak, awan pay ni maysa a nakaipus."

"Mabalbalin pay la ngarud ti umipus no kasta!" nagtawa.

Diantre man!

"Leap year ita. No maammuan daydiay bakbaketem iti opissinayo, agpaikasar a dina oras!" kinuna ni Ernie idi umakar ni Frances iti yan dagiti sabali a makiseminar.

Timtimbangek ni Frances iti panagkakaluganmi a nagpa-Manila. Saan a madleg. Gusgustona a kasarita dagiti cats.

"Agunika met, a, honey!" Numona ta ikidagna pay. "'Maykanto agpasiar iti kaserak, wen? Wenno idiay eskuela. . . a? Wenno siakton san ti umay idiay yanmo pambarak nga agresearch iti library workko. . ."

Kinunana a nagbasbasa iti eskuela dagiti madre ken padi iti elementaria ken high school ken eskolar pay iti unibersidad a pagad-adalanna idiay Manila.

"Sweet dreams, Jerry. . . Goodnight. Napintas la ketdi ita dagiti maputarmo a daniw," kinunana idi dumsaagkami ken Ernie iti bus.

"One click no armem daydiay, lakay," kinuna ni Ernie. "Panagkunak, no dinigaam idiay workshop, kukuamon itay addatay iti lugan. Napimpintas pay, a, ngem ni Milam daydiay. Pangromansa espesial ti pammagina. . ."

"Naks! Aarmen ngem saan nga aasawaen! Tarabitab. Sawenna ti kasdiayen, damomi pay lat' agkita. . ."

"Ibagana la ketdi a kaegka no dimo serken. Game isuna. Karkaritenna ti kinalalakim!"

ANIA ngata no armek? Diak patien nga awan pay nobiona iti daydiay a kinatarabit ken kinagarawna. No armek ket mapagtinnagko sanakto di palusposan, di ellekandakton dagiti nakauna. Ken maysa, addan ni Mila a kaopisinaak. Isut' ipudpudosak nga asawaento. Kasadoak koma itan no nayat idi kayatkon nga ikasar gapu kadagiti kinaribalko.

"Dita ti pakasubokam, lakay," kinuna ni Ernie iti naminsan.

"Saan a kas ken ni Frances ti kayatko a katakunaynay. . ." kinunak.

Nakigtotak idi sumarungkar ni Frances iti trabahok iti kabiernesan dayta a lawas. Naka-rugged. Simmingdat iti sippukel ti pammagina iti tisirt ken pantalonna. Nakakipis iti maong. Dumerderosas dagiti pingpingna iti pudot ti init. Adda kaduana. Kaadalanna kano. Nakaigpilda iti kuaderno ken libro.

"Adut' research workko ket nalagipka. Maysa pay, tagtagiuraykot' panagpasiarmo, ngem dika met immay," kinunana.

Inyawisna pay nga adda kano *ti-par* iti kaserada iti rabii. Saan a nagawid no diak winenan ti awisna.

Namaysaannak ni Frances. Nagkatawa a nangtapik kaniak idi addaakon iti ridaw ti kaserana a mangyaw-awat iti sagutko. Imlek met dagiti dua a babbalasang a kasinsinna kano.

"Mailiwak a makisrsarita kenka... Konserbatiboka unay ket kayatka a pagluposen," kinuna ni Frances.

"Manong Jerry, amangan no dimo pay am-ammo ni Frances. Kolektor dayta," insuldong ti maysa a balasang.

"Of course!" intudo ni Frances ti sangaestante a libro. "I'm a book collector..."

Iti di mabayag, dua a babbaro ti dimteng. Adda met iggemda a nabungon. Pinagaammodakami ni Frances.

"Naladawkamin, kunkunami la ketdin ngem nasapakam sa met," kinunada.

Immisem ni Frances sana binilin dagiti dua a babbalasang nga agidasar ta agsasangokami a mangrabii.

Saan a namati ni Ernie idi ipadamagko kenkuana ti panangawis ni Frances idi agkitakami manen.

"Ania pay la ngarud ti kueem? Nalawag a kukuamon! Bay-amon daydiay a Mila."

"Dikam agka-vives."

Kaska la di lalaki, Jerry, kinunak met la iti bagik. Armem man ketdi tapno agnakem!

Inawagak iti maysa a malem. Nagay-ayat iti awisko nga agpasiarkami idiay Rizal Park. Dinamagna pay no aniat' paboritok a kanen a balonenna.

Adut' binalonna. Sinutildakami dagiti kakaseraanna.

"Singdatam a singdanan, Frances, tapno di makatayab. . ."

"Numeruamton, wen. . ." insuldong ti sabali.

Nadekket ti panagkatugawmi iti taksi. Kasna pay ket igaggagara nga idennes ti barukongna iti takiagko.

Iti pannagnami nga agturong kadagiti tugaw iti igid ti baybay, siniketnak ni Frances.

"Ditoy kadi met Luneta ti pagpalpallailanganyo iti girlfriendmo, Jerry?" dinamagna idi agtugtugawkamin. Nalinak ita. Kasla

kumkumpasan dagiti allon ti nalamuyot a tokar a yay-ayug dagiti open juke box.

"No ita la nga umayak ditoy a sikat' kaduak," kinunak.

"Konserbatibo kad' la unay ta dimo maawis?"

"Awan pay nobiak."

"Dimo kunaen a patienka! Guapo ken mannuratka. Sa iti trabahom, dandani inaldaw a dagiti nalapsat a chicks ti kapulpulapolmo. . ."

"Sika met ngay? Manon dagiti boyfriendmo?"

"Kayatmo kadi ti agbalin a boyfriendko?"

Nagkatawaak.

Dimmenden. "Ammom, Jerry, naisupsupadika kadagiti naam-ammok. Saan la a tall, dark and handsome, nasariritka pay. And I really like you for your assets."

Saan a nagkedked idi bisongek.

Apay a kastoy ni Frances? Itulokna kadi ti bagina a paikastokastoy iti tunggal lalaki a magustuanna? Ania laengen ti makuna ti agbalinto a lakayna? Dagiti dadakkel ken kakabsatna, dida kadi biangan?

"Ammok ti pampanunotem, Jerry," kinunana a kimmayakay. "Ngem kitaem, saan kadi nga adda women's lib itan? No dakayo a lallaki ket maipeksayo ti riknayo iti babai a pagduyosanyo, apay ketdin a saan kadakami? Siempre, nasakit met ti nakemmi a makadamag a ni kastoy ken kasdiay ket nobiayo, di uray dakami, masapul nga ipeksami metten ti riknami? Kaniak, umanayen ti tallo a boyfriend a pagpiliak a.. ."

"Umanamongka kadi metten iti pre-marital sex?"

"No sika't pumili iti babai nga agbalin a lifetime partnermo, kayatmo kadi a naglasatannan dayta?"

"Saan la ketdi. . ."

"Man met laeng." Dimmenden manen.

Saanton a masunotan daytoy, inkarik idi addaakon iti iddak.

Nagimonan la ket ngarud ni Mila. Nupay naglibakak, dakkel nga ebidensiana ti naalana a surat ni Frances a nangawaganna kaniak iti Darling Sweetheart, Jerry.' Pappapanennak iti kaserana ta masakit kano.

"No pudno a dimo nobia daytoy a Frances, agkasarta itan!" kinuna ni Mila.

"Saan a pagdadaras dayta a banag. Ammom met a diak pay sisasagana. Diak kayat nga agbabawikanto. . ."

Nagsinakami ken Mila.

Nasangailik ni Ernie iti maysa a malem a panaggapuna iti trabahona. Adda surat nga impaw-it ni Frances para kaniak.

"Sincere a talaga 'diay tao kenka. Masakit. Inyunay-unayna a mapanka. Madi a payospital. Mayat kano no sika ti kaduana. Sangsangpet kano ni mamangna itay bigat ket agsangsangit. Madanagan unay."

Pinadanon ken pinagtugawnak ti mamang ni Frances.

"Sika la ketdi ni Jerry a padpadaanan ti anakko. Pangngaasim, uyotam a mapan iti ospital ket nakapsut unayen, nakkong. Makadominggon a kasta. Patptgennaka unay unay ti anakko."

Babaen ti ababa a pannalaysay ni Nana Conchita, spoiled ni Frances. Isut' buridek iti tallo a babbai, kapintasan ken kasariritan. Sigud a naestriktoda kadagiti dua nga inauna ket dakkel kano a leksion kadakuada ti imbunga ti kinaesriktoda. Isu nga iti panagadal ni Frances ti Manila, inikkanda iti wayawaya.

Nakapsut ni Frances. Napaisem iti panagtugawko iti iking ti kamana. Piniselko ti dakulapna.

"Inka idiay ospital. . . Agpadoktorka. . ." kinunak.

Rimmimat dagiti matana. "No sika ti agkuna, I am willing. Kuyogennak. Ammom, diak malipatan dagiti saludsodmo idiay Luneta. Ammok a dayta ti gapuna no apay a kasla ad-adaywannakon manipud idi. Agduaduaka kaniak. Ngem ammo ni Apo Dios, nga uray no nadekketak iti opposit sex ken diak madleg a mangibaga a magustuak, dina met kayat a sawen a ti kinababaik ket itedkon. No, Jerry. Ammok pay met la a saluadan ti bagik. Saan a game ti amin a banag."

Agsangsangiten ni Frances. Ket immirut ti panangpetpetko iti dakulapna. —0

Bannawag: Hunio 28, 1976.

Iti Pilid Ti Biag

NASANGPETAK ni kasinsin Lito, ti pinadakkel ken pagbasbasaen ni Papa, idi aggapuak iti eskuela. Baron. Pito a tawen a diak nakita. Diak nasarkedan ti riknak. Naginnapungolkami. Agbuybuya dagiti tallo nga annakko. Masmasdaawda.

"Nayaw-awanka, a," kinunak idi makatugawak.

"Pinasapul ni Tio ditoy yanyo, Manang. 'Bag ta nasarakak met laeng."

"Komusta ni Manang Sonia?" inggagarak a saan a ni Papa ti dinamagko.

Nabayag sa simmungbat ni Lito. "B-balasang pay laeng, Manang. Ni Manong Cesar ngay, Manang?"

"Kasdi latta, a, a Cesar. . ."

"Nabasa ni Tio ti naipablaak a write-upna iti Bulletin. Kasta unay ti ragsakna... Saannakay a kaguran. Umaykay kano nga umay inton birthdayna no Sabado!"

Husto 'di kunak idi maipablaak ti pannakaital-o ni Cesar iti trabahona. Sapulennakami ni Papa. Ngem apay a saan nga idi arigmit' makilimos iti tulong ken pannarabayda ti panangpasapulna kadakami?

"Amangan no ad-adda la a mapabainanda no umaykami. . ."

"Nagbalbaliwen ni Tio, Manang. Dakayo ti sangkakararagna a makita. No mailiw a makangngegen kadagidi toktokarem iti piano, agpaayab iti pianista. Ibagbagana pay a planona nga ited kadakayo ti papaabanganna nga apartment idiay Makati tapno as-asideg iti trabaho ni Manong Cesar."

"Saan a maaramid ni Papa ti kasta. Saan nga ipalubos ni Manang Sonia. Adda karida idi kaniak."

"Nagbalbaliwdan, Manang. Sangkadagullitna a makitana koma dagiti appokona. . ."

Nagpakada ni Lito idi agangay. Diak inkari nga atendaranmi ti kasangay ni Papa. Nakasingsingdat ti kayatda nga ipakita. Ayabandakami tapno ipakitadakami kadagii alta-sosiedad a gagayyemda sadanto kunaen: "Daytoy man ni Gloria, ti nasukir nga anakko ken ti mamirmiraut nga asawana a maysa itan nga executive."

Uray dagiti gagayyem ni Papa, inikayandak idi agasawakami ken ni Cesar. "Pagan-anom dayta mamirmiraut idinto a nagadu nga agar-arem kenka?" Saan pay ngamin idi a nagturpos ni Cesar iti komersio idinto a mangisursuroakon.

Kasla nailunod la ngarud ti panagdennami. Iti baet ti panangigaedmi nga agtrabaho, no ania ditan dagiti dimteng a parikut iti biagmi. Nagtinawenak a naganak. Natay ti katugangak a babai ket naipabaklay ti responsibilidad ken ni Cesar kadagiti tallo nga addina. Nautangak amin a gagayyemko. Pinabengbengko ti rupak ket immanay a pinangpapigsak iti nakemko a ti "biag ket maysa a pilid." Naanus, naayat ken naulimek ni Cesar.

Nakalutoakon iti pangrabii idi sumangpet ni Cesar. Nagkalumbitinan dagiti ubbing ket inunaandak a nangipadamag iti yaay ni Lito.

"Adda gayam Lolomi, 'pang. Birthdayna kano no Sabado ket aw-awisennatayo," kinuna ni Detdet.

Kinitanak ni Cesar. Nagtung-edak. "Malagipmo ni Lito, ti kasinsinko a tinartaraken ken pagad-adalenda? Pinatuntonnata ni Papa."

"Aniat' kunam? Intayo?"

"Diak ammo. . . Diak pay nalipatan dagidi. . ."

"Tapno awan masaoda, ken tangay ni Papa ti nagdisnudo a nangpasapul iti yantayo, di intayo."

"Ye-he! Ye-he!" naglaglagto dagiti ubbing. "Makitami ni Lolomin! Makitami ni Lolomin!"

"Ammok ti pampanunoten ni Papa," kinunak ken ni Cesar idi agid-iddakamin. "Ayabannata ta nangaton ti posisionmo. Ngem no saanka a naital-o, diak patien a patuntonnata."

"Ti nasken, isu ti panagkikitatayo. Dika mangipakpakita iti ania man a madi kadagiti madanontayo aglalo kada Papa ken Manang."

Tapno nawaya ti ipapan ken panagawidmi iti Laguna, aramatenmi koma ti kotse nga iggem ni Cesar iti opisinada. Madi ta amangan kano no ipapan dagiti madanonmi a nabaknangkami unayen. Nagbuskami.

Iti dalanmi nga agpa-Laguna iti aldaw ti Sabado, agsisimparat dagiti immapay kaniak. Bukbuklek ti rupa ni Manang Sonia. Iti naudi a panangsarakko kenkuna iti opisina a nagpapaayanna, kunam no asino a kondesa a nangitudo iti ridaw. "Apay a di dagiti kabagian ni lakaymo ti utangam?"

"Masakit ti anakko, Manang. Awanen ti mairemedio ni Cesar. Naasitganmin dagiti am-ammomi!"

"Sorry. Agtungtungpalak iti bilin ni Papa. Laglagipem a no saan a daydiay mamirmiraut nga Ilokano ti nakiaasawaam, adayo a kasta ti biagmo ita. Anusam ta isut' kinayatmo!"

Iti pamiliami, ti kasangay ti karagsakan a maselselebraran. Ammok nga adu ita ti sangaili ni Papa.

Nasapakami a dimteng. Kasla idi kalman la ti pito a tawen. Saan a nagbaliw ti itsura ti pagtaengan a pinanawak. Nagbaliw la dagiti muyong iti arubayan.

Ngem awan ti uray maysa a lugan wenno kotse iti arubayan.

Pinalagipan ni Cesar dagiti annakmi sakbay a talmeganna ti doorbell. "Aggigiddankayo a mangkanta iti 'Happy birthday, Lolo.' Kalpasanna, kiss!"

"Okay, Pop!" insungbat ni Leo, ti maikadua nga anakmi.

Adda timman-aw iti maikadua a kadsaaran iti pannakakiriring ti doorbell. Immayna inlukat ti ruangan.

"D-dakayo da *Manong* Cesar ken Manang Gloria?" dinamagna.

Nagtung-edak. "Ni Papa? Ni Manang Sonia?"

Ti piano ti immuna a sinapul dagiti matak iti salas. Adda pay la iti sigud a puestona, iti pannkasalon ti salas. Sinaggaysak nga inyam-ammo dagiti nakabitin a ladawan kadagiti annakko.

Madamdama, nagparang ni Papa iti agdan. At-atibayen ti katulongan. Agubanen. Indauluan ni Detdet ti kanta a "Happy Birthday" sada

inapungol a binisito idi makatugaw. Nagmano ni Cesar kalpasan ti panangarakupko ken ni Papa.

Napalua ni Papa. "N-nabayagen a pinasapsapulko ti yanyo manipud nakaaksidente ni Manangmo a Sonia."

"Nagyankami idiay Nueva Ecija, Papa. Nagsublikami la ditoy siudad iti panangidiaya kaniak ti kompania iti nangatngato a puesto," insungbat ni Cesar.

"Ket sika, Gloria, mangiursuroka pay laeng?"

"Wen, Pop!"

"'La, nasayaat unay, annakko, ta diyo met la inidian dagii trabahoyo. Kunak no ditay' makapagkikitan. Ni Manangmo a Sonia, manipud idi maaksidente, imbukboknan ti panawenna a tumultulong kadagiti nakurapay. Malemton no sumangpet."

Napaangesak iti nauneg. "Birthdayyo, ita, Pop, ngem awan sa met ti sangaili?"

"A-awan a talaga. Para kadatayo daytoy a panagsasango. Kaliwliwes ni Lito a napan nangala kadagiti pinaisaganak iti restauran. Kayatko a mapnek dagiti ubbing. Aniat' kunayo, appok? Adut' regalok kadakayo."

"Lolo, di imbagbaga ni Mama nga adda Lolomi," simmalingbat ni Joey, ti maikatlo nga anakmi.

"Agpianoka man ketdi, Gloria, bayat ti panangur-uraytayo ken ni Lito," kinuna ni Papa.

Nailiwan dagiti ramayko kadagiti teklado. Diak pay la gayam nalipatan. Husto dagiti tono. Innalak ti komposision a "Happy Birthday." Napunno ti salas iti makalunag-puso nga aweng. Agar-arubosen dagiti luak!

Idi taliawek ni Papa iti yanna, nakataltalna a tartaraisemen. Inasitgak. Dinamagko no apay a saan man la a nangliwat ni Manang Sonia iti daytoy nga aldaw. Kinuna kano ni Manang a tapno makapagwaywayaskami nga agpipinnadamag.

SUMARUNGKARKAYO koma a masansan, Gloria, Cesar," kinun ni Papa idi agpakadakami iti malem. Saggaysa a sobre ti impabolsana kadagiti ubbing. Inikkannak met iti surat. Dua a napunno a paper bag ti impabalonna.

"Umaykayonto met idiay balaymi, Lolo, tapno makitayo dagiti mula ni Mama ken dagiti taraken ni Papa a pugo," kinuna da Leo ken Detdet.

Binasak ti surat idi addakamin iti lugan.

Sapay koma, Annakko, ta adda kaimudingan 'toy sangkabassit a gated nga intedko kadagiti ubbing. Ibankoyo ta mabalindanto a pangrugian nga agadal. Ni Manangmo a Sonia, saan nga agpayso a kameng ti maysa a gunglo. Adda iti Correctional Institution manipud napatayna daydi nobiona. Ammok a ti napasamak ken ni Manangmo ti kadakkelan a leksion nga impaawat ti Dios kaniak. Iti daytoy a kinalakayko, sapay koma ta maawatandak. Maragsakanak unay unay kadagiti balligi nga adda ita ken ni Cear, ket ammok a didakto paayen no kiddawek kadakayo ti pannakaiturong ti sangkabassit a nabati pay a negosiotayo iti maysa nga aldaw.

Sarungkarandak koma a masansan. Makaikawa dagiti ubbingyo!

Kaasi met ni Papa, nayesngawko.

"Husto 'di kunak kenka a ti biag ket maysa a pilid!" kinuna ni Cesar. "Pasetna amin dagitoy itan. Siguro no saan a dagidi pananglalais da Papa ken Manang Sonia ken dagiti kabagiam kaniak, awanak koma iti agdama a saadko. Sarungkarantayo ni Papa, basta adda la ketdi panawentayo."

Kinitami dagiti sobre nga impabolsa ni Papa kadagiti ubbing. Tseke a sagsangaribu! —0

Bannawag: Marso 27, 1978

Rayos A Nasipngetan Wenno Komustaka, Dolly?

KASARSARITAK ni Dr. Telesforo Vicente, ti psychiatrist ditoy Pavillion 3, idi iserrek ti dua a nabaked a lallaki ti babai nga aggulgulagol ken sumkad nga umuli iti maikadua a kadsaaran.

"Awan ti bainyo! Demoniokayo amin! Mandiak kayat ti umuli! Saanak a bagtit! Saan! Ha-ha-ha-haay. Nanangkooo, isalakannak kadagitoy pasurot ni Satanas! Hu-hu-huuuu!"

Mapespespes ti barukongko. Kasla kayatko a tulongan ti babai. Insururotko ti panagkitak agingga a nailinged. Nangngegko ti pannakirinnimbaw ti ikkisna iti maikadua a kadsaaran kadagiti ikkis ken kanta iti ngato.

Natantanang dagiti adda ditoy baba a makilinlinnagod kadagiti social workers ken nurse. Inlawlawag ni Dr. Vicente kaniak itay sangsangpetko a nalimbongen ti isip dagiti adda ditoy, laeng ta under observationda. Grabe dagiti adda iti ngato.

"Mabiit laeng, Misis," kinuna ni Dr. Vicente idi ayaban ti social worker a nanguyog iti babai a sangsangpet.

Adda nangkalbit kaniak. Tinaliawko. Dua a babbai a nakaaruat iti rosas nga uniporme ti pasiente ti nangisem ken nangitaya kadagiti dakulapda.

"Good afternoon, Ma'am. Nagpintaskan, Ma'am! Ikkannakami man iti sagbibintingkami ta adda igatangmi iti sigarilio!"

Adda maikatlo nga immasideg. "Saan, Ma'am. Dimo ik-ikkan ida," kinunana.

"Awan bibiangmo! Umapalka!" nagdilat ti maysa.

"Agipulongak ken ni doktora," nagdardaras ti babai a simrek iti sabali a kuarto.

Immadayo dagiti dua a tumanabutob.

Nagpagnapagnaak bayat ti kaawan ni Dr. Vicente. Kinitak ti akinkanigid a pasilio a dumanon iti nalawa a kuarto. Ditoy, natâratar dagiti kama nga awan ti ikamenna. Adda dagiti agiidda. Nagpunganda kadagiti takiagda. Adda met dagiti agtutugaw nga agseselleng wenno dagiti agkumkumpas a kunam la no adda maipatpatayab a garampang a tokar. Naangseg ti angin a sumuknor iti agong. Makapadul-o.

Immadayoak iti pasilio. Sabali manen ti nangisem ken nangallawat iti dakulapna.

"Asino ti bisitaem, Ma'am? Siak, mailiwak unay 'ti umay mangbisita kaniak. Ngem awan pay ti immay uray no sumirip la koma nga agdamag no nalaingak met laengen."

In-inauna ngem siak daytoy iti panagkitak. Kusukuso ti buokna. Nalennek ngem naisem dagiti matana.

Diak ammo no ania ti nangkalbit iti dakulapko tapno luktak ti bagko ket inruarko ti balonko a sagaysay. Inyawatko kenkuana.

"Binting pay, a, Ma'am. Igatangko lat' sigarilio. Nabangsit ti iddami. Makapabakuar."

"Saan nga iparit dagiti social worker nga agsigariliokayo?" kinunak idi nayawatkon ti binting.

"Saan, Ma'am, basta saanmi la ketdi a dawdawaten kadakuada."

Natanang metten a makisarsarita.

"Nabayagkayo kadi ditoyen, Manang?" dinamagko idi imbagana a taga-Ilocos Sur.

"Innem a bulankon, Ading. Kayatko ngaruden ti agawid ngem didak sa metten malagip ti asawak ken dagiti annakko."

"Apay ngamin a naiserrekkayo ditoy?"

"Atiddog a salaysay. Problema ti pamilia. Problemak ken ni lakay. Problemak kadagiti biangot nga iipag ken kakatugangak. Siguro, nagdudugmoken. Diakon nadaeran. Kellaat latta idin a nagsipnget

ti panunotko. Kayatko a patayen amin ida. . .” Immanges iti nauneg sa nagsennaay. “Ngem itan, saanen. Agyamanak unay kadagiti adu a pammagbaga dagiti social worker ken nurse. Nalimbongen ti panunotko.”

“Ania ngarud ti ar-aramiden dagiti kas kadakayo?”

“Paglabaendakami kadagiti uniporme dagiti pasiente. Baumbaonendakami ket adda met sueldomi. Ngem diak al-alaen ti sueldok. Imbagak ken ni doktora a gulpiekto nga alaen no addanton umanay a pagpletek nga agawid.”

Simmublat a nagdamag no ania ti nakaayak iti ospital idinto nga awan met ti kabagiak nga umayko sarungkaran. Inlawlawagko a paset ti asignaturak ti kaaddak iti ospital. Umayak agobserbar ken aginterbyu kadagiti pasiente. Ammuek dagiti banag a nangiduron kadakuada a naiserrek iti daytoy nga ospital.

Apagisu a lumabas iti yanmi ti maya a nakapuraw. Sinitsitanna ti kasarsaritk. Adda inseniasna. “Innak pay, Ading, ket adda pangibaonanda kaniak,” kinunana.

Insursurotko ti panagkitak iti umad-adayo a pasiente. Rimmimbaw manen manipud iti ngato ti agduduma nga uni. Adda agar-ariwawa a kasla um-umkis a di maawatan ti sasawenna. Adda agkankanta; adda agdandaniw. Adda agkatkatawa. Adda pay agpatpatit iti lata.

Biag! nakunak iti nakemko. Kastoy kadi a talaga ti lubong daytoy nga ospital?

Nasaripatpatak ni Dr. Vicente nga umul-ulog manipud iti maikadua a kadsaaran. Pinayapayannak. Sinurotko iti lamisaanna. Adda iggemna a chart.

“Maikawalo a kaso ditoy pavillionmi daydiay sangsangpet, manipud itay bigat. No kuentaem dagiti pasiente a maawat iti inaldaw iti nasurok a duapulo a pavillion daytoy nga ospital, talaga nga agsakit ‘ta ulom. Hustuhusto ti kaaddam, Misis, iti isasangpet daydiay maikawalo a pasiente. Daydiayen ti aramidenyo a case study.”

“Dios ti agngina, Doktor.”

“Daytoy ti chartna.” Inyawatna ti iggemna a chart. “Basaem tapno maalam dagiti detalye a kayatmo a maammuan iti pasiente. Dawatek laeng a dimo ar-aramaten ti pudno a naganna.”

Nagtung-edak. Pinalabasak ti chart. Dolores de la Fuente ti nagan ti pasiente. Dolly ti birngasna. Duapulo-ket-innemna. Nakaigapuan ti sakitna: pannakapaay iti ayat iti padana a babai. Napamuraregak.

Kinitak ni Dr. Vicente a mangpalpalabas kadagiti dadduma a chart. "Doc, kayatna a sawen, kas nailanad iti daytoy a chart, tomboy ti pasiente?"

Immisem ni Dr. Vicente. "No apay ketdi, a, a mairaman pay dagiti tomboy a mapaay iti ayat iti padada a babai!"

"Awan kadi pay ti agasda, Doc?"

Nagwingiwing. "Sabali ti akinrebbeng. . . no addan makabael."

Idi makopiak dagiti nasken a banag maipanggep ken ni Dolly, dinawatko a kitaek daytoy sakbay a pumanawak.

"Masiripmo ngem dimo maasitgan," kinuna ti doktor.

Pinayapayan ni Dr. Vicente ti social worker a nakauniporme iti berde. Pinakuyognak iti ngato. Adda inkur-itna iti bassit a papel nga imbagana nga itedko ken ni Mrs. Bueno, ti nurse nga in-charge.

Simmurotak iti social worker iti agsikkosikko nga agdan. Nagsiddukerak a nakakita kadagiti nabaked a rehas a nakandaduan. Linukatan ti social worker nga adda iti uneg idi imbaga ti kaduana nga adda gagarak ken ni Mrs. Bueno.

Natitilengak kadagti aglalaok nga ariangga manipud kadagiti nakandaduan a nalalawa a kuarto. Simmuknor manen iti agongko ti agatibuor nga angseg—nakarkaro ngem iti baba.

Apay a kastoy? Tao kadi wenno ayup dagiti nakapupok ditoy?

Sinurotko ti kaduak a social worker. Nadalus t kuarto a sinerkanmi. Lima dagati nadanonmi a nakapuraw. Sabali dagiti lima a social worker. Adda babai ken lalaki a kasarsarta ni Mrs. Bueno. Dagiti kano nangkuyog ken ni Dolores de la Fuente. Kabsatna ti lalaki. Ipagna ti babai.

Manipud ditoy kuarto dagiti staff nurse, adda agsumbangir a tawa a tumannawag kadagti nalawa a kuarto a yan ti adu a pasiente. Iti makanawan a tawa, nailasinko ni Dolly a nakagalut dagiti ima ken sakana iti kama. Iti kaabayna a kama, adda pasiente a nakagalut dagiti takiagna ngem saan dagiti sakana. Agkuykuy-at iti angin a kunam la no agpedpedal. Nailukais ti badona agingga iti barukongna. Awan pantina. Agkankanta. Tunggal pedalna, ikumpasna ti narayok a kantana. Sabali

ti agkumkumpas a kasla adda kasarsaritana iti bobeda. Adda met agdandaniw iti aglalaok a pagsasao. Sibibiag kadi a tao dagitoy? nakunak iti nakemko. Apay nga adda kakastoy? Gapu kadi ta naulpit unay ti gimong kadakuada?

Mapespespes ti barukongko nga immadayo iti tawa tapno sumirip manen iti sabali a tawa. Nakarungiit dagiti timmungraraw a pasiente. Kayatda a gaw-aten ti imak. Adda dagiti agpagnapagna.

Pinagtugawnak ni Mrs. Bueno idi nakapanawen dagiti dua a kasarsaritana. Inyam-ammok ti bagik ken ti gagarak. Naanus a nangsungbat kadagiti saludsodko.

"Kas makitam," kinunana, "nasken ti adu nga anus ken pannakaawat kadakuada. Saan pay a nagpulang ti naan-anay nga isip dagiti adda ditoy no idilig kadagiti pasiente a nakitam idiay baba. Isu a kasda la ubbing. Adda dagiti awan pantina ket aglukaisda lattan. Ngem ditoy, awan ti malisia ta babbai amin dagiti pasiente ket babbai met amin dagiti socal worker ken nurse a mangtartaripato kadakuada.

"Ti la nakasaksakit a panunoten, ket ti kasla di pannakaawat ti gimongtayo kadagiti pasiente no aggapudan ditoy. Adda dagiti nalainganen a pasiente, a no mapagawiddan, agsublida pay la ditoy. Ti rasonda, katkatawaan ken lalaisen ida dagti kalugaranda. Ti dakesna, saan a malaingan dayta a pasiente, umad-adda ketdi. Adda payen dagiti agkuna a ditoyda laengen agingga a matayda. Ngem saan met a mabalin.

"No adda kas kadakayo nga umay agin-interbyu wenno mangsurat iti maipanggep kadagiti pasientemi, awan sabali nga igunamgunammi kadakuada no di ti panangidanonda kadagiti tao, a dagiti pasiente nga aggapu ditoy, maagasan ken malainganda a kas kadagiti ordinario a sakit. Ket iti panagsublida iti gimong karbenganda met ti maayat, mailala, ken maawatan."

Nagyamanak ken ni Mrs. Bueno iti adu a naammuak maipapan kadagiti pasiente. No kasano ti pannakamentenarda ken no ania ti kadakkelan a responsibilidadda kadakuada. Dinamagko no kaanonto a makasaritak a nasayaat ni Dolores de la Fuente.

"Agsublikanto kalpasan ti makalawas tapno nalimbongto bassiten ti panunotna," kinunana.

Iti luganko nga agawid, kasla diak patien a nakadanonak iti daydiay nga ospital. Asignatura nga inted ti propesorko daytoy. Kayatna ti maysa a case study. Kunak nga alaek la koman ti maysa kadagiti ubbingko iti maikamaysa ngem ni lakay ti nangkarit kaniak. Tapno kano naisalsalumina ti report nga isumitirko, nasken nga innak iti daydiay nga ospital.

Nalawa ti rungiit ni lakay idi impadamagko ti naggapuak.

"Naturedka met gayam, ken solo flight pay!" kinunana.

Nagsubliak iti ospital kalpasan ti makalawas, kas iti inkarik ken ni Dr. Vicente. Adda intugotko a makan para ken ni Dolly. Apagisu nga alas dos idi makadanonak ta adda klasek iti bigat.

Naragsakanak ta maysan ni Dolly kadagiti pasiente iti baba. Kinuna ti social worker a nagdamagak a lepleppas kano ti diagnostic test ni Dolly. Tallo a pasiente dagiti adda iti yan dagiti staff nurse. Napanak ken ni Dr. Vicente ket dinamagko no mabalinko a kasarita ni Dolly a dakdakami.

"Padasem bareng no mayat. Ngem panagkunak saan pay a nalimbong ti panagsungbatna," kinunana.

Pinaaayaban ni Dr. Vicente ni Dolly iti maysa a social worker.

"Mabalinyo a kasarita iti terrace," kinuna ti social worker. Intudona ti patio ti Pavillion 3.

Agkedked ni Dolly a sumurot kaniak iti patio. Laslasinennak. Nayat met laeng idi imbagak a maysaak a gayyem ket adda napateg nga ibagak kenkuana.

Nagtugaw a sitatalna. Inyawatko ti ginatangko a makan.

"Pinaited kadi ni Naty daytoy?" dinamagna. Mangus-usig dagiti nalennek a matana a nangperreng kaniak. "No saan a naggapu kenkuana, diak kayat a kanen."

Diak ammo ti isungbatko. Nagtung-edak lattan.

Binuybuyak ti nabattaway a panagkulisip ken panangngalngal ni Dolly. No dadduma, agmuttaleng. Adayo ti turong dagiti matana.

"Komustaka itan, Dolly?" kinunak.

Kinitanak. Nakapsut ti sungbatna. "Kastoy. . . agtugtugaw. Umin-inum. Sika, asinoka? Apay a kayatnak a kasarita?"

"Aniat' riknam. . . nasayaat met laengen?" dinamagko ketdi.

Immallikuteg dagiti matana. "Wen. . . kayatkon ti agawid. Mailiwakon ken ni Naty. . . Isu laeng ti mangipatpateg kaniak. Dagiti kakabsatko, pasigda amin a demonio! Pasurot ni Satanas! Pinaipupokdak ditoy. . . They don't understand me!"

Napamulagatak. Agsasarunon ti saona. Engllish. Tagalog. Kastila. Iluko. Binay-ak. Agingga a nauma.

Siak ti simmublat. "Komusta met dagiti dadakkelmo?"

Nagwingiwing a kasla napaksuyan. Nagmaratubbog dagiti matana.

"Natayen 'di Nanang. Nabayagen. Ngem. . . kanayonnak a sarungkaran. Kayatnakon nga alaen. Diak met pay kayat ti sumurot kenkuana. Kayatko, agkasarkami pay ken ni Naty."

"Agpadakayo a babai. . ."

"Mabalin, why not? I belong to the third generation. No adda nagkasar a dua a lallaki, apay ketdin a saan iti babai?"

"Ni tatangmo, komusta?" inturongko iti sabali ti saritaan.

Nangemkem ken immirut dagiti gemgemna.

"Ni tatang ti gapu no apay a kastoyak. . . Saan koma a nasapa a natay daydi Nanang no saan a gapu kenkuana!"

"Apay?"

"Binabaina ti buridek a kabsat daydi nanang."

"Ni tatangmo ngarud itan?"

"Adda 'diay probinsia. . . nangasawan iti sabali."

"Dina inasawa ti ikitmo?"

"Inungtan dagiti kakabsatko. . . Napanen idiay Hawaii. Inasawa met la ti nobiona."

"Awan ngaruden ti problema!"

"Adda! Isut' nangted 'ti dakkel a konsomison daydi Nanang. Isu ti nanggurguraak kadagiti lallaki. . . ken panagayatko iti padak a babai."

Nagtungtung-edak.

"Asino ni Naty?" sinaludsodko.

"Isu ti ideal womanko. Imbagana nga ay-ayatennak. Ngem. . . dagiti regalok kenkuana, in-intedna iti lalaki. . . Kayatko a patayen ida a dua. Ngem ay-ayatek ni Naty. No agpakawan kaniak, pakawanek. . . I love Naty. I really love Natyyyy!"

Binay-ak a sao a sao.

"'Maykan, itulodkan dita uneg."

"Urayek ni Naty nga umay agpakawan. Imbaga ni nanang idi rabii a sarungkarannak ita."

"Ungtandaka dagiti nars."

"Bekkelekto pay ida!"

"Madi dayta. . . Kas maysa a gayyem, ibalakadko a yagawam ti agpalaing ta umaykanto sarungkaran idiay balayyo."

"Balay?" nagngirsi. "Awan balayko!"

"Iti yan da manongmo," inyaturko.

"Dagidiay demonio? Didak maawatan! Adu ti ibagbagada a diak kayat. Madi ti tomboy. . . ti sigarilio. . . ti aginum. . . ti agpantalon. . . Demonioda amin!"

"Da manong ken manangmo, didaka kadi sarsarungkaran?"

"Uray dida um-umay no dida ikuyog ni Naty! Kari a kari ni Manang Marissa nga ikuyogna. . . dinak met pay sinarungkaran ni Naty."

Intulodko ni Dolly iti uneg. Nagtarusak iti lamisaan ni Dr. Vicente kalpasanna.

"O, ket?"

"Panagkunak, Doc, mapaspasublinan ti limbong ti panunotna."

"No dinanton dakdakamaten ni Naty ken ti natay nga inana. . ."

"Kasano ngata ti kapautna ditoy, Doc?"

"Dua, wenno tallo a bulan. Depende. Saanda a bastabasta mapalubosan nga agawid."

Agpakadaak koman idi mapasungadak ti maysa a babai nga agarup kataebko. Adda igpilna. Kasla isu ti ipag ni Dolly a nakitak idi iti opisina ni Mrs. Bueno.

"Komusta ni Dolly, Doctor?" sinaludsod ti babai.

"Under observation."

"Kaanonto ngata a mairuarmi?"

"Agingga a di agpulang ti naan-anay a panunot ti pasiente, saanmi a palubosan, Misis," kinuna ni Dr. Vicente. Binaw-ingannak. Pinagam-ammonakami.

"Siak ni Marissa, ti ipag ni Dolly."

"Siak ni Lita. . . Napilik ni Dolly a case study iti maysa nga asignaturak." Tinaliawko ni Dr. Vicente.

"Agdamagka ken ni misis iti maipapan ken ni Dolly," kinuna ti doktor.

Immannugot ni Marissa idi imbagak ti panggepko. Nagkuyogkami a rimmuar iti pabilion kalpasan ti pannangted ni Marissa iti inigpilanna a bungon ken ni Dolly nga addan iti kuarto. Nagturongkami iti kantina ti ospital. Nagorderkami iti saggaysakami a pagpalamiis ken makan.

Nagdamagak.

"Atiddog a salaysay," kinuna ni Marissa kalpasan ti nabayag a panagpanunotna. "Kinapudnona, awan kadakami idiay balay ti mangayon iti panagtumtomboyna, ta saan met a sigud a kasta. Adda met pamuyaan idi agbasbasa pay iti sekundaria. Adu ti nagar-arem kenkuana. Kayatmi idi a makaturpos iti ania man a kurso tapno dinto kakaasi iti masakbayan. Isu la ti saan a nakapagturpos kadakuada nga innem nga agkakabsat. Ngem naibarkada kadagiti tomboy. Dakesna, di pay agpakpakada no pumanaw. Itoy a panagsakitna, agarup makabulanen a di nagaw-awid. Naammuanmi ti kasasaadna idi immay ipakammo ti barkadana. Napasakitan kano ti gayyemna a babai."

"Sakbay dagita, awan kadit' ammom a napasamak kadagiti dadakkelna?"

"Adu. . . ngem very personal. Anyway, naammuak ken ni lakay a dimmakkel ni Dolly a pinampanuynoyan daydi nanangda. Amin a kayatna, uray no awan, pilit a mapaadda."

"Apay a nagbalin a tomboy?" Pinangpennekko iti nasao ni Dolly.

"Gapu ngata ta tomboy amin dagiti barkadana."

"Awan ngata ti naun-uneg a gapuna?" panangsintirko.

"Kuna ni lakayko nga amangan no ni Dolly ti nakatawid iti daydi ikitda. . ."

Nagwingiwingak. "Abnormal amin a tao," kinunak. "Patiek nga adda dagiti pasamak a mangaron iti kinaabnormal ti tao tapno kunatayo nga agmauyong. Ni Dolly kas pagarigan. Saan a sigud a tomboy. Nagbalin a tomboy. Nagarem iti padana a babai. Idi natakuatanna a lipliputan ti babai, kastoyen. . ."

"Nadusa ngata. . ."

"Di makedngan a kasta, Marissa," kinunak. "Kinapudnona, adda naibagana kaniak. A patiek a namagbalin kenkuana a tomboy."

"Ania daydiay?" kinitanak ni Marissa.

Inulitko ti imbaga ni Dolly: "Binabai ti Tatangda ti buridek a kabsat daydi nanangda. Isut' nanipudan ti sakit daydi nanangda, a bulon ti nakatayanna. Daydi met ti nanipudan ni Dolly a nanggurgura kadagiti lallaki. Ket nagbaliw ti kinataona."

Mangus-usig dagiti mata ni Marissa a naiturong kaniak. "Imbaga amin ni Dolly dagita. . . ket patiem met?"

"Agpayso kadi?"

"Adda kenka no patiem. . ."

Nagsinakami ken ni Marissa a di nalawlawagan ti saludsodko. Pinaayaban ni Dr. Vicente.

Iti karabiyanna, sinangalko ti reportko. Kinaritnak ni Lakay iti panagkunna nga agbalinto a naidumduma a case study no maammuak ti pagbanagan ni Dolly. No agbalbaliw iti ospital. No anianto ti reaksion dagiti kabsatna.

Simmarungkarak iti ospital kalpasan daydi panagranami ken ni Marissa tapno maammuak ti kasasaad ni Dolly. Apagbiitak la no daddma; agdamdamagak kadagiti social worker. Naammuak a namitlon a simmarungkar dagiti pasig a tomboy a gagayyem ni Dolly. Sapsapulenna ni Naty. Awan kano ni Naty iti grupo. Nagawid iti probinsiada ket mabalin a nagkasarda payen iti nobiona. Kimmaro ni Dolly. Inikkiikkisanna dagiti gagayyemna. Impuruapuruakna dagiti insarungkarda. Daydin ti naudi a panagparang dagiti tomboy iti ospital.

Agtallo a bulanen ti napalabas idi sarungkarak ni Dolly. Dakkelen ti nagbaliwanna. Isun ti agtugtugaw iti ridaw a para pastrek kadagiti sangaili.

Kalpasan ti panagpirmak iti logbook, inasitgak.

"Komustakan, Dolly?" kinunak.

Immisem. "Kastoy." Nababa ti timekna.

Immasideg dagiti dadduma a pasiente.

"Binting man, Ma'am. Igatang lat' sigarilio."

Kinusilapan ni Dolly dagitoy. "Dakayo a, awan lat' makitayo a sumarungkar, kanayon a binting. Dikayo la mabain. Ala, sumrekkayo. No saan, ipulongkayo. Binilinnak ni Ma'am, wen."

Nalimbongen ti isipna, nakunak iti nakemko. Naragsakanak.

Dinamagko ni Dr. Vicente. Adda kano iti uneg.

Nadanonko ti doktor a kasla agtutuglep a mangbasbasa kadagiti chart.

"Napuyatankayon sa met, Doc?" kinunak idi nakatugawakon.

"Nagpakaro ngamin ti maysa a pasiente idi rabii."

"Dakkelen ti namalbaliwan ni Dolly, Doc," kinunak.

"Makaparagsak ngarud. . . Ken adda karina. Saanton nga agarem iti padana a babai."

"Nagsayaaten!"

"First of its kind a pasientemi ni Dolly. Kinapudnona, pinili ti asosasionmi ti kaso ni Dolly a case study iti sumaruno nga Asian Conference idiay Japan."

"Kaanonto ti panagawidna, Doc?"

Nagwingiwing ni Dr. Vicente. "Dayta ti parikutmi. Dina kayaten ti agawid."

"Talaga?"

"Kasaritam ketdi, a."

Nalawag ti rupa ni Dolly nga inasitgak. Impakadak iti social worker ti panagpatangmi.

"Komustakan, Dolly?" kinunak.

"Nasayaaten, Manang," kinunana. "Ken ammom, sinarungkarandak da tatang ken ti asawana. Kasta met dagiti kakabsatko. . . Ngem awan ragsakda. Kasla kabutengdak. Naimbag ta mannakaawat ni Manang Marissa. . . Gapu iti nadlawko kadakuada, inkeddengko a ditoyak laengen tapno makapagserbiak kadagiti tao a nakariknaak iti panangilala ken pammateg. . . Dagiti social worker ti nakangngegak iti adu a pammalakad. Kadagiti kakabsatko, pulos! Diak ammo, ngem iti panagriknak, kayatko ti agserbi ditoy ospital. . . Dagiti tao ditoy ti nangisuro kaniak iti umno a direksion ti biag, ken no ania a talaga ti biag. . ."

Diak mailadawan ti riknak iti nangngegko. Sabali a talagan daytoy a Dolly iti daydi immuna a nakitak ditoy nga ospital.

"Dolly," kinunak, "saan a ditoy ti lubongmo. Ad-addanto a makita ken mariknam ti biag no rummuarka ditoy."

Nagwingiwing ni Dolly. Nakitak a nagmaratubbog dagiti matana. "Diak mabaybayadan ti pammateg ken kinaimbag nga impaayda kaniak, Manang. . ."

"Pagrebbenganda dayta," kinunak.

"Kayatko met ti agserbi kadagiti tao a sumrekto pay ditoy. . . Siguro, iti maysa nga aldaw, maibinglaykonto met ti napasamak kaniak. . . a silawda iti masakbayan."

Immisem ni Dr. Vicente idi imbagak ti palawag ni Dolly.

"Extraordinary a talaga ni Dolly," kinunana. "Isu la ti pasientemi a kasdiay."

Nagyamanak iti doktor sakbay a nagpakadaak. Innalak ti adres ni Dolly, iti balay dagiti kabsatna, ta bareng no masarungkarakto inton nakasublin ni Dolly iti sidongda. Imbatik met ti adresko.

"Kaasi met," nakuna ni lakay idi insalaysayko ti naudi a panagsaritami ken ni Dolly.

"A job well done. . . an extrardinary report!" kinuna ti propesorko, ken dagiti kaadalak idi nangnegda ti pakasaritaan ni Dolly iti panagreportko iti Sabado. Dida la ammo, adda masagsagid iti kaunggak. Para ken ni Dolly.

MAPANEN a dua a tawen ti limmabas kalpasan ti panangisuratko iti case study ni Dolly, idi, iti maysa nga agsapa ti Sabado a panagdaldalusko iti hardinko, diak napasungadan ti yaasideg ti sangkaasmang.

"Manang Lita. . . Manang Lita!" timmaray ti babai nga immarakup ken nangagek kaniak. Nagamangaak. "Siak ni Dolly, Manang! Dinak kadin mailasin?"

"My God, Dolly!" nayesngawko. "You're so beautiful. . . and sexy!"

Atiddog ti pagat-abaga a buokna. Nasileng dagiti kukona. Apagdillaw ti koloretena. Ni Dolly kadin a talaga daytoy?

"Manang, ni Nestor," inyam-ammo ni Dolly ti kaduana.

Inisemak ni Nestor. Pinastrekko ida.

"Addan sa ketdi napateg a gagarayo," kinunak idi nakatugawkamin.

"Diak agpalpallikawen, Manang," umis-isem ni Dolly a nagkuna. Kinitana ni Nestor. "Umaykayo imbitaran ken ni manong iti kasarmi. . ."

"Ha? Talaga?" bimmara ti rupak. Kinitak ni Nestor. Naanus ti panagruprupana. Kayumanggi. Agkabagayanda.

Nagtung-edda a nagkinnita.

Napasig ti isem ni Dolly a nangilawlawag no kasano ti panagam-ammoda ken ni Nestor. Nabasa ni Nestor ti nagan ni Dolly iti magasin a nakadanon iti Saudi Arabia. Ditoy ti nagam-ammuanda agingga a naabel ti ayan-ayatda iti sinnurat.

Minatmatak ni Nestor. Kayatko a tukoden ti kinataona.

"Awan ti inlimed ni Dolly kaniak, Manang," kinuna ni Nestor. "Nagkinnaawatankami iti laksid ti... ti napalabasmi... Kalpasan ti panagkallaysami, yawidkonton idiay balay. Sisiak ngamin nga inanak. Yaramidak iti bassit a pagtagilakuanna ta adda met bassit naurnongko. Ken siguro, mangipatakderakto metten iti bassit a talierko, ta saanakon nga agsubli idiay Saudi."

Napalabasmi, inulitko iti sipko. Ngem saankon nga inunton ti napalabas ni Nestor.

SUMSUMGARAK iti ragsakko idi addakamin ken ni Lakay iti simbaan a mangsaksi iti panagkallaysa da Dolly ken Nestor. Marmaratubbog dagiti mata ni Dolly idinto a di maruros ti isemna. Naulimek ti Tatangna ken dagiti kakabsatna iti akinsango a tugaw.

Inarakupnak ni Dolly idi malpas ti seremonia. Agsangsangiten.

"Dakkel ti pasetmo iti biagko, Manang!" inyarasaasna. "Dikanto malipatan..."

Nakaluaak.

Binuyak ni Dolly a nangawat kadagiti kablaaw idi nakapaginnibbetkamin.

Tinangadko ni lakay idi pislenna ti dakulapko. Naginnisemkami. Insadagko ti rupak iti abagana idi mayaguskamin a rummuar. —0

Maika-3 a Gunggona, Governor Roque Ablan Award for Iluko Literature (GRAAFIL), Agosto 2, 1982. Impablaak ti *Bannawag*, Abril 8, 1991 iti paulo a *Komustaka, Dolly?* Nairaman iti *Batonsileng*, Antolohia dagiti Sarita ken Daniw idi 1992.

Ansisit Kano

D IAK PAY naugasan dagiti platomi nga agiina iti dayta a pangaldaw idi awagannak ni Nanang.

"Umayka man ketdi ditoy ta sikat' makisarita itoy sulpeng a laklakayan!" kinuna ni nanang.

Ammok a ni Manong Peding ti sulpeng a laklakayan a kuna ni nanang. Maysa a bayog dita Daang Bakal a ti la adda nga iregregalona ditoy balay. Mangmangngegko a kursonadana ni Bascion, ti buridekmi. Tagalog ni Manong Peding.

Simmiripak. Ni Manong Peding nga agpayso. Nakabisikleta ket adda bitbitna a paper bag. Rimmuarak.

"Naimbag nga aldawyo, Maestra," kinunana ket naisipar iti init ti balitok a ngipenna.

"Apay, 'ya, nga inal-aldawyo met ti nagpakastoyen?" kinunak.

"Ngamin, Maestra, ta nawadwad bassit ti naalak a lames iti ipapanmi dita Wawa Dam, isu a nalagipko nga umay ikkan ni Sally. Sangkakunana ngamin a makasidsida iti sadiwa a lames." Sally ti birngas ni Bascion ditoy Montana Subdivision, Montalban, Rizal, a yanmi.

Inyawat ni Manong Peding ti bitbitna. Linukatak. Udang, kappi ken sumagmamano a buntiek. Nabayagen a diak nakaraman iti kastoy a lames.

"Nagimasen, Manong," kinunak. "Mano ngay ti bayadna?"

"Ni Maestra met. Pabayadak, aya. No kayatmo ketdi, a, ket intayto agpipiknik dita Wawa Dam. Adda kubomi iti bantay. Adut' mulami iti aglawlawna."

"Ita la a naibagayo dayta, a. Di nabayag koman a napantay nagpipiknik. Kayatko a makita ti Wawa Dam."

"No adda panawenyo, intayo. Nas'yaat kadagitoy a panawen ta nalames ti karayan."

Nadlawko a saan nga agang-angaw ni Manong Peding. "Ba'anyo ta planuek pay a nasayaat, Manong," kinunak. "Paibagakto lattan kenka."

Nakamisuot ni Nanang a nagtugaw iti sopa idi sumrekak.

"Itedna a libre, di alaen. Inkay ket lutuenen," kinunak.

"Isu nga agruam daydiay ta awatenyo amin nga itedna."

"Narigrigat no mabainan," inkalintegak.

"Kasla isulsulsolmon 'diay adim!"

Timmakder ni Nanang a tumanabutob. Intuloyko nga ininnawan dagiti plato.

"Naluton, 'Nang?" kinunak idi makainnawak.

"'Maymo ramananen, a," kinunana. "Sabali a talaga ti raman ti sadiwa ngem iti ilado.'"

"No diak inawat ti intedna, di saantay' koma makaraman ita iti sadiwa."

"Agasintarka ketdi, a. Amangan no sika ti kursonadana ta ammona nga awan ni lakaymo. Diak, wen, magustuan ti panagruprupana. 'Bag koma met no di naisapawen ti ubanna."

"Isu la ngarud a para kadakayo, 'Nang. Panagkunak, agkataebkayo ken ni Manong Peding."

"Papispisakto pay no siak ti pormaanna."

Nalamiisen ti init ngem awan pay ni Bascion. Pinasiarko ti kanatengen iti likudan ti balaymi. Sinukayko dagiti kaimmulak a tarong.

Adda anabaab iti kalsada iti sango ti balaymi. Ni Manong Peding. Adda kaduana a nataengan. Nakabisikletada. Nakalawlawa ti isem ni Manong Peding.

"Manong Peding, thank you manen, a, iti intedmo itay malem," kinunak.

Kinudkodna ti ulona. "Ni Maestra met, dayta la ketdin. Ba'anyo ta dobliekton no maminsan," kinitana ti kaduana.

"Addan sa ketdi papananyo, Manong?" kinunak.

"A-awan. . . Pinakpakastoymi man ta kayatna kano met a makita ni Sally."

Nagpormalak. "Kayatyo a sawen, Manong, baro pay a kas kadakayo 'toy kaduayo?"

"Napili ngamin unay idi, Maestra, isu a kasta ti nagbanaganna," nagkatawa ni Manong Peding.

No kasta unay ti gura ni nanang ken ni Manong Peding, sa adda manen sabali a Peding nga umay agpasar ditoy balay, ad-adda manen.

"A, e, dika koma gumurgura, Manong Peding. Amangan ta saan ketdi a sumangpet ni Sally ita a alem ta kunak kenkuana itay bigat nga umianto laengen iti kabsatmi dita Sta. Mesa no adda eksamenda."

Nagkinnita dagiti dua. Simmugpet ti rupa ni Manong Peding.

"Dikam' ngarud agbaybayagen, Maestra," impakadada.

Nasiputak ni nanang a sumirsirip iti tawa idi agsubliak. Dinagadagusna ti pimmanaw iti yanna idi nadlawna ti iseserrekko.

"'Nia manen ti nagsaritaanyo iti daydiay nga ansisit?" Pandek ni Manong Peding isu a birbirngasan ni Nanang iti ansisit.

"Imbagana nga umaynaka kano pasiaren. Intugotna daydiay padana a baak ta ipakitanaka kano ngem diak pinastrek ida," kinunak.

"Laglag. . . balasangak, aya, nga umayda pasiaren? Bekkelekto pay no siak ti ibagana a pasiarenna."

Kastoy ni nanang no suronenmi nga annakna. Arignat' balasang nga agdadamo a maarem. Nabayag ngaminen a balo.

"Dakes, aya, no agkinnursonadakayo tapno adda agnanayon a mangted iti sadiwa a sidatayo?" kinunak laeng.

"No panggepnak a yasawa, panawankayon nga agiina. Agawidakon idiay Subek."

Tallo a bulanen nga am-ammomi ni Manong Peding. Kadua idi ni Mr. Uy a presidente ti Homeowners nga immay ditoy balay nga agimbestiga iti panangipulongko a napukawanak iti pito a manok. Inkari dagiti miembro ti barangay a tiliwenda ti mannanakaw. Ngem agduanton a bulan awan pay met ti resultana. Nagboluntario idi ni Manong Peding nga isu laengen ti agronda iti kalyemi. Kameng ngamin ti Barangay Tanod.

Nasayaat ni Manong Peding. Nadayaw. Naangaw. No damagem no aniat' trabahona, ibagana a jack of all trades. Mabalinnat' agkonstruksion, agtarimaan iti silaw, makina, t.v., stove, mannalon ken mangngalap. Ngem gusgustona kano ti agbarbero no awan iti umana. Sukina kano amin dagiti adda ditoy Montana. Awan puestona ngem house service ti ar-aramidenna.

Gapu ta bulbuloden sagpaminsan ni Bascion ti bisikleta ni Manong Peding, agkursonada kano metten ken ni ading.

Mariknak ketdi a ragsak ni Manong Peding ti mangipapaay iti padana a tao.

Sumipngeten idi mapasungadak ni Bascion a nakalawlawa ti rungiitna. Kunam no asino nga agmarmartsa iti kalsada.

"Nagbayagkan, 'ya?" kinunak.

"No nakitak ketdin ni Manong Peding dita waiting shade nga adda kaduana a Peding kano met la ti naganna. Naggapuda kano ditoy itay."

"Ket nakituttotkan, ampang," simmalingbat ni nanang.

"Inyam-ammona ti padana a baak."

"Manipud ita, saankan a makisarsarita iti daydiay nga ansisit," kinuna ni Nanang. "Damagko nga adut' drug addict ditoy Montana. Amangan no maisagmakka met ketdi."

"Dakayo met, Nanang. No ania ti sumsumrek iti uloyo. Ba'anyo kad' latta no adda am-ammo a kas ken ni Manong Peding. No lakay ti naituding a para ken ni Bascion, di anusanyo ti agmanugang iti Lolo," kinunak.

"Siak? Pakpakawan! Innak la agbekkelen, a," inallawat ni Bascion. "Sika ti akimbagay kenkuana, 'Nang."

"Garampingat! Dinak idikdiklawit iti dayta a banag, a. No kayatkot' nagasawa, di idi ubbingkayo koma pay."

MAESTRA, adda koma ibagak," inkablaaw ni Manong Peding iti maysa a malem a panagkarkartibko kadagiti bermuda grass iti arubayanmi.

"Ibagayo latta, a," inyasidegko ti tugaw ngem kinaykayatna ti nagtugaw iti karuotan.

"Awan kadi ti pannakaikarik kadakayo, Maestra?"

"Dikayo maawatan, Manong. . ."

"Ni Sally. . . no adda pannakaikarik."

Immangesak iti nauneg. Saan nga agang-angaw ti baak. Nagwingiwingak.

"Panagkunak, saan pay a panawen nga asikasuenna dagita a banag. Agbasbasa ket kayatko met a makaturpos."

"Makaurayak, Maestra."

Nailabegak. Kastoy kadi a talaga ti kinaserioso daytoy a lakay?

"Apay a diyo napanunot ti nangasawa idi kabambannuaganyo, Manong?"

"Kabutengko ngamin idi ti agpamilia. Kunkunak idi nga apay koma a mangalaak iti sabali a tao a pakanek?"

"Pulos a diyo napadasan ti nakinobia?"

"Arem mata, bain baga, a." Nagkatawa. "Ne, Maestra, innak pay ngem diyo koma ibagbaga ken ni Sally ti imbagak."

Inarikumkomko dagiti napukis a ruot ken bulong. Intarapnusko dagitoy iti basura. Nataldiapak ni Nanang nga agsaksakdo iti poso. Kitkitaenna ti likudan ni Manong Peding nga umad-adayo.

"Aniat' imbagbaga daydiay nga ansisit kenka?" kinuna ni Nanang idi agbuggoak iti puso.

"Naku, 'Nang, nagkompable no adda kano met la pannakaikarina kadakayo," insutilko.

"Dinak man sutsutilen a kasta amangan no talawankayo nga agiina."

"Mabain kano kadakayo. Pinaspasablogak laeng iti kinasayaatna."

"Kunak ngamin a dimon kasarsarita."

Simmangpet ni Bascion a kasta unay al-alna iti maysa a malem. Impusotna ti bagina iti sopa iti beranda.

"Apay a kasta ti itsuram?" kinunak.

"Adda tallo a lallaki a nangsursurot kaniak. Ipilitda nga umaydak pasiaren. Diak met am-ammo ida."

"Taga-anoda kano?"

"Dita kano Daang Bakal. Am-ammoda ni Manong Peding. Nagtartarayakon, a."

Apagisu met a lumabas ni Manong Peding a nakabisikleta. Adda manen bitbitna a supot. Dimsaag ket nakarabrabuy ti isemna nga immasideg.

"'Bag a malemyo, Maestra," inkablaaw ni Manong Peding.

"Awan ti naimbag a malem ita, Manong Peding. Mangisarsarak dagiti kapurokam," insungbat ni Bascion.

Sinaritak ti imbaga ni Bascion.

"Ammokon no asino dagidiay. Kanayonda a damdamagen no nobiaka. Saan, kunak met, a, ta dayta met ti agpayso. Imbagana a kursonadanaka kano."

"Daydiay kasla agruprupa a jeproks?"

Tinaliawko ti sangili. "Addan sa ketdi naimbag a damag iti dayta a paper bag, Manong," kinunak.

"'Maykayo ngarud paramanan iti bunga ti mulak iti umami idiay bantay," inyawatna ti paper bag ken ni Bascion.

"Wow, sarap!" kinuna daytoy. "Sandia, papaya ken singkamas. Husto a sukaan. Adut' mulayo, 'ya, Manong?"

"Makitayonto, a... Di met nakunam idi, Maestra, a kayatyo a makita ti Wawa Dam?"

"Nabayagen a kayatko," kinunak.

"Areglado, Maestra. Inton Domingo. Agpakalapak iti sida. Umaykayo amin. Itugotyo ni mother ken dagiti ubbing."

Apagisu a nalpaskami a namigat idi dumteng dagiti dua a traysikel nga imbaga ni Manong Peding a mangala kadakami.

Nagkalugankami ken nanang ken dagiti dua nga annakko iti maysa a traysikel. Da Bascion ken dagiti tallo pay nga annakko iti maysa.

Nakadanonkami iti yan dagiti kasla uong a kubo. Adda sumagmamano a pagtagilakuan ken nakaparada a jeep. Adu ti tao kadagiti kubo. Adun ti agdidigos iti karayan. Nangpiliak iti bakante a kubo ket inserrekmi dagiti kargami. Adda nalawa a papag iti uneg. Nagbayadak iti sangapulo a pisos.

Dinamagko no sadino ti yan ti penned. Intudo ti lalaki iti kanigidna.

"Umulika iti dayta a bantay ket makitam ditan, Ma'am, ti dakkel a dam. Paset ti dam ti pagdidigosan."

Natukay ti pannakisarsaritak iti panangawis dagiti ubbing ken ni Bascion nga agdigosda kano. Pinalubosak ida ngem impaganetgetko ken ni Bascion a bantayanna a nalaing dagiti ubbing.

"Innak agkammel iti udang ken kappi," kinuna ni nanang.

Awan ngata pay sangapulo a minuto idi mapasungadak da Manong Peding a kaduana ti dua a lallaki.

"Nabayagkayon, Maestra?" kinuna ni Manong Peding idi maidissoda dagiti bitbitda.

"Nabiitkam' pay, Manong," insungbatko.

Innak koma ayaban dagiti ubbing idi adda nagiikkis iti nagturongan ni nanang. "Nin sa nanang daydiay!" kinunak.

Nagdardaras ni Manong Peding a napan iti yan dagiti agiikkis. Simmarunoak.

Agpayso, ni nanang ti lumned-tumpaw iti pangadalmen a paset ti karayan.

Tinaray ni Manong Peding ti timmapuak a napan nangarayat. Sinakroyna nga intakdang idinto a kunam no alimatek a kimmepkep ni nanang.

"Niat' napananyo idiay adalem?" kinunak ken ni nanang.

"Kasla adda nangguyod itay iti sakak," insungbat ni nanang.

Inatibaymi ken Bascion ni nanang nga inturong iti yan ti kubo. Simmaruno da Manong Peding.

"Mabisinkami a talagan," kinuna dagiti dua a lallaki.

"Sige, ibusentay' amin dagiti sagana. Bale doble a selebrasion daytoy nga aldaw," kinuna ni Manong Peding.

"No saan a gapu kenka, natayak koman," kinuna ni nanang idi agpalpalpan. Adda ni Manong Peding iti asidegna.

"Ni Apo Dios ti akinnakem iti amin. Siguro adda pay kayatna a paaramid kadakayo a diyo pay naaramid."

ITA, no umay agpasiar ni Manong Peding ditoy balay, saanen a kas idi a pampannaganan ni nanang iti ansisit. Isu pay ketdin ti mangpastrek ken makisarsarita ken ni Manong Peding.

Ah, biag, pamrayak laengen nga ikankanta no kasdiay a makitak ti panagsarsarita da nanang ken Manong Peding. —0

Bannawag: Hunio 20, 1983.

Adda Kenka Daytan

NAITEDEN ni Precy ti sumaruno nga asignaturana idi naggigiddan dagiti ubbingna a timmakder ken nagdaydayaw iti, "Good morning, Visitor. Please, come in. Please sit down!"

Naikuadro iti ridaw ti maysa a pamakeden a lalaki, nakarayban, umis-isem ken adda igpilna a regalo. Pugpugtuan ni Precy no asino daytoy mangis-isturbo.

"Thank you, Children," insungbat ti lalaki.

"You are welcome!" insungbat dagiti ubbing ket nagtugawda.

Isu pay laeng ti panagkuti ni Precy iti nagtakderanna ket immasideg iti ridaw tapno damagenna no asino kadagiti ubbing ti gagara ti lalaki.

"Happy birthday, Precy!" impasabat ti lalaki ket inikkatna ti raybanna.

"Ed... sika?" naklaat ni Precy. Dina ammo no ragsak wenno gura ti nagkubuar iti kaungganna "Please, sit down," intudona ti tugaw iti suli.

Imbes nga agtungpal, inyawat ni Ed ti igpilna a regalo. "Para kenka. Advance happy birthday. Adda dita dagiti paboritom."

"Apay nga immayka ditoy eskuela?"

"Let me explain. I came here to let you know I still care for you. Nagawidak ditoy Filipinas gapu kenka. Umayka alaen."

"Ni baketmo?"

"Nabayagen a natay. Awan pay dua a tawen a nagdennakami. I had already suffered a lot, Precy. Nagsakripisioak. Napundarko aminen dagiti arapaapta."

"Kasta kadi ti pagrukodam kaniak, Ed?"

"Siak pay laeng ti ay-ayatem iti laksid ti amin, Precy. Naammuak ti amin no kasano a naasawanaka ni Cesar. Dimo ay-ayaten ti asawam!"

"Saan a ditoy ti pagsaritaanta kadagita a banag, Ed."

"Ala wen, kalpasan ti klasem 'ton bigat. Urayenka iti Max Restaurant dita Cubao."

"Awanen ti nasken a pagsaritaanta, Ed."

"Kayatkot' agpalawag. Adu ti nasken a maammuam. . ."

"Pumanawkan. Kababain kadagiti co-teachersko."

"Urayenkanto ngarud no bigat. Same time, same place."

Nagdardarasen a rimmuar ni Ed. Nabati a maikulkuleng ni Precy. Nagtugaw iti sango ti lamisaanna. Apay a nagpakita ni Ed?

"Nalpas ti eksamenyon?" saan a napuotan ni Precy ti iseserrek ni Marissa manipud iti bangir a kuarto.

"Nalpasen."

"Sino 'tay pogi nga immay ditoy kuartom?"

"Ni Ed daydiay. Nagungar kalpasan ti walo a tawen."

"Ania?" Nagmulagat ni Marissa. "Adda pay rupana a nagpakita kenka kalpasan ti inaramidna?"

"Agkitakami kano dita Max inton bigat. Kayatko nga ipeksa ti sakit ti nakemko."

"Makisinnarakka? No adda ngay makaibaga kadagiti dadduma a kaduatayo ditoy eskuela?"

"Silulukat a libro ti pakasaritaanmi ken ni Ed ditoy eskuela. Ammoda amin no kasano ti iseserrek ni Cesar iti biagko."

"Diak dayawen ni Ed. Immay tapno rakrakenna ti urnosyo nga agassawa. Iti baet ti kinasayaat ni lakaymo, maaramidmo a liputan?"

"Look, Marissa. Saan a kasta ti kayatko a sawen. . ."

"Ba'amon daydiay nga Ed..."

RABIIN idi sumangpet ni Precy. Addan ni Cesar.

"Nasapaak a simmangpet ita, Mommy. Agsukatkan ta mangantayon. Addanto ipadamagko kenka," kinuna ni Cesar.

Kalawakaw ti ulo ni Precy a simrek iti kuarto. Pampanunotenna no ipudnona ti ipapan ni Ed iti eskuela wenno saan. Inyiladna idi

nakasukat. Nasakit ti ulona. Nangngegna ti kayaskas ti sinelas ni Cesar. Nagtugaw daytoy iti iking ti katre.

"Apay, 'ya? Madit' bagim?" dinamag ti asawana.

"Naulawak iti biahe. Ken simmakit ti ulok a nagtsek kadagiti test papers."

"Insangpetmo koma ngamin tapno matulonganka. 'Maykan ta mangantayon."

Bassit ti nakan ni Precy ta bumalballaet ti ladawan ni Ed iti mugingna.

Duduadan iti kuarto. Naulimek ni Precy.

"Ammom, Mommy," kinuna ni Cesar, "siak kano ti ibaon ni Mr. Reyes a mangibagi iti kompaniami a mapan makimiting idiay America 'ton umay a bulan. Makadominggo daydiay a kaduaka. Libre ti amin ket mangted pay iti pocket moneyta."

Saan a simmungbat ni Precy. Dina pay kinita ni Cesar.

"Dika kadi maragsakan, Mommy?"

"Kasano. . . baka didak palubosan iti eskuela."

"Siak ti makisarita iti prinsipalyo tapno palubosannaka."

Adalemen ti rabii ngem saan nga umapay ti ridep ken ni Precy. Makitkitana ti napalabas. Ti kaaddada a tallo, ni Ed, ni Cesar ken isu, iti maymaysa nga opisina. Agayan-ayatda idin ken ni Ed. Ammo ni Cesar daytoy ngem saan a nagbalin a lapped tapno ibisikna ti riknana ken ni Precy babaen ti regalo, rosas, ken panagpaspasiarna iti pagtaenganda nupay pulos a dina sanguen malaksid kadagiti dadakkelna.

Dimteng ti gundaway a nayalis ni Ed iti sabali a sanga ti opisinada idiay Kabisayaan gapu iti maysa a parikut sadiay. Gapu itoy, kiniddaw ni Ed ken ni Precy a mangisuron tapno maadaywanna ni Cesar iti opisina. Maysa a Maestra ken pasado iti serbisio sibil ni Precy ngem kinaykayatna ti nangopisina. Tinungpalna ti kiddaw ni Ed.

"Agsingsingpetka. Adaywam ni Cesar. Agkallaysatanton iti panagsublik," inkari ni Ed.

Ngem napikot kano ni Ed. Naammuan ni Precy nga addan da Ed ken ti asawana idiay America. Iti daydi a napasamak, ad-addan a simminged ni Cesar kadagiti kakabsat ken dadakkel ni Precy. No iriing

ni Cesar ti riknana, prangka ni Precy: "Natayen ti ayatko. Iti uray kaano man, dikanto maipateg!"

Ni met la Precy ti simmuko ken ni Cesar.

Dimteng ni Joel nga anakda kalpasan ti tallo a tawen. Ti ubing ti ad-adda a namagsinninged kadagiti dua. Nakagatangdan iti bukodda a balay, moderno nga alikamen, lugan ken addan naidulinda iti banko para iti masakbayan ni Joel.

Ngem iti puso ni Precy, sumalsallin latta ni Ed. Dina pay la maawat a liniputan ni Ed kadagidi adu a kari ken arapaapda.

Kabigatanna, imbaga ni Cesar a maladaw a sumangpet ta adda kano overtime iti opisinada.

"Imbagam kadi ken ni Cesar ti yaay ni Ed ditoy eskuela?" daytoy ti immuna a dinamag ni Marissa ken ni Precy.

"Panagkunak, saanen a nasken nga ibagak."

"No maammuanna ngay?"

"Bahala na. . . Isunton, a, ti panagpalawagko."

Nakisinnarak ni Precy ken ni Ed. Addan nga agpayso daytoy nga agur-uray iti Max Restaurant. Nataraki iti suotna.

Awan ganas ni Precy a nangan. Ni Ed ti kasta unay ti panagisubona ta nabayag kanon a di nakaraman iti paboritona a fried chicken.

"Okay, okay, nalag-an ti riknak. I'm so happy," kinuna ni Ed idi malpasda. "Makapagsaritata iti nalapat. Makapaglinnawagta. Adda dagiti banag ita a maammuam a dimo la ketdi namnamaen."

"No makapasakit, saanen, Ed. Saludsodek laeng, apay nga inaramidmo ti kasdi kaniak?"

"Gapu ta ay-ayatenka. Adda iti ngarab ti patay daydi Criselda idi naam-ammok. Dagiti dadakkelna ti arig nangiparintumeng nga ikallaysak ti anakda tapno makitada man la a rumagsak kadagiti maudi a kanito ti panagbiagna. Imbagak nga adda nobiak, a dandanitan agkasar. Adda kondision nga indiayada. Bugbugtong nga anak daydi Criselda. Isudat' kabaknangan a pamilia iti lugarda. Inkarida a kalpasan ti panagkallaysami, agyankami idiay America ta daytoy ti dawat daydi Criselda. Natay daydi Criselda kalpasan ti dua a tawen. Tinungpal dagiti dadakkel ni Criselda ti inkarida kaniak. Naited amin kaniak dagiti

tawiden daydi Criselda kadagiti dadakkelna. Isuda pay ti nagkuna a mabalinkon nga ikallaysa ti sigud a nobiak."

"Inaramidmo daydi a pulos a dinak pinakaammuan."

"Sinuratak ni Cesar. Impalawagko ti amin."

"Nagsuratka ken ni Cesar?"

"Binilinko a dinaka baybay-an ngem sabali metten ti inaramidna. Ngem okay laeng kaniak. Ti importante, natungpal aminen dagidi arapaapta a makapagnaedta iti ballasiw ti taaw. Addan bukodko a negosio sadiay. Umayka alaen."

"Kasta kadi ti kalakana? Immayka tapno alaennak ket sumurotak metten?"

"Dinaka igawid ni Cesar no ammona nga addaak. Ammona ti gagarak."

"Ed, you are kidding. That's not true," naipigsa ni Precy ti bosesna.

"Damagemto kenkuana no pudno wenno saan ti ibagbagak kenka. Idi simmangpet idi rabii, ammok nga adda impadamagna kenka."

"A-apay nga ammom?"

"Ammok ta makatawen itan a siak ti secret partner ti akinkukua iti opisina a yan ni Cesar."

"Ed, ay-ayamem kadi ti tao gapu ta baknangkan?"

"Inaramidko ti amin agsipud ta ay-ayatenka. Kayatko a kabingayka kadagiti suertek."

"Rummuartan, Ed!" Ket nagdardarasen a rimmuar ni Precy iti restauran.

Insayo ni Precy ti bagina iti kama idi makasangpet. Mariribukan. Tinimbangna dagiti balikas ni Ed.

Inggagara ni Precy ti di nagkir-in idi sumangpet ni Cesar. Ngem inagkan ti asawana.

Nagmulagat. "Nangankan?"

"Wen, nagpaala ni boss. Kunami no ania ti kunana nga overtime idi kalman. Tsibugan met la gayam ket iti pay nangina a restauran. Pitokami laeng. Nagbibingayanmi pay ti sobra."

Ania daytoy? Pakulo kadi ni Ed?

"Ken ammom, Mommy, diak man ammo no ania ti naknakan ti bossmi. Kinunana a no aggapuakto idiay America, siakto kanon ti ipanna a presidente iti maluktan a sanga ti kompaniami."

Bimmangon ni Precy. "Baka adda kayat a sawen daytan. . ."

"Suerteka, kunkuna ngarud dagiti kaduak. Sabagay, itedda man wenno saan kaniak daydiay a puesto, isu la nga isu kaniak."

"Adda ibagak ken damagek, Ces. Sit down."

"Kasla suspense ti itsuram, a," nagkatawa ni Cesar ngem saan a nagtugaw.

"No ibagak ngay nga immay ni Ed idiay eskuela?"

Nagarko dagiti kiday ni Cesar a kimmita ken ni Precy. "Ulitem man?"

"Ne Ed, immay idiay eskuela."

"Ket?"

"Adut' impadamagna. Adut' impalawagna. Agpayso kadi a nagsurat idi kenka?"

"That goddam bastard!" kinuna ni Cesar.

"Apay a dimo dinakdakamat ti surat iti unos ti walo a tawen a panagdennata?"

"Useless, Mommy. Ammok ti kayat a sawen ti panagparangna kenka. Tapno alaennaka kas insuratna."

"Aniaak? Ay-ayam a pagsusublatan? Ammom kadi a ni Ed ti secret partner ti bossmo?"

"Well, Mommy, ti nasurok a walo a tawen, kasla idi kalman laeng. Ammok nga iti laksid ti panangikarkarigatak a mapagbalin ti pamiliata a modelo, awan maaramidak no iti puso ken riknam ket adda pay la ken ni Ed. Adda kenka daytan a mangeddeng basta mabati iti sidongko ni Joel."

Nabayag a di nakatimek ni Precy. "No kasano ti kapateg ni Joel kenka, mas pay kaniak. Diak isukat ni Joel iti sanikua wenno ania man. Inton bigat met laeng, agikkatkan iti trabahom. Mangbangonta laengen iti kabukbukodanta a negosio."

Naarakup ni Cesar ni Precy. —0

Bannawag: Hunio 27, 1988

No Magatang La Koma Ti Biag

NASANGPETAK TI diak ninamnama a damag iti dayta a tengnga ti aldaw.

"Naaksidente ni Joey. Agngangabit. Intarayda itay agsapa iti East Medical Center kano," kinuna ni lakay.

"Serious, aya?"

"Nabuong kano ti ulona. . ."

"Nabuong ti ulona. . .? Kasano?"

"Kuna ni Nana Marcia nga imbales kano dagiti kameng ti karibal ti fraternityda. Minalmaloda sada intinnag iti derraas dita Tibag idi rabii."

"Mariosep! Kunakto pay la ngamin ken ni Lulu nga awan ti maganab ti anakna iti fraternity. Dinanto la ngamin ikkan ti atension."

Nagdardarasak a nagsukat ken kimmammet.

Dimmagasak iti balay da Lulu nga asideg laeng iti balaymi. Dimges manen ti apalko iti pannakakitak iti kasla palasio a patakder iti hardin. Anian a nagpintas. Tinalmegak ti doorbell.

Rimmuar ni Teresing, ti katulong.

"Sumrekka, Manang," inyawisna.

Nadatngak ni Nana Marcia, ti nanang ni Lulu, iti terrace. Inasitgak.

"Pangngaasim, Marissa, Nakkkong, inka bassit kaduaen 'diay gayyemmo idiay ospital. Kaasi met 'diay apok. Awan puotna nga inakupda," kinunana nga agbaningroten.

Pinikpikko ti baket. "Manangngaasi ni Apo Dios, Nana," kinunak.

61

Innalak dagiti kasapulan ti pasiente iti ospital ta saan kano a naitugot ni Lulu iti nerbios ken panagdardarasna.

Adu ti saludsod iti mugingko iti kaaddak iti lugan. Apay a napasamak manen ti kastoy ken ni Joey? Kapamitlo daytoyen no saanak nga agbiddut. Adda iti umuna a tukad ti kolehio. Is-isu a lalaki iti lima nga agkakabsat. Mannakiriri. Napudot ti panagul-ulona. No namin-anon a nagsennaay ni Lulu kaniak gapu kadagiti annakna.

"Marissa, apay a saan a kas kadagiti annakmo dagiti annakko a napasnek nga agadal? Itedko met amin a kasapulanda."

"Siguro. . . agsipud ta kurang ti atensionmo kadakuaa. Ad-adda a ti negosiom ti as-asikasuem."

"Ibagbagak met kadakuada no asino ti pagpaayan dagidiay a negosio. Ammom, kasla diak idan kabaelan a timonan aglalo ken ni Joey. Kasla agrebrebelde. No ania a gapu, diak ammo. Dinak dengdnggen."

"Apay a dimo kasarita? Agpalawagka."

"Useless, Marissa. Kaaduanna a rabiin no sumangsangpet. No sitarek, pamrayanna ti agpupok iti kuartona. Wenno saan, mapan iti yan da katugangak ket ti la ipulpulongna."

"Ni Fred, ania ti makunana?"

"Maysa met daydiay. Awan lat' bokabulariona no di kuarta. Agawidkan tapno tulongannak a mangtimon kadagiti ubbing, kunak, ngem sayang kano ti sueldona. Kayatna pay ti mangpundar iti sangapulo ti ridawna nga apartment."

"Nagadu la ngarud a paupaanyon."

"Diak ammo iti daydiay nga asawak. Saan a mapmapnek."

"Sabagay, awanen ti nasusuerte ngem sika. Adda amin kadakayo dagiti material a banag nga awan kadakami nga agassawa. Uray no kasano ti panangigaedmi nga agtrabaho, awan latta ti maurnong ta mapan amin ti teggedmi kadagiti agadal nga annakmi."

"Kinapudnona, Marissa, siak ti umap-apal kenka. Natulnog dagiti annakmo. Dida makiap-apa. Napasnekda nga agadal. Aggigiddankayo a makimisa iti Domingo. Naragsakkayo."

"Awan kaimudingan dagita no idiligmo iti estado ti biagyo. Sika ti akimbalay iti kapintasan ditoy subdibision. Adda agencyyo. Adut' paupaanyo a balay."

"Saanak a naragsak kadagita, Marissa. Kaslaak la robot a sumursurot ken ni Fred. Kimmayakayen ti kaaduan a sigud a gagayyemko."

"Mabainda ken ni Fred. . ."

"Saan met a kasdiay idi saan pay a dakkel ti sueldona. Basta kayat ni Fred nasken a mapaaddana."

Nakitak ti panaglupos ti biag da Fred ken Lulu. Sakbay a nakapan ni Fred iti ballasiw ti taaw, nangato idi ti takemna iti kustom. Adu idi ti saosao a maipparparaipus iti kellaat a panagbaliw ti biagda. Ngem ti saan a panagbalbaliw ni Lulu kaniak ti nangpukaw iti mugingko kadagita a saosao.

Diak napupuotan ti panaglabas ti oras, addaakon iti sango ti ospital. Immasidegak iti information. Adda da Lulu iti third floor, iti ICU. No kasta, talaga a serioso ti anakna.

Nadanonko ni Lulu a nakadumog iti mesita. Kaduana ti maysa a katulong ken maysa a kasinsinna. Inasitgak. Sinallabayko. Inyangadna ti rupana. Inarakupnak.

"Ni Joey, komusta?" kinunak.

Intudona iti nurses' station. "Sika man ti mapan agdamag. Kabutengko a maammuan ti ibagada. Inderetsoda iti operating room."

"Nasken a maammuan ni Fred daytoy."

"Inton makaruaren nga ipadamagko. Dinanto met la kayat ti agawid. Inka agdamagen, a." Agarup iduronnak ni Lulu iti nurses' station.

Pimmigsa ti tibbayok iti yaasidegko iti nurse's station. Nagdamagak. Intudoda ti agtugtugaw a doktora. Dinamagko ni Joey. Awan deretso a sungbat. Dinamagna ketdi no kapin-anok ti pasiente, wenno kapin-anok dagiti dadakkelna. Kalpasanna, kinunana: "Nabaybay-an ti pasiente, Misis. Naugotan iti dara sakbay a naitaray iti ospital."

"K-kayatyo a sawen, Doktora, saan a maisalakan?"

"Naoperaren. Nasuktanen ti dara a napukawna. Ngem ti utekna a nadaraan, diak ammo no ania ti resulta ti operasion."

"Aramidenyo ti amin a kabaelanyo, Doktora. Sindadaan nga agbayad dagiti dadakkelna iti uray no mano."

"Misis, prangkaak nga agsarita. Ngem ti makunak, ti Dios laengen ti makaammo nga agaramid iti milagro."

Serioso ti doktora. Intudona ti yan ti paciente. Dandaniak nagikkis a nakakita ken ni Joey. Benda amin ti ulona. Adda dara a rumrummuar iti agong ken lapayagna. Nakakidem. Sinubliak ti doktora.

"Doktora, apay nga adda dara iti agong ken lapayagna?"

"Saan la ngamin a ti ulona ti nadangran. Nakaro pay ti pannakabugbogna. Internal hemorrhage." Binilin ti doktora ti uppat a nars a bantayanda a nalaing ni Joey. Kiniddaw ti doktora a kayatna a kasarita ti ina ti paciente. Inayabak ni Lulu ket binay-ak ida a nagsarita. Ngem di man la immasideg daytoy iti kama a yan ni Joey.

"Diak kabaelan a kitaen ti itsura ti anakko, Marissa," kinuna ni Lulu. "Pangngaasim, dinak pampanawan. Agawidkanto no adda sumangpet."

"Serioso ti kasasaad ti anakmo. Nasken nga ipakaammom ken ni Fred."

"Umaykanto inton bigat ditoy. Kuyogennak nga umawag kenkuana."

Kasla labba a simgar ti ulok iti buya a nadatngak iti ipapanko iti ospital. Ar-arayatenda ni Lulu. Agik-ikkis. Agsangsangit.

"Pinatayyo ti anakko. Isublilyo ti biagna! Adda pagbayadko!" inriawna.

Ni Joey, natayen? Nagdamagak iti nurse's station. Itay kano alas dose a napugsat ti biag ti ubing.

"Inaramid amin da doktora ti kabaelanda ngem talaga nga orasen ti ubing. Dakes unay ti pannakapadara ti utekna."

Sinubliak ni Lulu. Saanen nga agsangsangit. Immarakup idi nakitanak. Agtigtigerger. Kasla ubing a nagsadag iti abagak. Naganug-og manen.

"Awanen ni Joey, Marissa. Diak ammo no ania ita ti kuna ni Fred. Apay a kasdiay? No magatang la koma ti biag."

Inakayko ni Lulu nga aglong-distance iti asawana.

No saan nga imbaga ni Lulu a maysan a bangkay ni Joey, saan a nagkari ni Fred a sumangpet. Agsangsangit ni Lulu ken napigsa ti timekna. "Aglusuloskan! Agawidkan ket dikanton agsubsubli dita!"

Binalakadak ni Lulu idi nakaawagen. Nasken a patibkerenna ti pakinakemna ket italekna aminen iti Dios dagiti sumaruno a mapasamak.

"Biag ti napukaw. Nasken a biag met ti bayadna!" kinunana ketdi.

Binayadan ni Lulu dagiti nasken a mabayadan iti ospital. Dina kayat a maimassayag ti bangkay iti puneraria. Kayatna iti salas ti dakkel a balayna. "For the very last time, kayatko a buyaen ti anakko."

Nagkuyogkami a nagawid. Nabati ti dadduma a kumuyog iti bangkay. Bayat ti kaaddami iti lugan, sinaggaysak a binilang iti panunotko dagiti am-ammok a gagayyem ni Lulu. Sadino ti yanda itan? In-inut a kimmayakay dagitoy idi ngumato ti biag da Lulu ket nagbaliw ti ugali ni Fred. Ammok, siak laengen ti nabati a nadekket kenkuana. No adda man dagiti makuna a gayyemda, pasigda nga alta-sosiedad nga awan ti as-asikasuenda no saan a dagiti negosioda. Kasta met ti lubong ni Lulu. Kinunana idi iti naminsan, "Ammom, Mar, naumaakon iti kastoy a lubongko. Napukawkon ti talinaay. Nabannogakon. Ngem daytoy a lubong ti kayat ni Fred."

Adu ti agsumbangir a kabagian ni Lulu ti nadanonmi iti balayda. Maysamaysa ti nakidamag no kasanon ni Joey. Nagagaran da Nana Marcia ken Tata Teban a makaammo no nakalasat met laengen ti apoda.

Ni Lulu ti simmungbat. "Awanen ni Joey, Mama, napanen. . ." ket bimtak manen ti sangit a nagalimpayang iti sibubukel a mansion. "Basol ni Fred ti amin. Pulos a dina inkankano ti anakna a lalaki." Naganug-og iti uray la nga.

"Awanen ti maaramidantayo no di mangawat iti kinapudno, Tata, Nana," kinunak kadagiti dadakkel ni Lulu. "Ti nasken, pasapul dagiti kriminal."

"Ammomin, Anakko, no asinoda. Immay dagiti dadakkelda idi rabii ket indiayada ti tulongda iti ospital. Ngem ania pay ita. . . awanen ti ubing."

"Makaammonton ni Fred, inton sumangpet," kinunak.

Inatibayko ni Lulu idi awanen ti sangitna a sumngaw. "Pakirdem ti nakemmo. Uray ania ti aramidem ita, saanen a maisubli ti biag ti anakmo."

"No mabalin la koma a gumatangak iti biag tapno isukatko iti biag ti anakko, arammidek. Ania ita ti serserbi ti sangkakuna ni Fred? A no adda kuartam, nabileg ken naturedka, ket awanen ti nagasgasat ken naragragsak. Ngem diak marikna dagita. Mabutbutengak. Mabatbatibatak iti tengnga ti aldaw."

"Lulu, isunan," kinunak. "Urnosen ken isaganatan ti pagyanan ti ubing."

Nagpakadaak a nagawid idi adun ti agsangpet.

"Isu a narigat ti agpaspasaw ken agpampannakkel," inulit-ulit ni lakay idi ipadamagko dagiti pasamak. "Ti ipapatay umay a kasla mannanakaw. Panagkunak, maysa nga adal daytoy iti komarim. Manipud addan negosioda, nabaybay-annan dagiti annakna. Adu ti katulong a mabalinda a bayadan, ngem sabali ti sapsapulen ni Joey. Mawaw iti pammateg ken asikaso dagiti dadakkelna."

Simmangpet ni Fred iti maikadua nga aldaw. Nasaksianmi amin a nadanonna ti kasla agmauyong a langa ni Fred a naganug-og a nangarakup iti lungon.

Diak nakatabuno iti pumpon ni Joey ta eksamenmi iti third grading period iti eskuela. Kasta met kadagiti simmaruno nga aldaw. Diakon nakitkita ni Lulu. Tunggal gandatek ti pumasiar iti balayda, lapdannak ni lakay.

Maysa a surat ti naawatko idi nadanon ti maikatallopulo nga aldaw ti panagtabon daydi Joey. Aldaw ti Sabado. "Marissa, awisenka, ta intayo amin iti balay ni Joey nga anakko," insurat ni Lulu.

Dinak napawilan ni lakay iti yaannugotko iti awis ni Lulu. Umis-isem ni Lulu a nangarakup kaniak. Impadamagna a naidanonen iti korte ti napasamak iti anakna. Naulimek ni Fred nga agtugtugaw.

Iti kosina, agkakaimas dagiti malutluto. "Bassit met ti bisitam ngem apay a nakaad-adu ti palutlutom?"

"Aduda nga agur-uray iti balay ni Joey."

"Balay ni Joey?"

Nagtung-ed ni Lulu. "Makitamto."

Saan a panteon wenno nitso ti balay ni Joey a kuna ni Lulu. Maysa a nadaeg a patakder a de marmol a nangrimbaw iti amin a museleo iti kamposanto. Dua a dadakkel dagiti kuarto. Adda banio, adda salas ken adda kosina. Kabarbaro ken kompleto dagiti muebles. Adda telebision. Adda prigidir. Nalamuyot ti sala set. Dekarpet ti salas. Iti maysa a kuarto ti yan ti bangkay ni Joey. Iti bangir a kuarto, adda dekutson a kama ken maysa a dakkel nga aparador. Adda amin ditoy dagiti aruaten ni Joey. Kasla sibibiag ti umis-isem a naipadakkel a ladawan ni Joey

iti salas. Segun iti estoria dagiti nagtrabaho, paspas ti pannakaaramid ti patakder. Nasurok a tallo a milion ti gatad ti balay ni Joey agraman dagiti alikamen iti uneg. Adu a kuarta! Anian a kadaeg!

"Bassit-usit daytoy no tungpalek amin dagiti inkarik kenkuana idi sibibiag pay. Pinaaramidko a kastoy ta no sumarungkarkami, kasla kaduami latta ni Joey. Mabalinmi ti mangan ken maturog ditoy," kastoy ti palawag ni Fred idi mangmangankamin.

Kasla diak matilmon ti kanek. Adda naulimek a kararag iti barukongko. Sapay koma, Joey, ta nakasaklangkan iti sidong ti Apo. Sapay ta adda ditan ti pammateg a sinapsapulmo idi addaka pay ditoy daga. —0

Bannawag: Hunio 26, 1995

Ti Arapaap Ni Tata Basil

KAPAMPANAW DAGITI kaarruba ken kabagian nga immay simmarabo iti isasangpetmi ken ni Grace idi adda aguni iti arsadanan ti agdan.

"Gasiiiing! 'Tay sarabooook. . ."

Nagtibbayoak. "'Sinno daydiay, 'Nang?" kinitak ni nanang a kasta unay ti dalukappitna iti lakasa nga agpaypayubyob iti pinadisna.

"Ni Tatam Basil. Naangotna la ketdi ti kaaddayo."

"Ipaaag! Gasiiiing! Marissa!" Napigpigsan ti raed a timek a bulon ti panangguttaguttadna iti tali ti agdan.

"Buisit a laklakayan. . . Mangibabain!" intanabutob ni Grace. "Iti kastoy nga oras nga umay mangkungkundinar. Nabannog ti tao. Kaawawid la dagiti sangareprep!"

"Saan a mamingga dayta no diyo paulien," kinuna da Bella ken Pedro, ti agassawa a kadua ni nanang ditoy balay. Agpada met dagitoy a kasta unay ti panagpayubyobda iti pinadis.

"Ania, pastrekek?" Kinitak ni nanang.

"Saan!" Nanabsuot ni Grace. "Umayto no bigat no mausawan."

"Loka, no naggapu idiay maikapito a bantay. Sigurado a nadamagna ti kaaddayo ket mailiw met a makakita kadakayo," kinuna laeng ni nanang.

"Paulienyon," kinunak.

"Agkibur. Saan nga agpakaturog dayta," kinuna met ni Bella. Napan ni Pedro nakiatag kadagiti lima a putotna iti laem idi maibellengna ti rungrongna iti tawa. Nagkukot met ni Grace iti papag.

Intangwa ni nanang ti iggemna a kingki idi mailukatna ti ridaw. Nangngegko ti katawa ni Tata Basil.

"'Bag a rabiim, Ipaaaag. Naimbag ta nasayaat latta ti panagpuspusom. . . a mangpasangbay kaniak. . . saan a kas ken ni kabagis dita. . . tianggi a mangbugbugaw kaniak. . . a kasla aso."

Nagranitrit dagiti pangal ti agdan.

"Kumpetka a naimbag amangan no matnagka," kinuna ni nanang. "Dayta ngamin ta kareggetmo unay ti agbartek iti kastoy nga oras. Nabannog unay dagiti ubbing."

Imbuang ti ridaw ti ayukos ken agdiwerdiwer a pakabulan ni Tata Basil. Rutrot ti badona. Takuptakop a butbot ti pantalonna. Tali ti barikesna. Lampong. Nagadiwara ti angot-basi. Diak nagtagtagari iti nagtugawak. Agbasbasaak pay la iti kolehio daydi naudi a pannakakitak ken ni Tata Basil.

"Tata, komusta," kinunak idi nagtalinaay a nagtugaw iti bangko a mangmatamata. Ammok a ni Grace ti sapsapulenna. Paboritona ni Grace kadagiti amin a kaannakanna idi babassitda pay.

"Ay, Marissakat'tay? Kastoy laeng, Balasangko. Napanawan. Maababi. Mauy-uyaw!" Ne, ket agsangit metten. Agdung-awen.

"Angkel, dika agdung-aw, a. Makariing dagiti ubbing," simngat ni Bella. "Agawidkan, 'la. 'Maykanton bigaten no mausawanka."

"Aniat' kunam?" Sinangona a kasla kayatna a duklosen ni Bella. "Agpapadakayo amin! Sangsangpetko, katugtugawko, pagawidennakon!"

"Ba'anyo kad' lattan. Ammoyo nga'd la ta ugalinan no mabartek," kinuna ni nanang.

"'Tay sarabok, Balasangko," kinunana. "Uray sapin ken kamisetak laeng. Ne, kitaennak kadi, a, mangrutayrutay."

Nagtung-edak.

"'Tay pay para basi, a, balasangko. . ."

"Saanen, husto daytan, kaasikayo met."

Kineddel ni Grace ti bakrangko. "Anusmo la ketdi a makisarsarita iti dayta a bartek. Pagawidemon, kunak!"

"Aniat' kunam, Gasiiing?" Nangngegna gayam. "Agawidak no didak pay pinasarabuan? Sangsangpetko, agawidak ketdin. Alla, lokoka, a, pumadaka met ken ni ulitegmo a kurimaong, kitaem."

"Kastakay' met 'tatta ngamin a bartek, Angkel. Nakababain ti itsurayo."

"Basil a bartek ngem ammok ti laud ken daya. 'La man, mangibagaka man no asino ti makaandur nga agindeg iti maikapito a bantay? No ibabainkayo a kunayo, apay ngarud nga adu ti um-umay a tao iti abongko?"

"Agawidkayon, Angkel," indagdag manen ni Bella.

"Alaem daytoyen ta imbag la a karemkemem a pagpausawam iti dalanmo nga agawid," kinuna ni nanang a nangyawat iti insupotna a tinapay.

"Pagawidanyo ngamin, Tata?" dinamagko.

Nagkumkumpas manen sana sinarigsigan nga inallawat ti supot a yaw-awat ni nanang. "Diak pagan-ano ti tinapay, Ipaaagg!"

"Diabloka ketdi! Agawidka man laengen ta dika mangis-isturbo."

"Pagawidanna kadi?" Ni nanang ti nagdamagak.

"Idiay Burador. Idiay maikapito a bantay. . ."

Kinitak ti relo iti imak. Alas dies media. "No agawid, anianto nga oras no makadanon?"

"Agtaraoktot' manoken, a."

"Naku, ba'anyon, kaasi met. Paturogenyon dita kosina. Amangan ta saan a makadanon idiay Burador a kunkunayo."

"Mandiak! Burakenna dagiti pinggan. Binuongna daydi maysa a malabimi idi pinaturogmit' naminsan a nabartek dita kosina," imsiag ni Bella.

"Dinatayo paturogen," kinuna met ni nanang.

Inyunnat la ngaruden ni Tata Basil iti bangko. "Sika a Bella, ti la tartarabitabem. Kasano a diak buongen ti pingganyo ket dinak met pakanen. Dakayo a kakaanakak, didak im-imutan tapno nasayaat ti biagyo. No didak ikkan ti sarabok ita, diak agawid."

Kinarawak ti limapulo iti bagko ket impapetpetko kenkuana. "'Toy sarabom kaniak, Tata," kinunak. "'Ton bigat, no mausawanka, agsublikanto tapno ikkanka iti sapin ken badom."

Bimmangon ni Tata Basil sana binisongbisong ti kuarta nga intedko. "Tengkiu! Tengkiu beri mats. . ." Timmakder. Naginat. "Agawidak

ngaruden ta hustonto a rummuar ti bulan a silawko no makadanonak dita Maramramot Dam. . .”

Idi awanen ni Tata Basil, kunam no asino a bimmangon da Pedro ken Bella ket binabalawdak no apay nga inikkak ni Tata Basil iti kasdiay a kantidad.

“Ti kasdiay a tao, masapul a maipupok idiay mental,” kinuna ni Pedro.

“No saan met nga agmauyong. . . Nalimbong met nga agsarita.”

“Mangibabain nga uliteg,” kinuna met latta ni Grace.

NAGRUBUATKAMI ken Grace a napan idiay ili idi nalpaskami a namigat. Insaganak ti kamerak. Adu ti kayatko nga alaen a ladawan. Adut’ kayatko a makita a tao a pasetto ti isuratko a libro. Kinapudnona, idiayak koma ili, iti balay daydi tatang, nga agtarus idi malem ngem diak nakumbinsi ni Grace ta mabain kano. Ket agsipud ta adda ni nanang iti away, ken nabayagen a diak nakita, isu a nagderetsokamin ditoy.

Adda tianggi a nalabasanmi iti pangalaanmi iti traysikel a mapan idiay ili. Nalasindak. Pinadagasdakami. Ti met la pangaw-awagdan kaniak. Maestra wenno Apo Mannurat! Nasayaat kano ta malagipko nga umay alaen ni nanang.

Iti presidensia, binisitami ni Ralph, ti inaudi nga anak daydi Manang Seniang ken paborito nga apoko daydi tatang. Diak pay nakita manipud panagtakemna a mayor iti ilimi. Nakitanak.

“Ni lakaymo, yanna?” dinamagna.

“Adda iti ballasiw ti taaw. . .”

Nagpipinnadamagkami. No kasano ti panangriendana iti ili. Rimmang-ayen ti ilimi manipud panagtakemna. Adda pay ditan ti College of Fisheries, dandanin mabangon ti eropuerto iti tanap ken adun ti napipintas a buya a linuktan ti Turismo para kadagiti lokal ken ganggannaet a turista.

“Nasayaat,” kinunak. “Makitkitakon a no sibibiag ita daydi tatang, awanen ti sapulenna a pannakaipatungpal dagiti arapaapna a pagbalinan ti impatpategna a lugar.”

“Mannuratka ngem iti kaano man dimo pay naisurat ti mapapan iti ilim,” kinuna ni Ralph.

"Maysanto a libro ngem saan pay nga ita."

Impailayonko ti traysikel iti disso a dinakkelan ken nakaimulaan ti isipko. Awanen daydi balaymi nupay makitkitak ti kinaubingko a nagay-ayam iti nalawa ken napanayag a paraangan.

Diak ninamnama a masangpetanmi ken ni Grace a nakalangkapi ni Tata Basil iti paraangan iti panagsublimi iti away iti dayta a malem. Saan a nakainum. Nalawag ti rupana. Nadalus met ti badona nupay takuptakop.

"Naimbag a malemyo, Annakko. Immaykayo indaw-asan iti pangramananyo kadagiti bunga ti papayak. Ken pambarak a mangdamag no kayatyonto ti nateng a yawidyo idiay Manila."

"Kayatko, a, Tata. Ikkannakaminto 'ti bayadak."

"Isu pay a kurkurantongtayo nga agawid, Manang. Nagadu a nateng sadiay," inyarasaas ni Grace kaniak.

"Diak pabayadan, Balasangko. Itedkonto a balonyo. No mayan-anusyo koma ti umay idiay Burador, a, ket nagsayaaten ta makapilika iti kayatmo. . ." Adu kano ti mulana.

"Intan?" kinunak ken ni Grace.

Nagwingiwing. "Saan nga iti umuli iti bantay ti nagbakasionak no di ket mapan agdigos iti baybay. Ti ket anusmo a makisarsarita iti dayta nga artek."

Naikarik ken ni Tata Basil a pasiarek ti lugarna tangay diak pay napadasan manipud iti kinaubingko ti immuli iti bantay. Sangkakuna met da nanang ken ni Bella a napintas ti Burador a pagnaedan ni Tata Basil a kabbalayna ti maya a barito nga anakna.

Karabiyanna, nagdamdamagak ken ni nanang maipapan iti biag ni Tata Basil ken no apay a nagbalin a bartek. Naammuak ti gapuna: nakilalaki gayam ti asawana, kompadreda nga adda mabalinna. Aggigian kano iti tao dagiti tallo a babbai nga inauna nga annakda. Nabati ti maysa idiay Isabela a yan ti katuganganna ket ti maysa, nabati kenkuana. Daytoy kano la nga anakna ti nakaanus ken ni Tata Basil.

Kabigatanna, napankami idiay bantay. Ni Grace ti agbantay kadagiti annak ni Bella. Immay da Bella ken Pedro. Simmurot latta ni nanang nupay ipagelko gapu iti uyekna.

Inunormi ti naabbatan a karayan. Simmang-atkami iti bangir ti teppang. Adda paskil a naisurat. *This way to Maramramot Dam.*

"Sumang-attayo a kumalipkip. Agtanangka iti pannagnam," kinuna dagiti kaduak.

Umas-asidegkamin iti penned. Matantannawaganmin dagiti mula nga agsabsabong a nayalad iti natukantukad nga agdan a dumanon iti kasla conference house wenno guest house. Kuna dagiti kaduak a no kayatko a tannawagan ti danum ti dam, masapul a sumrekkami iti inaladan.

Nakaangesak iti nalukay idi addakami iti tuktok ti maikapito a bantay ket makitakon ti kapanagan ken sumaggamaysa nga agaaddayo a kalapaw.

Agur-uray nga agpayson ni Tata Basil iti paraangan ti kalapawna. Intugawko a sibabannog ket dimmawatak iti danum. Nagtarus dagiti kaduak iti kalapaw ket dita ti imminumanda. Inruarannak ni Bella iti sangabuyuboy a danum. Idi nakainumdan, binilin ni Tata Basil ida a mapan agpuros iti bunga dagiti mulana iti aglawlaw. Dagiti papaya a narnuoyan iti bunga ti nakaawis iti imatangko iti dayaen ti kalapaw. Kasla diak patien nga adda kastoy a buya iti ginget ti kabambantayan.

Nasiputannak siguro ni Tata Basil ket kinunana, "'Gurayka ta innak alaen ti nayon daydi inyegko idi malem iti yanyo."

Alisto a simrek iti kalapaw ket idi rummuar, iggemnan ti napisi a papaya a naibandehado. Nainanaanak iti sam-it ti naluom a papaya.

Sinaludsodko ken ni Tata Basil no apay nga adda iti daytoy a nasulinek a disso; ken no apay nga agbarbartek no kasta a makarugi.

"Inkarikon, Nakkong, manipud idi insukatnak ni nanam a ditoyak laengen. Adu't mangdurdurog kaniak a riputek ida a patayen, ngem saanen. Bay-akon. Ni tatam a kabagisko nga inauna, adu ti pananguy-uyawna kaniak. Imbes a siak ti kaasianna, ilunlunodnak pay ta mangibabainak kano iti pulimi. Saanna la nga ammo no kasano ti riknak no malagipko daytoy a napasamak iti biagmi. Diak met ngarud maako nga agbalinak a kriminal. Naglaka no kayatko. Ammok ti balayda. Mabalinko latta koman a dinamitaen. Ngem pampanunotek met ni nanam nga uray no kasdiay ti namay-anna kaniak, asawak pay laeng a nangted kaniak iti lima nga annak. Isu a ti la arak ken basin ti

kamangko no kasdiay a malagipko ti kasasaadko. No diak makainum, agmulmulaak iti uray ania. Adu met ti kakabagian a sumuksuknal ditoy nga awan la ti ammoda no di dumawdawat. No dadduma, adda met dagiti mangiranta nga umay mamakiaw. Isu, a, ti pangalaanmi iti pagbiagmi nga agama."

Awan kano ita ti baritona ta dinagas ti kaarrubada a napan naganup iti bangir a turod.

Binagaak nga idiannan ti aginum ta awan ti maited daytoy kenkuana no di maperdi laeng ti bagina ken saan a makatulong daytoy a mangrisut iti problemana.

Nakitak ti panagmaratubbog dagiti matana.

"No kasta la koma amin ti mangngegko a pammagbaga, Balasangko, nabayag koma siguron a naidiak ti aginum. Ngem, ala, wen, mabalinko nga ikari nga idiakon ti agbartek. . . adda la koma ngarud dawatek kenka no mabalin, Balasangko. . ."

"Ania daydiay, Tata?"

"Ibagaannak kadi, a, ken ni Apo Mayor 'ti taraknek a nuang. Agassawa koma nga urbon. Damagko nga adda programa ti Bureau of Animal Industry nga agit-itedda iti ayup kadagiti mayat nga agtaraken."

"Apay a diyo ibaga iti kapitanyo?"

"Balasangko, saan a tao ti pangibilanganda kaniak dita baba. Nangruna daydiay baknang a kabagisko. Kasla di malamut ti aso ti panagsaona kaniak no maidaw-asak iti yanda."

"Ti ammok iti dayta a programa, Tata, mangted ti Bureau iti taraknen nga ayup ngem nasken a saan a mabaybay-an. Nasken a paganakem ti babai. Ngem no kastakayo nga agbarbartek ket mabaybay-anyo, saandakayo la ketdi nga ikkan."

Nagrimat dagiti mata ni Tata Basil iti daytoy nga imbagak.

"Saanakon nga agbarbartek, Balasangko, no maibagaannak la ketdi iti taraknek a nuang."

"Ikannaka ni Apo Mayor basta makitana ti kinasaldetyo. Awisem met nga umay bumisita ditoy lugarmo."

"Kuyogennak, Balasangko. . ."

Diak napakadaan dayta a dawat. Ket no ngay saan a patgan ni Ralph? Kinitak ni Tata Basil. Napasnek. Ngem kasano a patiek a maikkatna ti panagbartekna idinto a naigameren iti lasag ken darana?

Ngem idi ibagak kada Bella, kasda la immingar nga ampo.

"Ibabainnaka, Marissa, uray kita'm!"

Apay a kastoy dagitoy? Apay a dida tulongan ni Tata Basil idinto a naglainganda met a dumawat kadagiti bunga dagiti mulana?

"Isu a kasdiay ni Tata Basil ta diyo maawatan. Awan kano ti makaawat ken mangipatpateg kenkuana kadakayo a kabagianna. Ba'anyo ta padasek nga idanon ken ni Apo Mayor ti dawatna. Padasek a dawaten ti tulong ti kapitanyo."

"No kasta, paypaysuem?" inamad ni Pedro. "Ket ibagaannak met, a, ngarud ken ni Apo Mayor iti taraknek a kalding."

Patay, naisarsarakakon. A, ngem padasek. Maysa a banag a dakkelto a kaipapanak kadakuada.

Impagarupko no saan a patgan ni Ralph ti kiddaw da Tata Basil ken Pedro. Ngem naragsakan pay a nakaammo a kas kadakuada nga adda iti away ti kayatna a patgan ken tulongan.

NABAYAGEN daydi, ngem agingga ita, no malaglagipko, kasla diak patien a napagbaliwko ti biag ti maysa a kas ken ni Tata Basil. Ulit-ulitenna kano nga ibagbaga kadagiti tao a dinakto malipatan agingga a sibibiag. Ti naudi a damagko, awandan idiay Burador. Nakaipatakderdan iti anakna iti asideg ti kabsatna ket napaadudan daydi inted ti Bureau a taraknenda. —0

Bannawag: Hunio 17, 1996

Ti Didiosen Ni Resia

NAALUMAMAY TI timek ni Ester, ti guidance counselormi iti eskuela, a nangayab kaniak iti lamisaanna. "Please, Marissa," kinunana, "agtaruska iti balay ni Resia iti panagawidmo. Ammuem no sadino nga ospital ti yanna ta uray no moral suport laeng ti maitulongtayo kenkuana."

Nakigtotak. "Why? What happened to her?"

"Serious. . . it's between life and death. Adda immawag ditoy eskuela a nasapa."

Kasano a mapanak ket dandani dua a tawenen a dikami agin-innuni?

Adu a co-teachermi ti agdengdengngeg itay agsapa. Maysamaysa ti naglibbi ken nagdayamudom. "Agsakit met la, aya, ti usurera? A, ngem kaaduanna a kanser ti sakit dagiti usurera!"

"Gunggonana! Kunam no asino a reyna no agsingir!"

"Marissa, I want to hear from your lips if you go to Resia's place or not."

"Yes, I'll go. . ."

"Thank you, Marissa. Ammok nga adda kenka ti nadiosan a panirigan. Saan a kas iti dadduma dita a kakaduatayo. No apay a kagurgurada ni Resia, diak la ammo. Dina met ida pilpiliten nga umutang."

Addaakon iti klasek idi immay da Rose ken Manang Libring, agpada a kaduak iti grade one. Diak ninamnama ti imbaga ni Manang Libring. "Saanka a mapan iti yan ni Resia. No kayat a maammuan ni Ester ti kasasaadna a kunana, apay ket adda met dagiti dianitor a baonenna?

Sika, no inka, kaguraka. Uray iti kaano man, diakto malipatan daydi aramidna kaniak. Nalipatamon daydi nasakit a panagsasaona kadatayo?"

"Ita la a madamagko nga agsakit," inyallawat met ni Rose. "Ngem uray no agsakit, awan problemana. Milion ti kuartana. Dayta laeng, a, no kanser nga agpayson ti nakakapet kenkuana!"

Yad-adayom, Apo! Ti ammok, nagbakasion ni Resia iti makabulan ta asikasuenna ti pannakairugi ti maipatakder a sangapulo ridaw nga apartment a nabayagen nga arapaapna sakbay a sumangpet ni lakayna manipud iti ballasiw ti taaw.

Agingga nga addaak iti dyip, diak pay ammo no agtuloyak wenno saan iti yan da Resia. No diak mapan, kaguranak ni Ester. No mapanak, kaguranak met ni Manang Libring, ti kasla imbilangko nga inauna a kabsat, nga isu ti ad-adda a tarayak no adda parikutko.

Nagkaadalankami ken ni Resia iti Northern Luzon Teachers College (Don Mariano Marcos Univerity itan) iti siudad ti Laoag. Taga-Ilocos Sur, taga-Norteak. Agpadakami idi a kandidata iti kinasekretaria iti student council. Iti miting-de-avance iti kampus ti nagam-ammuanmi. Maysa a napintas a kanta ti impangngegna idinto a bitla kaniak a diak pulos a binasbasa. Diak pulos ninamnama a mangabakak. Inasitgannak ni Resia nga inapungol sana imbaga a basbasaenna dagiti gapuanak iti *Bannawag*. Sana kinuna, "Panagkunak, saan a kinamaestra ti talaga nga ambisionmo iti biag. Kas kaniak, kapilitan laeng."

Maysa nga apir ti insungbatko kenkuana.

Kadagiti kanito a kaaddami iti kampus, ni naminsan dina dinakdakamat maipanggep kadagiti dadakkel ken kakabsatna, malaksid ti ulit-ulitenna nga arapaap. Kayatna ti bumaknang nga adu ti depositona a kuarta ken alahas iti banko. Kayatnanto pay ti aglatak nga international singer no maipamaysananto ti panawenna iti panagkanta. Dinanto kayat ti mangisuro apaman a makaturposkami.

Agpayso ta di nagbayag kalpasan ti panagturposmi, nakaawatak iti surat ni Resia a nagkunaanna a subokenna ti gasatna iti Manila ngem saan a tapno mangisuro. Nagkallaysakami ken ni Larry. Nupay kunak idi a diak kayat ti mangisuro kalpasan ti panagturposko, kinaritnak ti asawak nga aramatek ti kursok agsipu ta pasadoak met iti serbisio sibil. Masursurokto kano nga ipateg ti propesionko.

Sinurotko ti balakad ni lakay ket naklaatak laengen iti maysa nga aldaw a giddato a panagparang ni Resia iti eskuela a kasukat ti maysa a naglusulos a kaduami.

"Oh, what a small world!" kinunami iti baet ti nairut a panaginnarakupmi a buybuyaen dagiti co-teachermi. "My best friend in college," kinunak kadakuada.

Adda nagsaludsod. "Mannurat kadi met a kas kenka?"

"A singer," kinunak.

"No more," kinuna ni Resia. "A dream that didn't come true. I married after graduation."

"Agpadata met gayam," kinunak.

Ngem apay a kayatna met la ti mangisuro? "Gaga! Tapno matungpal ti arapaapko nga agbalin a milionario!" insungbatna.

Dimmakkel ti mulagatko. "Kasano? Ammom a sangsangkabassit ti sueldo ti titser."

"Marissa, dumngegka," kinunana. "Sakbay a nagpursigiak a mangisuro adun ti naadalko a pamususan tapno magun-odko ti arapaapko. Diak pay ibagbaga kenka ngem maammuamto."

Lima a tawen kano a nagtrabaho iti maysa nga opisina nga inaldaw a mapumpunno kadagiti rummuar-sumrek a mannursuro nga umutang. Maymaysa ni Gerry nga anakna. Agsublisubli ni Gerald nga asawana iti ballasiw ti taaw.

"Agingga a diak matungpal ti arapaapko, dinto aglunit ti sugat nga immula ti dua a kabsatko a nangirurumen kaniak. Kayatko ida a balsen iti kinatangsit ken kinaagumda."

"Dakes dayta," kinunak. "Ni la Apo Dios ti addaan iti dayta a karbengan."

"Dios?" nagkatawa. "Adda kadi Dios iti daytoy a panawen? Kuarta itan ti Dios ti tao. Kuarta ti Dios ti dua a kabsatko ken dagiti kabagiak a kasla aso nga agsakmal iti kuarta gapu iti politika."

"Sika laeng, ngem siak, saan. Nasken nga adda Dios iti puso ti tunggal titser, Resia."

"Santasantitaka met gayamen, Friend. Okay, lipatemon ti imbagak. Let me learn the ins and outs of our school. Do me a favor. Help me."

"Basta diak kayat a didiosem ti kuarta. . . for old times sake. I'll help you, okay?"

Ad-adda a nagbalin a karkarna ti ugali ni Resia iti panaglabas ti panawen. Saan a narigat ti panangyam-ammo ni Resia iti bagina babaen ti bukodna nga estilo. Natahor. Alahas ken appliances ti pagandarenna. Sinitarko iti naminsan. Kastoy ti insungbatna: "Pannakikadua dagidiay. Ammom, adda ngamin gunggun-odek a pabor."

"Business kadi? Monkey business?"

Nagkatawa. "Keep guessing. . . But this is not yet the time. Just keep quiet of what I'm doing."

Kasla nairanrana iti daydi a panawen, nagang-angawan ni Larry ti nagaplikar iti maysa nga advetisement a para Saudi. Ne, ket telegrama metten ti simmangpet a sungbat a pappapanendan iti opisina nga itugotnan dagiti papeles a kasapulan. Ket nasken payen nga agsapulkami iti akaranmi iti kabiitan a panawen ta makabulan laengen ti plaso a maited a pawayway a panagyanmi oras a makaluas ni lakay a mapan idiay Saudi. Ni Resia ti nangyopreser ken ni Larry nga iti asidegda a subdibision ti akaranmi ta adda offer a house and lot sadiay. Pinautangannakami pay iti tallo ribu a processing fee nga insublimi met laeng idi naala ni lakay ti kuartana iti GSIS.

Ad-adu pay ti naammuak ken ni Resia iti panagbayagmi nga agkadua iti eskuela. Dua kano ti papaupaanna a balay iti kabangibangmi a subdibision. Sa sabali pay ti sangapulo a ridaw nga apartment a marugianton iti mabiit. Adu kano ti agkakangina nga alahasna a naggapu idiay Saudi. Sa adda depositona a kuarta ken alahas iti nadumaduma a banko iti Metro Manila.

Ket bimtak ti damag iti eskuela a ni Resia ti agpuonan ken manarawidwid iti maysa a Teacher's Loan iti eskuelami tapno saankami kanon a mapmapan umutang kadagiti ahensia nga agpapautang.

"Agsugponta," inyawis kaniak ni Resia. "Uray ta adda ni lakaymo idiay Saudi."

Nagwingiwingak. "Resia, sorry, dita makatulong kadagiti kaduata iti kastoy nga aramid."

"Sangapulo la a porsiento ti interest a dawatenta a saan a kas kadagiti agpabpabulod dita a kinse agingga iti trenta a porsiento."

Ket adu ti immasideg nga immutang ken ni Resia. Saan laeng a dagiti padak a mannursuro, uray payen dagiti nagannak. Ngem adu ti napagurana gapu iti kinaigetna nga agsingir. Ket maysa ni Manang Libring kadagiti napasakitanna. "Grabe nga agsingir daydiay a gayyemmo, Marissa. Naladawak la iti dua nga aldaw a nagbayad, sao a sao. A no saan kano a gapu iti kuartana, saan kano koma a nakapagabrod ti anakko. Marissa, dimo tultuladen ti ugali daydiay a gayyemmo."

PINARAK ti dyip iti asideg ti balay da Resia. Bahala na, nakunak iti bagik. Pinasimbengko ti riknak. Nagdorbelak iti sango ti dua a kadsaaran a dakkel a pagtaengan. Talaga a nagun-oden ni Resia ti arapaapna iti panagbalinna a kastoy.

Linuktan ti maysa nga agtutubo ti ruangan. Nagmano. "Sumrekkayo, Tita," kinunana. Baron ni Gerry. Nabayag a talagan a diak nakita.

Dua a babbai ti adda iti salas. "Tita, antik ida. Kakabsat ni Daddy. Isuda ti manges-estimar ken ni Mommy a kadua ti dua a nars."

"Ni Mommym?"

"Kitaek, Tita, no siririing." Simrek ni Gerry iti maysa a dakkel a kuarto iti baba. Nakisarsaritaak kadagiti ikitna. Dinamagko no ania ti pudno a napasamak ken ni Resia ken no apay a dida impan iti ospital. Nagwingiwingda.

"Pinaawiddakamin, Ma'am, ken saanen a kayat ni Resia iti ospital. Sa graben ti sakitna. Bimtak ti kanserna iti uneg. Dina ngamin inkanknano idi. Imbaga ti doktor a dimi lattan ibagbaga kenkuana."

Nagarigenggenak. Bimtak ti kanserna iti uneg? No kasta ngarud, nabayagen a rikriknaen ni Resia daytoy isu a nag-leave? "Ni lakayna, ammonan a kastoy ti napasamak ni Resia?"

"Wen, Ma'am, ur-urayenmi ngarud ti isasangpetna. Idi pay la lawasna a dadaananmi ngem saan a basta makapanaw nga awan ti kasukatna."

"Mabalin a kasarita?"

"Wen, agsarita met. Yasugna ti sakit ti barukongna no dumuko. Adda latta nana ken dara nga agruar no aguyek."

"Awan kadi ti doktor a kumitkita kenkuana?"

"Adda, Ma'am. Kasibsibetna la unay. Dua pay, a, ti private nursena, ngem matmaturogda dita ngato ta napuyatanda. Ti met la doktorna ti nagkuna a ditoyna laengen balay uray ta kompleto met dagiti kasapulanna."

Rimmuar ni Gerry. Sineniasannak a sumrek iti kuarto. Diak ninamnama ti buya a nakitak. Adda dextrose a nakakapet ken ni Resia nga iti abayna, maysa a dakkel nga oxygen tank. Tallo a dadakkel nga agtutuon a pungan ti pagsadsadaganna. Adu a bakante a nagawangan ti agas iti lamisaan.

"Resia, apayen?" Diak napengdan ti riknak a nagtugaw iti iking ti kama. Inallawatko ti imana a nakatanggaya. "Apay a binaybay-am ti bagim a nagbalin a kastoy?"

Naalumamay ken agbeddal ti sungbatna. "Dios ti agngina ta immaynak binisita. Sika ti ur-urayek. . . diak ammo, diak ammo no apay a kellaat a dimteng daytoy kaniak. Basta natumbaak latta idin ket intaraydak iti ospital. . . ngem maragsakanak ta immayka, Marissa. . . Ammok a napakawannakon. . . Ammom no ania ita ti ulit-ulitek a kiddawen iti Dios? Ikkannak koma pay iti kabarbaro a biag tapno masulnitak dagiti nagkurangak Kenkuana. Dinusanak siguro. . . Malagipmo daydi kankanayon a kunak kenka nga awan ti Dios ket ti kuarta laeng ti diosko? Uray gayam no adu ti kuartam no dumteng ti kastoy a pannubok, apagbiit la a mapukaw. Dakkelen ti naibayadko iti doktor, sa dagiti agkakangina nga agasko. Dandani maibus aminen dagiti naidepositok iti banko."

"Basta patibkerem laeng ti panunotmo. Agkararagka Kenkuana. Agpakawanka. Saan a managbaybay-a ti Dios!"

Piniselna a siirut ti dakulapko. "Ita la a maamirisko ti dakkel a panagbiddutko. Please. . . tulongannak nga agkararag. Idawatannak koma iti pammakawan kadagiti napasakitak iti eskuelatayo. No malasatak daytoy, saankon a kayat ti agsubli iti eskuela. Ibukbokko aminen a panawenko nga agserbi iti Dios!"

Pagpaturog siguro ti agasna. Nakaridep ni Resia kalpasan ti panagtomarna. Diak nagawidan manen dagiti nagarimayang a luak. Iti panagkitak, kasla mabiiten a mapan. Nagkararagak a sililimed iti abayna.

SAANEN a nagbayag ti ipupusay ni Resia iti daydi isasarungkarko. Adu met ti dimmar-ay iti daydi pumponna. Dimteng met ti dua a kabsatna agraman dagiti kabagianna a nangato ti takemna iti probinsia. Baliktad ti panangiladawan ni Resia kadakuada iti pudno a biag. Kinapudnona, isuda pay ti nangyopreser ken ni Gerald a mangisayangkat iti gastos iti pamumpon—wenno no pudno man daydi inlatak ni Resia kaniak, plastik ti impakita dagitoy a tao kadakami ket ni pay Resia ti imparangda nga adda biddutna. —0

Bannawag: Hulio 15, 1996.

Adda Dios, Joan

MA'AM, PUDNO kadi nga adda Dios?" kinuna ni Joan. Sangapulo-ket-limanan. Agarup agkataytayagkami.

"Adda Dios, Joan. Apay, agduaduaka?"

"No pudno nga adda Dios, Ma'am, apay a kastoy manen ti mapaspasamak kaniak? Apay a pinanawannakon ni Sister Didi? Isu a nagkuna ken nagkari nga ikkannak iti silaw tapno diakton mayaw-awan."

"Siempre, pimmanawen ta nalpasan ti misionna ditoy Filipinas. Kayatna a sawen matungpalen daydi karina nga alaenaka idiay America. Subliannakanto kas iti imbagana iti daydi naudi a panagsaritami. Isu nga igaedmo ti agadal."

"Pagtaltalawennak ni Sister Leona iti boarding house, Ma'am. . ."

"Adda ngata, a, naarammidmo a dina kayat?"

"Ipapilitna a tinakawko 'toy anteohos ken relo nga us-usarek idinto nga inregalo ni Sister Didi dagitoy sakbay a nagawid."

"Dimo imbaga?"

"Imbaak, Ma'am, ngem saan a mamati. Saan kano nga agtatakkon ni Sister Didi nga igatangannak iti kastoy ti kinapategna. Ipapilitna a tinakawko ta napukaw kano ti gamit ti maysa a gayyemna a dimmaw-as idi iti boarding house isu a nasungbatak, Ma'am. Diak ammo no apay a kasdiay ti ugali ni Sister Leona. Agsupadi unay ti ugalida ken ni Sister Didi. Padpadaksenna pay ni Sister Didi, Ma'am, idinto nga agpadada met a misionaria."

"Padpadaksenna iti ania a gapu, Joan?"

"Maipanggep iti libro nga inaramid ni Sister Didi maipapan kaniak. Kuna ni Sister Leona nga isu nga inaramid ni Sister Didi ti libro tapno makakolekta iti dakkel a kantidad kadagiti kameng ti simbaanmi."

Ita la a nangngegko ti maipapan iti libro. "Libro, kunam, Joan? Adda kopiana kenka?"

"Adda, Ma'am. . ."

Inruar ni Joan ti asul ti akkubna a libro. Ne, ket ni met Joan nga agpayso ti nailadawan iti akkubna.

Pinalabsak ti umuna a panid ti libro.

"Adu gayam ti diak ammo maipapan kenka, Joan," kinunak.

"Ma'am, ket no dika met ngamin agsalsaludsod. Sa no malpas ti klasetayo, pagawidennak metten a dagus. Manmano laeng a makapagsaritata. Ita man laeng, Ma'am, nga awanen ni Sister Didi a malukatak ti riknak kenka."

"Ammok nga adu ti obligasionko iti boarding house isu a kasta ti ar-aramidek kenka. . . Ania, mabalin a bulodek 'toy libro? Isublikto no bigat."

"Amangan no awanak no bigat, Ma'am. . ."

"Ta apay?"

"Umakarak iti balay ti maysa a kameng ti simbaanmi."

Nabatingting ti maikasangapulo-ket-dua nga oras. Nalpaskon ti ar-aramidek. Orasen tapno agawidak. Absent ti para malem a Maestra a kaduak ditoy kuarto. Palpaliiwek ni Joan. Saan pay a nagkir-in iti tugawna.

"No adda pay mangburburibor iti nakemmo, ipeksam aminen tapno matulonganka," kinunak.

"Agingga ita, Ma'am, burburtia latta kaniak no apay a nayanakak, no apay a kagurguranak ni Tatangko, ken no apay a napasamak dagiti diak ninamnama a pasamak. Isu a no dadduma, umapay latta kaniak ti panagduadua no pudno nga adda Dios. No adda man, saan a patas ti panangipategna kadatayo. Adda dagiti kaykayat ken idaddadumana."

"Adda Dios, Joan. Ikkatem ti panagduadua iti nakemmo ta dakes dayta. No adda dagiti kunam a pasamak a dimo ninamnama, dimtengda agsipud ta adda mensahe a kayatda nga ipaawat. Awan ti ama a di mangipatpateg iti anakna."

"Siak ngarud dayta nga anak, Ma'am. Baliktad ti amak. Saan met ngarud a bagtit. Kagurguranak iti pannakayanakko a nakatayan ti inak. Dinak inay-aywanan ti amak. Impadawatnak iti maysa a baket, daydi Lola Basilia a taga-Badoc. Ngem idi dandanin matay daydi a baket, pinaayabanna ti amak ket insublinak kenkuana. Pito ti tawenko idi. Il-iliwek ti pannakaipategko a kas anak, ngem pulos a diak narikna dayta. Tinagabonak ti hostess a kabitna. Pinareypnak idi agtawenak iti walo tapno adda isugalna. Idi nagipulongak ken ni tatangko, imbes nga isakitnak, kinabilnak pay ket imbagana a padpadaksek ti kabitna.

"Naglibasak. Awan ammok a papanan. Nagsangsangitak. Kayatko pay idin ti tumapuak iti derraas. Ngem nakitadak da Lolo Asiong ken Lola Tina. Naasianda kaniak. Innaladak. Imbilangdak a saan a sabsabali kadakuada."

"Apay a didaka pinagbasa?"

"Adayo ti eskuelaan, Ma'am, sa kunada ngamin, a no nagaget la ketdi ti maysa a tao uray awan adalna a kas kadakuada, bumaknang. Uray kano no kursom amin a kurso no nasadutka met, awan asenso. Mannalonda. Nalawa ti bangkag a mulmulaanda iti Trinidad Valley. Insursurotdak iti sadino man a papananda. Aglaklakokami iti tiendaan. No adu unay ti nateng, agipapakiawkami."

"Ayanda itan?"

"Nabayagdan a natay, Ma'am. Inulidakami dagiti armado a lallaki iti maysa a rabii. Nakaabungotda. Pinatayda da lolo ken lola sada innala dagiti kuartada iti aparador. Didak nakita ta naglemmengak iti sirok ti katre."

"Kalpasan ti pamumpon, awan nangala a kaarrubayo kenka?"

"Awan, Ma'am. Imbagada a siak kano ti gapu a nagmalasan dagiti baket ken lakay. Iti tiendaan ti nangawisan kaniak ti maysa a kataebko a babai a nakaibagaak iti problemak. Inawisnak nga agyan ken ni Ate Celia. Adukami nga ubbing a tarakenna. Insuronakami nga agsipdut, aggilet iti bag, agrabsut iti kuentas ken aglako iti shabu!"

Simriamak kadagiti palawag ni Joan. No kasta, agpayso daydi ballaag ti maysa a nagannak kaniak idi nabiit pay a naglukat ti klase. "Annadam dayta kadakkelan nga eskuelam, Ma'am. Number one kano nga esnatser ken mannanakaw dayta a dati a taga-Baguio!"

"Nagustuam ti kasta a biagmo?"

"Saan, Ma'am, dakami amin, dimi kayat. Ngem kapilitan. Awan met sabali a mangipateg kadakami no di ni Ate Celia ken ti butiog a lakayna a manmano la a makitami. Kuna ni Ate Celia, naulpit kano ti tao. Ti namay-an dagiti tao kenkuana ti nangiduron tapno aramatenna dagiti ubbing a pagibalesna."

"Adut' kuartam nga it-itedna?"

"Para merienda laeng, Ma'am. Uray kano ta dikami met manglangan a mangan ken naimas ti sidsidami."

"Dagiti polis, didaka tiltiliwen?"

Intudo ni Joan ti dakkel a piglat iti takiag ken mugingna. "Kakaasiak idi damo ti namay-anda, Ma'am. Sinit ti sigarilio ti piglat iti mugingko ket gapuanan met ti dos-por-dos ti piglat iti takiagko. Limmabanak ngamin idi. Ngem idi agangayen, saandakamin a sagsagiden nga agkakadua ta mangmangted ni Ate Celia ti bingay kadagiti polis. Sinsinan ipresintodakami no matiliwandakami ngem no makalikuddan, awaganen dagiti polis ni Ate Celia ket umaynakami metten iruar. Dagiti pay, a, polis ti mangibaga no sadino ti papananmi pagsipdutan."

Nangemkemak iti daytoy nga impudno ni Joan.

"Kasano a nagkitakayo ken ni Sister Didi?"

"Magmagnada idi iti asideg ti Burmham Park, Ma'am. Talloda. Nalabsanda ti puestok. Inagawko nga intaray ti dakkel a bagna. Nagikkis. Apagisu met idi a limmabas ti maysa a highway patrol. Nakamatannak. Naiprisintoak. Ti dakesna, kabarbaro dagiti nakaduty a polis. Inawagak ni Ate Celia ngem imbaga ti kaduak a natiliw dagti NBI sa impa-Manilada ta natiktikanda nga agideldeliber iti shabu iti Manila. Pampanunotek no kasano a makalibasak idi. Lalo a naiturong ti gurak iti amak ken ti kabitna. No saan a gapu kadakuada, saan koma a kastoy ti kasasaadko.

"Maysa nga aldaw, nasdaawak idi imbaga ti guardia a napiansaanakon. Idi rimmuarak tapno maam-ammok ti nangpiansa kaniak, kasla timmakder amin ti buokko idi nabigbigko ni Sister Didi a nakaiggem kadagiti papelesko. Umis-isem idinto a kaslaak la marunrunaw nga asin.

"Inyam-ammona ti bagina. 'Joan, siak ni Sister Didi. Maysaak a misionaria iti relihionmi, a naibaon ditoy Filipinas. Tulonganka nga agbalbaliw nga agsubli ken ni Apo Dios.'

"Daydi pay laeng ti kaunaan a nangngegko a pammalakad nga immukuok iti barukongko. Nagsangitak iti sango ni Sister Didi. Nagpakawanak kenkuana.

"Intugotnak iti boarding house a yanna idiay Quezon City. Tinungpalna ti karina nga ipategnak a kas maysa a kabsat. Saan a nauma a namalbalakad kaniak. Inkarina a pagbasaennak agingga a makaalaak iti kurso. Sangapulo-ket-tallo ti tawenko idi inserreknak iti Grade One. Diak nagbain ta kayatko a suplian ti kinasayaatna."

"Joan," kinunak, "Ni Sister Didi ti instrumento ti Dios tapno makitam ti awag ken marikram ti pudno nga ayatna."

"Apay a saan a patien ni Sister Leona a nagbalbaliwakon?"

DUA A babbai ti nasangpetak iti batog ti kuartok iti maysa a bigat. Babaen ti naganda iti tag a nakakapet iti baruongda, ni Sister Leona ti maysa.

"Ania ti maipaayko kadakayo, Sister?" kinunak nga umis-isem. Nagtalinaed a napasnek dagiti rupada. Ammok lattan a ni Joan ti gagarada.

"Dakayo ni Mrs. Marissa del Prado a maestra ni Joan?" nagdamag ni Sister Leona.

"Siak, Sister."

"Napateg unay ti nakaidaw-asanmi ditoy, Mrs. del Prado. Kayatmi la a mangngeg kadagiti bibigmo no sumsumrek pay la ni Joan wenno saanen."

"Saan nga agliwliwat ni Joan, Sister," knunak.

"Makadominggo itan a di sumangsangpet ni Joan iti boarding house. Pimmanaw idi sinitarko maipapan iti relo ken anteohos."

"Inregalo ni Sister Didi kenkuana ti relo ken anteohos sakbay a nagawid."

"Saan nga agmauyong ti maysa a misionaria a regaluanna ti kas ken ni Joan iti kasdiay kanginana a relo ken anteohos. Nabayag ngaminen

a napukaw ti relo ken antehohos ti maysa a kaduami nga immay iti boarding house."

No kasta, saan nga ammo ni Sister Leona ti panggep ni Sister Didi a mangalanto ken ni Joan idiay America?

"Ni Joan t itudom a nangala, kasta kadi, Sister?"

"Pimmanaw a di nagpakpakada kalpasan daydi panangsitarko, di nalawag nga isu ti nangala? Ket no dimo pay ammo ken tapno agannadka, adalam ti maysa kadagiti kasiglatan a mannanakaw ken mannipdut a taga-Baguio! Isu a dimmaw-asak tapno ballaaganka, ken tapno kiddawek metten ti tulongmo a no mabalin, dawatem ti relo ken anteohos ken ni Joan."

"Kunak man no tulonganyo nga agbalbaliw ken tumakder manen a sumango iti biag ti kas ken ni Joan, Sister? Nagdamdamagkayo kadin no ania a gapu ti nagbalinan ni Joan a mannaanakaw ken mannipdut idi?"

"Saanak a kas ken ni Sister Didi a konsintidor. Nasken a maammuam, Maestra, a no saan a gapu iti mision, saan koma a tao daydiay a Joan! Tumulongak no tumulongak ngem piliek ti tulongak."

Rimmasuk ti riknak iti daytoy a nangngegko. Ania a klase a misionaria daytoy a babai? Nupay kasta, naalumamay ti timekko.

"Sister Leona, tapno ibagak kenka ti pudno, awan anteohos ken relo a tinakaw ni Joan. Ginatang ni Sister Didi ti relo ken anteohos a kas regalona kenkuana. Ken ammom, agsublinto ni Sister Didi tapno umayna alaen ni Joan ket ituloynanto ti agadal idiay America. Maymaysa nga inanak ni Sister Didi ket kayat dagiti dadakkelna nga alaen ni Joan tapno adaptarenda a kas anak."

"Uray gayam sika, Maestra, nabrainwashnaka metten ti mannanakaw nga eskuelam!"

Simleng ti panagkitak ken ni Sister Leona. "Naim-imbag pay ti maysa a Puraw a kas ken ni Sister Didi ta ammona nga ipateg ken isakit ti maysa a kadaraantayo a kas ken ni Joan. Naimbag pay kenkuana ta kasingin ti panagmisionna ti naimpusuan a panagserbi a saan la nga iti Dios no di pay ket iti padana a tao. Mabalinyon ti pumanaw, Sister Leona, no awanen ti ibagayo kaniak!"

AGPITO A tawenen ti napalabas manipud idi, naammuak laengen babaen ti surat a nasuroken a lima a tawen ni Joan idiay America. Kinapudnona, nalipatakon ni Joan manipud idi nagsubli ni Sister Didi ditoy Filipinas tapno ipagnana dagiti papeles ni Joan. Nangasawa payen ni Sister Didi iti maysa a Filipino a misionario met idi ket addaandan iti dua nga annak. —0

Bannawag: Nobiembre 11, 1966.

Pagbiagan No Malasat

RUMMUAR-SUMREKAK iti wangwang a patio ti bassit a trailer a pagnaedanmi a mangwanwanawan iti isasangpet ni Marla manipud idiay Coachella. Makasuronak ta imbes nga isu ti makitak iti ruangan ti balayda, ti ketdi dakkel a nangisit a bulldogda.

"No ager-errado daydiay a kaanakam, ipakitakon ti ilemlemmengko!" kinunak idi rabii iti duduogan a lakayko, ket inulitko itay makariingak. "No di gapu iti kinatarabitabna, di koma pimmampanaw da Siding ken Ibing. Siguro, kasdiay ti insursuro ni Manang Asiang a kabagismo!" Adda iti maikatlo a kalsada manipud iti yanmi ti balay ni Manang Asiang.

"Dimo iramraman 'diay tao, Baket. Dinaka met masagsagid," kinuna ni lakay. "Ken saanen a Filipinas ditoy. . . tiliwenda ti ap-apera!"

"Ayna, basta tandaanam, Lakay, ipakitakon ti ilemlemmengko, no kunak. Amangan no iti panagkuna ni Marla, gapu ta napanglawak laeng a naikamang kadakayo, kastoy lattan a di malamlamut ti aso ti panagsasaona. No saan a kasdiay ti ngiwatna, di koma nagliblibas da Siding ken Ibing. No ania ti biagda itan, diak la ammon. Amangan no inton bigat, wenno sanga'ldaw, addan polis nga umay mangibaga a naaksidenteda wenno nareypda. Wenno innala ida dagiti durugista. Yad-adayom, Apo!"

"Adu la unay. Dimo ket ikarkararag nga addada iti nasayaat nga ima. Ni Marla, uray no tarabitab, manangisagut. Inikkannaka iti microwave, sa adu pay a makmakan. Ala, agkararagka man ketdi, nasaysayaat ngem ti la pagtaltalawatawan ti panunotmo."

"Nalipatakon ti agkararag! Naibusen dagiti luak. Bagim lattan. Bagbagaymo ta ditoyka lattan trailer a nakadalukappit nga agmalmalem!"

Walopulo-ket-maysan ni lakay ngem gapu ta uppat-a-pulo-ket-maysaak pay laeng, narimat pay laeng dagiti matana a mangsirsirig kaniak.

Natannawagak ni Alona a nakabitbit iti timba nga agpakkapakkang nga umas-asideg iti yanmi. Adda la ketdi manen ipadamag daytoy a masikog nga agab-abang met iti sabali pay a trailer da Marla. Idi addaak pay idiay Filipinas, impagarupko no ania ti trailer. Balay gayam a kasla kaha ti bus nga adda pilidna a mabalin a paguyoden a yakar iti sadino man a kayat a pangipanan, saan a kas iti trailer a pagbumbunag dagiti negosiante iti tabako idiay Kailokuan.

"Apay, 'ya, a kasla Biernes Santo manen 'ta rupam? Bigbigat, dika ket koma umisem," kinunana. Inggiddanna nga insan-ek ti bitbitna a timba. Nagparasipis dagiti tilapia. "Ne, mangalakan. Adu ti nabanniitan ni Andy itay parbangon ket innak ipan iti yan da Nana Orang ta isu ti aglako."

Kasla diak nangngeg ni Alona. Nagbannikesak a timmakder iti nagtugawak. "Ammom no ania ti pampanunotek?" inwitwitko. "No awan ti nasayaat a damag iti napanan ni Marla, pagsasawak metten iti di malamut ti aso. Ipakitakon ti kinatarabitabko! Awan mangatiw kaniak idiay Nagbakuitan tapno ammom!"

"Apay, 'ya?"

"No mano a rabii itan a diak makaturturog a mangpampanunot no sadino a lubong ti yan da Siding ken Ibing."

"Aniakan sa? No kimmuyogda kano kadagiti kakaduada a nag-picking ti ubas idiay Moreno. Awan siguro ti telepono iti nagtarusanda isu a dida makaawag."

"A, basta! Apaek ni Marla no awan ti nasayaat a damag nga isangpetna!"

"Mangalaka ket iti tilapian ket aldawen. Tapno ibagak kenka, dimo kabaelan ni Marla. Awan pay ti nakabael a nangapa kenkuana. Abusta tarabitab, kasla aparador pay ti bagina. No gammatannaka nga igusugos sa pandagannaka, dika pay narim-it? Numona ket kaska la burrarawit!"

"Padasenna ta idarumko. 'Mangan no 'pagarupna a diak ammo ti kalintegak. Ken binulan nga agbaybayadak iti upa kenkuana! No kunak nga idarumko, idarumko!"

"Ayna, ba'am daytan. Inka ket mangala 'ti pangikkam 'toy tilapian, da. Aldawen."

"Awan pagbayadko. Awan pay kuartami."

"Bayadamto no sumangpet ti pension ni lakaymo."

Nagsennaayak idi nakapanawen ni Alona. Ilokana met a kas kaniak. Taga-La Union. Nakaumay ditoy America ta beterano ni Tatangna a kas 'toy duduogan a lakayko. Ti dakesna, nakasirpat ni Tatangna iti Mehikana nga ub-ubing ken napimpintas ngem ni Nanangna. Dida ammon no sadino a suli ti California ti paglemlemmenganda. Idi nakapagtrabaho ni Alona iti maysa a klinika idiay San Diego, nasirpat ni Alejandro a maysa met a Filipino, ket nagkinnaawatanda. Nagkasarda iti di pay nabayag idiay Las Vegas. Butiten ni Alona idi maammuanna a dua a babbai ti immuna a nakadenna ni Alejandro. Maysa ti Amerikana a naanakanna a pinanawanna idiay San Jose. Ti la adda a pangay-ayo ni Alejandro no kasta a makalagip ni Alona. Uray ta is-isu kano met la ti inkasarna.

Nasinga ti panagpampanunotko idi matapik ti abagak. Inayabannak ni lakay. "Nakalutoka kadin, Baket?" kinermannak. No kasta ti idiarna, dua ti kayatna a sawen.

"Nakaapuyakon. Nalutok payen ti sidaen. Mangankan no mabisinka. Urayek pay ni Marla."

"Ne, ket presko man dagita tilapia. Agkulkulagtitda pay a kas kaniak. Makasidsidaak man 'ti sinigang, Baket."

"Di agsinigangka no makasidsidaka. Dinak kurkuriruen no kastoy a kasla labba ti kadagsen ti ulok!"

"Ibabam, a, Baket, tapno lumag-an."

"Ay-ay, dinak man lamlamiongen a laklakaddogan ta madi a talaga ita ti ulok!"

"Inka nga'd agidasaren, a, ket mabisinakon."

Husto a sumangokami a mamigat idi adda nagbanurbor a simrek iti nalawa nga inaladan. Ni Marla nga agpayso. Ap-aprosannan ti bulldog nga asona. Kasla tao a makaawat iti sao ti bulldog. Isu ti para bantay iti

dakel a balay ni Marla. Tumakderak koman a mangengkuentro ken ni Marla ngem inatipanak ni lakay.

"Tutorem ti mangan tapno adda pamigsam nga iwasawasna," kinunana.

"Ay, saan nga ager-errado dayta a kaanakam ta makitana la ketdi ti ilemlemmengko!"

"Agtanangka kadi, a, Baket. Laglagipem a dita pay nakabayad iti utangtayo kenkuana. Ken di mabalin nga ipakitam ti ilemlemmengmo ta siak la ti adda karbenganna a makakita."

"Pilosopo a laklakayan!" Ngem imbes a kasuronko, kas kadagiti kallabes a nalunag ti riknak iti nalamuyot a panagsarsaritana. Ti la lagidawek itoy a duduogan ta no adda ibaga ni Marla, wen amin, a kasla dina ammo ti agsao't saan. Dina pay sinupring wenno inungtan la koma.

Di nagbayag, adda nanakraad iti abay ti trailer a yanmi. Simmiripak. Ni Marla a kasta unay ti rungiitna.

"Aniat' damag, Nakkong?" kinunak. Ninakkongko ta pangalay-ayko iti mangrugi manen nga agsibo a riknak.

"Pastrekennak pay, a, Anti, sakanto sungbatan."

Simrek a kasta unay ti dagsen dagiti paddakna. Naganit-it ti nagtugawanna. Am-amkek la a malupisak ti tugaw. Naituon dagiti matak iti akak ni Marla. Grabe a talaga. Kurang la a dumanonen iti barukongna.

"Awanen ti pagdanaganyo. Nasayaaten ti trabaho da Siding idiay Moreno. Isu a dida nakaawag ta awan telepono ti immuna a kaserada 'ti makadominggo. Ngem adda itan ta iti yan da Komadre Isang ti immakaranda."

"Nakasaom ida, Nakkong?"

"Wen, isuda a dua, Anti. Awagandakayonto kano no Domingo. Talaga kano nga inggagarada ti di immawag."

Nakaangesak iti nalukay. "Mano a bulanda kano idiay, Nakkong?"

"Agyanda kano't 'diayen!"

"A-ania?" naapputko pay ti lapayagko a nagliteng iti pigsa ti ngiwatko.

Natnag met ti timid ni lakay.

Nagpaggaak ni Marla; kurang la nagpallayog ti akakna.

"Saan kadi. . . Dua wenno tallo a bulan, kunada met, Anti. Leppasenda kano ti panagpipiking iti ubas tapno addanto met la yawatda a bayad ti il-iliwmo!"

"Kasta unay ti danag ni ikitmo," kinuna ni lakay.

"Anti, uray ta nasolbaren ti problemam, kuyogendakto man no malem. Duakayo ken Alona."

"Papanantayo manen?"

"Intay agtakaw iti sandia," inyellekna.

"Salve Ari. Mandiak la ketdi!"

"'Nia ketdin. Makapangpanganak la't kappisi."

Pagsasao daytoy a Marla ti agtakaw. Namin-dun nga imbusonakami ken Alona a napan nagala iti paria, utong ken saluyot iti arubayan ti diak am-ammo a pulano wenno pulana a padami met laeng a Filipino. Awan dagiti akinkukua. Ti dakesna, dakami laeng ken Alona ti padissaagenna iti kotsena a mapan agpuros. No agawidkamin, kasta unayen ti ellekna.

Imbagak idin a dina pay la ipakada iti akinkukua ngem ti kasta a liblibasenna ti panagalana. Kasla ketdin naim-imas a kabukabenna ti liblibasenna.

"No ipakadam, mangtedda ngarud?" irasonna nga itingig pay.

"Ania, mapanak manen iti ibagbagana?" sinaludsodko ken ni lakay idi nakapanawen ni Marla.

"Uray no dimo kayat, isunto met la ti matungpal," kinuna ni lakay. "Inka lattan tapno awan ti riri."

"Por dios. Pulos a diak napadpadasan ti nagtakaw bayat ti panagbiagko. Ditoy ketdin America ti pagtaktakawak! 'Bag no makasaklangak pay ken ni Apo Dios no matayak?"

"Uray ta saanto met a siksika, Baket. Kaduamto da Marla."

"Ay, ay, ay! Pakpakawan!"

"Dika latta agtagtagari ngaruden, Baket," nagkaradap iti luppok ti kasla trapal a dakulap 'toy laklakaddugan. "Ti naanus, isu ti anak ti Dios," ingkilitna ket kurang la matnag ti piwis a bibigna iti panangsirigna kaniak.

Winitwitak ni lakay. "Tandaanam daytoy, sika a laklakayan," kinunak bayat ti in-inut a pannakaalep-ep ti mangrugi koma manen nga agkubuar a riknak. Diak la maawatan ti riknak ta kaslaak la aglusdoy

iti lamuyot ti panagsasaona. "No isarsaraknak daydiay a kaanakam, makauray iti di nasayaat!"

"Inta pay ngarud aginana, baket. . ."

Agalas tresen iti malem idi mangngegko ti pukkaw ni Marla. Kaririingko iti pannakailibayko iti abay ni lakay. Bimmangonak ket nagdardarasak a rimmuar iti siled. Nasiripko a kasta unay ti pakkapakkang ni Alona nga immabay ken ni Marla.

Diak la koma talaga kayat ti mapan ngem utro ngamin ni lakay.

"Inkan tapno awan mangngeg a sao," dinagdagnak.

Medio agraed ti nalabaga a pik-ap ni Marla idi panurnurenmi ti kalsada a nagbaetan ti nalawa a kataltalonan nga awan tambakna, a kasla awan patinggana. Nalabasanmi ti nalawa a kaubasan sa dagiti sangkis a kasta unay ti panaggilap dagiti amarilio a bungada a namirrayon iti darang ti init. Iti umay a bulan, kasla kutonto manen dagiti agpiking iti tengnga ti gumayebgeb a disierto. Awan ti pakaikarian ti pudot ti Filipinas iti pudot ditoy. Nalpasen ti panagpipiking iti kaubuasan, a nakaibilangak. No namin-ano a nadalupoak gapu iti pudot. Ti sangsangitko idi. Inlunodko no apay a nakadanonak iti daytoy nga impierno.

Insardeng ni Marla ti luganna iti nalinged bassit a nagbaetan ti kasangkisan ken kasandiaan, a kunana a papananmi. Ania ket nga agpayson a nagdadakkel dagiti naluom a bunga ti sandia nga agkaiwara iti kataltalonan.

"Ala, dumsaagkayon, Anti, ta kargaanyon 'toy pik-ap. Alaenyo 'toy kutsilio, ney."

Naggudengkami ken Alona.

"No adda ngay makakita kadakami?" kinuna ni Alona. "Amangan no maanakanak a dina oras!"

"Dika pay aganak. Ngem no aganakka, paltotenka no kuan. Ammok ti mamartera, ibagak kenka. Ala, inkayon. Siak ti makaammo kadakayo!"

"Addaka, a, ngem saan met a sika ti agpuros ken agikarga," kinunak met. "No matiliwankami, ket ibaluddakami ngay?"

"Awan takrot nga Ilokano! No mabaludkayo, umaykayto sakaen. Am-ammok ni hepe."

Immuna ni Alona a rimmuar. Simmarunoak. Dinardarasmi a gineppas iti pupurosan dagiti dadakkel a bunga ti sandia. Nagdadagsenda ketdin! Di nakateppel ni butit. Pmmisi iti maysa. Ingguduaannak. Nasam-it ken nalamiis. Inimasmi ti nagkurab. Talaga a sabali ti sam-it dagiti sandia ditoy.

"Alistuam, intan!" kinunak idi addan duapulo a nabilangko a napurosmi.

Naganangsabak idi maisalpak ti dua kadagiti naudi a binagkatko iti likudan ti pik-ap.

"Aganakak san, sika!" pinagtulid ni Alona dagiti bukelbukel ti matana idinto a sinarapana ti bokstina idi maisalpana met ti maudi a sakruyna.

Kasta unay rungiit ni Marla. Siniputak ti panagbirrayon ti akakna. "Kasta ti biag ditoy," kinunana. "Pagbiagan ti sikap no malasat!"

"Ipatay no malas!" kinunak met.

Husto a paandaren ni Marla ti lugan idi adda nagbosina iti adayo a likudanmi.

"Adda nakakita kadatayo!" kinunak. Nagtambor ti barukongko.

Kasla nakirog a rasa ti rupa ni Marla. Di nakapagbuelo ta asidegen ti nangisit a pik-ap iti likudanmi.

"Apay a nagpuroskayo a di nagpakpakada?" makasuron ti maysa kadakuada. Daras a dimsaagda iti luganda. Dua a lallaki. Mehikanoda.

"Nalapsat ngamin ti bunga dagiti sandiam isu a naay-ayokami, pogi." Anian a naggayad ti isem ni Marla. "Naayatan dagitoy kakaduak a nagpuros. Nasam-it, kunada man, ta nanganda pay dita nagpurosanda."

"M-Marla!" nayesngawko. Apo, ta isarsaraknakamin!

Kasla nasukaan metten a bagsang ni Alona.

"No comprende Inglese?" intudo ti maysa kadagiti Mehikano ti karatula a NO TRESPASSING.

Nagbaliw ti maris ti rupa ni Marla. "Hey, wait!" kinunana a kasla adda naglawag a bombilia iti mugingna. "Saan a sika ti akinkukua. Am-ammok ti akinkukua. Yannan ti green cardmo?"

Kinita ti lalaki ti kaduana.

"Uray sika, yan ti green cardmo?" Dimsaagen ni Marla ket binannikesanna dagiti dua. "All right, awan ti green cardyo. Kayatyo ta ipulongkayo?"

"No senorita. . . no senora!" Naarakattot dagiti dua. Nagdardarasdan a limmugan iti pik-apda.

Intarus ni Marla ti luganmi iti trailer ni Manang Asiang a Nanangna. "Paramanantayo. Tapno awan met ti kunkunana," kinuna ni Marla.

Dayta met ketdi ti dayawek ken ni Marla. Managpaburiraw.

Nalawa ti rungiit ni Manang Asiang a nakakita kadagiti sandia a sakruymi ken Alona.

"Nagdadakkelen!" indayaw ni Manang Asiang. "Nangalaanyo?"

Intudok ni Marla. "Pinatakawna, Manang," kinunak.

"Salbagkayo! Diak la ketdi kayat ti mairamraman iti basolyo!" Nagsariwagwag. "Isubliyo iti luganyo!"

Husto met nga umasideg ni Marla. Ngimmato dagiti kidayna.

"Sika, Marla, mangisungsongka. Di met kasta ti insursurok kenka. . !"

"Dikay' ket agyaman ta umaydakayo paramanan," imbirakak ni Marla. "Dimo patpatien ni Anti. Dinawatmi dagita kadagiti Mehikano!"

"Met la gayam!" Nakagaygayad ti isem ni Manang Asiang. Makakatawa met a saan ni Alona a nangsurot ken ni Marla iti lugan.

"Komustanto la ni *Manong*en," kinuna ni Manang Asiang a nangipabolsa iti pantalonko iti nalukot a papel de banko. "Adda bassit inabakko iti kasino idi rabii," inkissiimna. "Dimo ibagbaga ken ni Marla."

Nadanonmi ni Franz, asawa ni Marla, iti balayda. Agpagnapagna iti arubayan. Dandanogenna ti angin.

"Napnapanam, aya, a babai ta dimo inkandado ti ruangan?" kinuna daytoy ken ni Marla. Kasla kumilaw dagiti matana.

"Apay, 'ya?"

"Awanen ni bulldog. Pati kawarna!"

"Ania?"

Kurang la agpallayog a nagtaray ni Marla a napan iti sidiran ti balayda. Idiay la ketdi ti nangibatianna itay iti bulldogda. Idi kuan, nagugaogen. Inlunlunodna ti asino man a nangala iti asoda. Awan sabali

a pabasolenna no di dagiti durugista a sinursuruan dagiti Filipino nga agsida iti aso. Maiparit ti agsida iti aso iti America ngem adu latta ti makalibas.

Nagsubli ni Marla iti yanmi. Binaw-inganna ni Franz. "Amangan no sika met la ti nangpapulpog ken ni bulldog!" inyikkisna. "Nalaingka nga agsida't aso. Pinatakawmo kadagiti gagayyemmo!"

"Tiritirekto pay 'ta tengngedmo no pabasolennak!" inwitwit met ni Franz. "Bimmabbabay-anka a ballog!"

Sinangonakami ni Marla. "Anti, mangalakayon iti sandiayo ken Alona ta innak agreport ken ni hepe!"

"Adda pay ita para bantay!" kinuna met ni Franz a kasla adda sabali a kasasaona.

"Dina nalasat, Baket," makakatkatawa met a makais-isem ni lakay a mangipipiano kadagiti ramayna iti luppok idi estoriaek ti napasamak. Kinermannak. —0

Bannawag: Agosto 6, 2001

2

LORENZO GARCIA TABIN, SR.

Tao Ken Panawen

DANDANI MALPASEN ti katkatamen ni Ama Valentin a paradipad ti karatela idi dumteng ni Manolito.

"Kunak no saankan nga agsubli?" kinuna ni Ama Valentin.

"Nagdigosak pay ngamin, Tata," insungbat ti baro.

Apagisu nga umulog ni Herminia, ti kakaisuna nga anak ni Ama Valentin, a mapan sumakdo. Kinerman ni Manolito ti balasang idi kumita daytoy. Linibbian ni Herminia.

"Isimpam bassit 'diay atepnan," nagtimek ni Ama Valentin. "Kitaem no agkurang ta mangagiska iti daydiay maysa a galba." Saanna nga insardeng ti aramidna ket dina nadlaw ti panangsipsiput ni Manolito ken ni Herminia.

"Wen gayam, Tata," kinuna ni Manolito idi ar-aramidennan ti naibilin, "nalabasak ni Mang Castor. Paibabawina ti paspasangalna. Awan kano pay ti kuartana ta nagastona kanon daydi isagsaganana."

"Nagastona?" nagkuretret ti muging ti lakay.

"Kua, tata... Nadlawko ket kasla pambarna laeng dayta ta agsasaritada itay kada Mang Timot maipanggep iti panagsangal iti karetela. Magustuanda ti aramid ni Cardo. Kabaruanan kano a modelo ken nasayaat kano ti pannakasangalna. Awan met ketdi ti nasaoda maipanggep iti aramidta. Napigsa a kakompetensiata ni Cardo. Kitaem laengen, awan pay makatawenna, nalataken dagiti aramidna."

"Manipud pay idi punganay, siakon ti agar-aramid kadagiti pangukuartaanda." Insardeng ni Ama Valentin ti panagkatamna. "Amin dagiti karatela ditoy, siak ti nangsangal. Naglasatda amin iti imak. Ket

no dida nagustuan dagiti aramidko... Ala, addan ni Cardo, kunam. Kabaruanan a wagas ti aramidna. Nasayaat met no kasta."

"Nadagsen kano dagiti aramidta, tata. Nababaked kano unay dagiti tarikayona, ket gapu iti dayta, kakaasi kano dagitui kabalio nga agguyod."

Immisem ni Ama Valentin. "Ammoda a diak kayat ti agaramid iti narasi. Iti dida maaramat iti napaut. Kitaem dagiti aramidta, aglabas ti adu a tawen sa masapul ti pannakatarimaanna. Ngem nupay kasta, maragsakanak."

Nasdaaw ni Manolito iti naudi a sinao ti lakay. Dina impapan nga iti baet ti kaaddan ti kabalubalda, maragsakan pay. Ammona nga adda kinapudno dagiti kinuna ni Ama Valentin. Ngem ammona met ti dakkel unay a pakaibabaan daguiti ar-aramidenda: ti kinadaan ti wagas a pannakasangalda a maigidiat unay iti aramid ni Cardo—a nabiit pay a nagturpos iti kinakarpintero.

Nabiit pay a simmangpet ni Manolito manipud iti ipapanna itutulong a nagtalon idiay Isabela, iti yan da kasinsinna a Mauro. Nakurang a makatawenna sadiay. Sigud nga agkatunosanda ken ni Ama Valentin ket idi ngarud agsubli, inayaban ti lakay a kas katulongan.

Malemen idi isardengda ti aramidda. Sakbay a nagawid ni Manolito, napan iti kosina a yan ni Herminia nga aglutluto. Nabayag a nagmattider iti ridaw, ta saan a dagus a nadlaw ni Herminia.

Nagsig-am ni Manolito a nangipadlawanna iti kaaddana. Nakigtot ti balasang ket nagistayanna naibbatan ti kutsilio a paggalgalipna iti tarong a dengdengenna.

"Managkigkigtotka gayam," inkatawa ni Manolito.

"Sika ngamin. Kunak no asino itayen."

"Dispensarennak koma, Herming. Makiinumak koma."

"Inka man la tumakon," kinuna ni Herminia.

Idinto a mapan koma ni Manolito iti yan ti paginuman, nagtugaw ketdi iti bangko iti asideg ti balasang.

"Pumimpintaska iti panaglabas ti aldaw," kinunana.

"Kunak man no uminumka?"

"Makasingaak sa met. Innakon..." Timmakder sa timmallikud ni Manolito.

Idi makaulog, timmaliaw ket nasiputanna ti panangsirip ni Herminia kenkuana.

MALPASTON ti sangsangalen da Manolito ngem awan pay ti umay agpasangal. Saan a kas kadagiti napalabas nga aldaw. Adu pay idi ti taga-kabangibang a purok.

Nadlaw ni Manolito ti kinaulimek ni Ama Valentin. Saan a sigud a kasta ti lakay. No dadduma, isardengna ti aramidna ket agilad iti ulnas.

"Malagipmo kadi idi dita magebgeban ti trabahota?" inamad ni Ama Valentin.

"Wen, tata. Adu idi ti..."

"Ngem baliktad itan," ingguped ti lakay. Immisem sa nagtungtung-ed.

Insardeng ni Manolito ti panagkatamna ket kinitana ti lakay.

"Ammom kadi a di pulos immapay iti panunotko ti kastoy?" nagtimek manen ni Ama Valentin. "Ngem dimtengen. Ket ita la a mautobko nga amin a tao, uray no ania ti agdama nga aramidna wenno kasasaadna, dumteng met ti panagbalbaliwna. Iti panagtulid ti panawen, uray ti aldaw laeng, addan panagbalbaliw."

Saan a nagtimek ni Manolito.

"Rumbeng a mapasamak ti kastoy," intuloy ni Ama Valentin. "Ket iti pannakaaramidko iti namnamaek a napateg a banag, mariknak ita ti ragsak ken pannakapnek gapu iti panagpaay a naitedko kadakuada. Ngem iti sabali a bangir, malidayanak gapu ta diak napanunot nga insaganaan ti idadateng daytoy a pasamak. Awan koma ti aniamanna no sisiak laeng. Ngem ni Herminia ti pampanunotek. Balasang pay laeng. Awan ti sabali nga ammona nga aramiden no di agtagibalay. Kakaasinto..."

NAGPAKADA manen ni Manolito tapno mapan idiay Isabela a yan da kasinsinna a Mauro.

"Pumanawka manen?" nalidayan ti lakay.

"Wen, tata. Panagani manen ket ingguunamgunam ni Manong Mauro ti ipapanko ta awan ti katulonganna."

Nagulimek ti lakay, panagulimek a naawatan ni Manolito.

"Ladingitek ti panangpanawko kenka, tata. Dimo koma ipapan a pumanawak gapu iti mapaspasamak iti trabahota. Awan nga agpayso ti katulongan ni Manong Mauro, tata."

"Dimo met imbaga idi nga awanen ti panggepmo nga agsubli sadiay?"

"Kasta ti nakunak idi, tata. Ngem kasangsangpet ti surat ni Manong Mauro a nangipagedgedanna iti ipapanko."

"Kaano ngarud ti luasmo?"

"Inton malem, tata."

"Dikanto koma mangliplipat, Manoling..."

"Mangnamnamakayo, tata. No saan la a gapu iti panangigunamgunam ni kasinsin, saanak koman nga agsubli sadiay."

NASUROKEN a makabulan ti kaadda ni Manolito idiay Isabela. Nalpasen ti panagani. Iti maysa a sardam a panagiladna iti ulnas iti sirok ti lungboy bayat ti panagpalpana, nalagipna ni Herminia. Pilpilitenna a lipaten ti balasang. Kinapudnona, adda koma idiay Kailokuan no saan a gapu iti kinapaidam ni Herminia. Kayatna a lipaten ti balasang.

Nakaawat iti surat a naggapu idiay balayda. Impadamag ni nanangna a natayen ni Ama Valentin.

Nagrubuat a dagus ni Manolito. Masapul nga agawid. Mapanna kitaen ni Herminia. Nadanonna ti balasang a malidliday nga agtamtamdag iti tawada.

"Makipagladingitak," kinuna ni Manolito idi agsangsangodan ken ni Herminia.

Saan a natengngel ni Herminia ti riknana. Nagsaibbek ket intakkabna dagiti dakulapna iti rupana.

"Nadamagko a panggepmo kano ti agpa-Manila, Herming," kinuna ni Manolito idi nagsardengen ti Herminia iti panagsangitna.

"Wen," nagbanarbar ti timek ti balasang, "innak mangged. Innak agbirok iti trabahok, uray no pababaon laeng."

"No sibibiag koma daydi tata, saanna nga ipalubos ti kasta a panggepmo."

"No sibibiag koma. Ngem awanen daydi tatang. Ket masapul nga agbiagak."

"Saankan nga agtuloy. No mayatka, no dimo tagidaksen, awisenka idiay Isabela, idiay yan da Kasinsin Mauro. Mabalinko ti umawat iti talonek idiay."

Nayangad ni Herminia ti rupana a sibabasa iti lua.

"Saanka dagdagen. Ammok a silaladingitka pay laeng. Kabayatanna, di la mabalin a kuyogennak a mapan idiay kamposanto? Kayatko met a masarungkaran daydi tata."

Dandani sumipngeten idi rummuarda iti kamposanto. Sidudumog pay laeng ni Herminia iti panagsangsangitna.

"Nagkariak iti daydi tata," kinuna ni Manolito. "Ket adda kenka ti pannakatungpal wenno pannakadadael ti karik kenkuana."

"Magusgustuannaka daydi tatang. Kinapudnona, sangkadagullitna idi ti ipapanawmo. Riniknana unay ti panagikay dagiti sigud a parokianona."

"Kinaguranak kadi met iti panangpanawko kenkuana?"

"Saan, ta ammona nga agsublikanto."

"Ngem awanen... ket sika laengen ti pagsubliak, no ipalubosmo."

"Bay-am a mangwaksiak koma pay, Manoling."

Pinerreng ni Manolito ni Herminia. "Wen," binirok ti kanawan nga imana ti dakulap ti balasang, "masapul a mangwaksita pay."—0

Bannawag: immuna a naipablaak idi Oktubre 4, 1965; sa idi Agosto 27, 2018.

Taaw Ken Daytoy A Babilonia

APAGISU a naguni ti sirena a mangipasimudaag iti maikalima iti malem idi tumamdag ni Willy Shaw iti andamio ti bapor. Nakitana dagiti aglulumba a trabahador manipud iti mabangbangon a pasdek iti sakaanan ti bantay tallopulo a metro manipud iti danum, nga agturong iti pagibellengan iti basura nga aggapu iti bapor. Uppat a dadakkel a lata, sagdudua a metro kuadrado, ti napagaabay a pagbasuraan. Sinipsiputanna dagiti mangmangged a nagiinnuna kadagiti naibasura a puraw nga unipormeda iri bapor; sumagmamano ti nagala iti makan, kas iti mansanas, sankis, tinapay, itlog ken karne nga imbelleng lattan dagiti kosinero ta mabalin a simmadutdan a mangisubli iti pagpalamiisan; ken, no ania pay ditan a mabalinda a kanen. Amin dagitoy nga innalada, ammo ni Willy Shaw a saandan a kaykayat iti bapor. No ngamin adda bassiten a mansa ti lupot, ibellengda lattan sada pasukatan—sumangpet latta ti abastoda kas kameng ti armada ti America. Manon dagiti imbelleng ni Willy Shaw nga unipormena? Adda pay daydi ginatangna a sibilian a lupot a dina pay nausar a pulos, imbellengnan agsipud ta bassit kenkuana. Dakkel ti pakaigidiatan dagiti Amerikano kadagiti Filipino, nautobna. Kastoyda gayam ditoy. Nabiitda pay a simmanglad ditoy Subic.

"Intayon, Willy," nasinga idi pagtimkan ni Roger Briant, ti gayyemna. "Dimo ikaskaso dagidiay," innayonna idi madlawna ti nakaiturongan ti panagkita ni Willy.

"Kakaasida met," inwingiwing ni Willy Shaw.

"Talaga a kastada. Inta ketdin."

Maysa laeng ti ruaran iti ruangan. Maysa met ti serkan, malaksid iti ruaran ken serkan dagiti lugan. Agpipila dagiti magmagna a rummuar. Addaanda amin iti pases. Marikisa amin dagiti rumuar.

Iti labes ti ruangan, sumagmamano a metro ti kaadayo, adda kinabiti a rangtay a kalalainganna iti kadakkel. Nakita dita ni Willy Shaw dagiti babbai nga iti langada dagitay 'mangliwliwa.' Babassit dagitoy no idiligna kadakuada. Kaaduanda ti pagatkilikilina laeng. Nalaingda nga agsigarilio, a tunggal sumusopda, maalian iti nalabaga ti aammolan ti sigarilio. Saanda a napintas iti langada. Ngem saan a nagsiddaawan ni Willy Shaw no apay a makaay-ayoda unay kadagiti Amerikano.

Naawis ti panagkita ni Willy Shaw kadagiti ubbing iti baba ti rangtay. Lamolamo dagitoy. Adda bassit a bangka dagiti dadduma. Saggaysada iti sayut. Agiinnunada a mangitanggaya kadagiti sayutda bayat ti panangipukpukkawda iti *"Hi, Joe! Some coins, Joe!"* Adda dagiti manangngaasi nga Amerikano nga umis-isem a mangipuruak iti dies wenno peseta wenno salapi—adda dagiti lumabas lattan. No di maipunta iti sayut ti ipuruakda, agiinnuna dagiti ubbing a mangbatok. Narugit ti danum—narurusok ni Willy Shaw.

Maysa a nangisit nga ubing a kulot ti buokna ti nakasulek unay iti imatangna. Iti pannakakitana itoy, kas man adda immapay a rikna kenkuana, a dina ammo no ania. Aglalo idi madlawna ti nakaay-ay-ay a langa daytoy. Naliday unay dagiti matana. Isu ti kabassitan kadagiti ubbing ket isu met ti kanumuan iti masippaw a kuarta. Saan a napupuotan ni Willy Shaw ti ikakautna iti bolsana ket impuruakanna ti ubing iti plata a salapi. Kasta unay ti ragsak ti ubing idi maipisuk ti plata iti sayutna. *"Thank you, Joe. Thank you, Joe!"* impukkawna. Iniseman ni Willy Shaw.

Iti dayta a kanito, simken ti ilawna ken ni Ram, ti agtawen iti lima a maymaysa nga anakda ken ni Sally. Mailiw met ken ni Sally. Dandanin makatawen a dida agkikita. Kasla mangmangngegna manen ti nasinggit a timek ni Ram nga agkunkuna, "Saanka nga agbaybayag, wen, Pa? Mangisangpetkanto iti ay-ayamko, a, Pa?" Kasla makitkitana met ti panagis-isem latta ni Sally. Awan pay makalawas daydi a bakasionna. Naliday dagiti agina idi agpakada. "Malmaldaykamto manen, Willy," kinuna idi ni Sally.

Immanges ni Willy Shaw iti nauneg iti pannakalagipna kadagitoy.

Nasinga ti panagpampanunotna gapu iti arimbangaw. Addada gayamen iti ngudo ti rangtay. Saan nga ammo ti aridenggan kadagiti agyawis iti panagpasuplida iti kuarta.

"Change, Joe... Change, Joe!" impasabat kadakuada ti nalukmeg a babai iti makanigid ti kalsada. *"Here, Joe,"* kinuna met ti nakuttong a babai iti sabali a pagpasuplian ket ginuyodna ni Willy Shaw.

Duapulo a doliar ti pinasuplian ni Roger Briant. Lima a doliar laeng ken ni Willy Shaw.

"Bassit dayta, Willy," indillaw ni Roger Briant. "Saanka a mapnek."

"Umanay daytoyen."

Nagpipila dagiti diepan iti bangir ti kalsada ket agiinnunada a mangawis kadagiti pasahero. Naglugan da Willy Shaw ken Roger Briant. Agaabay ken agsasango dagiti klab. Dadakkel dagiti pasdek ket naraniag dagiti agduduma ti marisna a bombilia.

Pinaisardeng ni Roger Briant ti diep iti sango ti *Paradise Club.* Saanen nga innala ni Roger Briant ti supli ti pisos nga inyawatna iti tsuper.

Nalidem iti uneg ti klab. Kasta unay ti pamsaakan dagiti agtoktokar. Narimat ti kawes ti babai a madama mga agkankanta. Adun kadagiti nadanon da Willy Shaw a padada a marino ti nabartek. Kaaduan kadakuada ti adda salsallabayenna a babai. Nakaar-arimbangawda.

Nagtugaw da Willy Shaw ken Roger Briant iti lamisaan nga agpaay iti uppat iti maysa a suli ti klab. Inasitgan a dagus ida ti dua a naaayamuom ken napusaksak a babbai.

"Enjoy with us, Joe," inlailo dagiti dua a babbai.

"Oh, yeah, honey!" insupli ni Roger Briant ket sinallabaynan ti nagbado iti rosas. Inasitgan met ti nagbado iti amarilio ni Willy Shaw.

Sineniasan ni Roger Briant ti maysa a serbidor. Nakakaammon daytoy a nangyeg iti masapulda.

"Kastoy ditoy, Willy," kinuna ni Roger Briant. "Alaem latta ti kayatmo!"

Nagkatawa dagiti dua a babbai.

"Basta adda kastoy!" pinagkatek ti kaparehana ti tammudona.

Nagkakaktawada manen. Umis-isem laeng ni Willy Shaw.

Sumagmamanon a botelia a serbesa ti tinumba ni Roger Briant. Dudua pay laeng ken ni Willy Shaw.

"Makidanggayka iti agus, Willy!" kinuna ni Roger Briant idi madlawna ti kinaulimek ni Willy Shaw. Intangadna manen ti basona. Dina imbaba agingga a naibus ti naguneg. "Mabayagto manen ti kastoy no addatayon idiay bapor. Agliwliwaka ita ta addaka ditoy."

Immisem laeng ni Willy Shaw. Iti panagnadnad ti ininumna, nariknana ti mangin-inut nga ibabara ti bagina.

"Dika kadi naragsak iti dennak, *Da'ling*?" inlailo ti kaparehana. Immakar iti tugawna ket napan nagpasaklot ken ni Willy Shaw. Nasay-up ni Willy Shaw ti ayamuom ti babai. Iti apagdarikmat, inagkannan daytoy.

Nagsarita da Roger Briant ken ti kaasmangna. Idi agangay, nagpakadada kada Willy Shaw. Immulida iti ngato. Kasta met ti inaramid da Willy Shaw ken ti kaasmangna.

AWANEN ti naguneg ti petaka ni Roger Briant idi rumuarda iti *Paradise Club*. Adda pay lima a pisos ken ni Willy Shaw. Itay madamada nga agliwliwa, linibas dagiti kinakuyogda a babbai a kinaut ti petakada. Saandan a nakapagkitakit itay agkatkatawa dagiti babbai a nangyaon iti naguneg. *"Money first, honey!"* pannakalualodan dayta.

Nupay kasta, naragsak ni Roger Briant. "Kasta ti biag, Willy," kinunana. "Masapul ti linglingay. Bassit a kanito laeng ti pannakaruk-attayo idiay bapor." Pinikpikna ti abaga ti gayyemna. "Umaytanto manen no rabii no bigat. Aglinglingayta!" nagkatawa iti nakasarsarangsang.

Adu dagiti nabartek a kadaraanda a malabsanda. Agsisinnallalbayen dagitoy a maipaspas-iraw iti igid ti kalsada. Adda dagiti dadduma a mangilaklako iti relosda iti menus presio.

Iti masanguananda, adda ar-aribungbongan dagiti tao iti kalsada. Idi maasitganda, nailasinda ti maysa a kadaraanda a daradara ken tapoktapk. Limmitem ti maysa a matana. Agay-ayus ti dara iti ngiwatna ket naslepen ti pagan-anayna. Tinulongan dagiti sabali pay a kadaraanda nga inlugan iti diep. Naammuan da Willy Shaw a linugoban ti sumagmamano a Filipino gapu iti babai.

Dandanin makadanon da Willy Shaw ken Roger Briant iti rangtay idi makita ni Willy Shaw ti nangisit nga ubing a nakitana itay idiay rangtay. Adda iti abay ti aglaklako iti *barbecue*. Langana ti mabisin.

Nasdaaw ni Willy Shaw idi kasaritana ta ammona ti Ingles.

"Ania ti naganmo?" inamad ni Willaw Shaw. "Apay nga addaka ditoy? Rabiin, dika pay agawid?"

"Nat ti naganko," insungbat ti ubing. "Adda bassit a balaymi ngem kaykayatko ditoy. Awan ngamin ti kaduak idiay... Ania met ti naganmo, Joe?"

"Willy Shaw... awan kadi ti nanang ken tatangmo?"

"Awan ti tatangko. Adda ni nanangko 'diay klab."

Pinikpik ni Wily Shaw ti abaga ni Nat kalpasan ti pannangtedna iti pisos.

"Agsingsingpetka," kinunana.

SAAN a makaturog ni Willy Shaw. Saan a maikkat iti panunotna ni Nat, ti ubing a nangisit. Malaglagipna met da Ram ken Sally a pinanawanna idiay California. Iti pannakalagipna ken ni Sally ken ti napasamak kenkuana iti klab itay, adda nangisit a banag a simmippayot iti panunotna. No mapanunot met ngay ni Sally ti mangsapul iti ragsakna a dina maipaay bayat ti kaawanna?

"Malmaldayak, Willy, iti kaawanmo," patinayon a kuna ni Sally no agbakasion. "Matektekanak nga agur-uray..."

Ngem ditoy ti nakaibaudanna. Ditoy ti pagbibiaganda. "Agiinnanustay laengen," pannakalualonan dayta. Ngem pagpatinggaan ngata dayta a panaganus?

Nadlaw ni Willy Shaw ti di met pannakaturog ni Roger Briant.

"Roger?"

"Hmmm?"

"Dika pay naturog?"

"Dandanitay manen aglayag," kinuna ketdi ni Roger Briant. "Makasael a panaglayag. Agturongtayo idiay Japan. Inton agsublitayo idiay America, isunto man laengen ti panagkitami ken ni Windy," ti asawana ti kayatna a sawen.

ITI naminsan, naam-ammo ni Willy Shaw ti maysa nga agtutubo a Filipino. Adda ni Ramon, dayta ti nagan ti agtutubo a Filipino, iti rangtay. Agur-uray kadagiti Amerikano nga adda itukonda nga ilako. Intugot idi ni Willy Shaw ti kamerana.

"Mano ti pangilakuam, Joe?" inamad ni Ramon iti Ingles.

"Diak ilako."

Nataer ni Ramon, nadlaw ni Willy Shaw. Iti panagkitana, saan a kas kadagiti dadduma a nakitanan. Nadalimanek ti panagkawkawes ni Ramon. Deadal la ketdi.

"Agad-adalka?" dinamag ni Willy Shaw.

"Idi. Ngem nagsardengakon. Awan ti kuartak."

Inawis da Willy Shaw ni Ramon iti maysa a panganan.

"Naragsakkayo ditoy," kinuna ni Willy Shaw bayat ti pannanganda.

"Kasta iti panagkunam. Narigat ti biag ditoy, Willy. Ammom, kayatko met ti agbalin a *navy*, kas kadakayo."

"Nasayaat, Rammy!" binagi met Roger Briant. "Adu ti maramanam a *luto*!" nakasarsarangsang ti panagkatawana.

"Kuarta ti masapulko, Roger," kinuna ni Ramon. "Pannakapnek iti biag. Kayatko nga adaywan daytoy marigrigat a pagilianmi."

Tinapik ni Willy Shaw ni Ramon. "Adda met laeng iti nakayanakam ti ragsakmo, Rammy," kinunana. "Dimo masapulan iti ganggannaet."

"Awan ti ragsakko ditoy, Willy. Pasig a pannakapaay..."

"Ammom, Rammy, maysakan a balud no ag*navy*ka."

"Kayatko a saraken ti ragsakko iti ganggannaet, Willy. Awan a pulos ti talinaayko ditoy."

Nagkatawa ni Roger Briant. "Pagsiddaawennak, Rammy," kinunana. "Nagadu ti paglinglngayam dita... Awan kuartam? Sumurotka kadakami."

"Saan a dayta a banag ti makaipaay iti pagragsakakak," inwingiwing ni Ramon.

SAAN a nagkuyog da Willy Shaw ken Roger Briant a rimmuar. Nadagsen kano ti rikna ni Roger Briant—masapul met a manglipat ni Willy Shaw sagpaminsan. Masapul a mangiwaksi iti saem.

Bayat ti panangurayna iti sabali pay a botelia, inruarna ti nakunesen a surat iti bolsana. Kaaw-awatna itay ti surat. Naggapu ken ni Sally.

"Sangkaawagnaka ni Ram, Willy," kinuna ni Sally iti maysa a paset ti surat. "Apay kano a dika metten sumangpet? Uray iti iddana kunkunana: 'Doktor, apay di metten sumangpet ni Papa? Nauma kadin kadakami ken ni Mama? Doktor, pagawidem man, a, ni Papa' sanak kitaen, Willy, ket kunana: 'Mama, no sumangpeten ni Papa, maimbaganak a dagus.' Sangkadagullitna dayta, Willy. Ket idi dandanin mapan, kinunana: 'Sumangpetton ni Papa, aya, Mama? Dandanin, aya?' Siinanama a sumangpetkan, Willy, agingga iti nakaturog, pannaturog a..."

Nagkayammet dagiti ramay ni Willy Shaw. Nakunes ti surat. Timmangken ti pangana. Binukbokanna manen ti basona. Intangadna.

ADTOY manen ti makasael a panagdaliasat—pumanawdan iti Filipinas.

Dinto malipatan ni Willy Shaw dagiti trabahador nga agsukain iti basuraan iti oras koman ti panaginanada... dagiti ubbing iti rangtay a mangipukpukkaw iti *"Hi, Joe! Some coins, Joe...!"* Ni Nat a mangur-uray iti inana nga agtratrabaho iti klab... ni Ramon, ti agtutubo a Filipino nga agpanggep a mangbirok iti rasakna iti ganggannaet.

"Agragsaktayo, Willy. Danggayantayo ti agus. Aglinglingaytayo..." sangkadagullit ni Roger Briant.

Ngem agpanaas ti barukongna no malagipna ni Sally nga agkunkuna, "Malmaldayak, Willy, iti kaawanmo. Matektekananak nga agur-uray..."

Mangin-inuten nga umadayo ti bapor. Bumassiten a bumassit ti Olongapo iti panagkita ni Willy Shaw. Imbaw-ingna ti panagkitana iti kasla awan patinggana a taaw. —0

Bannawag: Hunio 5, 1967; *Napili a Sarita dagiti Ilokano: pp.*103-108, c1968.

Ti Eden Iti Biagda

1

HI, guapo, agpapukiska? Sumrekka. . . Ha! Ha! Kaska met la naidarekdek ditan. Bay-am man dagita agdadama. Kastada no kastoy nga awan ti parokiano. . . Umaykan, Gayyem. Salapi laeng. . ."

"Nalaingka met laeng?"

"Ania a pukis? Flat top? Alpunsino? Beatles . . . Twiggy, wenno ania? Aha, ammok ti maibaay iti naamo a rupam, Gayyem."

"Kayatko a napintas ti pukisko. Daytay tumilmon dagitay babbalasang dita uneg. Nangruna daytay nars a natagtgapulotan ti isemna, a makitkita ti muldotan a luppona no agtugaw. Ken daytay babai a kaabayko idiay winding."

"Ha! Ha! Kabaelak amin a kayat ti asino man, Gayyem. Ania ti naganmo?"

"Hilario. Sika?"

"Banong. Ne, saan a dita, Gayyem. Puesto daydiay ludingas a barbasan a butiog a kasla buddha a nagsikkawil dayta. Ditoy. . . Kasta. Ammom, Gayyem, sika pay la ti katarakian a kinagayan daytoy puraw a kagayko. . ."

"Agbiddut dagiti agkunkuna a bulambulanenka."

"Saanda a nagbiddut. . . uray sika. Ha! Ha! 'Mom, Gayyem, ti biag, agtatapaw iti angin."

"Nabayagkan ditoy?"

"Makatawen. . . Kumurang a dupaulo a tawen metten a mamukpukisak."

"Ilokanoka?"

"No addaak idiay ilimi, wen. Ngem Tagalogak ditoy. No sadino ti pakaidakdakak, kasdiayak. . . Ha! Ha! Baliodong, kuna dagiti bumabatok idiay Mindanao, Samar, Palawan. . . Aha, atiddog nga estoria ti padpadasko. Amangan no dinak patien."

"Kayatmo a maisurat ti kabibiagmo?"

"Kabibiagko? Ha! Ha! Awan ti agmauyong a mannurat a mangisurat. Ha! Ha! Nasaysayaat ti agbiag nga awan ti pampanunotenna."

"Karkarnaka, kunak koma, ngem awan ti tao a nakaskasdaaw no ammona nga amirisen ti kasasaadna."

"Sika ketdi, a."

"Apay?"

"Nagartistaka koma. Wenno nagadalka. Dayta a langam. . . Saan a maikari kenka ti pabrika a pagtartrabahuam."

"Ibagam laengen a nayaw-awanak. . . Ngem awan ti trabaho a di mainumo iti asino man a mayat nga agbiag. Kas kenka. Saludsodem iti bagim no apay nga agtalinaedka a barbero idinto a makastrekka koma met iti sabali."

"Nasaysayaat daytoy ngem dagitay agak-akup iti kuarta iti rabii. Adda naitani iti tunggal maysa. Maag dagiti agarapaap iti dida kabaelan."

"Dimo mababalaw ida. Bay-am nga agarapaapda no isut' pagpatinggaan ti kabaelanda. No awan arapaapmo, awan met masakbayam."

"Awan ti tao nga awan ti masakbayanna. Sika. . . aniaka?"

"Tao a managarapaap. . . Propeta a salawasaw. Agmauyong a nataer. Bayanggudaw a nalaad. Ken mangit a di aglua. . . Ngem naragsakak. . ."

"Ha! Ha! No adu ti kuarta, wen. Dagiti babbai. . . ah, kitaem man dagidiay. Kunam lan' matnag ti patongda. Ken, asus! Makitkita ti kagudua ti luppoda. Diak la ammon no sadino ti pappapananda iti rabii."

"Iti trabahoda, sadino pay? Kayatko nga aggayyemta. Sadino ti dagusmo?"

"Dita la igid ti ayus. Dita amianan. Daydiay balay a kasiping ti duogan nga algarruba. . ."

"Nalpasen?"

"Wen. Urayennak dita ruar, no kayatmo ti umay. . ."

"Sige ngarud. Ne, kuamon 'ta suplina."

"Oy, Guapo. . . Nabayagkan a rimmuar? Nagsueldokan?"

"Nakapapukisak payen. . . Inggawidnakan sa ni ludingas?"

"Pila ngamin. Sueldo ngaruden, narigat pay nga alaen. Talaga nga… Ehem. . . dinak man kitkitaen ket marunawak ladagita matam. Dinak iseman ket alunosennak dagita bibigmo!"

"Asino dayta, Hil?"

"A, Banong. Isu ti kunak a kaabayko idiay winding. . . ni Lily. 'Su ti gayyemko a barbero, Lily."

"Ha, nabayagen a makakitkitaak iti baboy. . . He! He! Tsk! Tsk! Uray sadino ti pangsirigak kenka, guapoka latta, Hil! No kayatmo ti agpasiar, urayenka idiay balay. Okey, Boy?"

2

DAYTOY man ti lubongko, Hil. Dispensarem laengen. Naladawak a nakariing. Dayta, agkaraiwara ti alikamek. Awan agidalimanek."

"Apay a dika mangala iti kaduam?"

"Nasaysayaat ti agwaywayas. Kapatpatangko laengen dagita pocketbooks. Isuda't pagsangpetak. Diak pay agdaldalusen no dadduma. Nairuam metten ti agongko iti angot dayta ubong ti baboy—dayta abay ti ridaw. Baboyak met. Ha! Ha! Diak agdigdigos no kua ta manmano nga adda danum."

"Agbasbasaka gayam iti libro."

"Dagiti la makalinglingay ken makapadakkel iti ulo. Dagitay gapuanan da Hemingway, Tolstoy, Melville, ken dadduma pay a nalalaing a nobelista."

"Kunak man no kunam itay a salawasaw dagiti mannurat? Nagadalka?"

"Apagrugik iti kolehio. Nagsardengak idi awan kuartakon. Bassit ti mapukpukisak. . . kinaykayatko nga ituloy ti trabahok ngem ti agsapul iti sabali. Nadalus ngamin. Ken isun sa ti nakaikariak. Nagadalka met?"

"Maikadua a tawenko iti kolehio. Nagsardengak ta didak mapagtuloy da tatang. Napadasak ti nagdalus iti kasilia ti restauran. Idi kuan, nagtuberoak. Saak nagtarimaan iti silaw. Ngem awan ti dur-asan kadagitoy. Pinadasko ti nagsursurat. Di pay umanay a pangsilpok iti angesko ti ibayadda kadagiti gapuanak. Napanunotko ti sumrek dita pabrika. Ngem awan met gayam ti dur-asan dita. Mayan-anusko koman ngem kayatko a pagadalen dagiti addik. 'Mom, Banong, adda kaayan-ayatko a maestra—iti kabangibangmi a probinsia. Mannurat met; adda arapaapna ket makatubengak no saanak nga agsalukag."

"Husto 'tay panangipapanko—mannuratka. Ti kaayan-ayatmo... Napudnokayo iti tunggal maysa?"

"Ti la panawen ti makaibaga iti dayta a banag."

"Awan dadakkelko, awan kakabsatko, awan kaayan-ayatko, awan kakabagiak. . . awan mangipatpateg kaniak—awan ti isagsaganaaak. Ngem naragsakak latta, Hil. 'Mom, adda idi kinaluobko, babai nga impateg ken inayatko. Adda anakmi. . . maysa, ngem nasangpetak a natay iti maysa a malem—diak ammo no pinatay ni Lita. Awan metten ni Lita. Simmurot iti sabali a lalaki ngem. . . Ha! Ha! Bay-amon ti napalabas. Bay-amon dagiti dadduma a saludsod."

"Kasimbronko ti agdama a trabahok, Banong. Pagnaak a pagna. Agsakit ti barukongko, nangruna no agkarapugsat dagiti sinulid. Kakaasiak a mangkamkamat iti orasko. Natangsit dagiti dadduma a kaduak. Kasta unay ti rigatda ngem masangoda pay la ti agkukubalsing. Mapnekdan san. Dagidiay la ngarud dandani sangapulo a tawenen nga adda dita. Dayawek ti anusda. Kabutengda ti strike. Kabutengda daydiay Hudio a ludingas."

"Adut' kaarrubak a nadekket iti dayta a Hudio, Hil. . . Ngem kayatko nga agragsakta ita a rabii. Adda ammok a nasayaat a pagpasiaranta. Saggatlo a pisos laeng. Uray agpatpatnagta, di maibus ti sueldom. Adut' napukisak ita."

"Diak kayat dayta, Banong."

"Sika latta. Adda sabali a papananta. Ngem mangrabiita pay ditoy. Naimas ti sidsidak, Hil. No saan a laki, sardinas. No saan a sardinas, uray anian a delata. Nasaysayaat dagitoy ta ti laengen innapuy ti lutuek. Nasadutak, Hil. Nasadutak. Ha! Ha!"

"Dumagastanto pay ngarud idiay dagusko."

3

DITOY ti kunak, Hil."

"Awan gidiat iti yan dagiti saggatlo, a."

"Ha! Ha! Masapul a padasem amin a kita ti panagbiag, Hil."

"Oy, Hil. . . nayaw-awanka?"

"Ernesto, Lito. . . Lino. . . Jim!"

"Ha! Ha! Ditoy ti paraiso, Hil. Mamindua laeng iti makabulan. . . A, Banong, kinaduam?"

"Kayatko a pabuniagan, Lino. Ha! Ha!"

"A, sumrektayon, a, Lito, Lino, Ernest. Sangailientay bassit ni Hil."

"Agur-uray dagiti serbesa idiay lamisaan, Hil. . . Banong, umaykayon."

"Aguraykayo ta adda papanak."

"Agdardaraska, a, Lito. Itugotmon dagitay langit."

"Ha! Ha! Nabara latta ti daram, ha, Ernest?"

"Masapul a lipatek sagpaminsan ni Mila, Banong."

"Apay nga agwingwingiwingka, Hil?"

"Malagipko dagiti dua nga annak ni Ernest, Jim. Mano nga aldaw ti sinueldom, itay, Ernest?"

"Sangapulo ket dua. . . Ngem apay a dayta ti panunotem? Tapno saanka a lumakay a dagus, masapul nga aginanaka. . . Adda ditoy ti langit, Hil. Bay-am man dagidiay agur-uray!"

"Kasta unay ti rigattay' idiay pagablan sa maungaw iti maysa la a rabii ti nagrigrigatantayo iti mano nga aldaw?"

"Ha! Ha! Ha! Dimo ipadlaw a kaippasngayka, Hil. Manmano ti kastoy a gundaway."

"Aggigidiat ti lubongtayo, Jim."

"Addagitoyen dgiti langit, kakadua!"

"Ha! Ha! Nalalapsat dagiti pilim, ha, Lito. Ngem agkurang iti maysa.

"Kukuayo aminen ta mangalaak iti kuak."

"Saanen, Lito."

"A, saan a mabalin, Hil. Ne, apagisu. Addaytoy met gayamen ni Lily. . . Lily sikan ti makaammo ken ni Hil . . . Kakadua, nasam-it ti tokar. . ."

"Hil, pinagsiddaawnak!"

"Inkuyognak ni Banong ditoy impierno! Kitaem, kunam la no addadan a lima iti langit. Sika, apay. . ."

"A, honey, nasalimuot idiay pabrika! Awan ragsak sadiay . . . dandaniakon aglusulos. . . Impierno sadiay! 'Mayka ta paragsakenka. Nabara dagiti bibigko. . . makabiag ti barukongko."

"Lily. . ."

"Makitam dagidiay kakaduam? Immulidan. Napandan idiay langit. Ha! Ha! Dagitay pay met ngarud nasasam-it ti natiempuanda. Todasda. Ha! Ha! Kayatmo, Honey? No sika, libre. Kayatka. . ."

"L-lily. . . L-lily. . ."

"Idiay langit, Hil. . ."

4

LINO, malmaldayka?"

"Awan kuartakon, Hil."

"Kunak ngamin idi Sabado."

"Dinak maawatan. Awanak koma idi no saan a gapu iti diaske a kaayan-ayatko. Inan-anusak ti nangged ditoy ta kayatko a makaurnongak iti pagtugawanmi. Inton umay a bulan koman ti panagkasarmi. Ngem nakitaray ketdin. . ."

"Agyamanka ta itan ti pannakapasamakna. Da Jim, Ernest ken Lito?"

"Indarumda ni Jim gapu kadagiti utangna. Nagballog ni Ernest. Nabartek manen ni Lito."

"N Lily?"

"Simmurot kano idi kalman iti lakay a baknang. Dina kanon pagan-ano ditoy."

5

OY, Hil, apay?"

"Pumanawakon, Banong."

"Papanam?"

"Nakastrekak iti maysa a sanga ti gobierno idiay Manila."

"Naimbagka pay, Hil. Siak, ditoyak lattan. Barbero aginggat' punget. Ngem... Ha! Ha! Awan met masakbayak. . . Agragsakak lattan, a. 'Nia ngay, isut' gasatko. Banongakto lattan, a, a bulambulanen. . . Pumanawkan, ditanto ngatan agkita."

"Malaglagipkanto latta, Banong. Innakon."

"Adios. . ."—0

Bannawag, Hunio 17, 1968; *The Quezonian,MLQU School Organ,* Ang Eden sa Kanilang Buhay (patarus iti Filipino), Mayo 24 – Hunio 7, 1971.

Rupa

"AWAN met laengen," kinuna ni Baket Sepa a tinaldiapanna ti relo iti lamisaan. Maikawalo iti rabii, impasirna iti lawag ti bombilia ti listaan dagiti pautangna iti panaglakona iti ikan. "Kaasi met ti anakko..."

Agsolsolo ni Baket Sepa iti kuarto nga ab-abanganna iti duapulo ket lima a pisos. Nailet ti kuarto; adda bassit nga aparador ken dekutson a kama. Bassit ti lamisaan a pangananna. Iti paladpad ti tawa ti nakaibangkeraan dagiti gamigamna nga agluto.

Iti tianggi iti sirok, adda simmangpet a natayag ken nabaked a lalaki. Kulisapsap ken kasla agruprupa a Hapones. Agtawen ngata iti duapulo ket lima. Inisemanna ti tagibian a tindera sa nagbilin iti serbesa. Bayat ti panagurayna, sangkakitana ti agdan a kumamang iti yan ni Baket Sepa.

"Adda idiay ngato," kinuna ti tindera.

"Madamdama," insungbat ti lalaki.

Kasla awan kirkiras ti panangarub-obna iti nasanger. Nalidem ti rupana; sa la umisem no agsabat dagiti matada iti tindera.

Iti ngato, rimmuar ni Baket Sepa iti kuartona, simrek iti sabali a kuarto a yan ti agassawa. Nakaunnat ti narapis a lalaki iti kama iti panagbasana iti magasin. Idaldlalimanek ti babai dagiti lupotda. Patinayon a makisarsarita ti baket kadakuada no kasta a mumalem.

"Nasingpet ni *Engineer*, Totoy," inrugina manen ti bisiona. Totoy ti awagna iti lalaki. Nagtugaw iti sango ti lamisaan dagiti agassawa. "Basta adda dawatek, mangted latta... Bareng no umay no bigat." Kidday a kidday no agsao.

"Ket daydi lakay a kuttong nga immay idi naminsan? Ken daydi mestiso idi naminsan?" nagtalinaed dagiti mata ti lalaki iti basbasaenna.

"Awan kuarta ni kuttong... saur ni mestiso," naglibbi ti baket. "Imbag ni *Engineer*, uray lakay... aw-awisennak nga agkasarkamin ngem mandiak met," naglibbi. "Kakaasiak laeng no kua. Naimbag koma no awan annakna."

"Adda met annakmo, Nana," kinuna ti masikog. Impasirokna iti kama ti karton a nagipempenanna iti lupotda.

"Wen, dagidiay annakko. Ni Clarita, agpapaungar; nagadu ti annakna. Piman nga anakko, nasapa unay a nabalo... kasano ngata metten ni Rogelio? Naital-o ngatan? Kasano ngatan ni Cena nga asawana, ken dagiti dua nga annkda? Ni Nestor a *navy*... ah, nalabit nga adda itan... Dagiti appokok... kaasida pay... Ngem diyo ibagbaga kada Rogelio ni *Engineer*, 'Toy, a?" Inaprosanna ti ababa a buokna.

"Ket apay koma?"

"Ammoyon, a... dida kayat ti kasta. Ngem dida met maited ti pagnam-ayak, aya, 'Toy?" sinagidna ti nakiskidsan ken naugedan a kidayna. "Napintasak met ket idi..."

Napan iti kuartona. Innalana ti ladawanna iti bassit a kuarto iti tuktok ti aparadorna. Nagayuyang ti isem iti napalabbaga a bibigna.

Nagsubli iti yan dagiti agassawa. "Daytoy ti ladawak idi kalaplapsatak! Kitaem, 'Ne, di ngamin napintasak met?"

"Wen," aleng-aleng ti masikog ti timmaliaw.

"Nagar-artistaak met idi! Uray paspasurot," dagdagullitan nga ipakita ken ipadamag ti baket dagiti ladawanna. "Nagbalinak pay a WAC iti daydi Presidente Quirino... Ngem ti karagsakan a paset ti biagko, isu ti kaaddak idiay Olongapo. *Wise* dagiti Kano! Ngem adu ti kuartada. Bassit la a patsarmitsarming, mapanen 'diay dua gasut a doliar. Ngem kuidawda!" nagkatawa. "Kuarta nga umuna sakbay ti pakasdiakasdiay!" naggarikgik.

Timmakder ti masikog. Innalana iti palanggana ti sandia a di pay napisi. Pinisina.

"Kunak no pinisim itay aldaw, 'Ne," kinuna ti baket. "Nasam-it daytay nayonna. Naglaka idiay naggatangak..."

Nanganda.

"Nayanakko idin ni Rogelio," kinuna ti baket. "No kitkitaem daytoy a ladawan, ipagarupmo kadi a tallo ti annakko?" minirana ti ladawan iti raniag ti bombilia; nagkurarap. Sa limmidem ti rupana. "Sairo daydi ama ni Rogelio. Idi naaramidna ni Rogelio, nagpukawen a kasla asuk! Diak ammo no sadino nga impierno ti napnapananna. Nalabit nagawid idiay Japon, wenno linamut ti bala..." Inyangadna ti nalangeban a rupana. "Daydi ama ni Nestor, maysa met. Siguro, napan naguper kadagiti padana idiay America. Ngem adu ti kuarta daydi Jones. Bassit 'ta sangagasut a doliar nga itedna iti aysa a rabii." Immisem sa pimasnek ket kinitana manen ti masikog. "Ammom, 'Ne, nasingpet daydi laklakaddoogan a Kastila nga ama ni Clarita. Pulos a diak naramanan ti imana. Ngem nakapsuten." Nagkatawa. "Ngem saan a maudi iti kuarta iti daydi anak ti diablo nga ama ni Nestor. Itedna amin a kayatko..."

Nagkarasakas ti basbasaen ti lalaki iti kama.

Iti sirok, naibusen ti lalaki ti tallo a serbesa. Nagbilin pay. Kimmita manen iti agdan. Sana kinita ti tindera.

"Talaga?"

"Wen," kinuna ti tindera. "Ken saan la a maymaysa; saan la a Filipino."

Intangad ti lalaki ti basona. Adda inruarna a puraw a papel iti bolsana. Inukradna iti sango ti tindera.

Nagmulagat ti tindera. "Ngem—"

"Inkari ni Clarita nga umay ita, awan metten," binaledan manen ti kalman ti rupa ni Baket Sepa. "Siguro, adda nakatalaananna, wenno aglokoloko manen ti buridekna... Piman nga anakko! Nasapanto met ngamin unay a nabalo. Nagadu nga annakna..."

"Di met adda pagsapulanna?" kinuna ti masikog.

"Agtartrabaho idiay Balara. Saan a maudi iti matgedan ken ni *manong*na a Nestor. Ammom, *navy* ni Nestor." No namin-anon nga imbagana. "Ni Rogelio, PC met... Ngem laglag daydiay a Rogelio. Kadakuada nga agkakabsat, isu laeng ti makaitured a mangsangdo kaniak. Kakaasiak a nangpapaadal kenkuana..."

"Adda gapuna a kasdiay," kinuna ti agbasbasa.

"Ania pay ti sapulenna?" immulagat ni Baket Sepa. "Nakastrek, aya, iti trabahona no diak inrekomenda? Sanak pay la ikaskasdiay... No pinatayko idi sikogko adda kad' koma naaramidna? 'Nia, Totoy?"

Nalagipna manen ti *Engineer*! No namin-anon nga inulit-ulitna nga isu ti mangmangted iti pagbaybayadna iti kuartona. "Masapul nga umay no bigat ta panagbabayad manen," kinunana.

Dida nadlaw ti immuli. Lumablabbasit ti napudaw a lalaki a mara-Hapones. Agdindinukol ti siketna. Kiniddayanna ti lalaki iti kama, a kimmiday met.

Napanganga ni Baket Sepa.

"Agmanoak, Nanang," innala ni Rogelio ti dakulap ni Baket Sepa.

"Ti Dios ti mangisalakan kenka..."

Napanda iti siled ti baket.

"Nangankan?" kinuna ti baket.

"Didak kad' latta pagdanagan."

"Imminumka manen! Aniat' parikutmo? Apay nga addaka? Di met naidestinoka idiay..."

"Agtiltiliwak ita kadagiti managbasol."

"Hmmmm, ket, adda natiliwmon?"

"Inkay' man ketdi mangala iti sangabotelia."

"Nabartekkan!"

"Adda kad' mabartek a PC? Ken ammoyo, tenientak itan."

"Apay a dika naguniporme?"

"Nalaklaka ti agtiliw no kua."

"Awan ti mammartek nga agtiliw."

"Pasetna amin dayta... Alas otso pay laeng, nasapakay' man?"

"Ket, papanak koma? Ur-urayek pay ngarud ni manangmo a Clarita."

"Isu a nasapakayo... Husto," nagtungtung-ed ni Rogelio. Nagkuribnas iti mabalinna nga ipauneg. Kimmiddis iti nalingta nga ikan iti tayab, sa imminum. "Clarita... he!"

"Alas siete pay laeng no dadduma, matmaturogakon."

Nawagwag ti abaga ni Rogelio iti panagkatawana. Pinasulianna a kinita ni Nanangna.

"Ammom, 'Nang, adda manen sabali a babai iti biagko. Diak kayaten ni Cena. Bay-amon 'diay dua nga annakmi... Kitaem daytoy retrato ti baro a sukik."

"Kaasiam dagidiay annakmo, Rogelio... Daydiay asawam."

Rimsik dagiti mata ni Rogelio. "Kaasiak? Ha-ha! Ammoyo met la ti mangngaasi iti anak? Kinaasiandak kad' idi?" kinitana ti dekutson a kama. "Yanna, 'Nang?"

Kinusilapan ni Baket Sepa. "Nabartekkan, Rogelio... maturogkan."

"Awan ti mabartek a malalaki... awan ti tuglep a beterano! Yanna?"

"Agbiddutka, Anakko... baketakon..."

"Ngem diyo pay nabaketan ti ugaliyo..."

"Hammo a sawen ti kasta!"

"Didak man bulseken...! Kayatyo ta tiliwenkayo?"

Timmadem dagiti mata ti baket. "Itay awanka, naragsakak... Maturogkan, wenno pumanawka?"

"Ta didak ngamin anak... Ta ni la Clarita ti anakyo. Pue!"

"Pumanawkan!" imsiag ti baket. "Diak pagtatakkonan ti anak a di makaammo nga agbain iti inana... Pumanawkan! Dimon sa ammo no asino daytoy kasangsangom. Ha! Asawa ti heneral daytoy! Ni Heneral Santos...!" agtigtigerger, makarkarattot ti baket a nangiruar iti retrato iti maletana. "Kitaem daytoy... Bigbigem. Am-ammom? Isu dayta ti nobiok! Dinak mabalin a butbutngen. Uray sadino nga abut ti lubong ti papananta... Kunam sa ket a kabutengka? Ha, no namin-anon a naisaksaklangak, ngem awan pay ti nakabakak. Gagayyemko amin a polis. Maysa a saok laeng, todasmon! Kayatmo ta paikkatka iti trabahom ita met laeng? Anakka laeng—"

"Wen, anakdak laeng. Anakdak ngem didak imbilang nga anak... Anaknak laeng itan ta dakkelakon... Ngem dakayo kadi ti dinakkelak? Saan! Adda kadi intedyo bayat ti panagdakkelko? Awan! Imparangkapdak!"

"Isu nga intedka kadagiti agassawa tapno makatgedak iti abastoyo nga agkakabsat. Imbatika laeng kadakuada, saan nga imparangkap. Inik-ikkak ida iti pagadalmo. Ngem impasurotda ketdin ti naganmo iti naganda... Basolko ngarud no agsapulak iti iduolko kadakayo? Ha? Ha?"

"Didak kad' lokuenen! No patpatgendak, apay a ni la Manang Clarita ti kaykayatyo? Diyo pay ipateg ni Cena nga asawak."

"No sika ti di makalagip iti asawam, laglag! Idi la kalman, impaw-itak manen 'diay asawam iti duapulo. Sika, adda kad' naipaburirawmon? Idi naopera ni Clarita, dimo pay pinautangan iti pagpunnona iti pagbayadna iti ospital..."

"Huston!"

"Animal! Immamaka a karasaen! Naim-imbag koman no pinatayka idi sikogka!"

"Makitayo?" bimmanel ti panga ni Rogelio. "Anak kad' ti pangibilbilanganyo kaniak? Ngem sumurotkay' kaniak ta adda pagpasiarantayo."

"Patiliwnak? Ta ania ti basolko? Ania ti pagpampannakelmo? Dimon sa ngamin ammo ni Heneral Santos... dimon sa ammo no asino dagiti nobiok." Nagiwakrat kadagiti ladawan. "Addagita! Bigbigem dayta a Presidente... dayta a Bise Presidente... dayta a diputado... a senador..."

Nangemkem ni Rogelio. "Urayendak." Timmakder. Kiniddayanna dagiti nalinak nga agassawa idi rumuar. Nabuaken ti sangakaarrubaan. Adu dagiti sumanultip a ngumayemngem. Adu dagiti rupa iti tawa.

Kasla agbusi ti ngiwat ni Baket Sepa apaman a nakaulog ni Rogelio. Aglalaok ti pammadakesna ken ni Rogelio ken panangidayyawna kada Clarita ken Nestor. Immulog pay ketdin, ket impandana kadagiti tao. Ngem awan ti nangikaso kenkuana. "Wen" laeng ti sungbat dagiti agassawa iti ngato.

Di pay nagmawmaw ti pungtotna idi dumteng ni Clarita. Natayag ken napuaw ni Clarita. Kimmastila.

"O, apay, ania ti napasamak?"

"Daytay awan ti bainna a kabsatmo a Rogelio ta immaynak riniribuk!" nagpulong ti baket. Ngem immalumamay. "Nangankan...? Komusta dagitay appokok?"

"Nagliblibasak, a, nga immay. Agpailista ni Boy no bigat."

"Manot' masapulna?"

"Singkuenta. Ngem... naggapuak a naggatang..."

Simmangpet da Rogelio ken Nestor. Agkataytayagda. Nabakbaked ni Nestor ngem naluplupoy. Natundiris ti agongna; bugagaw dagiti

matana. Immamerikano. Nagmano ken ni Baket Sepa. Nagalingasaw ti nasanger.

Apagkita ti baket ken n Rogelio, imsiag manen.

"Aniat' ar-aramidenyo, 'ya?" sakit ti nakem ti naibinggas iti ayug ni Nestor. "Immay ni Rogel idiay balay... nakababain."

"Ket no isu ti immay nangriribuk."

"Nakababain ti ar-aramidenyo. Kitaenyo dagiti tao. Ania laengen ti sawenda kadakayo?"

"Ha, ta ibaindak gayamen? Naglaingkayon! Kalpasan ti panangyanak ken panangpadakkelko kadakayo, kastoyen ti ipaayyo... Pumanawkayo!"

"Agtalnakayo!" naunget ti arasaas ni Nestor. "Nakababain kunak ket! Kayatmi nga agbalbaliwkayon. Bakbaketankayon."

"Adda kad' ar-aramidek?"

"Adu kano ti um-umay ditoy a lallaki... Panunotenyo, ania lat' rupamin kadagiti gagayyemmi?"

"'Su ngarud ti kunak itay," insalpika ni Rogelio. "Kaslanto met la pagdaksanda ti ibagbaga."

"Sika, Rogelio, patayenka, no kunak, patayenka!"

"Dikay' aglaaw!" minedmedan ni Nestor.

"Adda kadi ar-aramidek? Saak la rumuar iti bigat a mapan aglako iti ikan... Dakes ketdin ti mangged? No diyo kayat ti iruruarko... Diyo met ngarud maited ti abastok. Ti masapulko... Awan ti ar-aramidek... No dakesak man idi, gapu kadakayo... gapu iti masakbayanyo."

"Namin-anon nga imbagak nga umaykay' idiay balay," inngetnget ni Nestor. "Ngem kaykayatyo ti agukop ditoy... ta nawaywayakayo..."

"Umayak, tapno maigalutak kadagiti ubbing? Dagiti ubbing... dagiti ubbing..." nagdumog ti baket.

"Saan a rumbeng a pasakitanyo ni Nanang," inyallawat ni Clarita. "Baketen... apay nga ipaidamyo ti pagragsakanna...? Nalabes ti ipabpabadoyo..."

"Nalabes!" inngernger ni Rogelio. "Nalabes kadi ti pangikalakag iti pakaibabainan?"

"Kaska la agut-utek a paltat, Rogelio," inyanges ni Clarita.

"Kunam ti kasta, a, ta kutkutkotam!" inridis ni Rogelio. "Kunam siguro a diak ammo ti inalatmo. Dagiti makibkibkiban ni Nanang,

maysaka met a manglamut... Ken sika kano laeng ti anakna. Dinakam' ibilang nga annak ken ni *Manong* gapu ta inkasar kano daydi Kastila nga amam! Ket daydi Tatang? Apay, awan kad' la a pulosen ti pakaipadisan ti Hapones iti Kastila? Ken daydi Tatang ni *Manong*, gapu ta Amerikano..."

"Rumbeng koma a maawatanyo ni Nanang..."

"Agsardengka!" nangmesmes ni Nestor. "Dimo ayonan ti inaayup a pagduyosan ni Nanang. No awan ti bainmo, awan laeng!"

"Masapul a mapagnakem ni Nanang..." kinuna ni Rogelio.

"Agsardengka!" inyikkis ni Baket Sepa.

"Awanen dagiti ammatayo," makasangsangit ni Clarita. "Ket saan koman a rumbeng nga agapaden ida. Agkakabsattayo; maymaysa ti inatayo. Biddutna kadi no nagbalin a kastoy? Biddutna kadi ti panangyanakna kadatayo? Biddutna kadi ti kaada ti gubat a nakaigapuan ti kastoy?"

Nalabbaga dagiti marmaratubbog a mata ni Baket Sepa a naiturong kada Rogelio ken Nestor. Agtigtigerger dagiti nakeppet a bibigna. Timmallikud ket nagrikab ti rikep ti kuarto a ginuttana. Naigusod dagiti paddakna iti kuarto dagiti agassawa.

Naem-em dagiti bibigda, insursurot lattan dagiti agassawa ti imatangda iti baket nga inalun-on ti agdan.

"Ikkannak iti nasanger, 'Ne!" parpar ti nagubsang a timek ti baket iti tagtagibian a tindera iti sirok.

Awan sintimek a nagtungpal ti tindera.

"Dagiti annak ti diablo nga awanan iti bain a karasaen!" intangguap ti baket ti nasanger. "Dida ammo ti agsubad!"

Idi maibusna ti sangabaso, nagbilin manen. "Dida ammo ti agsubad!" indanogna iti eskaparate. —0

Bannawag: Hunio 23, 1969; Marso 12, 2018; *Tagumpay,* (patarus iti Filipino) Mga Mukha Sa Basag Na Salamin, Marso 17, 1971; *24 a Napili a Sarita:* 1969, pp.43-50.

Ditoy Gloria: Pagbaludan

AWAN duma iti ubong ti baboy daytoy nailet a siled a sangpetanna iti kada sumipnget. Sumkad ti riknana a sumangpet ta masemsem iti angot ti nabangles a makan, takki ti bao ken sipet, naangpep a lupot, nabungsot a danum iti suli a nakayaripingan ti buong a tubo a pagayusan ti rugit dagiti adda iti maikadua a kadsaaran. Masusungegen kadagiti di maidaldalimanek a gamigamna a panawanna lattan iti agsapa iti panagdardarasna a sumrek iti trabahona; kadagiti mapampag a rugit iti maikadua a kadsaaran. Aggagatel ti bagina ta manmano a makadigos. Uray ngamin no masapa nga agriing, no saan nga alas kuatro, saan a makasublat iti banio ta makumikom dagiti serbidor iti restauran a kasiping ti siledna ket awan ti agubo a danum. Masisilengen iti awan ressatna a patokar iti jukebox, iti ariwawa dagiti mangan, iti garakgak dagiti agiinum. Makaulaw ti angot ti arak ken serbesa.

Sakbay a simrek, kimmita iti restauran, riniknana dagiti arimpadek iti maikadua a kadsaaran.

Kasano nga agtalna iti kastoy a lubong? Nagsakuntip a nangkalbit iti switch ti bombilia. No makitada ti silaw, umayda la ketdi ngem agarikap ngarud iti kasipngetan? Intupakna ti nagbalunanna iti lamiseta a nakapakleban ti dua a kublakublang a plato, maysa a nagannaan a tasa, botelia ti kape, selopin ti asukar, nagawangan ti sardinas, kaha ti sigarilio, napis-it a kaha ti gurabis, pagyarsangan a botelia ti pomada, ken napadata a buong a sarming. Adda daan a kosinilia iti suli. Pinampagna ti rutrot a kama. Naganit-it iti panagtugawna. Naguksob. Pinasutna ti rutrot a sapatosna. Nagliad iti nalamiis a semento. Inapputna ti rutrot

a sapatosna. Nagliad iti nalamiis a semento. Inapputna ti rupana sa immanges iti nauneg. Nabungsot a biag! Nagbanang-es. Sal-it ketdi!

Nalagipna ti nadalus a kuarto idiay Espana Extension, ti nabanglo nga angsen, ti garakgak dagiti ubbing nga agkikinnamat iti asileng a baldosa, tinapay, karne, kalluto nga innapuy, stereo. Ti kabagianda a babai a nalaing a mangiwanwan kadagiti dua a katulonganda, ken mangdigos kadagiti annakna. Ti lakayna a kullapit a mangdumdumog kadagiti plano iti lamisaan nga awan ti mangsingsinga no di ti sagpaminsan a panaguyekna iti namaga.

No manangkami, a, ket manganka metten, kunada kenkuana. Kukuam amin a matgedam. Ngem no umadanin ti panagsueldo, ti la adda ditan a paggastuan nga agalen ti babai. Mangted metten, a, iti sangapulo, duapulo, wenno nasursurok, ket agkatkatawanton ti kabagianda a babai a mangidaydayaw ken mangidasdasig kenkuana kadagiti baliodong a nalaokan iti patiray-ok. Dida ibagbaga a tumulong ngem makaammo lattan nga agibelleng iti basura iti sardam, ken tumulong kadagiti dadduma nga aramid uray no nabannog iti trabahona, ta dina mairusok dagiti pasagid a nadagdagsen ngem iti bugkaw no baonenda koma.

Kinautna ti pitpit a kaha ti sigarilio iti bolsa ti pantalonna. Dandani natukkol ti sangkadubla a natda. Ginaw-atna ti posporo iti lamisaan. Maymaysa ti palito. Nanindi. Innalana ti buong a sarming sana minuraregan ti natadol a rupana, ti imingna, ti basengna, dagiti nalesseb a mata, ti atiddog a tengngedna, ti kullapit a barukongna...

Ama, kaska la aglanglangan nga al-alia! nakunana. Indissona ti sarming. Napan nagtakder iti ridaw.

Iti sango ti siled, iti likudan ti restauran—maymaysa a pasdek daytoy iti nagsulian ti P. Paterno iti abagatan ken ti Evangelista iti laud ket adda pannakadibisionna a namagdasig iti restauran ken iti pagaramidan iti korona iti laud ti siledna, nga akin-uneg—makumikom ti tallo a lallaki nga agurnos, agreppet, agubon, agsibog, ken agsangal kadagiti sabong ken palatang ti sinan-aba nga agpaay kadagiti agkasar, wenno matay. Agsisinnutilda.

Dida ngata, aya, mauma iti aramidda? naisipna.

Nagariangga ti jukebox. Nalagipna ti Bisayano a manedyer ti restauran. Ti Pampanggenia nga agpakasera ken ti napintas a balasangna a nasiripna iti naminsan a panagdigosna—unay ketdin a barukongna, a puseg, a pus-ong! Ti Ilokana a tindera idiay tianggi dita laud ti Evangelista. Dagiti utangna kadakuada. . .

Tinallikudanna ti ridaw. Simmusop iti sigarilio. Nagilad iti kama. Iti nalitem a bobeda, agsalsala ti ginggin-ed iti saputna. Dua nga alutiit ti mangsibsiblok kadagiti legleg. Nagkidem. Nakitana iti isipna ti bagina, iti pagtagilakuan iti libro, papel, pluma, amin-amin a pangopisina. Mangngegna ti pandek ken balkat a baket nga agmammandar. Makitana dagiti kaduana nga agkalkalimduosan. Maulaw no kasdaiay a dina ammon ti sanguenna. Lumag-an ti barukongna no makakita iti balasang a napintas ken nasam-it ti timekna, nadayaw ken saan a managinkukuna.

Dua a tawennan iti bookstore nga imbilangna a pagbaludan. Naganus, nakiin-innem, sa nakiwalo. Walo a pisos ti mailista iti payroll, ngem bagi ngata, a, ti di ammo a demonio ti dua a pisos! Manupulo a pisos ti makalawas? Sa ti maksay para iti no ania ditan a kontribusion. SSS pay.

Nagsardeng nga agadal. Pinadasna ti agurnong. Ngem tallopulo a pisos ti pagbayadna itoy lubong a pagnguynguy-aanna. Ti kanenna. Dagiti dina maliklikan a gagayyem. Lumag-an a lumag-an ti bagina. Kape nga awan gatasna iti bigat ken dies a pandesal. Gudua ti sopa ti apuyenna a balonenna a bulonanna iti naasinan a napettak a kamatis, ken dies a toyo. Sa la aglinab ti boksitna no kasusueldona. No buslonanna ti aggasto, todasna.

"Naumaka kadin ditoy?" mangegna manen ti baket a kabagianda. "Wenno adda kinaguram?"

"Saan, Nana," kinunana. "Kayatko la ti mayasideg iti trabahok. K-ken kayatko a padasen ti rigat ti agsulsulo. . ."

"Adda kenka," kinuna ti lakay. "Ngem no masapulnakaminto, agsublikanto latta. Ken no adda masaoda idiay probinsia, a, ket awan ti pabpabasolem. . ."

Idi kalman, nakaawat iti surat ni tatangna. Sumrek kano ni adingna iti panaglukat ti klase. 'Tay kuartam bassit, Nakkong. . . Imbagana idin

a di pay la makaipaw-it ta yur-urnonganna ti pagbasana. Agaasem, idi nagbasa ni Adingna itay napan a tawen, isu ti pinakilda. Mano kadi ti magasto ti aghaiskul? Aganuska, Barok, kunada, ta ania ngarud ket sika met la ti maararawanmi.

Simmusop manen. Apay ngamin, aya? Nagkidem. Malagipna manen ti kabagianda a babai nga agkunkuna: "Naumaka kadin ditoy? Wenno adda kinaguram?" Saning-i dagiti kakabsatna. Dagiti agbutbuteg a kasinsinna: dida kano pay namigat idinto a pangngaldaw manen; dida pay nagdigos ta gapgapuda iti kadilian; rutayrutayda. . . Ti ikitna nga arig matukkol ti bukotna iti kuttongna nga aglaga iti ikamen wenno basket tapno adda panglitupna iti kaawan ti gasat ni lakayna a nagbanniit idiay Puro. Ni nanangna a masaksakit ngem agkudit latta. Ni tatangna a pilay ta nabungbong ti gurongna, ngem agbatok pay la no kua, ken pasaray pay la suminit iti dinamita.

Nakatok ti ridaw. Mailasinna ti uppat a nagsasaruno a tik-ol. Ti bruha ta addan! Nangemkem. Dina la koman ginanggangtan ti silaw. Sabado ita, ngem dida nagsueldo. Nakidiablo ketdi a kapitalista! naingayemngemna.

Saan a nagkuti; minatmatanna ti samutsamot iti bobeda. Sinusopna ti rungrong sana inridis iti diding.

Naulit ti katok, napigpigsa, ad-adu. Bimmangon. Linuktanna ti ridaw.

"Sika gayam, Nana." Naginlilidlid kadagiti mata. "Nairidepak. Umuliak koma itay, ta ammok nga ur-urayendak. Kinapudnona, sakbay a rimuarak itay bigat, naikeddengkon nga itedko amin ti sueldok kadakayo..."

"Nagsayaaten ta adda igatangko iti irengrengreng 'diay garampingat!" Nabullad dagiti mata ti nalukmeg a baket.

"Isu a nasapaak a nagawid ta dandaniak naisarsarak idiay panggedak. No ti suronko iti daydiay kapitalista, ayna. Agaasem, nangnamnamakayo, ket mabainak unayen kadakayo, ngem didakami ketdin sinuelduan. Panggepmi payen ti agwelga. . ."

"Ay, masapul nga agbayadka! No awan ti pagbayadmo, pumanawka!"

"No dakdakkel la ti sueldok. . . Diak igaggagara ti di agbayad. Ngem talaga nga awan ti kuartak. . ."

"No dika makapagbayad agingga 'ti agsapa, pumanawkan!"

Nagariangga ti jukebox agingga iti siledna. Nagkaradukod dagiti adda iti ngato ket nagtinnag ti tapok.

Nakidiablokayo!

No agpungtotka, agsagawisiw wenno agdayyengka, kunada. Ket nagsagawisiw. Nagkiraus ti boksitna. Nanaklaang ti pagbagasan a linuktannna. Sangsangarakem ti bagas. Awan ti kilabban iti kaldero. Awan posporo. Awan kape. Awan iti uray ania a mabalinna nga ipauneg.

"Pansit. . . adobo. . . gisado. . . mami. . . siopao...!" Natibong ti garakgak dagiti nabartek.

Natuktok ti ridawna iti namindua a sagdudua. 'Tay manedyer daytoyen! nakunana.

"E, komusta, Amo?" kinunana nga umis-isem. "Siguro umaynak singirenan, 'nia?"

"Nabayagen daydi kinnanmo. Naitakki ken nailing-etmon. Ngem agingga ita, diak pay nakaawat 'ti sentimo manipud kenka."

"Kua ngamin, Amo. . ."

"Apay ngamin no ibagam a dimon kayat a bayadan bareng maikkanka pay iti kanem? Adu ti naluto ken di pay naluto. . . Saan a kasta nga agkarika sa met di matungpal. . . Kastakay la ketdi nga Ilokano!"

Tumanabutob ti Bisayano a timmallikud.

Nagkidem, immanges iti nauneg, nangmesmes.

Kinuentana ti utangna iti tianggi dita ballasiw. Adu! Ngem bareng no ikkanda pay. Uray ket Ilokana ti akintianggi.

Makumikom pay laeng dagidiay tallo a lallaki iti pagaramidan iti korona. Korona ti natay ti ar-aramidenda. Nalidem dagiti bombilia kadagiti narugit a bobeda. Adu latta ti maisagud a bumiding kadagiti korona.

Kinablaawanna ida. Inyisemna ti panagkiraus ti bitukana. Nabasa ti semento ken agkaiwara dagiti nagrugosan iti palatang ken bulong ken nalungsot a sabong. Iniseman ti pandek a kasla butiti.

Nagtakder iti bangketa. Kasla natatadem a mata iti kasipngetan dagiti silaw dagiti lugan iti kalsada. Iti kanigidna, makapabisaleg ti angot dagiti taraon iti panganan, ti kalangiking ti kutsara ken pinggan, ti panagipapel dagiti mangan. Iti kanawanna, um-umkis dagiti natagadtad

a pagaramidan iti lapida, ken no ania ditan a rebulto. Adu ti aggatang iti rebulto—babaknang, a pangitanggayaan dagiti agsusublat nga agbutbuteg, rutayray nga ubbing, kadagiti babassit a dakulapda.

Adu ti tao iti tianggi. Idi rumasay dagiti lugan, bimmallsiw. Inasitganna ti tindera nga Ilokana.

Nagrimat dagiti mata ti tindera. Naimbag kano ta immay, ta saanen a dumandanon idiay dagusna. Naimbag la kano nga inayonna iti igatangna iti lakona.

Masapul nga agdrama, no saan, di mangrabii. "Nagsayaat idiay Ilokos," innayonna iti palawagna, "ta uray no maibusanka, sitatallugod dagiti kaarruba a mangiburay iti kaasida. Kastatayo nga Ilokano, di ngamin?"

Nakaala iti sangasalup, sangalata a ligo, sangakaha a Bataan, gurabis, ken no ania pay a babassit a masapsapulna. Nakasublat iti sangapulo a pisos ta inkarina ti sueldona inton Lunes. Naimbag la a yunana iti pagkaseraanna.

Nakaanges iti nalukay idi makagteng iti siledna. Nagluto. Nangan. Nagsigarilio.

Idi makapalpa, immuli. Agsanud koma ta adu ti tao iti dakkel a lamisaan a pagsusugalan ti agpakasera ken dagiti sangailina, ngem nakita ti baket ken ti balasangna. Iti sango dagiti sangaili, sinaludsod ti baket ti gagarana. Imbagana nga agbayad. Sangapulo a pisos.

"Sangapulo?" Nabutuag ti kiday ti baket. "Di pay umanay nga ipustak iti maminsan!"

"Dayta laeng a gatad, Mama, bay-amon!" Naglibbi ti balasang.

"Alaek koma, ngem amangan no dikan mangan. Alaem pay laeng!" kinuna ti baket.

Simleng ti panagkitana. Timmangken ti gemgemna. Bimmara ti amin a paset ti bagina. Nagteppel. Agtigtigrger ti imana a nangibolsa iti sangapulo a pisos sa nagdardaras nga immulog a dina tinaliaw dagiti agina a nakalibbi.

Nadagsen ti barukongna a nangipusot iti bagina iti kama. Nagtayyek ti isipna.

"Naumaka kadin? Wenno adda kinaguram?"

"'Ta kuartam bassit, Barok. . ."

"Pasublatanka, ngem laglagipem ti agbayad inton Lunes. . ."

"Apay ngamin no ibagam a dimon kayat a bayadan ti linamutmo bareng maikkanka pay iti kanem?"

"Sangapulo? Di pay umanay nga ipustak iti maminsan!"

Immanges iti nauneg. Madamdama pay, imalmaletanan dagiti lupotna. Nalakananton ti mangikeddeng apaman a makaruar iti daytoy a siled. —0

Bannawag, Hunio 28, 1971; *Pakpakawan, Berde!* pp. 129-135.

Estero: Iti Maysa A Panawen

AGTANTANAMITIM. Narimat dagiti matana iti silnog ti langit iti panangtangadna iti unibersidad. Maayatan kadagiti estudiante a tuman-aw iti estero. Pasaray maisurot iti nasarangsang a katawada. Laslasinenna dagiti agsisinnallabay a lallaki ken babbai. Aglalo no agsisinnusopda iti sigarilio, wenno agsisinnuboda iti makan. Kagurana dagiti lallaki ta at-atiddog payen ti buokda ngem isu. Sa nalayak ti pagan-anayda.

Ngem ad-adda a maay-ayo kadagiti libro ken kuaderno nga igpil dagiti estudiante. Pasaray tuladenna ida ket agpagnapagna a kasla nakaigpil iti libro, sa agtugaw ket kasla adda ukradenna iti saklotna. Dagusenna ti agtan-aw no mangngegna ti kiriring iti unibersidad a mangipalnaad iti panagsukat ti oras. Buyaenna dagiti rumuar ken sumrek. Makitana ti bagina a makipulpulapol kadagiti estudiante. Makikinnatawa. Makidinnaer iti sirib.

"Ting . . . Ting? Addakad'ta, Apok?"

"Agruardan, Lola. . . nangngegmo 'tay kampanilian?" kasla anghel ti timek ni Ting. Nariknana ti agkarkarawa a dakulap iti abagana.

"Aduda manen, Apok?"

"Wen, Lola. . . ne, dagidiayen dagiti nagbinnisong idi rabii!"

"Iti sigud?" Naglupisak ti baket iti abay ni Ting.

"Wen, Lola, ket agsinsinnanggolda manen."

"Kaasi pay dagiti nagannak kadakuada."

"Di met dagiti napanglaw laeng ti nakakaasi, Lola? Nagbabaknang dagidiay, ne! Nagpintas 'diay bado ken sapinda. . ."

"Ania manen dagidiay agaariwawa?"

Adda agipukpukkaw iti di maawatan ti ubing ken ti baket. Agdadanggay ti pukkaw. Madamdama, nakita ni Ting nga agdadarison dagiti estudiante a rumuar iti ruangan ti pagadalan, iti asideg ti rangtay. Nabakiro ti tao a nagkawes iti asul ken nagtagibatuta. Inirik-irik ti sangapulo nga estudiante.

Iti laud, binallasiw ti sangapangen nga estudiante ti rangtay a kayo. Adda pirgis a lupot nga imbarabadda iti uloda. Adda wagaywayda a nalabaga. Darupdarupenda ti ruangan ti pagadalan. Agpupukkawda.

"Addada manen, Apok?"

"Wen, Lola. Ket ad-aduda ita. Naung-ungetda ngem idi kalman."

"Kumarodan sa ketdi."

"Wen sa. Adda pay agpidut iti bato. Kayatda ti sumrek dita eskuela. Apay ngata, Lola?"

"Di pay siguro napatgan ti kuna ni Inangmo a dawat dagiti estudiante. Maipanggep kano iti matrikula. Awan la ti di nguminan."

Nagsasaruno ti kiriring ti kampanilia. Nagruar dagiti estudiante. Nairikep dagiti tawa. Dagiti ruangan. Nabati dagiti guardia. Nagkirpa ti ariwawa dagiti estuiante iti ruar ti pagadalan. Ngem dida pimmanaw.

Nagkuretret ti muging ni Ting. Tinangadna ti init. Mabayag pay bassit sa lumnek. Sakbay ti maudi a kiriring mabayagto bassiten a nayaplag ti sipnget, ken nasindian dagiti narangrang a silaw. Ngem apay a nasapa ita? Nalidayan ni Ting. Impapanna a saan a mapasgedan dagiti bombilia. Ket awan ti anaraar kadagiti barongbarong.

"Isardengda kadin ti klase, Apok?"

"Wen, Lola."

"Kaasi pay dagiti estudiante."

"Lola, kaano nga isangpet ni inang ni amang?"

"Kua, basta adda ni Amangen, kunamton, a, no isangpetna. . ."

"Kada rumuar, kunana nga isangpetna ni amang. Mangloklokon sa met laeng. . . 'Mom, Lola, kayatko a sumangpet koman ni amang tapno adda mangpagadal kaniak."

"Makapagadalka met ket uray no awan ni amangmo. Di met kunam a kayatmo ti agbasa: tuladem daydi Doctor Rizal, daydi Marceo H. Del Pilar, daydi Emilio Jacinto, daydi Mabini. . ."

"Ken daydi Presidente Quezon, Lola. . . ken amin-amin a sinaritam a masirib. Kayatko ti agbalin a masirib. Ti agbalin a presidente. No presidenteakon, bumaknangtayo no kuan, Lola. Bumaknang amin a... politiko, kunam sa idi, Lola? Maam-ammodak pay dagiti tao. Kunam pay a dayta nga eskuela ti nagbasaan ni Apo Mayor. Ni Apo Senador. Ken kunam pay nga adu ti masirib a nagbasa dita. . ."

"Agawaam ngarud ti dumakkel. Dika aglokloko. Surotem amin nga ibagami ken Inangmo. Ammom, talaga a kayatnaka a pagbasaen ni inangmo."

Nagtugaw ni Ting iti bangsal. Simmango iti abagatan a pangpaspasungadanna ken ni inangna. Nangur-it ti baket iti laem.

"Awan met laengen ni inang," nayesngaw ni Ting. No sadino ti paggapuan ni inangna, dina masinunuo.

No adda agkakatawa kadagiti agkikinnamat nga ubbing kadagiti kalantayan, maisursurot ni Ting. Agmurareg no agbugkaw daydiay masikog a nagigpil iti di pay natawenan a tagibi, wenno umsiag daydiay kutongi nga adda umip-ius iti gaybang a bestidona. Kumkumpes ni Ting tunggal layatan daydiay nakakamiseta a lalaki a nasaknap ti bagina iti tato daydiay ubing a kataebna. Idiay bangir a barongbarong, nakita ni Ting dagidiay agkabsat, in-inaudi ngata ngem isu ti inauna, nga adda iggemda a pitpit a plato. Sangkaballing nga ittip ti pagin-innagawanda. Idi agrungaab ti ub-ubing, rimuar ti ina a nakaammal iti nangisit a sigarilo ket ginagarana a linabak ti inauna.

Ti laeng barongbarong a kaaripingda ti naulimek ita. Naisip ni Ting nga awan ti balasitang a sursuroten no kua dagiti babbarito. Awan met ti ina daytoy. Dida pay siguro simmangpet.

Napatit ti orasion iti simbaan iti plasa iti laud. Nagtaray ni Ting a limmaem. Nagparintumeng iti sibay ti baket. Nagugis, kas iti panagugis ti baket. Inkararagna a mangisangpet ni inangna iti adu a kuarta a pagbasana. Innayonna ti panangisangpet ni inangna ken ni amangna. Idi malpas, nagmano ni Ting iti baket.

"Saluadannaka ti Dios, Apok. . ."

Napanunot ni Ting ti mangisaang. Ngem kawaw ti pagbagasan. Napanda nagpalabas iti oras iti bangsal. Namituen ti asul a langit.

Saggaysa ti tao iti kalantayan. Awanen dagiti estudiante iti sango ti pagadalan.

"'Mom, Ting, kastoy ti kalamiis ti pul-oy idiay probinsia. No kastoy a sardam idiay away, naragsak dagiti aglilinnemmengan iti sirok ti kumanagkag a bulan. . ."

"Agpayso kadi ti kuna ni inang a napintas ti away, Lola?"

"Wen, a. Adu ti bayyabas, santol, sua, saba, mabolo, kulkulang, mansanita, allagat. . . amin nga agbunga iti makan. Idi ubingak, agum-umakami iti lamut. Uray kano ditoy idi. Adu met ti mula idi sakbay a dimteng dagiti Kastila. Naulimek. Awan dayta eskuela. Nalawa daytoy estero. Nadalus. Nalames. Adu ti agdidigos."

"Agpayso kadi a nasingpet dagiti tao idiay away?"

"Wen, a. No adda rigat ti maysa, rigat ti sangapurokan."

"Apay ngarud nga immaytayo ditoy. . .? Ken sabali kano ti lugarmo kada inang?"

"Agpayso. Saanko a kabkabagian ni inangmo. Ngem nasingedkami. Ammom, naragsak kano da inangmo idi. . . iti sidong daydi lola ken lolom. Bisayana daydi lolam. . . Ngem idi rumsua ti riribuk iti daga, nairamanda a natay. Nagpa-Manila ni inangmo. Isu a nayanakka ditoy."

"Ket sika, Lola?"

"Taga-Lagunaak. . . napanglawkami. Nalaadak, awan a pulos ti nagarem kaniak. Immayak nakigasanggasat ditoy. Natay dagidi dadakkelko a diak nakita. . . Adu a rigat ti napasarak. Agingga a napukaw ti lawag dagiti matak. . . Inton dumakkelka, maammuamto amin a palimed ti biag. . ."

Simmungad ti sangaparis iti kalantayan. Nailasin ni Ting ti balasitang iti kaariping ti barongbarongda. Lumakayen ti lalaki. Aggargarikgik ti balasitang idi sumrekda iti balay.

"Daytay kadi balasitang daydiay, Apok?"

"Isu, Lola. Adda lakay a kaduana."

"Kaasi pay."

Narikna ni Ting ti panaggunggon ti barongbarong. Sa ti panagareng-eng ti balasitang. Sa naunday nga ulimek.

"Kaasi pay," inulit ti baket.

Simmungad ni Inangna. Adda kakibinna a lalaki. Nagsardengda iti sungaban idi makitada ni Ting. Limnek ti lalaki ket nagpukaw iti kasipngetan.

Timmaray a simmabat ni Ting. Inawatna t supot. Nagsarunoda ken ni inangna iti kalantayan.

"Nagrabiikan, Inang?"

Immmisem laeng ni Inangna sana kinuso ti buokna.

Simrekda. Nangan ni Ting ken ti baket iti pansit. Nagbuya ni Inangna a nakipatpatang. Madamdama ginaw-at ni inangna ti buong a sarming ket sinirigsirigna ti bagina.

Rumuar kano. "Dimo baybay-an ni Ting, Nana, a?"

"Wen, a… mabayagka kadi?"

Saannan a nangngeg ti sungbat ni inangna. Nakapapel pay laeng iti pansit. Naimas, ket nalipatanna ti nagsaludsod.

NARIING iti ariwawa iti unibersidad. Idi bumangon, nakitana ni Inangna a narnekan iti maysa a suli. Nagin-inayad a rimuar. Iti bangsal, nadanonna ti baket nga agkarkarawa iti diding.

Napamulagat ni Ting. Reprep ti tao iti pagadalan. Adu ti maiwagwagis a nalabaga a bandera. Adda akaba ken atidog a lupot a nakaisuratan ti dadakel a letra. Dina maawatan ti ipukpukkaw dagiti estiduante. Itudtudoda ti agak-akak a lakay nga Amerikano ken ti karantiway a lakay a Filipino nga akinkukua iti unibersidad. Agtantan-awda iti lobby ti maikatlo a kadsaaran. Ditoy ti yan ti laboratorio ti kimika.

Limnek ti Amerikano ken ti Filipino.

Rimmungsot ti pukkaw dagiti estudiante. Adda nanabraang iti uneg ti pagadalan. Nagtataray dagiti adda iti uneg. Nagsasaruno ti kanalbuong. Sinaruno ti ikkis ken pukkaw.

Iti laud, immaweng ti sirena. Tallo a dyip ti polis ti dimteng. Nagtataray dagiti esdudiante.

Iti malem, adda manen dagiti demonstrador. Iti bangsal, nakipagbuya metten ti inang ni Ting.

Narungrungsot itan dagiti estudiante. Kuna ni inangna nga adda kano nailaok a di estudiante kadagiti agik-ikkis. Nabayadanda kano. Kuna pay ni inangna a dawdawaten dagiti estudiante a di maingato ti

matrikula. Ngem nasubeg kano ti Amerikano a nakisosio iti Filipino nga akinkukua iti pagadalan. Sursuroten kano ti Filipino ti amin a kayat dayta nga Amerikano.

Maikatlo ngatan iti malem idi agkanalbuong iti maikatlo a kadsaaran. Simgiab ti laboratorio ket nagkayamkam ti apuy iti bara ti malem. Nagtataray dagiti estudiante.

Nakamulagat ni Ting a nangbuya iti agdildilat nga apuy. Nagtayab dagiti dalipato. Dadakkel dagiti agtupak iti estero.

Nagdanag ti inang ni Ting. Nagiikkis dagiti agindeg kadagiti barongbarong. Nagtuloy dagiti alipaga.

"Agsaganakayo. . . Umadayokayo. . .!" adda nagpukkaw.

Inarikumkom ti inang ni Ting dagiti lupotda. Rimuarda. Saanen nga agsusurot ti kararag ti bulsek a baket a kimmibin ken ni Ting.

Addadan iti kalantayan a pagdudupudopan dagiti tao idi marsuod ti sumsumgiab a kayo iti estero. Nagiikkisda. Narsuod ti kalantayan. Naipabatokda iti estero. Nakakapet da Ting ken ni Inangna iti naguyaoy a kalantayan. Kimmalipkipda iti pader. Nabati ti baket a bulsek iti estero. Ken ti balasitang a kadua ti lakay idi sardam.

Nagdissuor ti dakkel a dalipato iti tuktok ti barongbarong. Linamut ti apuy dagiti karton a diding ken atep. Nagkayamkam ti apuy kadagiti barongbarong.

Nagrusod ti kasla balay nga apuy iti estero. Nagiikkis dagiti agbuybuya. Inludek ti apuy dagiti nailumlom iti pitak. Nagkidem ni Ting ta nairaman ti baket a bulsek.

Tinangad ni Ting ti unibersidad a nakainaigan dagiti arapaapna. Marmarbibi ni Ting. Lumablabbaga dagiti matana. Nagayus ti lua iti agsumbangir a pingpingna.

Awanen, nayesngawna. Awanen. . .

Nariknana ti dakulap ni inangna iti abagana. –0

Bannawag: Hunio 19, 1972; *Pakpakawan, Berde! Ken 22 a Sarita:* *c*1977, pp.147-153.

Tallo A Tugot

"Three passions simple but overwhelmingly strong, have governed my life: the longing for love, the search for knowledge, and unbearable pity for the suffering of mankind. . . Love and knowledge, so far as thy were possible, led upward toward the heavens. But always pity brought me back to earth."—Bertrand Russel.

KAYATKO a mangsuratka iti nobela a moderno ti sukogna, Hil," agan-annineng iti isip ni Hilario Garcia ti kinuna ni Valerio Castillejos, ti publisista ti *Mata*. "Ipakitam ti pakabuklan ti puli a tinirtiris ti biddut a sistema ti bileg. No kasano nga agdappuor ti bales dagiti gemgem iti igid kadagiti landok a makinaria a tanikala ti wayawaya. No ania ti posible a mapasamak no saan a maguped ti di panangipirpirit ti agsumbangir a bileg. Kayatko nga ipakanmo ti tadem ti plumam iti kabiitan a panawen tapno bumangon ti kinapudno. Itan ti panangipamatmatmo iti pudno a kabaelam!"

Napigsa a karit ken ni Hilario Garcia. Ngem naadat ti panagramanna iti balikas ni Valerio Castillejos. Apay, panagkuna ni Castillejos, dina ammo ti mapaspasamak?

Naituon ti panagkitana iti lampshade iti lamisaanna.

Linuktan ni Hilario Garcia ti uyosen ti lamisaan. Inruarna ti asul a kuaderno. Linukibna ti umuna a panid . . .

I. Langit

MAYAT ti dalukappitmi kada Anong ken Edwin iti bangsal iti maysa a sardam a namituen ti langit.

"Bituenko daydiay kadakkelan!" intudo ni Anong ti rimmuong dagiti bituen iti daya.

"Bituenko!" kinuna ni Edwin.

"Bituenko!" kinuna ni Anong.

"Bituenko ngarud daydiay!" intudo ni Edwin ti agsolsolo a bituen iti laud.

Kitkitaek ti bituen a sinaklot ti simmagaysay a bulan.

"Sika?" diak inkaskaso ti kalbit ni Anong. Pampanunotk nga addaak iti saklot ti bulan.

"Oy, nakaturogkan?" kinalbitnak manen ni Anong.

"Pampanunotek," kinunak, "no apay nga adda bituen iti saklot ti bulan. Ania ngata no adda payakko ket tumayabak a mapan 'diay bulan? Adda kano ni Apo Dios 'diay langit. Siguro adda 'diay bulan. Kasaok no kua, dawatek a patubbogenna 'diay bubontayo tapno saantayon a mapan agsaksakdo 'diay Kinwang. Bulodek no kua 'tay pagal-ala ni Angkel Disiong 'ti retrato ta retratuek ni Apo Dios . . ."

"No siak, dumawatak 'ti adu a paltog!" kinuna ni Anong. "Sumurotak no kua ken ni Manong Iyac nga agpaltog 'ti billit!"

"No makitaka, timbutenka!" kinuna ni Edwin.

"Apay met?"

"Kaasi dagidiay billit!"

Iti pataguab, umanet-et ti ruedo iti panagtiritir ni Lelong Iroy iti lapnit. Kumutikuti ni Lelang Andiang iti sagumbi.

Iti kapan-awan iti laud a labes ti bubuga, napigsa ti masagsagawisiw a Mona Liza. Ni Angkel Aling daydiay sumungad; naggapu iti Kinwang a nangpasagadanna iti dua burnay a danum.

Agkakabsat ti ammami kada Anong ken Edwin. Natayen dagiti dadakkel ni Edwin. Natay metten ti nanang ni Anong; adda iti siuad ni Angkel Moding a tatangna ket addan sabali nga asawana. Adda da tatang ken nanang idiay San Marcos ta papaagasanda ni ading.

Agkakasadarankami a tallo, bulan la ti nagbabaetanmi. Siak ti inauna, maikadua ni Edwin, kaubingan ni Anong. Agyankami iti balay da lelong iti tuktok ti Bantay Baybayyabas a hinomstedda iti nasurong a paset ti Santa Monica.

"Oy, tallo a tiltillayon, umaykay maturogen!" kasla agpaguyod iti bulo ni lelong a nangayab kadakami.

Maysa a bigat nga agpakpakankami iti manok, kasta unay ti rungiit da Anong ken Edwin a mamagpalpallot iti dua a manok. Linibasak ida ket tinarayko nga inuli ti sangapuon a katuday iti amianan ti balay. Kasla manen addaak iti langit. Insimpak iti sanga ti nangbuya iti Karayan Parsua iti amianan a baba ti Bantay Baybayyabas. Impasurotko ti panagkitak iti ayus nga aggapu iti Burayok Kimmandela iti Bantay Bullagaw iti daya. Nagsaltek ti panagkitak iti Pangasaan Elementary School iti sakaanan ti Bantay Bullagaw. Kasla sulsulken ti silap ti sim ti eskuela ti Kimmandela. Nakunak idi iti nakemko: inton pitokon, agbasaakto met dita Pangasaan.

"Hoy, tiltillayon, addaka man gayam ditan!" dandaniak nakaibbet iti itatangad ni Edwin.

Tinapuakko ti immulog ket kinamatko ida. Kinamangda ni lelong a manglaglagda iti barawid ti burnay iti pasagad.

"Anian sa dagitoy a butillog!" nakasuron ni lelong ket linapigosna ida.

"Beee!" dinilatak ida.

"Maysaka met," kinuna ni lelong ngem nagtarayakon.

"Intay agsakdo idiay Kinwang," kinuna ni lelong iti maysa a nadagaang a bigat. "Isangolmo ni Sawak kadaydiay dakkel a pasagad, Edwin. Sika, Anong, bagim ni Pango. Annadanyo a di mapakbo dagiti pasagad ket awanen ti reserbatayo a burnay. Sika, Ayong, sakayam ni Sikkubeng."

"Yaho, nagganasen!" naglagtit ni Edwin.

"Agay-ayatka ta lumabaska manen 'ti yan da Adela!" kinuna ni Anong.

"Lalanggong, dikay pay nagmata ket agaremkayon!" inkusilap ni lelong a makais-isem.

Nagpasalogkami iti abagatan. Agdaldalluyon ti nalawa a kapanawan. Linabsanmi ti narukbos a mansanita a narnuoyan iti bunga.

Nagtakderak iti bukot ni Sikkubeng ket gimmaw-atak iti insakmolko iti nagruyag a sanga. Timmulad ni Anong. Naikaglis ket nagsirko iti daga.

"O, dayta ti maal-alam!" kinuna ni lelong. "Kaskay la di mangmangan!"

"Kayatmo ti bayyabas, Dela?" kinuna ni Edwin idi malabsanmi da Adela nga agkalkali iti ubi iti gayadan ti Bantay Kimmabalio a hinomsted dagiti Olliero . . .

"Inigges dayta!" kinuna ni Anong. "Pinidutna la 'diay sirokna . . ."

"Patpatiem, kappurosko daytoy!" kinusilapan ni Edwin ni Anong.

"Agarem sa met 'ta apomon, Ama!" inrungiit ti tatang ni Adela.

"Saan met, 'ta," kinun ni Edwin. "Magustuak laeng ni Adela."

Immadani ti panagtutudo; dimi nadlaw ti ilalabas ti kalgaw. Aggurgurruoden iti nauneg. Agtiakoktiakok metten dagiti kakok iti kasamsamonan. Makumikomen da lelong ken angkel nga agipungdol ken aguma.

"Agiinnadutayo 'ti mabunag a pungdol," inkarit ni Anong iti naminsan.

Nakalima pay laeng idi madin ta natupakanna ti tangan ti sakana.

Kumkumpitis ti adu a mauma. Nagiinnunakami a nangala iti natadem a badang. Napuskol ti kudilmi, dimi inkankano ti gatel ti sabawil.

"Siak ti manindi," kinunak idi nagangon ti inumami kalpasan ti sumagmamano nga aldaw. Ginaikanmi ti igid tapno saan nga agkayamkam iti saan a nauma.

Kasla adda kanta iti barukongko iti risak ti gil-ayab kadagiti nagango a bulong ket kasla maisursurotak nga agpalangit iti agkutikot a dila ti apuy a mangibel-a iti nangisit nga asuk. Sinul-oyko ti bang-i a kumutikot iti agong.

Ket iti sardam a naulimekkamin iti balay, imasek a denggen ti sagawisiw ni angkel, no saan nga agtantanamitim, idinto a sursurotek ti nabuntog a pannagna ti ulep a kasla magawgaw-atko. Agkubkubalsing ken agrikrikiar da Edwin ken Anong.

Agur-urnongen ti langit iti ulep ket saan a mabayag, yabayabnan ti pakpakauna ti tudo. Iti kastoy a panawen, adu ti asad ken tubong nga insagana da lelong ken angkel.

Agkikinnidday ken agkikinnidol dagiti babbaro ken babbalasang a taga-Baba nga umay makipagmula. Danggayan ti risak ti ngiwatda. Kasla adda bituen kadagiti matada.

Nasapa a simmangpet ni angkel iti naminsan.

"Dimo pay la napagtinnag ni Caring?" dinamag ni lelong.

"Dandanin."

"Dandanika a dandanin. . . dimon sa met ammo ti agarem. Amangan no maunaandaka . . . ibagam, a, ta yaremka no kua," kinuna ni lelong.

"Laklakayan a kunam la no kalaingan!" kinuna ni lelang. "Dina pay nayarem ti bagbagina!"

"Ni baket met . . ."

Nagsubra ti angsot da Edwin ken Anong iti naminsan. Nagboksingda. Nagdugolda. Saan nga inanawa ni lelong ida. Manipud idin, saandan nga agang-angsot.

Simmangpet da tatang ken nanang iti saan a nabayag. Ngem awanen ni ading. Nagpatakder ni tatang iti balaymi iti abay ti balay da lelong. No dadduma, matiltiliwak nga agsangsangit ni nanang.

Ngem asideg latta ti langit iti Baybayyabas. Kasko la magawgaw-at. No manen, uliek ti katuday ket tannawgak ti Pangasaan Elementary School.

NATUKTOK ti ridaw ti siled ni Hilario Garcia.

"Papa, mangantayo kanon, kuna ni mama," timek ti buridekna.

Imbaba ni Hilario ti asul a kuaderno. "O, sige, sumarunoakon," kinunana. Nagintek ti imatangna iti lampshade iti lamisaan.

Linukibna ti kuaderno; nanglibtaw iti sumagmamano a panid. . .

II. Daga

APAMAN a nagturposkami iti maikanem iti Pangasaan Elementary School, nagsisinakamin. Innala ni Angkel Moding ni Anong idiay Manila. Napankami iti San Marcos kada tatang. Nabati ni Edwin kada lelong iti Baybayyabas.

Nagbasaak iti San Marcos Institute. Saanen a nagtuloy ni Edwin ta agbasa kano laengen iti bukot ti nuang. Diak mababalaw ta pullat idi

nagturposkami. Manmano a madamagko ni Anong. Ngem agbasbasa kano.

Nagraira dagiti mangrabrabii. Ngimmato ti presio dagiti magatgatang. Dimmagsen ti damag maipanggep iti riribuk iti pagilian. Saan a makaidna ni Tatang.

Idi makaturposak iti sekundaria, nagpa-Manilaak. Nagadalak iti panagiwarnak iti University of the Philippines. Sinapulko ni Anong iti address nga impaw-itna. Diak nasarakan ta napan kano nagenrol idiay Baguio, iti Philippine Military Academy.

Saanen a rimmuar ni Edwin iti Baybayyabas. Lakay ken baketen da lelong ken lelang ket dina kayat a panawan ida. Adda met ketdi ni angkel ngem adda kano dagiti gundaway nga agmutmuttaleng manipud idi nangasawa ti sabsabongenna. Nadamagko nga intuloy ni Edwin nga armen ni Adela Olliero. Kunak, sapay koma ta agkatuloyanda. Imbagak pay nga agawidak no agkasarda.

Iti naminsan a panagbakasionko, rinantak ni Edwin iti Baybayyabas.

"Ammokon no apay a natay 'di tatang ken 'di nanang," kinunana. Naliday. Uray idi yawatko ti sangaparis a tisert ken maong a pasarabok, kasla katamnay ti dinengdeng nga awan bugguongna ti panangawatna. "Aramid ti tao!" intuloyna. "Dagiti annak ti . . .!"

Tinapikko. "Bay-amon," kinunak. "Maisublim kadi pay ti napasamak?"

"Saan. Ngem adda maaramidko. Am-ammok ida. Makitkitak ida. Agburek ti darak no kua!"

Rinamesda kano daydi Anti. Nakita 'di angkel. Nagpagunggan. Pinatayda ida a dua. No apay a di nabalud dagiti nagaramid, napigsada kano iti daydi sigud a mayor.

"Daytoy ti laglagipem, Hil," kinunana sakbay a nagsinakami. "No saan nga agsardeng ti agdama a mapaspasamak, addanto agayus a dara iti Karayan Parsua!"

"Hey!" kinunak. "Sayang, insan, nagbasaka met koma. Linia ti mannaniw dayta!" Kayatko a kerrasan ti dagensenna.

"Saanak nga agang-angaw!" kinunana.

Rumabraban ti di panagkikinnaawatan ti gobierno ken dagiti aktibista. Umad-adu ti rally. Uray iti U.P. ket masansanen nga awan

ti klase gapu iti dumagdagsen a di panagkikinnaawatan. Agingga a limmatak dagiti grupo a kumangkannigid iti turay. Masansan ti panagbettak dagiti pilbaks ken panagpugsit dagiti tirgas. Iti kalsada, nadagsen ti danapeg dagiti estudiante, tumibtibong ti pukkawda. Pumuspuskolda. Umatipukpok ti kup-ayda. Kasla matattatek ti daga iti aglawlaw ti pagadalan.

Adu ti kaadalak a mangsugsugsog a kumappengak kadakuada. Ngem diak maalimon ti ideolohiada. Sabali ti turong ti panunotko. Kayatko ti aglatak a mannurat. Nagsakdoak iti sirib dagiti intelehente iti nadumaduma a paset ti pagsiriban. Pannakabalayko ti U.P. Main Library. No dadduma, dandaniak la makulong no mangrikepen ti dianitor ta addaak pay la iti suli nga agkalkali iti baro a pagsiriban.

Saanak pay a nagturpos idi rinugiak ti agsurat ta saanen a makatutor ti panagwerret ti utekko. Adun ti nasakdok ket aglipiasen ti ammok a nasken a makerrasan.

Iti naminsan a yaawagko kada Angkel Moding, nairana nga adda ni Anong, wenno Jan itan. Dandanikamin agturpos ket agpadakami a nasdaaw iti dakkel a nagbaliwan ti bagimi. Talaga a takderen ti militar ni Jan. Nangato kano ti ranggona iti akademia ket mangnamnama a maikkanto iti nangato a ranggo no agturpos.

"Adda ipabasak kenka," kinunana idi agmawmaw ti inniliwmi. "Ammok a magustuam."

Autobiography ni Bertrand Russel ti inruarna. Kinagiddan ti panangyawatna ti panangbulodna iti umuna a binatog ni Russel. Ti tallo a pasion ni Russel: *longing for love, search for knowledge,* ken *unbearable pity for the suffering of mankind.* Naimula iti panunotko ti pasetna a nagkuna: *love and knowledge, so far as they were possible, led upward toward the heavens. But always pity brought me back to earth.*

"Panagserbi, Hil," kinuna ni Jan. "Naadalko dayta iti panagindegko iti akademia. Saan nga umdas ti katawa a mangitag-ay iti kinatao; dagiti ragsakktayo idiay Baybayyabas, ladawan a saanen a nasken a sublian. . . Kitaentayo ti agdama a mapaspasamak. Ania ti maaramidtayo?"

Iti maysa nga aldaw a panagawidko iti kaserak, nasangpetak ti surat a naggapu kada tatang.

"Awanen ni Edwin, Nakkong," kinuna ti surat. "Nagkamangen iti bantay . . . simmurot kadagiti mangankanigid. Saanen a nagbayag manipud idi nagbekkel daydi Adela Olliero kalpasan ti panangrames ti kabsat ti mayor . . ."

Nalagipko ti kinuna ni Edwin iti naudi a panagsaritami: "no saan nga agsardeng ti agdama a mapaspasamak, addanto agayus a dara iti Karayan Parsua!"

Adda lamiis a nagkarayam a nagpangato iti durik.

Ad-addan ti panagbulanos ti utekko idi makaturposak. No ad-adu la ti extra curricular activities a nakaikappengak, saan koma a cum laude laeng ti nayalatko. Ngem saan a dayta ti napateg. Dandani inaldaw nga adda rummuar a gapuanak kadagiti aginaldaw a pagiwarnak, sabali la ti rummuar kadagiti aglinawas. Adda dagiti pagiwarnak a mangididiaya iti panagkamengko kadakuada, ngem kinaykayatko ti nag-free lancer. Nawaywayaak nga agdakiwas. Saanak a nakakahon. Maaramidko ti kaykayatko. Total, saan met a makapabisin ti matgedak.

Napusgan ni Jan a teniente idi damo. Ngem nadaras ti pannakaitalona. Awan pay makatawenna iti serbisio idi maingato a kapitan. Captain Januario Garcia! Naidestino iti Northern Luzon. Dandani naggiddankami a nangasawa. Nagnaed ti pamiliak iti siudad.

"Komanderen ni Edwin, Nakkong," kinuna ti surat ni tatang iti naminsan. "Saan la a bastabasta a komander. Nalatak unayen. Ananupen ti turay ta awanen ti ikabkabilanganna iti amianan. Adun ti soldado a napatayda iti teritorioda. Awan ti makaasideg. Kasta unay ti liday da lelongyo . . . limmanlan la ngarud ni angkelyo . . ."

"Aglablabesen ni Edwin," kinuna ni Jan iti naminsan a panagsaritami. "Saan koma a mapasamak. Ngem addan nangngegko a bilin ti turay a maikkanen iti ultimatum. Awan ti maaramidko no siak ti pusganda a sumarang kenkuana."

Inkeddengko a kasaritak ni Edwin. Kayatko a tulongan ida.

Nagpaitulodak iti karison ti am-ammok iti baba agingga iti gayadan ti Baybayyabas. Diak ammo no sadino ti yan ti kampo da Edwin ngem namnamaek nga ammo da lelong. Ammok a napateg da lelong ken ni Edwin ket dina maitured a di sarungkaran ida.

Adda pay la ti katuday iti amianan ti balay da lelong. Ngem lakayen. Kasla immilet ti arubayan iti panagkitak. Napuskol pay la dagti bulo iti abagatan ken iti laud. Nabengbeng ti kapan-awan. No adda nagbaliwan ti lugar, nalabit a ti kaawan ti ubbing nga aggagarikgik.

Aglulua ni lelang nga immarakup. Nasakit met ti riknak ta ita la nga agkitakami kalpasan ti adun a tawen. Adda pay la rimat dagiti matana. Nakadikkumer ni lelong iti suli. Nakapsuten, saanen a makailasin. Adda kano ni Angkel idiay Kinwang.

"Daydiay kasinsinyo . . . apok, aya!" Nagsaibbek ni lelang idi agapadek ni Edwin.

"Sarsarungkarannakayo met laeng?"

"Binulan . . . ngem di pay immay itoy a bulan."

Di ammo da lelang ti kampo da Edwin. Sumagmamano nga aldaw laengen sakbay nga agtapos ti bulan ket inkeddengko nga urayek.

Naklaat ni Edwin idi dumtengda iti maysa a rabii. Dandani diak nalasin, iti karaber ti barbasna. Imbagak ti gagarak. Ken ti panggep ti gobierno.

"Naladawen," kinunana. "Adun ti naisakripisio a biag, gapu iti kinaagum dagiti nabileg. Ti kunam nga isusukok, nalaka a sawen. Ngem ammom kadi ti riknak? Ammok kadi ti rikna ti mailupitlupit? Kasla kadi kalaka ti agmama ti mamakawan? Ti inaramidda kadagiti dadakkelko . . . ken ni . . . Adela . . . Sumukoak tapno katawaandak laeng?"

"Para iti pagimbagan ti pagilian, Ed," kinunak.

"Wenno pagimbagam?" manglalais ti isem ni Edwin. "Nalatakkan, Hil. Uray ni Anong. Ammok met ket. Ala wen, panggepnak ti turay a tiliwen. Saanakto a masdaaw no agsarangkami ken ni Anong. Ngem inunaam ida tapno sika ti aglatak. No sumurotak kenka . . . Saanak met ket a napaidam. Maitedko kenka dayta a sagut. Ngem ammom kadi ti gapu ti kaadda dagiti kas kaniak? Aglemlemmeng, pakamkamat a kumamkamat, kasla pusa ken bao. Nalatakkan. Adun ti nasuratmo. Ngem napanunotmo kadin nga imutektekan ti kapay-anmi? No naimutektekamon, asinokami iti panirigam?"

"Maysa laeng a di panagkinnaawatan ti nanipudan amin dagitoy," kinunak. "Ket patiek nga adda kadatayo, a makatulongtayo iti pannakarisut ti parikut."

Nagwingiwing ni Edwin. "Patiem kadi nga uray sumukoak ket agtultuloyto latta ti tignay?" kinunana. "Malagipmo kadi daydi kinunak nga agayus ti dara iti Karayan Parsua? Diak kayat a mapasamak ti kasta. . ."

"Isu nga immayak . . . a sinapulka," kinunak, "tapno agpatulongak. Agtinnulongta. Patiek a ti maaramidta, agpaayto a tulbek a mangrisut kadagiti parikut . . ."

Adda danapeg nga umasideg. Sinaruno ti panagtabbaaw ni Edwin a nakaawat iti senias. Natadem dagiti matana a nangilap kaniak.

"Traidorka, Hil!" kinunana.

"Nagbiddutka, Insan," kinunak. "Awan ti ammok . . ."

"Appok . . ." nakapsut ti arigenggen a timek ni lelong. Inabay ni lelang nga aglulua.

Nagtakder ni Edwin iti sango da lelong ken lelang. Impatayna dagiti dakulapna iti abagada. Sa nagdardarasen a timmallikud. Ginaw-isna ti armalite iti suli.

"Dikay pumampanaw ditoy, lelang," kinunak. Immulogak.

Naslag ti bulan ket nakitak dagiti anniniwan iti aglawlaw a simmapideng kadagiti pinuon. Nagarudok ni Edwin a kimmamang iti amianan a muging ti Baybayyabas a tumannawag iti Karayan Parsua. Kimmamangak iti dakkel a pinuon ti kumkumpitis. Insaganak ti kamerak. Maalak la ti maalak. Iti dayta a kanito, diak ammo ti rumbeng nga aramidek. Pampanunotek da lelong ken lelang. Mariknak nga adda ni Jan, nga isu ti nangidaulo iti iraraut; nalabit naangotanda da Edwin iti Baybayyabas. Ngem diak sigurado.

Iti adayo a laud, nakitak ti agiddep-agsilaw iti langit. Nakapsut ti wanengweng idi damo. Pimmigsa a pimmigsa. Helikopter!

"Edwin! Ammok nga addaka dita! Sumukokan!" nalasinko ti timek iti megaphone manipud iti gayadan ti Baybayyabas. "Ikarik a dika baybay-an. Ipagpagapum kada lelong ken lelang . . ."

"Naladawen!" impukkaw ni Edwin. "Naim-imbag no agawidkayon!"

Adda nagparatupot iti laud. Naladawen idi ibilin ni Edwin nga awan ti agpaltog kadagiti kaduana. Nagpukkaw met ni Jan ngem inalun-on ti ranipak ti timekna manipud iti ngato ken iti baba iti langit, asidegen ti helikopter. Pagam-ammuan, adda imbun-ayna a lawag a sinaruno ti ranipak.

Naudi a lagipko ti pannakakitak iti igigil-ayab ti balay da lelong. Nagkidemak. Nagtuloy ti ranipak ken asug, kimmapsut iti panagdengngegko . . .!

NATUKTOK ti ridaw ti siled ni Hilario Garcia.

"'Pa, apay, dika pay mabisin?" timek ni baketna.

"Umayakon," kinunana. Indissona ti asul a kuaderno. Naituon dagiti matana iti lampshade iti lamisaan.

Inukradna pay ti kuaderno, iti sumagmamano a panid . . .

III. Panagsubli

NAGSUBLIAK iti Bantay Baybayyabas kalpasan ti adu a tawen tapno ilangaak, ken kitaek ti kasayaatan a maaramid iti lugar a nagubingak a nabaybay-anen idi naisibet ti gil-ayab.

Isu pay la daydi Karayan Parsua, ti kuna daydi Edwin a pagayusan ti dara, laeng ta dakkelen ti nangananna iti dapan ti bantay.

Isu pay la dayta a muging ti Baybayyabas. Adda nagduogen a kumkumpitis, ngem adu ti narungdo a dinalapus ti panawen. Iti kusayanna, adu idi ti napasag. Diak nakita ngem nangngegko a maysa kadagiti sirok ti kumkumpitis ti nakapasagan daydi Captain Januario Garcia. Wen, ni Jan, ni Anong.

Kunak no diak kabaelanen nga ulien ti muging ti Baybayyabas. Saanen a siak daydi Hilario nga agtaray pay a sumang-at.

Ngem simmang-atak latta. Ket dita, wenno idiay, insimpak idi ti naglinged, dimngeg kadagiti paratupot, nangisagana iti kamerak. Nakitak idi ti isusungad ti helikopter manipud iti laud. A sinaruno ti parakapak iti ngato ken iti baba a muging ti Baybayyabas. Ken ti igigil-ayab ti balay.

Wen, Edwin, Januario, nagayus ti dara. Ti darayo. Ti darak. Ti dara da lelong ken lelang. Ti dara dagiti Garcia! Ni angkel . . .

Immunakayon. Ket nabatiak. Naikari ngata a mabatiak kalpasan daydi gil-ayab. Idi makariingak, hospitalen ti yanko. Awankayon . . .!

Ket nagtakderak iti nabati a pungdol ti katuday. Nagkaruotanen daydi disso ti balay. Awanen dagidi umarikiak a manok iti agsapa. Awan ti mangngeg nga ungak ti nuang ken baka. Awanen daydi Mona Liza ni angkel. Nakabasbaseng metten ti kabuluan. Ti kapan-awan a sigud nga agdaldalluyon, kasla naangrag a minuyongan. Ti rebba a kamanian ken kasandiaan nagblinen a kasamsamonan. Awan metten daydi bayyabas iti abagatan iti abay ti bubon a sa la agdanum no agtudo.

Adayo unay ti Burayok Kimmandela, saan a makadanon ti danumna iti Karayan Parsua. Saan metten a nasilap ti tuktok ti Pangasaan Elementary School. Adda pay ngata agbasbasa?

"Kalpasan daydi engkuentro," kinuna ti lakay a nagsaludsodak iti Karayan Parsua, "awanen ti immuli iti Bantay Baybayyabas. Saanen a sinublian daydi . . . angkelmo gayam. Saan kadi a nakaruar iti Mandaluyong?"

"Saanen. Idiay a natay . . ."

Nariknak ti kinakawaw ti lubongko, ti kinaeppes ti pagsiriban a sinakdok iti mano a tawen.

Ket dumges latta daydi ayat iti sinnutilmi kada Anong ken Edwin, ti nasakdomi a pudpudno nga adal iti inaldaw a panangsang-atmi iti Baybayyabas . . . Ngem awanen daydi sigud a Baybayyabas; awanen daydi langit. Kasano ti agsubli?

NAGANNINENG iti isip ni Hilario Garcia ti kinuna ni Valerio Castillejos: ipakitam ti pakabuklan ti puli a tinirtiris ti biddut a sistema ti bileg.

Ket nakitana ti aglawlaw . . . kasla nakaad-adu ti agkukuyamkuyam!

Simmiplot iti mugingna ti binatog ni Bertrand Russel: *But always pity brought me back to earth.*

Nalagipna ti baton-lagip a pabangonna iti Bantay Baybayyabas, iti sigud a nagtakderan ti katuday: sumango iti laud ni Captain Januario

Garcia; iti daya, ni Ka Edwin; iti sakaananda, agin-innarakup ti nagdalukappit a lakay ken baket a tumangtangad iti langit.

"'Pa, umaykan . . ." timek ni baketna.

Inrikep ni Hilario Garcia ti asul a kuaderno. —0

Umuna a Gunggona, ETTI 1988; Bannawag, Disiembre 19, 1988; *Daton: 1991, pp237-246.*

Agsardeng Koma Ti Lubong Ta Dumsaag Ti Tao

Prologo

SAAN a nabatad ti pakabuklan ti biag a kayat ni Abraham, Sr. nga iparang iti kambas. Agsasala iti panunotna dagiti agsasanggala nga imahinasion nga impinta da Kierkegaard, Sartre, Nietzsche, Jaspers ken Merleau-Ponty kadagiti sinuratda a nairaman iti *Reality, Man and Existence: Essential Works of Existentialism* nga inedit ni H. J. Blackham. Kayat ni Abraham, Sr. nga imutektekan ti pammati ni Kierkegaard iti Dios, ti namkuatan ni Nietzrsche a nagkuna a natayen ti Dios; kayatna a kutkoten ti kaipapanan ti ayat nga inladawan ni Sartre, ti kaibatogan ti penomenolohia nga inaon ni Merleau-Ponty manipud iti pinespesna a persepsion ken karirikna iti bukodna a padas. Ken dadduma pay a kapanunotan dagitoy a pilosopo. Kayatna nga iparang iti kambas ti agpang ti isip dagitoy a managpanunot tapno babaen ti kambas, agparang ti dagem a makitkita ken marikriknana nga imet ti pagilian. Kayatna a natingra dagitoy a maris tapno madlaw a dagus ti gimong a makaimatang iti dara dagti kailian a manglaylayus iti parmatana. Ngem kasla kulintaba nga agsilaw-agiddep ti ladawan ti realidad, ti tao, ken ti pannakaparsua a pagwerretan ti eksistensialismo. Makiin-innagaw iti mugingna ti aktibidad ni Filipinas Isabel, ti asawana. No dadduma, adda napigsa nga awis kenkuana a mangipinta iti sibubukel a ladawan

ni Fililpinas Isabel a pakaigameran ti eksistensialismo nga inladawan da Nietzsche, Sartre, ken dadduma pay.

NAGTUGAW ni Abraham, Sr. iti butaka ket nagkidem iti nairut. Inyallin ti parmatana dagiti ladawan nga agdadarison iti mugingna. Dagiti agkikinnamat ken agiinnuna nga agbitin iti luganda nga agawid iti naladawen a malem ken sardam. Dagiti kumunulkunol kadagiti dadakkel a pagtagilakuan a kunam la no di makunkunatan nga agsirigsirig iti tagilako—ipapanna nga adu kadagitoy ti mapan la dita tapno agpalamiis, wenno mangbussog kadagiti matada ta saan a kabaelan ti bolsada ti dagsen ti presio. Dagiti nalang-ay nga estudiante a di makarikna iti dagsen a yab-abaga dagiti dadakkelda iti panagadalda gapu iti ngina dagiti masapsapulda. Dagiti agiinnisiag. Dagiti nakamulagat a damag iti periodiko—pinnatay ditoy ken idiay, NPA ditoy ken idiay, natambang a soldado ken polis ditoy ken idiay, nagsikog ditoy ken idiay . . . Nakail-ileten ti siudad a nagbakuitan dagiti naggapu iti probinsia gapu iti panagturay dagiti Manangannigid. Kangrunaanna ni Filipinas Isabel a marimonen iti patienna a pannakaikalkalilisda a mannursuro ken dagiti padada a nababa nga empleado ti turay. Aglamiis no dadduma dagiti dakulap ken dapan ni Abraham, Sr. a makalagip iti aktibidad ti asawana a maibusor iti agdama a bileg: isu ti maysa a dadaulo dagiti aktibista a mannursuro.

Idandanag ni Abraham, Sr. dagiti lima nga annakda, da Filipinas Rosal, Abraham Joselito, Abraham Solomon, Filipinas Linglingay, ken Abraham, Jr. Nga agtawen iti sangapulo-ket-pito nga agpababa iti sangapulo-ket-maysa . . . ti masakbayanda.

1. Lubong

TALAGA kadi a saankan a mapawilan?" binaw-ingan ni Abraham, Sr. ni Filipinas Isabel a mangur-urnos kadagiti alikamenna a mangisuro. Insab-it ni Abraham, Sr. ti katartarimaanna a kuadro ti ladawanda a sangapamilia.

"Imbagak la ngaruden," kinuna ni Filipinas Isabel. Sinangona ti tokador ket kinitana ti rupana.

"Ania pay la ngamin ti pakiramramanam?"

"'Nia ti kunam?"

"Amangan no sika pay ti mangilunglungalong iti tignayyo," immalsem ti rupa ni Abraham, Sr. Sinangona ti bassit a biblioteka iti salas ket rinugianna nga urnosen dagiti libro. Inuksotna ti libro da Nietzsche, Sartre, ken dadduma pay.

"Ania koma ti dakesna?"

"Saan a sika ti akinrebbeng . . ."

"Asino ngarud? Dagiti politiko? Dagiti soldado? Dagiti NPA? Awan sa ngamin ti riknam ket."

"Apay a di ti panangisurom ti asikasuem?" kinuna ni Abraham, Sr. Indissona ti libro iti lamisaan. Nangala iti trapo.

"Apay, ania ti ar-aramidek 'ti panagkunam? Saanak a mangisursuro?"

"Iti kalkalsada?"

"'Pa, kaanonto pay nga agriingtayo? Adda pay ket ladladawkon, a. Kitaem daytoy . . . di maputpot ti karkari . . . nga awan met ti pagmatmataanna. Kasla aso a taul a taul dagiti adda iti poder. Umanaw-aw met dagiti adda iti ruar. Kasano ngaruden ti asug dagiti mairurrurumen? Amangan no aginkukunaka met a dimo ammo ti di panangipirpirit ti agsumbangir a bileg iti kondision a mangpatpatay iti sangapagilian. Malaglagipko pay no dadduma, nga ubbaw sa ketdi ti pammati ti tao iti Dios ta no lumablabasak iti simbaan wenno kapilia, nakaad-adu ti makimismisa, ngem diak la ammon ti ikarkararagda. Panagkunak, no kappia ti ikarkararagda, awan ti kastoy a riribuk iti pagiliantayo. Sayang, nakaad-adu pay met ngarud a pammati . . ."

Nagwingiwing ni Abraham, Sr. a di nalapsi ti panagkitana iti asawana. "Pampanunotek," kinunana, "nga adu unayen ti tao ket kasla adda bileg a mangdurdurog kadatayo tapno agsisinnida . . . datayo nga agkakabsat. Ar-aramatennatayo dayta a bileg a kasla makinaria iti inaayup nga arapaap!"

"Ket, ania ngarud ti aramidem?" tinaldiapan ni Filipinas Isabel.

"Mariknak ket maar-aringamon dagiti annakmo . . ."

"Nasayaat tapno mariingda iti kinapudno. Ket makidanggayda iti agdama a tignay. Diak kayat a tumanorda nga agdaldalikepkep lattan

agingga nga agkubboda. Kayatko a makipagmulida iti masakbayan. Kayatko a tumakderda nga adda sangina."

"Kasta?"

"Rumbeng koma a sika ti adda iti saadko. Masiribka . . . a frustrated writer and artist. Ngem awan man la ti panangipirpiritmo iti agdama a kasasaad. Kasla saanka a paset ti gimong."

"'Ma . . ."

"Dimo la ngamin marikna ti rigat ti makunkunatan ta saan a sika ti makititienda. Nakanginngina ti magatgatang. Marigataankami unay a mannursuro. . . ngem didakami met la pulos taliawen dagiti agrebbeng. Nalipatandan a tinagabodakami idi eleksion. Inngatoda kano ti sueldo. Ngem apay a saan a mapnek dagiti tao? Dimon sa ammo dagitoy ta dayta la kambasmo ti sangsanguem. Dimo payen maestimar ti bagim, atiwmon ti ermitanio. Agparparangka nga abalbalay dagiti elitista, 'Pa. Dagiti elitista nga agmamauyong iti kambas . . . koma met no bigbigendaka. Ngem awan sa pay ti makapidua a mangsirig kadagiti gapuanam."

"Naladawak ngamin a nakariing. Naladaw a naamirisko a naulimek nga ekspresion ti kappia ti arte. Adda dagiti kayatko nga ipinta a binatog da Nietzsche, Sartre, ken dadduma pay, nupay kuna dagiti dadduma a parparawpaw laeng ti ipakitada. Para kaniak, no awan dayta parparawpaw wenno kudil no tao koma . . . wen, awan met ngarud ti nauneg nga ilemlemmengna. Panagkunak adda met la iti tao ti kunkunada nga eksistensialismo. Ngarud, no adda kudil adda met lasag, ket no adda lasag adda met tulang, no adda amin dagitoy, taon, ket adda metten biag nga aglangoy iti realidad."

"Dagitanto ketdi Nitnitsi kada Sarsartre ti pampanunotem. Uray no kutkotem amin a di mangan-ano iti kararuam, mabiagnaka? 'Pa, kitaem ti aglawlawmo!"

"Namin-anon nga imbagak nga awan ti sabali a pampaunotek no di kappia . . . talingenngen? Dimo, aya, maawatan a diak kayat ti makiramraman iti nariribuk a lubong? Dimo la ammo, kayatko ti maipusing itoy a lubong. No koma lugan, kayatko ti dumsaag. Ngem diak pay kayat ti matay! Makauman ti mapaspasamak. Agkakabsat, agsisinnida. Apay a kastoy? Adu ti sabali a pagilian a mabalin a papanan.

Ngem diak kayat ti kasta. Kaykayatko pay ti agsubli iti probinsia. Ngem awan metten ti nasayaat a damag idiay."

"Ket?"

"Sanguentayo ti kinaudno, "Ma. Nariribuk ti pagiliantayo. Ngem laglagipem nga addaka iti poder. Empleadonaka ti gobierno, uray ania nga anggulo ti panirigam. Nasken a maysaka a makipagtengngel iti pagimbagaan ti umili, nangruna dagiti ubbing a sumaruno a bagnos ti kaputotan. Dimo ituloyen ti panggepyo nga agwelga. Saanyo koma a dagnayan pay ti parikut ti pagilian."

"Naladawen," kasla aleng-aleng ni Filipinas Isabel.

"Awan ti naladaw."

"Bay-annak lattan. Nairugikon ket nasken a leppasek. Uray ta saan la a ti grupomi ti mangayat itoy. Adun. Uray saankami nga aggunay, sisasaganan dagti dadduma. Panagkunak, iti saan a mabayag, adda mapasamak a nadara a yaalsa."

"Kasano ngay dagiti annakmo?"

"Annakkonto latta, a."

"Ket asawakanto latta met?"

"'Nia pay koma?"

Immanges ni Abraham, Sr. iti nauneg idi makapanaw ti asawana. Naituon dagiti matana iti libro ni Blackham, iti yan da Nietzsche, Sartre, ken dadduma pay.

2. Ididissaag

ISAWSAW koman ni Abraham, Sr. ti pinselna iti paleta idi agtaray ni Junior, ti buridek, nga umasideg.

"Daddy, Daddy . . . ni Mommy, adda 'diay t.v.!"

Nagsakuntip, indissona ti pinsel ket simmurot iti anakna iti salas. Adda dita dagiti uppat pay nga annakna a nakanganga a mangsangsango iti telebision, da Filipinas Rosal, Abraham Joselito, Abraham Solomon, ken Filipinas Linglingay.

"Daddy, ni Mommy," kasla naisab-it ti timek ni Filipinas Linglingay.

Awan gagar iti rupa ni Abraham, Sr. Sakbay a rimmuar itay nariwet ni Filipinas Isabel, binallaaganen ni Abraham, Sr. a saan nga agtuloy.

Ngem addaytan, iti sango, ket maysa kadagiti makipagik-ikkis ken mangiwagwagayway iti nalabaga a sangkapirgis a lupot idinto a kasla agar-aruyot a dara ti naimarka iti puraw a wagayway dagiti welgista a nakaisurtan ti dawatda. Nakapuspuskolda iti agmatuon, iti kalsada a mangdusang iti Malakanyang. Mangisursuro dagita, nakanipormeda . . . elementaria, sekundaria ken kolehio. Sangsangkamaysadan, naisip ni Abraham, Sr.

Nayakar ti kamera iti kanigid. Reprep dagiti estudiante. Umumkisda met. Sabali pay a grupo iti sabalil a bangir, sa iti akinlikud a paset, grupo ti empleado ti gobierno. Nabengbeng ti nakaigam a trensera ti turay iti sango.

Nadlaw ni Abraham, Sr. ti itatallikud da Filipinas Rosal ken Abraham Joselito. Second year ken first year dagitoy iti kolehio. Nalidem ti rupada.

Inyakar ni Abraham, Sr. iti sabali nga estasion. Isu met laeng ti pabuya. Agpapada ti pabuya iti amin nga estasion. Maymaysa ti kayat a sawen daytoy, naisipna: nadagsen ti isyu.

Iniddepna ti telebision.

"Daddy, kayatko a buyaen ni Mommy," kinuna ni Junior.

"Saanen," kinuna ni Abraham, Sr. "Agay-ayamkayo laengen iti Atari."

Sinangona manen ti kambas. Napigsa ti kidag ti nakitana iti telebision ket timmayab ti buya a nakabatbatad itay iti mugingna a kayatna nga iparang iti kambas. Napagtutugmokna itayen dagiti ladawan a kayat nga ipaduyakyak ti antolohia ni Blackham a nangbiaganna kada Nietzsche, Sartre, ken dadduma pay.

Pinidutna ti paleta. Immay manen iti panunotna ti pakabuklan ti pagilian. Dagiti tao iti siudad. Dagiti pasamak a mangtirtiris iti sangkatawan, ti mabukbukel a parmata iti mugingna. Dagiti naisakripisio nga inosente a makipagili. Dagiti naipatli a kameng ti armada. Ti bitek ti barukong ti paglilan. Kayatna nga iparang amin dagitoy iti maymaysa a dakkel a kambas.

Maudin a panangpadas iti daytoy, naisipna manen. No saan nga agballigi, idissonan ti arte ket nalabit nga agpaing laengen. Ngem nasken a paneknekanna iti asawana, ni Filipinas Isabael, nga adda imnas ti biag

iti laksid ti gimong iti bukod a panirigan, iti naulimek nga ilulugan iti parmata; iladawanna a nagsardeng ti ubong ket dumdumsaag dagiti nataengan, wen, dagiti nataengan a nautoyanen nga agdaliasat . . .

Addayta manen ti ikkis dagiti agrarali iti telebision.

Timmakder ni Abraham, Sr.

"Kunak nga agatarikayo laengen!" kinunana ket minulagatanna dagiti tallo iti salas. Iniddepna ti telebision.

"N-ni mommy, Daddy," nakadumog ni Junior.

"Bay-anyo ni mommyyo."

"Agraramboldan," kinuna ni Abraham Solomon.

"Bay-anyo nga agrarambolda."

"Nakaad-adun ti soldado," kinuna ni Filipinas Linglingay. "Adda payen puor.... agpapaltogda payen . . ."

Nangemkem ni Abraham, Sr. Nagsubli iti yan ti kambas.

Awanen dagiti maris iti mugingna. Indissona ti paleta ket nagilad iti butaka. Maudi daytoyen. Maudi daytoyen! Kasla mapisi ti pispisna iti agwerwerret a buya.

Sadino ti yan ti talna? Ti panagwaywayas? Ti imnas ti panagbiag? Kasano ti mailaksid iti daytoy a lubong dagiti tirtiris? Dagiti managinkukuna . . . dagiti antukab . . . dagiti natiri?

Nagkidem ni Abraham, Sr. Apo . . .

Nalukag iti arimbangaw iti salas. Linidllidna dagiti matana. Timmakder. Nagturong iti salas. Nakitana iti telebision dagiti agkakaribuso; adda kanalbuong, ken gil-ayab. Makumikom dagiti reporter ken retratista. Agkaragilap dagiti kamera. Saanen nga ikaskaso ni Abraham, Sr. ti sasawen ti anaunser. Sapsapulen dagiti matana ni Filipinas Isabel iti pagtarayan ti kamera. Kasla nawara a bunar dagiti welgista ket awan ti masnop a turongenda, ngem dida met pumanaw iti sango ti Malakanyang. No dadduma, maipakita ti sabali pay a grupo iti sango ti Kongreso, iti EDSA, iti arubayan ti estasion ti telebision. Adda mangrugrugi a gil-ayab iti dandani amin a suli. Adda ikkis.

Apo, daytoy kadin? naisip ni Abraham, Sr. Ket aglulupoy a nagtugaw iti sibay dagiti tallo nga annakna. Iti telebision, kumarkaro ti riribuk. Iggemen dagiti welgista ti estasion a pagbuybuyaanda. Awanen ti pabuya

kadagiti dadduma nga estasion. Ipakpakita dagitoy ti kunada a bunga ti panaglablabes.

Nagkarayam ti lamiis iti dakulap ni Abraham, Sr. idi maipakita ti pannakadarup dagiti mannursuro ket rapukrapoken. Nakitana ni Filipinas Isabel, ti asawana, iti sango, a kaduana dagiti dadduma a pangpangulo ket kasda la Gabriela Silang a mangitgtag-ay iti takiagda.

Piling! nayesngaw ni Abraham, Sr. iti unegna. Piling!

Iti ragup dagiti estudiante, sinapul dagiti mata ni Abraham, Sr. da Filipinas Rosal ken Abraham Joselito.

Timmakder, nagdardaras a nagrubuat.

"Dikay rumrummuar, a? Uray ania ti mapasamak, dikay rumrummuar ditoy balay." Kinitana ti pagorasan, dandanin alas sais iti malem. "Mangankayto lattan. Sika, Linglingay . . . sikanto ti mangisagana iti pangrabiiyo. Agannadkayo laeng. Didak urayenen. Dikay agpaspastrek iti sabali a tao."

"Papanam, Daddy?" dinamag ni Junior.

Kinuso laeng ni Abraham, Sr. ti buok ti buridek.

Dandani di nakalugan iti dyip iti ipapanna iti Cubao. Awanen ti agbiahe. Nangala iti taksi iti Cubao ket nagpaitulod iti Sampaloc. Madi koma ti tsuper.

Iti Rotonda, nasabatda ti sangapangen a tao nga umariwawa.

"Ti Malakanyang . . . Ti Malakanyang!"

Iti langit a batog ti Malakanyang, agdildilat ti apuy.

Ti la nangiserserkan ti tsuper iti taksi agingga a nakadanonda iti Legarda. Dita pay laeng, saanen nga ammo ti aridenggan. Binayadan ni Abraham, Sr. ti taksi ket nakilaok kadagiti tao a di masnop ti turongenda.

Lumanitog ti gil-ayab. Idi makadanon iti rangtay ti Mendiola, nakitana a mangrugin a marpuog ti Malakanyang. Saan a kabaelan dagiti bombero ti makapungtot a gil-ayab. Agkaraiwara dagiti naudatal iti kalsada nga as-asikasen dagiti agrebbeng. Mannursuro ken dadduma pay dagiti naipatli. Agtibtibbayo ni Abraham, Sr. a nangilasin kadagiti nakauniporme a mannursuro. Sapsapulenna ni Filiplinas Isabael. Awan ti asawana. Iti grupo dagiti naudatal nga estudiante, awan da Filipinas Rosal ken Abraham Joselito. Napananda ngatan?

Kasla agbettak a bulkan ti Malakanyang. Bumegbeggang dagiti rurog ti pasdek a mangsudsudak iti barukong ti langit. Idi kuan, adda bimtak iti kabangibang a pasdek. Ket agsaknapen ti gil-ayab. Nagtaray nga immadayo ni Abraham, Sr. a nakarikna iti bara ti dila ti apuy.

Tunggal adda masalawna nga ambulansia, wenno ania la ditan a lugan a nagkarga iti nadangran, ikagumaanna a kitaen weno ammuen no adda dita da Filipinas Isabel, Filipinas Rosal, ken Abraham Joselito.

Adu ti inawaganna a hospital. Kayatna a maammuan ti yan dagiti patpatgenna. No addada iti hospital, ammona no kuan ti napasamak. No awanda, dina ammo no nagawiddan, wenno kimmappondan kadagiti naglibas, wenno asino la ditan. Dina kayat a kasta. Uray ania dagiti nagsubsubanganda nga agassawa, ken panangung-ungetna kadagiti annakna, marikna ita ni Abraham, Sr. a patpatgena pay la ida.

Natuntonanna ti asawana iti Medical Center. Kaisimsimpada iti emergency room idi sumangpet. Dina makasao; ipawil dagiti doktor. Grabe ti sugatna. Impasiripda laeng. Nakasuero ni Filpnas Isabel. Nakakidem. Adda litem iti kanawan a pingpingna. Adda dara iti pispis ken kanigid a gurongna.

Awan dagiti annakna, da Filipnas Rosal ken Abraham Joselito.

Adu ti pasiente ket napunno pay ti pasilio iti agur-uray nga awan ti pakaipuestuanda a kuarto. Agatibuor ti agas.

Immawag iti balayda ket imbagana a di makaawid. Kinomustana dagiti annakna. Awan kano pay da Abraham Joselito ken Filipinas Rosal. Nangemkem ni Abraham, Sr. Sadino ngata ti napananda? Indawatna nga awan koma ti dakes a napasamakda. Dina mapanawan ni Filipinas Isabel, aguray laengen iti damag kadagiti annakna.

Adu pay ti nagsangpet a damag. Agtultuloy ti agsangpet a nasugatan. Narebbek ti kastoy a lugar. Iti amianan. Iti abagatan. Dimmapo ti kastoy a pasdek. Natay ni kastoy, ni kasdiay. Agtultuloy ti gil-ayab iti siudad. Saanen a matengngel dagiti agrebbeng dagiti makapungtot nga umili. Agdudupudop dgiti grupo nga aggapu iti dandani amin a paset ti paglian. Uray ti kampo dagiti soldado ket nastreken dagiti makipagili. Nakautibon ti sekretario ti depensa.

Immalsan dagiti umili!

Ket daytoy ti kangrunaan a damag: nagpukaw ti Pangulo!

Apo! nairut ti kidem ni Abraham, Sr. iti pagtugtugawanna iti pagurayan dagiti agbantay. Apay a kastoy metten ti napasamak?

Agsardeng koman dagiti kailian, nayesngawna. Agsardeng koman ti oras, ti kanito . . .

Agsardeng koma ti lubong . . .!

Epilogo

IDI damo, kasla saan a patien ni Abraham, Sr. ti adda iti sangona: dakkel a kambas a paggargarawan ti kasla pudno a biag, ken rebba wenno rurog—idi damo adda saggaysa a nangbabalaw iti obrana, ngem dina inkaskaso ida, agingga a nagturay dagiti positibo ti paniriganda a nakaawat iti mensahena. Iggem ti kanawan nga ima ti nakadeppa nga ina a nadigos iti dara ti amin a paset ti bagina ti sangabukel a lubong a kasla pilpilitenna nga agsardeng ket tumaptapuak dagiti tao. Iti amin a paset ti bagi ti ina, iti aglawlana, addagita dagiti agduduma a pasamak a nangbungon iti maudi a kagudua ti maikaduapulo a siglo a pakasaritaan ti pagillian.

Ita, sibsibet manen ti sabali pay a naayat iti pintura, a nangtawar ken agpakpakaasi a gumatang iti kambas iti uray ania a kantidad a kayatna. Maymaysa ti sungbatna: "Ladingitek, diak ilako daytoy kakaisuna nga Obra Maestrak."

Saannan a mabilang ti nalakona a kambas manipud iti daydi immuna a solo exhibitna a damo a nangiparanganna itoy kadakkelan, ken patienna nga Obra Maestrana, a kambas kalpasan daydi yaalsa. Tunggal exhibitna, adda latta a mairagragpin daytoy a kambas, a patienna a nangted iti gasatna.

Adun a pammadayaw ti naawatna. Agingga a nagbalin a gagangay unayen, ket no dadduma, ni laengen Filipinas Isabel a nabiit pay a nagretiro iti panangisurona ti pusganna nga umawat ta saannan a masango, ken pangbigbigna metten iti patienna a dakkel nga akem ti kaingungotna gapu iti pannakigamulona iti daydi a yaalsa. Ket uray no agpigsupigsol ni Filipinas Isabel, nalawag ti rupana ket dina malipatan a dakamaten ti puon ti nagbungaan dagiti arapaap ti asawana.

No pampanunoten, awanen ti sapulen ni Abraham, Sr. Nakapagsimpan dagiti lima nga annakda, da Filipinas Rosal ken Abraham Joselito nga agpada a nakalasat iti daydi nadagem a pannakairamanda iti maysa a paset ti yaalsa; da Abraham Solomon, Filipinas Linglingay, ken Abraham, Jr. Maipagpannakkel ti propesionda nga agkakabsat. Ket adun ti appokoda.

Ngem adda lattta kinakawaw a mariknana iti biagna, nanguna no maisagud dagiti matana iti libro a yan da Nietzsche, Sartre, ken dadduma pay, a dina inikkat iti daan a salansan. Saan a makaidna a mangpadpadaan iti mangrugin a panagmawmaw ti nakasamsam-it a pannakailibay ti pagilian. Adun a tawen kalpasan daydi yaalsa a makapelleng ti ulimek. Ngem adda manen maririing, nga isu ti tagtagiurayna a kasla kadagiti taraok iti nasapa a parbangon.

Iti suli ti panunot ni Abraham, Sr., adda dita ti Pangulo a simmukat iti daydi Pangulo a nagpukaw—naammuan idi agangay nga intalaw ken pinatay dagiti kanigid—a saan pay a nasukatan manipud idi naipatugaw ta di pay nauma dagiti umili iti panangiturayna.

Kasla kayat ni Abraham, Sr. ti mangipinta iti baro a ladawan ti historia ti agdama a siglo, a paggargarawan ti Pangulo. Ita ta kabaelanna pay nga iggaman ti pinselna.

Ket adda manen iti sango ti dakkel a kambas, a mangpampanunot iti sabali nga anggulo; kallabayna ni Filipinas Isabel idinto a naisagud dagiti

matana iti naisurat iti kusayan ti dakkel nga ina iti kambas: 'GOD IS DEAD"—Nietzsche.

Natayen dagiti didiosen! naisip ni Abraham, Sr.

Iti isipna, iti gayadan ti sabali a kambas, naisurat ti: "RESURRECTION"—Abraham, Sr.

Panagungar.

Inawid ni Abraham, Sr. ni Filipinas Isabel. —0

Maikadua a Gunggona, ETTI, 1989; *Bannawag*: December 25, 1989; *Daton: 199,* pp306-314.

Mangmatimati Dagiti Bituen Iti Eskopa

1. Adtoytayo, Dalen, iti Escopa

1. *Ket kunak itan, Dalen: bulsek a talaga ti lubong ta dina makita dagiti agkukunail nga agun-unnoy;*

2. *Wen, simamata a pudno, ngem pagimbubulsekannan sa man, aya, ti panagar-aruyot ti nadangro a gita dagiti saongan iti takdang a sisasagana a sumarubsob kadatayo.*

3. *Ta daytoy ti maysa a kinapudno, kunak manen, Dalen: ti bulsek makakita ket ti simamata ti pudno a bulsek.*

4. *Manen, kunak, Dalen: ti lubong aglanglangoy iti law-ang a napno iti kinatiri.*

5. *Mamatika, ayatko: bumangonto latta dagiti bulsek, ket agmulagatdanto iti nabengbeng a sipnget a pagmatimatian dagiti bituen ti Escopa.*

6. *Indanto karawaen ti kinapudno, ket saandanto nga agbabawi iti pannakaipasngayda iti Escopa, iti baet ti di aglabbet a tuok;*

7. *Ket ay-ayto pay, ayatko, dagiti makakita nga agimbubulsek. Ay-ayto pay ti lubong. . .*

Kapitulo 1

NARIING manen ti Escopa.
Nariingen ni Kosep. Ken ni Dalen. Ken ni Djona. 40, 30, 13. Ama.
Ina. Anak.

Isuda ket ngata ti immuna a nakariing. Di pay itay agbanatabat. Di pay agdungsa ti gagan-ayan. Ti barukbok. Nagsarsarita da Kosep ken Dalen. Nagin-innarasaasda. Inap-aprosan ni Kosep ni Dalen. Kadagiti nalamuyot a paset ti patpatgenna. Idinto a naisaluket dagiti mata ni Dalen iti regkang a pagpakpakadaan dagiti mangmatimati a bituen. Nauneg ti angesna.

Kimmita ni Djona iti yanda., sa timmalikud. Simmango iti diding; nagkukot. Nagpulpuligos dagiti matana iti aragaag a diding: papananna manen ita?

Papananda manen ita?

Manipud iti Escopa, rimmuarda. Iti J.P. Rizal.

Rimmuar met ni Julian Manglicmot a bulding.

Isuda amin, rimmuarda.

Manen. iti daytoy naalibuyong nga agsapa ti Lunes, umuna nga aldaw ti lawas, rummuarda. Mangngeg dagiti nalag-an a danapeg kadagiti baet dagiti pagtaengan a kaaduanna ti takuptakop, haloblaks a natakupan iti aglatlati ken buttabuttaw a galba. Ken karton. . .

Agdanapegda. A mangrugi iti umuna a pitik ti agsapa. Wenno panagbukar ti lawag. Addan ap-ap ti boksitda; adu dagiti awan pay ti naisakmolna.

Addan naisakmol ni Kosep. Ni Dalen. Ni Djona.

Uray ni Julian Manglicmot. Ta di maaw-awanan iti isakmol.

Saggaysa a kibin ti agruar iti sungaban iti laud. Dagiti aggudeng a tadek. Sumalpotda iti J. P. Rizal.

Adda isem iti rupa dagiti pakibkibin; adda alimuteng iti muging dagiti mangibkibin. Dagiti pakibkibin, takuptakop; dagiti mangibkibin, rutrot.

Iti muging ni Kosep, naipinta dagiti balikas ni Dalen. Ngarud, isuda ti lubong, isuda dagiti takuptakop ken rutrot. Iti daytoy a paraiso. Iti Escopa. Isuda dagitoy.

Lakay ken ubing. Baket ken ubing. Agpada a nataengan. Nalabit agama. Nalabit agina. Nalabit agassawa. Mata ti mangiturong. Iti ama, iti ina, iti asawa, dagiti mata ti silawda a paiturturong.

Kuna ni Kosep: agpapadatayo a lubong; maymaysa ti lubongtayo; maymaysa ti paggargarawantayo; maymaysa ti pagbibiagantayo. Isuna laeng a dakami awan init wenno bituen a masiripmi iti laksid ti nabengbeng a sipnget a naikumot kadakami; pasig nga arapaap ken tagtagainep nga awan kapaypay-anna. Dakayo, ti tagtagainepyo magawgaw-at, ta uray no adayo asideg. . .

Adda dagiti naisem. Adda dagiti Biernes Santo ti rupana.

Ngem ad-adu ti Biernes Santo. Kanayon a nagpanes dagiti aglabas nga aldawda.

Ta ti Escopa, nasipnget a lubong. Kasta ti estoria ni Dalen ken ni Kosep. Ken ni Djona. Ti Escopa, isu ti lubong a nasipngetan.

Kagudua laeng ken ni Julian Manglicmot. Ta nalawag ti bangirna. Iti panagkuna da Kosep ken Dalen.

Isu a nasipngetan ta nalikmutda iti nabengbeng a wayawaya. Sipnget nga iladawan ni Kosep a sangagpa ti kabengbengna. A di masarut ti katademan a mata. A kayat ni Djona a bawbawan. Tapno makitana ti ladawan iti bangir a lubong. Awan duma dayta a wayawaya iti bartolina a kanayon a nakakandado.

Ngem saan ken ni Julian Manglicmot. Ta adda Pajero a sipsiputanna.

Nawaya ti amin nga agibelleng iti natay a pusa. Natay nga aso. Natay a bao. Natay (wenno pinis-it) a sikog, no dadduma. Ken no ania la ditan a mitsa ti biag. . .

Wayawaya ta nawaya a pagtarayan dagiti mannibbarut. Namin-adun a nakasippadong ni Kosep.

Wayawaya ta makapagpataray dagiti drayber iti um-umada iti J.P. Rizal. Iti Aurora. Iti Katipunan. No adda maladditda a pakibkibin—dandanin ni Kosep—Dios laengen (wenno Satanas?) ti makaammo iti akin-Pajero.

Wayawaya. Ta nawaya dagiti sumrek-rummuar iti Escopa nga agikamat iti sumilsilap a batanggas wenno dos por dos wenno paltik ket madamdama pay agayusen ti dara iti natapok ken nangisit a kaldsada.

Ta awan ti umasideg a lallaki a tsokolate. Nalaka, aya, naisip ni Kosep, no isuda ti sumaruno a masudsodan iti nasilap a batanggas, numona ta awan metten ti pateg ti medalia, a, ta nanapriing metten. Piman, kuna ni Kosep a manglangit.

Wayawaya latta, Dalen, kuna ni Kosep; ken Djona, kunana pay, ta nawaya a sumrek ti Pajero a siputsiputan ni Julilan Manglicmot, ken ipus-ipusen ni Silbato. Wen gayam, ni Sarhento Anghel Guardiano, ti silbato. Agirub ti rupa ni Pajero; natangatang ti ulo ni Silbato; kanayon a sumirsirig ti maysa a mata ni Manglilcmot.

A, nawayada. Isuda amin.

Ibati da Dalen ken Djona ni Kosep iti maysa a nagkurosan a nabengbeng iti tao. Sadiay nga agtugaw. Wenno agtakder. Agunnoy. Umararaw iti itinnag ti langit.

Ngem adu dagiti adda silbatona; kasuronda dagiti kas kenkuana. Ngem agan-anus ni Kosep. Uray ta dagasento manen dagii patpatgenna.

Nagturongan kadi met da Dalen ken Djona?

Saan nga agsalsaludsod ni Kosep. Mangnamnama lattan a dagasendanto. Adda latta sampagita a yukkor kenkuana ni Djona. "Ti amak nga ipatpategko unay-unay." No ammona la koma ti pudno. "Ti anakko a kakaisuna a silawko," ammo ni Kosep a saan nga agsasao iti pudno. Ngem pudno kadakuada ken Dalen.

Ket agayamuom latta ti sampagita. Iti panangarakup kenkuana ni Djona. Ti anak. . . ti akin-anak.

Ni Dalen?

Natadem ti bangbanglona no rummuar. Ngem nagmagmagen no agsubli. Awan masasao ni Kosep. Apay koma pay? Addadan a mangipatpateg kenkuana. Simmangpetda a kasla milagro. Ni Dalen a naluom iti parikut nga impalay ti lubong. Iti ruar ti paraiso ni Kosep.

Pudpudnoka a tao, Kosep, kinuna ni Dalen. Saanka nga aginkukuna. Makitam ti di makita dagiti agimbubulsek.

Apay ngata? Naisip ni Kosep. Ngem dina sinaludsod. Adda laeng tibbayona. Namak payen no mapukawdanto met laeng?

Kapitulo 2

"DALEN, sika kadi dayta?" insarang ni Kosep ti pitpit a kanawan a lapayagna iti nailukat a ridaw.

"Buisit!"

"Ne, apayen?"

Insaltek ni Dalen ti bagina iti butbot a tugaw. "Awanen ti kasairuan nga ayup!"

"Ni Silbato kadi manen?" nalagip ni Kosep ni Anghel Guardiano. Nagrupanget a timmakder. Sinarapana ti bakrangna. Inarikap dagiti dapanna ti rutrot a sinelasna. Immasideg ken ni Dalen. Kinarawana dagiti abaga ti babai ket piniselpiselna.

"Naumaakon a makisarsarita. Ti la ddda nga ipampambarna. Dida pay la diretsuen no adda maganab wenno awan."

"Kunak met ngamin, bay-amon. Dida makita ti napasamak kaniak. Kitaem, awan pay maaramidan ni Julilan Manglicmot a masasao a pangulotayo ditoy. Ta nasilsilap ti rimat ti tsedeng a nangdungpar kaniak. Isu a didakon makita. . . Bay-amon."

"Dimo ngamin ida makita. . ."

"Makitak amin ida, Dalen. Uray dagiti di makita ni Silbato, ken ni Julian Manglicmot. Kas ken ni Mister Pajaro a mangkurkuriro kadatayo. Ken dagiti aliporesna. . . makitadatayo kadi?"

Mamutbuteng pay ti sairo!"

"Isu ngarud a sairoda. . . ken alingo pay."

"'Nia ngarud ti aramidek?" nanindi ni Dalen iti sigarilio. "Ikayangko kadi lattan, ket iduyayyatko a kasla tapa?"

"Apay met a kasta?"

"No isu't dawdawatenna!"

"Dika la maum-uma nga agsigsigarilio. Sika pay a tumulong a mangpapuskol iti polusion. . ."

"Dimo man yaw-awan. . . Shit!"

"O, Lubong. O, tao. O, Escopa."

"Sugsugsogannak pay 'diay animal. . ."

"A panawannak?"

"Uray no kastaka laeng, saanka a sairo a kas kenkuana!"

"Masdaawak ngarud kenka no apay a maanusannak pay laeng. . . Ngem nasken nga awaten ti tao ti kinaasinona."

"Uray no maagrabiadon?"

"Nasakit nga awaten. . ."

"Dayta ket!"

"Ngem nasken."

"Saan! Adda pagpatingaan ti amin! Isu a kastada ta awan ti makaitured a sumangdo kadakuada."

"Adda ngarud isangdotayo? Awan met ngarud ti panagkaykaysatayo."

"Saan la a ti bagik ti pampanunotek. . . Ni Djona, balasitangen. Madi ti panagkitkita ni Silbato!"

Insardeng ni Kosep nga inilut ti abaga ni Dalen. Kinarawana ti maysa a tugaw iti suli.

II. Ne, Apayen, Escopa?

1. *Siak, ni Kosep, iti nakaisakabak a ridaw daytoy agannatay a lubong. . . a lubongmi kada Dalen ken Djona.*

2. *Sumagibar iti agong ti nadangri nga alingasaw ti agmatuon.*

3. *Awan man dumam, Escopa, iti naangrag a biag a linamut ti gil-ayab.*

4. *Agtibtibbayoak. . . diak maawatan.*

5. *Gapu kadi ta awan dagiti ipatpategko?*

6. *Dumagdagaang ti lubongko. . . aggurigorka kadi, Escopa?*

7. *Kasla masirsiraman ti barukongko.*

8. *Isu a pinagbatidak dagiti patpatgek. . . aginanaak kano.*

Kapitulo 1

"IKKANKAYO iti sumagmamano nga aldaw!"

"Ne, apay a kasta, Mister Pajaro?"

"Ung-ongkayo a talaga. Kukuak daytoy a daga, diyo maawatan? Angel Guardiano. . . ditoyka, Sarhento."

"W-wen, Mister Pajaro."

"Daga ti gobierno daytoy, Mister Pajaro. Ngem dagamin ta nabayagkamin ditoy."

"Linteg dagiti attit!"

"Linteg dagiti bulsek a makakita. . . Kaaduanna kadakami ti naipasngay ditoy. Ditoyen a natay dagiti appomi, adun a tawen ti limmabas. . ."

"Awan bibiangko kadagiti appoyo. Ti ibagak ti surotenyo! No kunak nga agsaganakayo, agsaganakayo. No saan. . ."

"Rinuker a panunot!"

"Saankami a pumanaw ditoy!"

"Mataykami pay nga umuna!"

"Dakayo nga agum, nga alingo iti siudad. . . yan ti konsensiayo?"

"Julian Manglicmot. . . Julian Manglicmot!"

"S-sir. . ."

"Kitaem dagita. . ."

"Kakabsat. . ."

"Nagsara!"

"Nagsaong!"

"Buaya!"

"Agannadkayo. Addaak ditoy a pannakabagi ti linteg!"

"Sika a Sarhento Silbato?"

"Agtalnakayo, kakadua. Saan a marisut ti napudot nga ulo ti parikut."

"Ay, Kosep. Pagmulagatem 'ta konsensiam!"

"Laglagipem da Dalenmo. . . ken Djonam."

"Nasken nga irupirtayo ti kalintegantayo!"

"Ti Escopa ti parikuttayo. . . ania ti aramidentayo? Addayta ni Mister Pajaro. . ."

"Pajaro. . . Baldomero Caesar Pajaro!"

"Dispensarem, Mister Pajero, ay Pajaro. . . Ngem siak kad' laengen, a, ti mangisao kadagiti kapurokak. . ."

"Saan a mabalin. . . ni Julian Manglicmot ti panguloyo!"

"Julian Manglicmot?"

"Wen, kakadua. . . addaak ditoy. . . bay-anyo kadi ta kasaritak ni Mister Pajaro."

"Sao dayta ti bulsek a simamata!"

"No dikayo dumngeg. . ."

Kapitulo 2

"MAMATIKAYO kadi ken ni Julian Manglicmot?" nadagsen ti timek ni Dalen a naibansag ti panagkitana iti nabingngi a tawa. Nalidem iti ruar; umas-asimbuyok dagiti bubongan iti naladaw a malem, sumagibar iti agong ti mapiprito a tuyo iti kaarruba; manmano dagiti agranetret a karkariton kadagiti eskinita.

"Sika?" inaprosan ni Kosep ti abaga ni Dalen.

"Siak? Napukaw san ti pammatik iti amin a tao. Balasubasda amin!"

"Adda pay met nabati. . ."

"Dagiti inutil. . . dagiti mauma a paabalbalay. Dimo mangngeg iti radio? No mabalin laeng, tumayabak nga agpangato, daytay awan makitkitak a sairo."

"Panawam ngarud ti Escopa?"

"Shit!" immanges ni Dalen iti nauneg. "Panagkunak, dinatayo attanan daydiay a Pajaro. Napigsa iti ngato."

"No agkaykaysa ti Escopa. . ."

"No agkaykaysa ti Escopa! Kaanonto nga adda panagkaykaysa? No ultimo a Manglicmot bekkel ni Pajaro. . ."

"Kumarapettayo iti Dios, Dalen."

"Pakawanennak laengen. . . Panagkunak, adda ti Dios kadagiti nabileg. . . Laglagipem daytoy. Narugianen ni Pajaro ket saanen nga agbayag sanatayo ukomen. Laglagipem dayta!"

"Ania metten. Awan la kadin ti makitam a nalangto iti aglawlaw?"

"Yanna koma? Naangragen ti lubong, Kosep. . . no makitam la koma."

"Malang-abko. . . Ni Djona. . ."

"Ni Djona, wen. Malagipmo ni Silbato? Ni Anghel Guardiano? Talaga a dinak attanan 'diay sairo. Ni la unay Djona ti pampanunotek."

"Rummuarakto metten no bigat. Tapno matulongankayo."

"Ditoyka pay laeng. Amangan no ania ti mapasamak iti Escopa."

Kapitulo 3

SAANDA a dimngeg. Dagiti mangurkuranges iti Escopa.

Uray asino ti agdepdeppa!

Uray agsusukot a Pajaro.

Nga Angel Guardiano.

A Julian Manglicmot!

Kapitulo 4

ITAY agsapa, nasapa nga immulog da Dalen ken Djona.

Saan pay a simmurot ni Kosep. Saan pay a nakaungar.

Nagasatak metten. Uray kaskasano, naisip ni Kosep. Uray no dina maawatan no dadduma no apay a kastoy lattan ti panangipateg ni Dalen kenkuana. Ania ti adda kenkuana?

Dimo ammo? kinuna naminsan ni Dalen. Adda kenka ti mata nga awan kadagiti nabileg. Dimo maawatan? Bay-amon. Siak laengen ti makaawat. Ammom, adu ti kinadatdatlag iti lubong a di maawatan uray dagiti agar-aramid a mismo. Kasta no maminsan ti ngayed ti lubong. Adu dagiti di maawatan. Sika, maawatam kadi no apay a kastoy ti panagsasaok? Adu ti dimo pay ammo maipanggep kaniak. Kayatmo a maammuan? Saan laengen. Uray siak, diak ammo no dadduma ti bagik. Isu a burburtiaak met no dadduma. . . bay-am nga agtalinaedak a kasta.

Nadagaang ti aglawlaw. Ket dumagdagaang pay. Kasla makasiram.

Naisip ni Kosep: ania ngata no kellaat lattan a gumil-ayab ti Escopa?

Inwaksina ti mangal-aliaw kenkuana.

Adda dagiti aglabas: Kosep, komustaka?

Nasayaat met.

Ania ti damag?

Dandani kanon mangukom!

Kadi. . . ngem kunada met nga inaldaw kano a manguk-ukom.

Nagkiraus ti boksit ni Kosep. Saan sa ketdi nga agawid dagiti agina. 'Dan sa pay met la makan dita.

Ket nagkarkarawa. Nalamiis ti kilabban, ngem napipia.

Nagpalpa kalpasanna. Narigat met ti kastoy a nakapupok lattan a kasla natayen a sibibiag, naisipna. No mannuratak la koma, wenno pintorak. . .

Nalagipna dagiti ipadpadamag ni Dalen. Iladawanna koma ti lubong a paggargarawanna. Ngem apay ngata nga ammo ni Dalen dagitoy?

Kosep, komustaka?

Kastoy latta, agur-uray.

'Mangan no didakan sangpetan.

He, dika man lumablabas ditoy!

Ngem no pumayso ngarud?

Yad-adayom, Apo!

Limmukneng ti dagaang. Mangrugin dagiti taraketek iti eskinita. Immagibas iti agong ni Kosep ti angot iti kosina dagiti kaarruba.

Naipatayab dagiti damag iti transistor. Ne, sumipngeten.

Awan pay dagiti agina.

Nagtibbayo. Apay ngata?

Nagkarawa iti kosina. Mangisaang, pagpalabasanna iti oras. Apagisunto a makaluto no sumangpetda.

Ngem limmamiis a di nagaraw ti linutona. Saan pay a nagidda ni Kosep. Nakalukat pay la ti ridaw.

Awan pay dagiti agina. Apo, dimo ipalubos!

Kapitulo 5

APAGRIDEP ni Kosep idi malukag iti agdardaras a kayaskas iti ridaw. Intangwana ti rupana iti nagtugawanna.

"Ne, dika pay nakaturog?"

"Inur-uraykayo. . . Ni Djona?"

"Sorry, Kosep. 'Diay ngamin animal a Silbato. . . sairo a talaga!"

"A-apay?"

Nagsaibbek ni Djona.

"'Ta anakmo. . ."

"Dagiti kas kenkuana ti rumbeng a maukom!" adda saem iti barukong ni Kosep.

"Inukomkon," nababa ngem natangken ti timek ni Dalen. "Inukomkon!"

Pagam-ammuan, gimmil-ayab iti daya, iti tengnga ti Escopa. Nagsasaruno ti tapliak. Nagsasaruno ti panagsultop ti apuy. Kadagiti diding.

Nalukag ti Escopa.

Imkis ti aglawlaw.

"Uram! Uram!"

"Adda nagibuyat iti gas!"

"Kamatenyo!"

Pagam-ammuan, nasaywan ti balay da Kosep. Simmaruno ti gil-ayab.

Aggargarakgak ti gil-ayab iti parbangon.

III. Nagbang-ikan, Escopa

1. *Nagsaemen, Escopa, ti ladam;*
2. *Ta ti kakaisuna a paraisomi inda man ginamgam, ket adtoy ita ti rurogmo. . . ay, piman.*
3. *Makitadaka, Escopa, uray mangmatimati dagiti bituen;*
4. *Dagitoy ipatpateg. . . adtoykami nga umimatang, ngem dinakamin maimatangan.*
5. *Agriingka, ipatpateg, ket innakam arakupen, maudi a bara saem inka kad' ep-epen;*
6. *Dayta bang-i agkutikot nga insenso. . .*

Kapitulo 1

NAGSASARUNO ti sirena. Dagiti bombero. Lumanitak dagiti kamera. Nariing dagiti transistor. Nakibur dagiti agikamakam iti damag. Asino ti akin-aramid?

Kapitulo 2

NAGIINNAPUNGOLDA. Isuda a tallo. Ni Kosep. Ni Dalen. Ni Djona. Iti saklot ti rurog ti Escopa.

Timmangad ni Dalen: mangmatimati dagiti bituen. Nasaem ti ladam. Anian, tumulang!

Nailuganda iti ambulansia.

Wumanengweng dagiti nalabaga ken puraw a lugan. Gumilapgilap dagiti silaw.

Kadagiti pagiwarnak, idi makatangkayagen ti init:

Naiwalang ni Sarhento Angel Guardiano. . . Nageppas ti mabagbagina. . .

Natiliw ni Julian Manglicmot. . . iti paraangan ni Mr. Pajaro. . .

Kapitulo 3

ITI panagkidem ni Kosep, nakitana dagiti mangmatimati a bituen iti Escopa, segun iti panangiladawan ni Dalen.

Nakitana ti nasam-it nga isem ni Dalen.

Nakitana ti naliday nga isem ni Djona.

Nakitana ti bagina, ken ni Dalen, ken ni Djona, iti tallo a puraw a kama.

Natalnada. Nargaanda. —0

Bannawag: Pebrero 22, 1989; 2nd Prize, Kokua Lima Hawaii No Awards, 1993; *Saguday:* c2000, p.137-147.

Kasanon No Agsardeng Ti Lubong, Taraki?

e-mail 1: prologo

I

APAGLABES ti ngalay daytoy a siglo idi tumaud ti computer. Manipud idin, adun ti nagluposan ti lubong. Naglupos met ti Filipinas manipud iti dapo dagiti gubat. Adayo pay idi a napanunot ni tatang (Taraki I) ti agtalaw iti Filipinas ket umay agpasaklot iti America, ti daga ti Gatas ken Diro a makunkuna, ken impatomi a pasista ken nagwelwelgaanmi a radikal nga estudiante kadagiti unibersidad ti Kamanilaan, kas ti Unibersidad ti Daya, Unibersidad ti Filipinas, Politekniko nga Unibersidad ti Filipinas, ken dadduma pay.

Namin-anon a nagsukat ti presidente manipud idi nangrugi ti agpakpakadan a siglo ngem manmano ti nagtakder a maikari a tangaden; kaaduanna ti napilaw ta nagbalin dagiti karida bayat ti eleksion a kasla narayok a bugguong ti Kailokuan wenno inigges a buro ti Kapampangan.

Kasla nagtubo nga uong dagiti pagadalan, immadu dagiti estudiante—mabutengda a mailupitlupit inton dumteng ti panawenda. Naglako dagiti dadduma iti nuang. Adda nagpatagabo iti Manila. Nagadal dagiti dadduma a nagsibbarot kadagiti nasipnget a lansangan iti Tondo ken Quiapo, ken nagkayang kadagiti naangpet a siled iti Santa Cruz ken Missiricordia ken Felix Huertas ken Pandacan

177

ken Malate, ken Culiculi ken Calumpang, ken makisinsinnanggol iti Luneta sadanto mapan iti linged dagiti ladrilio iti Intramuros a nakaray-aban ti kakaisuna a puraw a kawesda. Adu ti nagbalin nga abogado, doktor, mannursuro, politiko—adu ti nagbalin a gamgam ta naaringanda kadagiti buaya a dinanonda iti siudad. Dagiti dadduma a nagturpos, nagpilida iti trabaho—ania, graduadoak, kastoy ti trabahok, inlibbida. Ngem nagangayanna, nagtinnagda a para gaik kadagiti nagkurosan.

Ngem adu latta met ti nabati iti sirok ti kamantiris wenno damortis nga agpaspasabeng; wenno iti sellang dagiti pay-as ken barukong dagiti sinilong ket karissabong ken karamukomda pay laeng ngem nakasursurodan nga agaw-awir ta nabengbeng ti sipnget ti sardam iti Abbarit ket nasam-it ti kanta dagiti kuriat ken andidit a nangilili iti riknada a timmangad kadagiti agkiremkirem a bituen iti labes ti langit—bay-am man dita ti adal-adal, nagbiag met da Lelong a palpal ken witiwit laeng ti inda kinain-innarakup, ken ubbog ti baresbes ti inda pinamedped iti wawda, saan a kola nga adda kapinna. Anak ditoy, anak idiay; awan ti anien, awan ti yapuy. Ngem nasam-it latta dagiti sardam; adda dagiti sinnutil a di magatgatadan iti doliar, nupay tumiltilmonda met no makangngegda iti berde nga isem ni Angkel Sam—ngem ti arapaapda adda iti likud ti langit.

Adu a ladawan, adu a pelikula ti pudno a biag. Ta ti lubong, saan a makaidna. Adu ti dara a nagayus ken umang-anges a rurog a bingbingrawen kadagiti nangisit a lansangan, ken naiwalang kadagiti kimmarayan iti sellang dagiti bantay ket agpipinnabasol dagiti napusgan nga agrebbeng. Awanen ti maisakmol ta dimteng ti krisis iti lubong. Awan ti panggedan. Umad-adu ti ngiwat a mabisin, ti boksit a lussulussok. Ket naigiddato pay dagiti didigra ti nakaparsuaan—ginggined, bulkan, layus, el nino: makaunget san ti lubong!

Adda nagarapaap a makaruar iti impierno a nakaikursonganda. Aglalo idi ngimmato ti doliar, ken bimmaba ti pisos, adun ti nagpanggep a mangtraidor iti inada a daga. Nagpayakpakda iti lugar a makairusok iti angrida. . .

II

ADDA kadi met angri nga insangbayko ditoy yanko ita, a pangus-
usarak iti sinakdok nga adal iti Unibersidad ti Filipinas? Siak, ni Taraki
San Diego II, saanak kadin a maikari a mangawag iti inak a Pinang iti
Nanang? Daydi nanangko nga imbati ni tatangko a Taraki San Diego
I idiay Abbarit idi inkeddengna a gundawayanna ti diaya ti gobierno a
mabalindan a beterano ti Maikadua a Gubat ti Sangalubongan ti agbalin
a makipagili iti America. Saanka a mapan, kinuna daydi nasingpet a
Nanangko a Pinang. No mapanka, diak sumurot; no matayak, matayak
iti nakayanakak a daga.

Ket kasdiay ti napasamak. Nagbalin ni tatang a kayumanggi a
makipagili iti America, nagbati daydi Nanang ket saan a napalubosan
ni tatang ti bangkayna idi maitabon idiay Abbarit.

Imbaonnak ti trabahok nga agadal iti Brigham Young University,
iti estado ti Utah kas iskolar ti pagilian. Nagsubliak met la iti Filipinas,
ngem saanakon a nagbayag ta kinamakamko ti puesto a programmer
nga indiaya ti Microsoft iti Orem, Utah a pangkutkutingtinganmi
ita iti y2k. Iti maysa a panirigan, nalabit a trinaidorko ti trabahok iti
Filipinas. Ngem maminsan la a dumteng iti biag ti napintas a gundaway.
Mababalaw kadi ti tao a mapan iti lugar a pakausaranna iti saguday nga
inted kenkuana ti Dios?

Ditoy, nakaadalak iti adu a banag a diak naadal iti UP. Adal a
magun-odko iti pannakipulapolko iti nadumaduma a puli a naggapu
iti uppat a suli ti lubong. No agtultuloy ti rinuker a pannakapataray
ti gobierno, ti yaadu dagiti politiko nga awan ti adda iti panunotda
no di ti bukodda a pagimbagan, nga agparparangdan a kaarngi ti
bampira iti panangsepsepda iti dara dagiti kadaraanda; no agsiwarak
ti panagidadanes iti bukod a dara, panagpipinnatay ti agkakabsat, ti
panagraira dagiti mangangkannigid, ti pannakaiwaras dagiti maipawil
nga agas iti Manila ken kabangibangna, ti itatayok ti presio dagiti
magatgatang gapu iti panangiludek ti doliar iti pisos ken panagbaybay-a
dagiti agrebbeng iti pagilian, adda met dagiti dadakkel nga isyu a
sangsanguen ti UN ken America, kas iti gubat ni Sadam, gubat iti Bosnia,
tension iti Chechnya, Ukraine, gubat iti politika, ken nadumaduma a

domestic ken sangalubongan a problema a makita kadagiti pagiwarnak ken social media.

No paggagampuren amin dagitoy, dakkel ti posibilidadna nga agsardeng ti lubong!

e-mail 2: tallo a Taraki

From: Taraki San Diego II /sandiegota@worldnet.att.net\
To: sandiegoba@mail.asiandevbank.com
Date: Thursday, March 4, _____, 8:40 PM
Subject: surat ni Taraki II

Dear Manong,

Napintek ti tiradam iti editorialmo iti *Bullalayaw*. Kuminnit dagiti balikasmo. Ti panangiladawam iti pangulo kaarngina ti butit a buaya iti takdang. Aglulua a mangsaksakroy iti naganus a rurog nga agtungtunglab iti ingel ti arak nga inarub-obna, ti pangulo, iti kallabes a rabii a selebrasion ti aldaw ni Rizal—agtedtedted ti lua (wenno dulno?) iti imingna. Kunam, nalaing nga agartista—adda kadi ngata kas kenkuana ti di makaammo nga agarte? Isu ngarud nga agtungtunglab ti sangapagilian—wenno sangalubongan—gapu kadakuada. Ti garakgakda umanayen a mangalimpayeng kadagiti inosente nga anghel. Arigna ti Pinatubo ti agsapri a sang-awda—adda kadi pay pakakitaam iti agtakder a maigidiat kadakuada? Dagiti adda iti kanigid, patiem kadi nga awan ti gamgamenda no di maikkan iti naan-anay a bileg a mangrippuog met iti lubong? Dagiti agpampanaas a barukong awan ti inda isansaning-in no di ti agalingasaw a buyok dagiti nalaesen a kari iti aggibgibusen a siglo. Addanto kadi pay agtakder a Moises wenno Cristo iti pagsaipan ti Disiembre ken Enero? Wenno agsardengto kadi ngata ti lubong iti maudi a pitik ti computer? Kasano a rakepem ti sangalubongan a kari ket kawesam iti natarnaw a puraw, sika nga editor, a mangidandanon kadagiti taom iti balikas a mangriing iti agtutuglepen a namnamada? Ik-ikkam ida iti namnama, ngem patiem kadi nga adda pay namnama iti lubong nga inladawam iti pagiwarnakmo? Ti panagtutudo dita Manila, kaarngi kadi pay dagidi panaglawlawintayo iti dalag ken paltat kadagiti

kinelleng ken waig idiay Abbarit, ken panagbambanniittayo iti ar-aro
ken gurami idiay Limas, panagsilsilotayo iti alimukeng ken pagaw
ken barog idiay Labut? Wenno linakub kadin ti nangisit nga angin ti
kalgaw ket agnguy-an ti lubong? Wenno nalabes kadi ti agwerwerret nga
imahinasion iti mugingko, gapu met laeng iti panangriingmo kaniak?

Magustuak ti kidag dagiti sinurat nga insaangyo iti kallabes a
bilangyo. No la koma mabalinda nga igam a mangduprak iti palasio
dagiti nagunggan. Ngem adda saludsodko: kayat pay ngata dagita a
nagunggan ti agbasa, wenno awanen ti panawenda, wenno kasda la
aglallalaten a rino ket saanen a kanen ida ti katademan a balikas?

Piman!

Ngem sakbay nga aggagampur ti panunotko—amangan no diak
maileppas 'toy nobelak a pangtratarak iti aggibusen a siglo—inta biit
iti nalaglag-an a topiko.

Nasaok idin a namitlon a naregregan ni Dayag, ket ita,
iti kamaudiananna, iti arinunos daytoy agpakpakadan a siglo,
nakabukelkami met laengen. No awan la ketdi ti nakaro a makatubeng,
maikapitonto ti Abril ti Panagsusulbod no tumao ni Taraki III nga umay
patenneb ditoy a lubong. Wen, Taraki III ti nagannanto ta ammomin
a lalaki ti saksakloten ni Dayag, segun iti ultrasound. Maseggaankami
unayen nga agur-uray, siak ken ni Dayag. Ngem sumangkasegga pay ni
tatang, wen, ni Taraki I. Nagbakasionen ni Dayag tapno masaganaanna
ti itatao ni Taraki III, uray ta adu met ti sick leave a dina pay naaramat.

Wen ni tatang. Kasdi latta. Aggagatel kano dagiti dakulapna nga
awan ti ub-ubraenna. Kasla adda kayatna a paneknekan wenno sulnitan.
Awan ti ar-aramidenna no di agkuditkudit ita ta nakalikuden ti Winter.
Panagkitak, di pay umdas a gamuluenna 'toy dandani maysa nga acre
a bangkag ditoy likud ti balay. Naguduanan a sinukay ket ur-urayenna
laengen ti umno a panawen a panagmulana iti tarong, kamatis, petsay,
sili, karabasa, kamotit, okra—wen, kaskami met la adda iti Ilokos no
kasdiayen nga agpuroskami iti bunga dagiti mulana. Ti nakaay-ayat, no
manen damagenna no kaano nga agpasngay 'toy ipagmo—idi imbagak a
Taraki III ti naganto ti apokona, minatmatannak sana imbaw-ing dagiti
matana iti agregreg a tartaraudi ti niebe iti ruar ti tawa iti laud.

Sangkadamagna met no kasanon dagiti appokona dita Filipinas—
agtukeng no kua a kasla manglagip. Uray no nabataden ti nagnaan ti
panawen iti rupana, madlawmo latta daydi bileg ti pakinakemna iti
panangyunana nga immay ditoy. Ngem ammotayo a ti panawen umay
a ditay madmadlaw. Ita ta agpakpakadan ti Winter—inton Marso 21
ti isasangbay ti Spring—mangrugi metten nga agsulbod dagiti lilies a
naglemmeng iti daga bayat ti panagurayda iti daytoy a panawen. Di
mabayag, lumangto manen ti aglawlaw ket agbukar dagiti nadumaduma
ti marisna, kas iti bullalayaw, a sabsabong ken bulbulong iti aglawlaw.
Kasla paraiso! Umayto manen ti Summer, ti Fall, ken ti Winter. . .

Umadanin ti pannakaipasngay ni Taraki III!

Kas iti yaadani ti panaggibus ti siglo, ken ti y2k...

Isuna laeng ta maipasngayto ditoy ganggannaet a lubong; adayo iti
nakaipasngayantayo, ken ti nakaipasngayan ni tatang.

Ngem asidegkaminto a dadakkelna. Siputanminto ti panagsulbodna.
Kas iti panagsulbod dagiti naganus nga uggot ken agbukar a sabong
iti Spring. Ammok a di masinunuo ti dana a surotenna ta awan ti
makaibaga iti dayta nupay uray no kaskasano, mabalin nga iturong, ita
ta nasapa pay, iti kasayaatan a pagbanaganna. Kas iti naganus a sanga
ti aruo, ti kayo nga agbiag ditoy kaniebean iti uppat a panawen—
Spring, Summer, Fall, ken Winter—agbiagto met ditoy iti uneg dagitoy
a panawen nga adayo iti polusion dita Cubao nga agpaut iti unos ti
makatawen. Adayo iti kidag dagiti di mangikankano nga agrebbeng—
uray no kasano ti panangisakit dagiti uken iti palasio kadagiti amoda,
agawaaw ti dangroda a kas iti narayok a bugguong; awan la ketdi ti
manannugot kadakuada ti kas iti imbutaktakmo iti editorialmo, ngem
saan a mailimed kadagiti makipagili ta saandan a bulsek a di makailasin
iti langa ti artista ken dagiti aggargaraw iti pudno a biag.

Ala wen, saan a maputpot ti kayatko nga isurat, uray man ketdi no
kasano ti kapaut ti panangusarko iti e-mail basta maibagak ti kayatko.
Ngem addanto manen sabali a panawen ta adu pay ti agur-uray a sabali
a sanguek.

Awan san ti panawenko a mailiw dita pagiliantayo—dakayo laeng
ti diak malipatan. . .

Masinunuok nga adu pay ti maawatmo nga e-mailko sakbay nga aggibus ti siglo.

'Toy adingmo,
Taraki San Diego II

e-mail 3: Bagnos San Diego

From: Bagnos San Diego /sandiegoba@mail.asiandevbank.com\
To: sandiegota@worldnet.att.net
Date: Wednesday April 7, _____, 9:40 P.M.
Subject: malmesen ti pagilian!

Nabayag bassit a diak nakapag-e-mail, Taraki II, Adingko. Saanen a nasken nga ibinsabinsak. Nakumikomak kadagiti kallabes. Sa medio nagloko daytoy e-mailko. Nalabit nga adda nakasirip kadagiti burias iti palasio kadagiti ipatpatulodko. Amangan no linappedanda ti pannakaiwarasda. Diak ammo. Sika ti makaammo amin a kinarakaran ti computer. Naimbag laeng ta dida pay impaulog ti pannakasensor dagiti pagiwarnak. Sapay koma ta awan ti makabasa itoy suratko kenka. A mangsensor. Tapno maammuam ti kayatko nga ilanad.

Malagipko gayam. Nasaom idi nga ita nga aldaw ti itatao ni Taraki III. Sapay koma ta makailusotda nga agina. Tapno umay met padasen dayta kaanakak ti makigasanggasat nga agkunail ditoy nariribuk a lubong.

Nalabit nga aggidiatta ti panirigan iti maysa a rupa ti biag. Ngem iti bangir, awan ti pagdumaanta. Agkaarngi pay ti estilota. Agpadata a makaawat iti tunggal linabag dagiti balikas nga ikurkur-itta. Agpadata a naayat kadagiti nasabsabongan ngem nagita a balikas. Ngem aggidiat ti lubong a paggargarawanta. Nalabit a nasaysayaat ti kastoy. Ta ad-adda a tumingra dagiti isuratta. Ngem husto ti kunam. Di ammo no basbasaen dagiti agrebbeng a begbegbegek kadagiti isursuratko. Ngem ammok nga adu kadagiti agbasbasa ti masilsilian ti kararuada. Inda la ketdi ilunlunod dagiti iladladawak.

Kasano koma a mapagimbubulsekanda ti mapaspasamak iti aglawlawda? Dida makaangesen iti panangkamatda iti itatayok ti pateg dagiti magatgatang. Kasano a mapagintutulnganda ti saning-i dagiti naganus a bungada? Napakilen dagiti piskelda iti tuokda nga agkaramut iti panilpoda iti anges dagiti patpatgenda. Makitada. Uray no dida mabasa. Iti lennek a matada. Dagiti atipukpok iti aglawlaw. . .

Adda manen rinangrangkayda idi sangaldaw . . .

Kuna ti mapagtalkan a naggapuan ti damag. Nga ama ti innem a babassit nga ubbing ti narangrangkay. Impakadana kano iti asawana a mapan agsapul iti isaangda. Ngem patay ti nasarakanna. Adda dagiti nagkuna a natiliwanda a nagtakaw iti sangakilo a bagas. Ngem awan ti pammaneknek.

Adda pay laeng dagiti agkidkidnap. Kasla awan ti maaramidan dagiti tsokolate. Adu ti makapaneknek nga adda kaduada kadakuada. Isu nga awan ti matiltiliw kadagiti aglablabsing iti linteg. Ti la agpapaimas ti paglainganda. Kunada, no ania ti aramid ti ama isu ti tuladen dagiti annak. Isu nga adu ti sugador. Adu ti babairo. Dida matandaanan no mano ti annakda iti ruar. Immadu kanon ti mangibagbaga nga isu ti ama ti anakda. Ngem dina met matandaanan no kaano a naginnimasda iti ina dayta nga anak.

Isu nga adayon dagiti mangurkuranges iti palasio. Kasla tagtagainep laengen kadakuada ti kaadda ti balay ti pagilian. Nalabit a madurmenda payen a makalagip. Nga adda kasta a pasdek iti lubongda. No la ngata mabalin nga iputong ti Abbarit kadagiti agatibuor a siudad. Naim-imbag koma nga amang ti agarapaap sadiay iti singin a bullalayaw. Ngem sadino pay ti pakasarakan iti singin a bullalayaw? Uray iti pannaturog, adu ti umay a ladawan. Pasig a nakadardara. Aragaag dagiti nagkautan a mata. Kinelleng dagiti pingping. Marmarba nga abaga. Kulay-ong a buksit. Sikkubeng a gurong. Nagango a buok. . .

No sangsanguek 'toy computer, kasla bangkay dagiti agparang a ladawan kadagiti sursuratek. Addanto ngata panawen a no sangsanguem ti computermo pagamuan lattan ta lumsot ti taom iti monitor ket darupennaka sakbay a maitalmegmo ti buton a delete.

Naagapadmo ti y2k. Adda kano parnuayenna a didigra iti nagsaipan ti Disiembre itoy a tawen ken ti Enero ti umay a siglo. Ngem no

ania man dayta a didigra a kunkunada, saan nga isu ti nakaituonan ti panunotko. Mannakabalin ti computer, kasla Dios pay ketdin no maminsan. Kunkunak no nakulkolen ti panunotko, nga ania koma no daytoy ti aramaten nga igam a mangrippuog kadagiti nagunggan a di mangipirpirit nga agrebbeng? Saan laeng a kas kadagiti robot iti pelikula. Ngem isu koma ti maaramat a pagdalus kadagiti ruker a buaya iti takdang.

Sika man ketdi ti mangaramid iti programa a kastoy. Total addaka iti ikub ti Microsoft. Mangpartuatka iti chip a mangwanawan iti lubong. Nga uray no sadino ti paglemmengan dagiti demonio sapulenna. Ket ipanna iti plasa a pangbuyaan kenkuana dagiti tao bayat ti panangibambandona nga isu ti karasaen ti pagilian. Ket awatenna ti ania man a pannusa dagiti makipagili. . .

Anian ti mapampanunotko, Taraki II, Adingko? No addaka ditoy, makitam a pudno ti ibagbagak. Ala wen, mabalinko koma nga iladawan dagiti kumunulkunol a tao kadagiti mall. A ladawan ti kinadur-as. Ta dimo madlaw nga adda problema dagitoy. A kasla mamitloda amin a mangan iti agmalem. A kasla dida parparikut ti kuarta ta nakaim-imas met ti panangsirsirigda kadagiti agkakangina a tagilako. Wenno buybuyaenda kadi laeng dagitoy? Adda met singin a bullalayaw kadagiti alintataoda! Inda sipsiputan dagiti nabubun-as nga adda bilbilangenda a nasisikkil a papel de banko. A pagbayadda iti balitok a pantalon wenno tisert. Nalabit a kunkunada: apay nga adda papel de bankona ket awan kaniak? No ngata sibbarutek?

Nakaadayoakon . . .

Ni manangmo a Sam-it. . . Wen, linumoten iti pangisursuruanna. Ti sueldoda? Dinan pampanunoten ta timmayaben dagiti adu a kari para kadakuada. Isuda a bannuar ti pagilian. Nga adigi dagiti tumanor koma a sarikedked ti pagilian. A pagangayanna a dida matimonan a nasayaat dagitoy ket imbes a nasayaat ti pagbanaganda, adu metten kadakuada ti adda kadagiti nasipnget a lugar a mangsussusop iti mitsa ti biagda. Dagitoy innem a kaanakam, bangbangolanda metten. Ngem naimbag ketdi ta binigbigda met ti kaipapanan ti naganko. Awan kadakuada ti naisiasi wenno naikuyog kadagiti mangsinsindi iti mitsa ti biagda. Dandanida agturpos aminen iti kolehio. Adda trabahon ti dadduma.

Kas kenka, dua met ti maul-ulaw iti computer. A kasla ketdin dida agbiag no awan daytoy nga amo ti tao. Pati ngamin siak ket addan daydi nagbibiagak a makinilia idiay bodega. Nalaklaka met ngaminen ti agsurat ditoy computer. . .

Ipadamagmo met ken ni tatang a Taraki I, nga awan ti pagdanaganna kadagitoy appokona ditoy a pinanawanna. Babai man wenno lalaki, tinawidda ti tangken ti sangina. Uray dagidiay bagi da kabagis a Taklin ken Angie. Tarakida latta a napeklan. Dayta ti mabalintayo nga ipagtangsit. Masaok a nagballigi ni Taraki I a tatangtayo iti panangpatanorna iti pamiliana. Saan a kas kadagiti kakabsatna a nagbalin a barrairong dagiti kakasinsintayo. Kunak itan: saanen a sayang ti nagrigatan ni tatang. Natalnanto la ketdin ti nakemna nga agsubli iti ina a daga.

Wen, isagsaganamin daytoy sumaruno a bilang ti *Bullalayaw*. Immadu dagiti mannurat a siaayat a makisinnarakuy. Mabigbigdan a rumbeng nga asaenda ti plumada tapno nabilbileg nga isarangmi kadagiti bukatot a kabusor.

Wen, saan pay a panawen nga agsuratkami kadagiti nasam-it a binatog. No kaanonto dayta a panawen, kunak nga inton sisasaganan ti pagilian a madaniwan iti naimnas a binatog. Sayang dagiti nasam-it a balikas. No arusibsiben met laeng dagiti tukab. Ngem ammok a dumtengto ti panawen. No saan, mabatinto dagitoy a tugot iti pakasaritaan 'toy agpakpakadan a siglo. Diak panggep ti agbalin a bannuar a kasla Rizal. Kayatko laeng ti agbalin a puling kadagiti natadem ngem agdudungsa a mata.

Nakaadayoakon. Ngem adu pay ti kayatko nga idanon kenka. Adu pay ti panawen. Adayo pay ti panungpalan. Ngem nasken met nga agsaganaak. . .

'Toy Manongmo,
Bagnos

e-mail 4: spring ken winter

From: Taraki San Diego II /sandiegota@worldnet.att.net\
To: sandiegoba@mail.asiandevbank.com
Date: Thursday, April 15,____; 9:30 p.m.

Subject: sungbat ni Taraki II

Manong,

Talaga a nataraki ni Taraki III! Immala kadakami ken ni lelongna a Taraki I. Ngem adda met naalana ken ni Dayag, kas iti matana. Nagguduaanmi iti inana ti uha ti rupana. Ita pay laeng, maitugotanen ti tibker ti pakinakemna—sapay koma ta pumudno ti pattapattak.

Naragsakkami a tallo—siak, ni tatang, ken ni Dayag—a nangpasangbay kenkuana. Ngem kadagiti napalabas a sumagmamano nga aldaw, nadlawko ti itatamnay ti rikna ni tatang. Kasla adda rikriknaenna ngem kinunana met a diak pagdanagan idi damagek no apay. Sigsigud a no kastoy a dumteng ti Spring, nakasarsaranta a mangsangsango kadagiti mulana a nateng. Nakaragragsak a makisarsarita kadagiti nalangto a muyong a kunam no maawatanda ti ibagbagana.

Wen, Spring manen. Nakalanglangto manen ti saringit dagiti naglupos a mulmula iti aglawlaw. Nalangton dagidi bangkay a sangsanga a mangpalamiis iti panagkita. Adun dagiti sabsabong a nagbukar. Awan dumana iti maysa a paraiso!

Maayatanak man iti kunam maipanggep iti computer. Agpayso nga adda iti imami a programmer ken technician ti masakbayan dagitoy a ramit, ngem adda met pagpatinggaan ti ammomi. Nalabit a makaaramidkaminto iti kas iti kunam, ngem saan pay nga ita. Ti panagkunak, tao, kas kadagiti politiko, ti mangar-aramid iti masakbayanna. No aramidenmi ti kunam, dakkel ti posibilidadna nga amin a bidduttayo ket 'dillawen' ti computer ket amangan no agbanagto a bekkelnatayon daytoy a ramit. Ngem diak kunaen a saan a balido ti kapanunotam. Mabalin a mapasamak ti kasta. Ngem adu a panawen ti nasken a busbosen sakbay nga adda nabatad a pagmataanna. Kabayatanna, ikagkagumaananmi, dakami a programmer, nga aturen ti biddut ti immuna a programa. Kunada iti Texaco a saan nga amin a pagam-amkan ti lubong maipanggep iti kapasidad ti computer, kas iti y2k, ket balido. Addan dagiti naatur a biddut nupay agpayso nga adu pay ti nasken nga aturen.

Diak ammo no ania ti pudno a rikna dagiti makipagili a Filipino dita Filipinas maipanggep itoy a kaso ti computer. Ditoy America, nangruna

ditoy Utah, adda naulimek a panagsagana dagiti makipagindeg. Nupay saan a nabatad ti pannakakumikomda nga agsagana, wenno ti danagda, adda dagiti maiwarwaras a polieto, nangruna iti kongregasion dagiti pammati, a mangisuro, wenno mangbalballaag kadagiti kamengda, nga agsagana. Nupay awan dagiti agtutungtong kadagiti alsong wenno sango ti temtem maipanggep itoy a parikut, adda met dagiti dida kayat ti makigasanggasat ket kaykayatda ti agtungpal iti patigmaan dagiti liderda. Kunada, awan met ti dakesna nga isaganada dagiti kasapulanda iti di mapakpakadaan a didigra, total maaramatda met dagiti pempenenda no kas pagarigan di dumteng ti insagsaganaanda. Adda agkuna nga agsaganada iti abasto iti makatawen, wenno makabulan, kas iti danum, naipagango a taraon, pagaron, ken no ania payen a kasapulan, nangruna ditoy a sakupen ti winter ti Disiembre ken Enero, a di ammo no nabengbengto ketdi ti agtinnag a niebe. Saan a gapu ta maamakkami, ngem nagnaminganmi ken ni Dayag a sumurotkami iti agus.

Ngem adu met ti di mangipirpirit. Adda dagiti anounser iti radio nga agkatkatawa, nga agkunkuna a maag dagiti mabuteng iti y2k. Awan ti makaammo iti talaga a mapasamak, pasig a pattapatta. Ngem dakami iti computer, adda bassit pamattapattaanmi, nupay ikagkagumaanmi a di mapasamak, wenno maliklikan dayta dumteng a didigra, wenno bassit a problema.

Malagipko idi addatayo pay idiay Abbarit. Adu ti agiinnarasaas maipanggep iti mapaspasamak iti aglawlaw, kas kadagiti agraira a mangangkannigid, wenno sakasaka a mangiwalang kadagiti kabusorda iti politika, wenno mangrabrabii. Ubingak pay idi, ngem nakaddadanag man ketdi ti kasdiay nga innarasaas, a kunam no adda talaga maiwalang manen iti kabigatanna, ipalnaawda iti sirok ti algarruba, wenno inulida a pensionado. Adu met ngamin no kua ti pumudno a bunga ti innarasaas. Adda pay dagidi panagraira ti damag nga asideg ti panangukom ti Dios, no namin-ano, ngem di met napasamak ti naiwarwaras a damag. Adda pay daydi nadamagmi ditoy, a sekta ti pammati dita Filipinas a nangiwarwaras iti damag a mangukomen ket imbagada pay ti petsa dayta nagasat nga aldaw. Inlakoda dagiti napateg kadakuada, total didanto kano met laengen kasapulan. Ngem saan a napasamak ti nagam-amkanda ket nagangayanna nagpakamatayda gapu ngata iti

bainda. Ngem adda met istoria iti nasantuan a kasuratan maipanggep kadagiti masirib a birhen. Nagsaganada iti lana tapno adda pagsilawda no dumteng ti sipnget. Adda nangkatkatawa kadakuada ta dida ida pinati. Ngem dimteng ti pasamak, ket awan dakes a napasamak kadakuada ta nakapagsaganada.

Isu nga adda iti tao a mangsurot iti kayatna. Ket isunto met laeng ti agsagrap iti bunga ti aramidna. No agbiag pay iti napapaut gapu ta sinurotna ti nasaysayaat, nagasat. Ngem no matay gapu iti kinasubegna, malasna.

Ne, kasta pay ket ay-ayabannak ni Dayag. Innak kano itemplaan ni Taraki III iti gatasna—kastoy ditoy, awan ti katukatulong.

Adingmo,
Taraki II

P.S.—Naguduakon nga isakab ti nobelak, ngem awan pay ti paulona; pampanunotek a pauluan iti **Maudi a Siglo**.

Komusta gayam ti *Bullalayaw*. Sapay koma ta agtultuloy ti tadem ti plumayo.

Siak met laeng.

e-mail 5: adu ti bulsek

From: Bagnos San Diego /sandiegoba@mail.asiandevbank.com\
To: sandiegota@worldnet.att.net
Date: Saturday May 1, _____; 9:32 P.M.
Subject: adu ti bulsek

Taraki II,

Dua a banag ti mabalin a mapasamak: agballigikayo a computer wizard a manglapped iti mabalin a mapasamak. Wenno mapasamak ti pagam-amkan iti teknolohia.

Maringguran dagiti pannakamata a kas kenka iti naulimek a gubat iti siensia. Kunayo a sangalubongan daytoy a parikut. Seknanna amin a computerized a ramit iti lubong. Kas iti banko. Koriente. Danum. Eroplano. Bapor. Telepono. Telebision. Ken dadduma pay. Datayo nga adda kadagiti siudad ti makaammo ti mabalin nga ibunga daytoy a

parikut. Nupay adu latta met ti di mangipirpirit. Adu ti agintutuleng ken agimbubulsek. Ngem dagiti dadduma, talaga nga inosente kadagitoy a banag.

Maysa ti ammok a kinapudno: awan ti bibiang dagiti adda iti probinsia. Nangruna dagiti taga-gingginget. No ania man ti mapasamak kadagiti naagapadko iti ngato. Ta adu kadakuada ti awan ti alikamenna a kasta. Nalabit nga adu pay kadakuada ti di makaammo ti maipanggep iti computer.

Iti panagpalpaliiwko, saan unay a maringguran dagiti makipagili. Uray no kaipapananna ti pannakapukaw ti computer. Nasnasken kadakuada ti pangalaanda ti isakmulda iti sumuno a pannangan. Pakaringguranda ti kinangato ti presio dagiti magatgatang. Dagiti sangatarayan-sangaapuyan ti kayatko a sawen. Iti panagkunak, adun ti manglanglangan a mangan. Makaallilaw ti kabengbeng ti tao nga agkukunulkunol kadagiti dadakkel a pagtagilakuan. Kunam la no adu ti makukuarta ti tao. Kinapudnona, adu kadagitoy ti naikkaten iti trabahona. Nalabit nga addada kadagita a lugar nga agar-arapaap laeng. Wenno umam-ambing. Adu ti awan ti trabahona ta naikkatda iti puestoda iti gobierno. Wenno napilitan a pimmanaw iti pribado a trabahona. Ta awanen ti panueldo ti akinkukua.

Agbisin ti tao, kabsat. Dagiti la unay ubbing. Isuda koma ti namnama iti masakbayan.

Mababalawmo kadi no inaldaw nga adda damag iti pagiwarnak maipanggep iti panagtambang wenno panagtakaw?

Mababalawmo kadi ti maysa nga ama no patayenna ti sangabukel a kaamaanna gapu iti pannakapukawnan iti namnamana?

Asino ti akimbasol?

Paset kadi ti kunkunada a pakpakauna ti maikadua a panangukom amin dagitoy? Didigra iti amin a suli ti lubong.

Ngem mapunno met latta dagiti disco houses. Kanayon nga agbilbil-a dagiti dyip iti kaadu ti pasahero nga agbitin tapno makapanda iti kayatda a papanan.

Kas itay nakunakon, adu ti nangnangruna a pakaituonan ti imatang dagiti makipagili. Para iti aginaldaw a kasapulanda.

Panagurnong? Ania ti urnongen dagiti tao? Pangalaanda? Nalabit a dida kayat ti agurnong ta no matiktikan dagiti nakarkaro nga agbisin, amangan no mitsa pay ti biagda.

No malausak ti mangamiris iti agdama a kasasaad ditoy, angsabenak. Kaslaak la mabekbekkel. Masaludsodko: daytoy kadin daydi Perlas iti Daya?

No adda urnongenyo dita, nagasatkayo. Ditoy, awan. Adu ti daksanggasat. Husto ti ipapanawmo. Naitarayam ti agdama a gawat. Ngem ammok a dimo maitarayan ti anniniwanmo.

Adu ti sumina. Ngem ad-adu ti maipasngay.

Kaasi laeng dagiti maipasngay ta umayda iti biddut a panawen. Naipasngayda koma idi kaburnok pay ti dalag. Ken paltat. Ken ar-aro. Ken gurami. Ken tokak. Ken nadumaduma a natnateng idiay Abbarit. Saanda koma nga agbisin. Ngem ita, umayda a polusion ti taraonda. Agsidada iti segseg ti bugguong. Agsepsepda iti ungel ti nagtebbaan iti saba. Naimbag no adda pay mayapuyda. Wenno makalida a kamangeg. Wenno atap a singkamas. Wenno makilawda a busel ti tarong. Kas iti panagkilaw dagidi nagunggan a Hapon idi maikadua a gubat ti lubong.

Ala wen, agsurattayo. Ginabsuon a sinurat. Bareng no dagitanto a libro wenno magasin wenno pagiwarnak ti taraontayo inton dumteng ti pudpudno a gawat.

Agsurattayo ta bareng no mailusotantayo daytoy a pannubok iti ngudo ti siglo. Ta addanto basbasaentayo bayat ti panagkirpa ti panagsiglusiglot dagiti lalaemtayo. Addanto itag-aytayo. Ket ipukkawtayo iti langit: DAYTOY TI DOKUMENTO TI NAPALABAS A SIGLO!

Diak ammo no mano ti bulsek. Diak ammo no mano ti tuleng. Ngem adu iti lanlansangan. Nasken laeng nga agbalintayo a propeta. Tapno makitatayo ti sasawentayto. Tapno mangegtayo ti saning-i ti lubong. Datayo a mannurat. Ta awan ti makaawat kadatayo. Iti pudpudno a punto. Bareng no makitanto ti tao ti gapu ti kaaddatayo ditoy a lubong.

Wen, ni tatang a Taraki I. Sika a Taraki II. Ni Taraki III. Adda bukodtayo a panawen. A naggarawan. Pasetnatayo amin ti sangabukel a siglo. Daytoy agpakpakada a siglo.

Adu, Taraki II, adingko, ti nasken nga awatentayo. Tapno agbukeltayo a tao. Ituloymo ti nobelam. Ileppasmo. Ilibrom. Uray no di mabasa ita, mabasanto iti masakbayan. Mabatinto a tugotmo.

Kastan. Kitaek no kasano nga isaangmi daytoy sumaruno nga isyu ti *Bullalayaw.*

Manongmo,

Bagnos San Diego

Pakamakam: Adda inplasda ditoy tv. Adda gerra iti abagatan. Adu ti natay ngem agtultuloy ti rupak. Soldado ken sibilian. Sa naigiddato ti layus. Layus iti kalgaw. –Siak met laeng.

e-mail 6: Paripirip

From: Taraki San Diego II /sandiegota@worldnet.att.net\
To: sandiegoba@mail.asiandevbank.com
Date: Saturday, May 22, ----, 9:44 P.M.
Subject: Paripirip ti fall

Manong,

Naragsak a kasangaymo, patgek a kabsat—no mano ti tawenmon, saan a bilangen iti tawen a limmabas ngem babaen dagiti tugot a nabatim, ket kunak nga adun ta nabengbengen dagiti binulong ti *Bullalayaw.* Kablaawanka, patgek a kabsat.

Dandanin aggibus ti spring. Agarup nakidseren dagiti nagrusing a sanga, ken dagiti bulbulong ken sabsabong. Kapades ti nakaparsuaan ti mangala iti pigsana para iti umadani a fall.

Nasurok la a makabulan ni Taraki III ngem nairuten ti petpetna. Natangken dagiti gemgemna. Mangrugi metten nga agilasin. Nakarit no agsapul iti gatasna. Saan nga agpakatutor. Puyatannak no dadduma. Ngem magustuak man ta adda ikarkari ti ibitna a masakbayan. Saanak a mabannog a mapan iti Food-4 Less, wenno iti Sams, no kasdiay a dandanin maibus ti gatasna—diak kayat a makunatan. Isu ita ti nakaitalimudokan ti imatangmi, ti panagsalsalukagmi ken ni Dayag. Makunak nga isu ti rupa ti San Diego iti sumuno a siglo. No isemannak, agandap ti singin a bullalayaw kadagiti natarnaw a matana. Naganus

pay dagiti gurongna ket agmimminar ti dara ni Ilokano nga agtartaray kadagiti uratna.

Ni Taraki III ti masakbayanmi ken ni Dayag! No ay-ayamenmi kadagiti balitok nga orasmi, kasla awankami ditoy a lubong ket malipatanmi nga adda pangta ti agpakpakada a siglo. Ipalnaad dayta a pangta dagiti ladawan ti panagsagana a nakaintar kadagiti dadakkel a pagtagilakuan ditoy Siudad ti Salt Lake. Awan ti mangngegmo a balikas ngem adda nakasurat. Umel a ballaag! Wen, awan ti agsasarita maipanggep iti dayta a pangta ti siglo. Ngem adda dagiti surat. Kas iti kaaw-awatko a surat ti bankok. Awan kano ti pagdanaganmi—ipatok lattan a saan a sisiak ti sinuratanda—ta mano a tawenen nga insagsaganaanda dayta nagasat a rabii.

Uray no kasta, sumipsiplot latta ti negatibo a panunot, kas iti di maliklikan nga idadateng ti fall wenno ti sagubanit ti bagi uray no kasano ti panagannad.

Maipalagip kaniak ni tatang, ni Taraki I. Natibker a talaga ta kasla dina kayat ti kumna iti aglabas a panawen. Ngem itay bigat, nakasaganaakon a rumuar ngem di pay rimmuar iti kuartona. Sigsigud nga umuna a makariing ket addan nga agkuditkudit iti plotna, a makisarsarita kadagiti mulana. Napanko kinita iti kuartona sakbay nga immulogak. Imbagana a kasla naberberdeng dagiti ur-uratna.

"Kitaem ta 'panka no kua pa-check-up, 'Tang," kinunak. Nalagipko nga idi kalman, agsay-asay-a.

"Kabaelak daytoy. . . uray mano a doktor no orasmon, orasmo lattan."

Kastan. Agsuratakto manen.

'Toy kabsatmo,

Taraki II

e-mail --: epilogo

ADUN NGA aldaw ti limmabas—agngalayen ti Winter ket masansan nga agtinnag ti niebe; ti parais ti nalamiis nga angin inna pagbibinegen ti rikna ngem ti puraw nga aglawlaw iladawanna ti maysa a paraiso iti sellang ti dua a bantay a nangsaklot iti Great Salt Lake—ngem ti kaaduna

kasla kaano laeng ti naudi a pannakaawatko ti surat ni Manong Bagnos, a nangipadamaganna iti kaadu ti nagawid a Filipino, segun kano iti damag a nagwaras, gapu iti yaadani ti y2k. Kunada kano a kaykayatda ti aguray iti mabalin a mapasamak iti nagbaetan ti Disiembre ken Enero, a panagsina ti daan ken baro a siglo. Kayatda nga addada iti sidong dagiti patpatgenda iti Filipinas sakbay a dumteng dayta a panawen. Diak masinunuo no agpayso ti damag ta ditoy yanmi iti Utah, naulimek dagiti kadaraan. Nalabit a dimi kayat a maammuan ti tunggal maysa ti danagmi; kayatmi nga iparikna iti tunggal maysa nga addakamin iti America, daga a tangtangaden ti sangalubongan. Innayonna pay nga agngangabit ti *Bullalayaw* gapu iti di napakpakadaan a panagngato dagiti materiales iti panagiprinta; kangrunaannan ti ibibiang dagiti adda iti poder. Kunana man nga adda uleg iti sidong ti pagiwarnakna ket nalabit a napamelmelan iti ulo ti Pangulo. Ngem adu met ketdi ti mangisaksakit, ngem di la ammo no pagpatinggaan ti tangken ti sangida a mangirupir iti kalinteganda.

Aggibus met laengen ti daan a siglo ngem di pay naatur ti pakasaritaan. Agtultuloy dagiti gubat. Pinnatangken. Awan ti mayat nga agpakumbaba. Awan ti mayat a maabak.

Manon a bulan ni Taraki III? Mangrugin nga agpasok. Mabalikasnan ti mama. Ngem adda dumukduko a danag iti barukongko gapu ta amangan no mariinganna ti riribuk ti sangalubongan. Amangan no umunanto a madlawna dagiti kanalbuong iti aglawlaw.

Ni tatang Taraki I, adda iti LDS Hospital iti downtown ti Salt Lake City. Intaraymi itay malem, ngem kapilitan a pinanawak ket sinarakusokko ti nabengbeng a niebe iti I-15 nga agpaabagatan nga agturong iti Orem ta adda napateg unay nga ikamakammi iti trabaho, para iti y2k. Naka-red alertkami amin a programmer ken technician ti Microsoft. Imbatik da Dayag ken Taraki III idiay balay ngem no manen, awagak, ket ipatpatigmaanko iti asawak, ti panamagkalmana iti riknana.

Awanak iti sidong ti pamiliak.

Awanak iti sidong ni tatang a makiin-innagaw ken ni patay.

Addaak iti trabahok ta pasungadenmi ti isisina ti daan a siglo.

Naaramidmin ti amin a kabaelanmi para iti computer. Panagkunami, nakasaganan ti lubong iti ania man a mapasamak. Naaturmi dagiti

nasken nga aturen. Kas iti padamag ni Manong Bagnos, adu met ti agsagsagana iti Filipinas. Wenno agur-uray iti mabalin a mapagteng.

No dadduma, masaludsodko: Kasanon no agsardeng ti lubong, Taraki? Iti ngalay ti makabibineg a Winter?

Nasken koma a naileppaskon ti **Maudi a Siglo. . .**

Bayat ti panagur-uraymi iti naituding a kanito, pamrayak nga isursurat daytoy. Nalabit nga aramatekto a paggibusan ti **Maudi a Siglo.**

Ania ti langa ti lubong no kellaat nga agsipnget iti katengngaan ti rabii? Ania ti mapasamak kadagiti hospital, uray no kunada a nakasaganadan?

Ni tatang, a makiin-innagaw ken ni patay. . .

Ni Taraki III. . .

No manen, tangadek ti dakkel a pagurasan iti diding iti sangok. Naannayas ti panagpallayog ti tillayonna, naulimek. Naulimek ti aglawlaw iti opisina. Kasla awan mayat a dumngeg iti radio. No manen, awagak ni Dayag. No manen, umawagak iti LDS Hospital. Ngem idi awagak koma manen ni Dayag, inkeddengko a saanen. Kayatko a matmaturogda ken ni Taraki III no agsabat ti daan ken baro a siglo.

Mano nga oras pay?

Napanunotko: umun-una ti oras iti Filipinas.

Sinangok ti computerko. . .—0

Saluyot: December 1999.

Wadsapani

T I NAGANNA: Policarpia Camangeg. Ti birngasna iti Kilkillabot: Carpia. Idi nakadanon iti Indio, California: Claire--nabangsit kano ngamin ti Carpia, kuna dagiti kabagiyan ni lakayna, ket awan ti agnagan iti naangdod iti America; isu a dina am-ammo a dagus dagiti imbagada nga agnagan iti Josh, Susie, Ernz, Madz, Nesty, nga idiay Kilkillabot timmangken a Kosep, Simang, Istong, Inyang, ken Sintang. Ti timekna: nasinggit nga umal-alimpatok ket isu ti reyna dagiti dadakkel ti ngiwatna idiay Kilkillabot— kasla armalayt nga agbusi no marugianna. Ti kudilna: nangisngisit ngem kayumanggi— nalabes met no kunaen nga atiwna pay ti likud ti pariok. Ti tayagna: pagattengngedna ni lakayna nga Apo Tabs (Gustavo wenno Usting) Camangeg ket mabalinna la a kulintitingen no kayatna. Kasla kanayon a masinsinit, wenno kasla naputotan a lawlawigan. Ti nakakayaw ken ni Apo Tabs? Siguro ti kasla binagsol a bangbangir a kallidna no umisem a kas iti karasay ti kabus a bulan. Ti nakapuraran dagiti nagannak kenkuana a nangyaso ken ni Apo Tabs, nga in-inauna pay ngem ni Nanangna? Ti pension ti lakay kas beterano idi Maikadua a Gubat ti Lubong ta dida ammo a battikuting laeng ti aw-awatenna. Sa idi agangay, nadumaduma nga agas ti mangririing kadagiti nagangon a parpariana.

Gapu iti panagsitisen ni Apo Tabs, naipuruak iti America ti pamiliana, isuda nga agassawa, ken ti tallo nga aburoy nga annakda a da Gretzie, 18; Totzie, 17; ken Latzie, 16 nga idiay Kilkillabot Trudis,

Sitang, ken Saling—nagdua a tawenda iti Mecca, California ket agtallo a tawenda metten iti West Valley City, Utah.

Idi sangsangpetda iti Indio, California a nagtarusanda manipud iti Kilkillabot, kimmalkalay-at ken nagkarkaradap dagiti mata ni Claire iti uneg ti balay ni Mang Rosie, ti ipagna nga adien ni Apo Tabs. Iniletna la unay dagiti kuarto ken salas, ken linetlet iti kayumanggi a karpet. Semento la ngamin ti basar ti balayda idiay Kilkillabot. Dina nabilang no mano dagiti sinangpetanda, ngem naulaw iti panagkukukunulkunolda.

Nagpakbet ni Mang Rosie iti paria, tarong, ukra, ken bagas ti puraw a kamotit a napakaptan iti bugguong-Dagupan a ginatangda iti Oriental Store idiay San Bernardino. Kellaatenna ngata ti kunana dagiti sangsangpet ta ipagarupda la ketdi nga awan ti taraon ti Saluyot iti California. Ngem idi sanguendan ti pangmalemda, napanganga pay ti baket iti naduktalanna: kinimkimkiman da Gretzie, Totzie, ken Latzie ti kanenda uray no madlaw ti kasta unay a bisinda.

"Apay a dikay' mangan?" immulagat ni Mang Rosie.

"Di ngamin agsidsida iti nateng dagita, Manang," insinggit ni Claire. "Dida pay kayat ti ikan. Kanayon a karne ti baboy wenno baka. . ."

"Ne, dida, 'ya, nayanak 'diay Kilkillabot?" ad-addan ti mulagat ni Mang Rosie. "Dakayo man pay la ti Ilokano a di agsidsida iti pinakbet! Apay nga inruammo ida iti kasta, Manong?" binaw-ingan ti baket ti kabsatna.

"No isu met ti kayatda, kabagis," marmaratamnay ni Apo Tabs. Kas karasay ti kabus a bulan nga agsao.

Kas iti kapartak ti angol a nagwaras kadagiti Pinoy iti Indio ken Mecca ti napasamak iti dayta a pangmalem, nangruna ta immuna a nakasagap ni Maribel nga inauna nga anak ni Mang Rosie nga adda ti balayna idiay Mecca a dumna iti Indio ken nagbedngan ti California ken Mexico. Uray no kasla insaltek a kuribot, nasinggit met ni Maribel ket kas ken ni Claire, aributantanenna ti agsao.

Nagdakkel ti nganga ni Claire ken arig sumalto dagiti matana iti panagarmalayt ni Maribel a kurang la nga aglabutab ti ngiwatna. Tinangad ni Apo Tabs ti asawana, a nakananga met, a kasla kunkunana: nakasarakkan, Baket, dayta ket ngatan!

Sakbay a nagiddada iti daydi a rabii, immawag ni Dennis, ti inauna nga anak ni Apo Tabs, a sibsibetna iti Indio ta nakaala iti trabaho iti West Valley, Utah. Adu koma ti ipadamag ni Claire ngem kasta unay ti panangisarang ni Mang Rosie iti lapayagna a kasla kudkudidit, isu a nagkikinnumostada lattan.

Idi agiddadan, insinggit ni Claire iti lakayna: "Ay, maustelak la ketdi a dina oras, Hani, no agbayagtayo ditoy! Daydiay kaanakam a burnay, diak magustuan ti tabas ti ngiwatna!"

Inin-inayad ni Apo Tabs a kinita ti ngiwat ni Claire sana met la inin-inayad nga inyadayo dagiti matana iti asawana.

"Dimo kunkuna ti kasta, Hani, amangan no panaganannaka met. . ."

"Padpadasenna ta makasarak iti dina pay nakitkita!"

Iti kabigatanna, inukkon ni Maribel da Gretzie, Totzie ken Latzie ken dagiti dadduma a kaanakanna a mapan tumulong nga agdalus iti balay ni Wally, ti amona idiay Palm Desert, pambaranna ti agpatulong a mangiserrek kadagiti tallo iti trabaho.

"Agdalus?" kasla naulpan ti rupa ni Claire.

"Ay, awan lugar ti sadut ditoy, Anti!" insippaw ni Maribel a nakadlaw iti panagtukiad ni Claire. Agkataebda iti nasurok nga uppat-a-pulo-ket-pito a tawenda.

"Awan ti ammo dagita ubbing a trabaho. . . Idiay balay, pulos a dida nagtatrabaho. . ."

"Ne, saankay' koma ngarud nga im-immay ditoy! Awan ti agbiag ditoy America a dina ammo ti agtrabaho!"

Napaltingan ni Claire. Naungap ti ngiwatna ngem sakbay a nakapagsao, inaributantan manen ni Maribel.

Immulo ti dara ni Claire. Idiay Kilkillabot, awan ti nakaitured a nangngiwat kenkuana. Isu ti ngiwat ti sangakaarrubaan.

Idi simmangpet dagiti napan nagdalus, ad-addan ti arikiak ni Maribel. Impadamagna ti panangal-alunggigit dagiti agkakabsat kadagiti pagdalus, ken ti panagsangit ni Totzie idi isurona nga agdalus iti kasilia, ken ti dina yaannugot a para balay da Wally.

"Apay, baknangkayo, aya, tapno agpilikayo iti trabaho?" inyagyag ni Maribel.

Maysa nga aldawda la iti balay da Mang Rosie. Iti simmaruno nga aldaw, inyakar ida ni Maribel iti balay ti natay nga ina ni Wally idiay Mecca nga asideg iti balayna. Tulagda nga upaanda ti maysa a kuarto. Imbirakak ni Maribel nga aganusda no kayatda ti agbiag ta no addanton green card da Gretzie, Totzie, ken Latzie ket addan trabahoda, bareng no agbaliwto met la ti biagda.

Pinanggep da Claire nga awagan ni Dennis idiay Utah ngem yinagyagan ni Maribel. Nangina kano ti bayad ti telepono. Kellaat a limmabba ti ulo ni Claire ket dandanina la siggawaten ti kulot ni Maribel sana ingubngob iti agkiamkiam a disierto ngem tinengngel ni Apo Tabs.

"Agparbengka laeng, Hani," pinikpikna ti patong ni Claire. "Agparbengka laeng . . ."

"Laslasek la koman ti rupa dayta a bornay!" imbanang-es ni Claire.

Bimmara ti aglawlaw ta dandanin agngalay ti kalgaw iti Mecca. Kasla dumardarang ti kiamkiam ti aglawlaw ket saanen nga agsardeng ti kapapaid ni Apo Tabs ta ipawil ni Maribel a paandarenda ti koler. Nangina kano ti bayad ti koriente.

"Kastoy gayam ti America! Makirog ti tao a sibibiag!" inkabukab ni Claire iti maysa a rabii a kurang la nga agdigosda nga agassawa iti ling-et iti kama a para maysa. Nagidda da Gretzie ken Totzie iti basar a karpet, nagidda ni Latzie iti dakkel a daan a sopa.

Adu ti nakakarton a ramramit a napanawan kano daydi baket nga akimbalay iti bangir a paset ti dakkel koma a kuarto. Iti tengnga ti kimmamarin a balay ti kuarto daydi baket ket saan a nasagid dagiti gamigamna, ken kanayon a padaldalusan ni Maribel ta isu pay ti pannakaopisina ni Wally--naammuan ni Claire idi agangay nga an-anusan ni Maribel ti ar-aramidenna ta dakkel kano ti nakadulin a tawidna, amangan la ketdi no agbalukattit ti panunot ni Wally a kakaisuna nga anak ti baket nga agtawid. Maluklukag da Claire no dadduma ta pagammuan la ta adda agar-arimpadek wenno mangilukat iti ridaw ti kuarto uray no awan met ti tao. Al-alia la ketdi ti baket, makasursuron nga ikabukab ni Claire ken ni ApoTabs.

Naduktalan ni Claire, ket ad-adda a pakasuronanna, a masansan a mapan mangan ni Wally iti yanda ket dida mabukodan ti gunayda. Di

nagbayag isun ti turtoran ni Maribel nga agluto ta magustuan ni Wally ti lutona. Ti la babbabawina a nangibagbaga nga ammona ti agluto. Numona ket sada la makapangrabiin no makaawiden ni Wally uray no kaipapananna ti panagurayda agingga iti tengnga ti rabii. Pamrayanda ti agkurinikon iti suli a mangpispisel iti rusokda, ket apaman a maisibet ti baknang, kasda la nabulosan a pusa a mangsango iti nabati a pangrabii.

Adu ti am-ammo ni Maribel iti Mecca ken Indio ket dagitoy ti nagpatulonganna a mangiserrek iti trabaho kada Gretzie ken Totzie apaman a naawatda ti green cardda. Immuna ni Gretzie a nakastrek nga ag-picking iti ubas. Ngem simmaruno a dagus ni Totzie. Adayo ti pag*picking*anda ta idiay Delano nga asideg ti puseg ti Calilfornia nga amiananen pay ti Los Angeles. Idi damo, di koma kayat ni Claire a palubosan dagiti annakda, kasta met ni Apo Tabs, ta dida pay napadpadasan ti naipusing, ngem yinagyagan manen ida ni Maribel. Nabati ni Latzie ta ituloyna ti high school iti Mecca.

"Agbiagkayo, aya, no agtitipkelkayo lattan! Palubosanyo ida, Anti, tapno makasursuroda nga agbiag!"

Idi mangrugidan nga agawat iti green money, nangrugi metten a singiren ida ni Maribel iti impautangna a pinagpleteda a naggapu iti Kilkillabot.

Gapu ta pannakalualo ni Apo Tabs ti kinailet ti pagpisipisanda a kuarto, imbaga ni Maribel nga upaanda ti maysa kadagiti trailer iti uneg ti lakub ti dakkel a balayna. Uray ta nayakaren ti pension ti lakay manipud iti Kilkillabot.

Apagakarda, pinakabitan ida a dagus ni Maribel iti telepono. Immawag kadakuada ni Mang Rosie apaman a nagkurri ti telepono.

"Kas met la balay ti billit-tuleng daytoy yanmi ita, Kabagis," inyangaw ni Apo Tabs nga agtigtigerger ken paypay a paypay ta pudoten kano. Nawalat ti trailer ken babassit ti tawana. "Adda pay ti pagpaknian iti tengngana. Idiay Kilkillabot hammo a kabbalay ti kasilia..."

Kasla simgar nga ampo ni Mang Rosie. Ni Claire ti nagipapasanna iti pungtotna ta amkenna no aghayblad ti kabsatna. Isu gayam ti akintrayler.

"Kaskay met la baknang unayen!" agtigtigerger ti timekna iti pungtotna. "Napia koma no diak ammo ken nakitkita ti lugaryo 'diay Kilkillabot. Nagbassit 'diay balayyo sa rutrot pay!"

"Agang-angaw kano met la ni lakay, Manang," inkarigatan ni Claire a tenglen ti riknana. Dina la ketdi kayat ti mangiwngiwatan.

Ad-adda pay ti seggar ni Maribel.

"Tultulongandakayo nga agbiag, kasta pay ti sasawenyo. Tapno ammoyo, ad-adu pay ti nakarkaro ti panagbiagda ditoy America, ta matmaturogda iti kalkalsada. Kasla awan ti ut-utangyo a naimbag a nakem!"

"Saan a kasta ti panagsasaom, a, Maribel. Uray no taga-aw-awaykami laeng, adda met riknami a masaktan!" saanen a nakapagteppel ni Claire. "Ti la ngamin nakailawlaw-ananmi nga immay 'ti America! Tapno ammom, awan pay ti nagsasao kaniak iti kasta! Daytoy ti laglagipem: no adda ngiwatmo, adda met kaniak!"

Napanganga ni Maribel. Dina impagarup nga adda met gayam ngiwat ni Claire.

Kayat ni Claire ti maaddaan iti kuarta tapno adda met maipaw-itna kadagiti kakabsatna a nabati iti Kilkillabot. Ta ngamin, makaaw-awat iti surat ken awagda iti telepono a dumawdawat iti kuarta. Nabudian iti patiray-ok ti tonoda, isu nga adda met masagid iti lingka ti puso ni Claire. Wen nga agpayso, addadan ditoy America, a kayatna a sawen kadagiti napanawanda, baknangdan—imut kano dagiti Pinoy nga adda iti America nga agkunkuna a narigat ti biagda.

Ngem tunggal irengrengna ti panangpanawna ken ni Apo Tabs iti aldaw tapno mapan agtrabaho, agtigerger ti lakay ket adu la unayen ti marikriknana a nasakit. Agkakapsut kano ket kurangna la a matayen.

"Saanka pay a matay, Angkel!" ilaaw no kua ni Maribel. "Adu pay ti basolmo a nasken nga ipakawanmo!" pasarunuanna iti nalab-ay a katawa. Naaliwegweg ngamin ti lakay uray idi sibibiag pay 'di nagawan a naanus nga immuna nga asawana, a nangputotanna iti dandani pasig a propesional.

Kinuna met ni Mang Rosie a kabuteng ti kabsatna ti bukodna nga anniniwan. Kunana nga ilalaen la unay ti lakay ni Claire, a kunam met la no di kuggangi.

Dandani pimmayso ti atap ni Apo Tabs ta iti maysa nga aldaw kadagiti manmano a panangpalubosna ken ni Claire, nagpulong daytoy nga adda nangsutil kenkuana ken nangapros iti patongna.

"Ket, nayatka met, a, Hani?" impasagidna nga agtigtigerger, a kasla laglagipenna ti panangkurkurimesna iti balasitang a nagyan kadakuada idi sibibiag pay ti immuna nga asawana.

"Ay, saannak nga ipadpada kadagiti sisikkaruden, Hani!"

Saanen a nagun-uni ni Apo Tabs, ngem iti kabigatanna, madi ta dina lattan palubosan ni Claire a mapan makipagburas iti sangkis iti nalawa a pagtatalunan iti daya.

"Matayakon no panawannak ita nga aldaw, Hani," inyarasaas ni Apo Tabs iti kasam-itan pay laeng nga arasaasna, a sinagidna pay ti kutit ni Claire. Kaano pay daydi naudi a panangsagidna iti asawana? "Ket no matayak gapu kenka?" inkilitna pay. "Saan a siak ti umay mangal-alia kenka, ngem ti konsensiam a mismo."

Kapilitan nga impambar ni Claire iti nangdagas kenkuana a kimmaro ti sakit ni Apo Tabs isu a di makapan.

Iti panagbayag da Claire iti trailer, uray no kanayon nga agsupanget ti dilada ken ni Maribel, mayat man met laengen ti saritaanda no dida agpakaro, ket adu ti estoria ti kaanakan ni lakayna maipanggep kadagiti lallaki a naglasat iti dayagna. A ti inauna nga anakna ket saan a pudno a putot ti kunkunada nga immuna a nobiona idiay Kilkillabot no di ket ti Mehikano nga akinkukua iti pagtagilakuan iti asidegda iti Mecca. Sa ti doktor a nangikasar kenkuana iti America tapno makaala iti green cardna, insinana ta awan met a talaga ti simgar a dutdotna ta dina malipatan ti immuna a nobiona. Sa idi karikut ti biagna, nakinaig iti asawa ti maysa a gayyemna, sakbay a nakidenna iti agdama nga ama ti dua pay nga annakna.

No dadduma a panagkuyog da Maribel ken ni Claire nga agpidut iti lata wenno botelia ti kola, sursuruan ni Maribel daytoy nga agpidut iti ania man a naiwara a banag, a kasla agtakaw, sana dardarasen ti umadayo no adda makitana nga umasideg a tao.

Naminsan a panangkuyog ni Maribel kada Claire iti doktor ni Apo Tabs iti panagpaagas ti lakay idiay Indio, insaluksokna ti ules ti hospital iti tugaw ti wheelchair ket imbilinna a di gargarawen ti ulitegna ti

kutitna. No dadduma pay a panagkuyog da Claire ken Maribel a mapan iti K-Mart wenno Wall Mart, adda dagiti ikurimedna nga iruar a di masipsiputan dagiti tindera.

Isu a no agsubangda manen ken ni Claire, kuna ni Claire ken ni Apo Tabs: "Di ager-errado dayta nalaing a kaanakam ta iburandisko ti sangabukel a buyokna idiay Kilkillabot. Ammok aminen ti kinaibbongna!"

"Dimo pay ketdin tubaen ti sangabukel a Kilkillabot, Hani," kinuna ni Apo Tabs.

"Ay, saanak nga agang-angaw! No dakkel ti ngiwatna, dakdakkel pay kaniak, tapno ammom!"

"Agpayso ti kunam ta makitkitak met. . ."

Nakaanges ni Claire iti dakkel idi malastaranda a bayadan ti utangda ken ni Maribel. Nagtutungtongda a sangakabbalay ket plinanoda ti mapan iti West Valley idiay Utah a yan ni Dennis tapno mayadayoda ken ni Maribel. Di kanon mairusok ni Claire ti ngiwat ni Maribel. Ken nalaka kano ti agsapul iti trabaho iti yan ni Dennis, saan a kas iti Mecca a maksetka nga agpikpiking iti ubas wenno sangkis no panawaenna, ket no naisibeten dayta a panawen, awanen ti trabaho.

Immuna a nagpa-West Valley ni Gretzie. Simmaruno ni Totzie. Pinalpas pay ni Latzie ti klasena iti Mecca sakbay a simmarunoda a tallo kada Claire ken Apo Tabs.

DANDANIN maisibet ti ipus ti Summer ket sumreken ti Fall idi sumangpetda iti Harvey Street iti West Valley, Utah. Nasayaat ti panangsarabo kadakuada da Dennis, Marie nga asawana, Rina a balasangna, ken ni Josuah a barona ngem kasla agirob ti rupa ni Claire. Apartment la ngamin ti up-upaan da Dennis a dudua ti kuartona, maysa a kosina, maysa a pagpaknian, ken panakkelen a salas.

"Nalablabestayo payen ngem sardinas, Hani!" inyarasaas nga inkabukab ni Claire.

Inserrek ni Dennis da Gretzie ken Totzie iti Deseret Industries a pagtatrabahuanna. Inserrekna ni Latzie iti Granger High School a pangituloyanna idi adalna. Idi damo, maay-ayatanda ta idi la a nakapagtrabahoda iti nasayaat bassit a pagtrabahuan iti America.

Nupay kasta, saan a napnek ni Claire. Adu ti madildillawna uray iti aglawlaw ti apartmentda ta adu ti tao a kasla warang laeng iti kalkalsada ta nagpuniponan ti nadumaduma a puli ti Harvey. Idi kuan, sangkadagullitnan ti babawina a napnapan iti Utah.

"No am-ammok la kastoy ditoy, diak la ketdi im-immay. No apay ketdi, nagpintas ti awis ti kaanakak idiay Modesto 'diay California, ditoy ketdin ti im-immayanmi!" inkabukabna iti sango ni Marie.

"Uray, a, ta didakayo met pinilpilit nga immay," kinuna met ni Marie a kasla napikaranen.

Nakakita ni Dennis iti napimpintas a trabaho ket pinanawanna da Gretzie ken Totzie iti Deseret Industries. Ngem di met nagbayag dagiti dua ta nakastrekda iti trabahoda iti Salt Lake International Airport a kas agtagilako kadagiti panganan. Pimmintas ti teggedda ket saanen a nagpabatubat ni Claire a nangirengreng iti yaakarda iti bangir nga apartment.

Di nagbayag, nakagatang metten ni Gretzie iti kotsena ta kasapulanna iti iseserrekda iti trabaho. Kasta unay ti tirad ti timid ni Claire ta nabarbaro ti kotse ti balasangna ngem ti kotse ni Dennis. Ngem iti karabiyanna, nagtatakkonan dagiti durog iti kaarruba a binarsak ti sarming ti kotse. Inaributantan ni Claire ti agsao ngem awan met ti makaawat kenkuana ta di makapagsao uray sangkaputed nga Ingles wenno Espaniol la koma. Naimbag ta adda insurance ti kotse ket daytoy ti nagbayad iti pannakatarimaanna.

Manipud idin, nagtutulagda kada Dennis nga agsapulda iti gatangenda a balay. Adda gayyem ni Dennis a timmulong kadakuada a gimmatang iti balay iti asidegda. Ngem imbalakadna a da la Dennis ken ti asawana ti agpirma iti kontrata ta kasta ti kayat ti linteg.

Madi ti rikna ni Claire a di nairaman ni Gretzie a nakipagpirma iti kontrata. Ngem dida kayat ti mabati iti Harvey isu a kapilitan a simmurotda met laeng idi umakar da Dennis. Ti tulag, tumulongda nga agbayad iti balay a kasla pannakaupada total nalaklaka met nga amang ngem iti pagbaybayadda iti apartment. Ken napimpintas nga amang ti lugar.

Idi damo naragsak dagiti lima nga ubbingda ta agkakataebda ken siguden nga agaammoda idiay Filipinas nupay idiay Montalban ti dimmakkelan da Rina ken Joshua.

Mautoyan ngata nga agbambantay ni Claire ken ni Apo Tabs ta awan met la ti aramidnan iti agmalem no di agbuya iti telebision ken mangpakan ken tumulong a mangpadigos iti lakayna ta idi agbaybayag, adu manen ti madildillawna. Gapu ta nalamiis iti baba a yanda. Gapu ta kumalimbatog dagiti tao iti ngato. Gapu ta nagdakkel ti bayadanda iti danum ken koriente, a pakiguduaanda. Pagsusiudotanna dagiti annakna no sumro.

"Awan serserbi nga agbibiag ditoy!" ikabukabna. "Awan pay pulos maiggaman a kuarta. Para balay latta dataon. Tagabo iti balay! Sumrekak metten iti trabaho, Hani!"

"Saan kadi, a Hani. Dinak pampanawan. Inton matayak, ala wen, agumakanto nga agtrabaho."

"Kaanonto pay?" immulagat ni Claire. "No kastoy laeng ti sasaadek, amangan no umun-unaak pay a matay!"

"Saan, Hani, dandaniakon matay. . . Isu nga an-anusannak lattan."

"No nakaad-adu ti agasmo. . . masangom pay ti kumalbit."

No dadduma, agkakarambolada nga agiina iti baba. Adu la amin a pagsisiudotan ni Claire. Masemsem no kua ni Dennis. Natalnada a sangapamilia iti ngato ta nasingpet dagiti annakna, ken nasayaat nga ina ni Marie.

No manen irengreng ni Claire nga iserrek dagiti annakna iti trabaho.

"Makastrekka, 'ya, ti trabaho ket dimo met ammo ti agingles!" nakasuron naminsan ni Gretzie.

"Agbasaak!" inyagyag ni Claire idi nadamagna nga adda pagadalan iti asideg dagiti nataengan a di nakaadak iti eskuela. "Iserrekdak ta agbasaak. Uray ta maysa nga oras met la iti maysa nga aldaw, ken rabii."

Kapilitan a ginastuan da Gretzie iti matrikulana. Idi kuan, rengrengenna ni Marie a mangisuro kenkuana ta nangisursuro ngamin daytoy idiay Quezon City sakbay a nagpa-Utah.

Ngem kas iti lulot a buneng ti utek ni Claire ta marigatan la unay a mangiselsel iti utekna ti ad-adalenna. No kuan, pagpambar ni Marie ti kaadda ti ar-aramidenna ket dina masango nga isuro. Agkabukab no kua ni Claire ket ipulongna ken ni Apo Tabs ti paidam ni Marie.

Idi agturpos iti umuna a panagbasana, addan sa met nakurang a sangapulo a balikas a natandaananna.

"Ituloyko pay!" impilitna kadagiti annakna.

Ket nagenrol manen. Kaskasdi, manmano a balikas ti nainayon iti bokabolariona. Pabasolenna pay ketdi dagiti titserna ta dida kano ammo ti mangisuro. "Agtittitserda la nga awan ammona!" imbirakakna.

Ngem nauma da Gretzie a mangigasgasto iti panagbasana ta sayang la kano ti gasgastuenna ket awan met ti masursurona. Nagsapulda ketdi ti maikadua pay a trabahoda ket dandani awanen ti panawenda nga agkikita nga agiina. Nagtrabaho met ni Latzie bayat ti panagbasana.

Idi kuan, addan Puraw a mangip-ipus ken ni Totzie no agawid iti naladaw a rabii, ken pumaspasiar iti Domingo.

"Kostumerko 'diay airport," kunana no adda agsaludsod.

Naammuanda idi agangay a diborsiado ti Puraw. Ken dandani kagudua ti tawen ni Totzie ti kalakayna. Kalbo payen, ken adda tallo nga annakna.

Idi agangay, saan laengen a sumarsarungkar, ngem umian payen. Sinitar naminsan ni Marie, ta di kayat ni Dennis nga adda kasta a mapasamak iti balayna. Ngem kinuna ni Totzie a gayyemna laeng.

"Ditoy America, awan ti aniamanna ti kastoy, Manang," kinunana.

"Saan ngamin a kayat ni manongmo ti kasta ditoy balay," kinuna ni Marie.

Ni Claire ti kasla simgar nga ampo idi maammuanna ti inaramid ni Marie.

"Saan a kasta-kasta ti anakko. Nadalus ti anakko. Awan aramidna a maikaniwas iti lubong, tapno ammoyo!" inlaawna uray no awan met da Dennis ken Marie iti sangona.

Ni Dennis a mismo ti nakisarita ken ni Totzie. Ti imasna, baribar ti sungbat ni Totzie.

"Saanak a puta! Ammok ti ar-aramidek!"

Imbes a sumungbat ni Dennis, namrayanna nga inem-eman ti pungtotna ket nagkamang iti siled. Manipud idin, saannan a kasarsarita ti kagudua a kabsatna.

Adda agassawa a gayyem ni Marie a nakipakaasi nga agupa iti maysa a kuarto iti ngato. Gapu ta nasayaatda met idi damo, inawat ida dagiti agassawa. Nagbalin a nasinged a gayyem ni Claire ni Pam. No saan la ketdi a sumro ni Claire, agkakatungtonganda a tallo a babbai.

No dadduma da laengen Claire ken Pam ti agsarsarita no kasdiay nga awan ni Marie.

Pagamuan, iti maysa a sardam ti Huebes, nagpakada da Pam nga umakardan iti kabigatanna, a sumurotda kada Claire ta nakagatangda kanon iti balayda iti saan unay nga adayo.

Naklaat da Dennis ngem awan ti naaramidanda. Naammuanda met la idi agangay a di kayat ni Totzie ti masitsitar iti aramidna, ket nagpatulong iti Puraw nga agsapul iti gatangenda a balay.

"Umakarkayo, umakarkayo lattan a di agpakpakada," kinunana.

Nupay kasta, saan unay a naapektaran ti panaglangen da Marie ken Pam. Di la kayat ti immun-una ti kasla pananguleg dagiti agiina kadakuada.

Nupay masao a naipusingdan, makadkadanon pay la kada Marie ti aramid dagiti agiina. No masansan nga um-umian ti Puraw idi addada pay iti yan da Dennis, ad-addan idi addan balayda.

Nagbakasionda iti Filipinas. Ket idi agsublida iti Utah, nadamag laengen da Marie a natulagen ti kasar da Gretzie ken ti nobiona a pinanawanna idiay Kilkillabot.

"Baknang daydiay mangasawa ken ni Gretzie," impannakkel ni Claire, a maam-ammuan met ni Marie.

Ngem pagamuan lattan ta agwaras ti damag nga agkasaren da Totzie ken ti Purawna. Awan ti planoda a kasta ta paunaenda koma pay da Gretzie.

"Naim-imbagen ti kasta," kinuna kano ni Claire, "ta amangan la ketdi nga agsikog a dina oras!"

No maladaw la a sumangpet ni Puraw, sangkasegga ni Claire.

"Wadsapen," kunana no dadduma.

Ilutuanna ti naimas a taraon ti manugangna, a no daddduma, nangruna iti Sabado ken Domingo, kaduana a mangan dagiti tallo nga annakna. Kasda la mabisbisinan unay ket masansan nga awan ti mabatbati a kanen da Claire. Ngem awan sidsidunget ni Claire. Gapu ngata ketdi ta Puraw ti manugangna.

Naistrikto nga agsingir ni Claire iti upa da Pam. Pakibianganna amin a panagusarda iti washing machine ken danum ken silaw.

"Kastoy ti aglaba, Pam," isurona ni Pam a bakbaket nga amang ngem isu, ken bakbaknang ngem isu idiay Filipinas.

"Hangka nga agdadrayer, Pam...

"Hangka nga agsilsilaw iti agdan, Pam...

Naminsan, makasidsida la ngata unay da Pam iti toyo isu a kapilitan a nagprito. Dina pay nalnalpas ti prituenna idi umarimpadek ni Claire nga immulog.

"Wadsapani!" inlaawna.

Napanganga ni Pam. "Ania ti kunam?"

"Wadsapani, kunak!" imbannikes ni Claire. "Kuna dagidiay ubbing, wadsapani. . . Saan a makaanges ni Troy iti bangsit ti lutlutuem!"

"A, what's up, honey!" immulagat ni Pam.

Nakadanon kadagiti dadduma a Filipino iti Utah ti wadsapani ni Claire.

Nakagayyem da Gretzie iti maysa a Pinoy iti Beehive Clothing ket impetteng ni Claire nga iserrekda nga agtrabaho iti pagdaitan. Uray kasta unay ti pakaasi ni Apo Tabs a dina pampanawan, awan naaramidan ti lakay. Uray no dina ammo ti agingles, gapu ta ammona ti agdait, nakastrek. Saan a nagbayag, pinatapuaknan da Pam. Saannan a kasapulan ti pagupada.

Di nagbayag, naala ni Gretzie ti lakayna manipud iti Filipinas ket naglasinda a dagus. Di kano kayat ti lakayna ti makiludludon iti adu a tao.

Nagpukaw a kasla asuk ti Puraw a manugang ni Claire, ket isu ngata ketdi ti ad-adda a nakadagdagan ti ipapatay ni Apo Tabs.

Adu dagiti sardam a panagmaymaysa ni Claire a kasla mataltalimpungaw nga agtamtamdag iti tawa. —0

Bannawag: Disiembre 3, 2001.

Sangabukel Nga Init, Sangkailgat A Bulan, Ken Lima Gantilia A Bituen

Happy heart and happy faces,
Happy play in grassy places
That was how in ancient ages,
Children grew to kings and sages.
—Robert Louis Stevenson
"Good and Bad Children,"
The Book of Virtues, pp. 23

APATOT. Saan a bassit a subdibision. Saan a dakkel. Adda iti agtengtengnga, kas koma iti butil iti tangga wenno tatsing. Nalaka a sapulen. Saan met a narigat a papanan. No ammom ti agtukma iti tokak, matumpongam met a di masasaan. No nakakitakan iti adu a pinuon ti apatot, isu daytan ti sapsaplem. Bassit a lugar. Ngem napuskol ti taona. A kaaduanna ti ubbing. A pasig a naragsak.

Narabaw ti kakatawaanda. Ket no agkatawada, agkatawa met amin a matada, ket kas man la nakaad-adu a bituen ti maruros kadagiti naraniag nga alintataoda. Uray ti nakamisuot nga aginaw, wenno bakka nga agpaspasikal iti lima a singin, mairayrayo nga agkatawa. Awan sa ketdi ti parparikut dagiti agindeg.

Kanayonda ket ngata a mabsog, saanda a mabisbisinan. Amangan no nagagetda unay. Nangruna dagiti inna. Ta kanayon a dadakkel ti tianda. Narawet ket ngata dagiti lallakayda a mangan iti apatot. Uray ngata met dagiti inna. Ta awan ti taltallo ti anakna.

Saanda met a sigud a kasta ket. Kinapudnona, saan idi nga inkankano dagiti lallakay ti apatot. Agatsabon ngamin. Di pay kayat a taliawen ti nuang wenno baka. Ngem idi nasumokan ti maysa, adda nairayona a kaduana, a nakarayo met iti sabali, agingga nga ammon ti sangalugaran. Immimas la ket ngarud ti panagkikibinkibin dagiti agassawa. Ken simmapa ti pannakaiddep dagiti silaw. Ken dimmaras ti panagdul-odul-o dagiti inna, ta kanayonda pay ketdin a nakamake-up. Dimmaras ti panagtartaray dagiti amma, a sakroyda nga ilugan iti traysikel ti asawada ket ikamakamda a mabtakan iti sinusuon idiay sentro a yan ti klinika ni Doktor Palpaltot, a nakalawlawa met itan ti isemna ta dakkel kano ti parabur kenkuana ti Dios ta napadakkelnan ti klinikana gapu iti nalabes metten no kunaen nga inaldaw nga adda agpapaltot kenkuana. A no agawiden ti pinaltotna, ipakamakamna a nakaat-atiddog ti isemna: "Umaykayonto manen no umay a tawen, wen?"

Gagangay ngamin nga uray no di pay naruros ti bulong ti kamantiris wenno dangla iti sirok ti dalagan, no labsen ti manao, no agdalagan koma ti ina, mabalin manen ti mawaw unay nga ama ti sumagpat.

Ngem saan a mapunno ti Apatot. Kas iti tambur no napunnon iti danum, aglibbiang. No adda mailaw-an a rummuar, kas man la malipatandan ti dalanda nga agawid wenno agsubli iti Apatot. Makasarakda ket ngata iti nalalaing nga agtrabaho iti rabii iti paraiso (wenno impierno) a pakaipalladawanda, ket didan kayat ti umaon pay! Idiaydan nga agnunog.

Ngem adu met ti kaykayatdan sa ti lumoten iti Apatot Subdivision. Didan sa ketdi mayadayo ti pantalonda iti puon ti apatot. Ket kanayon a tangtangadenda ti sangkailap a bulan, wenno siraraten ti sangabukel nga init, a kas man la kunkunada, nagbayag ketdin a lumnek!

Ala, rummuar-umuneg, kunada ngarud, ta kasta met ti tao. No adda mapan adda met sumangpet. Ket iti Apatot, ad-adu ti sumangpet. Nga ubbing.

Ngem adda naipangpangruna a pamilia iti Apatot. Ti pamilia Paraiso. Buklen da Papa ken Mamada, ken da Bingbing, 12; Bongbong, 10; Dangdang, 9; Tingting, 8; ken Yengyeng, 6.

SAAN a dakkel, saan met a bassit, ti pamilia Paraiso. Ngem saan a maatiw ti bilang ti annakda a nainaw amin iti nasapa a sardam. No kasdiayen a tinakderan ni Papada ti agngadal sa payen a makiniliana, nangruna no nakangusab iti apatot ket adda nga aglagudlagod ni Mamada no simmangpeten a naggapu iti kabangibang nga ili a pangisursuruanna iti maikamaysa—nasuroken a sangapulo a tawen a mangisursuro iti maikamaysa, ngem kasla dina kayat nga adaywan ti panagaw-awirna iti ubbing—saanen a mamingga a kumalbikalbit ken ni Mamada, ket no di la nagpakaponen daytoy, saan la koma a limlima ti nainawda iti saklot ti sardam. Ni Papada, masansan nga adda iti balay—kunkunada, isu ti agtagibalay. Nga agmalmalem a kubkubbuanna ti makiniliana. Adun ti napagsangitna a nakapagukraden a babbalasang ken kattungbol a babbalasitang. Ken napaarapaapna a damona ti agtaraok a babbarito wenno kawwetanen a babbaro. Ken napagarakgakna a sallayusay a lallakay ken nakulbeten a babbaket, a dumdumngeg ken mangbasbasa kadagiti sursuratenna. Kasla agayus a manteka ti utekna ket uray no kidkidemanna ti makiniliana, ammo latta dagiti ramayna ti pagkarayamanda, a kasda la makilinlinnailo met.

Nupay adu ti mabasbasa ken madamdamag ni Papada a balitok (kano) iti ruar ti Apatot, kaykayatna ti agkukot a kunada iti sirok ti apatot, ngem ti mapan iti lugar a pulos nga awan ti maang-angotanna nga uray no nalungsot la koma a bunga ti puon ti biagna.

Saan a nangato ti arapaap ni Papada; nalaklaka kano a gaw-aten ti nababa. No agrimat ti mata dagiti uriesda ken ni Mamada, kasla metten ginantilia a bituen ti karkarut-omenna ket mapunno iti nasarangsang a katkatawa ti bunggaloda a kasla kumkumleb a pag-ong. Kasla aglawag ti sangabukel nga init kalpasan ti pananglubbon ti sangkailap a bulan no aglinnagid dagiti matada ken ni Mamada.

Iti maysa nga aglaladut nga agsapa ti Sabado, nga umis-isemen ti init iti mumukatan ti Bantay Kayang ken kaguduan ti dagup dagiti uries iti Apatot Subdivision ti nakaimukat, tumarakatak manen ti makinilia

ni Papada iti murdong ti ekstension ti kusinada iti laud nga amianan idinto nga agkirudkirod metten ni Mamada iti kadaklan ti kusina. Uray agdudungsa, adda a pasalsali ni Tingting ken ni Mamada a mangsipsiput iti panaglutona. Iti salas, nalawa pay la ti kayang ni Bongbong iti sopa. Adda umas-asibay a bingraw iti apaggudua a ngangana, a no dadduma umisem ket lumsot dagiti wasay a panungadna, ket kunam no nakariingen ta saan a makelleban ti kalub dagiti matana dagiti makaluslusoten sa a bukelbukelna: kasla adda agsasala a bituen kadagiti alintataona iti pakaisaranganda a lawag. Kepkepna a kasla makatalaw ti nabengbeng a libro nga uray la a pinarbangon a nangbasbasa.

Iti maikadua a kuarto ti pag-ong a bunggaloda, kunam no aglinlinnailo ti kinnawil da Bingbing, ken Dangdang iti dakkel a kayo a katre nga awan kutsonna a katawen ni Bingbing. Iti akinngato a kadsaaran ti dobeldek iti dayta met la a kuarto, mangmatamatan ni Yengyeng iti magawgaw-atna a nalitem a bobeda, a salikepkepna ti gameboyna.

"Dimo pay la riniing dagidiay mamanteka a buriasmo!" insinggit ni Mamada a simmirip iti nalitem a kortina ti opisina ni Papada.

Kasla saan a nangngeg ni Papada ta mayat latta ti kubbona nga agmakinilia a no dadduma agmuestramuestra sana ituloy ti tarakatakna. Arig lumsoten ti durina ngem agrungrungiit pay la no dadduma, sa no kuan agtabbaaw sa manen agrungiit.

Nagin-inayad nga immasideg ni Mamada. Nagtingigtingig a nangsipsiput ken ni Papada.

"Nakatuknokan sa metten, Papada?"

"Aysiay, ti laya ti dapanna a baliena, aysiay!" kasla nakatugaw iti beggang a timmal-o ti kutitna ni Papada. "Aniakan sa a laya, ay baket. . . Nakatalawen 'diay tiltiliwek a sabong, ay nuang!"

Nagulimek ni Papada idi maisalat dagiti naridam a matana iti sab-ok ni Mamada. In-inut a nagkarayam dagiti matana iti nabaknang a barukong ni Mamada. Nagukkang dagiti kullapit a takiagna a kasla umarakup. Agan-andar pay la ti tallo bukel a naluom nga apatot a nginubngobanna idi sardam. Nagkilitkilit a pinagatiddogna ti subsobna a kasla umarusibsib.

"O, o, ania manen? Kastonay la nga'd ti namsaakam 'di rabiin. . ." nagsanud kampay idi ni Mamada. "Agkarakaankanto met ngamin 'ti apatot. . .Inka riingen dagidiay buriasmon, aldawen."

"Bay-am... kairutda nga agdakkel. Umayka ketdi, Mamada."

"Inka riingen ni manongmo a Bongbongen, Tingting," immandar ni Mamada idi umasideg ni Tingting. "Darasem ket aldawen. Riingem met dagidiay tallon."

Nasabat ni Tingting ni Yengyeng nga iggemna ti gameboyna iti ekstension.

"Inka kano riingen ni Manong Bongbong, Yengyeng," napasnek ti rupa ni Tingting.

"Apay, mabutengka ken ni Manong Bongbong? Dinaka met sidaen, ket."

"Kitaem man dagita matana," insungo ni Tingting idi makaasidegda ken ni Bongbong. "Siririing, wenno matmaturog?" sinirigsirigna. "Agurayka," kinunana. Nagtiltil-ay a napan iti kusina. Idi agsubli, iggemnan ti bassit a botelia a pagasinan. Inyawatna ken ni Yengyeng. Insungo ni Tingting dagiti mata ni Bongbong.

"Ay, sikan, a!"

Nagin-inayad ni Tingting nga immasideg iti nakataltalna a Bongbong. Imbatogna ti pagasinan iti mata ni Bongbong.

"Hoy!" bimmaringkuas ni Bongbong.

Dimmalagudog da Tingting ken Yengyeng a simmapideng ken ni Mamada nga apagisu a rummuar iti opisina ni Papada. Kinamat ida ni Bongbong.

"Asinanda ket ti matakon!" kinuna ni Bongbong idi agdamag ni Mamada. Arig lumsot dagiti matana.

"Diak imbaga nga asinanyo!" inungtanna da Tingting.

"Kasla ngamin sumirsirip a bisukol. . . Naimas ngata a maasinan, 'ya, Manong?"

"Hey!" Ad-addan a kasla kumilaw dagiti mata ni Bongbong. Insamirana a kinudkod ti kutitna.

"Ala, inkay riingen dagidiay duan ta mangantayon. Sabado ita, adu ti trabaho ditoy balay. . . Awan ti agbalballog."

Nagtaray da Tingting ken Yengyeng a simrek iti kuarto.

"Dikay' agbirakaken. . . nakariingkamin!" impasabat ni Bingbing ket nabati a nakanganga da Tingting ken Yengyeng a di nakaituloy iti pukkawda koma. Naginat met ni Dangdang iti iddana.

Madamdama pay sangsanguendan ti pamigatda a kinirog nga innapuy a nabawangan ken nabudian iti nawarawara a lungganisa. Agal-alisuaso ti nagatasan a soya a pannakakapeda. Nagiinnuna dagiti uppat, malaksid ni Bingbing, a mangitakal iti kutsarada. Ngem inatipa ida ni Mamada, ket nabati a nakatanggaya dagiti kutsarada iti angin. Urayenda kano ni Papada.

Simmungad ni Papada, a langana ti mangbilbilang kadagiti lima, a naituon amin ti matada iti agal-alisuaso a taraon. Iti sirok ti lamisaan, alisto ti kalawikiw ni Bronson nga aguy-uyaoy ti dilana a mangsipsiput kadagiti amona, a kasna la kunkuna, adda koma matnag a bungkol!

Apaman a nakatugaw ni Papada iti murdong ti lamisaan, mangala koman dagiti uppat iti kanenda, idinto a nakataltalna latta ni Bingbing nga agbuybuya, ngem inatipa ida ni Papada.

"I-blessmo pay, Bongbong," kinuna ni Papada.

Dinamag ni Mamada no asino ti aginnaw sakbay a malpasda a mamigat.

"Ni Dangdang ita," kinuna ni Bongbong a kastaunay ti panagisubona. "Siak idi Sabado, isu met ita, inton maminsan ni Tingting." Lunes ti batang ti inauna, nga agpababa iti Biernes. Agsisinnublatda iti Sabado ken Domingo.

Saanen a nagun-uni ni Dangdang. Ngem isu ti immuna a nagleppas. Idi malpasda amin, didan makita. No namin-ano a pinukkawan ni Mamada sakbay a simmungbat. Adda iti pagpaknian.

"Ayna, agtakki manen 'ti tali dayta!" kinuna ni Bingbing, nga iggemna ti journalna, a kanayon a dina maidisso. Isuratnan sa amin ti mapasamak iti tunggal darikmat nga aglabas iti biagna.

Nalabes metten no kunaen nga uray ti ar-aramidenna iti uneg ti pagpaknian ket nakasurat amin.

SINARUNO ni Bingbing da Dangdang, Tingting, ken Yengyeng iti ridaw. Aw-awisenda ngem dina kayat ti sumurot.

Idi sumrek ni Bingbing, nakitana a kaykayangan manen ni Bongbong, nga isamsamirana a kudkoden ti sellangna, ti mulmulagatanna a libro, a no dadduma ayek-eken ket ad-addan a di malapsi dagiti kasla lumsot a matana. Dina pay nadlaw ti ilalabas ni Bingbing iti sangona.

Inrikep ni Bingbing ti kuarto. Pidutenna a saan ti journalna. Ngem no kuan, mataliawna ti kuadernona, ken ti albumna iti suli ti kama. Agin-innagaw dagitoy no ania ti pidutenna. Makasuron iti panangsutsutil dagiti kakabsatna kenkuana. Ngem no maarapaapna ni Jerry, mabain pay iti bagina, ta kasla agpayso ti kunkunada. Dina maawatan no apay nga adda riknana a kastoy. Nabiit pay, ket mabain pay ketdi iti bagina, ngem makarikna no kua iti bara nga agkarayam iti pingpingna no iseman ni Jerry ket saknapen dayta a bara ti amin a paset ti bagina. No dadduma, salsaludsodenna iti bagina no mabalinna ti makiraman iti sakramento iti Domingo iti sacrament meetingda. Dina met kayat ti agdamdamag, uray ken ni Mamada, ta mabain la unay.

Nabiit pay a nayakar ni Bingbing iti klaseda iti Primary. Addan iti Young Women, idinto nga adda metten ni Jerry iti Young Men Organization.

Agkaseksionanda iti Grade Six iti Apatot Elementary School. Ipaspasnek ni Bingbing ti agbasa ta dina kayat ti paatiw ken ni Jerry. Kayatna nga ipakita a nalaing, ket bareng no ad-adda a maawis ti imatang ti barito kenkuana. Madlawna a di met paatiw ni Jerry. Isuda ti agin-innagaw iti umuna a puesto. No dadduma, madmadlawna a kumitakita ti barito kenkuana, sana met la ilisi dagiti matana, ket saludsodenna iti bagina: kayatnak kadi? Mabain kadi? No dadduma, kunana met la iti bagina: ubbingkami pay.

No dadduma, agkuyogda a magmagna nga agawid, no dida makauray iti paglugananda. Ngem manmano ta suronen ida no kua dagiti dadduma a kaklaseda.

Nasinga ti panagar-arapaap ni Bingbing idi mailukat ti ridaw. Ni Mamada ti simrek. Inrikepna a dagus ti journalna.

"Addaka gayam dita nga agpadpadakkel ti bakkana. Dika ket koma mapan agsagad dita ruar," kinuna ni Mamada. "Nakaad-adu ti naregreg a bulong ti kaimito. Didak la pulos matulongan, kakaisuna a bakasion. . . Ania dayta ilemlemmengmo?"

"A-awan. . ." impatallikud ni Bingbing ti kuadernona.

Kasla nagkeppet a bainbain ni Bingbing idi pinilit ni Mamada nga innala ti kuaderno.

Pinarimriman ni Mamada a makais-isem. Sana kinuna: "Ubingka pay, Iha. . . saanak nga agunget. . . Ngem ubingka pay." Immabay ni Mamada, sana impatay ti dakulapna iti abaga ni Bingbing. "Idi siak ti kas kenka, adda met idi barito. . . Ngem diak inkaskaso. . . Impasnekko ti nagbasa agingga a nagbalinak a maestra, ken nagkitakami ken ni Papam, a mannuraten idi. Isu a kastoy ti kasasaadtayo ita. . . Ipasnekmo ti agbasa. Inton naan-anayen ti kinabalasangmo, kas 'tay sabong a nakapagbukaren, no adda magustuam wenno makagustonto kenka, ibagam kaniak ta tulongankanto nga agpili. 'Tay kas ken ni Papam. . ."

"Ay! Diak kayat ti kas ken ni Papa! Kubbo! Kalbo pay!"

"Saanak a sigud a kubbo!" kinuna ni Papada nga itay pay nga agdengdengngeg iti ridaw. "Ken saanak a sigud a kalbo. Kinubbo ken kinalbonak ni Mamayo."

"Adu unay a sasawem a laklakayan. Inka ket agdigosen, 'mangan no malipatam manen; kastonayto manen ti agregreg a lasim!" Timmakder ni Mamada. Nagkibinda ken ni Papada a rimmuar.

ALDAWEN ngem di pay tinakderan ni Bongbong ti basbasaenna a libro ti dangeon. Isamsamirana latta a kudkoden ti sellangna, nga ad-adda nga aggagatel iti ayamuom ti nabugguongan a manok a sinagpawan ni Mamada iti bulong sili ken narekaduan iti laya ken salamagi; agtutubbogen ti ngiwatna ket aggaradugod payen ti tianna ta nabayagdan a di nagsida iti manok. Sada la makasida iti naimas no makasingir ni Papada iti bayad ti nobelana iti radio wenno iti Anaraar. Ngem dina kayat nga ibbatan ti basbasaenna, ken dina kayat ti umasideg ken ni Mamada nga aglutluto ta tinto man la pakaibabaonannan. Ni Tingting ti adda latta a pasalsali ken ni Mamada. Kaykayat ni Bongbong ti agbasbasa, uray agmalmalem wenno agpatpatnag. Isun sa ketdi ti dumakdakkelan dagiti matana.

Dina nadlaw ti iseserrek ni Dangdang, nga itay pay a mangsipsiput iti panagkudkodna. Nakanganga ni Dangdang ket saan a malapsi dagiti matana iti kudkudkoden ni Bongbong.

"Manong, apay a nagngisit 'ta sellangmo?" nakanganga ni Dangdang a nagmasngaad iti sango ni Bongbong. "Aggudgodka, ala!"

"Bastos!" immulagat ni Bongbong ket nagbaragsot a timmakder.

"Ma, aggudgod ni Manong Bongbong!" kinuna ni Dangdang a kimmamang ken ni Mamada.

"Husto daytan," kinuna ni Mamada. "Di met ngamin kanayon nga agdigdigos."

Nagin-inayad ni Bongbong nga immasideg iti likudan ni Dangdang a makalidliduken iti pangaldaw nga isagsagana ni Mamada. Kinellaatna a kinugtaran ti lakko ni Dangdang, sa nagintatan-aw iti lutlutuen ni Mamada. Napasarukigkig ni Dangdang.

"Kunana siguro, nakakatkatawa!" immisuot ni Dangdang. Adda met busi kadagiti matana.

"Hmm, nagimasen, 'Ma!" kinuna ni Bongbong a nagling-iling-i. Adda manen bituen kadagiti matana. "'Mangan no adda bunga 'ta sili, 'Ma, a."

"Agidasarkan, Tingting. . ." kinuna ni Mamada.

Itay pay la nga agkalkalawikiw ni Bronson iti sirok ti lamisaan. No kua, taliawenna ni Bongbong sa agsaepsaep sa agsuyaab.

Nagsisinnuron dagiti tallo bayat ti panagpusposda iti kusina.

"Inkay' agayaben ta mangantayon," kinuna ni Mamada.

Di pay nangangaan da Bongbong, Dangdang, ken Tingting ti pukkawda, addan nga agtartaray ni Yengyeng manipud iti paraangan, nga iggemna ti Gameboyna. Nagtarus iti puestona. Rimmuar met ni Bingbing manipud iti kuarto a salikepkepna ti journalna. Nagtarus iti puestona iti kanigid ni Papada, a sarunuen ni Bongbong. Mangabisera ni Papada, a tumarakatak pay la iti opisinana. Iti kanawan ni Papada ni Dangdang, sa ni Tingting, sa ni Yengyeng. Ni Mamada iti sabali nga ungto.

Tunggal agsidada iti manok wenno ikan, ammoda lattan no asino ti pakaidasaran ti ulo. Kuna ni Mamada, gapu kano ta ni Papada ti ulo ti pamilia. Ken tapno kano ad-adu ti masuratna a pangalaanda iti igatangdanto manen iti sidada a naimas. Uray kayat ni Bongbong ti ulo, saan nga agriri basta ni Papada. Kunkunana iti nakemna, agbalinakto met nga ulo.

Nakasangoda aminen. Malaksid ni Mamada nga adda iduldulinna iti oven. Nabingaybingayen ti sidada. Saggaysada iti malukong. Naited amin a pilida. Ni Mamada, no ania ti nabati, isu la ti sidana, kas koma iti puso ken batikuleng. Arig lumsot dagiti matada ket mapno ti lamisaan iti bituen. Ur-urayenda laengen ni Papada a rummuar iti umokna. Pukkawan koma manen ni Bongbong ta talaga nga agtutubbogen ti ngiwatna. Dida mabalin ti umuna a mangan no di kumpleto ti lamisaan, no addada amin iti balay. Ngem agar-arukongen ni Papada a sarsarapaenna ti siketna a sumungad iti panganan.

Madamdama pay, kumalangikingen ti kubiertos iti panganan. Kasta unay met latta ti kalawikiw ni Bronson iti sirok ti lamisaan.

Pagammuan la ta timmakder ni Bongbong. Nagtaray a simmalpa iti lababo. Naglagtulagto.

"Puah! Puah! Puah!" Kurang la nga agsabat ti buteg ken luana.

"Kukueemon, 'ya?" timmakder ni Mamada a mangtulong koma ken ni Bongbong.

"Yay hiyi. . . yay hiyi! Mungaya!"

"Ay ay, mungaya, ay Bongbong! Sili't sairo laeng. . . Kaska la amitaw," kinuna ni Papada. "Wenno inikkat ni Doktor Miguel ti ukelmo idi pinakapon, ay pinakugitnakayo ni Mamayo?"

Nagkakatawa dagiti uppat. Sinipsiputan ida ni Papada: kasla makitkitana ti adu a bituen nga agburayok kadagiti matada. Nasiputanna a linibas ni Dangdang a kinittaban ti sida ni Tingting a kumitkita ken ni Bongbong. Sana met la insubli a dagus.

Nagmurareg ni Tingting idi madlawna a bimmassit ti sidana.

"Nangalaka, 'nia?" kinusilapan ni Tingting ni Dangdang. Inagawna ti sida ni Dangdang sana kinuraban.

Nagsubli ni Bongbong iti tugawna idi agmawmaw bassit ti gasangna. Intuloyna a nginutngotan ti luppo ti manok. Mabisin la unay. Pagduaanna pay ti agkinnit. Pagammuan, naibbatanna ti luppo. Nagdumog. Naidungpar ti mugingna iti lamisaan. Sakbay a napidutna ti luppo, nasippawen ni Bronson. Intaray ni Bronson ti luppo iti ruar.

Kinamat ni Bongbong ngem nagsubli ta nakalemmengen ni Bronson. Makaliblibbi.

"Kayatmo ti manok, Manong?" kinuna ni Yengyeng. Intanggayana ti bingayna. Ngem idi awaten ni Bongbong, insubo ni Yengyeng sa nagtingigtingig a pinadakkelna dagiti matana.

"Bay-amon ta sukatak," kinuna ni Mamada.

Ni Bingbing, nga awan timtimekna, a napasnek a mangmangan, a makipagkatkatawa met, no manen taliawenna ni Bongbong.

URAY mapan salimpawer ti timek ni Dangdang, magustuanna ti agkankanta no agdigos.

Magustuanna a tultuladen ti estilo ni Jolina Madrigal. Idi kuan, binaliwanna ti kantana.

"Diatdiatteng arigudon, ni Manong Bongbong nga aggudgod!" inraed ni Dangdang bayat ti panaglidlidna.

"Sarampiting!" imbales ni Bongbong a nairana a napan imminum iti kusina. "Agbibisin nga agkanta. 'To no kuan agginggined!"

"Diatdiatteng arigudon," indueto ni Yengyeng a simrek iti ridaw ti kusina iti likud.

". . .ni Yengyeng nakakimmot!" insuldong ni Bongbong. "Dar'sem ta siak met ti agdigos," impukkawna ken ni Dangdang.

"Ayna, Manong. Uray no agmalmalemka nga agdigdigos, dinto malkab amin 'ta gudgodmo," kinuna ni Dangdang. "Inka agnateng ti bulong ti gabi wenno bunga ti sili't sairo ta isu't taltalem a pagsapsapom!"

"Ang-ang, di ad-addan nga agbusingar!"

"Kalpasan nga agbusingar, malkabto aminen a kudilmo, maikkatto metten ti gudgodmo."

"Suyatam lat' agburburek a danumen, Manong!" binagi ni Yengyeng nga agrungrungiit. "Ibagam no masuyatam ta umayka tulongan nga aglekkab, kaasika met. Ay, saan gayam, maakaranakto pay!"

"Maakarankanton! Pinagkansunsiliok 'tay briefmo!"

"Ay-ay!" nagdusngi ni Yengyeng.

Nakasukaten ni Dangdang idi rumuar iti banio. Mayat ti kinikinna a simrek iti kuartoda.

Idi rimmuar, inummongna da Tingting, Yengyeng, ken dadduma nga ubbing iti kaarrubada.

"Adda gimikko," kinunana, a linawlaw dagiti padana nga ubbing. Bassit no idilig iti dua a kasla kawayan nga ubbing, ngem isu ti dengdenggenda.

"'Mangan no ania man daytan, Darangdang," kinuna ni Tingting. Dangdang kuna latta ni Tingting uray no sarsarunuenna ti tawen ni Dangdang. "Ammok ti inalatmon, wen."

"Di uray diakto nagan ti Dangdangen. Daytayto napintas a nagankon. Dardanella da biuti!"

"Biuti 'ta rupam a pimmariok!" inlibbi ni Tingting.

"Makitayo daydiay sangapuon a kayo dita daya?" kinuna ni Dangdang. "Nasam-it daydiay."

"Nasam-it ti bungana," insippaw ni Yengyeng, a nagtingig pay a kasla nagpannakkel. "Adun ti nakanko a bungana."

"Korek ni Yengyeng. Uray maymaysa ti Yengyeng no kas ken ni Yengyeng a kimmot!" kinuna ni Dangdang. "Ammoyo ti adda iti panunotko? Saan ta diak pay imbaga. . ."

"Ammokon!" kinuna ni Tingting.

"Kunak a diyo ammo ta diak pay imbaga. Kaslattay' kunkuna ni Papa, a mangmangngegko no kua, kasla kano luto ni Apo Dios ti kaimasna. . ."

"Ania't aramidentay' ngarud?" masemsemen ni Tingting.

"Intay agala't bungana. Awan ita da Lakay Tanas. . . Ti madi sumurot, saan nga anak ni Apo Dios. Diyo kayat ti agbalin a di anak ni Apo Dios, di met?"

"Intay agtakaw?" nabutuag ti kiday ni Yengyeng.

"Saan. Dakes dayta. Intay la dumawat."

"Kunam nga awanda. Kasano a makadawattayo?" kinuna ni Tingting.

"Ibagatayonto no sumangpetda."

"Sika laengen," kinuna ni Tingting.

"Makakkakaanenkayo unayen, di ngamin?"

"W-wen. . ."

"No sinno ti sumurot kaniak, saan a takrot."

"Saanak a takrot," maysa maysa ti nagkuna.

Nagsasarunoda a simmurot ken ni Dangdang.

"Sige, uli," kinuna ni Dangdang idi makaasidegda iti puon ti mansanita.

"Sika?" kinuna ni Tingting.

"Agbatiak ditoy ta siak ti agbantay," kinuna ni Dangdang. "Dikay agdanag. No sumangpet da Lakay Tanas, siakton ti mangibaga iti idadawattayo."

Kasla nabisinan a sunggo dagiti ubbing a nagiinnuna nga immuli. Arig la maspak dagiti sanga a nagbitinanda. Agsinsinnublat ti sanapsapda nga agisubo ken ti alistoda nga agibulsa.

Mayat ti dadayyengan ni Dangdang iti baba, no manen dumawat ngem awan mangikaskaso.

"Tingting, dayta ney, naglabbasit. . . Ney, dayta pay. . . Ney, ney. . . Yengyeng, dayta addad'ta tuktokmo." Ti la nagitudo ti kinua ni Dangdang. "Kaaduenyo ti agala. . . isakibotyo. Ayna, nagiimas ngatan! 'Kannak man met, da!"

"Umulika met, a, ta di la 'ta agmammandarka!" pinuruakan ni Tingting iti dua bukel.

"Dayta pa-pay. . ." nasimbalud ti sanapsap ni Dangdang ta iti amianan, nakitana nga agpakkapakkang a sumungad ni Lakay Tanas. Nagsidduker. Dakesen, nakunana iti nakemna.

Saannan a tinangad dagiti adda iti aringgawis. Nagar-arudok nga immadayo.

Kasla mapurin a pinuon ti mangga ni Lakay Tanas ti panagdardarasna nga immasideg. Adayo pay agwitwitwiten.

"Hoy, mannanakawkayo nga ubbing!" kasla gurruod ti timekna.

Nakigtot ni Tingting. "Ay, Nanangko, addan ni satanas, ay Lakay Tanas!" dina masursurotan ti aramidenna. Kayatna ti tumapuak ngem nangato ti yanna.

Asidegen ni Lakay Tanas.

Nagsasarunoda a nagkaruskos. Agkaranabtuogda a nagdisso iti daga. Adda mangil-ilut iti tumengna, iti sikona, ken no ania payen a nasakit. Naitupa ti kutit ni Tingting iti nagtamburog a daga. Nagpug-apug-aw a sarapana ti kutitna a nagtaray. Timmapuak latta metten ni Yengyeng ket nagsagkisagking nga insiweten a nagawid. Nawarawarada ket ti

la nagturturongan dagiti dadduma. Naiburburandis dagiti nasam-it a bunga ti mansanita a sinab-okda.

"Aguraykayo!" kinuna ni Lakay Tanas. Makapungtot a makakatawa iti langa dagiti ubbing.

"Bastoska, Darangdangdang!" umanangsab nga insalangad ni Tingting idi makaawid, a sarapana pay la ti kutitna. Mayat ti lallallay ni Dangdang a nakasikkawil iti tugaw a pagbasbasaanna iti komiks.

"Nagbayagkayon. . .Yannan 'tay bagik?" kinuna ni Dangdang.

"Bagim 'ta rupam!" imper-ak ni Tingting. Kinarawana dagiti bolsana. Nangrakem iti nalabbasit a bunga ket nangpili iti isakmolna. Napukaw ti ut-ot iti kutitna iti panangnanamna iti mansanita.

"Ney, 'diay alutiit!" intudo ni Dangdang ti bobeda.

Sinalikepkepan a dagus ni Tingting ti saklotna. Dina tinaliaw ti intudo ni Dangdang. "Ammok ti istrokmon, oy!" inlibbina, a nagsanapsap manen. "Nagimasen! Hmm!" Pinaludipanna ni Dangdang.

"Maltotanka koma!" inkabukab ni Dangdang.

ADDADA a lima iti salas. Nakasikkawil ni Bongbong nga agbasbasa iti librona a dangeon. Agsursurat ni Bingbing iti journalna. Agtingigtingig ni Dangdang a mangkumkumpas iti kanta ni Jolina Madrigal iti cdna. Tangtangaden ni Yengyeng dagiti agpaparang a waya ti koriente a kimmamang iti doorbell.

Saan a makatalna ni Tingting, a kasla di makaanak a pusa. Nakadumog a kasla adda sapsapulenna a dagum iti nalitem a karpet. Nasurotna ti agpa-ekstension. Sa iti kusina. Nagtangadtangad. Nagsaltek dagiti matana kadagiti estante a pagik-ikkan ni Mamada iti kasapulanna nga agluto.

Linuktan ni Tingting ti maysa nga estante. Nagmusiig a naglisi nga insaripdana ti imana iti sangona idi agtaray ti payakan a sipet sa nagtayab iti sango ti agongna. Binutelia a bugguong, soy, pamienta, asin, betsin, bawang, ken no ania la ditan a rekrekado ti nakita ni Tingting. Linukatanna ti sabali. Adda babassit a karton ti arina, maaramid a cake, pagtempla, ken no ania payen dita. Ginaw-atna ti maysa a karton. Imparabawna iti lamisaan. Nagsapul iti masapulna. Iti uyosen ti oven. Kadadagiti pagipakpakleban ni Mamada. Nagsapul pay iti itlog. Iti

pagtemplaanna. Iti asukar. Iti manteka. Idi kuan, agkankantan a simmango iti oven.

Adda agtiltil-ay nga immasideg iti likudan ni Tingting. Insardengna ti nagkanta. Sana met la intuloy.

"Hoy!"

"Hoy 'ta rupam!" inlibbi ni Tingting.

Puted ti he-he ni Dangdang. "Apay ti kurita, kuna ni Papa, no makigtot agpadara nga agunnat nga agtaray," immisuot ni Dangdang.

"Kayatmo't masuyatan 'ti manteka?"

"Oy, nabanglo man 'ta lutlutuem, Ting. . ."

"Mmm, mmm, nakaangotka lat' malamut, pinapintasmon ti naganko. . .Tsu! Tsue!"

"Ting naman! Sa'nak met nga aso. . . Paraman man, da."

"Paraman 'ta rupam!" pinat-il ni Tingting ti ima ni Dangdang idi pumidut iti naluto. Ngem nakakiddisen ni Dangdang.

"'Nia't nagan daytoy?"

"Bibingki."

"Bibingki?"

"No dakkel, bibingka. Ngem gapu ta bassit, bibingki, tange!"

"No dakkel, Tangtang; no bassit, Tingting. . .Hmm, kasla naimas. Maysa man pay. . . Hmm naimas a talaga ti. . .kim, bibingkim. Nalaingka nga agluto, Ting," kimmiddis manen ni Dangdang. Dakdakkel itan. "Nakasursuruam nga agluto?"

"Tultuladek la ni Mama. . . 'Ta imam!" pinat-il ni Tingting ti ima ni Dangdang.

Nasaktan ni Dangdang. Idi maikabil ni Tingting ti naudi nga adawna, linibas ni Dangdang nga intaray ti bandehado, sana kinuna iti nakemna: "Kurita!"

Naglaaw ni Tingting idi madlawna nga awanen ti bandehado. Idi mapanna sapulen iti salas, naibusen dagiti uppat ti nagyan.

"Awanen, Tingting?" kinuna ni Bongbong a kasta unay ti panagkabukabna.

"Maysa man pay, Tingting," kinuna ni Bingbing nga indissuna ti journalna ket nagduaanna ti nagsubo.

"'Ka pay mangluto, Manang Ting," kinuna ni Yengyeng a kinawalna ti ngiwatna a nakaipilutan ti pancake.

"Awan bainyo! Linamutyo aminen! Saan met a dakayo ti linutuak!" kumanabukab ni Tingting a nagsubli iti kusina.

"Mangyegka pay!" dandani naggigiddan nga impakamakam dagiti uppat. Sada nagkakatawa.

Ni Papada ti napan inikkan ni Tingting iti pagkubkubbuanna nga agmakinilia. Kasla saan a nadlaw ni Papada ni Tingting ta tumarakatak ti makiniliana.

Im-imasen ni Tingting ti naudi a lutona, a bidbidingenna sakbay a mangisakmol, a kasna la kunkuna, nalaingakon nga agkik!

Idi simmangpet ni Mamada manipud iti naggapuanna, dinaras ni Tingting nga impakita ti indulinna a bibingki.

"Ma, kita'm 'toy lutok. Ramanam, naimas!"

"Hmm, naimas nga agpayso, Anak," kinuna ni Mamada idi makaisakmol. "'Gawaam ti agsursuro nga agluto tapno adda kasinnublatko no diak masango. Dagidiay kakabsatmo, 'diay la agpadpadakkel ti sellang ti ammoda. . .'"

"Kasano a dumakkel ti sellang, Ma?"

"He!"

Napan nakirayo ni Tingting kadagiti uppat. Mayat ti gargarikgikda iti salas, a no ania la dita ti malaglagipda a pagsasaritaan, ket no agdadanggayda nga agkatawa, kas man la ginantilia a bituen ti mapusi kadagiti matada ket mapno ti balay iti lawag. Uray ni Papada iti umokna, mairayrayo nga agkatawa ket mapukaw ti trrrrrrrrrrrrrrrrrrrk ti makiniliana. Uray ni Mamada nga agkuditkudit iti kusina, mairayo met, ket no agdanggayda ken ni Papada, kasla agtipon ti silnag ti sangabukel nga init ken ti sangkailgat a bulan. Kasla maysa a paraiso ti pagtaenganda kadagiti kasta a gundaway.

Ngem naputed ti katkatawada idi agngiwat ni Mamada. Manmano nga agngiwat ni Mamada, ket no agngiwat adda dakes a partaanna. Nakanganga dagiti lima. Adda la ketdi nagbasol kadakuada. Nagurayda iti sumaruno nga eksena.

Irubuaten ni Tingting ti rumuar, ta kasla ammonan ti mapasamak. Ngem nagngiwat manen ni Mamada.

"Tingting!" inrayok ni Mamada. "Nangipanam 'tay arina ditoy!"

"Binibingkina, 'Ma!" insalingbat ni Dangdang. "Imbagak a dina gargarawen, binibingkina met latta. . ."

"Suitikka!" immurareg ni Tingting. Kinusilapanna ni Dangdang. "Kinnan amin da Dangdang, Ma. 'Su ti nagpaluto. . . Kinnanda amin, 'Ma."

Ket kasla di maputpoten ti pinnabasol.

"Lutuek koma a miki daydiay. Linamutyo metten. . ."

"Uray ta naimasanka met, Mamada," makais-isem ni Papada.

"Gapu iti dayta, awan sidayo a mangmalem. Agsimutkayo iti bugguong!" kinuna ni Mamada.

"Ay!" kellaat a kimmaro ti gagatel ni Bongbong a nakangngeg iti bugguong ket insardengna ti basbasaenna. Nagduaanna ti nagkudkod. "Sika ngamin a kurita!" kinusilapanna ni Tingting.

DI pay simmangpet da Papa ken Mamada manipud iti inatendaranda a miting dagiti mannurat. Nakauldang da Bingbing, Dangdang, ken Tingting iti iddada ta nabannogda a nagay-ayam iti iskrabel. Nagsubli manen ni Bongbong iti puestona nga agbasbasa; saan unayen nga agkudkudkod ta adda ginatang ni Mamada nga agas ti gudgodna. Isu ti nangabak iti ay-ayamda; kanayon nga isu ti mangabak ket di kayat no kua dagiti uppat a kaay-ayam. Ngem kasla awan ti ania man ken ni Yengyeng, ta kanayon nga isu ti kultab. Ad-adda ngamin a sipsiputanna ti gameboyna, no adda iti balay, no saan adda iti ruar nga agtiliw iti tuwwato, kulibangbang, wenno agpidut iti kuting nga agwalangwalang iti kalsada, wenno imbelleng ti akimpusa.

Idi mauma, rimmuar nga awan masnop a Papananna.

Pinasiarna dagiti dua a barkadana a da Leo ken Bimbo. Awan mapanunotda nga aramiden. Nagpapatangda lattan a pangpatayanda iti oras. Idi kuan, inkeddengda ti agpagnapagna iti Apatot Subdivision. Aggagarikgikda. Agikup-ay iti masagangda a tansan, wenno ania man a banag iti kalsada. Rumabsotda iti bulong a madalapusda iti igid. No saan aglulumbada. No kuan, agtugawda iti igid ti kalsada. Wenno agiladda iti karuotan ket tangadenda ti asul a langit. Wenno agkikingkingda. Wenno

aglulumbada a saggaysada iti saka. Wenno agkikinnallabayda a tallo sada agtingigtingig nga agkanta iti puted. Adu la amin a pagsasaritaanda.

Adda sumagmamano a kapuon ti tawwatawwa iti murdong ti subdibision iti daya. Adda naluom a bungana. Nagang-angawan ni Yengyeng ti nangpuros iti maysa. Inukisanna.

"Oy, kitaenyo," kinunana. "Kasla bagas ti bunga ti lugo."

"Wen, aya."

"Naimas ngata met?"

"Ramanantayo," kinuna ni Yengyeng.

Bassit la idi damo. Ninanamda, inimasda. Ket nakaaduda.

Madamdama, nagawis ni Bimbo a nagawid. Isu ti kaaduan ti nakan.

"Wen," kinuna met ni Yengyeng. "Makaturturogak. . ."

Ket nagsisinada iti puon ti tawwatawwa.

Idi makaawid ni Yengyeng, nagtartarus iti pagpaknian. Nagparatupot. Namin-ano a nagsubli. Idi kuan madi ti riknanan. Aglamiisen. Maulaw.

Isu met a sumangpet da Papa ken Mamada.

"'Sinno ngamin ti nagkuna a mangankayo iti bunga ti tawwatawwa?" kinuna ni Mamada idi maammuanna ti kinnanda.

"Kasla ngamin mani. . . lugo," kinuna ni Yengyeng. "Ken naimas met."

"Saan nga amin a naimas ket naimas, ay, ket nasayaat a kanen," kinuna ni Papada.

Tumakki, sumarua kano met ni Leo idiay balayda.

Ni Bimbo, intarayda iti ospital ket nakadekstros kano.

Naminsan, napan manen nagpasiar ni Yengyeng. Sinapulna da Bimbo ken Leo. Ngem awan dagiti dua. Idi agawid, nakasalaw iti agngingiaw a kuting. Napintas ti labang ti kuting, kalanglanga ti ladawan ti Himalayan a nakitana iti libro.

Pinidut ni Yengyeng ket inyawidna.

Idi makadanon iti balayda, nakitana ti waya ti koriente, a naiwara iti kusina. Tinarimaan ni Papada ti plansa ket nalipatanna nga impakni ta nagtarusanna manen a kinubbuan ti makiniliana.

Nabayag a minulenglengan ni Yengyeng ti waya, sana kinita ti pagiselselan iti diding ti balay. Sana kinita ti sinalikepkepanna a pusa a nakataltalna kalpasan ti panangpakanna.

"Napintas man 'ta kutingmo," kinuna ni Bongbong nga apagisu a mapan uminum. "Dinno man ti nangtaktakawamon?"

Kasla saan a nangngeg ni Yengyeng ni Bongbong. Innalana ti waya. Inselselna ti maysa a murdong iti pagiselselan iti diding, sana insunel iti pusa ti dua a sabali a murdong ti waya.

"Ney, ney, an-anuemon?" napamulagat ni Bongbong.

Nagkulipagpag ti pusa ket simgar amin a dutdotna. Napadata met ni Yengyeng.

"'Nia't kukueenyo, 'ya?" kinuna ni Papada a nangtakder iti makiniliana.

"Kinuriente ni Yengyeng 'diay pusa, Pa!" kinuna ni Bongbong.

Agrungrungiit ni Yengyeng a nangap-apros iti napabutngan a pusa.

"Adu unay a paglukolukuam. To no kuan 'ta lukditmo ti nakorientem!" kinuna ni Papada.

Naminsan, masan-aran ngata unay ni Yengyeng a mangkitkita iti aguy-uyaoy a waya ti doorbell. Nangala iti tugaw sana ginaw-at ti waya ta tarimnenna ti kunana. Sabali ti napagdekketna a murdong ti waya ket limmanitog ti kahon dagiti fuse. Naiddep amin a silaw, pati ti dekoriente a makinilia ni Papada. Nagariwawa dagiti kaduana iti balay idinto a natnag ni Yengyeng iti basar gapu iti pigsa ti koriente a kasla nangkidag kenkuana.

Inungtanda amin ni Yengyeng. Nagrungrungiit la ni Yengyeng.

"Oy, saan nga ang-angaw ti ar-aramidem!" kinuna ni Mamada. "Inton maminsan, amangan no sikanton ti maasar a sibibiag! Yad-adayom, Apo!"

SARDAM ti Domingo. Dinanon da Bingbing, Dangdang, Tingting, ken Yengyeng ni Bongbong iti puestona nga agbasbasa iti salas. Saanen nga agkudkudkod, ngem nakakayang pay laeng ket sirsirigen ni Dangdang ti sellangna a ngimmisit; napiaan kadin ti gudgodmo, Manong, kunana koma ngem dina kayat ti manutil itoy a sardam. Natalnada amin, a kunam no anghelda a natnag iti daga. Addan dagiti libro a masapulda iti rabaw ti bassit a lamisaan iti tengnga ti salas, pati dagiti libro ti himno.

Ur-urayenda ni Mamada nga agkutikuti pay la iti kusina.

Ken ni Papada a pumarasapas iti banio.

Madamdama pay, addan da Papa ken Mamada iti salas. Kunam no nakukkokan a bisukol dagiti lima. No dadduma, agkikinnitada. Ngem dida kayat ti agkikinnita iti napaut ta amangan no adda makairugi nga agrungiit ket mapurosto man aminen a bituen kadagiti matada.

"Sinno ti conducting ita?" inrugi ni Papada.

"Ni Manang Bingbing, 'Pa," kinuna ni Dangdang.

"O, sige, rugiamon, Bingbing," kinuna ni Papada.

"Good evening. . . naimbag a rabiyo amin. Siak ti conducting itoy a Family Home Eveningtayo. Ket ni Papa ti presiding. Ni Dangdang ti mangted iti panglukat a kararag, ni Bongbong ti mangted iti scriptural thought, ni Tingting ti chorister, ket ni Yengyeng ti mangted iti pangrikep a kararag. . .Ti opening hymn, There is Beauty All Around, ket ti closing hymn, Count Your Blessings. . ."

Idi madanon ti batang ni Papada a mangted iti pamagbaga, ad-addan ti ulimek dagiti lima. Awan payen ti mangyangad iti rupana. Kunam no managbasolda amin a mapatawan iti dusa. Imbes nga ibaga ni Papada ti biddutda iti napalabas a lawas, isuda ti nagdamaganna no ania ti nasayaat ken madi a naaramidda. Inrugina ken ni Bingbing.

"Diak unay natultulongan ni Mama ditoy balay," inrugi ni Bingbing. "Ken, nakikaanak iti bibingki ni Tingting, ta kunak no dina tinakaw iti arina ni mama..."

Agreklamo koma ni Yengyeng ngem kumitkita kenkuana ni Papada, ket nagdumog laengen.

"Awan ammok a basolko," kinuna ni Bongbong. "Agbasbasaak laeng. Ken nakiramanak gayam iti luto ni Tingting. . ."

"Insungsongko da Tingting a nagtakaw iti mansanita," kinuna ni Dangdang. "Ngem inimasda met ti nangan. . ."

"Linutok ti iduldulin ni Mama," kinuna ni Tingting. "Ngem uray ta naramananyo met amin."

"Kinurientek ti pusa. . ." kinuna ni Yengyeng.

Binagbagaan ni Papada dagiti lima. "Agrepentkayo," kinunana. "Dagiti inaramidyo ita a lawas, agbalinda koma nga adal kadakayo. Diyonton ul-uliten."

"Ken ibagam, a tulongandak, Papa. Dumakdakkel dagita annakmo, ngem sumadsadutda."

"Nangngegyo ni Mamayo?"

Maysa maysa ti nagwen.

Idi maited ni Yengyeng ti pangrikep a kararag, imbaga ni Mamada nga adda insaganana a pagsasanguanda.

"Yipeeey!" maysa maysa ti nangitag-ay iti takiagda. "Uray maymaysa ti Mama no kas ken ni Mama!" nagduduetoda.

"He, balbalatongendak ketdin!" kinuna ni Mamada.

"Saan a balatong, Ma," kinuna ni Dandang. "Mais!"

"Asino ti aginnaw?" dinamag ni Mamada.

"Ni Papa!" nagdudueto dagiti lima.

"Very good, children!" kinuna ni Papada. "Ita, paminduaenyo ti ag-repent!"

"Ayyy!"

Madamdama pay, nagari manen ti gargarikgik, ket kas iti dadduma a gundaway nga aggigiddanda nga agkatawa, ginantilia manen a bituen ti naruros, ket napno ti pagtaengan dagiti Paraiso iti lawag ken nasarangsang a katkatawa.

Ket bayat ti panagregreg ti bituen kadagiti mata da Bingbing, Bongbong, Dangdang, Tingting ken Yengyeng, kiniddayan ni Papada ni Mamada.

Sakbay a simrek ni Mamada iti kuartoda ken ni Papada, kinunana: "Inkayto maturogen ket 'diay panagbasayo no bigat."

Napan ni Papada iti umokna nga agmakinilia. Idi rummuar, addan ngusngusabenna nga apatot.

Simrek ni Papada iti kuartoda ken ni Mamada.

Idi matnagen ti kalub dagiti mata ni Yengyeng, timmakder ket nagturong iti kuarto da Papa ken Mamada.

"Hoy, matmaturogdan!" intubngar ni Bingbing.

"'Nak la aggudnait," kinuna ni Yengyeng. Ngem nagsubli a nakanganga.

"Apay?" dinamag ni Bongbong.

Nagngilangil ni Yengyeng. Kinudkodna ti teltelna.

"'Tay maturogen," kinuna ni Bingbing.

Nagsasaruno dagiti uppat; nabati ni Bongbong iti salas nga agbasbasa. Idi makabatogda iti kuarto da Papa ken mamada, nagsarimadengda. Nagallingagda.

"Bastoskayo!" induron ni Bingbing dagiti tallo iti kuartoda.

Madamdama pay, natalnadan. Naglemmeng metten ti ginantilia a bituen kadagiti matada, kas iti panaglemmeng ti init ken bulan da Papa ken Mamada. —0

Enero 1, 2002, 2:11 P.M. (Draft)
Enero 6, 2002, 12:12 A.M. (Final)
Bannawag, Hunio 24, 2002

Puon

1. Maudi nga Aldaw

AGMAYMAYSA manen. Saan a makaturog manipud iti nasapa a ruar ti maikadua nga asawana a napan nagtrabaho—nangala manen iti kapunganna makatawen kalpasan ti ipupusay daydi nadungngo a kasimpungalanna. Agur-uray ti pamigatna iti bassit a lamisaan iti kusayan ti kamana. Manganto lattan no agkiraus ti boksitna, no mariknananto pay. Uray dagiti agasna nakasaganada amin iti lamisaan.

Winter ket makapakutimermer iti ruar aglalo no kastoy a sibsibet ti isno. Nupay kasta narenren ti venetian blind ken kortina ti tawa iti kusayanna. Maalep-ep ti kebbakebbana no buybuyaenna, uray no aragaag, ti naumbi a panangilili ti pul-oy kadagiti nalangto a bulong ti weeping willow no agngalayen ti spring, iti sangabukel a summer, ken iti autumn a panaglupos dagiti bulong iti nadumaduma a maris sakbay nga agaludaid ti winter a mangidateng iti sagpaminsan nga isno. Ngem kasla ilado ita a di pay naakasan kadagiti naidalungdong nga isno iti nagsulian ti Market Street ken 3800 South, ket kasla adda yelo a dumges iti barukongna. Nasugpet ti kiremna ta agur-uray iti anniniwan ti billit, ngem awan ti uray no aragaag ti agbatay kadagiti lamulamo a sanga, saan a kas iti spring wenno summer wenno autumn nga aduda nga agkakanta a no dadduma agbatayda iti barandilias ti tawa sada tuktoken ti sarming a rikep, sa kumitada iti uneg. Idi adda pay pigsa dagiti piskelna, pasarayna puruakan dagiti billit iti maregmeg ti tinapay wenno inapuy, isu ngata a masansanda a sarungkaran.

Awan ti naurayna a billit. Dina payen mangngeg ti areng-eng ti heater, nangruna ti angin a mangarakup a mangindayon kadagiti sanga ti weeping willow.

Ti inauna a barona iti daydi nagawan dita Yorkshire, kasanoda ngatan iti pamiliana? Kaanon daydi naudi nga isasarungkarda iti manugangna, ken dagiti appokona? No makabangon la koma, ken makapagna iti adayo, masansan la ketdi a pasiarenna ida ta asideg laeng ti Yorkshire iti Market Street. Ngem dina payen makuti ti kanawan a sakana ta inarado ti bala ti Hapon ti luppona idi Maikadua a Gubat ti Sangalubongan ket no manen agut-ot ket kurang la a mapugsat ti angesna no tumangken, nangruna no kasdiay nga agsulsulo, kas ita.

Tatang?

Dina no kua mangngeg ti nagtengnga a balasangna a nagsanguanda iti agdama nga asawana, a nakamanuganganna iti Puraw. Isu ti agbantay kenkuana iti aldaw agingga a sumangpet ti asawana, sa met sumukat ti balasangna a mapan agtrabaho iti rabii. Aldaw ti panagtrabaho ti inauna, kas iti inada, ket agtrabaho iti aldaw ken agbasa iti rabii ti buridek. No ania ti aramiden kenkuana ti balasangna, kasla tagtagainep amin ket bay-anna lattan a pulinglingenda ti kasla nateng a bagina.

Adda met dagiti gundaway a makakarawa iti diding a mapan makirayrayo kadagiti tallo a babbalasangna iti salas, kaduada ti inada, ngem no kasdiay a rumasok ti panagsusupanget ti saritaanda, pamrayanna ti agkarkarawa manen iti diding nga agsubli iti si*led*da nga agassawa ket idiayen nga ukopanna a lagipen dagidi naraniag nga aldawna. Agtayab ti panunotna ket ti la adda a pagam-ampayaganna. No manen agampayag idiay Pagasa, sa idiay Poblasion Sur, wenno idiay Labut ken Panay-ogan, wenno idiay Baybayyabas, wenno idiay San Isidro, wenno Guimod Sur, wenno idiay Abbarit. No manen idiay Tarlac, wenno idiay Bataan, wenno Corrigidor. Iti Death March, wenno idi sabsabongenna pay daydi nagawan. Daydi nagawan a baggak ti Guimod Sur ken sab-ok dagiti tagtagainepna manipud iti damo a pannakakitana iti paganian iti bimmalitok a kataltalonan iti amianan ti Cabanayan. Wen, saan a mapakil nga agampayag ket no kasdiayen nga adda ti lagipna iti law-ang, malipatanna amin nga adda iti lawlawna ket umisem dagiti raya ti bannawag iti rupana, ken nalamuyot ti agek

ti agpakpakada nga init iti malem. Adda pay dagiti gundaway nga isiwet iti law-ang ket mapan makiinnisem kadagiti bituen. Uray ania a kanito ti panagampayagna makitana ti nayaplag a tanap ken taaw iti baba, dagiti langana ti napakleb a balbalay, kataltalonan a naaplagan iti balitok a nadeppes a pagay, nalangto a bakir ken sumiksiksik a perlas a baybay. Nakalaglag-an man ti bagina a makirayo kadagiti tumatayab a mangtantan-aw iti pakabuklan ti lubong. Dina no kua mabigbig ti misuot iti aglawlaw, ti laaw dagiti tawataw: kas man la napasag a bangkay ti lubong.

Ngem no dumikar ti ut-ot ti sakana, masulnot iti pagam-ampayaganna ket agsubli iti pudno a lubongna. No agkirpa ti ut-ot, agaludaid manen ti lagipna iti sabali a lubongna ngem masansan a ti nasaem a buya ti agparang iti alintataona. Mangngegna dagiti damag manipud kadagiti bibig dagiti annakna. Ti mapaspasamak iti puseg ti ingungotenna nga ina a daga. Ti di makaidna a gimong. Dagiti saem iti barukong dagiti makipagili a gubuayen ti panagbaybay-a dagiti natudingan nga agaywan. Insebbada idi ti biagda para iti masakbayan ti patpatgenda a pagilian, idi panawen ti Maikadua a Gubat ti Sangalubongan, ngem daytoy kadin ti supapak dagidi nagayus a dara iti kabakiran ti Bataan ken iti kaunasan ti Tarlac; dagidi adu a naisebba a biag iti Death March? Daytoy kadi ti bunga ti napalabas? Daytoy panaglupos nga inyeg ti baro a panawen? Daytoy panagtatalaw dagiti nalinteg a makipagili tapno agsapul iti nataltalna a lubong, a kas iti nakapay-an ti biagna? Adda ita ditoy ti maikadua a paset ti pamiliana gapu iti dayta a panagbaybay-a, a no saan a nagbaybay-a dagiti diosen iti pagilianna, saan koma a nasayya ti pamiliana ket awan ti parikutna a sumina kadagiti patpatgenna. Saan koma a naisebba ti dayaw dagiti adu a Contemplacion iti lugar a nakipagbatbatnaanda iti iduolda kadagiti patpatgenda a bunga. Saan koma ita a kayarigan ti pagilianna iti bangkay a rinangrangkay dagiti nadangkok nga agila iti siudad. A nakaigapuan ti namin-adu a yaalsa dagiti agtutubo kadagiti dandani amin a pagadalan iti siudad, ken dagiti adu a napnuanen a makipagili. Ken rimmaba pay ti panangkunkundinar dagiti adda iti ruar nga aginlalaing, kasta met dagiti kutak a kutak a kunam no pudno a makipagrikriknada iti sakit ti gimong, ngem awan met ti maipaayda a pagimbagan ti pagilianda no di

pasig a buong ti ulo, ken pakaigapgapuan ti di mapekka nga itatayok ti presio ti mabekbekkel a biag ti sangapagilian. Awan koma ti biddut no saan a gapu kadagitoy nga aginlalaing ken managbaybay-a. Awan koma ti basol. Awan koma ti sulisog. Saan koma met a naisungsong iti kasta a parikut. Wen, isu a puon. . . isu a puon. . .

2. Sidir

BASOLKO, Inada.

Basolko.

Basolko.

Basolko!

Saanak a dimmawat iti pammakawanmo.

Ta ammok a dinak mapakawan.

Ket adtoyak ita.

Uray no adda sabali a barukong a pagsadsadagak, ti lagipko kenka dinto maumag.

Patpatgek dagiti bungata. Unay-unay. Ta isuda ti ladawam a sibibiag. Ngem anian ta maymaysa kadakuada ti asideg.

Kailiwko unay dagidiay nabati idiay Filipinas.

Manen, pakawanennak ta imbatik ida. Kuna dagiti dadduma, nasken nga isaganak ti masakbayan dagitoy tallo a nagsanguanmi iti insunok kenka. Kunada, awan ti masakbayanda iti Filipinas. Madamdamagko, Inada, ti rigat a sagsagabaen dagidiay bungata, dagidiay la unay dua a saan a naparaburan iti nawaywaya a gasat a kas kadagiti kakabsatda. Daytoy bungata ditoy Yorkshire ti napagasatan nga immay ditoy America. Ngem adu met ti appokom a bungada iti naimbag a manugangmo.

Adu ti appokom idiay Filipinas, ngem segun iti mangmangngegko a damag maipanggep iti parikut sadiay, maluyaan ti riknak a makasirmata iti nalidem a masakbayanda. Piman. Ngem ania ti aramidek? Awanen daydi sigud a pigsak, Inada. Masansan nga agut-ot daytoy luppok nga inarado ti bala daydi Hapon, ngem awan met ti makita dagiti doktor, no manodan a nangkita, a pambaranda a mangagas. Daytoy tengngedko ti sumkil no dadduma, ket masansan a diak makatilmon ta kasla adda agsullat a diak ammo no ania ket pengdanna ti ipaunegko a taraon, uray

pay ti inumek. Kuna kano ti doktorko, a ti ipaunegko agtartarus iti barak ta isu ti nakalukat. Kasta man ti panangilawlawag daydiay inauna a nagsanguanmi iti kadkaduak ita, ta isu ti makaawat ken makasao iti Ingles ket bagbagik la ti agngangnganga ken umawat iti ania man nga ibagada. Uray pay ket ngata no kunada a matayakon, wen kunak lattan ta awan metten ti maar-aramidak. Ti man panagriknak iti bagi ken kasasaadko ditoy, arigko ti sibibiag nga alis a sikkasikkaruden lattan ti panawen. Naimbag laengen, ket pagyamyamanak unay, ta saan a nagbalbaliw ti sidap ti lagipko; no lalausen ti manao, malagipko amin a di mangan-ano, isu a ti la pagdakdakiwasan ti panunotko.

Wen, Inada, kunada a paraiso ditoy America. Ngem paraiso kadi ti kas kaniak? Ti kadakkelan a lubongko awan sabali no di daytoy nailet nga uppat ti sulina a kuarto, a diak pay ket masiraratan a nasayaaten ta arigna angep ti aglawlawko. Ngem dayta ladawam, Inada, dinto pulos agkupas. Uray iti pannaturogko, kadagiti tagtagainepko, masansan nga agparang dayta ladawam.

Kunada, napintas kano ti aglawlaw ti Utah, nangruna iti spring, ken iti summer. Ken amin kano a panawen. Kuna daydiay barom dita Yorkshire a kaarngi ti biag ti panawen ditoy. Nga iti spring, ipasimudaagna ti panagungar dagidi nagaburan a mulmula ket agsulbod ken agsabong ken agrangpayada ket pagbalinenda a kaarngi ti paraiso ti aglawlaw; nalawag ti langit, naumbi ti apros ti angin ken naisem amin dagiti tao nga aglilinnagud iti inaldaw. Sa dumteng ti summer, wenno kalgaw idiay Filipinas ket tennebenna dagiti bulong, patingraenna dagiti agduduma a maris, a kas iti panagduduma ti puli dagiti nagbalinen a makipagili ditoy—idi nalawag pay ti panagkitak, nadlawko met ti nakaay-ayat nga agduduma a maris dagiti bulong, no apay a kasta, diak ammo. Intono kuan, umay ti panagreregreg, daytay autumn wenno fall a kunada. Makariknaak no kua iti dagensen, ta idi, no buybuyaek dagiti naannayas a panagaludaid dagiti agregreg a bulong iti barukong ti nakaparsuaan, mariknak a kasla 'toy bagik ti agaludaidto met iti dayta a nakaparsuaan— ngem nasaem a panunotek nga iti ganggannaet a daga ti pakaigameranto ti lasagko; kayatko, Inada, nga itinto koma sibay ti tanemmo idiay Filipinas ti paginanaanto met ti bangkayko. Ngem anian. Wen, Inada, agaludaid dagiti bulong ket di agbayag, maimuttalatton dagiti labus a sangsanga ket

kaarngida man ti adu a rurog a gumawgawawa iti kaasi ti langit. Wen, Inada, kas met agpanes ti aglawlaw ta madlaw latta ti kinaulimek dagiti tao. A kas man la amkenda unay ti paspasungadenda a winter. Ta ti winter ti mangidateng iti isno a mangitanem kadagiti nanukunok a bulbulong. Kasta man ti kalawag ti panangiladawan daytoy barom a nasagudayan iti kinamanagpaliiw iti aglawlaw a nakaparsuaan. Diak ammo, arapaapko met koma a makita ti kunkunada a kinapintas ti aglawlaw, ngem angep laeng ti makitakon ita. Ti katkatawa iti aglawlaw, kasla agtaud iti nauneg nga abut ta pati dagitoy lapayagko ket paidamandan ti riknak a mangnanam koma met iti kinaimbag ti lubong.

Ngem adda man nakalkaldaang a mapaspasamak kadagiti kadaraantayo ditoy, Inada. Imbes nga isuda ti agsisinnakit, gapu ta maymaysa ti nakaigapuan ti kaaddada ditoy, saan ta kurangda la ti agsisinnida iti panagpipinnadakesda. Adda dagitay di mangayat a dumngeg kadagiti makalais a saritaan, ken di makaibtor iti atibuor ti agsapri a pinnadakesda, ket saanen a makitatallaong kadagitoy napateg a kadaraan. Saan met ketdi nga isuda amin, ngem aduda. Kunkunak man, Inada, intugotda ti nalaad nga ugalida idiay Filipinas. Kunkunak pay, isu ngata a di dumurdur-as ti nakayanakantayo a daga gapu iti daytoy nga ugali.

Wen, Inada, adu ti dumakdakiwas iti panunotko nangruna no kasdiay nga agsulsuluak ditoy lubong a paggargarawak. Awan san ti aramiden ti panunotko no di agdakiwas ket adu la aminen a sumsumken iti ulok.

Isu ngata ketdi nga iti agdama a lubongko, Inada, saanak a makaanges no dadduma. Alimbabadawenak no kua ket no kuan, kasla agbalibaliktad ti lubongko ket agsasabat dagiti uppat a diding a nanglakub kaniak ket ipitendak. Agriawak no kua, ket sumkil ti bagik, ngem no malagipko a sisiak ditoy, nga awan daydiay sandim ta napan nagtrabaho, pakpakirdek ti nakemko ta no mabalin diak kayat a mapukawak ditoy gangganaet a lugar. Ti lubongko, Inada, daydi pay laeng lubong a sinangalta, napno iti katkatawa, mapnektayo iti kappuros a nateng. Awan makukuartatayo ngem naragsaktayo. Ditoy, adu ti taraon, ngem awan ti kappuros a nateng a nakairuamak idiay Abbarit. Adda met marunggi ken okra ken saluyot ken paria ken tarong ngem dandani pasigda a bimmato. Iniladoda dagiti bulbulong, ngem imasen lattan dagiti pada nga Ilokano ta naim-imbag laengen ngem ti dida pulos makaraman.

Diak ammo, no dadduma kayatko a babalawen ti Namarsua iti panangipalladawna kaniak ditoy. Ngem adda ngata karbengak a mangbabalaw iti namarsua kaniak, nangruna ti nasapa a panangyadayona kenka kaniak? Wenno daytoy ngata ti dusak iti adu a nagkamtudak kenka? Apay ngata nga impalubosna a naisungsongak iti sulisog, tapno agbasolak kenka? Basolna kadi, wenno basolko? Agsasaibbek ti pusok no malaglagipka, Inada. Ngem inumek man dagiti luak, maisublik kadi pay dagidi nalangto nga aldawta?

Wen, Inada, kunkunak no dadduma, nga impuruaknak ti panawen ditoy ganggannaet a lugar. Awan maawatak a pulos a panagsasaoda. Uray ti buybuyaek iti telebision, maawatak la bassit babaen ti ar-aramidenda, idi nalawag pay ti panagkitak. Nadagsen ti barukongko, Inada, ngem anian, anian!

Naragsakka kadi iti yanmo ita, Inada? Dagidi bungata nga immunan nga immay dita, kasanoda metten? Dagidi appokom a simmina a nasapa, dadakkelda kadin? Naragsakkayo kadi dita? Siak, masaok a saanak a naragsak. Agkakatawa dagiti kabbalayko, ket makipagis-isemak latta metten uray no diak maawatan ti pagsasaritaanda. Awan dumak iti bambanti wenno tirtiris nga awan kaipasanganna iti lubong a paggargarawak iti agdama. Wenno aggargarawak kadi pay, Inada? Amangan no bangkayakon nga aggargaraw?

Yanmo kadi, Inada? Apay a dinak man la sungbatan, wenno agpakita man la koma kaniak uray apagkanito? Mailiwak kadagidiay bungata idiay Filipinas, ngem mailiwak met kenka. Adu ti basolko, ngem mapakawannak ngata?

Yanmo, Inada, yanmo?

Nadagsen 'toy barukongko, Inada. Saanak a makaanges. Kasla adda mangbekbekkel kaniak. Malenglengngesak. Ti barkongko, kurang la nga agkupit. Apayen, Inada, apayen? Yawatmo man dayta imam ta saranayennak. No adda karbengak nga agpabitibit kenka, Inada. Saanak...

3. Iti Ngarab ti Lubong – 1

ANIA'T napasamakna?

Diak ammo man, basta lattan agririaw itay addaak dita salas nga agbuybuya iti DVD. Itay umayko kitaen, kasta unay ti wadagwadag ti kanigid nga imana sa tengngel ti kanawan nga imana ti luppona. Annay nga annay.

Ania't nasakit, Daddy? Daytoy kadi dunormo?

'Tan, aya? 'Tan, aya?

Dinno't papananta?

'Tan, aya. . .'tan, aya?

Apo Dios! Ania metten. Inawagam da *manong*mon?

Awan tao 'diay balayda. Rabiin no sumangsangpet ni *manong*.

Ania metten. Napan met ngarud 'diay kakam idiay Wendover. . . dimo inawagan 'diay cell phonena?

No addad'ta met.

'Tay adim?

Madama ti finalsda. . . Ne, agtantanamitim ni tatang!

Denggem man no ania ti ibagbagana. . . Nairut ti petpetna. . .

Tatang, Tatang. . . Di met sumungbat. . . Ne, kitaem, 'Nang, dina ginaraw 'ta kanenna. . . ken 'ta agasna. . .

'Su met laengen, a! Apay a dimo kinita?

Am-ammok, aya, ket saan met la nga is-isu ti asikasuek.

4. Basol

ANNAKKO, *pakawanendak kadi, a, iti ania man a babak a naaramidko. . . Annakko, Annakko, didak kadi mangngeg? Denggendak kadi, a. Ammok a nagbasolak kadakayo, nangruna iti daydi nanangyo.*

Wen, daydi Nanangyo. Daydi nanangyo a naasi unay. Nakaaramidak iti nadagsen a babak kenkuana.

Imetko iti sadino man a papanak ti babakko kenkuana. Awan nangibagbagaak kadakayo. Uray dagidiay addim, Barok, dida ammo; uray daydiay buridek a kabsatyo a dua la ti tawenna idi, diak ammo no naawatannan dagidi a pasamak. No malagipmo, um-umay idi daydi nanangyo idiay Manila, ket pambarna ti iliwna kadakayo, nangruna dagiti inauna nga appokona, nga isu dagiti annakyo iti naimbag a manugangko. Isu ti immuna a nakakita iti dagusyo idiay Balara, nga

immayna timmulongan a nangaywan iti daydi maikaduam. Sa idi kuan, idiay Times, idiay Sampaloc—malagipko latta uray no diak napadasan ti immadak kadagidiay a nagdagdagusanyo bayat ti panangisaganayo iti masakbayanyo. Diak pinanggep ti umay agbakasion, wenno kumita man la kadakayo. Kanayon a pambarko iti daydi Nanangyo nga agulawak nga agbiahe, ken adu ti aramid a mapanawak idiay Labut. Ngem kinapudnona, adda dakdakkel a banag a diak mapanawan. Isu dayta ti dakkel a sulisog. A diak kabaelan a yebkas uray kadagitoy a gundaway. Nadlawko ti gura iti barukong dagiti dua a kakabsatyo a balasitang idin, ngem diak inkankano.

Nadagsen a babak, Barok, ket mabainak a sumarang iti kayatko a 'apanan. Awan ti bileg ti pakinakemko nga agtuktok iti daydiay dakkel a puraw a ridaw, ta kasla adda mangigawgawid kadagiti sakak.

Gapu ngata ta diak dimmawat iti pammakawanyo?

Diak la ammo no adda nasasao daydi nanangyo, wen, daydi nasingpet a nanangyo. Malagipko ita, ket malunag ti nakemko a manglagip, ken bainek ti bagik. Wen, adda dagidi gundaway a madardarimusmosanna ti aramidko, ngem awan man la ti nangngegko a panagtukiad ti nakemna, ken gundaway a panangsalangadna iti daydiay a sulisog, a bunga pay met ngarud ti kabsatna. Pamrayanna la ti aglua bayat ti panangisaganana iti sanguenmi a taraon, wenno ubbaen ti di met agpapaubba a buridek a kabsatyo. Masalsalamaak ti panagluluana no kasdiay nga adda uray ania a babassit a kudkuditenna. Ammok a siak ti gapuna, ti aramidko, ngem timmangken ti nakemko, ket diak met pinadas ti dumawat iti pannakaawat, wenno panggep nga ilawlawag dagiti pasamak; ta ania koma ti ilawlawagko? Wenno kasano nga ilawlawagko?

5. Awis

LAKAYAKON, Barok, ania pay la ti innak kueen 'diay America? kinunana iti panagpapatangda nga agaama kadagiti annakna iti immuna nga asawana iti balitang iti sirok ti balasitang a mangga iti sidiran ti balayda iti Poblacion Sur. Nagbakasion dagiti annakna manipud iti Manila iti daydi a kalgaw.

Narigat unayen ti biag ditoy, kinuna ti inauna a barona. Nalabit nga awan unayen ti pategna kadakayo. Ngem napateg unay kadagitoy tallo. . . Awan nasayaat a masakbayanda ditoy.

Wen met ngamin, kinuna ti adien daytoy. Ta ipetisiondakaminto met. Diak koma kayat no mabalin a mariingan 'toy apoyo ti kinarigat ti biag.

Nabayag nga ibagbagakon, kinuna ti agsiuman. Dina met kayat. Libre la ngarud kadakuada a beterano ti agsitisen. Nabannogakon nga agtartaraken iti baboy ken agpaspastor iti baka. Kayatko met ti makaiggem iti grinbak a kunada.

Agpanunotka, Brader, kinuna met ti doktorna a padana a beterano. Agpayso ti kuna dagidiay annakmo. No ditoyka laeng, rigatto man met laengen ti tawiden dagita tallo a babbalasangmo—pasigto man met la aminen a nagtawid iti rigat dagiti maasawada. Total naikkantayo iti gundaway nga agbalin nga Amerikano, apay a ditay gundawayan? No awan la ti nadagsen a rikriknaek, nabayag koma metten a napanak nagpasaklot ken ni Angkel Sam.

Idi nagsubli ti inauna a barona manipud iti America a nangibaonan ti trabahona tapno agobserba, a nakaalaanna iti awan limitadona a bisa, inkeddengen daytoy ti nagsubli a nakigasanggasat. Daytoy a barona ti dinanonda kalpasan ti nadaras a pannakaaprobar ti papelna nga agsitisen. Kaduana ti asawa ken tallo a babbalasangna.

6. Iti Ngarab ti Lubong – 2

INAWAGANKA, Barok, ta daytoy amayo di met agsaon. 'Tan, aya a 'tan, aya ti yar-arasaasna. Ngem no kasaom di met sumungbat.

Adda kadi pay met la agasna?

Inggatanganmin.

Inggatangan? Di met adda medicaidna, aya?

Inikkatda ta adda met kanon trabahok.

'Tan, aya? 'Tan, aya?

Isu daydiay?

Agam-ammangaw sa metten, Barok.

Ipanyon idiay LDS Hospital, ta isu ti yan ti doktorna.

Awan met dagitay addiyo a mangitulod kadakami. . . dagidiay koma ubbingyo ngem awanda met 'diay balayyo. . .

Saanak a makapanaw ditoy trabahok ta busykami unay. Alas nuebe medianton no agretiroak.

Kasano ngaruden, Barok, agpapadakayo met a bisi? Diak met ngarud makasasao iti Ingles, ken awan met ti paglugananmi.

'Nia met ti pannakairanrananan. Ala, bay-anyo ta kitaek.

7. Pakada

KAYATKO nga iti sidongyo ti suminaak.

Dimo panunoten dayta.

Ngem kayatko met a palabsen ti maudi a kanitok iti sidong dagidiay ubbing idiay Filiplinas.

Mabingaymo ngarud ti bagim?

Kayatko ti maitanem iti ili a nakayanakak.

8. Pateg

MABATI man ti bangkayko ditoy, ti espirituk umay kenka, patpatgek nga Inada!

9. Iti Ngarab ti Lubong – 3

ADDAKAYO aminen?

Kompletokamin, Barok.

Isaganayo 'ta computeryo. . . luktanyo 'ta monitor, wenno t.v.yo ta dakdakkel. . . agkokomperensiatayo. . .Sige, umasidegkayo. . . agururaydan 'diay Manila.

Adda kadin gadgetda, Manong?

Inggatangak ida idi nagbakasionak.

'Tan, aya? 'Tan, aya?

Sinno ti kasarsaritam, Daddy?

'Tan, aya? 'Tan, aya?

Ne, addadan, Manong. . .

Nasayaat. . . dakayo dita Manila, addakayo met la aminen?

Addakamin, Manong. Pati ubbingmi, kompleto. . .

Nasayaat. Aramidentayo ti kastoy ta ditayo ammo ti sumaruno a mapasamak. Kas makitayo. . . makitadakami met laeng? Daytoy ni Tatang. Umang-anges, ngem kitaenyo ti langana. Kuna 'diay doktorna. . .

'Tan, aya? 'Tan, aya?

Ania kano?

Dayta la ti masaona.

Kaano pay a kasta?

Idi la kalman a nangrugi, nupay nabayagen a manmano a bumangon.

Adda agasna?

Kompleto, a. . . ditoyto pay ti kunayo.

Kasano ngarud?

Idi makasao pay, sangkadagullitna ti umay dita Filipinas.

Apay a diyo inkaskaso?

Saan a kasta ti kalakana. . . maawatanmi ti rikriknaenna. Ngem saan a kas iti agkaariping a kuarto ti nagbaetan ti America ken Filipinas.

Apay a nagbalin a kasta?

Dikami nagbaybay-a, Annakko. Uray no pampanawak iti aldaw, adda met 'toy maysa nga adiyo a mangbambantay. . . agrinriniliebokami. No sumangpetak iti malem, isunto pay la ti iseserrekna iti trabahona.

Uray no ti la koma maudi a kanitona met a makitami pay a sibibiag.

Mano kadakayo dita Manila ti awan trabahona? Mano kadakami ditoy America ti awan trabahona? Adda amin trabahotayo. Dagitoy ubbingmi ditoy, agtrabahoda iti aldaw sada sumrek iti eskuela iti rabii. Makumikomtayo amin. Nawaya koma nga ipanmi iti pagtaraknan, ngem kaykayatmi nga iti sidongmi ti yanna. Ammok nga agpapadatayo a mangipatpateg kenkuana, iti laksid ti. . . ti napalabas.

10. Iliw

AGAWIDAKON!
    Pagawidanyo? Ditoy ti balayyo!
    Adda met balayko idiay.

Awan balayyo idiay. Kinamkamen dagidiay nalalaing a kaanakanyo. Amin a pinanawanyo, sabalin ti agtagikua.

Awan papel a pakakitaan iti panagtagikuada. Awan dokumento. No awan dokumentom, awan ti maidatagmo iti pangukoman a mangpaneknek iti panagtagikuam.

Saanen a nasken ti dokdokumento idiay. No kayatda nga alaen ti kukuam, alaenda lattan.

Saan a pudno dayta!

Uray ania ti sasawenyo. Amerikanokayon nga awan surok ken kurangna. Saankayon a Filipino. Nawaswasen ti kina-Filipinoyo idi agpirmakayo iti panagbalinyo nga Amerikano.

Awan pinirpirmaak.

Nagdeppelkayo.

Amerikanoak kadin ket kayumanggiak pay met laeng a luppap? Awan kadin ti karbengak nga agsubli iti daga a nakayanakak? Awan kadin ti karbengak a mangbigbig iti kinakayumanggik? Ti puso ken kararuak, Filipinoak a di mapaginsasaanan. Ti kina-Amerikanok, papel laeng ket uray balbaliktadenda ti lubong, didanto mabaliwan ti maris ti kudilko, ti linaon ti isipko, ti dara nga agtartaray kadagiti uratko. 'Toy pusok ipitpitikna pay laeng ti nakayanakanna a panagayat, panangipateg, kultura, ken amin a kababalin a maipagtangsit ti patneng nga Ilokano a kas kaniak.

Ngem addakan ditoy America, 'Tang. Ania pay laeng ti pagsubliam idiay Filipinas? Addakan iti naimeng a dekutson a kama, kayatmo pay la ti agsubli iti natangken ken nalamiis a datar.

Awan mariknak a panangipateg ditoy. Awan ti am-ammok a kaarrubak. Awan ti mangngegko a taol. Awan ti mangngngegko a taraok dagiti kawitan nga agtatapuak iti parbangon. Awan dagiti nakairuamak a katkatawa. Kailiwko ti pinekkel nga inapuy nga isimutko iti napettak a kamatis a naasinan iti ginaramian no panagani.

Agkabawkayon.

Saanak nga agkabaw. Malagipko pay la amin dagiti napalabasko, uray ultimo a kababassitan a paset ti biagko, nalangtoda pay laeng.

Inkayo idiay ta umababa ti biagyo. Awan ti doktor a kas iti doktoryo ditoy.

No gasatmon ti matay, matayka lattan uray no kasano ti kalaing ti doktormo. Awan basol ti doktor no matay ti pasientena.

Asino ti kailiwyo idiay?

Dagidiay kakabsatyo. . . kaasida met.

Adda aminen assawada. . . Napatpategda kadi ngem dakami ditoy?

Panawandak ngarud a buridek a di pay nagsimpa?

11. Iti Ngarab ti Lubong – 4

KEN pampanunotenmi ti situasion ti medisina dita. No awan kuartam, matayka a dina oras. Ikkandaka pay iti agas a saan a para kenka. . . dakayo ti saksi iti dayta; laplapendaka a padaraen uray awan daram. Isu nga adu ti agtaray nga umay ditoy nga agpaagas.

Adda met bassit urnongmi. . . dimi baybay-an.

Baliktadentayo ngarud ti pasamak? Adda ni tatang iti kondision a kasapulanna ti kasayaatan nga agas, maitedda ngata dita? Uray kabaelanyo nga igastuan, magemgemanyo ngarud dagiti akin-iggem kadagiti ospital?

Nakapsuten ni amayo. Amangan no madagdag laeng iti dalan.

Kayatmi pay a makita. . .

Kayatmi met a makita ti maudi nga orasna.

Dayta ti dakkel a parikutna. Patpatgennakayo dita. Patpatgennakami ditoy. Kasano a bingayenna ti bagina?

Nabayagen a kinaludludonnakayo. No lalausen ti manao, binukodanyo ti maudi a kagudua ti biagna. Uray no ti maudi a kanitona laeng ti maimatanganmi. No ti pagpletena nga agawid, pagtitinnulonganmi. Kayatmi la a makita.

12. Umel a Balikas

KADAKAYO nga adda iti sibayko. . . Pinadakkelkayo. Inikkankayo iti gundaway. Inyegkayo ditoy yan ti masakbayanyo. Kabaelanyon ti tumakder

nga awan mangibin kadakayo. Dagidiay kakabsatyo, piman dagidiay
dua. . . dida ammo ti pangalaanda iti sumaruno nga isaangda. Ammok nga
awan ti anakko a di mangipatpateg kaniak. Ngem nasaksakit a panunotek.
Ammoyo, diak kayat ti maipusing kadakayo. Ngem kasta met kadakuada.
No umulogak ditoy a balay kas pagarigan, panunotenyo koma laengen a
nabayagen a pimmusayak. Patpatgenkayo, Annakko. . .

Kadakayo nga adda iti Filipinas. . . kayatkayo a kasarita, ngem ania
ngarud ti mamaayna ket didak met mangngeg? Agaaddayotayo, annakko,
agaaddayotayo.

13. Pangngeddeng

ANNAKKO, palubosandak man a mangipeksa iti nanumo a
kapanunotak. Saan a siak ti pudno nga inayo, ngem impategko
met 'toy amayo, a no di man makaartap iti pammateg daydi inayo,
pinadasko met nga inted ti amin a kasapulanna, 'toy amayo, bayat ti
panagdennami. Nalabit nga adda kunkuna ti panangawatyo kaniak kas
sandi nga inayo, ngem diak inkaskaso ta patiendak koma, ket sawek
itan, nga impategko 'toy amayo gapu ta isu ti pudno a nagtaud iti
kaunggak. No kasano nga ilawlawagko, diak ammo, basta mariknak
ket umdas daytan. Adu dagidi nangnangngegko a kunkuna dagiti
tao, a gapu ta adda aw-awatenna iti binulan kas beterano, isu kano ti
inalumanko. Nalabit nga idi damo, kasta ti panagkita dagiti nagannak
kaniak ta nagtaudkami iti marigrigat a kaamaan ket naawatak nga awan
ti adda iti panunotda, kas kadagiti amin a nagannak, no di ti nasayaat
a masakbayan dagiti annakda. Sinursurokto lattan ti pangngeddengda.
Ngem iti panaglabas ti panawen, nasursurok nga inayat ken impateg
'toy amayo, ket patienyo man wenno saan, arig la mapirpirsay met ti
riknak no adda pakasairan ti riknana, aglalo kadagitoy kallabes a paset
ti biagna. Narigat ti mangeddeng, annakko, ket dayta ti dadagsen iti
barukongna. Sangkakunana no kasano ti panangipategna kadakayo,
no kasano ti panangipategna kadakami, kadagitoy addiyo. No kasano
ti ayatna nga agsubli iti ili a dinakkelanna ket sadiay nga agipulang, iti
inay-ayatna a daga, a nakaibukbokan ti darada kadagidi kakaduana a
nagserbi iti pagilian. Ngem no manen, aglulua a mangkitkita kadagitoy

addiyo. . . Narigat a panunoten, Annakko. Uray siak, diak kabaelan ti mangeddeng. Isu a tulongandak kadi, a. Tulongandak a mangsurot iti maudi a kalikagum 'toy amayo. No ania ti pangngeddengyo, awatek a sipupuso, ta napategkayo metten kaniak, ta imbilangkayon a kasla pudno a nagtaud iti darak. Maysa laeng ti dawdawatek. Ditay koma pagbalinen a narigat unay nga awaten daytoy a kasasaad. Awan maaramidantayo no di mangawat iti naituding a gasattayo. Ammotayo a kayattayo man wenno saan, mapan ket mapanto latta daytoy amayo iti nakaikarianna. . .

Kakabsat, ania ti masaoyo iti nangeganyo? Dakayo dita Filipinas?

Sika man ketdi, Manong, no ania ti makunam.

Dakayo ditoy. . . dakayo a tallo?

Dakayo lattan, a, Manong. . . no ania ti pangngeddengyo. . .

14. Isusuko

SAAN nga agkirkirem. Maymaysa ti turong dagiti matana. No kua manen, agtantanamitim. No kua manen, adda sumngaw a balikasna, ngem awan sabali no di 'tan, aya? 'Tan, aya? Ket agkuti dagiti takiagna a kasla yawatna iti no asino, wenno kumarayo. Marmaratubbog dagiti mata ti maikadua a kaingungotna a di makaadayo iti sibayna.

Adda dagiti uppat a bungada, ti inaunaanda amin nga adda iti Yorkshire, ken dagiti aburoyda iti maikadua. Nakaul-ulimekda; kasla awan mayat a mangbettak iti ulimek. Adda met dagiti annak ti barona, ken ti manugangna nga inada. Dagitoy appokona a no dadduma, agkinnidol, a kasda la maangsan iti kinaulimek ti lubongda. Kayatda no kua ti agpakatawa ngem mingmingan ida ti inada ket pamrayanda ti kumita iti baba.

Nalabit a maymaysa ti adda iti panunotda bayat ti panangurayda iti pangngeddeng ti doktorna. Dina palubosan nga agbiahe.

Ngem pinalubosanna. A kasla dina met kayat nga adda sumina a pasientena. No awanen iti poderna, awan metten ti sungsungbatanna.

Kasla adda iti nauneg a lungog, wenno bubon, iti panagdengngegna kadagiti saggaysa a balikas. Uray iti naudi a balikas ti doktorna, a nangibagaan daytoy a mild stroke ti nakakapet ken kenkuana, saan

a nagliteng kadagiti lapayagna, nangruna ket dina met maawatan ti pagsasao ti mangngagas. Uray ti panagkitana, napudawen nga angep ti aglawlawna. Ngem nakaskasdaaw, para kenkuana, no makuna a kasta ta awan man ti mariknana a kebbakebba. Nalag-an man ketdi ti riknana. Uray ti masansan nga agut-ot a luppona, kasla nakalaglag-an. Kasla tumtumpaw iti law-ang. A no dadduma, adda umis-isem a ladawan, no ladawan daydiay, a kasla mangpaypayapay kenkuana.

Dina ammo nga intulodda iti Salt Lake International Airport. Nga inluganda iti eroplano, a kaduana ti maikadua a kaingungotna, ken ti inauna a nagsanguanda. Dina ammo nga insursurot dagiti mabati ti panagkitada aginnga a nakastrekda iti lubong nga andamio ti eroplano, aginnga a nagrikep daytoy. . .

15. Pammakawan

DIOS ti kumuyog kenka, Tatang. Sapay koma ta saanen a sumken ti liday kenka. Nalabit a saantayonton nga agkikita ngem lagipenkanto a maysa a pagwadan nga ama, iti laksid ti naaramidmo a bassit a biddut. Annugotek a nabayag a diak naawat a saan a bassit a babak ti naaramidmo, a nangmulit iti nadalus a papelmo. Annugotek met a napukawko ti panagraemko kenka kadagidi a panawen. Saan a gapu kadakami nga annakmo, ngem daydi la unay nadungngo nga inami. Panangliput. . . adda kadi sabali a panangiladawan iti naaramid a babak? No malagipmo pay, namin-adu a simmarungkar daydi nanang idiay Manila—nalabit a no mano ti immakaranmi a dagus, kasdiay met ti kaadu ti isasarungkarna. Iti daydi maysa a dagusmi iti Manila, a napunno iti kiteb. . . no kunak a napunno iti kiteb, awan surok ken kurangna. Iti daydi a dagusmi a simmarungkaran manen daydi Nanang, ti nangibagaanna idi agsarsaritakami a dua, nga adda sabali nga ar-aramidem. Kastoy ti kinunana, nga awan surok ken kurangna: 'Sabalin sa met ti ar-aramiden 'diay amayon, Barok.' Medio naawatak ti kayatna a sawen, ngem diak inikkan iti naun- uneg a kaipapananna, ket kinunak laeng: Saanyo a pampanunoten dayta. No saan a bumasol ti lagipko, awan kadagiti kakabsatko ti nangibagaak iti paliiw daydi Nanang. Inamakko a masabidongan

ti naganus a panunotda, ta nagduaduaak iti kinapudno ti kinuna daydi nanang.

Ngem agpayso gayam ti paliiwna. Nagmata idi pimmusay, ken inyegmo ti nakasulisogam iti Balara a yanmi. Kasla natupakan iti bomba ti pagtaengan a mulmulienmi, ket kurang la a nasayyasayya ti napintek a kaamaan a binangonmo. Adda dagiti pasamak a nakaigapuan ti di pannakatuloy daydi a gagem, agingga a naam-ammom ti naawatmi a suno daydi nanang.

Wen, Tatang, naikupinen dagidi a pagteng. Kangrunaanna, pinakawankan.

Wen, pinakawankan, Tatang. Nalukayen ti barukongko a mamalubos kenka. Sapay koma ta maipaltiing kenka ket sumlep dita barukongmo ti bara a marikriknak ita. Ita ta maipusingkan kadakami, isu ti pudno a pannakariknak iti kinapategmo. Dagidi sardam a napno iti sarsaritam sakbay a maturogkami, nalangtodanto nga agnanayon iti panunotko, ket ipasagepsepkonto kadagitoy appokom. Dagiti awid ni Ilokano nga intukitmo iti panunotmi isudanto met ti ipasagepsepmi itoy manugangmo iti panunot dagitoy appokom ket tumanordanto a pudno nga Ilokano ditoy ganggannaet a lugar a pangbangonandanto met iti bukodda a lubong. Uray no adayodanto iti daga a nagtaudan ti puonda, Ilokanodanto latta a nagtaud iti daram, iti puso ken kararuam. Sapay koma ta makapudnokami ket makitanto kadakuada ti ladawan ti puonda...

Dios ti kumuyog, Tatang. Dios ti kumuyog...

16. Intayon, Papa

NARIKNANA ti nairut a petpet ni kaingungotna iti takiagna.

Intayon, Papa, awanen da tatang.

Wen, intayon, 'Pa. Dimi pay nalpas a binuya 'diay A.I. ni Speilberg. Intayon...

Ket insursurotna ti panagkitana iti eroplano agingga a nailinged iti napudaw nga ulep.

17. Maudi a Kidag

KELLAAT a kasla adda nanggutad iti kanawan a luppona. Nalukag ti kaingungotna a kaabayna.

Anakko, ania ti kueen 'toy amamon?

Apay, aya?

Sabali met ti itsuranan! Nars. . . miss. . . Apo Dios..!

18. Intan, Dungngo

NE, sika daytan, Inada? Nagsayaaten ta addaka met laengen.

Ne, ania daytoy kasla napudaw a sinulid. . . sinulid daytoy, wenno ania, a kasla singdanko? Ania daytoy?

Bay-amon, Amada. Umayka ketdin.

'Tan, aya? 'Tan, aya?

Wen, intan.

Papananta? Kasla marigatanak. . .

Bay-am ta kibinenka.

Diak makaanges, Inada. Kasla mabembennat daytoy. . . daytoy singdanko a puraw. . . ne, uming-ingpis. . . uming-ingpis, Inada. . .

Dika agdanag.

Nagpintaskan, Inada. Nagpintaskan...! —0

Umuna a Gunggona, Palanca Memorial Awards for Literature; *Bannawag:* Oktubre 21, 2002.

Dana

I. Idi Punganay. . .

. . . **P**INUTOTNAK ni tatangko ket timmaoak ditoy daga. Pinutotna dagiti kakabsatko. Pinutot ni katugangak ni kaingungotko. Pinutotko dagiti annakko. . .

Nagallaallaak iti duapulo-ket-walo a lugar manipud iti puonko, iti nakaipasngayak, sa iti nadumaduma a lugar iti naunday a panawen ket kas iti kabengbeng ti angep iti agiwet-iwet a kalsada ti namnamak nga agtungeden—no daytoyen ti maudi—ti wanesko ditoy puseg ti siudad nga addaan iti panawen a nabingay iti uppat, nupay nabatad iti mugingko a ti kadakkelan a kalsada iti lubong awan ti puon ken ngudona. Nagkaliak kadagita a lugar iti padas a kaarngi ti gameng a gamgamgamen ti adu no di man ti amin a tao nga addaan iti natadem a sirmata nga agbukar manipud iti damo a lawag nga umisem iti muging ti kaippasngay a maladaga.

Diak ammo no manon a kabus ken bituen ti nabilangko iti adun a sardam ngem kas man la nakurang latta dagiti rabii ta agbukar manen ken manen dagiti aldaw a mangsinga iti naannayas a panagkalap iti arapaap, ta ngamin iti aldaw aglemmeng dagiti bituen ta natadem unay ti rungiit ti init ket inna pagikayen ti parmata nga umagibas iti natalinaay a lubong ti kappia.

Adu ti arapaapko. Natungpalen ti dadduma. Adu pay ti agbibitin iti angin.

Maigidiatak sa man la unay iti daytay nabiag a bato a lumlumoten iti kasla di umang-anges nga agus nga agpataaw—di man la ngamin agpasurong. Sinubak amin a dawel iti tunggal binulong ti nabengbeng a libro ti biag ti kaputotak. Ket napaneknekak a ti karikutan nga aramiden isu ti itataliaw iti likudan bayat ti panangsuba iti dawel: adun a kayaw-atko ti nagkabsiw.

6:00 P.M.: Iti Sango ti *Computer*—1

AGPUKAWPUKAW ti *cursor* iti murdong ti kaudian a balikas iti *screen*; agur-uray iti command iti nakamulagat a monitor. Pumudpudot ti bombilia a naimuntar iti sinantakiag a naiturong iti keyboard. Agan-andar ti oras iti baba a kanawan a suli ti *screen*. No manen agkidem ti monitor ket agparang ti *screen* saver. Dagus a tulnekanna ti space bar tapno agsubli ti *screen*.

Iti makanawan ti monitor, naiparabaw ti nakanganga a Nangisit a Libro: kirmakirman ti *cursor* iti *screen* ti maudi a letra ti binatog nga: ***addanto nalawa a pagnaan dagiti nabati a tao ti Apo...***

Iti makanigid, aglalaok dagiti naiwara a SandDisck ken PNY. Iti sirok ti lamisaan, nakapsut ti arasaas ti tower. Iti abay ti tower, nakagangat ti berde a *led* ti *printer*, nga iti ngiwatna nakasubo ti agarup sangaramayan ti bengbengna a puraw a papel.

Nakataltalna iti tugawna iti sango ti computer: kasla matmaturog, ngem naipiget dagiti matana iti monitor. Pagammuan agsala dagiti ramayna iti *keyboard* a mangdanggay iti *We've Only Just Begun* dagiti Carpenters manipud iti media player. Apagkirem nga agparang dagiti balikas a mangkamat iti *cursor*. Tulnekan ti kanawan a kikitna ti *delete* no narusanger ti panagsaad wenno biddut dagiti letra a mangbukel iti balikas. No manen pagpusiposenna ti swivel chair, sa kellaat a pagsardengenna iti sango ti computer, ket dagiti bukuan a ramayna agsalada manen kadagiti tekla ti keyboard, a kasla la makilumlumba iti pannakaruros dagiti darikmat. . .

*We've only just begun to live. So many roads to choose. . .*nalamuyot ti agarup arasaas nga ayug.

1. Isasangpet

NAGTUNGED manen ti sabali pay a biahem manipud iti bangir a lubong.

Nagtayabkayo a kasla nagtalaylay iti nagarko a bullalayaw iti nalawa a taaw a namagsilpo iti naggapuanyo ken iti papananyo; a kas man la adda iti tukot ti daga ti kagudua ti bullalayaw a mangbegkes iti lubong. . .

Dimo masinunuo ti immapay a riknam iti umuna nga addangmo iti daga a nakayanakam kalpasan ti adu a tawen a pannakaipusingmo. Mabingbingay ti panunotmo: kadagiti annakmo, ken ti pakabuklan ti sangpetam a pagilian. Ket nangmatamataka, a kas man la awan ni kaingungotmo a kaduam: ania ti pakaigidiatan ti lugar a pinanawam itoy baro a lugar a sarungkaram? Kasanon dagiti annakmo?

No saan la a gapu iti panagkun-os ti barom iti misionna—isu ti naudi kadakuada a lima—nalabit a dimo pay naisapar ti simmarungkar.

Timmayab ti panunotmo iti ruar ti eropuerto, kadagiti umay sumabat kadakayo. Ania ngatan ti langa dagiti tallo a bungayo ken ni kaingungotmo, naulitmo, a di idi nakasurot kadakuada ta nalabesen ti tawenda, ket dagiti la dua nga inaudi ti nakaumay? Adda kadi nagbaliwan ti barom iti walo a tawen a diyo panagkita?

Pagamuan addagitan dagiti sumabat.

Saan la a dagiti tallo a bungayo ken ni kaingungotmo ti simmabat kadakayo. Ti pay kabsatmo a lalaki nga akinkukua iti pick-up, ken dadduma pay a kaanakan ken kakabagyanyo. Makalulua a makiin-innarakup ni kaingungotmo.

Naginnarakupkayo iti barom.

Kinkinuamon? tinapikmo.

Kinessetnak ti dua a tawen iti kalkalsada, 'Pa, kinunana. Ngem nabunga met.

O, sika, kinunam idi arakupennaka ti inauna a balasangmo. Agpatpatiska lattan?

Ni Papa met. Next missionko dayta. Ammom, aya, amangan no subliek 'tay baknang 'diay nagmisionak!

Ket sika? Insublatmo ti nagtengnga a balasangmo.

Alaendak ngaminen ta umayak mangbanniit iti Puraw! inrungiitna.

Komusta ti negosiom? dinamagmo iti kabsatmo idi un-unorenyon ti natrapik a kalsasda.

Medio kimmapsut gapu iti agdama a kasasaad ti ekonomia. Apektado ditoy ti napasamak iti WTC. Ngem umang-anges pay met laeng. Bassit la a pannakisala iti transaksion. Nakaay-ayat ngarud ta uray no saanak a nagturpos, engineer ti awagda kaniak. Diak latta met agun-unin, a. . . Ne, dayta building dita kanigid, dakami ti nangipatakder.

Nagasatka.

'Tay kunakon, nasken nga ammom ti makilinnana kadagiti asitgam tapno mayasidegka iti kusina a kunada. Agyamyamankami ngarud ken ni baket gapu iti sasaadenmi ita. Adu la ketdi ti di mamati. Ngem diak pampanunoten idan. Kinapudnona, adda dagiti taok a mangipagna iti amin a masapsapul, siak laeng ti mangmanmanehar.

Kitaem la a talaga ti biag, kinunam iti kabsatmo. Atiwnakami pay a nagturpos.

Kurangmo ti naidarekdek idi agsardeng ti pick-up iti sango ti ulila a pagtaenganyo.

Kinnan kano ti anay ti adu nga alikamenyo, ken sumagmamano nga urnongmo a magasin ken libro, a yan ti dadduma a sinuratmo. Ngem ti estante nga inaramidmo sumagmamano a tawen sakbay a pimmanawka, saan a sinagid ti anay. Dagiti libro ken magasin ken manuskritom addada pay la iti sigud a yanda.

Kasla dakkel a rengngat ti birri iti tengnga ti kadaklan gapu kano iti ramut ti kaimito nga immulam iti sidiran ti balay. Ngem natakkaban iti alpombra nga inyawidmo iti naminsan a panagbakasionmo manipud iti Dhahran a nagtrabahuam iti mano a tawen.

Ti sigud a bassit nga opisinam iti ekstension, kurang la a marsuoden ti bubongna ket awanen ti nagmamaayan ti lamisaan a nagsursuratam. Ti steel cabinet a yan dagiti rekordmo, a dimo pay ket malagipen no ania, kinnanen ti lati. Adda dadduma nga alikamen iti uneg, ngem amin a naguneg iti opisinam, awan dumada iti basura. Dimo nagustuan ti kumurkurikor iti agongmo a sang-aw ti kuarto, ket dika simrek, sinirsiripmo lattan, ken dimo man la inammo ti naguneg daydiay kinnan ti lati nga steel cabinet.

Isu kadin daytoy daydi balay a pinanawak? naisipmo.

Nagdakkel ti pakaidumaan ti dakkel a balayyo iti naggapuanyo a kanayon a naimeng agbagyo man wenno panawen ti niebe, wenno kalgaw nga uray la a gumayebgeb ti kabakiran iti ruar ti siudad gapu iti napalalo a pudot; saankayo a makunkunatan iti taraon nga ipauneg, lupot nga aruaten, lugan nga agpasiar. . .

Ania lat' inar-aramidyon? pammabalaw ni kaingungotmo kadagiti bungayo.

Awan met ti pagpatarimaanmi, kinuna ti inauna.

No binulan nga agpaw-itak. Ken adda met trabahoyo.

Di pay umanay nga igatangmi iti pagbiagmi.

Agpayso, 'Ma. Adda pay saadko iti opisina, ngem bassit ti sueldo, sa adu ti ikkatenda.

Siak, di pay umanay a pagpletek ti sueldok, kinuna ti maikatlo.

Ania laengen ti serserbi ti inadalyo? Kurang la a naguyaoy ti dilami a nangisakad iti panagadalyo, kasta met laeng ti kapay-anyo!

Dakdakkel ti porsiento ti graduado ngem ti trabaho, kinuna ti inauna. Kitaenyo, tinawen nga adu ti agturpos—kurang la nga agkubbo dagiti nagannak a mangisakad iti panagadal dagiti annakda. Ngem di met manayonan ti trabaho a mabalin a serkan. Uray dianitor, nagturpos iti kolehio. Adu pay ti graduado a peon laeng ti trabahoda, wenno serbidor iti restauran, wenno drayber ti FX. Ti pay ngina ti plete, ken amin a magatgatang. Ken nalipatanyon sa a dua a tawen nga awan ni ading.

Alaendakamin, kunami ngamin, kinuna ti maikatlo.

Sangsangpetko, kinuna ti barom. Ngem dikay' agdanag, 'ton makatrabahoak, daytanto ti umuna a sanguek. . .

II. Alep-ep

URAY man la koma no apagapaman nga anem-em ti maiburayko nga innudo dagiti makasapul kadagidiay a lugar. Uray man la koma no sangkatedted a diro ti maipinas iti kimraang a bibigda. Uray man la koma no sangkapirgis a pranela ti inda pagkukotan.

Asino ti pabasolen?

'Toy pusok mabekbekkel iti tunggal paludip iti sirok ti init; iti tunggal mayaplag a niebe iti lubongko; iti tunggal agbukar a

sabong kadagiti parke ken paraangan; kadagiti agsulbod a bulong ken tumingra a maris, gapu kadagiti agsublisubli a ladawan iti sabali a paset ti lubong. . .

Gapu ta iti sarming ti lagipko adda sadiay dagiti makunkunatan a kararua; a nalabit a maminsan iti makatawen a malinaban ti bitokada; a nalabit nga iti tagtagainep laeng a makapanda kadagiti naranga a lugar a mapmapno iti turista; a makaumayda ditoy lugar a tagtagainep laeng ti bisin, ken lammin, ken alimbasag.

Gapu ta no dadduma matiltiliwak ti agkarayam a lua iti manggapun nga agkinelleng a pingping ti ina no kasdiay a mulmulenglenganna dagiti ladawan iti saklotna.

7:30 P.M.: Iti Sango ti *Computer*—2

NAGSUBLI iti sango ti computer. Tinulnekanna ti space bar ket nagpukaw ti *screen* saver. Nagparang ti agiddeiddep a *cursor* iti murdong ti maudi a balikas iti programa ti Microsoft Word. Nagkiremkirem a nangpalabas kadagiti naisurat.

Nataliawna ti Asul a Libro iti makanawan ti monitor. Madamdama pay, kirmakirmanen ti *cursor* ti baro a binatog a nalikudanna: **no maiturong dagiti ubbing iti umno a dana a surotenda didanto maikalilis.**

Nagsalasala dagiti ramayna iti kanigid, iti laksid ti keyboard, a nangdanggay iti *Top of the World* dagiti Carpenters manipud iti media player.

Adda sayamusom nga insangbay ti immasideg, nagbatay ti dua a dakulap iti agsumbangir nga abagana ket nariknana dagiti naitalmeg a bukuan a ramay.

Nagsabat dagiti uppat a nasneban a bituen.

Kadagita a bituen nagkallatik ti napalabas.

Ken ti masakbayan.

I'm on the top of the world lookin' down on creation, inyunnoy ti media player.

b. Sang-atan-Salugan

TALLO ti nagpilianyo a papanan sakbay a rinugianyo ti agbiahe iti amianan. Iti nagmisionanna ti pili ti inauna, a kenkuana maysa a paraiso; iti nagmisionanna ti pili ti maikatlo; iti siudad ti bantay, a nagmisionanna met, ti pili ti barom. Inkeddengmo nga iti naud-udi tiapananyo ta malabsanyo iti panagpaamiananyo. Ta adda nangnangruna a pakaigapuan ti panagturongyo sadiay: amangan no maudi daytoyen a gundawaymo. Naragsakan ti barom ta masublina dagiti nabatina.

Kasla awan ngudo ti camino real nga agpa-amianan. Apaman a simiasi ti luganyo iti Dakkel a Kalsada, nadlawmo dagiti kinelleng a natnateng, mais, unas, pagay, ken dadduma pay. Nuang, baka, kalding, manok, ken dadduma pay a dinguen. Nalangto ti aglawlaw, ngem iti nagbabaetan dagiti ili, nasulek dagiti matam kadagiti babassit ken daan a balbalay---kailiwmo dagita a buya ta ganggannaetda iti naggapuanyo.

Kinitam dagiti annakmo. Agang-angsot dagiti babbalasangmo, agkarapungngail ti ulo ti barom kadagiti malabsanyo, ket ibagbagana no ania dagita.

Sementado ti agsang-at ken agiwet-iwet a kalsada. Manipud iti nadagaang a baba, lumamlamiis ti pul-oy a subaen ti lugan. Manipud iti naangrag a buya, kunam la no umis-isem dagiti manglangitlangit a nalalangto a kayo iti agsumbangir. Naursa ti matangad a bakras ti bantay ken makaaliaw ti rangkis nga agpababa iti kanigid ken iti kanawan. Saan a napartak ti panagtaray ti lugan no idiligmo iti naggapuanyo ngem agkuy-os ti riknam tunggal kumitaka iti derraas wenno no agsikko ti lugan ket maisango iti teppang. No dadduma makasarunokayo iti dadakkel a lugan nga agan-anikki a mangisang-at iti kargada. Nadlawmo ti kasla di yaanges ti makina ti luganyo ta kaaduanna a nakasegunda wenno tersera laeng. No dadduma tumaliawka iti nalikudanyo ket kas man la diyo maadaywan ti naggapuanyo nga agiwet-iwet a kalsada. Agal-aligagaw dagiti babbalasangmo.

Di ngamin kasla paraiso? kinuna ti barom. Makitayonto ti nagsangsang-atak . . .

Iti maysa a pagpikoran, natalenten dagiti agsang-at a lugan, ket iti adayo a ngato, natangadyo ti maur-uram a trak. Dimo ammo no kasano

ti kaadayo ti kaasitgan a yan ti bombero, ngem inabutnakayo ti mano nga oras sakbay a nakalusotkayo iti dayta a buya. Maisursurat iti isipmo dagiti buya ken pasamak itoy a lugar a nalabit nga awan ti aniamanna kadagiti annakmo ngem para kenka maysa daytoy a kinadatdatlag ti nakaparsuaan. Kas pagarigan dagiti pasdek iti rangrangkis a kas man la takuptakop ti buttabuttaw a kambas ti pintura. Adu dagiti pasdek a langada ti agtutuon. Dadakkel ken babassit. A laklakay nga amang ngem sika iti aginnem-a-pulomon, ngem iti takderda natibkerda pay la a sumaranget iti ania man a karit ti nakaparsuaan.

Idi agtakderkayo iti ngarab ti rangkis iti maysa a parke a yan ti adu a tagilako nga aramid dagiti natibo, ti riknam kasla adda iti ngarab ti paraiso: dagiti natukantukad a bantay, a nalalangto ken ap-apungolen ti angep, a dagiti balbalay wenno pasdek iti bakrang wenno tuktokda arigda man iti pintora nga Obra Maestra.

Impasiarnakayo ti barom kadagiti napnapananna: sumang-at-sumalog. Inyam-ammonakayo kadagiti gagayyem ken iti pangulona iti mision—agduduma a puli.

Paraiso ditoy, kinuna ti barom a kasla nakabasa iti panunotmo. Ngem adda met nakas-ang a mapaspasamak. Makitayo dagita a bakras ken pasdek? Sobra ti ginggined. . .

Wen, naamirismo: Obra Maestra ti dua nga agsupadi a buya!

Dayta ti nangpasingked iti agum-umok iti panunotmo: iti daytoy a paraiso, adda leblebna a nasipnget.

Nagbalawka idi mariknam a lumamlamiis ken lumidlidem ti aglawlaw. Malemen. Nasken a sumalogkayon ta ituloyyo ti agbiahe. Nawatiwat pay ti dalan.

Ngem kas man la dinakayo palubosan dayta a lugar a pumanaw iti saklotna. Nakabengbengbeng dagiti lugan a nangsullat iti amin a kalsada. Kasda man la naitukeng ket kayatdan ti margaan iti yanda, a kasla ditoyen ti pagtungedan ti dalanda. . .

Nakalusotkayo iti nabengbeng a trapiko. Saanen nga iti sinang-atanyo ti saluganyo. Ngem agpadada a naursa. Nasipngeten ti kalsada nga agpababa.

Uray no ipalpalagipmo iti drayberyo ti panagannadna, iti panagriknam kasla maipampana ti lugan nga agpababa, sa aganit-it dagiti pilid no

agpreno no adda masabat wenno kadagiti pagpikuran nga adda matupar a derraas. Dimo kayat a panunoten ngem umagibas latta iti mugingmo: ania ngata ti pagmamayan ti bagi dagiti matnag iti derraas? Uray da kaingungotmo ken dagiti bungayo, naulimekdan, nalabit a kas kenka a dida kayat a panunoten nga addada iti lugan iti kasta nga oras iti kasta a gundaway ken iti kasta a lugar.

Adda nakamakamyo a bus ngem kasla dina kayat ti masaligan isu nga inip-ipusan lattan ti drayberyo.

Pagamuan ta nasinga ti panagdakiwas ti panunotmo iti ranipak iti masanguananyo. Kellaat met a nagpreno ti luganyo ket kurang la naipuruak iti nakarungaab a derraas.

Iti nagpikoran, natan-awanyo dagiti nasilawan ti luganyo a naspak a sangsanga iti ngarab ti derraas ket iti baba makatitileng ti ikkis ken asug, nga inalun-on ti bettak ket pinisang ti gil-ayab ti nabengbeng a sipnget.

Apo Dios! nayesngaw ni kaingungotmo.

Napanganga dagiti annakyo.

Napunno ti bus iti pasahero ket natayda amin malaksid ti tallo nga agngangabit nga intarayda iti ospital.

Naisipmo: panagsang-at. . . panagsalog. . .

III. Likud ti Rupa

NO apay ngamin a nasken ti itataliaw iti naggapuan—agsublisubli dayta a saludsod iti mugingko, uray no adda sungbat nga agiddeiddep, saanak a mapnek. No dadduma ammok a pudno ti sungbat ti saludsodko ngem into no kuan saludsodek manen ti isu met la a saludsod, a kasla batibat nga agsublisubli. Apalak no kua dagiti agtutubo ta kas man la awan iti panunotda ti adda iti panunotko. Wenno nalabes ngata ti panangiturturongko ti isipko kadagiti banag a pulos a di umapay iti muging dagiti agtutubo?

Adu unay ti ladawan nga umap-appayaw nangruna no ikidemko ti aguldag—yisemda ti agsasala manipud iti no sadino a ginget ti utekko ket kasda la manglukluko nga agawis iti nadumaduma a ladawan.

Ket addaytan, agaayawdan: ti napalabas, ti agdama, ken ti masakbayan. Maatil ti panunotko ket saanak a makaturog.

Umay ket umay dagiti rupa. . .

9:00 P.M.: Iti Sango ti *Computer*—3

ADDA ti Nangisit a Libro iti kanigid, napakleb ket kasla duri ti kubbo a nataengan ti nagsasaipan dagiti binulong iti likud. Kublakublang dagiti letra iti duri ken iti sango ti libro ngem langana pay laeng ti di sumuko iti basnot ti aglabas a panawen.

Nasulek dagiti matana iti balikas a kiremkireman ti *cursor*: Rupa.

Umir-irteng ti rupana a daddadangen ti bombilia a naimuntar iti sinan-ima a kasla manggawgaw-at iti monitor. Makaturturog ti arasaas ti tower a mangbibiag iti computer: nakagangat pay laeng ti *led* ti *printer*, a nakangangan ta naakasen dagiti naisubo a papel a naurnosen iti kanawan a sikigan ti monitor, iti uluanan ti *keyboard*. Nanayonan dagiti naiwara a diskette iti agsumbangir a sikigan ti monitor.

Adda anas-as nga immasideg: ti nakaduster a nagiggem iti tasa nga agal-alisuaso. Indissona iti abay ti Nangisit a Libro. Naawis ti imatangna iti *screen* a nakabasaanna iti binatog a linikudan itan ti *cursor*: **ti tao a nagna iti kasipngetan makakitanto iti lawag**. Piniselna ti agsumbangir nga abaga ti nakatugaw sa timmallikud.

Nagsala manen dagiti ramayna iti *keyboard* a nangdanggay iti *Solitaire* dagiti Carpenters manipud iti media player ket naglulumba dagiti letra a mangkamat iti *cursor* iti *screen*.

There was a man, a lonely man, inyunnoy ti media player.

c. Dapan

BABAEN ti silaw ti luganyo, napaliiwmo a kasla nabiit pay a nasemento ti nailet a kalsada a kumamang iti purok da tatangmo. Dandani met di makastrek ti lugan iti solar iti adu a mula nga agbunga, ken arig la nagrerekketan ti nakurang a sangapulo a balbalay.

In-inut a nagparang dagiti tao iti ridawda. Kakabagyanyo kano amin ida. Dimo ninamnama ti kaaduda. Apay a nagdadarisonda iti yan ni tatangmo?

Ti balay ni tatangmo, adda a mismo iti nagtungedan ti agduapulo a metro a dalan wenno paraangan. Naraniag ti hasag a naibitin iti sangapuon a mangga iti sidiran ti ridaw.

Napintek ni tatangmo a nangsirarat kadakayo.

Ti anakkon, Apo! simngaw kadagiti kirriit a bibigna.

Malasinmo pay 'toy manugangmo, 'Tang? Ken dagitoy dagiti tallo nga inauna nga agtawid iti naganmo. Nabati dagiti dua. . .

Nagmano dagiti annakmo.

Karuprupam kano unay ni tatangmo. Nataytayagka laeng, aglalo ta manggapun a tallikudanna ti langit. Isuna laeng ta kasla dina iginggina ti panangmulmol kenkuana ti panawen. Natangken pay la dagiti piskelna a tinenneb ti init ken tudo kadagiti tambak ken sinilong. Kasla awan nagnaan ti sinamirna a puyat ken utoy ken nagsayasay a darana idiay gubatan idi maikadua a gubat ti lubong. Iti nasuroken a walopulona, kas man la di kabaelan a daleben ti panawen.

Kinuna ni tatangmno idi makapagwayaskayo nga in-inut nga immasideg kenkuana dagiti kaarrubana idi rumikot ti panagbiagda. Naawatam a dagus ti kayatna a sawen, a sungbat ti saludsodmo.

Adda barito a kadkadua kano ni tatangmo, anak ti maysa a kasinsinmo iti murdong ti pagilian iti amianan. Isu kano ti napan nagbanniit ken naglawin iti dalag, buntiek ken paltat nga insaganada kadakayo. Bassit kanon ti makalapan ngem adda pay la maala no maanusam. Inimasyo ti pinulpogan a dalag nga insawsawyo iti artem a sili.

Nadlawmo ti naikuadro a ladawan da tatangmo ken daydi nanangmo iti sakaanan ti papag iti kuartona.

Nalitemen ti ladawan ngem nabiag latta agiti mata daydi nanangmo a di nakalasat idi ipasngayna ti buridek a kabsatmo.

Ammom lattan: diyo mabalin ti agtuloy nga agpaamianan iti dayta a rabii.

Uray no ita man la a rabii ti palabsenyo iti sidong ni tatangmo.

Ta amangan no dinton masunotan.

Natangken ti suelo a nagiddaanyo ket nupay narigatanka a nangyunnat iti likudmo idi damo, iniliwmo ti nakaisigudam nga idda--iti balayyo iti naggapuanyo, dakkel a dekutson a kama ti iddayo nga agassawa. Binakol nga abel Iluko ti inruar ni Tatangmo manipud iti daan a lakasa ket nailasinmo a dagus dagita uray no adun a tawen ti napalabas. Inim-imluyan daydi Nanangmo dagita, ket uray no agappempen iniliwmo a sinanggol--dimo pinagules ta dagaangenka.

Nalukagka iti taraok, a sinaruno ti nagsasaruno a taraok, ket inimasmo dayta a kas man la dayyeng nga indateng ti agbukar nga agsapa.

Sakbay a nagluaskayo, impasiarnakayo ni tatangmo iti kataltalonan.

Nakaranting ni tatangmo a nangyuna, a sinaruno ti barom, a nangtalaytay iti tambak kadagiti sinilong kalpasan ti panamigatyo ket kas man la nakalaglag-an ti riknana a mangitudotudo kadagiti nalangto a pinagayan. Inipusnaka ni kaingungotmo idinto a maay-ayatan dagiti babbalasangmo a no manen aggurnot iti nagtamed a dawa sada kutiman.

Nagsardengka iti ngalay ti maysa a tambak ket inwarasmo ti panagkitam iti nakayaplagan ti pinagayan iti daya. Ti sayamusom nga isangbay ti pul-oy-agsapa iti agongmo, inna palasbangen dagidi panagsaksakaymo iti bukot ni Sikkubeng kadagidi panagraraep ken panagani. Itayabnaka ti riknam nga agaliwaksay ket kas man la addaka iti bassit a paraiso a di magaw-at ti inaldaw a pulkok. Dagita a tambak, danada met a talaytayen dagiti mariing a dapan iti tunggal agsapa, a maisupadi kadagiti nagkurosan iti siudad a pangyab-abagaanyo iti inaldaw nga imetyo.

Kasano nga agpakadaka iti karuprupam unay nga ama? Kasano a panawam daytoy nagtaudam nga agsulsulo a mangyabaga iti aldawna? No isaadmo ti bagim iti bagina, paggapuan ngata pay ti agayuyang nga isem kadagiti bibigmo? Adda ngata pay isem nga agbukar kadagiti kirriit a bibigna?

Ditoy kadin ti pagtungedan ti bukodna a dalan itoy a biag?

Inkayon, annakko, kinunana idi agpakadakayo. Inkayon tapno makadanonkayo iti papananyo. Didak pampanunoten. Ti lubongko. . . ditoy. Ti lubongyo. . .

Dimo nayebkas ti balikas a nagbatay iti murdong ti dilam.

Nairut ti panangarakupmo ken ni tatangmo. Panunotem laeng no agkitakayonto pay malunagen ti riknam. Apay ngamin a kastoy?

IV. Nakusnaw a Ladawan

DUA a ladawan ti nakusnaw ngem agsublisubli iti alintataok. Iti tuktok ti bantay a kabayyabasan adda maysa a bassit a balay a nagtagipan-aw, nagtagibulo, ken nagdatar iti inakilis a kawayan. Iti tengnga ti bangkag iti amianan, narnuoyan iti sabong ti katuday. Iti abagatan, nabengbeng ti kabuluan nga agpababa--kinalatkatan ti nalangto nga ubi a narnuoyan iti bunga ken agbirbirri ti daga a bumbumkongan ti bagas dagiti pinuon.

Apagtangkayag ti init iti daya. Iti sidiran ti balay, adda sangapasagad a dua a burnay a danum a nasakdo iti adayo nga abagatan. Digdigosennak daydi a simmantamaria, nga idi la a nakitak. Naanus ti timekna; sumangkaanus pay a nanglidlid iti kimbaal a kabkabko.

Naruros ti binulong ti kalendario ket sabali pay a nakusnaw a ladawan ti agampaampayag. Idiay bassit a purok, masmasnaayan a mangyab-abaga kadagiti lima a naadiadi a bunga nga imbati daydi nagawan.

Padpadasek nga ilangaan kalpasan ti no mano a tawenen. Isu ngata pay daydi rupa a simmantamaria? Awanakon idiay, Anakko, insuratna iti naminsan. . .

10:30 P.M.: Iti Sango ti *Computer* --4

AWANEN ti tasa a pagal-alisuasuan ti mainum iti abay ti keyboard. Nayalis manen ti Nangisit a Libro iti kanawan, ngem nakaukrad latta dagiti binulongna. Salasalaan ti *cursor* ti maudi a binatog: **nailet ti dana a kumamang iti biag.** Awan ti nakatugaw iti sango ti computer, agub-ubo ti danum iti pagpaknian. Umang-anges pay laeng ti tower ken nakagangat latta ti *led* ti *printer*. Pagamuan nagari ti *screen* saver iti monitor, agbaliwbaliw ti buya.

Bimmengbeng dagiti naurnos a papel a naakas manipud iti *printer* iti abay ti keyboard.

Iti bangir a siled, iti masters bedroom, awan ti mangngeg nga anasaas.

Nailukat ti ridaw ti pagpaknian, sa nairikep. Nailukat ti ridaw ti siled a yan ti computer ket simmabat ti nakamulagat a monitor. Nasam-it ti *Only Yesterday* dagiti Carpenters.

After long enough of being alone, inyunnoy ti media player.

d. Kabagis ti Ina

NASAPA pay ngem agdudungsan dagiti babbalasangmo idinto a naulimek ni kaingungotmo a mangisursurot iti panagkitana iti aglawlaw; sangkakalbitnaka ti barom a mangitudotudo iti malabsanyo. Maysa kadagiti nalabsanyo ti rangtay a di pay nalpas a natarimaan ta rinebban sa kano idi ti dakkel nga ayus wenno ginggined, wenno ania man a didigra. Sa idi kuan, malabsanyon ti purok a linamut ti apuy idi panawen ti nadawel a politika. Sa ti simbaan iti tuktok ti turod. Saan a mabayag, addagitan dagiti sinilong a napno iti natnateng. Malagipmo a nakurang a sangagasut a porsiento ti dagup dagiti ili iti daytoy a paset ti pagilian ti agnagan iti nadumaduma a santo wenno santa.

Ibagbagam amin dagitoy kadagiti annakmo, tapno, kunam, maikkanda iti pamalpalatpatan ti lugar a nagtaudan ti puonda. Naraniag dagiti mata ti barom a dumngeg idinto a mapaspasurot dagiti babbalasangmo.

Ti lubongko, anak. . . ditoy. Ti lubongyo. . . *balikas dagita ni tatangmo.*

Ket nakadanonkayo iti ili a dagasanyo. Dayta ili a dagasanyo isu ti puon ni tatangmo. Ngem awan ti ammom nga am-ammom, no adda pay nabati kadagidi nabatbati. Awanen ti nakadamdamagam. Nangngegmo laeng idi es-estoriaen daydi Lelongmo a daytoy nga ili ti nagtaudanda. Ngem in-inut a nagwarasda: iti amianan, daya, abagatan. Idi kuan, iti ganggannaet. Ne, agkakabagiantayo gayam, pagamuan ta adda masagangmo nga agkuna. Wen la ketdi, kunam met lattan ta ti kaputotanyo babassit kano amin.

Ditoy nga ili ti nagtaudan ti sumagmamano a malalaki iti literatura, ken iti pagbabakalan.

Saan a puon ni tatangmo ti pakaigapuan ti dagasanyo. Ti nabatbati a kabsat daydi Nanangmo, a naipadpad laeng ditoy ta iti kabangibang nga ili ti nakaipasngayanna, ti gapu.

Nasarakanyo iti dayaen ti poblasion. Ti rupa daydi sigud a simmantamaria nga adda iti isipmo, maigidiaten iti adda iti sangom. Inangragen ti panawen, kinessen ti adu a dagensen daytoy nga ina..

Anian a rimat dagiti matana ken isem dagiti kirriit a bibigna ket inarakupnakayo idi makitanakayo..

Ay, ti anakkon, Apo, ti anakkon! Nalapunosen dagiti matana idi tangadennaka.

Napintas gayam ti lelangmi no aglua! kinuna ti barom.

Marmarbibi nga immisem ti ikitmo; nagkatawa dagiti babbalasangmo iti puted.

Nagtalaytay a nagsubli ti isipmo iti adun a panawen a naikupin. Donia idi idiay siudad, saan nga agtatrabaho ta dakkel ti tegged daydi lakayna nga Electrical Engineer. Agbasaka, uray no bokasional laeng, kinunana idi, ngem dina inkaskaso. Idi pinarmek ti sarut daydi lakayna, a babassit pay dagiti annakda kapilitan a nagkarkarawa iti kasipngetan ket nagsubli iti bassit a purok. Sadiay nga inkaradapna dagiti babassit pay nga annakna. Nailakona amin a mabalinna nga ilako a napanawan daydi lakayna, ket idi naibusen, dagiti marabamban a ramayna kapilitan a naggatud iti napigket ken naingel a birhinia, nagtudok ken nagpuyat. Ket nasimpalungan ti maysa nga artek ken walay ket nagdennada agingga a binurak ti bala dagiti di mangikankano ti bangabangana. Dimo ammon ti adu a pasamak ta nabayag nga awan ti damagmo. Sumagmamano kapirgis laeng ti naipatpatayab kenka.

Narangtayan manen ti libbawangyo idi mabasana ti maysa a sinuratmo a yan ti addressmo, ket sinuratannaka. Manopulo a tawenen a dikayo nagkita?

Imismisaankayo, annakko, ta bareng no ipaay ni Apo Dios nga intay pay agkikita. Imismisaak daydi lelongyo, ken daydi lelangyo, ken daydi angkelyo. Nangruna daydi Nanangyo, daydi naanus a Nanangyo. Asino kadi pay ti innak kamangan ket sisiak metten ti nabati kadakami nga agkakabsat? Dagidiay kakasinsinyo? Dida pay mabiag ti bagbagida.

Dagita a balikas ti ikitmo inda linunag ti riknam. Nakaas-asi nga agpayso daydi Nanangyo, ngem naasi met daytoy nabatbati, ken uray daydi lelangmo a nanangna. Ngem ti panawen, apo, ta no mabalin la ngata ket

didan maturog tapno trabaho, trabaho, trabaho, agingga nga aguyaoy ti dilada.

Wen, daytoy nagangon a simmantamaria, isu nga adda ditoy, ta kayatna pay ti agbiag. Mangarkaramut nga agserserbi iti sabali a tao tapno masilpuan pay ti biagna. Nasuroken a pitopulona, ngem nakaranting pay laeng, wenno dina ket ngata iginggina ti ania man a bannog wenno utoy wenno ania pay a didigra ti panawen iti essemna nga agriingto pay iti sumuno nga agsapa.

V. Allon

MANON a tawen a diak nakita daydiay a lugar? Nasurok a tallopulo? No saanak a pimmanaw, ania ngata koma itan ti kasasaadko? Linadogak ngata koma met wenno kinesset ti apgad ti danum? Idiay koma latta metten ti nagpuspusiposak a kasla napiringan a nuang nga agdapil, saan a nagbaliw ti dalanko ket awan ti ammok a ladawan iti sabali a lubong malaksid iti saggabassit a madamdamagko. Nalabit a di koma met nagtugmok ti dalanmi ken ni kaingungot ket sabali la ketdi a kararua ti simrek iti biag kadagiti annakko. Maysaak koma kadagiti nabatbati a nanangadtangad laeng kadagiti bituen ken bulan ken init kadagiti regkang ket sagsangabukel nga ar-aro wenno pimmaltat wenno ragragutirit wenno pukpuklo, balbalulang ken kulot ti pinangep-epko iti sarsaraaw dagiti annakko. Ngem asino koma ti nangpappapudot iti ikamenko? Maysa a kinurkuriban ti kadilian ken tangrib ken ngiwat iti parparaangan a makitintinnukad nga agkarukay iti wakray a buok iti malem wenno agsapa wenno agmatuon. Kankantaak koma met ti kabus a bulan iti sintonado a di umabot iti paraiso. . .

11:59 A.M.: Iti Sango ti *Computer*—5

NAIBUSEN ti mainum iti tasa iti makanigid ti monitor ket iti makanawanna nakanganga ti Nangisit a Libro.

Iti likud ti *cursor* naiban-uyat ti: **mapunnonto ti daga iti sirib ti Apo, kas iti pananglapunos ti danum iti baybay.**

Nabengbeng manen ti papel iti ngiwat ti *printer* a nakamulagat latta ti *led* iti pispisna.

Nalamuyot ti kimmapsut nga ayug ti *For All We Know* dagiti Carpenters. Mabingbingay ti turong ti pispisna.

Ngem kaykayatna no kasta ta aggagampur dagiti pasamak nga ad-adda a mamagmaris kadagiti ladawan a maipinta iti ipus ti *cursor*.

So much to say and as we go from day to day, arasaas ti unnoy ti media player.

e. Nagtalawan

IMBILINMO iti drayber nga iparpartakna ti agpataray. Atiddog pay ti daliasatenyo, adda pay maysa a sang-atenyo sakayonto sumalog sa ituloyyo a panurnoren ti atiddog a camino real. Malabsanyonto ti nakaitamnan daydi Nanangmo iti daya ti kalsada sakbay nga agsikkokayo nga agpa-laud ket dita a pagpikuran, kas man la di kinnan ti panawen ti nagadalam iti sekundaria, dimmakkel sa man ket kasla ad-adda a timmangig iti turod a nagtakderanna. Napabaro metten ti merkado iti lauden ti pagadalan, ket awan ti mailasinmo kadagiti pasdek a linabsanyo sakbay a simrekkayo iti kalsada nga agturong iti lelennekan. Dita, awanen ti nakitam a kalesa, kabalio ken kutsero. Ketdi, traysikel ken sumagmamano a dyip ti agururayen iti pasahero.

Sementado ti kalsada. Nagluposen, nakunam. Ngem idi makasalogkayo iti sumina a sanga iti kanawan, nadlawmo a putedputed ti sementado. Ken lasunglasong ti kaaduan a pasetna.

Nagturposka iti maikanem iti nalabsanyo nga eskuela a nangsaedan kadakayo dagiti mangisursuro ta nakitanaka ti maysa kadakuada idi nagsardengkayo ta retratuem ti eskuela, ket naammuanna a sika daytay mannurat a paboritona. Pinadagasdakayo.

Nagtaruskayo iti igid ti kadilian ta linabsanyo ti purok a nangbuklam iti kinaagtutubom, ket iniliwmo ti isem ti tangrib ken kadilian a nagnunnunogam no awan ti klasem iti sekundaria. Awan nadlawmo a nagbaliwanna; kas man la dagidi allon a pinanawam isuda pay laeng a siaayat a mangsarabo kadagiti matam. Adu ti inabelmo nga arapaap iti sidong dagiti dalluyon.

Idi dumagaskayo iti purok, nagsubli iti mugingmo ti adu nga isem ti bulan ken kiremkirem dagiti bituen bayat ti panangimutektekmo iti nagluposen a lugar iti baro a takuptakop a buya ti kimmebkeb a kinakurapay. Awanen daydi regkang a pagtaengan a nangukopam iti adu nga arapaap. Kasla matmaturog a bindog ti simmukat a pagtaengan.

Pinurokdakayo dagiti rutayrutay a kinirog ti apgad ket nagmarikadkad dagiti annakmo. Adda terrem iti mata ni kaingungotmo.

Kitaem ti pinanawanyo, anakko, kinuna ti ulitegmo a nakatultulang. Pimmanawkayo. . .. Nalipatanayo ti lugar a dinakkelanyo. Nabatikami, a matayto met a kas kadagiti immunan. . . a mangipatpateg itoy a lugar.

Naipas ti riknam. Uray no nanumo dagiti pinanawanyo adda met riknada a mangimutektek.

Agpayso kadi, 'Pa? Saan a naisina dagiti mata ti barom iti sango ti lugan idi ituloyyo ti agpadaya. Inawidmo ti abagana.

I. Karayan

MASANSAN a sungbatak ti saludsodko iti *diak ammo* sakbay nga agpanunotak. Kas man la diak kayat nga umatiddog ti kanito a di agandar ti panunotko.

Nakulkol? Ngata ketdi. No kitkitaek, kasla nakulkol a sinulid dagiti pasamak nga inabel ti kaputotak. Ti karayan ti biagmi, saan a kas iti Karayan Parsua a manipud iti Kimmandela iti bakrang ti dakkel a bantay iti daya, nagtartarus ti ayusna aginga iti baybay iti laud, malaksid ti bassit a sangana a kimmamang iti waig iti amianan sa met la nakitipon iti laud.

Ti biagmi? Nadumaduma ti turongna. Kasla koma daytay kuitis nga agbukar a sinansabong iti ngato sa kasla petalo a mapursing iti ungkayna.

Ti la adda a nakaipurpuruakanmi. . . Nasayyasayyakami.

1:43 P.M.: Iti Sango ti *Computer-6*

NAYABAY iti Nangisit a Libro dagiti kaak-akas a papel manipud iti *printer.*

Nakamulagat latta ti *cursor* iti murdong ti naudi a balikas ti maudi a binatog iti *screen*: ***ti nasayaat a kayo agbunga iti nasayaat, ti rinuker a kayo mangted iti dakes a bunga.*** Nalamuyot ti arasaas ti tower. Nalamuyot ti arasaas nga ayug ti *(They Long To Be) Close To You* a kanta dagiti Carpenters nga aggapu iti media player.

Di pay nagbaliw ti darang ti bombilia iti ngatuen ti monitor. . .

f. Puon ti Pakak

NANGMATAMATAKA iti agsumbangir ti camino real. Palpaliiwem ti nagbaliwan dagidi ammom a lugar. No adda nanganan ti panawen. Dagiti nagtubo a pasdek. Ken narpuog. Isu pay laeng a kalsada. Isu pay laeng nga akasia--ti ket tibkerda a nangsuba iti saanen a mabilang a saplit ti panawen.

Isu daytoyen ti ili a nakaipasngayan daydi naasi a nanangmo. Nga iti uluananna iti daya a nagtakderan ti Kimmandela, sadiay ti puon ti lagipmo: iti Pangasaan Elementary School.

Ibagbagam amin dagitoy iti kaingungot ken kadagiti annakyo.

Intudom ti tiendaan iti kanawan. Dita ti immuna a nakaramanak iti sorbetes, kinunam. Ice cream, inyaturmo ta didan sa maawatan ti sorbetes. Nga insublim ti apa ta nadadael iti panangdildilpatmo sa nagtartarayka nga immadayo a nangsapul ken ni nanangmo amangan no agunget ti sorbetero.

Nakadanonkayo iti karayan ti nakaparsuaan. Impaisardengmo ti luganyo iti sangi ti rangtay ket inlawlawagmo a dayta a karayan ti pinasurong ken pinababayo iti panamagsilpoyo iti kabayabasan iti surong ken iti bassit a purok iti baba. Adda paset ti kinaubingko sadiay, kinunam, nga ad-adda a naiturong iti bagim.

Intay' man kitaen, kinuna ti barom.

Makapagnaka, aya? kinuna dagiti babbalasangmo.

Awan panawentayo, kinuna ti kaingungotmo.

Nagulimek dagiti kaduam idi nakadanonkayo iti sungaban ti kalsada nga agpalaud.

Nasemento bassit--kasla nasaywan laeng iti subsobra a semento. Nailet ta marigatan ket ngata nga agsabat ti dua a lugan. Nadagaang ti angin a

yap-apros dagiti kayo ken kawayan iti agsumbangir. Manopulo a tawenen? naisipmo. Adda pay ngata dagidi sakasaka; dagiti maipalpalnaaw idi kabudo ti politika? Awan kadi ti nakalagip iti daytoy a ginget ti lubong? Dagidi nagtatalaw nga annakna, yandan, naisipmo. Ngem yanmo kadi metten? Nalaglagipmo, ngem kasano ti pananglagipmo?

Iti pattapattam kapatas ti kalsada ti natirkagan a karayan iti amianan a sikigan. Nadamdamagmo idi a no agdinakkel ti karayan lapunosenna ti sangabukel a sitio ken ti kataltalunanna ket makisinnabat iti danum nga ibil-a ti dakkel a waig iti abagatan.

Iti abagatan ti kalsada malabsanyo ti lugar a nakaisuratan ti maysa a paset ti biagmo, ngem imbagam a labsanyo pay laeng sayonto dagasen no agsublikayo, tangay dikayo met agbayag. Adda kangrunaan a paset ti kinataom a kayatmo a makita, nga isu ti ad-adda a nakaigapuan ti panagpa-amiananyo.

Daydiay lugar nga immuna a nakakitaam iti lawag. Daydiay lugar a sinirsirmatam iti adu a panawen. Daydi maab-abel a ladawan iti mugingmo, maigidiat unay iti nasaksiam. Immadayo ti karayan iti amianan. Nalangto dagiti mula iti aglawlaw. Ngem ti kalsada, ama, ta lipit laeng iti panagkitam. Dagidi sumaggapat a balbalay, awanen ti nabati. Nagkaruotanen.

Daydi pakak, nakitam, babaen ti panangipatuldo dagiti tao a nadanonyo. Dakdakkel ngem sangarakepan ti puon a ngimmisit iti nakadalebanna.

Ti siddaawem, nakitam pay laeng dayta a puon. Kalpasan ti nakurang nga innem-a-pulo a tawen, adda pay laeng dayta napuri a puon daydi pakak. Ket pakak laeng, saan a maibilang a nalagda wenno makipinnaut iti panawen. Ngem addayta.

Iti sirok daydi pakak nga isu dayta a pakak, nagtakder ti bassit a balay, wenno kalapaw ket iti uneg dayta a pagtaengan, isu ti immuna a nakakitaam iti lawag. Dita ti immuna a nakangngegan ti lubong iti timekmo. Ken dandani nakatungdayan ti apagsipasip nga aldawmo idi timmayab ti maysa a dakkel a bala ti Hapon a simrek iti nakalukat a tawa sa limmumlom iti sakaanan ti tallo ti tukadna nga agdan. Uray daydi nanangmo dandani met napukaw iti daydi a kanito ta ad-adawennaka

iti indayon idi kimmay-ab ti kasla layap a beggang iti sango ti rupana nga isu dayta ti bala.

Kabagianyo kano pay la dagiti tao a nangipatuldo iti puon ti pakak. Dagiti tao nga inagapadda, isuda ti namagsilpo kadagidi nariingam a nagan, nga adu kanon ti pimmusay.

Dagidi a tao ti kinapulpulapol ni tatangmo. Am-ammoda unay ni tatangmo gapu iti kinabeteranona iti maikadua a gubat ti sangalubongan. Inlemlemmenganna idi dagiti kabusor iti maikadua a gubat. Intaraytarayna kano idi daydi manongmo nga inaunaanyo nga agkakabsat iti daydi teppang ti karayan dita amianan. Kadagidiay kinawayanan iti daya, intartaraynaka met daydi nanangmo ket nasiitan pay iti siit ti kawayan dayta alipusposmo gapu iti panangigagana kenka kadagiti nagdakiwas a makapili ken Hapon.

Nagkidemka a nanglagip ket ad-adda pay a limmangto dagiti buya iti mugingmo iti nalamiis a pul-oy a nangapiras iti rupam a nagtugotan dagiti naglabas a panawen. No awan koma ti kaduam, ita, yuldagmo iti linong ti kayo iti abagatan ti nabual a puon ti pakak ket bay-am nga agannurot dagidi panagbasbasayo iti pagadalan ti elementaria; dagidi panagiinnubor dagiti ubbing iti purokyo kadagiti ubbing iti sabali a purok; daydi panangkagat ti dadauloyo ti lapayag ti dadaulo ti sabali a grupo. Dagidi panagtakawyo iti kamas, wenno panagpuriyo iti garit, banila, wenno gagangay nga unas no agawidkayo iti aldaw wenno iti malem.

Ditoy kadi a talaga ti nakayanakam, 'Pa? Kinuna ti barom.

Wow, naglangto ti aglawlaw! Nayesngaw dagiti babbalasangmo. Ngem apay nga awan balbalay?

Nagreretratokayo sakbay a nagbueltakayo nga agpa-daya. Inalaannaka pay ti barom iti solom iti abay ti puon ti pakak, nga adda agpadpadegges a rikna iti kaunggam.

Iti idadagasyo iti purok a maysa a paset ti kinataom, nakitam ti dakkel a nagbaliwanna. Awanen dagidi dua kapuon a bakkalaw iti abagatan ti solar. Awanen dagiti balay nga ammom. Babassit met la ti naisukat, a kasla kumkumleb a piek. Awan nakitam a ladawan ti panagdur-as.

Nakakitaka iti sumagmamano nga am-ammom, a dandani dimo ida nailasin uray no agaraup agkakaedadkayo, gapu iti adu a nanganan ti panawen iti rupada.

Kakaasi ti tao, kinuna ti maysa.
Manmanokamin a nabatbati, binagi ti sabali.
Dagidi pimmanaw, saandan a timmaliaw. . .
Awan dumngeg iti ararawmi. . .
Tulengda. . .
Dumtengto ti panawen nga agsabat ti dua a karayan a mangyanud
itoy a lugar.
Ayaunayen, kimmebkeb iti panunotmo.

VII. Mangyaw-awan

PADPADASEK nga alat-aten dagiti pasamak. Ngem nautoy ta atiddog ti nakaiban-uyatanna. Maibuston ti orasko ngem atiddogto latta ti mabati a sinulid a pagduaduaak no addanto anus dagiti annakko a mangkatikat ta ti lubongko maigidiat iti lubongda kas iti pannakaigidiat ti lubong ni tatang iti lubongko. Makasalawdanto iti mangyaw-awan a kas iti nasalawko.

3:51 A.M.: Iti Sango ti *Computer*--7

NAIPARABAW ti tasa nga agal-alisuaso mamen iti Nangisit a Libro iti makanigid ti monitor a pangsalsalaan ti *cursor* iti: ***iturongnatayo ti Dios iti dalanna, ket magnatayo iti danana.*** Nalamuyot ti naliday nga ayug ti *A Song For You* dagiti Carpenters iti media player. Napartak ti lagtit ti *cursor* a kamkamaten dagiti maipinta a ladawan iti *screen*.

g. Nagsangaan

WEN, naggapukayon kadagiti sinarungkaranyo a ladawan ti napalabas.
Kinitam iti napaut dagiti annakmo.
Nawatiwat ti camino real nga unorenyo nga agsubli. Naulimekkayo
amin.
Inabutnakayo ti sipnget iti ngalay ti tallo a nagsangaan ti kalsada:
kanigid, kanawan ken iti tengnga.

Diyo nasurot ti umno a turong, nga isu koma ti mangitunda kadakayo iti papananyo. Nabayag kano ngaminen a di nagpa-amianan ti drayberyo, sa rabii pay. Atiddog daytoy a kalsada a pakayaw-awanan, naisipmo. Namak payen a bannog ti drayber, ken ti maibus a gasolina. Napawingiwingka a nakaisip a mayaw-awankan iti sigud a pagud-udaudam... ta maysakan a ganggannaet. Kababainka pay, nakunam iti bagim.

Inabutnakayo ti napaut nga oras a nagiwes-iwes iti nakayaw-awananyo. Idi makadanonkayo iti umno a dalan, sinadanakayo ti patrol ta dadael ti silaw iti likud ti luganyo. Ket nagbayadkayo sada pay innala ti lisensia ti drayber.

Yes! Intag-ay pay ti barom ti dua a takiagna idi makadanonkayo iti balayyo. Parbangonen.

Ay, salamat! Nayesngaw dagiti babbalasangmo. Immanges met iti nauneg ti kaingungotmo.

VIII. Ti Kaasi. . .

. . .TI Apo ti adda koma kadakayo amin. . .

Nadagsen a panunotek ti pannakaipusingmi kadakayo, Annakko. Dagensen nga imetko iti inaldaw nga angsek. Ngem ipapantayo kadi laengen, a, a biktimanatayo dagiti pasamak iti amin a panawen. Dakayo ti puon ti kaaddami iti yanmi ita. Dakayo met laeng ti puon ti di pannakaidna dagiti darikmatmi ken ni nanangyo. Ti papelyo agan-andaren. Ngem no kaanonto a makadanon iti naituding a panawenna, ni la Apo Dios ti makaibaga. . .

Adu ti pagteng ti biag a narigat a maawatan. Iti panagabeltayo iti masakbayan awan makaibaga no umno ti addangtayo—mangnamnamatayo laeng a magun-odtayo ti kayattayo a tun-oyen. . . iti kabiitan a panawen.

5:00 A.M.: Iti Sango ti *Computer*—8

NAISALANSAN ti Nangisit a Libro iti pagsalansanan iti uluanan ti monitor, iti abay ti takiag ti bombilia a mangtantan-aw iti keyboard ngem iti *screen* kurkuridemdeman ti *cursor* ti: **napintas ken nagloriaan**

ti sanga ti Apo. Nalamlamuyot manen ti ayug ti *Where Do I Go From Here* dagiti Carpenters manipud iti media player. Nakamulagat latta ti *led* ti *printer* nga agbilbil-an iti papel. Naurnosen dagiti diskette iti abay ti monitor ket maysa laengen ti nakasubo iti ngiwat ti tower kas ipasimudaag ti nagrungarong a butonna. Saanen nga agsardeng ti lagtit ti *cursor* a tiliwtiliwen dagiti balikas iti *screen*. Napartak met ti yuuli dagiti limbang, a kasla adda oras a kamkamatenda sakbay a maungpot ti papel. . .

   Where do I go from here. . . tell me, damdamagen ti media player.

h. Ipapanaw

ADTOYKAYO manen. Iti maudi nga aldawyo. Maikawakayonto manen. Ibatiyo dagiti annakyo a narimat dagiti matada a mangisursurot iti yaadayoyo. Didakayo maitulod agingga iti iluluganyo, ngem ti panunotda, ken ti panunotyo, agtugmokdanto kadagiti tagtagainep ken parparmatayo.

   Makitamto ti pakak. Ti karayan. Dagiti kinelleng. Ni tatangmo. Daydiay ladawan daydi nanangmo. Mangngegmonto ti saning-i dagiti dalluyon. Makitamto dagiti magmagna a tulang. Atilento amin dagitoy dagiti sardammo.

   Iti uppat a suli ti balay a sangpetanyo, iti uppat a panawen a mangtenneb iti kinataoyo, agtagimaristo ti tunggal darikmat. Ta natingranto nga agnanayon ti maris dagiti ladawan iti agsumbangir nga ungto ti bullalayaw.

   Iti sirmatam, agsasanga dagiti lansangan a pagwiwinnidawidan dagiti tao a magmagna ken pagtatalentenan dagiti lugan nga agtartaray, ngem addanto latta dagiti Dadakkel a Dalan a daliasaten dagiti agganggapat. Addanto dagiti eropuerto a mangitayab iti agduduma a maris ti tao iti agduduma a turongda iti agduduma a panawen. Addanto maisurat a pakasasritaan ti tunggal maysa. . .

   Adda dagiti annakyo a sangpetanyo, ngem ad-adu dagitoy ipusingyo a dinto maminngga nga umar-araraw iti sirok ti init.

   Agtayabkayo manen. No sadino ti pagtungedan ti dalanmo, awan ti makaibaga.

Ngem denggemto latta dagiti ayug ni ayat a mangsebseb iti iliwmo a mangitayok iti kararuam a tumulong kenka a manglipat a maysaka kadagiti di makaidna, ta ti pusom napno iti di mayebkas a panangipateg, uray pay iti mannakaawat a kaingungotmo.

Dimonto malipatan ti agarup agpapada a pammakada dagiti annakmo: agyamankami, 'Pa, iti panangipasiarmo kadakami—diminto malipatan.

Am-ammokan, 'Pa, kinuna ti barom.

Ken ukrademto latta daydiay a Libro a pagubbogan ti bileg ti kararuam.

Agtayabkayo a kasla agtalaytay iti nagarko a bullalayaw iti nalawa a taaw a namagsilpo iti naggapuanyo ken iti sangpetanyo—a kas man la adda iti tukot ti daga ti kagudua ti bullalayaw a mangbegkes iti lubong.

No kasano ti kapautyo nga agtayab, ammom nga agtungedto, ken ammom no apay. . . no apay nga addaka iti yanmo. . .

Inawidmo ni kaingungotmo ket silalailo nga insadagmo ti ulona iti abagam idi nakapagsimpan ti luganyo iti law-ang.

Nayesngawmo ti maudi a binatog: ti kaasi ti Apo ti adda koma kadakayo amin...—0

Petsa a pannakaisurat, ken pannakaidalusna: *1/19/03, 5:51 P.M; 1/23/03, 12:52 P.M.; 1/28/03, 10:58 A.M.; 2/9/03, 11:49 A.M.; 2/10/03, 1:23 P.M.; 2/11/03, 11:8 A.M.; 3/9/03, 7:49 A.M.; 3/12/03, 10:49 A.M.; 3/14/03, 2:25 P.M.*

Dagiti Anghel
Iti Saklot Ti Kinerker A Garami

I. Paskua 1962

KASLA palsiit ti taliaw ni Ayong idi mapasungadanna ni Angela. No apay ketdi nga iti sumurok-kumurang a siam a tawenna, kasla lumagto ti pusona tunggal makitana ti dua a nauneg a kallid ni Angela. Agpangato daydiay rikna a lumagto ket pagamuan la ta agkidkiddayen ti kanigid a kidayna. Dilatan ni Angela a mayat latta ti kinikinna nga umasideg, ket kas man la makalbit a bulong ti baimbain ti rikna ni Ayong ket kunam no agkurinikon ti lagto ti pusona iti no sadino a suli ti barukongna.

"Apay a kiddakiddayannak?" inkusilap ni Angela idi makaasideg iti yan da Ayong, Abat, ken Ansit iti abay ti karaang. Ken ni Ayong ti kusilap ni Angela kasla apagbukar a sabong ti baimbain.

"D-diak man ammo," pinilit ni Ayong ti immisem. "No ngamin malagipko ti kidday ni *manong* Boni ken ni manang Paring no agsabatda, daytoy matak tumulad met!"

"Agbunga kano 'ti kasla gemgem ti agkiddakidday a mata!" inlibbi latta ni Angela.

Naggarikgik da Abat ken Ansit.

"Apay ngamin a kiddakiddayam ni Angela, Yong?" inrungiit ni Abat ket nagparang ti kasla wasay a rukapina.

Nagplastar nga agkanta ni Ansit ket inlangitna ti ayug ti Manang Biday.

"*Manong* Ayong agkiddakidday, 'ta. . . 'ta. . . 'ta kidaymo napuskol unay!"

"Dagitoy a tiltillayonen!" imbugtak ni Isio a tatang ni Ayong a makais-isem. "Dikayo man pasalsali. . ."

Kasla di nangngeg dagiti uppat. No manen, siblokan da Ayong, Abat, ken Ansit ti lugsot dagiti tinubong a matuntuno iti karaang; agbuybuya laeng ni Angela, agkatawa iti nasinggit nga agkinni iti apagballing, a nagsabat dagiti dakulapna iti likudna. No manen tiliwen dagiti mata ni Ayong dagiti kakasla baballing a bituen a mata ni Angela. Dilatan latta met ni Angela. No manen, bugtaken ida da Isio a tatang ni Ayong, Masong a tatang ni Abat, ken Kanor a Tatang ni Ansit. Agkabsat da Isio ken Kanor; kabsat ni Pinang nga asawa ni Isio ni Masong. Tumultulong ni Ibiang a Nanang ni Angela kada Pinang nga agidaldalimanek kadagiti naggamayan iti bellaay (nagpukaw a kasla asuk daydi Bantor a Tatang ni Angela idi naisurot a nakipaggapas idiay Pudtol ket awan ti makaammo no nakursonadaan ti baket nga Igorot ket intarayna iti kabakiran ti Santa Maria.) Agkakasadaran dagiti uppat. Agkakaarrubada iti solar iti amianan a pingir ti Abbarit. Agkakaadalanda iti maikatlo iti San Isidro Elementary School.

Kinalbit ni Ayong ni Abat, a di nalapsi dagiti matana ken ni Angela.

"Bat, apay ngata a no kitaennak ni Angela agbisaleg ti baba ti pusegko?" insanapsap ni Ayong.

"Damagem kaniana, a," di tinaliaw ni Abat ni Ayong. Naimas latta ti kabukabna iti nasippawna a lugsot ti tinubong.

"Oy, A-angela," inkusilap nga intingigtingig nga immusimusiig ni Ansit. Naginawan kano di Nanangna iti ariwaiw a makalapan idiay kadilian ti Timmippang isu nga aggilabgilab ken agtung-etung-ed, ken putedputed no agsao. "K-kuna ni. . . ni A-yong. . .yong. . .apay kano a no kitaem, a-agbisaleg ti. . .ti baba ti pusegna?"

"'Mok, 'ya, diak met sagsagiden ti pusegna!" immisuot ni Angela.

"Lalanggongkayo!" imbugtak ni Masong nga agtartarukboy ti isemna. "Awan pay kawwetyo, ti la addan a tantanawtawenyo. Immapokayon sa ketdi iti daydi nagawan!"

"'Madayokayo ngamin ditoy ta dikayo pasalsali!" kinuna manen ni Isio. "'Kay 'diay. . . 'mangan no dakayo ketdi ti maisarabasab dita karaang.. ."

Nagtataray dagiti tallo a kimmamang iti pasagad iti sirok ti narukbos a bakkalaw iti abagatan. Kasta unay ti ngusab da Ayong ken Abat iti lugsot. Tinaray ni Ansit a napan ginaw-at ti bandiona a naaramid iti lalat ti banyas a naisab-it iti abulog ti balayda.

Uray tungtung-ed ken aggilabgilab ni Ansit, nalaing nga agbandio a widona laeng. Kabaelanna pay ti agpondar iti kanta bayat ti panagkantana a yayugna iti tono dagiti nalatak a kanta, wenno ania ditan a malagipna. Saan a putedputed ti panagbalikasna no agkanta.

Isubo koma manen ni Ayong ti lugsot ngem nataliawna ni Angela a kumitkita.

"Kayatmo?" indiaya ni Ayong ti lugsot ken ni Angela.

"S-saan," kinuna ni Angela, ngem dina insina dagiti matana iti lugsot.

"Dika agimbabainen!" inrungiit ni Abat ket nagparang manen ti wasay a ngipenna iti panangipapelna iti lugsot. "Madi a mapabpabainan ni Ayong, allaka. Dinakanton ik-ikkan uray dumawatka. . . wenno kayatmo ti itedko?"

Sakbay a nayawatan ni Abat ni Angela, inawatnan ti yaw-awat ni Ayong, a pinaludipanna pay.

"Oy, kaykayatna ni Yong, yos!" kinuna ni Abat.

Dinilatan la ni Angela ni Abat sana pinarimriman ni Ayong.

Nagkulibagtong ti puso ni Ayong. Iti panunotna, immisem ti apagbukar a sabong ti baimbain iti panagsabat dagiti matada ken ni Angela.

Agtartaray a nagsubli ni Ansit iti yan dagiti tallo.

Inyuldag dagiti tallo iti pasagad. Nagpungan ti teltelda iti bangir a paladpad, sa ti lakkoda iti sabali a paladpad. Nagtugaw ni Angela iti sangol a naiparabaw iti ulo ti padapan ti pasagad.

Kinurengreng ni Ansit ti bandiona. Mayat ti aweng ti bandio a maidanggay iti agtrimtrimulo a timekna.

"Pamulinawen, ni Yong a timmangken," intungtung-ed nga imbullabullad nga insungisungi ni Ansit. "Uray no taltalem. . ."

Kasla nakapayat iti beggang a bimmangon ni Ayong. "Langgong!" kinatusanna ni Ansit.

"Dinto a lumukneng!" imparaipus ni Abat.

"Maysaka met!" nagngarietan ni Ayong a linapigos ni Abat.

Um-umlek ni Angela a mangbuybuya kadagiti tallo.

"Adda ammok," kinuna ni Ayong. "Tay makipaskua no rabii?"

"Wen, 'la," kinuna ni Abat.

"S-siak ti para kanta. . .si-sika ti kargador, Bat," kinuna ni Ansit.

"Siak ti mangibaga no papanantayo," kinuna ni Ayong. "'Nia, sumurotka, Angela?"

"Diak kayat. . ."

"'Bingayandakanto 'ti mapaskuaanmi. . .tayo. . . intayonto paskuaen ni Apo Marta. . .itedminto amin kenka a mapaskuaantayo kaniana."

"He, inkayo laeng," ad-addan ti panagkedked ni Angela. "Manggagamud kano isuna."

"Dinakanton kidkiddayan ni Ayong. . . no sumurotka."

Nagdilat ni Angela.

"Ibbongka a Bat!" pinateltelan ni Ayong ni Abat. "Ad-addan, a, a madi sumurot ni Angela."

Naggarikgik ni Abat. Naggilap ti wasay a rukapina

"Talaga nga awanton mangkidkidday kaniak," kinuna ni Angela. "Pumanawkaminton ken ni Nanang."

"Papananyo?" kinuna ni Ayong. Dina naituloy ti subona.

"Inkamto kano 'diay. . . Capay-odan."

"Ay, a-aasi pay ni A-Ayong!" imbullad nga intingig ni Ansit. Kinurengrengna ti bandiona sana inkanta iti ayug ti Manang Biday: "Ay Angela, 'pay a pumanawka, awanton ti inkam kadkadua; agpaneston ti Abbarit, ni Ayongton, ay, agsangsangit!"

"Langgongka a Sit!" inkusilap ni Ayong. "'Tay ket 'diay sapaw agpraktis 'ti pakipaskuatayo."

"'Mayka, Angela?" kinuna ni Abat. "Dimon sa pay nakita 'diay sapawmi a kinerker a garami. . ."

Nagsasarunoda nga uppat. Immuna ni Ayong. Simmaruno ni Abat. Maikatlo ni Angela. Adda iti kutit ni Ansit a saan a madlaw ti tingigtingigna ta kumkumpasanna ti en-ensaywenna a pakipaskua a

kanta. Danggayanna pay iti kingking. Pati dagiti tallo nga immuna, maisursurotda iti panagkanta ni Ansit.

Adda ti sapaw iti tengnga ti bangkag iti laud ti bassit a purok, nga asideg iti balay da Ayong. Bassit ti ridawna, a marikpan iti dua a mapagabay a kinerker. Naaplagan iti napuskol a garami, a naparabawan iti rutrot nga ikamen. Kinerker met la a garami ti pannakaatepna, ngem adda dagiti libbawang a pangsirsiripanda kadagiti bituen no agiiladda nga agsisinnutil. Masansan a kantaan ni Ansit dagiti bituen, a segsegundaan ni Ayong ken terterseraan ni Abat. Manmano a sindianda ti bassit a pagsilawan a naiparaw iti nagbaetan ti dua a dadakkel a bingkol nga adayo kadagiti kinerker ken awan garami nga aplagna. Kanayon nga ibilbilin da Tatangda a dida liplipatan nga iddepen ti silaw amangan no malitsonda a dina oras.

"Daytoy ti nadaeg a pagarianmi, Angela!" intangig ni Abat. "Sumrekka," inlugayna.

Arinkedkeden ni Angela a nagtungpal. Nagapput idi makastrek.

"Naangdod!" immusiigna.

"Dagita ngata ules. . .ules ni Sit dayta," intudo ni Ayong ti nadaluson a nalitem a napagsasaip a supot ti arina. "Ules ni Bat dayta rutrot nga abel-Iluko. . . Awan ulesko," kinuna ni Ayong idi ipalawlaw ni Angela dagiti matana. "Dagaangenak no kua isu a diak agul-ules."

"Saan nga agdigdigos isu a pannakaulesna ti kimbaal a kabkabna!" inggarikrik ni Abat.

"'Suda, a, makatawen san a dida nagdigos isu a nakaang-angdod ti ulesda!" kinuna ni Ayong.

"N-nalamiis ti Paskua, k-kunayo man!" inkurengreng ni Ansit iti bandiona.

"Naimas ti maturog ditoy?" dinamag ni Angela.

"Nagangganas ngem 'diay balay!" kinuna ni Ayong. "Kanayon a tapatan ni Ansit dagidiay bituen, ken 'diay bulan. . ."

"O, naraniag nga abut!" indayyeng ni Ansit. "Napalawlawan ti. . . ti bituen." Kinurengrengna ti bandiona a nanglangit. "Ania ti inkam masakbayan, sika a tangtangaden."

". . .Ni Ansit a nabangsit!" inrayok nga insuldong ni Abat.

1. Umuna a Tapat

"AGANNADKAYO," imbilin ni Pinang a nanang ni Ayong. "Dikay umas-asideg 'diay yan ni Baket Marta a manggagamud."

"Dika agdanag, Anti," kinuna ni Abat. "Adda sumangko. . ."

Nagpayabyab ni Ayong. Nagkipis ni Abat. Nagbistukol ni Ansit, nga adda paratimidna, tapno di matnag no agling-i a kumusilap. Naggigem ni Ayong iti linaga a silag a basket nga us-usarenna no mapan agbasa. Inyabaga ni Abat ti dakkel a langgusti a pagsuksukat ni Tatangna a Masong iti irik no agwagwagda. Sakbat ni Ansit ti bandiona, ket no manen, kurengrengenna; ngem pasardengen ni Ayong tapno di kano madlaw dagiti tapatanda. Nasilnag ti bulan, agkiremkirem dagiti bituen. Naraniag dagiti saggaysa a parol a naisab-it kadagiti tawa.

Nagaabayda a nangtalunton iti nailet a desdes nga agpaabagatan iti kabalbalayan. Nagtengnga ni Ayong, akinkanawan ni Abat ket akinkanigid ni Ansit. Iti adayo a laud, ken abagatan, ken daya, adda mangngeg nga agtaptapat. Adda pay kumbatsero.

"Unaentayo 'ta yan da Angkel Kilin," kinuna ni Ayong. "'Saganam 'ta langgusti, Bat. Sigurado nga adu ti ipapaskuada. Nagadu ti bulo a pinaguyodda a naggaput' surong."

"Nagimut ni Anti Pasing!" kinuna ni Abat.

Angkel ken anti ti awagda iti dandani amin a kaarrubada iti Abbarit. Dandanida agkakabagian amin.

Naganaw-aw ti labang da angkelda a Kilin idi makaasidegda iti agdan.

Kinurengreng ni Ansit ti bandiona. Nagplastar da Ayong ken Abat. Ad-addan ti anaw-aw ti aso.

"Dienggel bels," inrugi ni Ansit.

"Dienggel," insegunda ni Ayong.

"Bels," intersera ni Abat.

Ket tinarastasdan.

"Dienggel bels, dienggel, bels. . . Ni angkelmi dakkel ti. . . dakkel ti kuana."

Nagtaguob ti aso.

Kinidag ni Ayong ni Ansit.

"Ti pusona," insuldong ni Ansit.

"O, anian, sangalanggusti," saan nga inkaskaso ni Ansit ni Ayong. Ket sinulonan. "Ti 'tedda nga 'ginaldomi."

Nagtaguob manen ti aso.

"Dienggel bels," sinulon ni Ansit. "Dienggel bels, da Angkel naasida. Ikkandakam, ikkandakam, sangakaban nga 'ginaldomi!" Agtrimtrimulo ti ayugna.

Nagareng-eng laengen ti aso.

"Paskuayo, Angkel," impukkaw ni Ayong.

"Ni Abat, ni Abat, agur-uray 'ti inna isakbat," imparaipus ni Ansit.

"'Ka agkantad'ta bangiren ta urayenmi ti 'tedda," kinuna ni Ayong.

Sakbay a nakatallikud ni Ansit, nagparangen ni angkelda a Kilin a nakakarsonsilio iti manta. Tallo nayon a tinubong ti iggemna. Atiddog ti isemna.

"Napintas ti kantayo," kinunana. "Ulitenyo man pay."

"Awan tawarna, Angkel," kinuna ni Abat. "Ken agdardaraskami. Ngem no..."

"Ala, nayonak ti aginaldoyo," kinuna ni angkelda a Kilin.

Nagsay-a ni Ansit. Kinurengrengna ti bandiona. Ket impatayabnan ti trimulona. A pinaspasarunuan da Ayong ken Abat. Kasda man la suksukdalen dagiti bituen ken ti naslag a bulan.

Nakangangada a naguray idi malpasda nga agkanta.

"Napintas. . .!" nagpalakpak pay ni angkelda a Kilin. "Nalaingkayo a talaga nga agkanta. Dakayon ti kalaingan nga agkanta nga ubbing," kinuna ni angkelda a Kilin idi malpas nga agkanta ni Ansit. "Ala, utangko ti nayon ti aginaldoyo. Agsublikayonto no sumaruno a Paskua ta doblenton ti aginaldoyo." Ket inrikpenan ti ridaw.

"Su-suitik a la-lakay!" inggilab nga intingit ni Ansit.

Naganeng-eng a nagkalawikiw ti aso a naguyaoy ti dilana a kasla umis-isem. Kinugtaran ni Abat. "Buisitka!" kinunana. Naganang-ang ti aso.

"Hanabale ta adda met tallo a tinubong," kinuna ni Ayong. "Adu pay ti paskuaentayo."

Nagpaabagatanda iti ka-Farinas-an. Nanglabasda iti tallo a balay. Pinilida ti kalalainganna a kadakkel.

"Padasentayo ditoy," kinuna ni Ayong.

Tinangad ni Abat ti balay. Agkurkuridemdem ti lawag ti pagsaingan iti salas.

"Matmaturog san da Mang Itok," kinuna ni Abat. "Kita'm, nakataltalnada."

"A-awanda si-siguro," kinuna ni Ansit. "N-nabiitda p-pay a nagkasar."

"No adda silaw, adda tao," kinuna ni Ayong. "Kurengrengem ketdin 'ta bandiom, Sit!"

"'Guraykayo," inyatipa ni Abat. "Nangngegyo 'diay nangngegko?"

"'Nia koma?" kinuna ni Ayong. "Kaska la ngamin aglaplapayag nga aso!"

"Denggenyo!" kinuna ni Abat. "Ne, kitaenyo, agsalsala ti lawag 'diay pagsaingan da Mang Itok! Aginggined sa! Agan-anit-it 'ta balayda.."

Nagallingag da Ayong ken Ansit. Nagkinnitada iti lawag ti naslag a bulan.

"Agpimpinnaskuada ngata," kinuna ni Ayong. "Agar-aramidda 'ti adingda."

"Kasano nga ammom?" dinamag ni Abat.

"Nangngegko 'ti maysa a rabii nga agsarsarita da Tatang ken Nanang. they

"Nga agaramid da Mang Itok 'ti adingda?"

"'Garamidta ti ading ni Ayong,' inyarasaas ni Tatang ken ni Nanang. Idi kuan nagginggineden."

Nagayek-ek ni Ansit. "Ging-ginggined, ging-ginggined!" inggilabna.

2. Maikadua a Tapat

NAGSARDENGDA iti nasungadda a balay. Adu ti aso dagiti kaarruba ket umanaw-awda.

"Kitaenyo 'ta gurongyo 'mangan no pagpaskuaan a kuraban dagita aso!" kinuna ni Ayong a sangkataliawna ti agsumbangir a sikiganna.

"Kilawekto pay ti dalemna!" kinuna ni Abat.

"'Saganam 'ta langgusti, Bat. Agparparikna kaniak a dakkel ti ipapaskua da Tang Bosyong. 'Tay kapintasan a kanta ti kantaem, Sit."

"Kaska met la ken ni Mam Insiang nga agmammandaren, yos!" kinuna ni Abat.

Kinurengreng ni Ansit ti bandiona.

"Daytoy a balay," inrugina. "Paipusanyo, a," kinunana kada Ayong ken Abat.

"Daytoy. . ." insegunda ni Ayong.

". . .a balay," intersera ni Abat.

". . .a masungadmi," intuloy ni Ansit, a tunggal agpenal ti kantana, segundaan ken terseraan da Ayong ken Abat. "Balay da Tang Bosyong a nataraki, daytoy ngatan ti pangulpianmi 'ti nawadwad nga aginaldomi. Ala, Abat. . ."

"Dimo 'bagbaga ti naganko, a!" inkidol ni Abat.

". . .umasidegka," saan nga inkaskaso ni Ansit ni Abat. "ta 'watem 'diay ited ni Nana. No bassit agpanayonka. No adu panayonam latta."

"Ay, dagiti gayam tallo a tiltillayon!" kinuna ti baket a nangyawat iti aginaldoda a tupig. "Dikam' nagtinubong. . . tupig la ti adda," kinunana.

"Saan a tiltillayon ti naganmi, Nana," kinuna ni Ayong. "Siak ni Yong, ni Bat daytoy kargadormi, ket ni Sit ti gitaristami. Ti nagan ti grupomi, Yong-Bat-Sit. . ."

"Ay wen, dagiti tallo a tiltillayon!" kinuna latta ti baket.

"Bakbaketan a kumkumbet!" intanabutob ni Abat idi makalikudda.

"K-kasla ub-ubet ti pariok ti rupana!" kinuna ni Ansit, a pinigsaanna a kinuragrag ti bandiona.

"Tagtagarin," kinuna ni Ayong. "Dakes kano ti agpungpungtot 'ti paskua."

"Nagkuna man kenkan?" inkabukab ni Abat.

"Natagtagainepko," kinuna ni Ayong.

"T-tag-tagainep n-ni A-yong a naangpet!" inyayog ni Ansit.

"Langgong, saanak a naangpet!"

Naggarakgak ni Abat.

Nagsarugaddengda iti maikatlo a nasungadda a panakkelen a balay. Tinangadda. Nagsardeng ni Ayong.

Ngem nagna met laeng.

"Apay?" kinuna ni Abat.

"Diyo malagip?" kinuna ni Ayong. "Saan nga agpappapaskua da Apo Bantor."

"A-apay n-ngata?" kinuna ni Ansit.

"Imutda," kinuna ni Ayong.

"Nagkuna?" kinuna ni Abat.

"Kunak ngaruden! Apay, dikay' mamati? Ti pudno, awan paskuada!" kinuna ni Ayong. "Kuna ni Nanang, saanda kano nga. . .. nalipatakon 'tay kunana. . . basta awan paskuada."

3. Maikatlo a Tapat

NASUNGAD da Ayong, Abat, ken Ansit ti kabaruan a balay iti abagatan. Nabitinan iti saggaysa a parol dagiti tawa iti akinbaba ken akinngato a kadsaaran. Daytoy ti umuna a balay a nagatep iti yero iti Abbarit. Saan unay a kaimuan dagiti tallo ti akinbalay. Kuna dagiti dadakkelda a kabagyanda ida ngem nabayag nga awanda iti Abbarit ta napanda idiay Hawaii ket sada la nagsubli idi nagretiro ni Apo Porong iti trabahona a pagtubbuan. Umaripapa dagiti tao nga umasideg ta bainenda ti bagida a mayabay kadagiti baknang.

"Agpapaskua ngata da Apo Porong? kinuna ni Ayong.

"Apay, awan kadi met ti Paskuada?" kinuna ni Abat.

"A-mangan n-no n-nabatida 'diay Ha-Hawaii," kinuna ni Ansit. Kinuradradna ti bandiona sana met la dinakulapan.

"Padasentayo?" kinuna ni Ayong. "No dida mangted. . ."

"K-kantaek 't-tay bulong ti apatot, paskuayo a naimut, umulog ti makarurod ta pang-orek 'ti sarukod!" kinuna ni Ansit.

"Satayto sublien a puoran," kinuna ni Abat.

"Madi, a, dayta, langgong!" kinuna ni Ayong.

"Dagiti imut, saan nga anak ni Apo Dios. 'Su a masapul a mapuoranda!" kinuna ni Abat.

"Nagkuna met?" kinuna ni Ayong.

"Kunak ngaruden!" kinuna ni Abat. "Kuna ni Nanang, maipanda iti impierno. Ti impierno, apuy kano a dumardarang. 'Su a litsonentayo ida a sibibiag!"

"Litsonen a sibibiag!" inyayug ni Ansit iti Hark the Herald. "Ni Apo Porong nga imut!"

"'Tay ngaruden!" kinuna ni Ayong. "'Tay ul-ulsam 'ti naangdod ti 'pasaksakmo, Sit. Pimpintasem. . ."

Kinurengreng ni Ansit ti bandiona. Nanglangit, a kasna la suksukdalen dagiti bituen ken ti bulan. Naitalimudok dagiti matana iti barukbok iti tengnga ti langit. Impatayabna ti pondarna a pamaskua a katan nga inayugna iti O Naraniag A Bulan. Sakbay a sinegundaan ken tinerseraan da Ayong ken Abat, dinamag ni Ayong no apay a kasta ti ayugna.

"Siak ti nangpondar," kinuna ni Ansit. "N-no d-diyo kayat, dikay agkangkanta!"

Kapilitanen a pinasurotanda.

"*O, naraniag a bituen, a nagparang 'diay Belen, 'toy kantami inka denggen, ta 'ginaldomi inda itden; No ni Apo Porong nayridepen, inka kad' riingen, ta yawatna 'tay doliaren, langgusti ni Abat inna punnuen.*"

Kinidag ni Abat ni Ansit. Dina tinerseraan ti naudi a linia.

"*No indan nakariing,*" intuloy ni Ansit, "*ni Abat nakaranting, mangawat 'diay doliaren, nga inkam aginalduen; Da 'Po Porong nabaknangda, adut' inda ipapaskua, tapno pumintas ti biagda, 'matiddog pay ditoy daga.*

"*Inkam itan agyaman, 'papaskuada a kinabaknang, tapno 'kam met mairanud, ita a paskua ni Apo Jesus!*"

Di pay naipukkaw ni Ayong ti Paskuayo, Apo, nailukaten ti dakkel a ridaw ti balay. Naibuang ti natayag, ludingas, pamulladen a lakay a nagbado iti labunglabong a sabongan. Kurang la dumanon ti gigisna iti agsumbangir a piditpiditna iti atiddog nga isemna. Pinayapayanna a pinastrek dagiti tallo.

"Magustuak ti kantayo," kasla agkamkamat iti susuit ti paninggiten a timek ni Apo Porong. "Sumrekkayo!"

Aringkedkeden dagiti tallo. Nakangangada, nabullad dagiti matada, mabilbilang ti addangda a nanangadtangad.

"Apo Dios! Apo Dios!" nagsawaw ti siddaaw ni Ayong. Bombilia ti silawda, nakananga dagiti dadakkel a pagtugawan a nalukneng. Marmulisado ti basar. Puraw dagiti naguyaoy a kortina.

Awan simngaw a balikas da Abat ken Ansit. Nalipatan sa pay ketdi ni Ansit ti gilab ken tung-edna.

"Praning," nagtimek ni Apo Porong.

Kasla agin-iniin nga itik ti baket a naibuang iti dakkel a ridaw iti kanawan. "Yes, Dear?"

"Adda sangailita a tallo nga. . . anghel!" kinuna ni Apo Porong. Di pay nalapsi ti isemna iti nakaisab-itanna a piditpiditna. "Ikkam ida iti pagpapudot da . . . aniat' naganyo, ken dagiti nagannak kadakayo?"

"Siak ni Yong nga anak da Isio ken Pinang," kinuna ni Ayong. "Siak ti ulomi a tallo . . ."

"Ta dakkel ngamin ti ulona," insuldong ni Abat. "Siak met ni Bat a putot da Masong ken daydi nanang. . . No saan la a daytoy rukapik, siak koma ti katarakian kadagiti padami nga ubbing ditoy Abbarit."

"A-angsit, ay Ansit t-ti n-naganko," kinuna ni Ansit. "Pu-putotnak ni Tatangko . . ."

"Yong-Bat-Sit ti nagan ti grupomi, Apo," kinuna ni Ayong.

"Appokokayo pay la gayam!" kinuna ni Apo Porong. "Nakakaykayakaykayto met, di ditay agaammo!"

Nagsubli ni Apo Praning a nagtapaya iti bandehado a yan ti tallo a tasa a pagal-alisuasuan ti nabanglo a tsokolate. Angotna pay laeng agkaratilmonen dagiti tallo.

"Dikay agbabain," kinuna ni Apo Porong.

Immigup a dagus ni Abat. Nakalua a nangyula. Inapputna ti ngiwatna. "N-nalamaw san ti dilak!" sawaw ti arasaasna ken ni Ayong.

Inyasideg ni Ayong ti tasana iti ngiwatna. Simmimsim iti battikuting. Inaw-awanna ti tasa. Simmimsim manen iti battikuting. Inimasna! Indakdakkelna ti nangaw-aw. Indakdakkelna ti simmimsim. Nagimasen, Apo! kinunana iti unegna. Ngem pudotnan, aya!

Nakain-inayad ti panangyasideg ni Ansit iti tasa iti bibigna, a guyabguyaban ken tingigtingiganna. No manen, yadayona. No manen, yasidegna. Sumuksuknor ti angot ti tsokolate iti luppap nga agongna. Tumtumbog ti katayna. Pinug-awanna sangkaballing. Kimmutikot ti asuk iti agongna. Nagkidem a nangnanam. Pinug-awanna manen. Ken manen. Ken manen. Tunggal pug-awna, sarunuen ti panangsay-opna iti

alisuaso. Idi kuan agsasarunon ti pug-aw ken say-opna ken sanapsapna. Nalipatannan ti naggilab ken nagtung-ed!

Kinidol ni Ayong ni Ansit. "Kukueem, langgong!" kinunana. Nakaguduan iti inumenna.

Idi narikna ni Ansit a limmamiisen ti inumenna, intangadnan nga inarub-ob!

Agkalkalimduosanda a mababain a kimmita ken ni Apo Porong a nagsabaten ti gigis ken dagiti piditpiditna iti sangadangan nga isemna.

Inruaran ida ni Apo Praning iti saggaysada a supot ti tsokolate a babbabassit ngem dakulapda ti kadadakkel. Pattapatta ni Ayong, agarup duapulo ti nagyan iti maysa a supot.

"Nalaingkayo," kinuna manen ni Apo Porong. "Sinnot' nakasursuruanyo nga agkanta ken. . . ken agbandio?"

"Ni Sit, Apo, ti nalaing nga agkanta ken agtokar," kinuna ni Ayong. "Tawidna kano iti daydi leloongna iti dapan. Ken sinursuruan metten, a, ni Angkel Kanor a Tatangna."

"Uray dakayo. . . magustuak ti panaggagampor ti timekyo."

"Dikam' agyamyaman, Apo, ta sunotanminto pay!" naguyaoy ti isem ni Abat.

Nagkatawa ti lakay. Umis-isem met ti baket.

"Lelong, kunayo lattan, loko. . . Gapu ta dakayo ti immuna nga ubbing a nasangailimi ita a Paskua, adda regaloyo. . . isu dayta inted ni Lelangyo a sinupot a tsokolate."

Adu pay ti sinarsarita dagiti agassawa sakbay a pinalubosanda dagiti tallo. Adda kano annakda a nabati idiay Hawaii, ken sumagmamano nga appokoda. Pinagkantada pay ida, ket maymayat manen ti panaggampor ti timekda, a konso muestrada pay a kasla adda suksukdalenda iti langit. Inulitda ti Naraniag a Bituen. Ninayonan pay da Apo Porong iti sangasupot a tsokolate ti paskuada.

Dida pay nakaad-adayo no ar-arigen, binulosanen dagiti tallo ti tengtenglenda a rikna. Naglagtolagtoda. Nagriawriawda. "Yos! Yos!" kinunada a nagiinnarakup. Sa kinuna ni Ayong: 'Nakto met Hawaii! Uray sinnot' agdepdeppa, 'nakto met 'diay Hawaii!"

"'Guraykayo," pagammuan ta pimmasnek ni Abat, nga apputna ti nagkabbibaw a bibigna. "Saggaysakami 'ti supot ken ni Sit, apay a dua kenka, Yong?"

"'Tedkonto ken ni Angela 'toy maysa," kinuna ni Ayong a timmangad iti langit.

"Ket no di met immay. . ."

"Kaasi met. Awan nangted 'ti Paskuana, di kano pay nagtupig wenno nagtinubong ni nanangna. . ."

"Yalismo man ti alipusposmin. . . 'wan met nangngegko nga imbaga ni Angela. . .'Da nangngegmo, Ansit?"

"'Ray no a-arasaas la k-komat' alutiit!" kinuna ni Ansit.

4. Maikapat a Tapat

NAKADANONDA iti dakkel a tambak iti daya ti purok. Nagtugawda iti sikigan ti tambak a sumango iti daya a mangtannawag iti pagtatalonan a naaplagan iti bugbugianen a pinagayan iti saklot ti Kabanayan. Nalamiis ti palayupoy ti lumakayen a sardam a mangidandanon iti sayamusom ti pinagayan kadagiti agongda.

Naiturong ti panagkita ni Ayong iti bassit a balay iti abagatan-a-daya ti purok. Makidinnakkel ti parol iti tawa a nakaibitinanna. "Napunno kadin 'ta langgusti, Abat?"

"Sampay, ngem nabantoten," kinuna ni Abat. "'Tanton basketmot' pagikkan..."

"Makitayo daydiay?" insungo ni Ayong ti bassit a balay.

"Balay ni Baket Marta a manggagamud," dandani naggiddan da Abat ken Ansit.

"Intay paskuaen," kinuna ni Ayong.

"Ay, sika laengen! Kuna ni nanangmo. . ." kinuna ni Abat.

"Diak p-pay k-kayat ti matay!" kinuna ni Ansit.

"Adda met sumangmo. . ." kinuna ni Ayong. "Kitaenyo, nagdakkel ken nagraniag 'diay parolna. Isu la ketdi ti kadakkelan ditoy Abbarit. Ur-urayennatayo."

Kinarawa ni Abat ti bolsana. "Diak gayam naitugot!"

Nagpanunot ni Ayong. "Intayo," impettengna. "Ti di sumurot, awan lategna. Ken kunak ngaruden a saan a manggamud."

No adda naibbatan ni Ayong a sao, tungpalenna, uray asino ti agdepdeppa.

"Dika mamati?"

"Mamatiakton no nagamudnatayon."

"Kasanonto pay no nataykanto metten?"

Nagkintayeg ni Ayong a nakalagip iti kamposanto.

"D-diak p-pay k-kayat ti m-magaburan!" nagtigerger ti timek ni Ansit. "'Nia ngatat' rikna ti magaburan, Apo?"

Uray no adda metten amakna, inyunan ni Ayong. Simmaruno ni Abat. Dua nga agpa ti nakaudian ni Ansit, nga itantanamitimna: "D-diak pay k-kayat ti m-matay. . . diak pay kayat!"

"Pintasem ti agkanta, Ansit," kinuna ni Ayong. "No saan, gamudennaka ni Apo Marta!"

Pinasikalian ni Ansit ti pamaskua a kantana nga inyayugna iti *Naminsan a Rabii Nagkabkabalioak.*

"Apay man a kastan?" inkidol ni Abat.

"Siak ti a-akimputar, s-saan a sika!" kinuna ni Ansit. "No dika agkanta, sika ti gamuden ni Apo Marta!"

Ket impatayabda ti *Nagkabkabalioak.*

Naminsan a rabii, nakipaskuakami, balay ni Apo Marta a kaarrubami; naraniag ti bitbituen a silawmi, tapno dikam magamud. . .

"'Ta ngiwatmo!" inkidol ni Ayong.

"Tapno dikam maitibkol iti papananmi. . ."

Di pay nagpenal ti kantada no ar-arigen, nanglukaten ti baket.

"Umulikayo, Appok! Umulikayo!" inyawisna.

Nagkikinnita dagiti tallo. Makabubuatitenen da Abat ken Ansit, ngem tengngel ni Ayong dagiti takiagda. Iti suli ti panunot ni Ayong, inkararagna: "Apo, kaasiannakami!"

"Agtugawkayo, Appok, agtugawkayo," intudo ti baket ti dulang iti kusina. "'Moyo, sangadungdong ti aroskaldo a linutok. Pinartik 'tay kakaisuna a dumalaga a manokko. Pagay-uma 'diay Kinwang ti bagas nga inlaokko. Ken nagpatupatak pay!"

"Pakanennatayo sanatayto gamuden!" nagsawaw ti arasaas ni Abat.

Kasta unay ti paragsit ti bassit ken narapis a bagi ti baket a naggao. Dadakkel a duyog a kayo ti naggaw-anna, ken kayo met laeng dagiti kutsara nga inruarna. Nalawag dagiti lesseb a matana, naisem dagiti naingpis a bibigna.

"Sige, mangankayon, Appok," kinuna ti baket.

Nagkikinnita dagiti tallo. Nabanglo ti aroskaldo ket nagkiraus ti boksit ni Abat.

"Dikay agbuteng. . . dikay. . .gamgamuden!" nagbanarbar ti timek ti baket.

Irubuaten dagiti tallo ti tumakias.

Ngem nagsaibbek ti baket. "Sige, Appok, mangankayon."

Naggiddan da Abat ken Ansit kimmutsara. Naggiddanda a nangisubo.

Kimmutsara met ni Ayong. Ngem saan a nangisubo. Binuyana da Abat ken Ansit.

Iti suli ti panunotna, no matay da Abat ken Ansit, agtaray nga agawid a mapan agpulong.

Nagustuan da Abat ken Ansit ti aroskaldo. Kasta unay ti sanapsapda. "Apay, Apok, a dika mangan?" kinuna ti baket ken ni Ayong. "Mabutengka kadi kaniak?"

"'Amman. . . saan, 'Lang," kinuna ni Ayong ket inkidemnan ti nangisubo. Kaasiannak, Apo! kinuna ti isipna.

"Nagsasaruno a natay daydi lakayko ken dagidi dua nga annakko idiay Tiktikrubong. Ubbingda pay idi," kinuna ti baket. "'Su ngata nga imbaga dagiti tao a manggagamudak."

Naisardeng ti kutsara dagiti tallo iti sango ti ngangada. Dadakkel dagiti matada a kimmita iti baket.

"Nagsanga ti dila ti tao. Sinurotnak ti saosao uray idi immakarakon ditoy Abbarit. No agpayso la a manggagamudak, ginamudkon amin ida!"

Pinaspasan dagiti tallo ti nagsubo. Agarup naggigiddanda a nagleppas; a nagtig-ab iti dakkel. Gaw-an koma pay ida ti baket, ngem inkadkadakkelda ti nagtig-ab, sada dandani naggigiddan a nangibaga a nabsogdan.

Pinabalonan ida ti baket iti adu a patupat. "Saganak dagita kadakayo," kinunana.

Rikriknaen dagiti tallo ti bagida iti nabuntog a panangtaluntonda iti tambak nga agpa-amianan. Makaibelbellengenda iti patupat ngem agkedked ti muging ni Ayong.

"Agaluadka no diakton makariing no bigat, Yong!" kinuna ni Abat. "No kunak nga umayka al-aliaen, umayka talaga al-aliaen!"

"No kunak nga awan mapasamak kadatayo, awan," kinuna ni Ayong. "Uray ringudandak." Ngem iti unegna, kinunana: Sapay koma, Apo, ta awan nga agpayso!

"Ri-ringudandaka, Yong-yong!" inggilab nga intung-ed ni Ansit.

5. Maudi a Tapat

"DUMAGASTAYO pay 'ta yan da Angela," kinuna ni Ayong. "'Tay paskuaen ida."

Madi koman da Abat ken Ansit ngem ingguyod ida ni Ayong.

"Di-diak kayaten t-ti agkanta," kinuna ni Ansit. "P-pasikalianka l-laengen."

Sinimpa ni Ayong ti nagtakder a nanglangit. Inilutna ti karabukobna, sana impatayab: Saalen nayt, ooli nayt, ol is brayt, ol is kam, ron yon birdyin mader en tsayld, oli empan so tender en mayld. . .

"Diak ammot' silponan!" inkidol ni Ayong ken ni Ansit.

Sakbay a nasilpuan ni Ansit, nailukat ti tawa ket timman-aw da Angela ken ni nanangna. Pinaulida ida.

"Dikami nagluto," mababain ni Angela.

"Agpayso, Annakko," kinuna ni nanangna. "Awan ngamin ti lutuenmi. . ."

"Saankami nga umay makipaskua, Nana," kinuna ni Ayong.

"Umay papaskuaan ni Ayong ni Angela, Nana," insuldong ni Abat.

Mababain ni Ayong a nangyawat iti sangasupot a tsokolate ken ni Angela. "Bingaymo iti napaskuaanmi 'diay yan da Apo Porong. . ."

"Daytoy pay patupat," inyawatan ni Abat ni Angela. "Napaskuaanmi 'diay yan ni. . ."

". . .Da Angkel Kilin," inalistuan ni Ayong nga insilpo.

"Nagsayaatkayo nga ubbingen," makalulua ti nanang ni Angela. "Maikawakaminto no awankamin ditoy."

"'Payso kadi a pumanawkayon, Nana?" kinuna ni Ayong.

"Kalpasan ti baro a tawen. Ngata. . ."

"A-agsang-sangitton, a, t-ti pu-puso ni Yong, N-nana," kinuragrag ni Ansit ti bandiona sana inyayug: "Bannatiran 'ta dutdotmo. . . puraw. Pumanawkan dinakam man la kaasian!"

"Puraw 'ya met!" inlibas ni Ayong a kinidol ni Ansit.

6. Iti Saklot ti Kinerker a Garami

INDAGAS da Ayong ti bingayda iti napaskuaanda iti balbalayda. Nakita ni nanangna ti patupat ket nangan a dagus ta paggugustona ngem dida nakaluto. Kaasiam ni nanangko, Apo! inyilling ti isipna.

Im-imasen da Abat ken Ansit ti mangngatngatingat iti sagsangabukelda a tsokolate. Saggaballing ti panangkurib ni Ayong iti bagina. Mayat ti uldagda iti saklot ti kinerker a garami a sapawda.

"Kanayon koma a Paskua, 'nia?" kinuna ni Abat.

"Saan a mabalin," kinuna ni Ayong. "Maymaysa ni Apo Jesus nga anak ni Birhen Maria."

"Aganak koma ni Apo Mayyang iti adu a Jesus tapno kanayon a Paskua," kinuna ni Abat.

"S-sinno a M-mayyang?" inggilab ni Ansit.

"Ti nanang ni Apo Jesus. Ni Baket Maria didiay Bacsil, Mayyang ti awagda, di Mayyang met ti nanang ni Apo Jesus."

"Lapigosennaka ni tatangmo no mangngegnaka, Langgong!" kinuna ni Ayong.

"A-apay ng-ngamin no P-paskua amin nga aldaw?" kinuragrag ni Ansit ti bandiona.

"Tapno kanayon a naragsaktayo," kinuna ni Abat. "Kuna ni tatang, no kanayon a Paskua, awan kano ti agpipinnungot a babbaket ken agbibinnadang a lallakay. . . Ken diyo kadi kayat a kanayontayo a mangan 'ti tinubong? Kanayon pay siguro nga ikkannatayo da Apo Porong 'ti tsokolate. . ."

". . .Ken patupat ni Apo Marta," insuldong ni Ayong.

Dinapadap da Abat ken Ansit ti boksitda.

"Nasakit sa 'toy tianko," nagsawaw ni Abat.

"U-uray siak sa," kinuna ni Ansit.

Nagkatawa ni Ayong. Ngem napugsat ta nalagipna da Angela ken ni nanangna a nangan iti patupat. No pudno a manggagamud ni Apo Marta, mataykami amin no kuan, Apo! inyarigengen ti unegna. Agbabawi koma ngem natangken ti ulona.

Sinirip ni Ayong dagiti bituen iti libbawang ti kinerker a garami. Apo, dimo kadi palpalubosan da Angela a pumanaw. . .

"Wen, Barok, diak ida pappapanawaen!" nabangag ti timek iti sikiganna.

Kasla nalastikuan ti tengnged ni Ayong a timmaliaw ken ni Abat.

"Abat a longat!" kinatusan ni Ayong ni Abat.

Naggarikgik ni Ansit a bulon ti panangkuragragna iti bandiona.

Nakariingda iti bigat a sumirsiripen ti init iti regkang ti kinerker a garami idi maiwangwang ti rikepna.

"Bumangonkayon, Tutur-og!" nasinggit ti timek a naggapu iti ruar. Ti naisem a rupa ni Angela ti naitangkarang kadakuada. Nagkikinnitada. Naggigiddanda a nangdapadap iti boksitda.

"Saan a nasakit!" nagsawaw ni Ayong.

"Saan a nasakit!" immulagat ni Abat.

"M-makaib. . .a-ay, s-saan gayam a n-nasakit!' inggilab ni Ansit.

"Ayooooong!"

Ad-addan ti atiddog ti isem ni Ayong a nakangngeg iti pukkaw ni nanangna.

Ket naggigiddanda a bimmangon. Naggigiddanda a timmakder. A limmagto.

"Meri krismas!" impukkawda.

"Adda 'padamagko," kinuna ni Angela. "Naimas 'diay tsokolate. . . ken 'diay patupat; inimas ni nanang. Ken kunana, saankamin a pumanaw. . .ta pinampanunotnakayo kano."

"Yippi, yippi!" naglagtulagto ni Ayong. Binuya apagbiit da Abat ken Ansit sada tinulad.

Narba ti sapaw a kinerker a garami ket nagaburan dagiti tallo. Um-umlek ni Angela idi itungraraw dagiti tallo ti uloda iti nagbabaetan dagiti kinerker, a nakaat-atiddog ti isemda.

II. Paskua 2003

"MERRY Christmas, Bat! Komusta ti Seattle? Ti pamiliam? Dakayo, Sit, komustakayo dita Canada? Nakisalbagkayo, kaskay' met la 'tay Hippo a bumbumladen!"

"Ay, Yong, Merry Christmas! Rimmuar kadin 'tay umuna nga apoyo ken ni Angela? Komustakayo dita Alaska? Salbag, nailadokayon sa ketdi ta mayat lattat' bagbagiyo!"

"Masapulyot' kinerker a garamid'ta 'Laska, Yong? 'Toy buridekko, salbag ta isun sa't nagtawid 'ti kina-Ansitko! Ngem computer wizard, dakayo!"

"Kitaenyo man lat' gasat. 'Nagkuna a makaumaytayo iti yantayo ita? Ken ne, computer payen ti pagkikitaan ken pagsasaritaantayo!"

"MERRY CHRISTMAS AND HAPPY NEW YEAR!" naggigiddanda a nangipukkaw.

(Inkissiim da Yong-Bat-Sit nga aginaldoda ti kaaddada ita iti yanda! He! He!)—0

2nd edition, 12-28-2002, 3:07 p.m.
3rd edition, 01/05/2003; 5:04 PM
Bannawag, May 26, 2003

Laud

Timek 1

A MMOK nga addakayo ditoy a biag sumurok a pitopulo a tawenen ti napalabas. Ngem sa la in-inut a simken iti panunotyo iti in-inut a panagbukar ti nakemyo. Sinursurotkayo iti sadino man a napnapananyo. Amin nga aramidyo. Amin a katkatawayo. Amin a sakit ti nakemyo a gubuayen ti pannakapaay. Amin a balligiyo. Amin a ragsakyo. Manipud iti saklot dagiti nadungngo nga innayo. Iti sappuyot ti manangngaasi a daga a nakaipasngayanyo.

Saanak a naaw-awan iti biagyo.

Ngem adu ti gundaway a diyo maamiris ti kaaddak iti sibayyo. Wenno manmano ket ngata nga umagibasak iti isipyo. Nangruna no agsagsagrapkayo iti nabuslon a parabur.

Awan ngamin ti timekko a mangngegyo. Awan ti ladawak a makitayo. Tapno koma kanayon a malaglagipdak.

Ta diak pagrebbengan ti mangipinta iti bukodko a ladawan. Saan a siak ti mangipangngeg iti timekko.

Dakayo ti rumbeng a mangbukel iti ladawak, uray no iti panunotyo laeng. Dakayo ti mangtimud iti timekko, nga agbalin a dayyeng wenno ayug iti puso ken panunotyo. Ta ti ladawak ken ti timekko ti agbalin a paratignay iti tunggal darikmat iti unos ti panagbiagyo.

Ngem ania ti ar-aramidenyo?

Pakauna

KASLA adda timek a mangyar-arasaas kaniak. . . agpayso gayam a dika pay nakadigos!" nailansa ni Tang Mike iti ridaw ti kuarto ni Tang Dave. "Playboy sa manen 'ta basbasaem?" siniraratna ti magasin a kurkuridemdeman ni Tang Dave iti iking ti kamana. Naiwangwang ti venetian blind iti daya ket nagaragaag ti naisapaw a buok ti gayyemna a nangtallikud iti tawa.

"*AARP Modern Maturity*," linidlid ni Tang Dave dagiti matana. "Napintas daytoy nga artikulo maipanggep iti kapanunotan ni Kofi Annan. Kunana: '*You don't hit a man on the head when you've got your fingers between his teeth.*'

"Sinno dayta a Kofi Annan?"

"Isu ti agdama a Secretary General ti United Nations. Kapaminduanan ti agtakem. Lakay metten ngem nagkaykaysa dagiti kameng ti UN a nangpili manen kenkuana apaman a naawatna ti premiona a Nobel Peace. Isaksakitnatayo nga. . .adun ti tawenna. . . Agbasaka ngamin met sagpaminsan tapno dinaka maadaywan ti panawen. Adayon ti nakaarusam, Miguel. . ."

"Mike, kunam kadi lattan, ta addata ngaruden ditoy America. Naikupinen daydi Miguel. Computer age sa ti awagdan ti panawen ita. . . ken lakay, kunam kadi lattan. Apay, aya, ket lakayka met a talagan. Pitopulomon."

"Pampanunoten ni Kofi Annan ti masakbayan ti sangalubongan a panaglakay."

"Ti kunam, matengngelna ngata ti panaglakay? Maisublina ngata ti pitopulom idi agkabannuagka pay?"

"Saan, ngem maikkannaka iti namnama nga agragsak kadagiti nabati pay nga aldaw a panagud-udaudmo itoy a biag."

"Ay siay, inka ketdin agdigos ket ti papananta. Amangan no nalipatamon," inkanuskos ni Tang Mike iti teltelna ket timmallikuden.

Minulenglengan pay ni Tang Dave ti basbasaenna sakbay nga inkupinna. Imparabawna ti magasin iti rabaw ti lamiseta iti sikigan ti kamana. Immanges iti nauneg sa timmaliaw iti daya a sinanguan ti tawa ti siledna. Inwangwangna itayen ti venetian blind ngem dina linuktan ti

nakatangep a sarming a rikep ti tawa. Uray no kasta, nabatad a makitana ti nadalus a langit iti daya. Ken ti globe willow tree iti abagatan-a-daya ti apartmentda. Nakapagbulongen ti narukbos a kayo ket nagminaren ti panagsinanlubong ti sukogna.

Serserrek ti Abril ket dandanin agngalay ti Spring wenno Panagsusulbod a maysa kadagiti uppat a panawen iti America.

Timmakder ni Tang Dave. Nagkayang a nagdeppa. Sa naglagtolagto. Nagbilang. Sa nagpug-apug-aw.

"Ania man ti. . ." timmungraraw ni Tang Mike. "Apo, aya, ta dikanto la mauma nga agek-eksersais!"

"Pangpaatiddog iti biag, Mike. Pangpaatiddog," kinuna ni Tang Dave a dina tinaliaw ni Tang Mike.

"'Nia ti kayatmo? Abutem ti tawen ni Metusalem? Purawton ti wak!"

"'Mom, aya, no agmilagro?" Saan nga insardeng ni Tang Dave ti aramidna.

"Sus!" nagkanuskos ni Tang Mike. "Ammom no apay a maan-anusanka?"

"Gapu ta maan-anusanka."

"No! No! Gapu ta padaka a Saluyot! Ken agpadata iti gasat. Dimo kadi mapampanunot no apay a nairanrana la unay ti panagtugmok ti dalanta ket naglawa ti America? No di la nakapimpiman ti langam idi damoka a makita idiay City Park... No dika inawis, pagyanam koma? Kalpasan ti panangpatapuak kenka ti ubing a Puraw nga asawam. . . Ngem bay-amon ti napalabas. . . ipapanta laengen nga agpadata a nagasat iti panagtugmok ti dalanta. Malagipmo a kunak idi, nga adu ti mayat nga umay makikabbalay kaniak, ngem managpiliak a tao? Idi damo pay la a makitaka, ammokon nga agkapudosanta. Ngem, ne, umaldawen. Dika pay namigat. . ."

"Apay ngata, Mike, a magusgustuan dagiti lallakay a lagipen ti napalabas?" pinarimriman ni Tang Mike ni Tang Dave.

"He!" kinusilapan ni Tang Mike ni Tang Dave. "Aggunaykan, kunak. . . kaska la ubing a dagdagdagen."

"Narigat ti naganat, Mike, aglalo no lakaykan," kinuna ni Tang Dave. "Urnongem ti nabati a pigsam para kadagiti dumteng nga aldaw."

"Sige man laengen. . . Inka agdigosen. Inton makadigoska, agtaruskanton 'diay kosina ta isaganakon ti pamigatta."

"Agyamanak unay, Mike. Gapu iti ar-aramidem kaniak, malaglagipko la ngarud daydi nagawan nga immuna nga asawak."

"Langgong a lakay!" kinuna ni Tang Mike ket timmallikuden a napan iti kosina.

Nangala ni Tang Dave iti pagsukatanna. Simrek iti banio. Naannad a nangpusipos iti dua a ballugo ti bath tub ta dina kayat a nalamiis wenno napudot unay ti pagdigosna. Narigat ti agsakit, kanayon nga ipalagipna iti bagina.

Idi sanguenda ti kinirog nga inapuy a nabawangan, saggaysada nga itlog ken saggaysada a longganisa nga insagana ni Tang Mike, binidingbiding ni Tang Dave ti taraon sakbay a nagsubo.

"Nasken a balanse ti ipauneg a taraon, Mike," nalamuyot ti ayug ni Tang Dave. "Saan a mabalin nga inaldaw nga itlog. Saan a mabalin nga inaldaw a karne. Kasta met a saan a mabalin nga inaldaw a nateng."

Timek 2

KANAYON a siririingak. Ammok ti kaipapanan ti tunggal karasakas dagiti pinanid a maukrad. Ammok no natingra wenno nakusnaw dagiti balikas a nailanad. Addaak iti alintataoyo, Dave a David idi addaka idiay Sabang a pinasukatam idi nagbalinka nga Amerikano. Nupay naan-anaykan a makipagili iti America, sika pay laeng daydi kaippasngay a David a sinursurotko. Ti isipmo pinessaan dagiti balligi ken pannakapaaymo. Iti man trabaho wenno iti ayat. Iti labes dagiti malukot nga aldaw ken mayaplag a rabii, agriingka latta iti sumuno nga agsapa a kanayon a sumangoka iti daya. A singisingan ti init. Iti uray ania a panawen.

Kaslakayo la agkasingin, Dave ken Mike, a Miguel idiay Saud, manipud idi nagsabat ti dalanyo. No agkuyogkayo, kasla dakdakayo ti tao iti lubong. No adda kanen ti maysa kanenyo a dua.

Maysa la ngata a nginabras ti uratyo ti di nagsilpo: saan a masnop ti sanguam, Mike, no agriingka, daya man wenno laud, abagatan wenno amianan. Agpadakayo a nakadata no maturogkayo. A kas man la tangtangadenyo ti bobeda ti langit. A tunggal rabii a panangsappuyot

ti iddayo iti naduri a bukotyo, kas man la mapespessaan ti agbukar nga
agsapa. Saan a mailinged kaniak nga adda banag nga im-imluyan ti
mugingyo, a kas man la tagtagiurayyo ti adu pay nga agsulbod nga aldaw.
Nasalun-at ti panangarakupyo iti agbukar a lawag. Sika, Dave, sanguam
amin malaksid ti pananglikliklikmo iti laud; agingga a kabaelam dimo
kayat ti sumango iti laud. . .

1. Panagsusulbod: Main Street Plaza

NI Tang Mike ti pinagmaneho ni Tang Dave iti kotsena a Thunderbird
77. Di kayat ni Tang Dave ti agmaneho ita ta malaglagipna manen ti
Puraw nga asawana a nangpanaw kenkuana. Kas iti panagsulbod dagiti
uggot ken panagbukar dagiti sabong, nalasbang nga agsubli iti lagipna
ti Puraw iti kastoy a panawen.

Nagsikkko ni Tang Mike iti kanawan nga agpadaya iti Lancer Way
manipud iti Kalye Harvey a yan ti apartmentda. Saanen a mailinged
ti kaadda ti Spring (Panagsusulbod) iti panagsulbod ti nadumaduma a
saringit dagiti kayo a nataratar iti igid ti kalsada, kasta met ti nabun-as a
panagsampaga dagiti tulips nga amarilio, bioleta, puraw, wenno nalabaga
ti sabongda iti paraangan dagiti balbalay. Adda pay la ti lamiis nga imbati
ti napalabas a winter (panawen ti niebe, nga ad-adda nga ammo dagiti
Filipino iti America nga isno, saan a niebe), a mangpaspasalibukag iti
rikna ni Tang Mike.

Magustuan ni Tang Mike ti agmaneho ket kaykayatna pay a suroten
dagiti side streets ta makarit ti kabaelanna iti sango ti manibela. Ken
maadalna dagiti lugar, uray no masansanen a pagpagnaanna.

Nagsikko ni Tang Mike nga agpaamianan al iti 2700 West a
nagbaetan ti City Hall ken ti Valley Fair Mall, sa nagpadaya iti
3500 South a kumamang iti Freeway I-215 nga agrikus iti county.
Nagpaamiananda iti I-215 sada simmiasi iti I-80 a mangbeltak iti puseg
ti siudad sada kimmamang iti 600 South ken nagpaamianan iti 200
West. Nagparada ni Tang Mike iti ikub ti Dees' Restaurant iti North
Temple ket nagnagnadan a nagpadaya a kumamang iti Main Street
Plaza iti nagbaetan ti Salt Lake Temple ken ti Church Office Building.
Iti amianan a sikigan ti North Temple, nabileg ti takder ti Conference

Center a mangtannawag iti Temple Square iti abagatan ken makidinnaer iti kapitolio iti amianan a daya. No makitkita ni Tang Mike dagitoy a buya, aglalo iti Spring, malagipna nga idilig ti Saud a kabakiran ti aglawlaw. Sinukog ti Nakaparsuaan ti Saud idinto a tao ti nangsukog itoy siudad a nagbalinen a lubongda.

Iti dayta nga agsapa ti Sabado, adun ti nadanon da Tang Dave ken Tang Mike nga agpalpalabas iti oras iti plasa. Nalalangto dagiti pandaka a kayo a parparungbuen dagiti namaris a tulips iti aglawlaw. Iti tengnga ti plasa, nalitnaw ti bassit a sementado a dan-aw a paglalanguyan dagiti agduduma ti marisna nga ikan a dandanuman dagiti babassit a fountain iti aglawlaw ti dan-aw. Paggugusto dagiti turista a sarungkaran daytoy Main Street Plaza a dua a tawenna pay laeng. Agduduma ti puli dagiti tao nga agisaw-isaw.

Iti nagtugawanda a sementado a banko, insursurot ni Tang Dave ti panagkitana kadagiti agpa-amianan ken –abagatan iti plasa. Agsisinnabat, agsisinnibbaingda. Dagiti ubbing aggagarikgikda a kibin dagiti nagannak kadakuada. Dagiti agkikibin nga asmang adda bituen iti agsapa kadagiti matada.

"Dekahon a biag," kinuna ni Tang Dave, nga awan ti masnop a nangituronganna.

Tinaliaw ni Tang Mike, ngem nagtalinaed a naem-em dagiti bibigna.

"Mike, ammom kadi a dekahon met ti biagta?"

"Amangan no kunam pay a delungon?" kinuna ni Tang Mike a dina tinaliaw ni Tang Dave.

"Paggapgapuan ken pappapanan ti tao?" insungo ni Tang Dave dagiti tao.

"Kasda met kenka, a. Apay nga addaka ditoy? Apay a dika nagnunog 'diay San Juan? Adu a gapu ti panagtawataw ti tao. Ngem kas kenka, kas kaniak, diak maawatan no apay a ditoy ti nangipalladawan ni gasat kaniak. Kalpasan ti ipupusay daydi nagawan, nga awan ti naibatina a bunga a katakunaynayko koma, ti la addan a naturturongko iti America. California, Delaware, Florida, sa ditoy Utah…"

Pimmuskol ti tao iti plasa. Manipud iti Salt Lake Temple, naragsak dagiti apagkallaysa a Puraw ti nobia ken Nangisit ti nobio a rimmuar iti inaladan ket nagturongda iti plasa, a kaduada dagiti kabagian ti

agsumbangir. Nagreretratoda, ken saan a maymaysa ti mangibidbidio kadakuada.

"Nasayaat a panaglaok ti puli," nakuna ni Tang Dave.

Naulimek ti grupo dagiti apagkallaysa a simrek iti ikub ti templo.

Immakar da Tang Dave ken Tang Mike iti laud a ligason ti Main Street Plaza, nga aw-awaganda iti Temple Square, iti pingir ti Salt Lake Temple iti abagatan, nga abagatan met ti Tabernacle Building a kas la napakleb a kagudua ti dakkel a lubong---nasuroken a sangagasut ti tawen ti pasdek. Kas iti plasa, nalasbang ken namaris dagiti tulips ken dadduma a kaykayo. Naumbi ti ayug ti kanta dagiti kameng ti Tabernacle Choir nga agen-ensayo iti kantaenda iti sumuno nga agsapa ti Domingo. Dinomingo nga ipabuya ti Bonneville Communictions iti telebision ti Tabernacle Choir.

"Kas man la paraiso ditoy, Mike!" nagkidem ni Tang Dave a nangnanam iti maipatpatayab nga ayug iti Tabernacle Building.

Iti South Temple, iti ruar ti Temple Square, adda bassit a grupo nga agididiaya iti polieto ti pammati a maigidiat iti itaktakderan ti Salt Lake Temple. Nadagsen ti nabanayad a litaklitak ti landok a sapatos ti nangisit a kabalio a nagguyod iti karuahe iti South Temple.

Timek 3

AWAN gawayko a mangtubeng iti gagemmo, Dave. Adda dagiti paltiing iti isipmo, babassit a timek, a kayatko a timudem. Ngem dayta a bileg nasken a sika a mismo ti dumngeg. Adda paglintegan iti biag a nakaitalimudokan ti rebbengek ket aginga la dita ti agpang a pagaliwaksayan ti kabaelak.

No kayatmo a gaw-aten dagiti bituen a naririmat iti panawen ti kalgaw a pannakatubay dagiti baro a padas, awan gawayko a mangtubeng. Ammok nga adda pagpatinggaan ti kabaelam a gaw-aten. Ngem no adda bilegmo nga agtayab iti tangatang, ala ket surotenka iti sadino man a turongem. Tangay tumadtadem ti panagriknam iti kaaddak.

Nalaglag-an a tenglenka, Mike, ta no ullawka koma, nababa ti tayabmo. No ania ti adda a makan isu ti isubom. Awan dumam iti nataengan a bulong iti kalgaw nga agur-uray lattan iti agek ti sumuno nga aldaw.

2. Kalgaw: Timpanogos Cave

KAS paset ti panagsagana da Tang Dave ken Tang Mike iti ipapanda iti Timpanogos Cave National Monument iti Sabado, napanda naggatang iti masapsapulda iti NPS. Gimmatang ni Tang Dave iti Noni Gold, ti nakabotelia a tubbog ti apatot a naaramid kano iti Hawaii, a pagpakiredna, malaksid iti binotelia a danum kas balakad dagiti nagdamaganda.

Sangkarengrengna ni Tang Mike a gumatang met iti ania man a masapulna, ngem nagkedked ti naud-udi. Awan arisgarna a sumang-at iti Timpanogos ket no di la gapu iti adu a panangpilit kenkuana ni Tang Dave, adayo a mapanunotna ti mapan iti dayta a lugar.

Dandanin agngalay ti Summer ket mariknan ti kinnit ti darang ti init. Tumingtingra metten ti nadumaduma a maris dagiti bulong—amarilio, berde, bioleta, nalabaga, ken adda pay asul, ken puraw. Uray ti globe willow tree iti sidiran ti apartmentda, pinatayengtengen ti Summer ti berde a bulongna nga apagapaman nga indayonen ti nalanay a pul-oy.

Nasapa a nagriing ni Tang Dave. Nasapa a nagdigos. Nasapa a nangisagana iti masapsapulna—insakemanna metten ni Tang Mike, a pangay-ayona a mangkadua kenkuana. Sigud nga isu ti dagdagdagen ni Tang Mike, ngem baliktad ita.

"Dimonto pagbabawyan ti isusurotmo kaniak," kinuna ni Tang Dave bayat ti panagmanehona nga agpaabagatan iti I-215 a kumamang iti I-15. "Dakkelto a padasmo iti unos ti panagbiagmo ti isasang-atmo iti Timpanogos."

"Unos ti panagbiagko?" nagarko ti kiday ni Tang Mike. "Naimbag koma no ubingak pay. Ngem daytoy nga edadko. . . Masdaawak no apay nga arisgaram pay la ti sumang-at."

Imbes a sumungbat ni Tang Dave, inyintekna ti panagkitana iti masanguananda a nakaiban-uyatan ti I-215. No dadduma, kumita iti agsumbangir a sikiganna. Bay-anna lattan a saligan dagiti kaskasero; maysa pay amkenna nga agpalia ti Thunderbirdna a 77 iti ngalay ti freeway. Pengpengdanna ti agdungsa, ta dina maliklikan no kasta nga

agmaneho iti nawatiwat. Dina impilit a ni Tang Mike ti agmaneho, amangan no ad-adda a di sumurot.

Pinunnona itay iti gasolina ti tangke ti luganna ngem dandanin nagudua idi dumanonda iti pagawatan ti sangaili ti Timpanogos Cave National Park nga inipit ti dua a kalbo a naursa a dadakkel a bantay. Kasla umuli nga uleg ti kalsada ket dayta ti ammona a nalaka a nakaibusan ti gasna.

Adun ti nadanonda a turista nga agur-uray iti kaduada a mangbuya iti videotape maipanggep iti Timpanogos. Ti rasonda a mangipabuya: tapno adda gundaway dagiti turista nga agsanud no kas pagarigan ipapanda a dida kabaelan ti sumang-at. Ngem makaay-ayo ketdi ti panangilawlawag ti natudingan a mangilawlawag ket awan ti nagtukiad malaksid ni Tang Mike.

"Diak patien a kabaelak pay nga ulien," kinunana idi maibaga a maysa a milia-ket-gudua ti kaatiddog ti akikid a desdes nga umuli. Agarup a tallo ribu a kadapan ti kangatona. "Sika lattan ti agtuloy, Dave. Urayenka laengen ditoy. Awan duaduak a diak kabalen ti sumang-at."

"Addata la ngaruden ditoy," kinuna ni Tang Dave. "Sumang-attan. No kabaelan dagita babbai, dita ketdin kabaelan?"

"Ubbingda. Data ngay?"

"Kabaelanta, ania ketdin!"

Ket gimmatang ni Tang Dave iti tiketda uray di pay nag-wen ni Tang Mike. Napan nangala iti kotse iti sagduduada a botelia ti danum ket impabitbitna ken ni Tang Mike ti dua.

"Imulam iti panunotmo a kabaelam," kinuna ni Tang Dave idi rugiandan ti sumang-at. "Ken dimo pampanunoten ti kaatiddog ti desdes nga agpangato."

Kasla naikitikit nga uged ti desdes a kimmalipkip iti naursa a bakrang ti bantay. Bato ken saggaysa a kayo ti adda iti kanigid a bakrasna a no tangaden kurang la marung-ad ti tengnged. Kakaykaywan iti derraas a kanawan a di mangngeg ti pagdissuan ti bato nga agtulatid.

Dida pay nakaaddang iti duapulo, agranetreten dagiti tumeng ni Tang Mike.

Awan ti ranetret dagiti tumeng ni Tang Dave, gapu ngata iti binigat a panagwatwatna, ngem mariknana metten a kasla umer-erteng dagiti piskelna.

"Agsardengta pay!" inyanal-al ni Tang Mike. Timmangad iti papananda. "Adayo pay!"

"Dika tumangtangad," kinuna ni Tang Dave. Intuloyda ti sumang-at. "Italimudokmo ti panagkitam iti dalan. Dika kumitkita iti baba. . . iti derraas."

Adda dagiti pagestasionan nga agkuna no mano pay a kadapan ti sang-atenda.

Adda saggaysa a masabatda.

"Adayo pay?" no kua saludsoden manen ni Tang Mike iti masabatda.

"Adayo pay!" isungbatda. "But amazing!"

Nakamakam ida ti pangrapisen a lalaki nga adda sakbatna a gitara.

"Hello, guys!" kinunana. "Are you okay?"

"I'm dying!" inyanangsab ni Tang Mike.

"Asidegen, 'nia?" dinamag ni Tang Dave.

"Adayo pay," kinuna ti lalaki. "Ngem makadanonkayonto. Siak, maminduaak a sumang-at iti makalawas."

"Apay nga adda gitaram?" dinamag ni Tang Dave.

"Adda balasang idiay ngato a magustuanna ti aggitara," kinuna ti lalaki. "See you later." Ket pinartakannan ti simmang-at.

Napanganga ni Tang Dave. Iti askaw ti lalaki, kas man la magmagna laeng iti patad.

Awan sa pay sangapulo nga addang ti napagnada idi agsardeng manen ni Tang Mike.

"Diak kabaelanen, Dave!" inyal-al ni Tang Mike. "Naibusen ti angesko!"

"Uminumka," kinuna ni Tang Dave.

Nakamakam ida ti panglukmegen a babai. "Hi, guys!" inkablaawna. "Are you okay?"

"Yes, we are," kinuna ni Tang Dave.

"No, I'm not!" kinuna ni Tang Mike. "I'm dying!"

Nagkatawa ti babai. Imbagana nga adda la iti panagsanay. Mamitlo kano iti makalawas a sumang-at.

"Nasken laeng," kinuna ni Tang Mike a nangisursurot iti panagkitana iti babai nga agarup itarayna pay ti sumang-at. "Adu pay ti nasken a regregenna!"

Agkuy-os ti rusok ni Tang Mike no mailaw-an a kumita iti derraas iti sikiganna iti kanawan. Agkarawa iti kanigid a mangsapul iti pagkaptanna.

Agritturittuok metten dagiti tumeng ni Tang Dave ngem saan a nagpadpadlaw. Agkuy-os met no kua ti riknana, ken angsaben metten ngem adda timek iti isipna nga agkunkuna: *kabaelam, Dave, kabaelam!*

Agdua nga orasen a sumangsang-atda ta umas-assidegen ti panagsardengda. Adun ti nakalabas kadakuada a sumang-at, ken nasabatda a sumalog. Dandanin agmatuon ket pumudpudot ti aglawlaw, malaksid kadagiti pasetna a nagbalayan ti isno a di nabaelan a rinunaw ti kalgaw. Iti umuna a gundaway, immapay iti panunot ni Tang Mike nga asidegen ti pagtungedan ti biagna. Pabasolen ti panunotna ni Tang Dave, ngem babalawenna met ti bagina ta dina impetteng ti nagkedked iti awis ti gayyemna.

Nakadanonda iti pagpaknian a kasla agbibitin iti rangkis iti pangrugian ti nabati nga apagkatlo ti desdes. Aglamiisen ti ling-et ni Tang Dave ket saan a ganggannaet kenkuana dayta a rikna. Partaan ti pasungadenna a madi a rikna. Idalupisakna la koma ti kunana iti uneg ti pagpaknian ngem ad-adda a maulaw iti angot. Kinaaduna ti imminum. Dina impadlaw ti riknana ken ni Tang Mike idi rummuar.

"Asideg kanon!" kinunana nga umi-sisem. Iti unegna, indawatna a maikkan pay iti umdas a pigsa.

Nagtugaw ni Tang Dave iti ruar ti pagpaknian bayat ti isusublat ni Tang Mike. Inwarasna ti panagkitana iti amianan, daya, ken abagatan. Iti amianan, nababbaba ti bantay ngem iti yanda. Iti daya, naursa a derraas, ket iti ipapanna nga alimpatok, nakitana ti ipus ti dana a sursurotenda. Iti abagatan, nakarit dagiti tangkiran a kayo nga agbibitin iti bakras ti bantay. No kumita koma ni Tang Dave iti laud, makitana ti nagtamedan ti dua a bantay ket iti nagngangaanda, maitangkarang ti tanap ti Timpanogos ken ti nagsikogan ti Karayan Jordan. Ken inaldaw a lumnekan ti init. Matannawaganna koma ti sangabukel a laud a paginanaan ti agtulid nga aldaw.

Dina kayat a panunoten nupay ammona nga adda sadiay ti Karayan Jordan—no apay nga impasurotda ti nagan dayta a karayan iti Karayan Jordan idiay Israel, paset dagiti banag a likliklikanna a lagipen.

Nakatulong ken ni Tang Dave ti panagtugawna iti kayo a bangko bayat ti panangurayna ken ni Tang Mike. Idi sarunuenda dagiti padada a turista, adda bassiten kiredda a nangbilang kadagiti askawda. Dandanidan maibus ti sagsangaboteliada a danum. Ngem saan a kayat a sagiden ni Tang Dave ti maikadua a botelia ta saganana iti isasalugdanto.

Pinadasna a di panunoten ti panagsang-atda. Ketdi, pinagsalana ti panunotna iti Noli Gold nga imminumanna iti tallo a kutsara itay agrubuatda iti apartmentda. Ken dagiti naragsak a kalmanna. Ken liniklikanna ti kimmita iti ngato ken iti baba. Ngem kadarrato a taliawenna ni Tang Mike. Sangkakunana nga asidegdan. Ngem ammona nga ul-ulbodenna ti bagina ta uray isu ket maganatan metten a makadanon iti ngato. Nasuroken a dua nga orasda a sumangsang-at. Kasano pay ngata ti kapautda a sumang-at? Tangadenna koma ti init ngem dina kayat a maammuan a dandanin agmatuon. Ngem uray no kasta, ammona a kasta ta makitanan ti anniniwanna, a kayatna a sawen, nagparangen ti init iti naglingedanna a mungay ti bantay a sangsang-atenda. Madamdama pay, agligsayton; agin-inayadton nga aglemmeng ti init iti laud.

Nakapamin-anoda pay a nagsardeng. Dida metten mabilang no mano ti nanglabas kadakuada a sumang-at ken nasabatda a sumalog. Ita a nasaludsod ni Tang Dave iti unegna: ania ti maganabna iti nagpagusanna a sumang-at? A mapan mangkita iti nalatak a kueba iti tuktok ti Timpanogos? Apay ngamin nga iti pay tuktok ti bantay ti nagsaadan dayta a kueba? Ania a talaga ti adda iti uneg dayta a kueba?

Tinaliaw ni Tang Dave ni Tang Mike. Kasla bilbilangen ti naud-udi ti askawna, a nakadumog, a kasla awan tao iti asidegna.

"Welcome to the Timpanogos Cave National Park!" nasinga ni Tang Dave iti nabara a kablaaw ti naisem a babai.

Addadan iti pantok!

"Nakitam!" nagrimat dagiti mata ni Tang Dave a nangsipat iti abaga ni Tang Mike a kasla agdudungsa a ganador dagiti matana.

Iti ngiwat ti gukayab, narikna ti Tang Dave ti nalamiis a sang-aw nga aggapu iti uneg. Adu ti nakaskasdaaw a banag nga inlawlawag ti tourist

guide. Naglaon dagiti tallo a kueba iti ginasut nga agduduma ti sukogna a calcite wenno taredted a nagbalin a bato a pimmirak wenno bimmalitok ti marisna. Natitiradda. Kangrunaanna ti pannakadiskobre iti gukayab. Daydi bunggoyda ti immuna a nangdappat iti daytoy nga estado ti America. Awan ti danum idi iti aglawlaw ket ti la nagsapsapulanda agingga a nakadanonda iti dapan ti Bantay Timpanogos. Manipud sadiay, nakakitada iti tugot ti leon; adda pammati a no agsapul ti leon iti danum uray bantay ulienna. Sinursurotda dayta a tugot agingga a nakadanonda iti yanda ita. Bassit kano ti serkan idi punganay, ngem pinadakkelda. Tapno nasaysayud ti pannagna wenno yuusok dagiti turista, napanunotda a nayonan wenno ilawa ti abut ti kueba. Inikkanda pay iti silawna a bombilia. Maysa a nakaskasdaaw a bileg ti tao ti panagisang-atda kadagiti inaramatda. Adu ti tektites nga imbaga ti tourist guide a ditoy laeng a lugar ti pakasarakan.

Nupay talaga a nakaskasdaaw dayta a lugar, saan a naaw-awatan ni Tang Dave ti nangnegna. Ti napateg kenkuana, natungpalen ti panggepna a sumang-at iti dayta a bantay.

Sabali a ridaw ti rimmuaranda. Apaman a nakapagpipinnakadada kadagiti kaduada a simmang-at, ken kadagiti mangimaton iti kueba, immunan ni Tang Dave.

Nagsardeng iti wangawangan ti dana a sumalog—sabali ti sinang-atanda a nagturong iti sinerkanda iti dana a nangsabat kadakuada iti rimmuaranda, ngem agsabatda met la iti saan unay nga adayo. Nagbannikes ni Tang Dave a simmango iti laud: iti umuna a gundaway. Ket kas man la nalawa nga isem ti nagkayangan ti dua a bantay a nangsabat kadagiti matana.

Kinuna ni Tang Dave ken ni Tang Mike: "Makitam! Makitam!"

Ngem iti panagsalogda, kasla nakabirkakak a buaya ti derraas a makaalimpayeng ti kaunegna.

Timek 4

NAIMBAG la ketdin ta sabali ti naikudi a rebbengek. Iti lubong a paggargarawak saan nga agtulid ti oras ket diak pampanunoten ti panaglakayko a kas kadakayo, Dave ken Mike. Awan reklamok iti tunggal

darikmat a pannakipulpulapolko kadakayo. Diak sintiren ti kettang ken pulkokko agur-urokkayo man wenno agkatkatawa.

No man is an island, *kunada. No baliktadek ngata, a* no island is a man? *Hmm. Saan a nasken kadakayo a nasinged nga aggayyem, ngem ammok nga ammoyo a kasta, ta no dadduma ket denggenyo ti nakapsut a timekko a manmano ti makaammo a dumngeg. Wenno makaammo nga adda kasta a timek a ti kaunggan ti pudno a makangngeg.*

Maawatak no apay nga alusiisenkayo. Ngem diak la ammo no maawatanyo a nasken a masurot ti linteg ti nakaparsuaan. Narigat kadi nga awaten ti panagtulid ti panawen? Ti gundaway a pannakaipusing iti sangkatawan?

2. Autumn: Antelope Island State Park

AGLUOMEN ti bulong dagiti kayo iti igid ti freeway iti dandanin agngalay ti Autumn wenno Fall wenno panagreregreg ti bulong, iti arinunos ti Oktubre. Pati ti globe willow tree iti abay ti apartmentda natangkenanen dagiti bulongna ket saan a mabayag agregregdanton. Kadagiti uppat a pannakadasig ti panawen iti America, daytoy a panawen ti di magustuan ni Tang Dave. Awan ganasna nga agpasiar, kaykayatna koma ti agkumeg iti apartmentda, ngem napaut unay ti tallo a bulan a dina panagaliwaksay. Saan nga umdas ti binigat a panagwatwatna tapno maiwagsakna ti pulkok nga agpilit nga agukop iti mugingna. Ken ti lamiis a mangmulmulmol kadagiti dakulap ken dapanna.

Sursuroten ni Tang Mike ti 65 m/hr a pagsurotan iti partak ti panagpataray iti Freeway I-15, ngem kayat ni Tang Dave a nabumbuntog koma.

Saanda nga agin-innuni, nagintuturog ni Tang Dave. Dina la koma kayat nga iti Antelope Island State Park ti pangpalabsanda iti sumagmamano nga oras, wenno iti sangabukel nga aldaw ti Sabado, kas ita. Ngem bagi ita ni Tang Mike a pinilit a sumurot kenkuana. Agarup sangapulo a milia ti kawatiwat ti I-15 a panurnorenda manipud iti Harvey a yan ti apartmentda sadanto sumiasi nga agpalaud iti bassit a kalsada a kumamang iti pito a milia ti kaatiddogna a rangtay

a namagsilpo iti parke ken iti siudad ti Syracuse iti nalawa a Great Salt Lake.

Ania ti adda ditoy a parke a mangparasuk iti regget? Naisip ni Tang Dave. Naiputputong ti Antelope Island State Park iti tengnga ti Great Salt Lake. Awan ti nalangto a buya iti uray ania a panawen. Disierto ti kaaduan a pasetna, malaksid kadagiti ruot a paggugustoda ti agbiag iti kasta a lugar. Ngem adda pagpastoran, wenno ranso, nga isu ti Fielding Garr Ranch. Adda pay visitor's center. Adu kano ti turista a sumarsarungkar apaman nga agngalay ti spring agingga nga aggibus ti autumn.

Nasinga ti panagpampanunot ni Tang Dave idi agbanurbor ken agaludaid ti Thunderbird 77. Namulagatanna ti pananglukat ni Tang Mike iti sarming iti batogna ket adda yaw-awatna iti tao iti gate. Addada gayamen iti pagentradaan.

"Enjoy your stay!" kinuna ti tao.

Enjoy? Naisip ni Tang Dave.

Nagbanurbor manen ti Thunderbird 77. No dadduma agsaiddek ket dandani la maawanan iti anges.

"Dinatan sa met maidanon 'toy Batmanmon!" angaw ni Tang Mike.

"Nasayaat tapno saanta nga agtultuloyen," saan nga immisem ni Tang Dave. "Dita pay nakadanon, nabannogakon!"

"Nabannogkan? No magmagnaka nga agawid, dika ngata mabannog? Laglagipem, nasurok a duapulo a milia ti kaadayo ti Harvey. Naimbag koma no adda lumabas a Greyhound wenno UTA ditoy. Awan mayat nga agilugan kadagiti dida am-ammo."

Saan a nagtimek ni Tang Dave. Naalsem ti rupana a nangipalladaw ti panagkitana iti abagatan ken no dadduma iti amianan a sikigan ti rangtay—sabali a kita ti rangtay ti daldaliasatenda; awan adigi ken paradipadna ta ginaburan dagiti nagaramid ti nakaiban-uyatanna. Inrantana ti di kumita iti laud a masanguanda, a pangipadlawna ken ni Tang Mike ti isesekkad ti riknana a mapan.

"Bagim idi idiay Timpanogos, bagik met ita ditoy," bangbangir ti isem ni Tang Mike. "Amanusta laengen, Gayyem. 'Tay kunadan, give and take."

"'Nia pay koma ti maaramidak?" kinuna ni Tang Dave. "No adda la koma kabsatko, wenno kabagiak nga asideg ditoy, wen man, ta pagananoka met a kadua!"

Nagpaggaak ni Tang Mike. "Dayta ket!" kinunana. "Awan kabsatmo, awan kabagiam. . .. kastaak met. Di kapilitan a datan ti agkabsat. Kayatmo man, wenno kayatko man wenno saan."

"Malas!"

"Oy, saan. Nagasatta ketdi. Apay, kunam? No sika ti maibusan, wenno siak ti maawanan, addaka a sumaranay wenno addaak a pagsadagam. Malagipmo 'di pannakapukaw ti pensionmo iti koreo? Ken ti panangputedda iti SSI-ko gapu iti biddut ti gobierno? Kasano koma ti biagta no awan ti tunggal maysa kadata?"

Idi makadanonda iti Antelope Island State Park, nabayag a nagrikusrikosda sakbay a nakadanonda iti Visitor's Center. Nasdaaw ni Tang Dave ta iti baet ti pannakaiputputong ti parke, saan a kasta ti ipasimudaag dagiti adda iti sentro. Awan dumana kadagiti babassit a pasdek a masarakan iti siudad. Kompleto dagiti masapsapul dagiti turista.

Ken adu ti tao! Putputong a lugar ngem adu ti tao? Ubbing, nataengan, ken adda pay agsisinnannggol nga agpaparang ti pusegda. Nagmurarareg ni Tang Dave. *No man is an island?*

Ad-addan ti siddaaw ni Tang Dave idi mapanda iti Fielding Garr Ranch. Iti panagkitana, iti tanap a nalabsanda awan met unay ti kasano a ruot a kanen dagiti bison, mule deer, nuang ken kabalio iti pasto, ngem nalulukmegda. Kasano nga agbiag dagitoy iti kastoy a lugar? naisipna. Wenno adda ngata mangip-ipan iti kanenda? Kasano ti biagda iti winter?

Napanda iti linong ti maysa a pagtutugawan ket sadiayda a nangaldaw. Natangkenen ti darang ti init ngem alep-epen ti pul-oy a pakpakauna ti winter. Makapasaguyepyep ti pul-oy ket in-ut a tininnagna dagiti kalub ti mata ni Tang Dave, a dinuayya pay ti nakataltalna a rimat ti agin-iniin a bukot ti danum. Nakaul-ulimek ti aglawlaw, a manmano a singaen ti nasinggit a garikgik dagiti ubbing iti sabali a pagtutugawan.

Naisip ni Tang Dave: nargaan ti Antelope iti saklot ti Autumn iti puseg ti Great Salt Lake!

Timek 5

ADDA imeng ti barukong a pabaraen ti tunggal pitik ti darikmat. Kasko met marikrikna ti saligemgem iti kaungganyo, Dave ken Mike, iti kas man la kaawan ti mangipatpateg kadakayo no di dakayo met la a dua. Ti timekko nga ipalpaltiingko kadakayo sumagsagepsep iti panunotyo ta kasapulanyo ti anem-em iti tunggal maysa. Ipitpitikko kadakayo a nasken a pagkaysaenyo ti panunot ken riknayo ta dakayo la ti makaawat iti bagbagiyo.

Agingga a dumteng daydiay napateg a panawen. Kayatko nga awatenyo ti paltiingko a tallopulo-ket-maysa laeng ti aldaw ti Disiembre.

3. Winter: Park City

"DAYTOY panggepko a papanan, nasken a saanko a bukbukod a pangngeddeng," kinuna ni Tang Dave iti maysa nga aldaw a panagbuybuyada ken ni Tang Mike iti telebision. "Nasken a pagtulaganta. No dimo kayat, saan a matuloy. Ngem nasken met a mangisingasingka iti papananta. No ania ti kunam, isuratmo iti papel ti panggepmo, kasta met kaniak, satanto pagdiligen. Iti kasta maliklikan ti pinnabus-oy."

Kasta ti napasamak. Ket iti maysa kadagiti manmano a panagtunos ti kapanunotanda, nagkasurotanda a mapan iti Park City.

Agpadada a di pay napan iti dayta a siudad a kangrunaan a pagii*ski*an iti winter, aglalo no nabengbeng ti nagtinnag nga isno.

Ken ni Tang Mike, kayatna a makita a personal dagiti nalaing nga agiiski. Mano a tawennan ditoy kunkunada nga estado ti isno ngem di pay nakabuya a personal.

Ken ni Tang Dave, kayatna a padasen ti agiski. Tunggal makabuya iti agiiski iti telebision, agungar ti riknana a mangpadas met. Nakaim-imas ngamin ti riknana nga agbuya, ket iti isipna, naim-imas pay ngata no isu a mismo ti adda idiay nga agtayabtayab. Patienna a saan a paglalakayan ti ania man nga aramid no napigsa ti ragutmo a mangaramid. Kayatna a paneknekan a saan pay a naladaw iti kas kenkuana.

"Sika ti agmaneho a sumang-at," kinuna ni Tang Mike.

Saan a nagkedked ni Tang Dave. Ipakitana ken ni Tang Mike a saan a maaliaw nga agmaneho uray iti nabengbeng nga isno. A kabaelanna nga iturong ti Thunderbird 77 iti baet ti kinalakayen ti luganna.

Iti aldaw sakbay ti isasang-atda iti Park City, napan gimmatang ni Tang Dave iti Deseret Industries iti segunda mano nga ski boots. Dina imbagbaga ken ni Tang Mike; dina impakpakita. Kayatna a surpresaen ti gayyemna.

Nupay aggidiat ti pampanunotenda, agpadada a nasaranta a nagrubuat. Agpadada a nasaranta a limmugan iti Thunderbird 77. Iti panangunor ni Tang Dave iti I-80 nga agpadaya nga agturong iti Park City, nagdanggayda a nangpasurot iti *Top of the World* a kanta daydi Karen Carpenter a maipatpatayab iti stereo. No manen, agdespasio ni Tang Dave no madlawna nga agkabsiw ti pilid ti lugan no makadalapus iti nagbalay a yelo. Natangken ken nagalis ti ngimmisit a yelo ket adu ti maak-aksidente a motorista no agkibaltang ti panagmanehoda.

Dandanin agtindek ti init a simmirip iti ulep a nabati iti limmabas nga isno iti napalabas a rabii idi makadanonda iti Park City. Adun ti turista ket kurang la nga aglibiang dagiti convenience stores iti wangawangan ti parke.

Bayat ti panangbuya da Tang Dave ken Tang Mike kadagiti agiiski nga agpangato ken agpababa kadagiti galunggalong a pagandaren ti koriente, nadlaw ti naud-udi ti sakbat ti gayyemna. Saan a nagtagtagari ni Tang Dave, a nagpamarang a napasnek a mangbuybuya kadagiti agtayab nga agiiski.

Kaaduanna a turista ti adda ramitna a para ski, malaksid la ti nabengbeng a pagimeng a nangbalkot iti bagida.

Adda met pagimeng dagiti dua a lallakay ngem saan a kas kadagiti dadduma. Nagboneteda, ken nagguantista.

No adda agtayab nga agiski, maipaspasurot ti bagi ni Tang Dave, a kunam no agilus-ilos met. Idi kuan, inruarna ti ginatangna nga ski boot ket insukatna iti sapatosna.

"Ay, ay, dika agar-aramid!" nalagawan ni Tang Mike.

"Padasek laeng," kinuna ni Tang Dave. Iti unegna napinget a nagkuna: *kabaelak, ania ketdin!*

Ket nagna iti kayeluan. Idi damo, sinintirna ti bagina. Mayat! Agarup sangapulo a kadapan ngata ti kaadayona iti dapan ti kayeluan.

"Saan, Dave, saan!" naglagaw ni Tang Mike idi irubuat ni Tang Dave ti agpakuyasyas.

Ngem nagkuyasyasen ni Tang Dave.

Timek 6

ALA wen, Dave. Ala wen, Mike. Itoy a gundaway ammok a nalawagen iti mugingyo no aniaak.

Imdenganyo ti timekko. Imdenganyo: Addaak kadakayo, addaak iti tunggal tao. . .

II. Pangrikep

NAULIMEK ni Tang Mike a mangbuybuya iti gayyemna a natalna a matmaturog iti kama a nakaulsanna iti puraw. Maikadua nga aldawnan iti LDS Memorial Hospital. Nakatalupak ti kanawan a takiagna a naipalek iti nabuntuon a timmangken nga isno idi maipakuyasyas. Di pay manamnama ti doktorna no kasano ti kagrabe ti tengngedna. No kaskasano, amangan no napalsian ti spinal cord iti teltelna. No kasdiay agnanayonton a baldado.

"Kaasiam ti gayyemko, Apo!" nagraed ti timek ni Tang Mike a giddan ti panangpiselna iti kanigid a dakulap ni Tang Dave.

Dandanin lumnek ti init iti laud idi agkuti ni Tang Dave. Napataliaw ni Tang Mike nga agdudungsa iti tugawna. Bassit la ti naiturogna manipud idi kalman a panangitarayda iti gayyemna iti hospital.

Nagmulagat ni Tang Dave.

"Dave. . . Dave!" napalua ni Tang Mike.

Namaga ti isem ni Tang Dave. "Dika agdanag, Mike. Kabaelak daytoy," apagasngaw ngem napnuan namnama ti timekna. Kimmita iti nakalukat a tawa iti kusayanna a sumango iti laud. Kasla adda natimudna a bassit a timek a nagkuna iti bagina: adda met laudmo, Dave.

"Agawaam ti agpalaing, Dave. . ."

"Napintas ti laud, Mike," nalukay ti isem ni Tang Dave.—0

Disiembre 31, 2002, 3:45 p.m.; Enero 5, 2003, 1:46 AM; Enero 5, 2003, 3:37 PM; Abril 26, 2003, 10:11 AM; Hunio 16, 2015, 2:51 AM. Immuna nga impablaak ti *Rimat*, Mayo 2003.

Pagawidam, Felipe Abraham?

Pakauna

Naggapuam, Felipe Abraham?
Nawatiwat sa ti dinaliasatmo ta langam ti napaksuyan.
Wenno agawidka kadin, sadino ti pagtaengam?
Wenno balaymo kadi amin a papanam?
Adda kadi kaamaam a sangpetam?
Wenno mangipatpateg kenka nga agur-uray?
Asinoka iti lubong a paggargarawam—
Maysa a gabat a naiwawa wenno nalipatan?

-I-

"MAYMAYSAN sa ti papananta, Kabsat," kinuna ti kayumanggi a lalaki a nangtangad iti sarsarunuenna. Kasla nadagsen ti guyguyodenna a maleta. "Maymaysan sa pay ti naggapuanta. . ."

Kasla saan a nangngeg ti masarsaruno a nagarukong iti iseserrekna iti ridaw ti eroplano. Kamkamatenna ti angesna. Adayo ti pinagnana manipud iti nagdissaganna a Delta Airlines iti Los Angeles International Airport, nga akaranna iti Philippine Airlines. Nabannog unay ti langana ken kasla di naturog iti no mano nga aldaw. Bassit ti *knapsack* nga agarup pimmakep iti panadulen a bukotna ngem kasla nadagsen pay a sakbatna.

"Kabsat... Kabsat." Mamitlo ti addang ti sumarsaruno iti maysa nga addang ti sarsarunuenna a padpadasenna a kamakamen.

Kasla bulldog iti likudanna ti panangtaliaw ti naabay iti nangabay kenkuana. Nalesseb dagiti nalanay a matana iti immatiddog a rupana. "Siak kadi ti kasarsaritam. . . Kabsat?"

Nagkatawa iti puted ti immabay. Tinangadna ti inabayna. "Naangawka met, Kabsat. Dinnod'toyka 'diay Pinas, Kabsat?"

Kinuti ti naabay ti abagana; nagling-i iti apagapaman.

Dinnod'toyak 'diay Filipinas? Sadino ti nakayanak? Naipasngayak kano iti ruar ti kamanilaan, kuna 'di tatangko. 'Di tatangko, patneng nga Ilokano. Uray 'di Nanangko, wenno ni Nanangko—diak ammo ti yanna, no sibibiag pay. Agpadada a naidaknir iti nagsarakanda. . .

"Your attention, please. Palagip kadagiti pasahero: maysa laeng ti mabalin a hand cary ti tunggal pasahero." Natibong ti bilin a naggapu iti boarding area.

"Apay a kastakayo ket pinalubosandakami la ngaruden itay nagtsek-inkami?" Makaunget ti reklamo iti ruar.

"Nangngegmo, Kabsat?" kinulding ni Miguel Arcadio ni Felipe Abraham. "Agreklamoda ket dida met ammo ti sumurot iti linteg. Ammom no kasano a nakalusot ti hand carryda? Dida intugot iti mismo a pagpatsekan. Imbatida iti immay nangitulod kadakuada. Saur a talaga. . . Pinoy a talaga!"

Nagsikko ti naabay iti kanawan a nanglabas iti stewardess a nangkablaaw kenkuana. Simmurot ti immabay.

"Siak gayam ni Miguel, Kabsat. Miguel Arcadio. Mike ditoy America. Ilokanoak. . .taga-Norte." kinuna ti immabay. "Pasensiakan no medio nauntonak. Agsapsapulak ngamin 'ti makaawat kaniak. . . Sika?"

"Felipe Abraham," nauneg ti balikas ti naabay. Nagsay-a iti namaga.

"Felipe Abraham. . . napintas a nagan. . .Taga-Norteka met, Felipe?"

"Makasaoak iti Iloko."

"Nasayaat man. . . Pagawidam?"

Kinuti ni Felipe Abraham ti kanigid nga abagana.

Pagawidak? Tagaanoak kadi tapno adda pagawidak? Sadino ti yan ti balayko? Sadino ti yan ti agur-uray kaniak? Ngem adda kadi agur-uray?

Nakisinneksek ni Felipe Abraham kadagiti tao nga agsapul iti tugawna.

"Good morning, Sir," inkablaaw ti stewardess ken ni Felipe Abraham. "Ditoykayo, Sir," kinunana idi makitana ti boarding pass.

"Thank you." Nagsay-a iti namaga.

Nagsardeng ni Felipe Abraham idi nadlawna ni Miguel Arcadio.

"Adda problemam, Miguel?"

"Pasensiakan, Kabsat. Makasingaak kadi?"

"Kayatko ti agsulsulo . . ."

"Ngem kayatko ti adda kaduana. . ."

Nagwingiwing ni Felipe Abraham iti apagapaman.

Filipino amin dagitoy. Awan ngata ti Puraw a mayat a makikalugan kadagiti Filipino? Wenno dida ngata mabalin ti aglugan iti PAL? Nabayag la idin. Dakkel kadi unayen ti nagbaliwan ti Filipinas?

Daytoy kabsat a sumursurot. . . Kanayon ngata nga agawid? Pagawidanna met ngata? Adda ngata asawa wenno pamiliana nga agur-uray kenkuana? Napiaka pay, kabsat, no kasta.

Dika pay nagawid wenno nagbakasion iti Filipinas, Felipe Abraham, nasurok a duapulo a tawenen ti napalabas. Malagipmo kadi pay no apay nga immayka iti America, ken no apay a napanka idiay Utah ket naglemmengka idiay Provo idi naumakan iti Upland, California? Kayatmo pay kadi a lagipen dagidi nga aldaw? Ala, bay-amon. Lipatemon a piglat dagidi a pasamak. . .no kabaelam.

"Addada la ngaruden iti uneg, agdadarisonda pay laeng, Kabsat," kinidol ni Miguel Arcadio ni Felipe Abraham a nakadlaw kadagiti padada a pasahero.

Di la makauray dagitoy a tao. Maganatanda la unay. Adda numeroda ket sigurado nga awan ti mangagaw iti tugawda. Apay a maganatan la unay ti tao a makadanon iti papananna? Ania la unay ti paggangganatanda? Dida latta koma urayen ti orasda total madanonto met a di bumurong.

Ania ngata no matnag ti luganda iti taaw, di kasla kinamatda metten ti patayda? Tao a talaga. Pappapanan ngata dagitoy nakaad-adu a tao? Di ngata maibus ti kuartada? Wenno adda bubonda iti kuarta?

"Ania ti numero ti tugawmo, Kabsat?" kinidol ni Miguel Arcadio ni Felipe Abraham.

"13-A..." nagsay-a ni Felipe Abraham.

"Ne, agkatugawta gayam! 13-B kaniak. . . 'Nia met a nagalas ti numerotan, Kabsat! Diak kayat ti trese. Saanak a nayanak idi ugma ngem madi ti pagkitkitaak itoy a numero. . ."

"Mabutengka kadi a matay, Kabsat?"

"Hangka nga agang-angaw, Kabsat! Ammom, manmano nga agbakasionak 'diay Filipinas gapu iti dayta. Kasla natayakon iti panagriknak no addaak iti ngato."

"Mabutengka kadi a girsagirsayen ti yo dita taaw?"

"Ni Kabsat met!"

Dika kadi met mabuteng a matay, Felipe Abraham? Ania koma pay ti pagbutngam, ket awan metten ti pangilalaam iti bagim? Di ngamin? Ilalaem kadi pay ti bagim, Felipe Abraham? Apay pay? Mamatika kadi a ti tao ket marunrunot bayat ti panagbiagna? Mamatika kadi a no maipasngayen ti tao sumaruno metten ti patayna? Ala ket no dika mamati, adda la ketdi dakkel a gapuna. Ngem no ania man dayta a gapu, ipakitana laeng ti kinatakrot ti tao. Ngem awan ti takrot nga Ilokano; sika a patneng nga Ilokano awanka koma, wenno dika koma nakapan kadagiti adu a ganggannaet a lugar no di gapu iti kinatangken ti pakinakemmo, di ngamin? Adda kadi sabali a gapuna? Malaksid no adda intartarayam, a nadagsen a basolmo. . . Ngem ania koma a basol? Pimmatayka kadi? Sumagmamano kadagiti rituer iti pagilian? Ne, ket bannuarka no kasta, kuna dagiti nasionalista ti panagpampanunotna, wenno radikal a kas iti kunayo idi panawenyo ti agtataray ken aglilinnemmengan iti sulsuli dagiti unibersidad iti kamanilaan, sayo tupraan ti liklikudan dagiti kunayo nga uken dagiti butit iti palasio. Kunayo idi a saan a basol ti ar-aramidenyo. Ania ngarud ti ilemlemmengam? Babbai? Adu a babbai? Naminsan, wenno namin-ano nga inlunodmo dagiti babbai ta isuda ti mangdaddadael iti kinalalaki dagiti amma. Nalipatam a babai met ni Nanangmo...

"Daytoyen ti trese, Kabsat. Papanam, aya?"

"Sorry, Kabsat." Kinelkel ni Felipe Abraham iti namaga nga uyek.

"Nagdakkel nga eroplano ngem bassit ti pasahero. Dinamagko iti maysa kadagiti Stewardess no mano ti capacity daytoy ket 474 kano.

Ngem 121 la ti pasahero ita. Isu kano a direct flight daytoy imbes nga adda koma stopover idiay Honululu. . . nasayaat met tapno nabibiittayo a makadanon 'diay Filipinas. . . kayatko ket addatay koman idiay!"

Ania ngatan ti langa daydi a lugar? Dakkel ngata ti nagbaliwannan?

Napno iti katkatawa ti pagtaenganyo, Felipe Abraham. Awan dumana iti bassit a paraiso. Umdas laeng ti matmatgedan ni tatangmo iti imprenta ti unibersidad ket saanen nga agsapul pay iti dakkel a sueldo. Total taltallokayo a pakanenna. Saan met nga agrekreklamo ni nanangmo ta saan a nangato ti arapaapna. Adda bassit a telebision iti suli ti bassit a balayyo iti akindaya a paset ti kamanilaan. Bassit a radio. Bassit a bentilador no kapudotna. Saankayo a makunkunatan iti taraon nupay mangrugi idin nga agpangato ti presio dagiti magatgatang.

Napintas ni nanangmo. Nagmutia iti lugarda ket adu ti immapal iti gasat ni tatangmo. Uray dagiti dadaulo iti pagilian a makaam-ammo kadakuda. No apay a nagkagasat da tatang ken nanangmo, di mailawlawag ni tatangmo. Bulsek kano ni ayat. Kinuna ni nanangmo: ni tatangmo ti kataknengan a tao a naam-ammok. . .

Nalaing a manarita ni tatangmo iti sardam sakbay a maturog. Adu ti nakaay-ayat nga es-estoriaenna, ket uray ni nanangmo, naragsak met a dumngeg. Gapu ngata ketdi iti panagtratrabahona iti imprenta, adu ti nabasbasana a libro a nagadawanna iti sarsaritaenna.

Idi kuan, nadlawmo nga adda lallaki a masangsangaili da tatangmo. No makaulog dagiti lallaki, nakalidliday ken makasuron ti rupa ni nanangmo. Ngem uray no adda pulkok iti rupa ni nanangmo, napintas latta. Isu ti kapintasan a babai nga am-ammom. Dimo pay ammo idi ngem natimudmo iti naminsan a sardam a panagsarsarita da tatang ken nanangmo maipanggep iti maysa a politiko iti probinsia. Dimo pay ammo no kasano ti langa ti makasuron ngem idi pay la a nangngegmo a nagtabbaaw ni tatangmo.

Iti saan a nabayag, pagamuan lattan ta dimteng ti politiko nga adda badigardna ket iti imatangyo a dua ken ni tatangmo, rinamesna ni nanangmo. Idi rumkuas ni tatangmo, pinalekda ti teltelna sada pimmanaw nga intugotda ni nanangmo. Gasatmo ket ngata ta nalipatandaka ket imbatidaka a nakanganga.

Saan a nakapagreklamo ni tatangmo. Awan dimngeg kenkuana. Nabusalan sa amin a makaammo iti napasamak. Awan gaway dagiti tao. Ngem manipud idin, masansanen a nakamuttaleng, a no kuan, agsangit a kasla ubing.

Daydin ti naudi a pannakakitam ken ni nanangmo. Impanawnaka ni tatangmo iti daydi a lugar ket pinadakkelnaka iti siudad. Saanen a nagasawa pay ni tatangmo. Ngem awanen dagidi aldaw a napno iti katkatawa. . .

Dagiti sairo!

"Ania ti kunam, Kabsat?"

"Ha?"

"Ladies and gentlemen. . . welcome aboard. Thank you for using the Philippine Airlines."

Napataliaw ni Felipe Abraham iti naggapuan ti timek. No saan nga isu, katimtimekna la unay daydi pinanawanna nga imnas. . .

Manmano ti gundaway a natalna ti lubongyo ken ni Agrippina, Felipe Abraham. Kanayon nga addakayo kadagiti nagkurosan uray no kuminnit ti darang ti init iti aglinteg. Kasla saan a mabannog dagiti takiagyo a mangitagtag-ay iti wagayway ti kalintegan dagiti nakurapay ken mailupeklupek. Uray no parparen ti karabukobyo a mangyik-ikkis iti kunayo a kalintegan, uray no agkiamkiamen ti aglawlaw gapu iti nalaus a bisinyo, nasikkil pay la dagiti gurongyo a mangitaktakder iti ilablabanyo a prinsipio a mangkarit iti rinuker a paglintegan ti rugak a kagimongan. Para kadakayo, atiddog pay ti panawen ket nawaya pay ti gundaway ti panagbalbaliw ti panawen ken ti lubong; nalawa pay dagiti tay-ak a pangpatakderan iti baro a lubong a mangilili kadagiti nakurapay iti natalna nga indayon ti biag. Dakayo, Felipe Abraham, ti maysa kadagiti dadaulo iti itaktakderanyo a prinsipio, ket kurang la nga awanen ti panawenyo ken ni Agrippina nga agpinnerreng ken aginnisem iti sirok ti bulan no kasdiay a kabus ken lutuad iti daya ken naumbi ti pul-oy.

Adda kakaduayo a nagkunkuna a di mabalin nga agreppeng ti idiolohia nga itaktakderan ti tignayyo ken ti rikna nga ipitpitik ti pusoyo. Ngem naturay dayta a pitik ta mabalinna a dupraken ti ania man a prinsipio nupay dina kaipananan a no sumgiab ti darang dumapo metten ti

namnama a mangrubrob iti panangipateg kadagiti agur-uray a paisalakan iti kuko ti nadawel a kagimongan.

"Nadagsen ti barukongko no masirmatak ti kapay-an dagiti lesseb ken tulang iti lanlansangan ken dagiti kumibkibkib kadagiti agrungrungaab a rengngat iti ragangirang a kataltalonan," nadagsen ti timekmo, Felipe Abraham. "Ngem mabingay dayta a rikna no addaka iti sibayko, Agrippina!"

"Diak kabaelan a pursingen ti nagtubo nga ayat iti pusok, Felipe," nabara ti barukong ni Agrippina nga aggitgiteb iti barukongmo iti panangyet-etna kadagiti takiagna iti tengngedmo. "Adda pagrebbenganta kadakuada ngem adda met pagrebbenganta iti tunggal maysa a di mabalin a dita ikkan iti pategna . . . kabaelam kadi, Felipe?"

Agbalin a melodramatiko dagiti kanito nga agpitik iti lubongyo, Felipe Abraham, ngem mapengdanyo kadi? Naturay unay ti rikna a mangad-adipen kadakayo. Ket dayta a rikna ti mangbingay iti itaktakderanyo a prinsipio. Kabaelanyo ngata?

No kasdiayen a sumged ti mamedmedmedan a darikmat, bukodanyon ti kanito ket bay-anyo a malmeskayo iti agliblibiang a panangipategyo iti tunggal maysa.

"Ayatko, siksika laeng!" adda tumrem a lua ti panangipateg kadagiti bituen a mata ni Agrippina ket lemmesennaka.

"Siksika laeng, Ayatko!"

Dagita a darikmat ti kapapatgan iti biagyo.

Ngem tinaktakaw laeng dagita. Ta ti tinakderanyo nga idiolohia kasla saan nga agkirpa ti darangna agingga a di madalusan ti nagkabakiran a gimong tapno sumantak dagiti nabaybay-an a muyong. No nagkirpan ti darang iti nagbaetanyo, sabali manen a darang ti maarunan ket isu dayta ti darang a manguram kadagiti ruker. Di pay nagtaraok ti naiwawa a kawitan agsagsaganakayo manen nga umaridakdak iti Mendiola wenno Bonifacio wenno Ayala wenno Edsa segun ti lugar a napagnanaminganyo kadagiti kameng ti tignayyo . . .

Sadino ti yanmon, Agrippina? Daydi maladaga kasano metten? Nagbaaw kadin dayta barukong? O, Agrippina, adayo unay ti Norway. Adayo unay, Ayatko!

"Ania ti kayatyo nga inumen, Sir?" nasam-it ti isem ti stewardess a mangkitkita ken ni Felipe Abraham.

"Ne... pannangan kadin?" kinelkel manen iti uyek ni Felipe Abraham

"Wen, Sir. . . Okaykayo met laeng?" nagalikuno ti kallid ti imnas.

Diet a soda ti inorder ni Felipe Abraham. Nabuntog ti wingiwingna a nangisursurot iti panagkitana iti patong ti stewardess. Intangadna ti pumait a pagpalamiis a nangalep-ep iti namagmagan a karabukobna.

Mayat ti urok ni Miguel Arcadio iti akinsango a tugaw—immakar ta nawaya dagiti tugaw. Saanen a riniing ti stewardess.

Kimmita ni Felipe Abraham iti tawa a dumna iti tugawna. Ginudua ti labanag a lumlumnek nga aldaw ti tangatang—nangisit iti baba ken amarilio iti ngato, a kasla nagtakkab a nangisit a pariok ken balitok a malukong.

Dagidi nadara a sardam. Dagidi nasipnget a rabii.

"Dakes ti damag, Felipe . . ."

"Marikriknak, Agrippina. Marikriknak."

"Nagpukaw ni Jun."

"Pakpakauna ket ngatan. . . Dagiti sairo!"

"Amangan no isarunoda ni Cesar. . . sa. . . yad-adayom, madananganak. Ita la a mariknak daytoy. Saan pay a nagbiddut ti ania man nga agparikna kaniak."

"Natennebkan kadagiti pasamak. . . pagduaduaam kadi pay ti bagim?"

"Taoak laeng nga adda met riknana. . . kasanon no pumayso ti agparparikna kaniak?"

"Napukaw kadin ti panagtalekmo iti Dios?"

"Felipe. . .Felipe!" adda nagtuktok iti ridaw.

"Asino daydiay?"

Simmirip ni Agrippina. "Ni Dario. . ."

Inlukat ni Agrippina ti ridaw.

"Felipe. . .dakes ti napagteng ni tatangmo. Sinapuldaka kenkuana. Isu ti pinagikaroda."

"Dagiti sairo. . .dagiti sairo!" Simged dagiti matam, Felipe Abraham.

"Felipe. . ." tinengngel ni Agrippina ti takiagmo, Felipe Abraham.

"Nakaikeddengen ti tignay, Felipe. Agpaknika pay laeng."

"Ita pay? Ita pay nga ad-adda a kasapulannak ti tignay? No matayakto met laeng, daytoyen ti kasayaatan a gundaway."

"Saan. Ad-adda a kasapulandaka iti masakbayan. . . saan pay nga ita. . . naisaganan amin a kasapulam. Laglagipem, napategka unay a mapukaw ita. Adda panawen a naisangrat kenka. Agsublikanto."

"Ladies and gentlemen fasten your seatbelts," timek ti kapitan.

Nabaringkuas ni Miguel Arcadio. Nagtaray nga immallatiw iti yan ni Felipe Abraham.

"Kabsat, day-daytoyen ti paggibusanna!" agtigtigerger ni Miguel Arcadio. "A-ammok, i-isu daytoyen. . . Agsublitayo la koman!"

"Yan ti itlogmo, Kabsat?" saan a tinaliaw ni Felipe Abraham ni Miguel Arcadio. Nabitin ti isemna ta kinelkel manen iti namaga nga uyek.

"F-Felipe. . . s-saanak nga agang-angaw. . . m-masakitka kadi?"

"Hey, Miss, ikkam man 'toy gayyemko iti pagpakalma," saan a sinungbatan ni Felipe Abraham ni Miguel Arcadio. "Nabatinan sa ketdi ti balonna 'diay Utah!"

"Agbaudkayo, sir, tapno dikayo pay matay!" agkatkatawa ti Stewardess a timmallikud. Idi agsubli addan mainum ken agas nga intugotna.

Saan a nagbayag timmalna met la ti panagkatugkatog ti eroplano. Naiddep dagiti silaw a nangipakdaar itay iti di nasayaat a panawen iti tangatang. Natalnan ti eroplano a sinab-ok ti sipnget.

Saan a makaturog ni Felipe Abraham. No manen tumaliaw iti tawa, nga awan ti makitana no di pasig a sipnget, wenno iti telon ti dakkel a telebision iti tengnga a sangoda. Ngem awan ti mayulona iti pabuya. Maisagsagud ketdi dagiti matana kadagiti stewardess nga aglabaslabas iti pasilio ti eroplano. No manen kelkelen iti namaga nga uyek.

Ania ket daytoyen. Pagpatinggaanna ngata? Nakaad-adun nga agas. Awan dagitoy a dudoktor. Pagalada met la ti kuarta. Hanabale koma no... Yanmo kadin Agrippina? Daydi ubing yanna metten?

"Daytoy ti diak kayat, Felipe," natalnan ti timek ni Miguel Arcadio.

Tiniped ni Felipe Abraham ti uyekna. Tinaliawna ni Miguel Arcadio.

"Mabilbilang ti panagbakasionko 'diay Pinas, ken adda latta kaduak," intuloy ni Miguel Arcadio. "Dakkel ti pobiak iti eroplano, numona ket adda bassit diperensia ti pusok, ken ti darak."

"Pasensiakan no medio rinabakka bassit itay," kinuna ni Felipe Abraham. "Diak ammo nga adda sakitmo." Inturongna manen dagiti matana iti tawa.

"Ubingak pay idi innalanak ti ikitko idiay Provo, Utah," kinuna ni Miguel Arcadio. "Nariribuk idin 'diay Pinas. Nabati 'di Tatang ken 'di Nanang ken dua a kakabsatko. Mannalon 'di Tatang ket umdas ti apitna iti nataba a taltalonenna a pagpakanna kadakami. Ngem dimteng ti nakaro a didigra kadagiti mannalon. Nagruar dagidi dudon a dua ti sakana ket nagarianda ti bassit a sanikua dagiti mannalon. . . dumdumngegka, Kabsat?"

"Ituloymo."

"Adu a ginagaramugam ti inaramid dagidi a dudon. Ammom ti kunkunada a dudon?"

"Ammok."

"Nagpautangda. Nagpaanakda. Ti la adda a ginuyguyodda idi no di makabayad ni pobre a mannalon. Sumilsilap ti tuktok ti balbalayda idinto a matumtumoyen ti pan-aw nga atep dagiti kalapaw dagidi pobre a mannalon. . ."

"Awan kadi ti masaritam a napintas a ladawan ti Filipinas?" Timmangken ti sangi ni Felipe Abraham. Makauy-uyeken manen. "Kas koma iti. . ."

"Rice Terraces? Buracay? Mount Makiling? Baguio? Hundred Islands? Taal Volcano? Chocolate Hills? Ha-ha!" nalab-ay ti katawa ni Miguel Arcadio.

Kinelkel manen ni Felipe Abraham.

"Kayatmo a denggen ti estoria dagiti beaches a pagkikinnamatan dagiti moderno a dudon? Ha-Ha? 'Nia, dumdumngegka pay, Kabsat?"

Immanges ni Felipe Abraham iti nauneg. Mulmulenglenganna manen ti nangisit a tawa.

Isuda laengen ti siririing—natalnan dagiti pasahero. Malaksid iti agtultuloy a pabuya iti telebision, ken ti naannayas itan nga aneng-eng

ti makina, awanen ti sabali nga aggargaraw a mangted iti biag iti uneg ti eroplano. Uray dagiti stewardess nagsardengdan nga agisaw-isaw.

"Idi saanen a mairusok 'di Tatang ti atibuor dagiti dudon," intuloy ni Miguel Arcadio, "inkeddengna a yeg ti pamiliana iti America, babaen met la ti nabayag a pananguy-uyot ti ikitko. Inlakona amin a bassit a pagbibiaganda ket sisasaganan nga agtayab. Nalaka pay la ti mangala iti visa idi."

"Kas kenka, imbaagna met ti ipusna ket tinarayanna dagiti kabusorna?"

"Saannan a naitarayan ida!" nadagsen ti timek ni Miguel Arcadio. "Sinurotda ida agingga iti airport—saan nga isuda a mismo. Aduda a naglugan idi iti daydi a biahe. Malagipmo, wenno nangngegmo daydi bimtak nga eroplano a di pay nakangato iti airport no ar-arigen? Minulaanda iti bomba. . ."

"Adu ti gagayyemko a naglugan iti daydi. . ."

"Awan a pulos ti namidutanda iti daydi Tatang ken 'di Nanang ken dagidi dua a kakabsatko. Adu ti namati a sinabotaheda daydi. Ngem ania ti maaramidan dagiti natay? Ita, sisiakon a nabati. . . sisiakon!"

"Dagiti sairo!"

"'Nia ti kunam?"

"Adu ti naisebba a biag. . ."

"*Nakiraten ti tignay, Felipe,*" kinuna ti surat ni Dario a naawatmo *idiay Amsterdam, Felipe Abraham. "Arigmi ita iti bao a sibsiblokan dagiti musang iti rabii. Adun ti nayaw-awan. Manmanon ti makontakko. Nagsitakias dagiti dadduma. Napanda iti nadumaduma a paset ti lubong. Dagiti nagtalinaed iti ideolohia nga itaktakderan ti tignay, nagtalinaedda iti sidong ket nagasatda a di nariput dagiti mangngalap iti takdang. Maib-ibuskamin, Felipe Abraham. No kas pagarigan ta ti gasatko ket agpatingga laeng ditoy, laglagipem a diak tinallikudan ti pagrebbengak kas makipagili. Kas nasaok idin, nagayatan ti tignay ti ipapanawmo ket agsublikanto no adda nasayaat a gundawaymo ta sika ti mangituloy a mangaron iti tignay. Mabilbilang metten ti aldawko. . . diak ammo no makapagsuratakto pay . . .*

Pakamakam: Awanen ni Agrippina. Dikami nakapagsarita sakbay a nagpukaw. Damagko nga intugot ti maysa a Norwegian idi nagawid

idiay Oslo. Nabun-as daydi ubing—karuprupam la unay—nga intugotna.
Kurang ti detalye no kasano a napasamak.

"Saanak koma nga agbakasion," nagtimek manen ni Miguel Arcadio.
"Nariribuk kano ita idiay; amangan no bumtak ti rebolusion. . .Ngem
inawagannak ti ikitko, ti kunak a nangala kaniak idiay Provo. Baketen.
Isu ti masansan nga agbakasion. Adda ita idiay Pinas. Adda kano
napasamak ket nasken a mapanko sukonen tapno adda kaduana nga
agsubli idiay Provo. Isu laengen ti nabati a kabagiak. Isu a nasken a
mapanko alaen."

"Nagasatka, Kabsat. . ."

"Iti maymaysa a kabagiak?"

"Sinaludsodmo itay no pagawidak. . ." kinelkel manen ni Felipe
Abraham iti namaga ken nauneg nga uyek. "Awan ti masaok a
pagawidak," intuloyna idi agkirpa ti uyekna.

"Good!" nagkatek ni Miguel Arcadio. "Sumurotka kaniak. Ipasiarka
'diay Paoay Lake. . .uray no sadino ti kayatmo. Nabayagkan a di
nagawid, iti panagkunak. Maragsakan la ketdi ni Anti a makaammo a
nakasarakak iti gayyemko nga Ilokano. . . Idiay Provo, awan ti masao a
nasinged a gayyemko. Manmano ti Filipino idiay. Awan nasarakak nga
Ilokano."

"Agyamanak unay, Miguel. Ngem. . ."

"Awan pagdanagam iti pagyanam. Siak ti makaammo!"

"Adda sakitko, Miguel. . ." kinelkel manen ni Felipe Abraham iti
uyek. "Mabilbilangen ti aldawko."

"W-what?"

"Mabilbilangen ti aldawko, wenno oras ket ngata. Awan makaibaga.
Agawidak ta sadiay ti nakaitamnan 'di tatang. Ken kayatko ti maitanem
idiay. Ken nadamagko a sibibiag pay ni nanang. Asino ti makaibaga,
bareng ketdi no ikkannak ni Apo Dios iti at-atiddog nga aldaw ket
makapagkitakami pay. Ti piman nga inak. . ."

"Awan kadi ti pinanawam 'diay. . ."

"Logan, Utah. . . Awan. . ."

Idiay Amsterdam, idi kairut ti panangipampanesko iti
pannakaipusingko kadagiti napateg kaniak iti Filipinas, adda
maysa nga imnas a nakipagrikna kaniak. Naawatanna ti parikutko.

Indiayana ti tulongna. Agingga nga uray ti bagina. Nasayaat a babai, adda met darana a radikal. Apagapaman a nalipatak ni Agrippina. Diak sinursuratan gapu ta isu ti kuna ti tignay ta amkenda nga adda makasiim iti yanko. Ngem apagbiit la dagidi a darikmat. Uray no awanen ti kontakmi ken ni Agrippina, isu pay laeng ti naguneg ti panunotko. Isu ti nabati a paratignayko.

Ngem saanak a nagpaut idiay. Mano a tawenko laeng. Adu a paset ti Europa ti nagakar-akarak. Adu met ti nasuratko, uray kaskasano, ket sumagmamano ti naipablaak. Wen, nakasursuruak a nagsurat iti kaaddak iti gangannaet ta nasken nga adda pangiwagsakko iti iliwko. Ngem tepo ti journal ta isu ti asideg iti riknak. Naimbag la nga adda pagpalabsak iti oras. Malaksid, a, dagiti babbai a nagsisinnublat iti biagko.

No addaka iti ganggannaet nasken nga agpanunot iti banag a mangtulong kenka a manglipat iti dagensenmo. Adu ti banag a sumangbay iti biagmo ket gapu ta masapulmo ti pagsanggiran agsanggirka iti ania man a makitam a mabalin a makatulong. Uray no kaskasano.

Iti panaglabas ti tawen, iti panagur-urayko iti gundawayko nga agsubli iti Filipinas, naamirisko a marigatanak nga agsubli nga awan ti maisakripisio a prinsipio. Idi la ngaruden naawatko ti surat ni Dario, daydi Dario, nga awanen ni Agrippina, napukawen a namimpinsan ti essemko nga agsubli iti Filipinas. Asino koma pay ti pangisagutak iti panagsakripisiok no awan metten ti kakaisuna a pudno nga ipatpategko?

Idi maikkanak iti gundaway, inkamangko ti dagensen ti barukongko iti America. Bareng ketdi, kunak, no idiay ti pakasarakak iti tipping ti nabatbati a namnamak iti biag. Maysaak kadagidi nangtuptupra iti ladawan ti America. Ngem ti prinsipio ken ideolohia no agluomen ti biag agluom met amin nga itaktakderan ket baliwanna ti pagirayan ti pammati. Maysaak kadagiti kimmannigid a kas iti pammati ti tignay a nangibukbokak iti nalabon a ling-et ken panawen.

Nagdakiwasak iti America. Iti California. Iti New York. Iti Florida ken dadduma pay agingga a naidakdakak iti Utah. Kadagita

a panawen, paset ti biagko ti babai. Nagpalpalabasak ida. Wenno siak
ti nagpalpalabasanda. Iti America, napno iti pannakigasanggasat.
Napno iti ganggannaet. Ammom ngata met, makuna a pasig nga
immigrant dagiti tao. Nadumaduma a puli. Dagiti Puraw, no sadino
man a suli ti lubong ti naggapuan dagiti nagannak kadakuada,
nawayada nga agaramid iti kaykayatda. Bukodda amin a gunay,
pati nagannak kadakuada dida ida mabalin a sagiden uray no
paltingen la koma ti kikitda no makaaramidda iti babak. Awan
babai a nagpaut iti biagko. Wenno awan kadakuada ti nakairusok
a mamagpaut kaniak iti biagda. Nageksperimentuandak la ngata.
Wenno ramittayo la kadi iti lubong a pamadasan?

Adda maysa kadakuada a nagpaut met iti biagko iti
sumagmamano a tawen. Tallo, uppat a tawen. Adda dua nga
annakmi. Idi kuan, indeborsionakon. Naabakak iti kaso ket napan
kenkuana dagiti ubbing. Babai ken lalaki. Isuda ti pappapanan ti
kuartak. Alimony.

Awan ti masnop a pagyanak. Awan balayko. Ngem diak
mailemmengan ti turay ti America. Surotennaka uray no sadino a
suli ti America ti papanam.

Nakaalaak iti sakitko, mano a tawen itan ti napalabas. Wenno
iti ababa a pannao, diak ammo nga adda sakitko agingga nga
intaraydak iti ospital ket naammuak nga adda sakit a nangikeddeng
a saanakon nga agbiag iti mabayag . . .

"Ladies and gentlemen. . ." agarup nalukag ti amin iti natibong
a timek ti kapitan. "Ladingitek nga ipakaammo a ditayo mabalin ti
agtuloy iti Manila International Airport."

"What!" agarup naggigiddan dagiti pasahero a nagkuna.

Napanganga ni Miguel Arcadio.

Naem-em dagiti bibig ni Felipe Abraham, a mangtiptiped iti
uyekna. Nga idi agangay imbulosna ti nakamagmaga nga uyekna a kasla
di agpulsot ket uray la a nagrukob a nangapput iti ngiwatna.

"Ladingitek," intuloy ti kapitan. "Adda bimtak a rebolusion idiay
ket kanselado amin a biahe. Awan ti mapalubosan nga aglanding.
Imbilinda nga agsubliak. . ."

"Pordios. . ."

-II-

AGSUBLIN ti Philippine Airlines iti naggapuanna. No sadino ti pagsardenganna, awanen iti panunot ni Felipe Abraham. Nadagsen unayen ti barukongna.

Makalulua ni Miguel Arcadio.

"Ti ikitko . . . ti ikitko!"

Nagkidem ni Felipe Abraham. Iti nairut. Dina kayat a tumbog dagiti matana.

Ni nanangko . . .

Ni Agrippina. . .

Ni. . . ania ti nagan dayta ubing, Agrippina?

Dagidiay ubbing ti alimony . . .

Nagsasaruno ti panaguyek ni Felipe Abraham. Kinelkel iti uray la nga. Arig la agkupit ti barukongna. Pimsuak ti dara iti agong ken ngiwatna. . .

Nagsam-iten, Agrippina. . . Agawidakon. Mailiwak unayen iti naikari a taengko. Adda met taengmo, Agrippina. Awan makaibaga no pagawidan ti tunggal maysa kadatayo. No maymaysa ti pagawidantayo, nasayaat unay. No maymaysa ti pagawidanta, siak koman ti karagsakan. Ngem kayatko ti agawid iti minuyongan a napno iti sabsabong, sabong a di malaylay. Iti tanap a no winter maaplagan iti niebe a kasla kapas—kas man la paraiso iti panagkitak, Agrippina—ti lamiisna alep-ep ti nasaem a sugat. Wen, agawidakon, Agrippina. Agawidkanto met. Agawidtayo amin. Ni Junior—Junior kadi, Agrippina? Kayatko man a kallabayen . . . Agrippina, o, Agrippina!

Matartaranta dagiti stewardess. Adayo pay ti sangladan ti eroplano ngem addan agur-uray nga ambulansia.

Pakamakam

Dios-ti-kumuyog, Felipe Abraham
Sadino man ti inka papanan
Naungpotmon ti nailet a dalan

Naunday a panawen inka nagnagnaan
Agpakadakan iti rumiet a sangkataw-an
Agpakadakan iti amin a nakaluganam
Agpakadakan iti nabengbeng a niebe iti Logan
Agpakadakan iti adu a libnos a nagpalabsam
Agpakadakan kadagiti tirtiris iti law-ang
Agpakadakan, Felipe Abraham, agpakadakan
No sadino man ti inka pagawidan
Sapay koma ta awan tubengmo a sumaklang. . .—O

Rimat. Pebrero 2004; 1ˢᵗ Honorable Mention, *Sirmata Literary Award*, 2001.

Adtoyak, Ni Tranquilino Tacneng: Iti 28 Kadsaaran A Lubong

9:50 ti Bigat, Mayo 22, ---

NAGADU a taon. . . immay sa metten ti sangabukel nga empleado ti Cosmopolitan Office Building. Napunno ti nagdakkel a Conference Room ditoy COB 26 ngem adda pay la agtatakder iti ruar. Makapatunglab man.

. . . Asinokami la unay, aya, nga agretiro?

Asinoak kadi la unay a mairaman kadagitoy a Puraw?

Ilokano. . . Brown American, a naipasngay iti maika-22 ti Mayo innem-a-pulo-ket-lima a tawenen ti napalabas, iti arigna kalapaw iti abay ti dakkel a pakak iti bibig ti Karayan Biag iti amianan a sinipingan ti lipit. Nataratar dagiti nalayug a kawayan iti agsumbangir ti lipit nga immuluan iti Kamino Real iti daya a nangbisngay iti Bacsil. Nagkusay ti lipit iti San Isidro nga asideg ti Saoang nga ab-ab-aban dagiti allon iti laud.

No apay ketdi a nasken pay nga agamerikana ti tao. Kasla la datao mabekbekkel itoy salbag a nektay! Kas man la 'tay agsagsagana a mabitay, nga itedda ti ania man a taraon a dawatenna.

Naimbag pay dagitoy dua a kaabay ta maay-ayatandan sa la unay. Adadda pay ti bessagda iti nangisit nga Amerikanada, kontra iti naisapaw a

buok 'toy maysa, ken ti nakasilsileng a tuktok 'toy maikadua—naimbag
ta di pay namki 'toy buok iti tallopulo a tawen a yuuli-yuulog ditoy
duapulo-ket-walo kadsaaran. . . a nagbalin a lubong...

Tallopulo a tawen a panagyan iti Heber. . .

Ket ditoy Cosmopolitan Office Building, wenno COB?

Tallopulo?

Kasano ngatan ti Abbarit?

Mapanka kadi lattan, Kilin?

*'Nak met sapulen ti gasatko idiay, Inang. Masirsirmatak a nalidem ti
masakbayak ditoy. . . bareng ketdi no nasaysayaat sadiay.*

*Saanakon nga umubing, Barok. Awan met ngaruden daydi amayo.
Nasakit ti nakemko a mayadayoka. . .*

Nasakit met ti nakemko a mayadayo ditoy Abbarit, Inang. . .

*Lipatem kadin, a, ti napasamakyo ken ni Idot. Talaga a dikayo
agkagasat. . . kinurimes kano ngamin daydiay. . . siguro, dina kayat a
sikat' agtakup.*

*Gapu ta seaman ni Teodoro. . . Ngem paseten ti napalabas ni Idot,
Inang; saan nga isu ti gapu. . .. 'Tay kunakon, awan masakbayak ditoy. . .
Kakaisuna nga adda naasi a tao a tumulong kaniak. . . Laglagipenkayonto
a kanayon, Inang. Kanayonto a suratankayo. Agbakasionakto kalpasan ti
makatawen. . .*

"Congratulations, Quiel!" nairut ti dakulap ti pangulo idi kalman.
Quiel ditoy; Kilin idiay Abbarit.

Maysa kadagiti tallo a Distinguished Employee of the Year? Iti
agtallo ribu nga empleado?

Distinguished?

"Thank you, sir. . ."

Anibersario? Mayo 22 . . .

Kalpasan ti COB, sadino?

Maudi nga aldawen no bigat . . .

9:52 ti Bigat, Mayo 22, ----

"ARE you okay, Quiel?" ti naisapaw.

"Ha, e... What do you think?"

"Langam ti nayaw-awan iti disierto!" ti nasileng ti tuktokna.

"Enjoy! This is our last hurrah!"

Maudi?

"Naragsakkayo kadi? Aniat' panggepyo nga aramiden kalpasan ita?"

"Lawlawenmi ken ni baket ti lubong. . . ibusenmi ti naurnongko!" inggarakgak ti naisapaw.

"Innak sapulen ni Bin Laden. . . uray 'diay yanyo . . . 'diay Filipinas!" ti nasileng ti tuktokna. "Kidding aside, I really don't know. Awan kasano a naurnongko. Siguro, agsapulakto ti pagpartaymak. Kayatko pay ti agtrabaho, tapno saan nga umababa ti biagko. . . Sika, Quiel?"

"Siak. . .?"

Kailiwkonto ngata 'diay mail room. . . ti 1LL—akinngato nga underground, kunadan sa 'diay Filipinas, saan a First Lower Level?

Tallopulo a tawen. . . sumagmamano nga aldaw a bakasion. Sakit ti ulo? Gurigor? Sakit ti tian? Ay, adu ti agas. Dua a tableta laeng tumayaben ti ania man a sagubanit. Mabalin latta ti agtrabaho, agmalmalem nga umuli-umulog iti 28 a kadsaaran ti COB, babaen ti freight elevator met ketdi a.

Sinno ngatat' nangtedanda kadagiti di nausar a bakasion? Sayang met. . . dagidi sobra, innayonda la koman iti gatad iti panagretiro. Ngem, ala, naimbag met no maminsan ta nakatulong kadagiti nakasapul. Adda ngata lima gasut nga oras? Sobra?

Manon sa ketdin ti nabati 'diay banko?

Saan a maud-udi 'diay kaanakam 'ti klaseda, manong. . .

Sangagasut. . . dua gasut. . . Mano idin daydi kadakkelan? Lima gasut? Nagkasar idi ni Manuel a kabsat a buridek.

Dandani binulan. No dadduma, mamindua pay iti makabulan.

Uliteg. . .

Kasinsin . . .

Ipag. . .

Kayong. . .

Agan-anuska, Angkel. Agsubsubalitkaminto. No mairuarko ti board exam, addanton engineer a kaanakam inton umay a tawen! Ni Angkel Salaknib . . .

Sinno daydin nagturpos iti kina-Maestra? Ken daydi nars? Ken daydi commerce? Manodan sa ketdin? Lima? Walo? Sangapulo?

Asinoda idin? 'Pay ket malagipen ti naganda. Yanda ngatan? Addan sa nakapan Hawaii. Alaskan sa pay. Adda kad' idi nakapan Canada? 'Dan sa pay Australia. Manot' nangasawa kadakuadan? 'Dan sa uppat a napaw-itan 'ti pinagkasarda.

Dagiti ngata annak ni Salaknib?

Kasanoda ngatan? 'Pay ket malagipen no kaano ti naudi a panagsuratda; wenno nakangngegan 'ti damag 'papan kadakuada. Wenno sinno kadin ti nagsurat kalpasan ti panagturposda. . . ti panagasawada?

Wen gayam, 'da kasinsinda a nag-email 'di naminsan. Sangagasut kano manen.

Ngem kasano pay?

"It's a company's policy, Quiel. . . We hate to lose you, but we have to give way to younger generation. . ."

65, lakay kadin?

Angkel idi. . .

Angkel ita. . .

Angkelto latta nga awan patinggana. . .

Ne, ket awan met lat' maurnong a pagplete nga agbakasionen, a!

Ngem. . . dagidiay annak ni Salaknib, dida man la agsurat. Bilbilinen ngata ida dagiti dadakkelda? Uray koma no naidaddadumada, a, ket. . .

Mailiwak unayen kenka, Kilin, anakko. Adda met ketdi dagiti kakabsatmo ditoy, a, ngem in-inutda metten nga agtatalaw. Adda napan idiay Mindanao. . . Kaanonto, aya, nga agbakasionka? Nakapsutakon. Kanayon a maitagtagainepko daydi amayo. Nakaragragsakkami kampay idi a magmagna iti nakapimpintas a minuyongan. Kas man la nakalaglag-an ti panagriknak iti bagik, kasla awan saksakitko. Ayna, no dadduma pay, aya, no makariingak ta mariknak ti ut-ot dagiti susuopko, kaykayatko pay koman no diak maluklukag iti tagtagainepko. Ngem diak ammo man, barok, no tagtagainep daydiay, ta kas man la agpayso. Nakalanglangto ti aglawlaw. . .

Wen, naawatko daydiay impaw-itmo a para iti kompleaniok. Ngem awan 'tay kas sika a makita ken mangngegko ti timekna. Dagidiay suratmo . . .

Nalanglangto kadi ti aglawlaw dita ngem ti nalawa a pinagayan, wenno kanatengan iti nagbaetan ti Limas ken ti Karayan Biag? Awan kadi ti agdalluyon a dawa dita? Adda kadi kakkalap a buntiek, samsam-it, araro, dalag, lagdaw? Singkamas, sandia . . . marunggi, adda kadi? Saluyot? Tokak?

Agtudo kadi met dita, wenno niebe lattan nga umatiberret? Kaasika pay, Kilin, anakko. Naimbag no di agbibineg amin a bagim iti ultimo a lamiis? Ay, apo aya. . . Naimbag koma no adda asawam. Apay ngamin a dika mangasawa tapno adda katakunaynaymo iti rigat?

Wen, no kunam a makanmo amin a kankanen ti babaknang dita. . . ditoy, dagiti la agtaud iti sangadakulapan a suksukayen dagiti kakabsatmo ti masao a libre, ngem dagiti nasken a magatang, apo aya, anakko, tumukno ti presioda iti langit a kunada. No dadduma a makaud-udongenak ket sumurotak iti asino man a mapan makitienda, dandani diak mayawid ti bagik iti nalaus nga ulawko iti naipanurok a kaadu ti tao. Ay, apo, ta adu latta ti agriringgor, lallaki wenno babbai.

Wen gayam, ni Kapitan Ladio, pimmusayen. Nakitada ti bangkayna a naipalnaaw iti teppang ti Karayan Biag. Adda pamalpalatpatanda no asino ti akinggapuanan. . . ngem nakaul-ulimek dagiti kakabagianna. Ammomon, a, no ania ti pampanunotenda. Ay, apo, Anakko, aya.

Ngem diak ibagbaga a dika agawid . . . Ni Salaknib nga adingmo, pulos a di pay immaridakdak iti sabali a lugar. Ammom metten 'diay adim. Ditoyak, kunana, ditoy kano lattan. Kunana man, no adda dagiti di napudno iti lugar a nakayanakanda, ta dida ammo nga ipateg. Kunana: siak, diakto pulos bag-oten ti ramutko ta ditoyak a timmao ditoyakto met la a dumaga . . . No makapagbakasionka koma, makitam ti ar-aramidenna; kunana ngamin a diak sagsagiden iti suratko kenka. Ngem. . . isu man ti kasla di mangitulok nga iludek ti rigat. Kanayon nga adda iti talonna. Diak ammo man, napnapan pay agsemseminar no dadduma.

Malagipko ni Idot. Duanton ti annakna. No masabatnak, ikarkarigatanna ti mangliklik. Ayna, Kilin, Anakko, kasla balay a nagrakayan ti bagi 'diay tao. Nagdudupudopan ngamin ti bisio daydiay lakayna. . . ken saanen a siman. Patartaraken lattan ken ni Idot, sa kanayon kano pay a mansuenna. . . Piman ti biag, aya, anakko?

Ne, kasta pay ket adda kano papanan 'toy naanus nga ubing a pagpaspasuratak. . .

9:55 ti Bigat, Mayo 22, ----

IDI kalman:

"Howdy, Quiel?"

"Ha-e... I'm fine, Kellie. . .!" Saan a pudno daydiay.

Huebes. Panagdedeliber ti papel dita 3WW—adda ngata met Third Floor West Wing dagiti building 'diay Makati? Ken 4WW. . . ken dita 1NW. Manot'tay a cases ti masapuldan? Lima iti 4WW. Maysa. . . dua. . .tallo... uppat, lima. . . innem iti 3WW. Sa manot'tayen iti 1NW? Uppat met. Naimbg ta awan 'diay 2EW.

Tallo pay la dagidi cart a 6-wheelers. Di pay la ketdi napan nagideliber ni Don iti rotana. Ni Kevin, alas diesto pay la no sumangpet.

Ooops! Kurang la a matukkol ti salbag a siket. 'Gasem met ngamin ti sangapulo a rim ti maysa a karton? Mano a libra? Duapulo?

Naimbag met ta 9:10to no sumangpet ni Lynn. . . saan a problema ta manmano nga adu ti isangpetna.

Ni Eric, 9:40 no sumangpet. Daydiay ti kanayon nga adu ti bagahe nga isangsangpetna, nga iwaras met ditoy COB, ken kadagiti dadduma a departamento iti ruar. Agarup mawarasan ti intero a 28 a kadsaaran iti no ania la ditan a pakete. Nasakit a talaga ti salbag a siket. . . di koma mangisangsangpet ni Eric iti adu a kinahon a computer. Kaanon daydi nasurok a sangagasut ti naideliber a computer?

Ngem sigurado nga adda latta isangpetna a di nakurkurang ngem sangapulo a kahon wenno kahita ti micrographics para ken ni Gloria Frances dita COB 2. Ken FCH para ken ni Adriane Candelaria dita COB 5. Idiay COB 25, inaldaw latta met nga adda agpaay ken ni Roberta Appell. Idiay COB 28, ken COB 12, COB 3 ti sigurado nga awan ta di pay nalpas ti renovationda.

Ita man pay. . . makipagrikriknan sa metten dagitoy gurong. Kasda met la sumsumkilen ket apagsibet la ti spring no ar-arigen. Tinto met ngamin buntog daytoy nga elevator, arig la dagitay lugan 'diay Manila nga agin-iniinda uray 'diay EDSA. Di pay ngata nagbaliw ti trapiko?

Mano ti pakete a para iti COB 4? Daytoy kadi laeng para ken ni Linda Clawson? Idiay COB 6? Para ken ni Jullie Attridge kadi laeng? Nabayag met dagidiayen. Adda met ngata 20 a tawenen ni Linda. Ni Jullie, siguro 15 a tawen. Napanan ngatan dagidi nadanonko idi? Dandani tinawen nga agsukat dagiti tao. Agpababa agpangatoda a kas iti elevator. Adun ti awan.

COB 4 gayamen.

"Hi, Linda. . ."

"How're yah doing, Quiel?"

"Great. . ." Manen! Apay ngamin a great latta wenno fine uray no saan? 'Nia ti kunada no kunam a not so good? Sorry! Agpayso ngata met ti riknada?

"Damagko nga agretirokan, Quiel. . . agpayso kadi?"

"S-saanak nga agretro. Pagretretiruendak. Lakayak kanon. Lakay kadin ti 65, Linda?"

"Napigsa pay la ti langam. . . Ngem, dimo kadi kayat tapno makapaginanakan? Inka agpasiar. Around the world. Inka 'diay Israel. . . idiay Jerusalem. . ."

"Idiay Afghanistan. . ."

"Inka sapulen ni Bin Laden? No way, Quiel! Pagkatkatawaennak. . ."

Around the world? No ultimo a Park City ket namnaminsan la a napanak. Ti Lake Powell, damag laeng. Antelope Island, naminsan. . . Dayta, a, Great Lake, ta matantan-awan iti COB 26. . .

Iti COB 26. . .

Ni Salaknib: ni Nanang, manong, napanen. . .

Duapulo a tawen idin iti Heber. Umuna nga isasarungkar iti Abbarit. Nakaskasdaaw ti nagluposan ti napanawan a lugar.

Ti naganmo ti sangkaulitna, kabagis, sakbay a nagsatan.

Apay, ket kanayon met a sursuratak, ken pawpaw-itak.

Ni Salaknib pay: Dagiti suratmo ti sangkakepkepna. Dagiti impaw-itmo, nalabit saan nga isu ti napateg kenkuana. . . kitaenna maminsan sa manangad nga agkuna: daydiay kabsatyo, kaasi met. No manen, saludsodenna: dina ngatan mapanunot ti mangasawa, ti agsubli ditoy? Sana met la sungbatan: kunana nasarakanna kanon ti lubongna iti yanna. Kaasi pay.

Nanang, pakawanennak. Ti kinatan-ok, napaneknekak nga adda iti sadino man a yanmo no ammom nga ipateg ti kinataom. . .

Ni Miguel: Dimo man la sinarungkaran uray no naminsan laeng, kabagis.

Ti sabali a kabsat: Kaska la nagpasugnod a baed, kabagis. Nalipatam a namimpinsan ti Abbarit.

Ti ipagna itoy: Ania ngay ti serbi ti kaaddam ita, kayong, ket awan metten ti inayo a makakita kenka?

Ditay koma pagsasaritaan dayta iti sibay ti bangkay ni nanang. . . Ngem ammoyo no apay? Awan urnongko a pagpletek. Ammoyo no apay? Ammoyo? Saludsodenyo iti bagbagiyo. . . Ngem yandan dagiti nagturpos nga annakyo? Yandan? Itoy maudi a gundaway a pannakakitada koma itoy apoda. . . Yanda? Yanda? Dakayo, sadino met ti yanyo kadagidi aldaw a pannakailiwna kadatayo?

Asino ti makaawat kaniak?

Nagaawid dagitoy kalpasan ti pumpon. . .

Ne, nagadun a plake? Salacnib Tacneng. . . kukuam met amin dagita, kabagis! Diyo man la impadpadamag.

Nasken kadi, kabagis. . .

Ne, apay, dika maragsakan, kabagis?

Kunam, kayong, ket agunget pay nga ipadamagmi kenka.

Nasaysayaat koma no dimo nadlaw. . .

Kunam ket naminsan la a napan immawat, kayong. Malaksid iti dayta plake a Distinguished Filipino Farmer of the Year, a napilpilit pay a napan immawat, siakon ti pinatudonna a napan nangawat kadagiti dadduma. Outstanding Citizen of the Year. Distinguished Farmer of San Juan. Ken dagita. . .

Dika maawatan, kabagis.

Kaniak la a maysa, ti natan-ok a makipagili isu daytay saan a mangisukat iti kinasiasiona iti ania man a banag—kinabaknang, dayaw. . . Ania koma dagiti plake no saanka met a napudno iti bagim? Gabsuonandaka man iti plake wenno sertipiko no dimo ammo ti kinasiasinom, ken no dimo ammo ti agserbi iti amin a kabaelam uray awan naragpatmo nga adal, ania ti mamaayna?

Dagita naawatmo a pammadayaw, di kadi pay umdas a mangipakita iti panagserbim...?

Nasken kadi dagita tapno agserbika? Agserbika a dimo pampanunoten iti yaawatmo iti pammigbig. . .

9:56 ti Bigat, Mayo 22, ----

"LADIES and gentlemen, we are honored to gather here in recognition of these three distinguished associates for their unceasingservices with the Cosmopolitan Office Building. . ."

Piman 'di nanang. . . piman. . .

Angkel. . .

Kayong. . .

Kasinsin. . .

Ni Idot. . . mano ngatan ti appokona? Di kano met nakapagadal dagiti annakna. Impalnaawda kano met 'di Doro a lakayna. Agpayso ngata a putot ti baknang 'diay ili ti maikatlo nga anakna?

Ne, naglangto daytan a paset. Mano nga ektaria dayta?

Aglima ngata, kabagis. Mairamanen dayta agarup maysa nga ektaria a pamupokan dita asideg ti Cabanayan.

Adda pay. . . poultry kadi dayta? Ken pamabuyan?

Agsangaribu dagita manok a nabennebenneg segun ti klaseda—adda white leghorn, kamanokan. . . Dagita baboy, agarup agdua gasut metten.

Dimo kunaen a kukuam dagita. . .?

Nain-inutak a napondar babaen met la ti tulong ti gobierno. Napanak met nagtrentraining. . .kayatko koma nga adda dagiti kakabsatta a katulongak, a, ngem kas kenka, ti met la nakaipalpalladawanda.

Apay dayta wangwang dita laud ti balaymo?

Kunak man, pagbalayanto ti mayat. . . no addanto mayat nga agsubli ta uray dagidiay kaanakam ket kayatda met a suroten ti tugotmo.

Iti rabii:

Asino dagidiay, kabagis?

Dagiti kakabsat iti ruar.

Addada pay laeng, aya? Apay. . . apay nga inikkam ida?

Diak inikkan ida. Isuda lattan ti napan nagala.

Kanayon?

No makalagipda.

Apay a dimo ida ipulong iti agrebbeng?

Awanak koma itan. Maysa pay, no adda kasapulan dagiti agrebbeng, umayda met mangibaga. Awan singsingirek kadakuada. No dadduma, ti la adda a mait-itedda. Diak prepresioan. Makaammoda lattan.

Ammo dagiti kaarrubayo?

Ammoda.

Kasla saan a nakappapati! Yal-alismon sa met ti alipusposko. . .

Agpayso a saan a nakappapati. Ngem mapaspasamak. Mamatika man wenno saan.

Ganggannaetkan iti Abbarit, Kilin. . . kadagiti kakabsatmo. Dimon am-ammo ni kabsatmo a Salaknib. . .

10:00 ti Bigat, Mayo 22, ----

IDI kalman:

"Congratulations gayam, Quiel! You deserve your award."

"Thank you very much, Linda. Kasta met amin a bitayenda, di ngamin? Pakanenda iti um-umana. Damagenda no ania ti kayatda sadanto bitayen. . ."

"Kasla dika maragsakan? Manmano la ti maikkan iti award for being loyal. Agaasem, mano a tawen a nagtrabahoka ditoy?"

"Tallopulo. . . Tallopulo a tawen nga inuli/inulogko ti 28 a kadsaaran ti COB. . . 'Mom, Linda, malaglagipko ni kabagisko a Salaknib. Pulos a di pimmampanaw idiay Abbarit. Nagtaltalon latta. . . Ooops! Adu pay gayam ti i-deliverko!"

"Good luck, Quiel."

COB 16? Sinno daytoy a Karilyn Moore?

Ne, apay nga awan met ditan ni Wendy Maugham?

"Good morning. . ."

"How're you. . . Quiel? I'm Karilyn Moore. Nagsinnukatkami ken ni Wendy iti lugar. Impanda idiay JSMB."

"Adda pakete ni Wendy, Karilyn."

"Thank you very much, Quiel. Ibatim lattan ta itedkonto. Ammom, adu ti imbagbaga ni Wendy maipanggep kenka. Sika kano ti kasayaatan kadakayo a mail carrier."

"Agyamanak unay, Karilyn. Ngem kuna ngamin 'di Nanang bayat ti panagdakkelmi, a saluadanmi ti kina-Ilokanomi. Sadino man a papananmi, ipakitami ti kinasiasinomi. . . nagaget daydi Nanang. Uray daydi Tatang. Nagaget amin a kakabsatda. . ."

"Nagasat la ketdi ti pamiliam. . ."

Kadi. . .?

Ne, dandaniak nailabesen iti COB 25. Manot'tayen ti pakete ni Roberta Appell? Uppat? Ne, kukuana gayam amin dagitoyen. Awanen ti para iti 27 a yan ti DTA, ken 28 a Security Department.

"Nasayaat ta immayka, Quiel. Mangrugi ti bakasionko no bigat."

"Kunak la ketdin no... pumanawka metten, Roberta."

"Saan. Awan pay tallopulo a tawenko ditoy! Mabayag pay sakbay nga ag-65-ak."

"Nagasatka."

"Nagasgasatka, a, ta agretirokan."

"Ammom metten?"

"Asino ti di makaammo, Quiel? Sikanto pay, nga am-ammo amin ti sangabukel a COB. Panagkunak, maikabesam amin a paset ti building. Amin nga opisina. Amin a tao."

"Adun ti kabarbaro, Roberta. Namin-adun a nagsukatsukat dagiti empleado. Kas iti aldaw nga aglabas, kas iti elevator nga agpababa-agpangato a diak matandaanan amin a pasamak, kasta met dagiti tao ditoy."

"Awanakto no bigat, Quiel. Sorry. Ngem alaem daytoy. Pagyamanmi iti kinatan-okmo. . . ti kinasayaatmo kadakami. Pulos nga awan napukaw, wenno naladaw la koma a nai-deliver kadakami a pakete bayat ti panagserbim. Dagiti busko ditoy, ammoda ti kinasayaatmo a tao. Awatem daytoy."

"R-relo?"

"Tapno malaglagipnakaminto tunggal kitaem ti oras. . ."

10:05 ti Bigat, Mayo 22, ----

"LAST but not the least, Tranquilino Tacneng. . .

"Kadagitoy a panawen, iti kaadu ti pannubok iti biag, nangruna iti ekonomia, saan la nga iti America ngem ammotayo amin a global ti parikut, manmano no adda man kas kadagitoy tallo a kakabsattayo a nakapagpaut ken naikkan iti gundaway nga agserbi iti COB iti kas iti kaunday ti panawen a binubosda iti departamentoda. Duapulo, duapulo-ket-lima, tallopulo a tawen agingga nga agretiroda.

"Iti kinadalus ti rekordda, rumbeng laeng a maipaay kadakuada ti kastoy a pammadayaw. Ditayo ammo no addanto pay kas kadakuada iti kinatan-ok.

"Saan met a panangidumduma, ngem kas makitayo, ni laeng Tranquilino Tacneng ti ganggannaet kadagiti tallo. Segun iti rekordna, pulos nga awan mantsa ti rekordna iti unos ti panawen a panagserbina. Diak ammo no kasano ti inaramidna, ngem dayawek ti andorna. . . Kasla kadi amin kenka dagiti kadaraam a Filipino, Quiel? Mangirekomendaka man iti kasukatmo!"

Natibong a sipsipat.

"Mapadayawanak ngarud a mangyawat kadakuada kadagiti sertipiko ken medaliada. . . Don Green, duapulo a tawen a nagserbi. . ."

Palakpak.

"Eric Barkbuster, duapulo-ket-lima. . ."

Palakpak.

"Tranquilino Tacneng, tallopulo. . ."

Natibtibong a palakpak.

"Ladies and gentlemen, agyamanak iti pannakaited kadakami iti gundaway a mangipeksa iti adda iti panunotmi.

"Adda pagsasao ti Intsik a kastoy: More talks, more mistakes; less talks, less mistakes; no talk, no mistake. Isu a 'tay kunak, ababa laeng ti sawek.

"Ti tao, saan nga agpatingga ti pagrebbenganna iti biag kalpasan ti panagretirona. Agtultuloy ti pannakigasanggasatna iti tunggal aldaw nga aglabas. Agyamanak unay iti naited kaniak a gundaway nga agserbi ditoy COB, kasta met iti panagtalek nga impaayyo.

"Kangrunaanna, agyamanak unay iti daydi nanangko a nangtubay iti kinataok iti nasapa nga ipupusay daydi dakkelmi a lalaki. Insuronakami nga agkakabsat daydi nanangko a mangtimud iti pitik ti kaungganmi; tinubaynakami iti galad ti pudno nga Ilokano, dagiti Filipino nga agindeg ti puonda iti Amianan a Luzon. Dagidi patigmaanna ti nagbalin a taraon ken bilegko nga immay nakigasanggasat ditoy America. Nagsagabaak iti nakaro nga iliw iti pannakaipusingko iti daga a nakayanakak ngem gapu iti bilbilin ti naasi nga inak a nagramut iti panunotko, saan a nabaelan ti tallopulo a tawen a pinukaw ti anag ti kina-Ilokanok. Uray no maysaakon a makipagili iti America, Ilokanoak a naipasngay, Ilokanoakto pay laeng nga agsubli iti tapok a naggapuak. . .

"Ne, ababa, kunak, ngem atiddog met daytoyen.

"Agyamanak unay iti panangipategyo kaniak kas kabsat. Napatpateg dayta ngem daytoy pammadayaw nga impaayyo kaniak. Balonekto dayta a pammateg inton agsubliak iti daga a nakayanakak. . ."

10:30 ti Agsapa, Mayo 22, ----

COB 26.

Maudi daytoyen. Awanton ti gundaway nga umay ditoy kalpasan daytoy a pasken. Ditoy kadsaaran a nairanta a pagawatan iti turista. Dita daya ti pakatannawagan iti adu a babbabassit a pasdek. Maibilang ti unibersidad ti estado nga iti bakrang ti bantay nayurit ti puraw a dakkel a letra U nga insignia ti pagadalan.

Iti akinlaud a pagtatan-awan, matannawagan ti agtallo a tawen a dakkel a Conference Center iti asideg a sakaanan ti COB. Iti abagatan-a-laud, nadumaduma a pasdek a pakaibilangan ti Delta Center, ti Marriott Hotel, ken ti Salt Center. Iti adayo nga amianan, iti bakrang ti bantay, nabaked ti kapitolio ti estado a langana ti mangtantannawag iti aglawlaw. Iti pangadaywen a laud, mailangaan dagiti aglanding ken agtayab nga eroplano iti International Airport. Iti labes daytoy ti yan ti Great Lake.

Nakaay-ayat man ti um-umay ditoy a kadsaaran tunggal adda panawen. No kairut ti panagregreg ti niebe, nakapurpuraw ti aglawlaw

ket dandani la awan makita a sabali a maris ta naaplagan ti intero nga aglawlaw. . .

Itinto laengen arapaap a matannawagan ti airport. . .. dagidiay agtayab nga eroplano.

Dagidiay agtayab. . .

Ay wen, Abbarit. Dagita sinilongmo a nalangto. Dayta pamupokan dita saklotmo. Dagiti nabatbati a naanus a taom. . . wen, awanen daydi pakak, napanen daydi ina, ngem ti Karayan Biag. . . kibkibkibanna kadi pay laeng ti bakrangmo? Ti lipit a simmiping iti karayan sibibiag kadi pay?

Ni kabagisko a Salaknib. . .

Ni Idot. . .

Ti pakabuklam. . .

Kailiwko ti umay agpasag dita saklotmo, Abbarit. . . Kailiwko ti umay agpasag. . .—0

Umuna a Gunggona, RFAAFIL, 2005; *Bannawag:* Nobiembre 7, 2005

-Dagiti Awtor

Naipasngay ni Lorenzo Garcia Tabin, Sr. idiay San Juan, Ilocos Sur idi Mayo 22, 1944; ni Sinamar Alos Robianes Tabin, Sr. idiay Pagudpud, Ilocos Norte idi Abril 20, 1945. Nabayagdan nga agipatpatarus ken interpreter iti The Church of Jesus Christ of Latter-day Saints; Temple Sealer ni Lorenzo iti Jordan River Utah Temple; nagretiro iti Mail Operations ti Church Office Building, ken iti Deseret Bookstore iti Salt Lake City, Utah. Adu ti nasurat ni Lorenzo a nobela, sarita, daniw, ken salaysay kadagiti magasin a Bannawag, Rimat, TMI Jornal, Asia Philippines Leader; adu ti naawatna a gunggona, kas iti UMPIL, ti kangatuan a pammadayaw a maited iti mannurat a Filipino; Pedro Bucaneg Award a kangatuan a maited iti mannurat nga Ilokano; Palanca, ETTI, GRAAFIL, RFAAFIL, ken dadduma

pay (para iti listaan dagiti sinurat, pammadayaw, ken dadduma pay, kitaen ti bibliograpiada a nairaman iti libro, iti nagbaetan ti orihinal ken ti patarus). Awan inggana a miembro ti GUMIL Metro Manila gapu iti panagpresidentena iti gunglo. Nairamanda ken ni Sinamar kadagiti nangbuangay iti TMI Global (Guild of Ilokano Writers Global) nga indauluan daydi T. Gabriel Tugade, a kaduada da Aurelio Solver Agcaoili, PhD. ken ni Cristino Iloreta Inay, Sr. Nagturpos ni Lorenzo iti AB Journalism iti Manuel L. Quezon University, sa iti MA Literature iti University of the Philippines iti Diliman, Quezon City. Adu met ti nasurat ni Sinamar a nobeleta, sarita, daniw, ken salaysay iti Bannawag, nagsursurat iti Normalite Bulletin nga school organ ti Northern Luzon Teachers' College a nagturposanna iti BSEEd, Ilokano Section Editor ti Ilocos Courier ti Laoag City, nagab-abak iti panagsuratan, nageditor iti Bangui Star ti Bangui Provincial High School. Nagretiro a maestra. Immuna a libro ni Lorenzo ti *'Pakpakawan, Berde! Ken 21 a Sarita.'* Rex Bookstore, 1977, 220 pp. Nagbuliganda ti libroda a *'Woven Strands of Roses / Naabel a Linabag ti Rosas,'* XLibris, 2014. Lima ti sibibiag a bungada: Loumarie Linglingay (Banking and Finance and Business Administration), Lorenzo II (BS Physics), Noami (Accounting), Sinamar II (Interior Designer), ken Marlo Bagnos (MS Business Administration). Agindegda iti West Valley City, Utah 84120 USA.